MEMOIRS OF A MANIC-DEPRESSANT

All inquiries should be addressed to:

Book Domain LLC.
543 E Louise Dr Phoenix, Az 85050

Ordering Information:

Amount Deals. Special rebates are accessible on the amount bought by corporations, associations, and others. For points of interest, contact the distributor at the address above.

Printed in the United States of America.

ISBN-13	Paperback	978-1-972696-70-5
	eBook	978-1-972696-71-2

Library of Congress Control Number: 2026917856

MEMOIRS OF A MANIC-DEPRESSANT

MICHELLE MCCONNELL

BOOK DOMAIN LLC

CHAPTER 1

1977: AGE 8

DECEMBER 29, 1977

I am Maddy Tanner. I am writing in my new diary I got for my birthday. My birthday is so close to Christmas and New Year's Eve, it feels like I don't have a birthday at all.

Katy and Karen couldn't come to my birthday party because they were visiting their grandparents in Missouri. They live on the Air Force base still where I used to live in a 32' camping trailer when mom first joined the Air Force. I met Katy and Karen in that trailer park. We played together every day. I usually went to their trailer after school instead of being by myself. I was really young then and shouldn't stay alone, even though mom and dad never seemed to notice. Katy and Karen's mom was my Brownie leader so I went to meetings at their trailer. Katy and Karen's parents were waiting for a house big enough for their whole family. Katy and Karen are twins, not identical, and they have an older, mean brother. Mom said there is a waiting list for people to get into base housing.

I live in Clarksville, California now. We couldn't get into a house that dad liked on base so we moved here. I think there were only one bedroom houses available. Mom has to drive a lot further to work now.

Diane was the only friend who could make it to my birthday party. All of my other Clarksville friends were out of town for Christmas, so it is hard to have a real birthday party with balloons and decorations. I haven't had a decorated birthday party since I was 3 years old, not that I remember. I've seen the picture. Diane is in Clarksville because her father is Jewish and doesn't believe in Christmas. She is the only Jewish person I have met, I think. She comes from Polish immigrants and she knows the best Pollack jokes. I thought the jokes would offend her, but they don't. Her dad tells her most of the jokes she knows. He says there is no reason to get angry when there is so much in the world already. Diane has the best dad in the world. I wish I had a dad like that. My dad is always mad.

We move around a lot so I have to keep making new friends. I have lots of friends here in my neighborhood who are the same age as me, so I like Clarksville a lot. Also, my real name isn't Maddy, it's Leigh. Everyone has to call me Maddy because dad says so. No one is allowed to call me Leigh anymore, not since I was 3 years old. I don't know why they changed my name to Maddy. I am not allowed to ask questions or dad gets super mad.

Another thing I got for Christmas and birthday is the lime green ten-speed bicycle that I really, really wanted, really, really badly. I didn't have the bike on Christmas, but mom gave me a small wrapped box with a note inside saying that I got a ten-speed bike for Christmas. Mom and dad took me to Sears to buy it yesterday. It was so exciting. I feel so grown up having a ten-speed bicycle. Dad bought the bicycle that was displayed in the store so he wouldn't have to assemble it. He asked the man who worked for Sears if he could get a discount for the display bike which was so embarrassing. The man went away to talk to someone and said it was okay, the bike could be sold for $110 instead of $120. It is a "combined" Christmas/birthday present. I don't like when I get "combined" Christmas and birthday gifts. Everyone else gets different gifts on their birthday, so why can't I get different presents on my birthday?

Now I will be able to ride bikes with my friends, which will be so much fun! I can't wait until everyone is in town again. It was hard to keep up with my friends when I was on my skateboard, unless it was down the big hill. I try not to go down the big hill after Christmas last year when I got my skateboard and went down the big hill. I made it down the hill and around the corner until I hit a rock and skidded in the street on my knees and hands. I got them all bloody and ripped my brand new red Ditto jeans. Mom wasn't mad at all like I thought she would be. She said she was a tomboy, too, and said she would buy a cute patch to iron over the hole in my jeans. I had to hide my ripped jeans from dad until the patch was ironed on because he gets very angry and scares me. Mom said she was glad that I didn't hit my head. She knows I don't want to wear a helmet because only the retarded kids wear helmets. None of my friends wear helmets. Mom understands.

I am still so happy to have that bike. It was really lucky that I even got it. I had to go to the doctor because my left knee cap keeps getting dislocated. My knee cap slides to the side of my leg and really hurts. It is also gross when it happens. My right knee has started doing it, too. The first doctor said I needed surgery, but recommended a knee specialist in Sacramento. Mom told dad that I had to go to the doctor so he took me because he didn't have a job then and she did. Dad doesn't like to go to the hospital much. He thinks doctors are full of (bad word goes here).

The doctor in Sacramento said I didn't need knee surgery, that too many people had surgery for no good reason. He said the ligaments are loose in my knees. He told dad that if I had a bicycle and it would solve my knee problems. I was so happy that dad heard it from the doctor that he had to buy a bike for me. The doctor said it will strengthen the muscles in my knees.

Oh, I also got the yellow Ditto jeans I wanted, some short socks with pom-poms, and days of the week underwear. Ditto jeans with the seam running around the back like a rainbow are so popular at school. I got a red pair for last Christmas, the ones I ripped when I fell off my skateboard and got an iron-on patch.

Gammy sent me another part to my Barbie set for Christmas. Barbie is kind of fun because she has so many clothes she can change into. Barbie can become a different person depending on the clothes she wears. The clothes are my favorite part. Gammy really likes Barbie because she used to get Barbie for my mom when she was little, so I like Barbie, too. This year, she bought me the townhouse with a tub and shower that really works when you add water, an elevator that goes up all three stories. I got Barbie furniture for my birthday. Each year at Christmas, Gammy buys more furniture and clothes for my Barbie set. Last Christmas, I got the tanning Barbie. You can lay her in the sun and she gets tan lines. It is so neato.

One time, I took tanning Barbie with me when dad went to see one of his creepy drinking friends. I was told to go play, so I took my Barbie into this big field out back, tanned her, and let it fade. Then I would tan her again but in a different outfit so she had new tan lines. The drinking friend had a Doberman Pincer that kept chasing me around. I didn't like that dog at all. I like most dogs, but not that one. I'll just try to keep away from dad's drinking friend with the mean dog. Mom makes me go with him to keep dad out of trouble.

DECEMBER 30, 1977

Mom said it is okay to write about things in my diary that happened a long time ago. I want to tell you about when I was super sad in June of 1976 because mom had to do Basic Training to join the Air Force. She was gone 6 weeks to San Antonio, Texas. Mom was 26 years old and said she had a hard time with the obstacle course. She felt old because everyone else was 18 or 19 years old. She said the hardest part were the pull-ups and the wall climbing. Mom didn't pass that part of the test for a long time and dad got really mad at her on the phone and told her to do it or they wouldn't let her into the Air Force. He really yelled at her. I'm sure she was crying. I went to my bedroom and played with my Barbies for a long time. I like to stay in my room when dad is home.

Dad wouldn't let me talk to mom because we didn't have our own phone back then. We were staying with Fred, some friend of dad's from the Air Force and Vietnam. Fred's mother and teenage daughter, Rebecca, lived in the house which was way out in the country in Washington state, up near the Canadian border. I didn't like Fred because he was so mean, like dad. I am afraid to be with dad by myself because he drinks too much and gets meaner with each drink.

Fred and Rebecca's favorite thing to do was drive into the mountains really close to the edge of cliffs. It was fun at first, but Fred drove faster and faster. Rebecca laughed and liked it but I cried and cried because it was so scary. Mom wouldn't have let Fred scare me like that, even if dad got super mad at her.

Dad finally told Fred to stop but he wouldn't stop. That was the day when dad got so mad at Fred, they got into a real fist fight! They were fighting in the front yard of Fred's house once we got back to his house. Dad said we were going to leave and hooked up our camping trailer and drove down to California, staying in some camp grounds on the way.

We were in a dumpy trailer park in Yuba City, California, when mom finally got back from basic training. It was what mom called the "seedy" part of town, next to lots of taverns and titty bars, as she called them. We didn't stay at that RV park long, especially when a woman who lived there kept inviting me over for dinner. Dad didn't care, but when mom returned, she got really mad about it. She told me not to see that woman any more because it was really strange so and even went to the poor lady's trailer and yelled at her until she cried. I don't think the lady was strange because she listened to everything I said and seemed to really care what I thought. She was a really nice woman who lived all by herself because she said she "lost" her children, which is really sad. I don't know how you lose children, unless they died or were taken by someone else.

CHAPTER 2

1978: AGE 9

JANUARY 20, 1978

Diane, my best friend in Clarksville, spent the night over at my house last night. She doesn't sleep over often because of dad, even though he likes Diane because she tells him Polish jokes. Mom said that Pollack isn't a nice term, that I should say Polish instead.

All my friends are afraid of dad and only stay the night once and never return. I usually stay over with Diane, plus she has a swimming pool. Karen was my best friend when I lived on the Air Force Base. I don't see her much any more since she lives too far, which makes me sad.

Diane and I were able to watch television here because dad was at the Royal Oaks Tavern until late last night. When dad is home, he won't let me watch shows that I like except *The Muppets* because he likes the Muppets. My favorites are *Mork and Mindy*, *Battlestar Gallactica*, and

Banana Splits. Dad says *Battlestar Gallactica* is the dumbest show he has ever seen. It hurts my feelings when he says that to me. Mom tells him to shush, the show is for kids. I usually pretend I don't hear him. It is easier that way.

Diane and I made Jiffy Pop on the stove. I love watching the aluminum top grow bigger and bigger until the popcorn is done. You have to keep shaking the Jiffy Pop or it will burn and smell bad. Mom helped us make the popcorn because our stove has a pilot light that needs to be lit every time you use it. She also made some Hawaiian Punch and set up the couch pillows like a fort. Mom sat in the fort, too, eating popcorn and drinking Hawaiian Punch.

When dad came home, we were still up late, laying in our fort watching tv. Mom was having so much fun with us, she forgot to get dinner ready for dad. When we heard his truck pull up, mom and I froze in terror. Since Diane was there, he said he wasn't angry and told us to keep playing. Diane stood up and told dad a funny Polish joke. She is the only one of my friends dad likes because she always makes him laugh.

JANUARY 30, 1978

Mom's Christmas present from dad blew up this morning. The Mr. Coffee pot was half filled with coffee when it made a really loud explosion, sending hot coffee and shattered glass flying everywhere in the kitchen. We were in the living room so no one was hurt. It was a terrible mess and dad swore a lot more than usual. Mom had to clean it up before going to work, even though she was running late. Dad isn't working right now so he could have cleaned it up. I wasn't supposed to sweep the glass because I might cut myself. Mom promised that she was going to take it back to the store and get a new one since we've had it for only a month. That seemed to make dad happy so he stopped yelling. It seems weird that she has to return her own Christmas gift. He should exchange the coffee maker for her.

Dad works odd jobs here and there. I don't know who he works for since the jobs are "under the table". He worked construction for a few months, then recently took another job as a crack inspector which he thinks is so funny because it sounds like he inspects butt cracks. He puts smoke into pipes to look for leaks which need to be sealed. He says it is the easiest job he ever had and it's a shame the job will only be for a few weeks. Dad doesn't have a steady job like mom. He never has since the Air Force. He retired in 1974. Mom works at the Travis Air Force Base hospital as a medical records technician and brings home all kinds of fun surgical and medical things for me to play nurse, like scrubs, blank patient files, even an old stethoscope. All my stuffed animals have medical records, Aphrodite being my favorite patient. Aphrodite is a two-humped yellow camel mom bought for me while pregnant, so I've had her all of my life.

Dad has been saying for years that he will take the postal exam but still hasn't done it. He said he gets extra "points" for being retired military and having a back injury from Vietnam, so he could probably get a good job. Dad is very lazy and does as little as possible most of the time, except drink.

I make money by doing chores around the house such as dusting, vacuuming, and cooking dinner, even though we have a stove that has to be lit with a pilot light every time we use it, which I don't like to do since my cousins, Tracy and Jack, died in a fire when I was six years old. Mom told me to stop being a baby and just light the damn the stove, so I don't complain any more.

I also have a secret way of making money. Mom buys the mega bag of various flavored candy sticks from the Air Force Base commissary. The bag has like 50 candy sticks in it, so I sell most of them to kids during recess at school for 5 or 10 cents, depending on who wants to buy one. Collette is charged 10 cents since she is so mean and is a big bully to other kids. I hate bullies. They make me really angry. Mom doesn't know I sell the candy sticks at school. She keeps buying me the candy in bulk because she thinks I really like them.

FEBRUARY 3, 1978

I got into a fight at school with Collette today. She is cruel, swears like a sailor and is generally obnoxious. Collette's mother died when she was a little girl. I feel sorry about that, but Collette doesn't need to be a bully. She likes to pick on kids who are younger or are really shy or different. It makes me furious when she makes little kids cry. I help kids she pushes around by telling Collette to go away and to leave them alone. Collette wouldn't go away today and turned on me for the first time. I got so angry that I blacked out and still can't remember what I did. It was like my soul left my body and went to a dark place. The first thing I remembered was after the fight was over, Collette was on the ground crying, holding her stomach and vomiting. I really hurt her but don't remember doing it. I have absolutely no memory of the fight. Maybe she won't pick on other kids now.

My friends told me that I started screaming profanity at Collette, spinning my arms like a windmill and kicking like a deranged kangaroo. I've done it before at another school, but wasn't caught by a teacher so I didn't tell anyone. The other fight was also with a bully who was picking on a little girl half her size. I blacked out during that fight, too, only realizing I had a fight when I saw the other girl on the ground, crying with a bloody nose. When I come back from blackouts, I am always shocked to see that I've been in a fight. It frightens me when I lose control.

FEBRUARY 6, 1978

Diane, is a year older and a grade ahead of me, so she attends Clarksville Middle School. I go to Clarksville Elementary School. Diane's mom raises rabbits, kills and eats them, which is horrible. One time, when I was invited for dinner, Diane's mom told me I was eating chicken. After I finished eating, her mom laughed evilly and told me I just ate the cute black and white rabbit that I liked so much. I felt like crying but didn't want her to see my tears. Diane knew it was rabbit before we ate, but she looked so sad and ashamed about the incident that I couldn't get mad at her.

FEBRUARY 9, 1978

Diane knows an old lady in our neighborhood, Mrs. Krantz, who used to be an actress and drinks a lot of alcohol straight from the bottle. She scares me the way dad does. She is mean when she drinks, I think.

We wash her cars and she pays us $5 each, which is a lot of money. That woman always wears a white silk robe with feathers, a bottle of vodka in one hand and a cigarette in the other. Mrs. Krantz wears white high heeled slippers that also have feathers. Every time I've met her, she is very drunk, like dad, and dominates her quiet husband. Mrs. Krantz's husband hardly ever talks and when he does, he tells me he is sorry. He reminds me of Mr. Olson from *Little House on the Prairie.* I love that show and often pretend Pa Ingles is my dad. It would be nice to have a dad who was nice to me and loved me.

FEBRUARY 15, 1978

I want to write about some other friends since I talk about Diane way too much. I'll begin with Rhoda. Rhoda is a skinny little thing with strawberry blond hair, lots of freckles, and acts like a princess in her frilly pink dresses. She looks wholesome, yet has a colorful vocabulary which would get me in hot water at home. She doesn't have many friends since she acts like the most important person in the universe. Sometimes, while we are playing, I pretend that I am possessed by evil spirits and use a deep, rattling voice to frighten her. Rhoda runs away screaming. Diane said it wasn't a nice thing to do. I only do it sometimes, when Rhoda is acting like a brat or picking her nose, which is disgusting. My parents play poker with her parents once a month, so when I go to her house, I bring my Barbies. She's a Barbie kind of girl. Rhoda's dad is a prison guard and is incredibly enormous. He is friendly and gentle and treats Rhoda like a princess, picking her up, kissing her and twirling her around. That is probably why she thinks she is a princess. I wish I had a dad like that.

Theresa is another one of my friends, even though she is a spoiled brat. She is taller than me and has short brown hair. Theresa's family is quite wealthy and she was adopted at birth. They live in a large house at the end of my street. Theresa likes to talk about how she was adopted to play the pity card. I don't feel sorry for her since she has a family who adores her and gets whatever she wants.

Theresa's bedroom is overly large and obnoxiously pink. I am not a pink girl. People think all girls like pink, but it just isn't true. Theresa's room is full of dolls in lacy dresses which adorn her pink canopy bed. Theresa's family has a large swimming pool but Theresa hardly ever lets anyone swim in it. Theresa is purposely selective when choosing playmates. Sometimes she invites Diane and other people over and not me, although she knows Diane and I are best friends. Theresa does it intentionally. She doesn't have true friends but her pool parties are the best on the block. There is always plenty of food and games.

The last time I was invited to the coveted pool party, I wore a bikini and when I dove into the pool, my bikini bottoms fell off! Kyle was there so I was totally embarrassed. They all laughed and said that I had a really white bum. I had to swim to get my bikini bottoms which were floating in the deep end. That was so humiliating.

Kyle is the cutest boy in all of Clarksville. He is a grade ahead of me, in Diane's class. I love him so much. Diane said that if you really love someone you can't see what they look like when you try to imagine them in your mind. I can't remember what he looks like when I close my eyes so I must love him. Kyle has brown hair but everything else goes fuzzy. He has a pool, too, and a really beautiful mom who has lots of wrinkles from laying in the sun too much. Kyle has a poster of Farrah Fawcett in his bedroom, on the inside of his door. He pointed out Farrah's nipple peaking out from the bikini top. He likes me as a friend, but that's all. Mom doesn't like me going to Kyle's house even though I only go over there with Diane. Mom told me never to play hide and seek with him, but it is okay because there are lots of kids playing. I don't know why mom gets so upset about Kyle and keeps asking if he has tried to kiss me. I wish he would, but he only likes me as a friend. I think it is because

I started growing breasts so mom is worried. Hardly anyone in my class has breasts.

On the opposite end of the spectrum is Todd Mallard. He is a hyperactive punk who lives across the street. Todd is two grades ahead of me and goes out of his way to push me around and interferes with games my friends and I are playing. Sometimes his mom babysits me when my parents go out with other people. They don't want people to know that I usually stay home alone. Todd's mom and sister are friendly. They watch C.H.I.P.S and Laura, Todd's sister, is in love with Erik Estrada. I don't know why. He looks average and his teeth are too big and white. I hate that show.

Mr. Mallard's brother has a boat and they sometimes go water skiing on the weekends. I was invited once and was so excited to go water skiing. I was about to go with them when dad stormed across the street, yanked my arm and wouldn't let me go. He didn't give any reason at all. It was so mean that I cried and cried for most of the day. Sometimes dad is so unfair. I think he likes being mean to me.

MARCH 3, 1978

Today I want to talk about a man we used to live near named Joe because dad has been especially mean lately, making me hide in my room and write in you, my diary. I loved Joe so much because he was so nice to me and never yelled or made fun of my like dad. He had one arm because he lost it in World War II. I asked him once if he ever "found" his arm and Joe laughed. Joe could roll his own cigarettes with his one hand. He tried to teach me how to roll a cigarette, but it was so hard. It was difficult to learn and I never really got it. He told me I might need to know how to do it one day. I don't know what he meant because I don't like cigarettes. My parents smoke all of the time and it makes me cough. I don't like riding in the car when they are both smoking. It makes my eyes burn and itch. When the window of the car is open, mom's cigarette blows burning ashes into the back seat that really hurt when they land on my skin. My parents continue smoking, even when I get burned. They tell me to wipe it off and stop complaining.

I remember going fishing with Joe in Washington state's Puget Sound a few times. Dad had a fishing boat which wasn't very good because it only had one motor. Joe said you should have two motors when going out in the rough bay. I was too little to fish so I sat with them. It started getting stormy and the waves got super big. Water was coming into the boat and the plug at the bottom wouldn't drain the water fast enough. Dad and Joe had been drinking and fishing all day and no one was wearing a life vest. Joe said that I should put on a life jacket, then dad said we all needed life vests. They didn't have a kid's size vest, so Joe helped me put on an adult one that was so big it covered my face. Dad was trying to get the water out of the boat, so he grabbed my bucket and ripped the handle off to use it as a scooper. I started to cry because I liked my little red bucket. Dad said he would buy me a new goddam bucket but since we were sinking, he needed to use it. The one engine didn't take us in to shore very fast because of the big waves. Dad told Joe to get his life vest on since he only had one arm. Joe was trying to get his life vest on which was hard because he only had one arm. I wanted to help him but Joe told me to stay seated and hold on to the beer cooler because it would float. Joe finally got his vest on but dad said it was on backwards and he had better turn it around. Joe said it was so hard getting the life jacket on in the first place that he wasn't going to try it again. Dad said that if we fell in the water, Joe would be face down and the life vest would drown him. Joe said he didn't care at that point.

I was really scared and cried because I didn't want Joe to drown. Joe said he was old and would be okay. He said he survived a war so he would survive a fishing trip. Finally, we were near the shore so dad jumped out of the boat and pulled us ashore with the rope. The boat was half full of water, but we made it. Dad told me not to tell mom, but he ended up telling her after he got drunk. They were drinking strawberry daiquiris so she was drunk and laughed about it. Mom said it was funny that a one-armed man had a life vest on backwards, dad was scooping out water with my little red bucket and I was using my shovel while crying about my bucket being broken. She laughed so hard she almost peed her pants. I guess it was funny although I never laughed. I was scared Joe would drown because his life vest was on backwards. I don't know why it was so funny, but I will always remember that fishing trip. Dad never bought me a new bucket.

MARCH 4, 1978

I got Shultz, a dachshund, because my hamsters died last summer. We went to San Francisco for vacation. I love going to San Francisco and walking through Chinatown. It is so colorful and the food smells good, even though dad never lets us eat at any restaurant. When we left for vacation, it was so hot, getting over 100° every day. I wanted to leave the air conditioning on, a little bit. Dad wouldn't let me. He said my hamsters would be just fine. I left lots of water for them because I was so afraid they would die.

When we were driving home, I said that I couldn't wait to see Abbott and Costello (my hamsters), dad said "oh, they are probably dead" and laughed about it. I got so scared and wanted to get home as soon as we could so I could check on them. He said it was a joke, but it really wasn't. We got home and they had died. They had lots of water still so they must have died from the heat. Dad didn't blame me for their death. He always gets mad at me when something bad happens. Dad says lots of bad things are my fault, but not that time. It was his fault. I cried so much when Abbott and Costello died. He brought home Shultz, a dachshund, a couple of weeks later.

MARCH 19, 1978

Today is Sunday and I learned how to shoot a rifle. Dad took me out to one of his deer hunting friend's house and let me shoot beer cans off a fence. It is so rare dad actually does anything with me, I felt special. Dad even laughed and said he would do the drinking and I'd do the shooting.

Dad told me a secret. It doesn't happen very often and I don't usually like his secrets. This secret was good. Dad likes to go hunting and camping with his friends, but he doesn't put bullets in his gun because he killed enough in Vietnam. That is why he has never bagged a deer. Dad doesn't like guns and doesn't want to kill a deer but wanted to teach me how to use one safely. He said that I should never point a gun at anyone, even if there aren't bullets in it. Sometimes I forgot, but dad always turned the gun to face the ground like it is supposed to be. I didn't shoot very well at first but got much better after dad gave me shooting tips. He is a good shot. Dad grew up on a farm and he had to shoot animals for food. He shot down all of the cans that I missed. I had a lot of fun. I hardly ever have fun with dad. I hope we do it again soon. Dad was really nice and did something with me instead of telling me to go off and play.

MARCH 24, 1978

Mom made me go to the bar with dad again last night. This is becoming a regular thing because I can go into bars in California, as long as they sell food. They don't have good food at the Royal Oaks Tavern, mostly potato chips and microwaved chili. They have Cheese Puffs and Shirley Temples, so that is okay. It was mom's birthday yesterday and she wanted to rest because she was really tired. I think mom sends me to the tavern with dad so he won't drink as much. I don't know if it works very well. I don't like to be alone with dad because he scares me and I am afraid to talk to him. I like playing pinball and shooting pool at the tavern.

It was illegal for children to go into taverns in Washington State, so I used to wait in the car while my parents went inside to have drinks. I was really young then. Mom told me to lock the car doors and listen to the radio and she would bring me out fish and chips and a Sunkist soda, my favorite. Our old car had a c.b. and I liked to use it. I started to talk on the c.b. when they were in the bar. My c.b. name was Baby Bear. One time, I talked to a man who I thought was really nice. He was a trucker and said he wanted to play with me and keep me company while I was alone in the car waiting for my parents. He asked me where I was, and I was about to tell him when another trucker got on the c.b. and told me I should not talk on the c.b. anymore. He said never tell anyone where I was located. The nice trucker said some people want to hurt kids like me. He made me promise that I wouldn't use the c.b. by myself again. I was afraid after that so I turned off the c.b. because the creepy trucker kept trying to talk to me. I kept looking around in the dark, afraid that trucker was coming to get me. It was so lonely in the car by myself for what felt like hours. I cried a lot when my parents went into the bar and left me in the car by myself, especially in the dark. I don't cry anymore because I am older now. I didn't tell my parents about the creepy man on the c.b.

because dad would probably blame me and hit me with his belt. Dad makes me pull down my pants to hit me and the buckle sometimes hits me and leaves welts.

MARCH 26, 1978

We visited Walt, dad's friend, after a day of drinking at the Royal Oaks Tavern. I think Walt is his friend. I can't really be sure since they often yell at each other. We went to Walt's creepy one-room shack deep in the woods which has no electricity and the "yard" is littered with old junk cars, rusted metal farm equipment, refrigerators and other trash piled everywhere. A lot of dad's friends have junk in their yards. Everything had camouflage covering it, even the junk. You wouldn't be able to see the place from any road or flying overhead.

Walt was chopping wood with an axe when we drove up. He is a very big and scary man with flaming tattoos all over his arms, wears black leather pants and drives a Harley Davidson. Walt hasn't been to the tavern for weeks and still had dad's metal detector, so after a day of drinking liquid courage, dad decided to go to Walt's place to get it back. He said Walt shouldn't be so intimidating with a kid around. Walt was not happy to see dad and started yelling right away and asked why he brought his goddam kid. I felt scared since Walt tossed down his axe, picked up a large stick and told dad to get the *bleep* out of there before he got his ass kicked. I secretly wanted Walt to hit dad. I can only tell you, diary, because I would get in real trouble if anyone heard me say that out loud.

After Walt picked up the stick and threatened dad, I was told to go wait in the car. I could see them and tried to hear what they were saying. Walt wouldn't give back the metal detector because dad owed him money. I'm not sure why dad owed him money, except maybe for poker or some other gambling. Walt is a foot taller than dad and very muscular, so dad didn't stay long. He said Walt can keep the metal detector. When dad got back in the car, he cursed at Walt but he looked afraid. He told me not to tell mom. He tells me that a lot.

MARCH 28, 1978

Mom has been going to the tavern with dad lately. She now goes one or two nights during the week, meeting dad there after work and sometimes on the weekends. Dad goes to the tavern every day, even when he isn't working. He goes to the tavern right after lunch and usually stays until after my bedtime. We hardly have enough money to buy food so I don't know why dad spends all of mom's work money at the tavern. Mom doesn't stay at the tavern as long as dad since she drives her own car from work. She likes to come home and have dinner with me. At first I cried, begging mom not to go to the tavern, but she said she needs to get out and promised she wouldn't stay out late.

Dad usually wants us to wait for him before eating dinner, so mom has to call the tavern and ask when he is getting home. She has the phone number memorized and it's written on the tack board next to the phone. Since he comes home so late, I don't know why he makes us wait for him to eat dinner. It's some sort of cruel game to him. Mom usually ends up making me dinner and making another dinner when dad comes home. Dad is a mean drunk, so I go in my room when I hear his truck pull up. Dad gets angry about everything when he comes home. His dinner is cold. Where's Maddy? Why isn't Maddy waiting for him? He quizzes mom about her day, seeing if he can catch her in a lie. Mom doesn't do things after work with the other employees at her work because dad won't let her. She doesn't lie to dad when he's drunk, except if she buys me clothes or a toy, then she will lie and say we didn't do anything even though we went to the store. He spends all of that money drinking and gambling but gets mad when I get new clothes for school. Mom hardly ever buys anything new for herself because dad will make her take her new clothes back to the store because they are too short, too tight, or too low cut. She is only allowed to wear a little foundation and mascara. If mom's makeup isn't just right, dad calls her a whore and makes her wash it off.

The Royal Oaks Tavern is a little far from our house. It is in the next town over. There are taverns in Clarksville but dad doesn't go to those because one is a restaurant and the other one has some people from our neighborhood. Dad says he doesn't want our neighbors "knowing our goddam business". The Royal Oaks Tavern is dirty and old. The taverns in Clarksville are much nicer, especially the Silver Dollar Restaurant with the big buffalo head in the front lobby. Dad says it is too expensive to go and drink there. I like the buffalo head and the restaurant. We only eat there on special occasions, usually when dad's mom visits, so we've only been there twice.

We have real buffalo that live on the edge of town. They are so big and gentle. I like to go and see them when I visit Heather. She lives right next to the buffalo farm. Buffalo won't come over unless we feed them grass, so we get handfuls of grass. Clarksville is a really small town. I can get from our house to downtown in a few minutes on my bicycle. I go every day to the post office to get our mail. We have a mailbox in front of our house but dad always uses a post office box. I asked mom why we do that, and she told me that's just what we do. Dad doesn't trust banks so he has cash all of the time. It is kind of strange, now that I'm getting older. We have always had post office boxes for our mail even though our houses had a mailbox. I go to the general store after getting the mail and get a Pixie Stick or some other 10¢ candy. There aren't many candies that cheap. Sometimes Diane goes to the post office with me so we can go to the general store together. It's fun because Clarksville is an old gold mining western town and has huge old houses along Main Street. I wish I could live in one of those houses or go inside to see how nice it must be inside. They look expensive and the paint is so colorful. Our house is better than a lot of places we have lived before, which were mostly trailers, so I am not complaining.

APRIL 8, 1978

Today, dad and I stayed at the tavern for a long, long time. It gets very boring. I can only play so much pool or pinball and have to get off the machine if a grownup wants to use it. Sometimes men in the bar will play pool with me since dad won't play pool. He says it hurts his back. Walt turned out to be really nice to me and played pool with me today. I don't think dad was happy about that since he still has our metal detector. Walt bought me three Shirley Temples and taught me how to play pool much better. I told him I don't want him to let me win, I want to win on my own. Walt lets me go first because he usually clears the table in one turn, he is so good. That's probably why dad doesn't play pool with him. I think he used to play pool but lost too much money betting on games. Dad isn't very good at pool. The best part of playing with Walt is no one asks me to get off the pool table. Walt lets me play as long as I want. I usually play three or four games and then want to stop. Dad told me not to play pool with Walt again. If Walt asks me to play pool, I will since dad is afraid of him.

After dad was done drinking, we went to another of his tavern friend's house. His name is Paul and he sells junk from his yard. Paul is very old and doesn't have many teeth. Dad gave me my allowance for the week so I could buy something. Paul sold me six little bottles of real alcohol they sell on airplanes. Miniature vodka and whiskey bottles. I thought they would be great for Barbie. The bottles were so cute. I also bought a white ceramic kitten playing with a ball of yarn. I like cats a lot. The man said he shouldn't sell me alcohol but since the bottles were for Barbie, it was okay. That made Paul laugh. Paul is nicer than most of the tavern friends. We never stay very long so I wonder why we drive all the way to people's houses only to stay twenty minutes. It is strange.

APRIL 12, 1978

Mom had her yearly exam two weeks ago and two days ago, her doctor says she has cancer of the uterus. That is why she has been so tired lately. She went into the hospital today. Dad says I am not allowed to visit her in the hospital. It is the same hospital where she works, so she knows all of the doctors and nurses. I know they will take good care of her. Mom has to stay in the hospital during treatment and may be there for months. She could die from the cancer. Mom is only 27 years old. She isn't supposed to die yet. Mom said she wouldn't die but I heard dad talking to her and she will have to get a hysterectomy. That was a big word so I looked up in one of mom's medical books. A surgeon will remove her uterus so she can't have any more children. She wanted to have another baby, but dad had a vasectomy a long time ago so he couldn't have kids. I didn't know what a vasectomy was, so mom explained it to me. They went to a doctor about reversing his vasectomy a few months, but it had been too long so it wasn't possible. I want a brother or sister, but I don't want one to live in my hell.

I am so afraid mom will die, then I would only have dad. I don't have much family so I would probably be forced to live with him. Maybe he'd give me up for adoption. I would like it better if he did. I don't want to be alone with him.

APRIL 15, 1978

Mom had the surgery to remove her uterus. Now she has to go through chemotherapy in case they didn't get all of the cancer in surgery. I don't know what that is for sure, except it is medicine she gets through a needle in her arm. Dad won't let me talk to her and he won't tell me anything about the medical stuff. I understand more than he realizes since mom has taken me to work at the hospital and shown me how to do her medical records job. I went to work on the Bring Your Child To Work day.

I really, really hope mom comes home soon. I don't like being alone with dad. He isn't here very much, which is good, but I have to make my own dinners and I don't like lighting the pilot for the stove. There isn't anyone else around to help and I'm not allowed to invite friends over while mom is in the hospital. I usually have a peanut butter and jelly sandwich so I don't have to use the stove or oven. Dad hardly ever cooks and hasn't bought any groceries. I have to search the cupboards for food when I'm hungry, but there isn't much. Some Campbell's soup, but I prefer tomato soup made with milk and have to light the stupid stove, which I hate. We have powdered milk, but it tastes gross. I wish dad would fix me a hot meal, but I'd rather he stay at the tavern than cook me a hot meal.

The first night mom was in the hospital, dad asked if I wanted to sleep in their bed. I didn't want to at first because it seemed weird, but did since dad is rarely nice. I ruined it completely. I sleep so soundly that I didn't wake up when I had to pee. I wet the bed and dad was really mad and used a lot of curse words at me. Their bed doesn't have plastic on it like my bed since I wet the bed almost every night. Dad doesn't know that. Later in the day, dad was nicer to me and said that it was okay, but he didn't ask me to sleep in their room again.

My bed has a giant trash bag cut along the seams and stretched across my mattress, tucked in. I hate the garbage bag so much because whenever a friend sits on my bed, it makes a loud crinkling sound. That is another reason I don't have friends come to my house, besides having a mean, unpredictable dad. I don't want my friends to know I wet the bed. Diane knows, but she is super nice about it. When I stay at her house, I don't drink anything after 4:00 pm so I won't wet the sleeping bag on the floor. It usually works. Only once, I forgot to stop drinking at 4:00 and wet my sleeping bag. After that, Diane helped remind me to stop drinking after 4:00 pm. She is a really good friend and doesn't make me feel embarrassed about it.

MAY 6, 1978

Mom is still in the hospital and I still can't go and see her. I have talked to her on the phone twice now, but she takes pain medicine so she doesn't feel like talking much. Dad said they got all the cancer but are still doing treatments just in case. He says she will come home soon. I am still so scared it is all a lie. I'm afraid that she is not getting better and will die and I will have to live with dad all by myself. Maybe Gammy could take me in or the Scotts, dad's sister's family in Washington who are really nice and normal and live on a big farm with horses and cows that uncle Fred keeps but doesn't kill because he is a city boy who always liked cows. I wouldn't want to stay with dad by myself. He scares me.

MAY 17, 1978

I got into another fight at school today. I don't look for fights. There are two or three bullies in school who pick on kids who are different and that makes me very angry. Collette kept calling Mike "Squarehead" (Square is his last name) which really hurts his feelings. Mike is very shy and doesn't take baths very often. I've been to his house and it is just him and his dad. Mike is fun once he starts talking. Poor Mike was staring at the ground and crying because of Collette and some other kids joined in the taunting. That is the last thing I remember because I blacked out and attacked Collette. I've been in two other fights with Collette for picking on other kids, and each time I black out before the fight and come around afterwards. I have no memory of fighting, but I win every time. It is hazy, then I realize I am standing up with blood on my knuckles. That is when I hear the crying of Collette as she rolls on the ground. Each time I beat her so badly she lays on the ground crying. This time, her nose was bleeding. I looked around and all the other kids were staring at me. Mike must have went home because I didn't see him. I was scared, so I ran to the school bathroom and cleaned Collette's blood off my hands. No teacher said anything to me, so I don't know if they saw it happen. If they did, the teachers didn't care since Collette is so mean to everyone. I don't like blacking out and I wish it would stop. I don't want to be in fights.

MAY 21, 1978

Mom is home! The doctors that she works with got rid of all of the cancer. I am so glad. Mom said joining the Air Force was fate because she hadn't been to the doctor in years. The Air Force makes her get a physical once a year.

Something bad happened before mom came back home. I am so ashamed. I was in the bathtub, getting ready for bed, when dad came home and asked me to get out of the bathtub and come into the hallway where he could see me. Dad asked to see me without my clothes. He said he had never seen a girl before puberty before. I was so scared, but got out of the bathtub without the towel. I opened the bathroom door and felt so ashamed that I looked down at my feet. I couldn't look at him. Dad changed his mind and said he was sorry for asking me to do that and thanked me for trusting him. I don't know why he wanted to see a girl before puberty. I hope he never asks again. Now that mom is back home, I'm sure he won't ask me to do that anymore. I am so glad mom didn't die.

JULY 10, 1978

Diane's dad is the opposite of my dad and is incredibly kind and gentle. He is "New Age" and believes in pyramid power. He does yoga and doesn't have much furniture or a television. He has lots of pillows around the walls of his apartment where we sit. I think it is the coolest place I've ever seen. When Diane and I stayed at his apartment one weekend, he gave us both foot massages because he explained that all nerves end in our feet are pressure points which relieve pain elsewhere in the body and help to center our auras. He took Diane and me to see *Grease* at the movie theater. We were so excited. I bought the 8-track soundtrack soon afterwards. I had been pleading with mom to take me to see *Grease*, but she never did. My parents never take me to movies anymore. I wanted to see *Star Wars* last summer so much since all my friends had seen it. Even dad's mom, Grandma Johnson, saw *Star Wars* and told him to take me to see *Star Wars*. Grandma Johnson told him that every child should go see it and he should be ashamed of himself for being a bad father. After she left, he never took me to the movies because the lines were always incredibly long, sometimes around the block, whenever we drove by the movie theater. There isn't a movie theater in Clarksville or I'd go by myself.

My parents used to go to drive-ins in Florida when I was 3 and only watched scary movies like *Exorcist*, *The Sinful Dwarf*, and *Twins of Evil.* Whenever I got too frightened, mom told me to lay down in the back seat and not watch the movie. That was difficult since I could hear screaming through the window speakers which made me peek my head up again to watch the movie. We don't go to the movies any more.

JUNE 14, 1978

I have braces now. Mom wanted me to get them while she is still in the Air Force and has dental insurance. Mom thinks I am too young for braces, but it is free so dad told her to do it.

I am going to the same orthodontist as Laura Mallard from across the street. Mrs. Mallard told mom about Laura's orthodontist, Dr. Jenkins. He is kind and told me he will give me laughing gas every time he works on my teeth. Dr. Jenkins' assistant puts a mask on me, turns on the gas and I start to see the walls move like I am in an elevator. It makes me feel good. I look forward to visiting Dr. Jenkins.

While mom was in the hospital, I think someone noticed that I was alone most of the time and must have said something to her, because now, I have to go to the Mallard's house after school for two hours every day. I don't like going to someone else's house to be babysat. I'm too old for that and want to be in my own room. I'm used to being by myself. I always had my own key to our house, no matter where I lived. I even had my own key in Sedro Woolley when I was in second grade. I keep it on a red piece of yarn around my neck. I know how to lock and unlock the door and go to our house when mom is working and dad is at the tavern, which is every day. I keep my key under my shirt so no one grabs it at school. It seems silly to now go to someone's house after school when I've been walking home by myself since second grade.

I come home for lunch, too, since I can't have cafeteria food like the other kids. Dad won't let me buy the cafeteria lunches because he says that they are too expensive. I am embarrassed bringing my brown bag when almost all of the other kids eat cafeteria food, so I go home for lunch. Usually only the poor kids bring a bag lunch. I guess we are poor. I don't know, but we are not as poor as we used to be, before mom joined the Air Force. Anyway, school is only three blocks away from my house. Mom asks me call her at work when I get home from school to let her know I made it home alright. Sometimes I call her at lunch, too. She doesn't mind. Mom says that she is happy when I call. I have the number to her work phone memorized. I'm happy that my mom loves me even if dad doesn't.

JULY 15, 1978

I played with Rhoda today because Diane isn't acting nice. We got into some stupid fight so we aren't talking right now which is really upsetting since it is summer vacation and Diane has a pool. Rhoda and I played at the kindergarten and first grade school playground, which is only two blocks from my house. We go there sometimes because it is so close and has a better playground. My school is another block further for grades 2-6. The kindergarten school has a very tall chain-link fence around it. Rhoda said it is 7 feet tall. She is better at guessing measurements than me, so she is probably right. The kindergarten has only one entrance through a main gate that is left unlocked for kids to play. The kindergarten school is in the middle of Main Street through Clarksville. The street splits and goes around the school, so the road circles around the entire school to form an island.

Something really, really bad happened to us there today. We were bored and wanted something different to do. Rhoda said that we should moon the cars going by. I thought it was silly, and maybe someone we know would see us. I didn't want to do it but Rhoda likes to do it and said it isn't any big deal. Rhoda said to shake my bum when I pull down my pants. I didn't pull my pants down very far, only half way down. It felt stupid. We saw it in on Happy Days, when some kids used to "moon" people.

We mooned a few times (I still was doing half moons because it felt wrong) when an old green car with a peeling white roof pulled up to the fence and a scraggly man with light brown, shoulder length hair and a green army jacket asked us if we wanted a ride. Rhoda said we didn't need a ride, but the man driving said he would just drive around and bring us back. I wanted to go for a ride and was just about to say yes when Rhoda said no. Her dad works at the prison and he told her not to get into a car with a stranger. I said no, too. The man driving said it would be fun because he could take us out of town and drive the car really fast. I looked at Rhoda since she seemed more experienced than me and she told him we wouldn't get in his car because her dad told her not to.

To our surprise, there was another dirty, skinny man we didn't notice before who got out of the passenger side and started climbing the playground fence to get us. The fence is so tall, he was having trouble climbing, so he jumped down and ran to the only gate in the playground. I was really frightened then because there was no way for us to escape. We couldn't get by the man at the gate and couldn't climb the fence fast enough. Plus, there was the man in the car who started to drive around the island. I felt a coldness in my heart that almost made me stand still like a deer. I have never felt such terror. I knew it would be horrible if the men caught us. I didn't know what would happen, but it felt like life or death.

Rhoda grabbed me, which shook me out of my trance, and we ran toward the gate anyway, in case we could get by the man. The man on foot spread his arms wide, blocking the gate, so we ran to the other side of the building to hide. The original man we saw was in the car, driving around the school island, really slowly, telling the other man inside the fence where we were. Rhoda and I were terrified because every time we tried to hide, one or the other could always see us. The school yard isn't very big so it was hard to find a hiding place. We tried the school doors but they were all locked. The man in the car parked in front of the gate so we couldn't leave the playground. Both men started chasing us inside the fence, one man staying close to the gate so we couldn't escape.

Rhoda and I kept running around the school, away from the men. For a brief moment in time, both men couldn't see us, so Rhoda whispered to me to climb into the giant holly bush. I did it right away, and the prickly holly leaves cut us up until we started to bleed, but we were so afraid of the men that we didn't care. It was Rhoda's idea to hide in the holly tree. It was a good idea. There were lots of holly bushes all around the school that are so thick and tall, you can't see into them.

We stayed hidden in the middle of the holly bush, afraid to breathe. Rhoda covered my mouth because I was breathing so hard and the man might hear me. One man stayed in the playground looking for us while the other man got back into his car. The car man drove around the playground slowly looking for us. The man inside the fence had a stick and was whacking the bushes. He came around and stood right next to our bush and hit it with his stick, almost making me cry out in fear. He was only a couple of feet away but couldn't see us. The men were yelling at each other, saying they lost sight of us. The man next to our holly bush was so angry, he yelled terrible profanity at us, describing how he would hurt when we were caught. I held my breath. The car man parked his car in front of the gate again and yelled at his friend that we were hiding somewhere since he didn't see us leave and told him to find us. The man standing near our bush was swearing, swinging his stick and was really angry we got away from him.

It felt like we were hiding for a year. Finally, an old lady who lived right across the street yelled at the men to leave us alone and told them she called the police. The men got scared, the stick man ran to the car and they drove away quickly, squealing their tires through town. We waited another minute or two to make sure they were gone, then slowly crept out of the bush. The woman saw us and motioned to come over to her yard, saying she would keep us safe until the police came.

It took a while for the police to come even though they were only a mile away and didn't help much. The old woman got mad at them because they didn't try to go after the men and didn't seem to care. We told the policeman that the car was green and had a white, peeling roof. The old woman yelled at the police because they didn't write down our story or ask us our last names. I will never moon anyone ever again. Rhoda said she won't, either. The woman didn't say anything to us about mooning, so I guess she didn't see that part. We didn't tell the police about mooning cars. I knew it was a bad thing.

The police left quickly and didn't try to find those two men. One of them said they were heading up the road toward Reno and would be long gone. It seemed like a poor excuse. I was bleeding from lots of scratches all over my body, was really tired and felt guilty and ashamed about the whole experience, so I just wanted to go home.

Rhoda told me not to tell anyone what happened. I didn't tell my parents. They might get mad at me and say it was my fault and spank me for being bad. As soon as I got my empty home, I ran to the bathroom and cleaned up the bloody scratches, changed into clean clothes (I ripped my shirt) and went back to acting normal. I won't even tell Diane. It was the most frightened I have ever been in my entire life. I hope those two men didn't hurt any other girls.

JULY 28, 1978

My braces broke and the wire is sticking the inside of my mouth. Since today is Friday, mom made an appointment with Dr. Jenkins for next Tuesday. That means I have to go all weekend with this broken wire. I have wax to put on the end of the wire so it won't poke into my cheek. It makes it really hard to eat. At least I'll get the laughing gas on Tuesday.

Last night, that mean boy Jeff Mallard from across the street (I used to go to his mom's house after school but mom doesn't make me go anymore) came over to my yard when a bunch of us girls were playing Blind Man's Bluff. I was playing with Diane, Rhoda, and Theresa and mom let me use her favorite scarf as long as I was careful. I was careful, but Jeff came up and ripped the scarf from my face and threw it up on top of the stop sign so I couldn't reach it. I got really mad and blacked out like I do sometimes at school when Collette picks on other kids.

Diane said I went up to Jeff and punched him in the stomach. I kept hitting and kicking Jeff on the ground. Jeff ran away, doubled over, crying and puking the entire way home. That is when I started to become aware of my surroundings. I don't remember hitting him at all, but everyone said that I was great. Jeff is two grades ahead of me and I beat him up.

Mom came outside when she heard Jeff crying. She is tall enough to get the scarf from off the stop sign and said that I did good beating up Jeff. Mom said she never liked him and called him a "little shit". We stopped playing after that because I was exhausted from the fight. I always feel very tired after a blackout. I didn't tell mom about the blackout. It doesn't seem like normal behavior, so I don't want her to know. I keep a lot of secrets.

AUGUST 8, 1978

Our second Mr. Coffee exploded just like the first one. It started smoking before blowing up. Glass and coffee exploded everywhere, just like before, so it felt like déjà vu. Mom went to the store and got a new Mr. Coffee maker, for the third time. She said she would switch brands if she wasn't getting so many free coffee makers. Mom said if it happens again, she'll call Joe DiMaggio on the phone. Mom says he used to play baseball ages ago, but now is in the Mr. Coffee commercials on TV.

AUGUST 20, 1978

Bad things seem to happen to me. Last night, I went through hours of fear. I feel like a giant bad luck magnet. My parent's friends, the Garcias, are from Mexico and Mrs. Garcia cooks really good, authentic, Mexican food. I love her homemade tortillas. We've going to their house lately while my parents and the Garcias drink, talk, and have dinner while I play with Jimmy and Timmy. Jimmy is aged 9, Timmy aged 11. Timmy is older but isn't very smart. He is fat and quiet and does everything his younger brother, Jimmy, tells him to do.

Other times, we all go watch motorcycle races in an ugly dirt pit, while Mrs. Garcia cooks homemade Mexican food, so it is worth going to a dirt pit watching motorcycles race. I never liked Mexican food before I had her cooking. Mr. and Mrs. Garcia are kind, generous people. Their sons are a different story.

Last night, my parents went to dinner with the Garcias, so they left Jimmy and Timmy at our house. It was the first time I had been alone with the boys and the first time they visited our house. Usually we go to their house, which is sunny, warm and friendly compared to our drab, brown and beige house. The three of us were singing and playing when Jimmy wanted to play tag. I said I didn't want to play. Jimmy told Timmy to get me. They grabbed me and fat Timmy sat on me while Jimmy tickled me so hard it hurt. I didn't laugh at all but started screaming because I was so scared, like the time when the men chased me at the playground. Timmy started to cry and got off of me because I was crying. Jimmy turned into some wild animal and began to chase me through the house, and kicked my bedroom door open before I could close and lock it. He was so fast. I ran out of my room and jumped over the couch, tried to reach the front door, but Timmy caught me because Jimmy told him to get me before I exited the house. Timmy did what his brother said, even though he was crying, too. I was chased by two weirdos, again, and it happened in my own house!

I was getting so tired from fighting with them, screaming, and crying that it was difficult to breathe. I hurt all over from being hit, punched, and sat on by Jimmy and Timmy. I don't know what Jimmy wanted to do, but he had an evil look in his eyes and was laughing. Finally, I pretended to run for the front door but instead turned and ran as fast as I could to my bedroom. I slammed the door and quickly locked it. Jimmy kicked the door and it looked like he might get in since the door only had the handle lock, so I pushed my big yellow dresser in front of the door. It was heavy, but I'm strong, especially when I'm scared. I piled my heavy toys on top of the dresser so they couldn't get in. Jimmy was yelling at me to come out and Timmy was crying like a big, fat baby. I wish Timmy helped me instead of crying since he is bigger than Jimmy.

I stayed in my room for a long time, waiting for mom to come home. I was too afraid to go out of my room even when Jimmy tried to talk really nicely and told me he would stop. I didn't believe him because he looked so evil earlier. I should have seen his bad ways because once, when we were visiting the Garcias, Jimmy showed me his blue parakeets. Jimmy told me that he had other parakeets before and liked to stomp them to death. I asked him why he hurt his birds and he said it was fun. Jimmy threatened me not to tell anyone. I didn't really believe him then, but I believe him now.

Our parents got home and dad told me to come out, but I wouldn't until Jimmy and Timmy left. I could hear through the door Jimmy acting super nice, but his dad was angry at him right away. The Garcias yelled at the boys, telling them to go and wait in the car. I moved my dresser and toys, slowly came out of my bedroom, and told them what happened. The house was a wreck because of the hour long chase through the living room. Dad told the Garcias that we would never visit them again unless Jimmy and Timmy were out of the house and said the boys couldn't come into our house again. I was relieved they believed me. I hope I never see Jimmy and Timmy again.

SEPTEMBER 10, 1978

Last night my parents and I went to Rhoda's house so our parents could play poker I didn't want to go play with Rhoda, but mom said it could be fun and I should bring some of my Barbies. Rhoda and I were in her bedroom playing, and it was the first time we really talked since the playground incident. We were avoiding each other at school after the two men tried to kidnap us. Rhoda was acting nice and was in a sharing mood, so it was fun. Sometimes she can be cool to play with, when she isn't being overly bossy.

It was getting late and I was sleepy but my parents were still playing poker and didn't want to leave. I don't know how long we were at the Richardson's house, but it had to be at least 3 hours. Rhoda and I were playing Monopoly in her bedroom when we heard yelling and sounds like chairs being knocked over. We ran into the living room and saw my dad in a fight with Rhoda's dad. They were playing poker and I don't know what happened because I was in the other room. Rhoda's dad is really nice, I can't believe he would get in a fight. Dad probably started it after he was drinking whiskey on ice. He gets so jealous and doesn't like any man talking to mom. That's probably what happened. A man talking to mom can send dad into a rage. Mr. Richardson is very big and works as a prison guard so I don't know why dad thought he could fight him.

Just after Rhoda and I came into the dining room, dad was soon flat on the floor with his arm twisted behind his back by Mr. Richardson. Dad was beaten so fast it made him even angrier. While he was pinned on the ground, dad yelled swear words and said he was going to kill Mr. Richardson. Mr. Richardson didn't look very put out, said he didn't think so, and told dad to get the hell out of his house. He literally threw dad out the door because Mr. Richardson still had dad's arm behind his back. I guess he knows how to tackle people since he works with prisoners. Mr. Richardson turned to mom and me and said he was very sorry, but we had to leave, too. I felt so ashamed. Rhoda and I looked at each other and said goodbye. She wasn't mad at me because my dad started a fight. I guess Rhoda is okay after all since she didn't make fun of me or my family and didn't tell anyone about it at school today.

When we got home after the fight, mom told me to go straight to my room while dad cursed, yelled, kicked, broke and hit things for a long time. He said cruel things to her and probably hit her, too. I put a pillow over my head so I couldn't hear anything. Mom is good at covering up bruises. She put makeup on my bruises once before a school play. She wears long sleeves and scarves a lot even though we live in the hot part of California because I think she is hiding bruises. Last night I fell asleep crying with the pillow over my head.

SEPTEMBER 16, 1978

It's a good day because it's dad's birthday, so he'll be at the tavern all day and late into the night. I had to give dad a gift mom purchased and sign a stupid birthday card. Mom made me write "I love you, dad". I'd rather vomit into my Wheaties, but did as I was told.

SEPTEMBER 24, 1978

My head is still spinning. This morning when my parents and I were going to the store, I decided to bring my dog, Shultz. I don't know why I wanted to bring him and I don't remember taking Shultz on any car rides before. Shultz growled and nipped at me when I tried to hug him. I told Shultz he was a bad dog. I wasn't hurt because Shultz didn't actually bite me, only nipped in my direction, but dad got overly angry. We didn't go to the store. Instead, dad told me to stay at the house and took Shultz away from me and to the country "to live". Dad said Shultz should live on a farm where he can't bite kids. I kept saying Shultz didn't actually bite me but dad wouldn't listen. I miss Shultz so much. It all happened so fast that I can hardly believe Shultz is gone. I hope Shultz is alright. Sometimes I wonder if dad hurts my pets just to be mean to me. My heart is broken. I don't think Shultz has a home. I hate to think of him out in the world all alone. I can't think about it because I will go crazy. I wish I didn't bring Shultz today and wish I had a nice dad, not an evil, cruel one. What can I do? Mom didn't help and I don't have any other family. Gammy is across the country in Florida and I'm not allowed to use the phone for long distance anymore. Dad doesn't like when mom calls her family so she stopped. I wish I had somewhere else to live. I don't want to be in my life anymore. I want a new life somewhere else.

OCTOBER 8, 1978

My parents have lots of friends who disappear from our lives, never to be seen again. I can't do anything about it so I keep quiet. What else can I do? It's depressing.

OCTOBER 19, 1978

I heard some talk about a Vietnam war. I have heard of the country Vietnam, but didn't know about a war. I didn't believe Collette since she lies most of the time, so we went to the teacher because Collette wanted to prove that she was right, and she was. It was called a conflict but was really a war, Mrs. Rodgers said. I asked, why it isn't taught in school since World War I, World War II, and Korean wars are taught in school? Mrs. Rodgers said it was a controversial war. She said it should be taught, said she isn't allowed to teach it to us and I should ask my mom about it.

When mom got home from work, I asked her about the Vietnam conflict to see if she had heard of it. She said dad was in that war and has medals from the Air Force. He got the Purple Heart, a very important medal, but dad threw it away and said he didn't deserve it. Mom got it from the trash when he wasn't looking and hid it in her jewelry box. He said a lot of people got the Purple Heart in Vietnam that didn't deserve it. He keeps his other medals that he thought he did deserve in a wooden box way back in the closet behind his big pile of Playboy and Penthouse magazines. I had seen the small wooden box when I snooped in their closet before but didn't look to closely at the things inside of it since it was just Air Force pins, medals and some pictures of people I didn't know.

Mom got the small wooden box that I had secretly seen before and showed me his Master Sergeant stripes and medals and said that he did a good job in the war even though he didn't want to be there. Of course, dad wasn't home while we were looking at his Air Force things. Mom said he was a jet engine mechanic and got Agent Orange dropped on him in Vietnam by American planes and sometimes has rashes and boils on his neck and shoulders. I have seen the boils before and remember he went to the V.A. Hospital for treatment, but dad doesn't usually talk to me so I don't ask. Mom said Agent Orange was a terrible chemical dropped from airplanes that burns plants and hurts people, even though the Air Force claims it never used chemical weapons in the conflict.

It makes sense now, when dad came back from a doctor's appointment so angry at the Air Force for telling him he couldn't have Agent Orange because it "wasn't dropped" on anybody in Vietnam. He told the V.A. doctors that they were lying to him because he saw it being dropped from airplanes, the same airplanes he repaired. The wind blew a toxic cloud back to where dad's airport in the Vietnam jungle in the early 1960s, so that is how his skin came in contact with the chemical. Mom said that one time, when dad went to the V.A. hospital for rash treatment, a young V.A. doctor said he sees a lot of other chemical burns from Vietnam veterans that "weren't" dropped in Vietnam. The doctor also told dad that he was forced by the Air Force to lie to patients and the doctor didn't like doing it but had to or he'd have stripes taken away and his pay cut. That made dad happy to hear someone finally believe him about his Agent Orange burns. Mom told me never to talk about it around dad. She didn't have to tell me, I'd never talk about Vietnam to dad. He can be mean for no reason at all and he scares me most of the time. Maybe being in a war made him mean. So Collette was right, there was a Vietnam war. I mean, conflict.

NOVEMBER 1, 1978

I was in the Halloween parade that went through town this year. In addition to kids in costumes, there were four firetrucks, one that was really old, from the 1920s, with a hand pump to a water tank. For the parade, I dressed up in overalls and sat in the hay wagon waving to people and throwing candy to the crowd. My pants were rolled up because they were my dad's overalls and a girl on our float made fun of my hairy legs. She said all girls shave their legs and that I needed to shave mine. I never thought about my leg hair before since it is blonde and can barely see it. After she said it, I wanted to shave my legs.

I asked to wear some pink lipstick for the parade, which mom applied to my lips. She put some on, too, to look nice when I went by in the parade. Dad saw the lipstick on both of us and got really mad. I feel terribly guilty since I asked to wear lipstick. In the past, I've heard him yell at mom for wearing too much make up and telling her to wash it off because she looked like a whore. I didn't know what he was talking about because she didn't wear much make up and I know what a whore is, and she is not one. Dad sometimes tells mom to change her clothes because her skirt is too short or her shirt is cut too low or something like that. Really stupid.

Anyway, after the parade, I went trick-or-treating with a bunch of friends. It was so exciting. Diane, Theresa, Rhoda and Kyle went to houses together. Mom said not to eat any fruit or homemade foods because it said on the news that razor blades were being put in apples and rat poison in cookies. I don't think anyone in our neighborhood would do that.

I dressed up as a black cat with whiskers and had my face painted black. Kyle was a pirate, Diane was Raggedy Ann (like I used to do when I was little), and Theresa was a princess (not much of a surprise there). Oh, and Rhoda was a butterfly with wings. My pillow case was almost half way full of candy by the time I got home. We visited so many houses, that is why I got so much candy. I've been eating candy all day. I traded some candy I don't like with some of Diane's candy she doesn't like. I traded my coconut and peanut candy for Pixie Sticks, wax lips, and Milky Ways. Diane won't give up her peanut butter cups.

I love Halloween so much!

NOVEMBER 10, 1978

Yesterday, I fell off the uneven bars at school during recess. I was practicing my gymnastic pike swings, going from the low bar to the high bar in the playground. I learned how to do that when I took gymnastic classes on the Air Force Base with Katy and Karen. I can't take gymnastic classes here in Clarksville because dad thinks it is a waste of good money.

Anyway, while I was trying to switch from a backward to forward pike, I fell forward because my hands were facing the wrong way. I tried to turn them in time, but wasn't able to and fell right on my head and was knocked out. Friends said my eyes were open when I was knocked unconscious. They said I was staring straight ahead like I was dead. While I was out, I had a vision that I went to Heaven. I floated into a light that felt warm and safe. Jesus was waiting for me in a seat next to a big throne. The light was coming from the big throne. That must have been God. He looked like a bright light to me. Jesus came over to me so I asked him if I was in Heaven. He laughed, bent down and said yes, I was. He touched my cheek. He was so nice, gentle and loving. Jesus wore a glowing white robe and told me that it wasn't my time to be in Heaven yet. I will be in Heaven someday, but not now. I wanted to stay with Jesus because I felt loved, but he sent me back. When I awoke on the playground, I could hear my friends screaming. They had all run away leaving me alone.

I know I saw Jesus. It was so real. It makes me happy that Jesus is looking after Tracy and Jack, my cousins who died in a fire when I was 6 years old. I got up from the ground, vomited and went back to recess which was over a minute later. No one told a teacher that I was hurt so I just went back to class. I didn't know what else to do. I didn't tell mom. She might take me to the hospital and dad hates when I go to the hospital and usually won't let me go. When I get injured, I hide it so I don't get yelled at by dad. He always blames me, says that I am a klutz, and tells me he had a lot worse when he was growing up on the farm.

I have felt dizzy on and off since yesterday. I hope it goes away soon. It is yet another secret I have to keep inside. I'm glad I have this diary or I wouldn't have any one to tell my secrets to.

CHAPTER 3

1979: Age 10

JANUARY 1, 1979

I feel so empty inside, Christmas wasn't very joyful. It is like I don't have a home where I feel welcome. I don't have a pet to help me feel less lonely. I still worry about them. Diane's dad told me about St. Frances of Assisi who gave away all of his worldly possessions and moved into a cave, wearing only a monk's robe. He said that St. Frances got very lonely by himself so he befriended the animals. St. Francis is the patron saint of animals, so Diane's dad said I should ask St. Frances to look after my lost animals since he helps sick and wounded animals return to health. It was a nice story. Diane's dad is very smart, listens when I speak and actually cares about my opinions. He is a perfect dad. My dad calls him horrible names behind his back, like filthy hippy, weirdo, those kind of things. Diane's dad isn't a weirdo at all.

JANUARY 9, 1979

I am shocked and saddened by the things my parents have been hiding from me for all of these years. Mom and dad have been having "secret" conversations for the past couple of weeks. I listen in on as many of their private talks as possible.

I feel like my life is crumbling around me, nothing seems real anymore. My parents have been lying to me for so many years. I finally know what all of the secret arguing and discussions are all about. Two months ago, I heard my parents talking about my real father in Boston. I never thought about Jim not being my real father. I know they married when I was three years old, but I thought they just had me out of wedlock and were too embarrassed to talk about me being a bastard. There has never been a mention of my real father. Never. Not from mom, even. Who am I? Jim probably doesn't like me because I'm not his "real" daughter.

I have always known that I was born in Boston because grandpa and my mom's brother still live there. My real father's last name is Maskrey. I couldn't hear his first name. So Maskrey is my real name? I went through all of my old family photos, trying to find anything about my real father. Nothing. The closest I got was finding my mom's hospital band with her first name, my date of birth, but our last name was cut out with scissors. Why even keep the hospital band if you are going to cut out my last name? I searched everywhere for my birth certificate but couldn't find it. I have never seen my birth certificate, now that I think about it. Did they burn it? Of course I did all this searching when the weren't home. I'd be beaten with the belt for going through mom and dad's closet. I'm never allowed into their room, even when they are home. Jim has told me to stay out of their bedroom, except for that one night I slept in there.

My parents still don't know I've been listening. Last week, they were sitting in the living room and thought I was outside playing. I came in through the garage because I was checking the mouse trap to see if there was a dead mouse I could dissect and look at under the microscope. I really love looking at things under the microscope and wanted to see a mouse's organs in detail. The dead mouse was stiff as a board. Literally. I held the mouse by the tail and it stuck straight out. Mom almost caught me with the stiff, dead mouse when I came in from the garage, so I hid it behind my back because I know she would think I'm a sicko for trying to dissect a dead mouse. I could see I interrupted a serious conversation, which made me suspicious, so I pretended to go back out to the garage but hid behind the dining room curtains instead with a dead mouse in my hand.

I heard my parents talking about how I could get an Air Force dependent card if Jim adopted me so I could have medical insurance once mom leaves in the Air Force in April. I don't know why mom is leaving since she is the only one working. Since Jim was in the Air Force for so many years, he has medical coverage for himself and his dependents even though he is retired. I was horrified to hear Jim say it is too expensive to adopt me, but doing a name change would be a lot cheaper and they were practically the same thing anyway. Mom said that a name change and adoption were not the same thing and she wanted him to adopt me because it means more than just a name change, but Jim said he wouldn't spend that much money for something that is only on paper. I am glad he didn't adopt me. I don't want him to be my dad. I have a dad somewhere who might be nice and love me.

It makes some sense about Jim changing my first name since they were lying about my last name. It isn't really Maddy Tanner, it is Leigh Maskrey. I've been registered at all of my schools as Maddy Tanner. Isn't that illegal? Shouldn't schools ask to see legal documentation showing my name?

FEBRUARY 8, 1979

I feel like I'm living outside of my body. Nothing seems real. Yesterday, I had to tell a judge in his chamber that I wanted to have my name legally changed to Leigh Tanner. I didn't want to change my name but was forced to lie to a judge. I told my mom I didn't want to change my name. Jim heard me say that and grabbed me so quickly I didn't see it coming. Jim threatened and intimidated me. I had to swear on a bible that I was telling the truth. I was terrified the judge would see through my lies. I really wanted to tell the judge the truth, that I didn't want my name changed and my step-father was forcing me to do this. I heard Jim say that I should change my first name to Maddy while they were at it. At least my mom refused to do it. She said she named me Leigh and wanted to keep it. She stood up to Jim in a small way. I was relieved to keep my real first name because I've always hated the name Maddy because it sounds like a small, yippy dog.

My parents were required by law to advertise my name change in the legal notice section of the Sacramento newspaper for six weeks prior to the name change. Apparently, my parents already ran the name change in the paper and the six weeks already went by. I wish my real dad saw the newspaper and will come and save me from my evil step-father. We live in California and my biological father probably still lives in Boston, so he would never see the legal notice in the newspaper. Jim knew that. I hate him even more now.

My name change happened so fast, I can barely think. My entire identity has been stripped away. I feel like I am falling into an endless abyss, like in a horrifying dream. This isn't a dream, it's my life.

FEBRUARY 23, 1979

I live in a house of sand. Nothing is as it seems. Something weird is going on and it isn't about my name change. Mom answered the phone but was quiet as she listened to someone on the other end. She barely spoke to the person, covered the phone, told me to go to my room and gave the phone to Jim. He looked like he was expecting someone so he took the phone and was quiet for a long time. I pretended to go to my bedroom, but stayed in the hallway so I could eavesdrop. After a few minutes, Jim started crying and was on the phone for almost an hour. I soon discovered that the person on the phone was his biological daughter, Tracy, from his first marriage. Jim has four kids, but I guess they are grown up now, from the sound of it. I heard him asking about his other children. Some of his children were married and have kids of their own. It sounds like they hate his guts. I don't blame them since he hasn't seen them in decades, not since they were toddlers from the sound of it. He joined the Air Force and went to Vietnam to abandon his first family. That has to be what happened. That is why we have moved so many times, Jim only gets jobs that pay cash, and we always get post office boxes even if there is a mailbox in front of the house. More lies. I don't know who I am anymore.

After Jim got off the phone, he called Tracy a terrible names. Jim said that Tracy wouldn't have called him if she didn't need help. He asked how she found our home phone number and it sounded like a private detective found us. Jim asked a lot of questions about his ex-wife and if she knew where we lived, too. I guess she does now. Tracy is coming to visit within a couple of weeks to get some money, I think. She is bringing her 2 year old son whose father is an American Indian in Washington. I am shocked to discover that I have a step-sister I didn't know I had. I don't know if I am happy about it or not. There is too much happening too quickly. I can't handle it but I'm not allowed to talk about it. It seems that what I say isn't important to anyone. Is this how everyone lives?

MARCH 8, 1979

Tracy was supposed to come visit but still hasn't shown up. I feel like I'm walking on broken glass because I will get yelled at if I ask about Tracy, Jim's children, my father, all topics I have been threatened not to discuss on penalty of beatings with the belt. The belt beatings are extremely humiliating since I must pull down my pants and underwear and get beaten directly on my bare skin. It's always done in my bedroom with the door closed and mom never watches. She always leaves the room when Jim hurts me so she pretends it doesn't happen.

Mom's birthday and my parent's anniversary were last week. Not much to celebrate. Their anniversary is only 3 days after mom's birthday. She always forces me say happy anniversary to Jim and give him a gift and personalized card. I don't want to give that mean bully a gift because I wish they weren't married. Mom is so beautiful, one of the prettiest mom's of all of my friends, so she could have married someone better. I wish I had a dad who wanted to do things with me besides taking me to the tavern. That isn't much fun, watching Jim drink beer after beer. I wish I had a dad who actually worked for a living instead of drink away my mom's money. Jim does not allow my mom to have her own checking or savings account. All of her work checks must be deposited into their joint account. Jim scours the deposit and withdrawals on the account and will question mom on any purchases he feels are not necessary.

We used to go camping once or twice a month when I was little and Jim, who was more of a dad then, would take me fishing for trout and we would walk along river banks, splash in the water, jump from rock to rock, climb over fallen trees and hike through the forest. We haven't done those things since before we lived in the Philippines. I haven't fished for four years. Jim has only one hobby now; drinking. What is wrong with me? Why doesn't Jim love me? I feel hollow inside, like an Easter chocolate bunny.

MARCH 22, 1979

Tracy, the mysterious, new step-sister, finally came and visited us last week when I was on spring break. She was supposed to arrive earlier, but I think she was afraid of meeting her father. It was strangely exciting to suddenly have family. She was really sweet and gentle and taught me how to play gin-rummy. We played when mom was at work and Jim was at the tavern, although he told Tracy he was at work. What a liar. He didn't want to spend time with his real or artificial daughters.

Tracy has a little 18 month old boy, Sam, who stayed in Washington with Tracy's mother, Jim's first wife. Jim didn't spend much time with Tracy while she was here. I know she went to the doctor, which was really the abortion, and had to call a taxi to get there because my mom hated seeing Tracy and Jim was busy drinking. Jim gave her money for the abortion and the taxi, but Tracy was very upset that she was doing it alone. Even though I really enjoyed playing gin-rummy and Yahtzee with Tracy, she was terribly sad about not seeing her father. The last time she saw him is when she was three years old. She is one of a twin, the other is a boy. Tracy said her three brothers despise Jim and didn't want her visiting. Poor Tracy called her mom almost every day.

Jim left four small children, all under the age of six, without a word to where he was going. I found out that a private investigator had been looking for Jim for over twenty years and finally found him when they placed the legal ad announcing my name change. Jim's name was in the notice. That was one determined detective. Good work finding Jim through one ad in a paper in another state!

MARCH 28, 1979

A terrible accident happened at Three Mile Island in Pennsylvania. There was a partial meltdown of a reactor and leaked radiation. It is the worst nuclear power accident in U.S. history. I don't have much information about it except President Carter will be visiting the area. They don't know how far the radioactive cloud will go and people were evacuated around the nuclear plant. It sounds like a full meltdown would have been more terrible, so I'm glad that didn't occur. I hope everyone involved will be okay. I'm glad it's on the other side of the country.

APRIL 16, 1979

The news says that radiation testing around Three Mile Island shows no contamination. It appears that nothing radioactive was released into the surrounding habitat. I hope the news is right. Dad says the government is lying to us. That's not surprising he'd say something anti-government and blames everything on President Carter. President Carter looks like a nice man. I believe his reports to the public. He seems honest to me.

MAY 3, 1979

Things aren't getting any better at home. The household seems to be spiraling into darkness. Jim stays at the tavern even longer than usual and mom goes with him more often. Ever since the Tracy visit, Jim, or really mom, has had to pay half her paycheck to his ex-wife for back alimony and child support from the 1960s. Jim doesn't have a job right now so the money can legally be taken from my mom's paycheck. I think that is why the lawyer kept calling when Tracy was visiting. Tracy probably got a lot of information about us during her visit. Maybe she was a spy the whole time. Tracy was very kind to me so I can't hate her. Once Lynnette found out where Jim lived, her lawyers descended on us like locusts, forcing Jim to pay all those years back child support payments.

Looking back now, I think Jim had us living in a camping trailer for a reason. It explains why we moved two or three times a year and why he works at jobs that only paid cash; so Lynnette's private investigator's couldn't find him. Mom hates Lynnette with a passion and doesn't feel like it is fair to take money from our family to pay for a family that is already grown up. I kind of understand what she is saying, but mom shouldn't blame Jim's ex-wife, she needs to lay the blame at Jim's feet. He left his family without any income or money. That is a really low thing to do. I think Lynnette has been angry with Jim for so many years, she is finally having her revenge. I don't know how long mom has to pay half her paycheck. Both of my parents are drunk and angry almost all of the time. I feel like a ghost in my own home. There is no happiness anymore, only darkness.

Last night, there was a heated battle about selling our house and moving into a trailer in Washington state. It sounds like they will pay Lynnette a lot of the money from the sale of the house, but I don't think we own it completely yet. The financial arguments are nightly, although it might be solved if mom stayed in the Air Force for another four years and Jim actually got a job. I don't want to move from Clarksville because I have so many friends here. We have a real house instead of a trailer. I will miss Diane so much if we move.

There has been so much turmoil, none of which I can talk to anyone about. Mom said I can talk to her, but she goes to the tavern after work, and I don't want to talk to her after she has been drinking. Mom gets as angry as Jim when she is drunk. I've gotten into at least two fights recently at school. One was with Collette and another was with some girl I barely know. I don't think I actually fought anyone else since I tend to frighten them away with my wrath. I am quick to anger and have been blacking out from my rage. Some of the fights are over stupid things where no one is even being bullied. Mom doesn't know about the fights. I haven't lost a fight so I don't have black eyes or other bruises. I fight like I'm possessed so the other kids don't want to play with me much.

Diane hasn't wanted to play with me lately. It is probably about my frequent flares of extreme anger. I am so alone. I wish there was someone who would talk to me and do fun things together. I want to go see a movie. I want to drive to Reno and visit Circus Circus again where my parents gave me money as they go to other casinos and gamble while I watched the acrobats. I wish we could drive to San Francisco and look at Alcatraz and walk through colorful Chinatown and see the beautiful dragons. I want to go swimming at a friend's house and have sleep overs. Those things aren't happening right now so it makes me really sad and depressed. There is no escape from this torment.

AUGUST 12, 1979

We came to Washington state for a long vacation. Jim signed some legal paperwork for Lynnette for payment of back child support. We drove to the house where she lives, the place she raised her four fatherless children alone, so Jim knew exactly where to find her. We took my new dog, Asker with us. I named her that because if someone asks her name, I say, ask her.

My parents also took all of the money from my savings account to pay Lynnette, even though mom didn't want to. Jim said he will pay me back, but I know that is a lie since he takes what he wants and mooches off mom. It was money I was saving for college. I had $1,423. That is a lot of money saved from doing chores, washing cars, and gift money for Christmas and birthdays. That money was hard earned, something Jim doesn't understand. I shouldn't say this, but I hate him. I wish he would die. He drives drunk daily, so why doesn't he die in a car crash? I would prefer a single car accident where no one else was injured. Run off the road and down into a ravine.

While we were waiting outside of Lynnette's house in the car, mom chain smoked cigarettes. I don't know how many cigarettes she went through, but she got angrier with each one. It built up to such a crescendo, that she finally jumped out of the car, threw down her cigarette, and ran up to the house and tried to go in the front door, which was locked. I reached for mom to stop her but all I got was air. Mom pounded and kicked on the door and screamed at Lynnette about her being a bitch and taking our money. Jim came out of the house with a red face, yanked mom's arm, threw her back into the car and told her to shut the fuck up and stay the hell out of it. (Sorry for using the "f" word.)

Mom didn't say a word on the drive back to Sedro Woolley, just smoking cigarettes with the window down, so every once in a while, hot ashes flew into the back seat, burning my skin and clothes. They didn't seem to know I was in the car with them. I'm an invisible nothing.

AUGUST 15, 1979

Lynnette finally set up a time yesterday when we could meet Jim's other adult children. Before our drive to Bellingham, I got in the car and was told to wait while Jim took mom behind grandma's garage for a "talking to". I can only imagine he threatened mom, sticking his fat finger in her face, spitting angrily, warning her not to act like a jealous harlot again and to shut up unless she is addressed. Jim is all about not speaking unless addressed by elders and I've heard him tell mom the same thing.

I met three of the four of Jim's children. They are all married, except for Tyler, Tracy's twin brother. James (aka Jim Jr.), the oldest of the Jim's kids, remembers the day his father left home, never to return, wouldn't come visit us at first, but finally came after his siblings kept calling him. It was awkward to the millionth degree, lots of fidgeting and small talk. Jim, as always, told me to keep my mouth shut. I cannot understand his reasoning for not allowing me to speak to my step-siblings. What could I possibly say that would embarrass him? It was incredibly boring. James obviously despises his father, mom and me since he barely spoke and looked at me like he wanted to break my neck, as if he should be jealous of any love given to me instead of him, since love has been lacking in our household.

James' wife, Katrina, was the most friendly of everyone, and went out of her way to treat me kindly. Katrina did most of the talking when conversation lulled and has a daughter from a previous marriage, Clarissa, who was the only child present, besides myself. Katrina is an American Indian, from the Swinomish tribe. That is the same tribe as Tracy's boyfriend, who did not attend our dreaded get-together.

AUGUST 18, 1979

When we drove back up to Bellingham yesterday to see Jim's children again. This time, James didn't show up but his wife and daughter, Katrina and Clarissa, stopped by for a short time and invited me to stay the night with them. I agreed, which turned out to be the most exciting part of the visit. We spent the night with Katrina's grandmother who lives on the Swinomish Indian Reservation. It appeared to be part of the original colony of Indian settlement, with painted totem poles and wooden long houses brightly painted with stylized animals. It looked like an extension of the ocean with drift wood benches and carved, wooden objects everywhere. Her home felt alive. I was told to call her Kalkal (I am guessing how to spell it).

Kalkal doesn't speak English, and Katrina appeared to be almost apologetic about it. Kalkal refused to speak the language of the people who demeaned her ancestors, that is what Katrina told me. Her language is like a melody I never tired of, and Katrina translated stories of ancient rituals which still occur on the reservation, one of which took place that night. I heard hours of stories about her mother, and her mother's mother, going back in history because Katrina's grandmother is very old, so I think she is probably her great grandmother. I don't know where Katrina's parents are, and didn't ask since it wasn't openly discussed.

The house was a living museum, with Indian artifacts, art, drums, wooden carvings and old photographs. I stayed the night there so we could all go to the Indian Pow Wow celebration. I don't know a lot about the rituals and elaborate dances, but almost everyone dressed in traditional Indian attire, headdresses made of feathers and paint on their skin. I discovered they danced for the sacred salmon, some chanted while others played what appeared to be seal skin drums. There were totem poles depicting salmon and whales surrounding the fire pit where they danced and played music. We were there watching the celebration for hours, until after the sunset. There was smoked salmon to eat afterwards which was delicious. I absolutely love salmon. It was smoked on the fires during the celebrations. Animals and nature are revered and animal gods were thanked for feeding their people. The salmon holds a high position on the totem pole in their tribe because it is the main industry they have on their reservation.

I didn't say a word through the entire ceremony because it felt so special, I didn't want to disturb the spiritual beauty. I had a sense of the sacredness of the place and was very respectful, especially to the elders, like Katrina's grandmother. I will never forget that ceremony as long as I live. I could feel the spirits of their ancestors watching the ceremony and looking on with pride. I would be proud, too, to be a part of such a beautiful ceremony. I am grateful for being a witness. Whites usually aren't allowed, but Katrina's grandmother vouched for me and said I was still a child, so the rest of the people let me stay. I am eternally grateful she did since it was something so ancient and will remain close to my heart. I have never felt so much happiness and love as I did that night. It was with a heavy heart that I returned to my sad existence.

OCTOBER 15, 1979

The thing I feared the most has happened. We moved from my beloved Clarksville, full of friends I finally acquired, pool parties, trick-or-treating, singing Christmas carols to the elderly, skipping, playing, biking, roller skating, skateboarding, hide-and-seek, sleep-overs, week-long summer camps full of adventure and fun, picking juicy pomegranates. I couldn't write about it before because my heart is broken.

My parents made me sell almost all of my toys at a yard sale before leaving Clarksville. I didn't want to sell, but was forced to get rid of my Barbies, the Barbie Townhouse, my microscope, train set, my Easy Bake Oven, bubble gum machine, dresser, desk, and so many other things. I couldn't bear to be there for the yard sale and went to Diane's house to play. The money probably went to Lynnette. One devastating heartbreak after another. Everything has been taken away from me, my name, identity, home, friends, and possessions.

I will miss Diane the most. I requested to live with Diane and asked mom if I could, but she laughed and said I couldn't live with Diane. Her laughter was cruel because I wish with all of my heart to live with Diane.

For the last few months of mom's tenure with the Air Force, we moved back on base, into free base housing. I have been going to my second 6th grade school this year. I have moved to a different school almost every year of my life. Only in the Philippines and Clarksville I stayed at the same school for two years in a row. I went to two second grade schools, two third grade schools, and three fourth grade schools while we bounced around from one side of Sedro Wooley to the other, avoiding prying neighbors and "busybody's," as Jim likes to call them. I am beginning to see the pattern and the reasons for moving. Jim's drunken fights with neighbors, his demeaning rants and abuse towards mom over some imaginary jealous rage, overheard by neighbors, who ask questions and doom us to flee our home.

I remember one of the worse fights I'd ever seen between my parents while we were living in Sedro Wooley before moving to the Philippines. I was in second grade and had Ms. Johansson as a teacher, the sweetest person I have ever had the privilege to meet. We had a neighbor who owned a peacock farm. One day, our peacock farmer neighbor, Mr. Brown, I'll call him because I can't remember his name, said that we could park our large camping trailer in his garage. Jim yelled at mom to come outside and help guide him into the spot using hand signals.

Jim tried to get the very large camping trailer into that small spot but couldn't get it. As usual, he got incredibly angry, swearing up a storm and yelled at mom to do the hand signals better. Mr. Brown was a quiet and gentle man and didn't like Jim yelling at my mom in front of me and politely asked Jim to leave. Jim was insistent that he could park the trailer. Mr. Brown asked Jim to go home, but Jim wouldn't leave. Jim flat out refused to let mom leave either, yanking her arm and spitting profanity into her face.

Mom looked broken and near collapse, pleading with Jim to stop. Mr. Brown began insisting that they both leave immediately, but Jim continued to ignore him. It reached such a fevered pitch that Jim backed the camping trailer right into the corner of the garage and ripped a big hole in our trailer and dented the garage rain gutters. The trailer had a hole all the way to the inside because you could see the insulation and torn metal. Jim jumped out of the truck and began shaking mom and yelling at her that it was all her fault. Jim apologized to Mr. Brown, but Mr. Brown told Jim to leave.

It was really bad for mom that night. I went to my room, laid on my bed and pressed my pillow to my ears. Jim was incredibly loud and mean to mom for hours. I never got lunch or dinner that day because I was afraid to come out of my bedroom. I remember wishing that I could fly so I could go up into the clouds an be a better place. Even then, I tried to make myself leave my body, so I wouldn't feel the pain.

NOVEMBER 1, 1979

I didn't go trick-or-treating because I didn't want to go alone.

NOVEMBER 12, 1979

The darkness in me continues to grow. Since we moved away from Clarksville and met Jim's children, Jim drinks even more than before. He often throws up all over himself or in his truck. Jim has passed out in his truck several times since we've lived here in this short amount of time. He has passed out on the living room floor, too. Mom always cleans him up and puts him to bed. I tell her she should let him lay in his own vomit. I would like to see him wake up on the floor with vomit all over his face and clothes. I know Jim would yell but it would be worth it. He probably doesn't remember passing out and thinks he made it to bed by himself. He is as helpless as a big, ugly, mean hairy baby.

Yesterday, I rode my bicycle to Katy and Karen's house, but they weren't home and had to come all the way back in the extreme heat. The hill seemed steeper than usual due to the heat, so I had to walk my bicycle half way up the hill to get home. I got extremely dizzy from the heat, and decided to climb into a bathtub filled with cold water like I'd done before. The hot California sun has made me pass out, or feel dizzy and get bad headaches. I was so dizzy I had to crawl home, leaving my bicycle abandoned on the side-walk. I vomited and had terrible leg cramps. I started feeling better but had a blazing headache afterwards. I had to do it alone because there wasn't anyone at home to help me.

NOVEMBER 15, 1979

The days continue to be bleak and I feel like I don't belong anywhere. I finally gave my bird a name and I seemed to have jinxed him. I named my bird Mork since *Mork & Mindy* is my favorite show. I still have my rainbow suspenders. Just days after naming my poor little green parakeet, he died of a cold. Mom called the pet store, and once she explained the symptoms, the man there said it was most likely a cold. Birds can get colds very easily, according to the pet store employee. The cold came on so suddenly, Mork was only sick two days. It crushed me when Mork died since I took such good care of him.

I was sitting on the couch, finishing my homework when Jim came home after a long day of drinking. Mom always relays the news of the day to Jim in condensed form as soon as he arrives home, to get all of his anger out of the way. Jim was in the door for twenty seconds when mom told him about Mork dying, thinking Jim would have sympathy in his heart toward me. Instead, Jim told me Mork's death was my fault because I "probably didn't feed the goddam thing." It was such a hurtful and cruel thing to say that I instantly burst into tears and ran to my bedroom. It isn't true. I took such good care of Mork. I cleaned his cage, gave him fresh food, clean water, and let him out of his cage every day to let him fly around the house for exercise. I did everything the pet store man told me to do.

I could hear mom telling Jim that it wasn't my fault and he should apologize for saying such a terrible thing to a child. It isn't any surprise that he didn't apologize. Jim immediately changed the channel on the show mom and I were watching to some stupid show he likes to watch, plopped down in his own personal easy chair, and told mom to bring dinner to his tv tray and a cold beer. Jim is so lazy, he NEVER gets his own beer. He sits in his easy chair, yelling for me or mom to get him another beer. We don't dare sit in his chair when Jim is home. Jim is so hateful and cruel. I am not coming out of my room for the rest of the night. I have to hide in my own home.

NOVEMBER 20, 1979

Shock and amazement. Jim purchased an Atari system that connects into the tv and plays video games. I have Space Invaders, Pong, Blackjack, Starship, Video Olympics and Breakout, for now. I didn't really think I would get an Atari system because they are expensive. It was the best gift he ever gave me and it isn't even Christmas yet! I know Jim only bought it because mom needled him for yelling at me and saying I killed my bird. I put Atari on my Christmas wishlist to mom. I think they are $199. None of my friends have one.

Since I don't have many friends on base (Katy and Karen have a lot of after school sports so are quite busy), playing video games is the only fun I get in life. Time flies by so quickly playing Space Invaders. I am so excited, I want to get more games.

DECEMBER 1, 1979

Thanksgiving was complete misery. Mom decided not to spend money and time actually cooking a Thanksgiving turkey, stuffing, mashed potatoes, yams, and pumpkin pie, but instead prepared three turkey TV dinners, eaten on tv trays in front of the television, watching football that Jim wanted to watch. We didn't have any guests nor did we visit anyone. This year continues to be the bleakest in human history.

DECEMBER 7, 1979

Two things of moderate interest occurred in my dismal existence this week. One was hitting a telephone pole on my skateboard. I was skateboarding on the sidewalk when I hit a rock, flew off the board and hit a telephone pole. I think I got knocked out again because I was really groggy and confused until I saw my ripped clothes, blood, skinned knees and hands. I sat still for a while until some of the pain and dizziness went away. I limped up the hill to go home and clean up. It took a long time to walk back home because I hurt all over. I didn't tell mom about the accident. Most of the skinned parts are places I can hide them. She doesn't need to know.

The other thing to happen was Alice spending the night. She is a friend from my new school on base. While she stayed over, there were several events which were strangely negative in nature, causing Alice to cry, saying she brought bad luck. The things weren't that bad and weren't even her fault. The bad luck thing is just plain silly, and I kept telling her, but she still cried.

First, Alice spilled her root beer on the couch but mom didn't get mad at her. We cleaned it up. It isn't like we have a nice couch. Afterwards, we played Space Invaders and Alice pulled the cord too hard while playing and the game console fell onto the wood floor. It didn't break, thank goodness. After that, Alice wanted to go back to my room and play. It was a good suggestion because Jim could come home at any time.

We were joking and having fun again when Alice suggested we jump on my bed and pretend it's a trampoline, like at gymnastics. Alice did a really good front flip and dared me to try it, too. I was in gymnastics before so I gave it a try. I did the front flip but bounced off the bed and landed on the wood floor, right on my tailbone. At first, I couldn't feel or move my legs at all. I felt extremely panicked because I couldn't move from the waist down. There was a pile of pillows on the floor to protect us if we fell, but of course I missed the pillows completely. Mom opened the door and asked if we were alright since she heard a loud thump, so I said I was fine. I told mom I fell off the bed and laughed about it, even though I was scared inside and still couldn't move from the waist down.

Alice wanted me to tell my mom about being hurt, but I insisted that Alice not leave the bedroom. Alice became even more distressed since she believed I should tell my mom about being injured. I couldn't move for a short time, and soon a tingling feeling came back to my legs a little at a time. I had to drag my legs when I moved, pulling my body with my arms. When I could finally move my legs, Alice put her head under a pillow and wouldn't talk to me for the rest of the night. She continued crying because she was worried that I was really injured. I told her that I was fine and tried to cheer her up, but she wouldn't. We had already set up a place on the floor for Alice to sleep, so I crawled up into my bed and finally fell to sleep. I doubt if Alice will spend the night again.

DECEMBER 11, 1979

Another humiliating moment in our lives. In the middle of the night, mom and I woke up to a car horn blaring. It wouldn't stop. It was so loud it must have woken up everyone in the neighborhood. Jim passed out onto the steering wheel, pressing down the horn of his old pickup truck with his face. The loud constant blaring horn didn't wake him up because he was so drunk. How he could drive home is beyond me. Mom went to get him but wouldn't let me help, telling me to stay inside.

I knew when she got to Jim because the horn stopped blaring. That was a relief since it was so jarringly loud and totally embarrassing as porch lights of houses clicked on up and down the street, knowing full well neighbors were gawking at the drunken spectacle. I watched out the window next to the front door, grimacing as mom pull Jim from his truck and half carried, half dragged him toward the house, one small step at a time. I opened the door when she got to the doorstep because she was using all of her strength to carry/drag him. Jim had thrown up all over himself and wet his pants. It was so gross and smelled like an open sewer. It was obvious from the odor that he consumed large quantities of whiskey. I wish he would have crashed into a telephone pole and died or got arrested for driving while intoxicated. That would be a welcome relief to me. No such luck. Thank goodness no one was run over by the drunken maniac.

Mom dropped him on the floor of the foyer with a dull thud, trying to catch her breath. He is heavier than mom, so I don't know how mom got him in the house. I am strong, too, so I guess it is possible. I believe her sheer embarrassment of having the neighbors' eyes drilling into her back gave mom super human strength. I told her to take him back to his truck and leave him (I offered to help carry him). Mom said she couldn't do that, he would be furious in the morning. I said that he deserves to wake up in his own mess so maybe he won't be foolish enough to repeat it.

Mom had a determined look on her face and began stripping the filthy clothes from Jim's lifeless body, telling me to fetch clean clothes for Jim. I told mom to leave him in his filth on the floor. She still refused, fearful Jim would wake up angry as a hornet, and take out his embarrassment and fury on us. I don't know how much he hits her because they go into the bedroom and close the door. I hear yelling and thumping but am afraid to listen. When mom is dragged back to the bedroom in a fit of rage, I flee to my room and cover my ears or listen to music with my headphones so I don't hear the fighting. Jim is extremely mean to mom. She doesn't deserve to be treated so badly, especially for problems that he caused.

DECEMBER 14, 1979

I had a special event at school. We had a 1950's dress up at school today. Mom helped me plan my outfit earlier in the week. One of mom's friends at work has a sweater and poodle skirt from the 1950's which she let me borrow. She is a small adult, so the clothes fit me perfectly. Mom tied a scarf around my pony tail in back. I already have black and white saddle shoes like they had in the 1950's. Mom told me to fold down my "bobby" socks.

At school I won first prize for dress up! That made mom and me so incredibly happy. I almost always win best prize when mom helps me. Mom took some pictures of me in the costume and one with Asker, who kept wanting to jump up in my lap. It was the most fun I've had in a long time.

When Jim got home, mom told him that I won first place at the school 1950's dress up and didn't I look cute? Jim walked by me without looking, grunted, turned on the tv, demanded dinner and ended up falling asleep in his recliner after he devoured his food. It deeply hurt my feelings to be treated as if I were an insect. Crying, I ran to my room, changed out of the 1950's clothes, and put my headphones on.

Later in the evening, when it was safe to come out of my room again, Jim was snoring incredibly loudly in his easy chair so I decided to get my cassette recorder, held a microphone really close to him and recorded the snoring. Mom thought it would be funny because Jim always says he doesn't snore, but he does. When he woke up, we played the tape for him, thinking it would be humorous and make him laugh. Instead, Jim got alarmingly angry and said that it wasn't him in the recording, that we made it up. Why would we make something like that up? Jim yelled at me and told me never tape record him again. He didn't want me "spying" on him. Mom tried to tell him it was supposed to be a little joke, but he didn't laugh. His anger frightened me, so I went back to my room and cried, again.

DECEMBER 23, 1979

I keep thinking this year has hit rock bottom yet keeps surprising me by getting even lower. I have no self esteem and feel like I have only half a life. Last night we went to a Christmas party at Dr. Lewis' house, a surgeon mom works with. I was invited to also attend the party and I wore my best red dress. Usually mom and Jim leave me at home by myself when they go out, but Dr. Lewis was adamant that it was a party for both grown ups and children. I haven't been taken to dinner or gone anywhere fun for so long, I can't remember the last time. To be invited to a party was extraordinary.

It was a cheerful party with twenty or so people from mom's work, mostly doctors and nurses, and their spouses. Dr. and Mrs. Lewis' party had so many delicious appetizers, soda and adult punch. They had Orange Crush, my absolute favorite soda in the whole world. It was a great party, in the beginning. Dr. Lewis asked how I was doing in school. He seemed to actually care about me, which made me feel really good.

Jim located Dr. Lewis' open bar immediately and began mixing his own drinks. Dr. Lewis is so kind, he was happy to share whatever he had with others. I knew it wouldn't be a good evening after that moment. As time went by, Jim's voice became louder and his comments seemed to make people feel uncomfortable because they moved away from him, like rats fleeing a sinking ship. He refilled his glass at an alarming rate.

By the second hour into the evening, furniture was pushed against the wall to make room for dancing. I absolutely love dancing and know how to disco dance. I have seen *Saturday Night Fever* with Diane and her dad, so I knew a few moves. I was shy at first, but then people heartily encouraged me to dance, so I got bolder and really started to groove. So many people were dancing, not just with their husbands or wives, so Dr. Lewis asked mom to dance (BIG mistake). Mrs. Lewis stepped in and asked Jim to dance, but quickly moved on to someone else who wanted to dance because Jim told her flatly, “no”. Mom hesitantly danced with Dr. Lewis and he spun her around, which made her laugh. The spinning seemed to be the fuse that lit the bomb in Jim, because that is when he started yelling at Dr. Lewis, telling him not to touch his wife.

Mom stopped dancing immediately and went over to Jim but he was red with anger and was stumbling around, yelling at Dr. Lewis. Mom tearfully pleaded with him to stop and for us to just go home. Jim roughly pushed mom aside and took a wild swing at Dr. Lewis. The doctor wasn't nearly as drunk as Jim and quickly stepped aside, missing the blow. Dr. Lewis simply refused to fight Jim, telling him he was being ridiculous and not to be jealous because mom is a nice person. I wanted to hide under the table while this was going on because the party was so much fun but all the fun stopped and everyone stared at Jim while he made a fool of himself. I was horrified. Jim really ruined it for us.

Dr. Lewis finally lost his temper and asked us to leave his house. He apologized to mom and me, but said he didn't want to ever see Jim again (I don't either!) Mom and I were so demoralized that we both cried as we left the party. Mom's work friends are so smart and friendly, I hated to end it like that. I wish my parents could keep these kind of friends instead of the creepy ones Jim hangs out with from the tavern.

Remembering last night is making me cry again. I have stayed in my room all day today. I don't want to go out and see Jim and mom's eyes are red and puffy from crying. I can't bear to see her so sad. I am signing off for now.

DECEMBER 27, 1979

It wasn't a particularly special Christmas because of the lingering effects of Jim's fight at Dr. Lewis' house. Mom was still sad about the party because she works with those people and had to see them after the party. I already got my "big gift" of the Atari system, so I didn't get much else. I got Concentration and Indy 500 for the Atari.

I still get sad every December because my close cousins, Tracy and Jack, died just before Christmas when I was six. The pain lingers since we don't discuss it, my parent's pushed it out of their minds, so they assumed I did as well. It hasn't ever healed. They died December 14, 1975. It was a fire at their house. Tracy, Jack and I just saw the movie *Jaws* together a week before they died. The movie was so frightening, I hid my face most of the time. We sat in the front row because that is what little kids like to do.

After the fire, we went to Jim's mother's house where she sorted through all of the pictures of Tracy and Jack. There were burned photo albums laying on a sheet in her living room and mom tried to save any photos she could. The smell of smoke from the photo albums was so strong it made me sick to my stomach knowing Tracy and Jack perished in the flames. I still think about them every time I smell smoked wood.

Aunt Linda blamed Uncle Phil for Tracy and Jack dying, but it wasn't his fault any more than it was hers or my parents, who were all out together for dinner and drinks while we had a slumber party. It was the metal screen on the fireplace, it wasn't closed like it should have been, and a log rolled out onto Jack's sleeping bag. I can't bear to think about the rest. One stupid metal screen destroyed so many lives. I saw the police photos of their burned bodies. Jim had to identify their bodies and left the pictures on the hallway table. I was curious and looked at the gruesome scene. Jack was curled up in a ball, completely blackened. Tracy was crushed under a wooden beam, partially burned, some of her skin still visible. Her photo was the worst since parts of her were recognizable. My parents never knew I saw the photos.

No one discussed the fire with me. During the funeral, I began laughing hysterically, not crying, but laughing and not able to stop. Collin heard me laughing and told me it wasn't funny. I knew it wasn't funny, but I couldn't stop laughing. I couldn't cry but only laugh uncontrollably. Collin hated me after the funeral because I laughed. It wasn't a real laugh, something more primal, a guttural sound. I'm still broken up about their deaths after all these years.

CHAPTER 4

1980: Age 11

JANUARY 2, 1980

Mom took me shopping today, so I bought a pair of gray Moon Boots and a Kodak 1-Step camera with my Christmas and birthday money I got from grandparents. Grandpa sent a lot of money this year, perhaps making up for never calling to actually speak to me. I think he is well off financially, and it must have been a good year for him, so he shared the wealth.

Mom and Jim went out for New Year's Eve while I stayed home by myself. I don't like staying home by myself because it is so boring, I want to be around people, not by myself watching tv. Mom bought me Orange Crush, my favorite soda for New Year's Eve. I watched the New York ball drop count down hosted by Dick Clark but didn't stay up until midnight. A new year is just a gimmick. Nothing changes. It is exactly the same as the day before. I don't know why people get so excited about New Year's Eve. Maybe if I was invited to a party, I'd like it better.

FEBRUARY 10, 1980

I had a good experience, which is rare lately. Last night I had a sleep over at Diane's house in Clarksville one last time before we move to Washington state. Rhoda also spent the night, because, apparently, she liked me more than I ever realized. I never said goodbye to any of the kids in Clarksville because goodbyes are too sad. We listened to a brand new album which came out February 7th, The Sugar Hill Gang, over and over again. It is super cool dancing music. Diane told me it is a new style of music called Rap. It's way cool. Of course I didn't drink any liquids after 4:00 pm to be safe from bedwetting. Nothing is more humiliating than waking up in a wet sleeping bag and everyone seeing the stain. I don't like to talk about my bedwetting, I only talk about here, where it's safe from ridicule. My diary has a lock so no one can read it.

Mom and I move to Washington within weeks. Jim will stay with some "new" friend in Yuba City and work at the post office a while longer. For some unknown reason, Jim got a job at the post office just a few months ago, even though we are supposed to move. I think it is an excuse for him to stay in California longer. I am quite suspicious of his motives. He claims to be getting close to receiving full retirement benefits with the post office, so he is going to finish up the time required. I'm not sure how he can get retirement benefits when he has worked there for such a short amount of time, but apparently the government adds that time to time served in the military. It doesn't seem right, but I guess it's legal.

Jim plans to transfer to whatever post office we live near when we settle in Washington. I wish he would stay in California and mom and I live in Washington by ourselves. Actually, I'd rather Jim move to Washington and mom and I move back to Clarksville. I bet she could stay in the Air Force. She had a great job as a medical records technician. She also had potential friends from work if Jim wasn't in the picture. Without Jim, she would probably socialize with people, invite them over for cookouts or go out to dinner. I would really like my parents to have normal friends, or any friends come and visit. It is like sunshine when Jim is away and a hurricane when he returns.

FEBRUARY 25, 1980

We are about to move to Washington state, so mom and I have to completely scrub the Air Force base house from floor to ceiling. Jim never helps clean any of our houses before we move. The Air Force is extra strict about cleaning. Someone comes in to inspect with a white glove and touches all surfaces, checking if there is any dust left behind. They'll make us re-clean the house if they find any dirt. Lazy Jim always goes to the tavern when we start cleaning.

After talking it over with someone for work, mom has decided to hire a woman who will scrub and wax the floors for $40. The wood floors are definitely the most difficult thing to clean. Jim would get mad spending money on cleaning when we could do it ourselves, so of course, it is yet another secret we must keep from Jim. He must spend a lot of money in the tavern, so he should be offering to hire a house cleaner for mom.

I'll be attending a third sixth grade school soon. Who knows where, exactly. We have no definite plans. I'm leaving all of my friends behind. It is the first time I had real, true friends. Everywhere else it has been playmates. I met some great people who, I wish, I could grow up with. I think that is the biggest tragedy in all this business. I won't have life-long friends.

MARCH 2, 1980

I can't stop crying and am soaking the pages of my diary from tears. Jim won't let me bring my dog, Asker, to Washington because he said it would be a "burden" on the Gillys. The Gillys have two dogs, a cat and a guinea pig. They used to have a small horse but it died of old age. Annie Gilly, already told mom that Asker wouldn't bother them at all. They live on 3 acres and have plenty of space. I miss Asker so much. She was my favorite pet in the history of petdom. Jim already took Asker away. Such a cruel, hurtful thing to do.

MARCH 13, 1980

Mom and I moved up to Tacoma, really a town called Winder which is just south of Tacoma, and are staying with the Gillys for a short time. Jim was pushing us to pack and move quickly. I know “hate” is a word that should not be said to anyone. It’s not good to hate, mom says. I won’t tell her how much I hate Jim. I loathe him. Jim drove us up to Tacoma and left us without a car. He sold the green Gremlin so we’re terribly restricted with all the rules we must follow. We can’t go to the grocery store or anywhere ourselves. It’s humiliating! It is too far to walk to the store so we have to wait until Annie does her shopping.

The Gillys live about twenty miles from Bean, where mom was told by Jim to look for property, for some unknown reason. While Jim was here for the briefest time, we drove around until he found the “right place” to look for property. After he made the decision where to live, he drove back to California immediately. It is a terrible prospect. Maybe he chose that area because there is an Air Force base nearby with a large hospital. Mom may be able to work there as a medical records technician. Annie really wants us to try and find a house near their’s so we could see each other on a regular basis. I told mom that was a fantastic idea and that I would rather live in a neighborhood than way out in the country. Bean is so small and far away from everybody and everything. They only have a population of 256!

Bean has a grade school, but no high school. Annie told us the high school burned down years ago from someone setting it on fire and was never rebuilt. Bean isn't the best place to live, according to the Gillys. I wish my parents would use reason. Jim wants to live three miles in the country, not even in the town of Bean, where there are forests, a few clusters of cheap trailers, and run-down shacks. Jim thinks the area around Tacoma has too many people around so we have to obey his rules.

There is absolutely nothing near Bean, no zoos, stores, not even a gas station. The gas station in downtown Bean still stands, but they stopped getting gas years ago and use it as a car repair shop. The Bean Grocery store still stands in the center of town but is boarded up and abandoned. The only businesses left in the town of Bean are the Bean Tavern, Bean Bar & Grill, an ancient granary, a one-room post office next door to a one-room police station. There is one flashing yellow light at the sharp curve entering town. The town isn't big enough for a stoplight. Jim probably chose Bean because there are two bars two doors down from each other. There were plenty of cars parked in front of the drinking establishments.

To get to Bean, you have to drive through 15 miles of thick forest where there isn't anything but road because the Army owns one side and the Air Force owns the other. There are no stores, gas stations, nothing for those 15 miles. It feels like you are going into another world, a secret, frightening place. I could hear bombing and gun shots because the Army practices artillery with their tanks, setting off bombs and improving their shooting skills in the forests that surrounds Bean. I saw a tank and a few men in camouflage carrying semi-automatic machine guns, walking near the road. It feels like we are moving into a war zone, which it really is. A war practice zone. I wish I had control over my life. I wish I was adopted by normal people. I am so alone, no siblings, no friends.

MARCH 13, 1980

I actually did something fun which helped take me out of this dark depression. I learned how to ice skate yesterday. Annie dropped mom and I off at the ice rink. I absolutely love ice skating. Soon, I was able to do turns and skate backwards. I used to roller skate and skateboard when I lived in California, so I think it was an easy transition. Ice skating is kind of like roller skating. I asked if I could get my own ice skates and take lessons but mom says that we'll live too far away to be able to do sign up for classes at the recreational center.

What am I going to do out in the middle of nowhere? If I could have a horse, then living in the country would be fun. Jim already said we aren't going to buy property large enough to keep a horse. He said that maybe I could get horse riding lessons once we move to Bean. I already know that will never occur. I need to have activities to keep me busy. I wish I was old enough to live on my own, or live with someone else who cares about me. I have no where to go.

MARCH 22, 1980

Oh goodness, something crazy happened in the news. While we were watching the local news at the Gilly's house, we saw a report that Mount St. Helens appears to be an active volcano again, with some steam rising from cracks in the mountain and fairly large seismic activity. Mt. St. Helens has been a dormant volcano for hundreds of years. The government is evacuating everyone on the mountain because scientists believe the mountain will erupt in the near future. There is no way to accurately predict when it will erupt, but scientists are fairly sure it will.

Most people don't want to leave their homes on Mt. St. Helens because there is nothing definite, no real eruption has taken place, and no signs of lava. The news reporter interviewed people who were distressed about where they would move and for how long. I understand their predicament, because the eruption may be in a year, yet I wouldn't want to be boiled in hot lava! They interviewed one very old man named Harry Truman (not the president) who said he wouldn't leave the mountain. I will give a direct quote from Mr. Truman, "If the mountain goes, I'm going with it. This area is heavily timbered, Spirit Lake is in between me and the mountain, and the mountain is a mile away, the mountain ain't gonna hurt me." I don't believe Mr. Truman fully understands the horrors of dying in a volcanic eruption. The excavations of Pompeii show people twisted in agony from the toxic fumes and incredible heat. He may be boiled by molten lava, burned in super-heated dust, or crushed in his home. The people living on the mountain don't seem to be taking the situation seriously. You can rebuild your home, but can't come back from the dead.

MARCH 19, 1980

I like staying with the Gillys even though we sleep on the floor of their empty family room. The room is empty for dance parties because Annie loves dancing so much. She is petite, at around 5'2", but has an incredible amount of energy and really lights up a room. Fred is the opposite and is quite tall, 6'4" and very gentle. Fred reminds me of Baloo from The Jungle Book. That is him, exactly.

With the Gillys, we have dinner together like a real family and watch TV together afterwards. Jill, mom and I enjoy watching M.A.S.H. Fred teases us about watching M.A.S.H. because he hates the show saying it's too liberal. He finally began to like the show after being "forced" to watch it by the "women". Jill teased her dad by saying how much she loved MASHed potatoes, and MASHed pears, and other things MASHED.

I have been feeling empty inside again. For the past week, I've been having another bout of bed wetting, or carpet wetting, in this case. Urine soaked through my sleeping bag onto the carpet, which I tried to hide by folding my sleeping bag on top of it, but mom discovered my ploy. Mom dried the spot with a space heater while Annie and

Fred were at work, then put down a plastic trash bag on the floor, underneath my sleeping bag. Mom sleeps on the couch now because the ground was causing her back pain. I think I have been drinking liquids too late at night, at 7:00 pm when we eat dinner. I need to stop drinking fluids after 4:00 pm. We'll see how that goes. It should work because it has in the past. A doctor once told mom that bedwetting is treatable and is usually caused by stress and anxiety. Mom chose not to seek treatment. That was three years ago.

APRIL 4, 1980

I feel like a fighter who keeps getting up only to be knocked down, again and again. Jim is forcing us move out of the Gilly's house. He strongly recommended mom and I move into an apartment so we don't "impose" on them. The Gillys honestly don't want us to leave, they pleaded for us to stay, but Jim insisted, via the telephone, that we were imposing on them. If Jim left us with a car, we wouldn't have been as much of an imposition. Mom buys food for us, so we aren't mooching off the Gillys for everything. I've been acting polite the entire time we have stayed here. In fact, I think they enjoy having us stay as guests. It is another one of Jim's sadistic demands to torture and control us. I know mom could get a job as a medical records technician. There are hospitals in every city where she could work. Mom could take control of her own life if she only got a job and had some confidence in herself.

Unfortunately, we moved our few, pitiful belongings into a run down efficiency apartment in a seedy part of Tacoma because that is all we could afford with the money Jim sends us. Annie nearly cried when she dropped us at the apartment since it is in the worst part of town, asking mom if she would change her mind. Mom stubbornly kept to Jim's demands, even though he isn't here to see the filth in which we live.

There is a horrid grade school nearby where mom is going to send me to finish the year, which is odd, because there was a school near the Gilly's house and I haven't been going to school for a while. Why send me now? The school yard is overgrown with weeds, the chain link fence is cut and bent in some places, paint is peeling from the building, it has only four swings, a couple monkey bars and two teeter totters which look more tottered than teetered. I am severely dreading attending that school. It is a block away so I will walk. Again, we have no car, so we are trapped like rats in this run down misery.

APRIL 8, 1980

Fear and depression rule my life. I'm constantly anxious and feel sick to my stomach. I now attend that filthy school in south Tacoma. It is as dark, dirty, and graffiti ridden on the inside as the outside. Large groups of mostly young Hispanic men gather up and down the block and play their boom boxes so loudly it shakes the apartment windows. It goes on throughout the day and night. They like to rev up their cars, even when they don't drive anywhere. The creepy men whistling and staring at me every time I leave for school and walk home bother me. They leer at me and I am eleven years old! I don't feel safe walking to school, and mom just stays in the apartment and won't walk to school with me. It is unbelievable she lets me walk through the rough gang of people to get to school by myself. We are living in a city slum, some place which is unfamiliar territory.

During my first day at the grungy middle school, a girl who I thought was a boy (but maybe a boy who looks like a girl, I'm not quite sure) started smoking a joint right in class. Even his/her name was confusing, Terry. I've met boys and girls named Terry. I've smelled marijuana before. I know I smelled it coming from Jill Gilly's room. The boy/girl who smoked the joint in class was asked to leave school immediately. He/she created a terrible scene before leaving the classroom. He/she threw a chair at the window, which just bounced off and didn't break the window because it was plexiglass, flipped over desks and yelled obscenities at the teacher. It was the most frightening way to begin a new school! We obviously live on the wrong side of the tracks.

The principal came and talked to me to see if I wanted to go on a week-long school camp in two weeks. Uh, no thank you. She said it would be fun. I'm afraid to see what kind of fun it would entail. To be honest, I've been so nervous and afraid of bedwetting, that is the main reason I declined. Also, I literally know no one at that school No one is friendly.

That dirty old school is only a block and half away from our apartment, but it feels like walking through three miles of land mines. It is creepy, for sure. Teenagers standing in small groups after school, smoking cigarettes and joints. Those groups are okay, it's the lone teenage boy that frightens me the most. The way boys stare at me makes my skin crawl. I can't help it if I grew breasts in sixth grade. I hold my jacket in front of me to cover my breasts.

Our apartment walls are so thin we hear a Hispanic family fighting every night. It is frustrating because they argue only in Spanish so we can't eavesdrop.

APRIL 15, 1980

I'm relieved to say that the constantly arguing Hispanics who lived next door got evicted. They played music so loudly, at 11:00 pm and later, every night. They hung out in the parking lot all day which made it uncomfortable to go outside. They always stopped talking and watched me when I walked by. I really didn't feel safe, especially since they were always drinking beer. I think six people lived in their efficiency apartment. I also caught them syphoning someone's gas from a car when I left for school. I turned away and pretended I not to see them and never told anyone about the incident. It wasn't our car because we don't have one.

Within a week of the Hispanic family moving out, a large Black family moved in. They are just the same as the Hispanics, hanging out in the parking lot, drinking and smoking all day, playing loud music all night, and getting into arguments. They also have nightly fights, making it nerve-racking and difficult to watch tv. The Hispanics couldn't speak English so we never knew what their arguments were about. Our new neighbors speak English so we can understand everything they are saying. A lot of "I'll kill you, mother fucker", "I'll get my goddam gun", and "I'll fuck yo ass up." Some frightening altercations. The men look at me in a lecherous way, too. Why do men stare at me? I am just a kid. I am fairly tall for my age, so they probably think I'm older than I am.

While walking home from school one day, a strange, swarthy man tried to lure me into his car. He drove his car really slowly beside me, talking to me with his window down, trying to convince me to go for a ride in his fast car. I told him no thank you (I am at least polite about it). I began to walk faster when the man got angry and told me to get into his car. That is when I started running. He followed me so I yelled at him to leave me alone. He wouldn't. I was trapped on the sidewalk between him and the tall chain link fence around the school. I was only half a block from the apartment, but I didn't want him to know where I lived, so I kept running until I got to the hole in the fence. I knew it was there since I walk by it every day. I leapt through the hole and ran back across the school yard, running toward some houses that are opposite our apartment. I pretended that I lived there. Once I got into the neighborhood, I hid, then peeked around the corner to see if the car was still there. It wasn't, but I didn't take any chances after that horrible experience in Clarksville. I snuck behind cars and bushes and made my way back to our apartment.

The only sunshine in my cloudy life is mom and I love to watch science fiction and monster movies, eat popcorn, and sleep on the convertible couch in our sleeping bags. That part of living here is fun, being without Jim. Mom wasn't very fun at the Gilly's house. She was quiet and sulky, but here she acts happy, which is twisted since we live in the ghetto. Sometimes we bake cookies. We never go out of our apartment unless we have to. We don't see the Gillys anymore, either, because Jim doesn't want us to bother them. Mom buys some basic food from a convenience store nearby, so meals are cereal, peanut butter and jelly, macaroni and cheese, and hot dogs.

APRIL 18, 1980

I have only a few weeks left of sixth grade before we can move from this horrible, run-down apartment. Jim came up for a short visit to bring more house supplies: pots and pans, some more clothes, a few small pieces of furniture we have to shove into the corner so we can walk around. The best part is he's leaving us a car. A beat up Mercury something which blends in nicely in our neighborhood. Unfortunately, mom and Jim purchased an acre and a half of land in Bean. There isn't a spot for a mobile home, so they'll hire someone to clear part of the land. Jim is taking the train back down to Yuba City immediately (hurray). Mom and I were given an assignment while Jim is in California, still working at a post office. We will be selecting a double wide mobile home. I suggested that we could build a house instead, even a small one, but mom likes the "extras" a mobile home offers. What could a trailer possibly have to offer? I'd much rather live in a two bedroom cabin than a more spacious double wide trailer. I strongly dislike living in mobile homes because people look down on us, as if we were disposable people. The cabin idea was quickly cut down, even after I mentioned Jim has construction experience, and I know there are pre-fabricated wooden houses out there to be purchased. That would require actual work for Jim, so we mustn't have that.

Before he left, Fred Gilly called Jim at our apartment to tell him that we could come back and stay at their home, but Jim refused, saying that I was already enrolled in a school and couldn't leave now. Did Jim even look at the school? Leaving it would be a pleasure. It sounded as if Fred said some bad words to Jim about making us stay in this apartment. I'm glad he stuck up for us, even if it didn't work. It sounded like Fred hung up on Jim.

APRIL 25, 1980

Today is a joyous day! Jim came up for his weekly visit to bring more boxes and returned with Asker! Jim gave Asker permanently to Leonard, a man from the post office. Leonard has a house in the country, so I suppose taking Asker to the country was true. Leonard planned on keeping Asker long enough for us to get settled in Washington, then return her to me. Jim didn't agree with that plan and was angry at Leonard for defying him. Jim didn't want to take Asker and Leonard must have said some choice words to a man who would take away a girl's dog.

After a long silence, mom opened a second pack of cigarettes which sparked Jim to start unloading furniture and boxes he brought in the truck. Boxes are stacked to the ceiling and a path has been made to the bathroom and kitchen. The efficiency apartment is almost filled, leaving little room for mom and I to live.

It is quite uncomfortable when Jim visits because he is always snooping around, looking at everything in our small apartment. I don't know what he is looking for, but he didn't find anything. We don't have much. Like mom would write love letters to some man. That would never happen.

Mom kept the beer flowing into Jim's fat belly to keep him satisfied. Jim actually said that our apartment wasn't that bad. What planet does he come from? Paper thin walls, men hanging out in the parking lot, drinking and playing boom boxes all day and night, yelling and fighting. Oh, yes, this is a wonderful apartment, thank you very much.

Now I have Asker, so I don't care if Jim is drunk and obnoxious. Maybe he would like to hang with our neighbors in the parking lot. I wish he would go out there and pick on them for a while. I don't think they would take his poor attitude very well.

APRIL 27, 1980

I am so anxious all of the time my stomach hurts, like the time I had the ulcer. Jim dragged us to the mobile home dealership to finalize the purchase of a lovely dog doo brown double wide trailer. Mom and I selected the trailer ahead of time but it needed the stamp of approval by Jim. Forms were signed, cash exchanged, and a date was scheduled for delivery to Bean. We had to drive way out to Bean in order to get the land prepared for the double wide monstrosity. The mayor, who also clears property for a living with his bulldozer, readily agreed to do the job, cash only. His name is Dick. His name sums up the town of Bean.

While Dick and Jim exchanged money and beer, Jim jabbing his fat finger at which trees would stay, I walked around the property, picking flowers and saying sorry to the gorgeous wildflowers which will soon be bulldozed over. There are so many colors of flowers: red, yellow, orange, gold, purple. I picked bouquets to make beautiful flower arrangements in our dismal apartment. Poor birds and squirrels, settled peacefully in their nests amid trees which soon will be annihilated. I boldly spoke up that only the trees for the trailer should be removed, and leave the rest standing. Dick and Jim looked at me like I was speaking Chinese.

While my parents were walking and marking the property perimeter, Asker and I wandered into the field behind our property and discovered an old, long-abandoned lumber mill. It was deserted and lonely and had a creepy feeling. It was really fun looking at all of the old equipment but it was strangely quiet. There was no breeze, no crickets, no frogs, nothing. I heard a lot of nature sounds when I walked to the mill, and there had been a nice breeze, but all went silent at the deserted mill.

A dark shadow came over my heart, a heaviness, a feeling of dread, like something terrible happened at that mill years ago. It felt like ghosts were closing in on me from all sides, pressing me, pulling me. Asker felt it too because she darted away and into the thick bushes. I called for her, tears streaming down my face, terrified I would lose my dog again. I was also frightened of the oppressive air and the feeling of a presence, so I ran as fast as I could back up the hill where our property was located. I decided I could look for Asker after returning to mom. I ran heedlessly with fear of being pursued by some angry spirit. I ran so fast that I didn't pay attention to the blackberry brambles, scratching me with their thorns, and ran head long into a patch of nettles, setting my skin on fire. The nettles burned my flesh but I didn't dare stop or look behind me because I felt the presence of something or someone.

When I returned to mom, I was crying about my ordeal and the pain I was suffering from my scratches and nettles. I was near hysterics over losing Asker, but just then, Asker walked out of the bushes. I couldn't believe it.

Mom pulled off some of the nettle clusters from my face and arms and tried to wash off the wounds the best she could with some Kleenex and a little water. It didn't stop the burning of the nettles. It felt like bee stings all over my face, neck and arms. The breeze returned, the insect and animal noises began their humming again. I was safe again.

MAY 2, 1980

Sixth grade ended rather abruptly and unexpectedly. The school announced it was now the end of the school year, closed its doors and cleared out. It seems a bit earlier than previously stated. Perhaps there were one too many assaults by students on teachers and they decided there had been enough completed school days, the students wouldn't make anything of their lives anyway, and called it a day. It's rather odd and unfair to those children who want to learn. Admittedly, there hasn't been much learning at this school, everyone is more on the defensive and trying to survive the day.

I suppose it is good that our property in Bean was cleared for the double wide mobile home. Mom told me not to call it a trailer, even though it is a trailer. The mobile home will be delivered to the property tomorrow. They'll put it up on concrete blocks. My parents purchased an aluminum "skirt" that goes around the bottom of the trailer to cover the cinder blocks. It doesn't fool anyone because we all know it's still a trailer. It won't look quite as junky as a trailer where you can see trash underneath.

The only good thing about getting the trailer is that we'll be moving out of this flea-ridden apartment. I was horrified to see the total destruction of almost all trees, plants and flowers on our property. Dick went overboard on the clearing, and even Jim thought it was too much. Jim thinks Dick sold the lumber and profited from the earth's misery. All of the colorful wildflowers I picked from the field are gone. It is all turned earth, which is mostly rock with only a little dirt. A few scrawny pine trees remain.

The town of Bean has a fairly long and sordid history. It is called Bean because Judge Roy Bean allegedly hung some men there. The original jail cell still stands in the Bean Tavern parking lot. It is a miserable confine, made of thick stone blocks with rusted metal bars for the door, only about 5' tall and 4' wide. That was the jail used during the mid to late 1800s. Not much room for a person to move, but I suppose they didn't care. You can't enter the jail since it has an old rusted lock without a key. Maybe the police still have the key but I'm not going to ask them.

The closest junior high and high schools are 16 miles away. That won't be a fun bus ride. There are a few other people scattered out there, but no one lives very close. The nearest neighbor is a quarter mile away and live in a modern wooden house with solar panels. I met the couple who live there, Mr. and Mrs. Cooper, who just got married and are very friendly and actually want me to visit them often. Mom said I shouldn't but I don't understand why. We should be friendly with our neighbors. They have a sweet dog that runs around outside whose name is Taxi. I think Taxi is a German Shepard mix. She gets along well with Asker since they both have the same temperament.

The Cooper's house is open and modern, with the master bedroom upstairs with a balcony overlooking the first floor. There are sky lights everywhere and is smells like cedar, which is divine. No smell of cigarette smoke in the Cooper's house. It's fresh and clean.

Their kitchen is the best I've ever seen because it has a large bay window filled with plants and herbs for cooking. The Coopers showed me how their solar panels transfer energy, where the energy is converted into electricity, which produces enough to run the stove and heat the water. There isn't enough sun in Washington state to get much more out of solar heating. But it saves some money on their electric bill. They are very intelligent and interesting people. Jim won't like them.

MAY 10, 1980

The stress of living in the ghetto has disappeared since we now live in our mobile home. It doesn't have the skirting on yet, and the front door is about four feet up from the ground, so the trailer installers stacked some very unattractive concrete blocks to make temporary stairs. They are precarious on the rocky terrain, so we use the back sliding door. You could actually break a leg if you fell from the front door.

Jim will build a front porch with stairs when he permanently moves up with us. There is no rush, really. It is so much nicer when Jim is not around. There isn't any stress, mom laughs and has fun and we do jigsaw puzzles for hours. I can only call him Jim in you, my diary, because I would get a back hand to the face if I called him Jim. I am required to still call him “dad”, which is so deplorable to me, I rarely say it. Instead, I don’t use any pronoun when addressing him. Pronoun, is that correct? I have missed so much education by moving to too many schools, my basic education has huge gaps. Often, I relearn what I already know when moving to a new school. They don’t teach the same curriculum at the same pace, so it is a mishmash education. The Tacoma slum school only required I memorize the states and capitals.

We have no electricity until the electric company comes and installs telephone poles and wires from the road next to the Cooper’s house. Yes, we live so far in the country, there aren’t telephones close enough to our trailer for electrical wires to reach. Some men came to see what work had to be done and told us that two telephone poles should do the trick. The warned us that it may be two or three weeks before the electricity is actually hooked up to our trailer.

We had to dig for a well, which was done immediately since running water is incredibly important in a First World country. Jim took care of installing a water well just before he returned to California. I’m relieved he did something useful. Since we live on a tall hill, they had to dig 118’ until they reached the water table. Once the water was reached, an ugly water device that shows water pressure and usage was placed on the well opening. Next, PVC pipes were installed to our house. It was a muddy, ugly mess. The well diggers said it was one of the deepest wells they had ever dug. Of course, none of these things from the utility companies are free. The well cost extra because it was deeper than usual. After so many feet down, they start charging per foot.

I think they covered up to 100', so it was close. We had to pay for the last 18'. The telephone poles and wires won't cost us anything except time waiting for electricity. One of the well diggers built a cute, wooden shed to disguise the well in a single day and even painted it for us. We decided on a green shed with white trim. It will probably look nicer than our trailer.

The septic pipes had to be laid down, too, when our road was officially installed. It was leveled and truck loads of rocks were dumped on the dirt. It's a rocky road to get to our home. We hoped to name the street, but the county assigned a number. Too bad. The septic pipe work was done before we actually moved into the mobile home. I never really thought about it, but I guess you can't just dig a hole for toilets to drain. It would mix with our drinking water in the aquifer. That is a nasty thought. I don't want to die from cholera.

I have to admit, the inside of the mobile home is nice, although a bit boring with everything being either beige or brown, with atrocious fake wood paneling in the living room. It's a new trailer, so it has the new carpet smell, although we technically purchased it "used". Jim purposely purchased the viewing model, which had people traipsing through it a few dozen times, so he got the price reduced. When we viewed this mobile home, it had plastic mats that you had to walk on so nobody ever actually walked on the carpet. If there is a way to save money, Jim will find it. The kitchen is fairly nice because it is open and has a cooking island in the middle and a dishwasher. It will be our first dishwasher, so I'm relieved since I do all of the cleaning around the house. It is part of my allowance.

There is a bar off the kitchen where we can put stools and sit at the counter. We only had a couple dozen boxes from the raggedy apartment which mom and I quickly unpacked. We sleep on the floor. The master bedroom is at the opposite end of the trailer from the other two bedrooms. There is an extra bedroom which can set up for guests, mom said. We don't receive guests, so I highly doubt it.

The trailer is situated on the top of large hill, so we have a view of Mt. Rainier from our living room on clear days.

I quickly discovered that I can't roller skate, skateboard, or ride my bicycle since we live so far up a gravel road. The gravel road must be a mile from the paved road, it is so long. The paved road is too dangerous to bicycle since drivers are reckless out here. I wish my parents would have noticed this before we bought the property. All activities I loved to do have been taken away from me. It is depressing seeing my roller skates and skateboard sitting in the empty corner of my empty room. There isn't even a park or parking lot nearby for me to take my skateboard. It's two and half miles just to get to Bean, so it isn't easy for me to get to civilization. Strange, there is no church in Bean. We don't go to church so it doesn't bother me, but towns usually have large church parking lots to skate board. Even the parking lots near the taverns are gravel, not paved.

We are alone, in the middle of this vast wilderness with nothing to do. Jim wants to be away from people so he can be mean and drunk without prying eyes. The only visitor we had was a retarded man who wandered into our yard the other day. I think he lives behind us, down the hill, in the direction of the abandoned mill. He has a strangely shaped head, like a cone, and he stood at the end of the road staring at our trailer, watching me and mom. Mom called the police after the third weird visit from the staring man with a conical shaped head. When the police got to our house, they told us that it was "only Charlie" who wouldn't hurt anyone. When he was a toddler, he was playing behind his dad's truck when he was accidentally run over. He didn't die because his head got pushed into the mud. That is why his head is a cone-head, like on Saturday Night Live, but without humor.

MAY 18, 1980

Mt. St. Helens erupted and I saw the entire breathtaking event. I was outside picking flowers from the Cooper's yard when I saw a big, black mushroom cloud climb up into the sky. Actually, I thought it was a nuclear bomb attack and went screaming into the house that we were being nuked. Mom laughed when I said it was a nuclear attack, although I don't know why she thought the idea so incredulous. There are after school specials about nuclear attacks sometimes. She turned on the radio and we heard it was Mt. St. Helens. I am quite relieved it wasn't a nuclear attack. That scares me because I wouldn't want to die like those poor people in Hiroshima.

It turns out the eruption was an explosion of hot gas and burning ash. No lava, but the eruption ripped off an entire piece of the mountain. The news report said rivers from the mountain turned to boiling mud that gushed with such force it uprooted all the trees in the area. The blast also leveled trees for many miles around, as if they were toothpicks. Some campers are missing and presumed dead, although they don't know yet. The flooding of the rivers filled with boiling mud and debris wasn't anticipated, it seems, since people at the base of the mountain weren't evacuated.

MAY 29, 1980

The isolation is starting to take its toll on my nerves. I feel sad and anxious again, although we now have our telephone poles and electricity. We haven't been able to take a warm shower or bath since we've lived here because there was nothing to heat the water. Apparently, we live too far in the country to get cable television like we had on the Air Force base, so our only option is to purchase a huge satellite dish which will be about 15' across and will receive over a hundred channels. Jim has demanded mom get the satellite installed before he moves up with us. Apparently, he can't live without television because of sports. I suppose we need television since there is nothing else to do out here. I wish we purchased enough property for a horse so I'd have an outdoor hobby. Without my skateboard and bike, I am bored stiff.

I've been having nightmares almost every night. Last night, in my dream, Jim became possessed and was able to do magic tricks, like levitate and move objects by using mind control. He did a lot of tricks of this sort for mom and me. I asked if he could do anything else. That is when Jim showed us the day and hour that he murdered a family. It was a mom, dad and little kid. I watched as Jim ran over the three of them in his truck. Mom didn't want to see the deadly memory, so she turned around and left me alone with Jim. I decided to follow her but she was gone, and instead I saw ghostly faces everywhere of people who were murdered, including the family Jim killed.

A masked murderer came running after me with a large bloody knife. I began running and saw a house and barn, so I ran to the house first, which was locked, then to the barn. I couldn't get into the locked barn, either, so I ran to an orchard where a playhouse appeared. I hid in the playhouse. I could hear the murderer's heavy footsteps and the knife scraping against the wall. Shutters, doors, and windows began opening and slamming shut while toys flew all around me.

Next, there was snow on the ground and I shivered from the cold. Mom saw our car and yelled at me to run to it. Of course, the car was locked with the keys inside. As the knife wielding man, axe carrying woman and the creepy child ran toward us, we pulled at the car doors until it finally opened on the passenger side. We climbed in and mom got the car started. The family that Jim killed were trying to murder mom and me.

The road was slippery and our car was fish-tailing from side to side. There was ice on the windshield so we couldn't see the road. As we continued to drive, the snow and ice started to disappear. Our car suddenly stalled, sputtered, and rolled to a stop. Mom tried restarting the car but it wouldn't start, so she told me to make a run for it. I got out of the car and ran as fast as I could.

Suddenly, the ghostly faces of the dead family were around us again, and mom and I froze in terror. I was actually still in the nightmare, but thought I was awake, I discovered that I somehow received magical powers. I showed Jim my new magic powers by making books fly off the shelves and crash into him. Jim cowered from my powers as books pelted him. That is when I really woke up. I was sweating from fear.

JUNE 9, 1980

Sadness is creeping in again since Jim moved up permanently from California yesterday. He brought the last of our few belongings with him. It was a sad day. Our giant satellite dish was installed a couple of days ago. Jim bugged mom about it, calling two or three times a day to make sure we had the television up and running by the time he arrived. What a jerk.

Jim's truck was loaded with boxes and his ugly brown recliner. It should blend in nicely with the brown walls of the trailer. Jim made certain to remove his chair first, forcing us to help lug the beast into the living room. Since we had the television already set up with satellite, Jim brought in his case of beer, sat down in his chair and started flipping through channels. To my disgust, he stopped on the Playboy Channel, the old pervert. He grunted every once in a while as girls in bikinis were splashing playfully in Hugh Hefner's swimming pool.

The truck was still loaded with boxes but Jim stopped helping us once he settled into his easy chair and satellite television. I was wrong, it doesn't have over one hundred channels, it has over three hundred. Mom and I unloaded all of the boxes by ourselves. It took us hours. Some boxes were so heavy, mom and I had to slide them over the rocky ground, around to the back door and into the living room. The concrete blocks for stairs to the front door are precarious, so we had to travel twice the distance to the back door. We really should have moved the truck closer to the door. I hate Jim. He is so lazy, too lazy, TOO LAZY. I wish he would die. I want to scratch his eyes out as he is leering at the bikini girls.

After all of the boxes were in the house, mom tried to cheer me up by saying they would get me a bedroom suite this week so I have a real bedroom. I sure hope so. I think she said it so I wouldn't stay angry about moving all the boxes while Jim sat on his butt. Jim didn't notice how mad I was, or pretended not to notice. Evil, lazy, selfish man.

JUNE 11, 1980

I woke up last night vomiting. Unfortunately, I didn't make it to the bathroom. I was ashamed so I cleaned up the disgusting mess. Mom is at the other end of the house and didn't hear me in distress. I am not sure why I vomited. It could be the return of Jim.

Jim was able to transfer to the Bean post office, but work is only part-time and he has to drive his own vehicle, sitting on the right side and driving with his left foot. Luckily, Jim's truck is an automatic. Unluckily, he needs to have a car to be at a lower level. Jim balked at taking mom's junker car he bought for us, so he will be looking for a new car for himself. For a part-time job. That pays hardly anything. The post office said they can wait until he has the proper vehicle. It should be soon since Jim is running out of beer money. Neither of them are working. I know he gets disability income and retirement from the Air Force, but I have no idea how much money that amounts to each month. Come to think about it, how did they pay for the new mobile home with cash, dig the well with cash, buy and install a satellite dish with cash? Where did this money come from? Mom didn't ask any questions. What was Jim doing in California when we were living meagerly in the slums of Tacoma? I am not allowed to ask any questions or I will get a backhand to the face. I do not exaggerate. I'm not sure mom asked, either. She probably doesn't want to know how Jim acquired thousands of dollars, mostly in large bills.

Jim put the screws on mom getting a job as a medical records technician at one of the hospitals, either on the Air Force or Army base, which are side by side. She's been applying for job positions while Jim spends his time at the tavern, until he finds a car that will work for his postal duties, of course.

Mom recently bought me charcoal and a sketch pad so I have something to do in this lonely life.

JUNE 22, 1980

I have to admit, the huge satellite dish in the back yard is cool. There are no commercials since the video feed is coming directly from the broadcaster. Jim was watching a Seattle Mariner baseball game, and in the spots which were supposed to show commercials, the video is still on the commentators. They don't realize that people can hear them talk, and they used profanity and said completely inappropriate comments about women in the stands.

We get HBO and a lot of stations from around the country. Apparently there have been heated discussions at the Bean Tavern about how long shows will be allowed to broadcast on satellite, especially because of the lack of commercial control. Some say satellite will fizzle out and we'll all be left with enormous yet completely useless satellite dishes pointed toward the sky like Cape Canaveral. Time will tell. It wasn't my money spent on the huge dish. It's fun watching horror movies when I'm home alone with all of the lights out.

Basically, my only source of entertainment is watching television or playing Atari, which I set up in the guest bedroom on our old, smaller television. Jim bought a large console tv when we first moved in to go with the satellite. Setting up the Atari in the guest room was genius since it gives me an excuse to leave the room if my parents are drunk and obnoxious. I got rid of my bike, skateboard and roller skates. There is absolutely no place to use them, so Jim got rid of them for me.

Since we get so many channels, mom and I have really gotten into watching *General Hospital* and *All My Children* soap operas. We tape the shows on the VCR so mom can watch them after work and drinking. *General Hospital* has the whole Luke and Laura drama going on. Laura is seeing Scotty and works at a disco, but Scotty works for the mafia. Luke is sent to break up Luke and Scotty's relationship and ends up forcing himself on her at the disco. I am confused because it seems like he raped her, but Laura seems to be attracted to Luke. It's totally weird. Mom prefers *All My Children* with the Tad intrigues between mother and daughter. Also, the Adam Chandler character who is a strong, forceful type, and her favorites, Erica Kane and the wise cracking Opal. I don't tell mom, but Opal gets on my nerves.

Mom got a medical records job on the Army base, so that's why we bought the VCR, to tape shows for her. Jim still works part-time with the post office and mom has suggested that he look for a jet engine mechanic job at the Army or Air Force base, since that is what he used to do in the Air Force. It would be a lot more money. I'd much rather

Jim get a jet engine mechanic job and stay away from home longer instead of lingering around barstools. I never know when he is coming home because he doesn't work full-time and when I casually asked about his work hours, he said it is none of my goddam business what hours he works. It seems unnecessary to treat me like a subhuman when I'm trying to have a conversation. This family doesn't know the meaning of conversation, only attack and defend.

JUNE 23, 1980

I've been seeing Dr. Scott about my braces. They will remain on for another year or two. Dr. Scott made an odd comment to me. He said if the police recovered my skull and had to identify my body, at first glance, he would say my teeth look like those of a 16 to 18 year old. Dr. Scott said he has done identification work with the police before and said my teeth look five to seven years older than they actually are. I blushed when he made the comment about examining a skull. I really don't know why I blushed, because he was talking about looking at dead people's teeth. I think I blushed because he talked to me about something personal. I don't get much personal conversation. He is very handsome. That is probably why I blushed.

JUNE 28, 1980

I built an obstacle course, stacking concrete blocks to run around, and a broom laid on top of some blocks to use as a hurdle. I ran with Asker through the obstacle course several times until I was out of breath. I stood there, looking at the makeshift course and realized how boring my life is.

JULY 1, 1980

I burst into tears the other day because I still don't have bedroom furniture and feel like I'm not important to my parents. I finally got bedroom furniture. As always with a large purchase, Jim had to tag along. Nothing would be bought without his approval. We drove the thirty plus miles to Ethan Allen and I selected a rather nice oak set, which included a desk, dresser, nightstand, headboard and footboard. To my surprise, Jim approved my choice, wrote a check this time (instead of the usual cash) and scheduled a delivery for tomorrow. I was surprised they delivered as far as our house. The salesman knew where Bean was located and had other business from people there, so we aren't the only humans in Bean.

When we returned home, Jim decided that since he spent so much money on my new bedroom set, I needed to go out to our front yard and remove rocks. The entire yard is riddled with rocks. Jim wants to use his riding lawn mower on the front yard to mow down the weeds that are returning. He can't mow until most of the rocks are gone. Seriously? I pulled up three wheelbarrows full of rocks, dumped them onto the empty lot next to ours. To my dismay, the yard remained filled with rocks. That was all I could do. Jim felt it was his duty to inspect my hard work. He got out of his arm chair, brought his beer, and went to the front to make sure I did sufficient work. I felt like I was on the chain gang requesting a break from The Man.

Jim took one look at the yard and something about it being shit, so I showed him the pile of rocks I dumped onto the adjoining lot. Only then did he believe I did any work. I explained that the yard is filled with rocks, so removing them all won't be possible. He disagreed and said I'll have to try again tomorrow. No, I gently reminded him, my furniture is delivered tomorrow. Yes, Jim said, I still had time to get two or three wheelbarrows of rocks out of the yard before my bedroom furniture arrives. Jim sold my bedroom furniture in California, and forces me to hard labor for requesting new furniture which was already promised to me when we moved here. Unbelievable! I have no one to complain to except you, diary. Is it just me, or is this completely unfair?

JULY 4, 1980

The 4th was so depressing I cried. My parents didn't buy any fireworks this year, not even sparklers. We used to purchase the small box of assorted fireworks and lit them off together, well, mom and I did the fireworks. Jim was never around for any Fourth of July celebration.

Today, mom asked me if I wouldn't mind her going to the tavern sometimes. I said okay because that is what she wants me to say. I am alone for this holiday, with no fireworks or friends. It felt ominous when mom asked my permission to go to the tavern. She's gone before, for a couple of hours, and comes home to eat dinner with me. It feels like a turning point. I am afraid that I am slowly losing her to Jim, to alcohol. It's really depressing sitting here by myself, but I didn't want to "guilt" her into staying home with me. If mom wanted to spend time with me, she would. I should have known she would eventually escape this boredom and leave me isolated and alone.

JULY 5, 1980

Mom stayed at the tavern with Jim until very late last night. It is a bad sign. Already today, Jim assigned me to pick up three wheelbarrows full of rocks before he and mom left for the tavern again. I got the manual labor out of the way as quickly as possible, watched some tv, then played Atari.

Around dinner time, I started wondering if I should eat another tv dinner. There was no word from mom. I was about to cook the disgusting dinner when I heard the car drive up. They were home. I nervously awaited their mood, not sure if it would be fair or foul. They stumbled in, mom saying "shit" as she always does when she has been drinking. To my surprise, they brought home a kitten. That was unexpected. Asker ran up to the kitten and sniffed her all over. The kitten barely moved, which made me believe she was not quite all there mentally. I feel sorry for her, so I love her more. Yet I wonder, did someone give away kittens at the tavern? Was there a left over brain damaged kitten no one wanted, so my parents drunkenly agreed to take the poor thing, out of guilt for abandoning me to this nothingness? I picked up the little furry thing and named her Samantha, from *Bewitched*, since I was watching it earlier on the tv.

JULY 27, 1980

I haven't written for a little while because I am unable to process everything that has happened. I am shattered inside and feel fragile, like a leaf in the wind. Last week, Jim stood up to go to work. Asker was right there with us. She must have ran out with Jim, because a few minutes later, there was a loud screaming yelp like I'd never heard in my life. I saw Asker running towards me from outside, and I noticed the screen door wasn't completely shut. Asker jumped into Jim's armchair, circling and whining and bleeding from her mouth. Jim ran over Asker with his car! She couldn't breathe, it was horrifying. I stood in shock, unable to move. Asker came running to me because she thought that I could help her. I gently touched her head, afraid to cause her more distress. Asker lost consciousness and died a few seconds later. I broke down and cried until I couldn't breathe. How could this happen? Why didn't Jim close the screen door? Why didn't he look behind him before he backed the car out of the driveway?

Only three days later, three days, Jim accidentally killed Samantha, in front of my eyes. She was climbing up the screen door, as usual, which irritated Jim. He pulled the screen door open with a brutal tug, causing the screen door to jump off the tracks and land right on Samantha's neck, breaking it instantly. Samantha was limp and lifeless. I was still grieving Asker, and was so shocked, no tears came to my eyes. Jim casually said, "it's better that it's dead since it was retarded." He called her "it". Jim decided it was time to go to the tavern, and my mom grabbed her purse, Samantha, and ran out the door, going to the tavern with Jim. I don't know what she did with little Samantha's body. They were all gone, just like that. No Asker, no Samantha, and mom ran away and didn't stay with me in my grief.

AUGUST 01, 1980

The news on every channel is about the Shah Mohammad Reza Pahlavi of Iran finally dying in Egypt from cancer. The 52 American hostages are still being held in Iran. It has now been almost 300 days since the hostages were captured in Iran in November 1979. From what I gather, the Iranians turned against their leader, the Shah, so he decided to flee Iran and came to the United States to hide from his unruly subjects. Apparently, the Shah was also dying of cancer. The United States said we were keeping the Shah to treat his cancer. The Iranians protested in the streets of Iran, burning the American flag, and blaming us for hiding the Shah from them. The people want him to stand trial for crimes against their citizens, but it appears that will not happen. In retaliation, a small group of angry, masked people captured 52 Americans as hostages.

The Shah fled the US in December 1979 and moved to Egypt. Apparently, he died in Egypt a few days ago from his cancer. The Iranians said that they are going to release the hostages because, according to the Iranians, there is a holiday where everyone in Iran has to release any hostages. On both sides. Nothing definite has happened, so I am unsure if the hostages will be released. We are supposed to put a lighted candle in the window as a vigil or prayer for the hostages safe return.

SEPTEMBER 4, 1980

I started the seventh grade. It is a long bus ride almost all the way to Tacoma. I have to wake up at 5:15am to get the bus stop, on the paved road where the mail boxes are located, by 5:50am. I have a bowl of cereal, make a peanut butter and jelly sandwich for lunch, with some chips and an apple. I make my lunch the night before and leave it in the refrigerator. Mom has been coming home rather late in the evenings, going straight to the tavern right after work. My parents are getting into a bad habit of making me prepare dinner for them to be ready at 6:30 pm. They aren't always home at that time, so I eat by myself and leave the food covered with aluminum foil.

The bus ride to school is almost an hour long, and the bus driver, a large, gruff, unattractive woman named

Pearl runs a tight ship. On the first day I got on the bus, after she picked up all of the kids and was driving the last 12 miles to school, she pulled the bus over, stood up and looked each of us in the eye, saying she wouldn't take any guff from any child. If anyone gives her a problem, she'll kick them off the bus, even if they aren't near their home. Pearl's voice is raspy from smoking too many cigarettes, and her bowl haircut appears to be done by herself. I was relieved that she didn't want any children standing up and causing problems so I wouldn't have to be stressed out by the commotion. It puts an end to bullying on the bus. Everyone talked in low, muffled tones, and whenever someone stood up, Pearl pulled over and yelled at them to sit their butt back down in the seat and don't move another muscle until we got to school. I rather like Pearl.

SEPTEMBER 8, 1980

I am getting used to using a locker at school. I've been writing the combination number on my wrist every day since I get nervous and forget the code. My locker is next to a girl who wears a back brace because she has scoliosis. Her name is Sam. She doesn't have friends so I've been nice to her. Sam was friendly to me until another girl, Shena, started teasing Sam about her back brace. I told Shena she was mean to make fun of Sam's back brace. I got really angry at Shena but Sam just ran away.

SEPTEMBER 12 1980

The locker situation is getting uncomfortable and awkward. Sam and Shena are good friends now and they both call me a weirdo and brace face (because of my braces). They both are being so mean to me, calling me a freak and slamming my locker closed. I feel hurt that Sam has betrayed me like this, so I don't say anything. I think I frightened them both when I yelled at Shena, thinking I was protecting Sam. I probably yelled too loudly and said some unkind things for them to call me a freak. I was trying to help. I go to my locker when they aren't there, hiding and watching until they leave. I can see them looking for me. I hate bullies.

SEPTEMBER 18, 1980

I forgot to mention that I was cast in a musical. I'm doing well in choir, so my teacher suggested I audition for *The Sentimental Scarecrow.* I got the part of a singing gypsy and have been lucky enough to have an excuse to stay after school and take the late bus home. There are only two buses going home, one after school, and one after sports. I get home around 5:00 pm, which is so liberating.

In the play, there is the main character, Scarecrow, 7 gypsies, 2 sisters, 1 brother and Polly (who falls in love with Scarecrow). I didn't get the coveted Polly role, although I am pleased to be one of the cast. I feel like I belong for the first time since moving to Bean.

Tonight was the show, and my mom made it just in time. Jim did not arrive for my performance, which was disappointing.

Before the musical, I tried out for cheerleader. I was in gymnastics, so I joined the after school cheerleading practice. There was a coach available who helped me build a routine. I chose to end the routine with a front walkover terminating in a forward split. Last year's cheerleaders were in their own group, with only one girl coming over to wish me luck and said she was glad to see a new girl trying out.

I practiced hours after school and at home. I performed in the auditorium in front of all the grades, seventh through ninth. I was one of two seventh graders to audition. The current cheerleaders were predicted to win, and they did. Rob, a very athletic boy who is in my grade and plays both basketball and football said I did a great job, he voted for me. I blushed furiously. He is so cute. He is one of a twin, Rick, the other. Rob's parents know my parents through the bar, we met once at an outdoor Bean keg party.

It was uncomfortable waiting for votes in my classroom, with all of the other kids watching me. One of the winning cheerleaders happened to be in my class. She is very popular and was the only seventh grader chosen. By sad coincidence, her name is Leigh, too, so when I heard "Leigh" announced as the cheerleader winner, my heart leapt with joy. It quickly plunged when the last name was not my own. Still, I'm glad I auditioned for cheerleading. So many other kids said they loved my routine, it makes me feel good. They said it was very brave of me to audition.

I did get a part in the musical, so I won something!

SEPTEMBER 24, 1980

I am starting to hate my new dog, Shasta. It isn't just because of her cowering and urinating on the carpet, which I have to clean up. It's mainly because Jim will feed him food from the table and treats Shasta with such love and affection, completely ignoring me at the dining room table. Meals are misery. I have to prepare a hot meal for my drunk parents, then Jim, knowing that I dislike animals being fed from the table, goes out of his way to feed the begging Shasta bite after bite. I made the mistake of asking him to not feed Shasta at the table since it instills bad habits of begging. Jim made a point to feed Shasta more often, looking at me as he did it. He is a cruel person. Mom sits there in her green robe, eyes half closed from intoxication, oblivious to my ill treatment. She seems to purposely pretend that Jim doesn't mistreat me. When he gets especially aggressive and mean to me, mom stumbles back to her bedroom, mumbling good night and closes the door. I am stuck with clearing the table, putting the food away in Tupperware containers, rinsing the dishes for the dishwasher, wiping down the dining room table, and putting away the placemats that I made in 4H when I was in fifth grade. Jim usually goes into their bedroom and either argues, gets disgusting with mom, or watches tv. Jim never helps clean up after dinner, even though I made the meal while they were at the tavern.

My parents don't ask about school. Nothing beyond, "how's school". I answer with, "fine" and leave it at that. Mom no longer asks if I have homework, if I like choir, if I've made friends, nothing at all. I am so sad and lonely. If I complain in the slightest, I am treated with such contempt and told to go back to my room. Jim has even gotten his belt and whipped me with it. I don't pull down my underpants anymore. That seems too creepy. I barely even pull down my pants so he beats me on my back mostly. I'm told I am disobedient and treated worse than the dog.

I am going to the Pumpkin Bowl on November first and to a birthday party at a girl's house a couple of blocks from school November 2nd. This Friday is a costume dress-up at school, so I'm going as a pirate. I have a poet's shirt, brown knickerbocker pants, tall brown boots, a hat and an eye patch I sewed myself. I love dressing up. There is a dance coming up which I may go to. We'll see.

There is one demented and drill sergeant style teacher who I can't stand. Mr. Patrick. I have him for three classes, and it is an utter disaster. He likes to pick on students, find the weak one and belittle them in front of the class. He hasn't picked on me, yet.

I am still doing very well at choir. The teacher has taken notice of my voice and puts me in some strong soprano parts. Our choir sang in front of the whole school the other day. I am fairly tall, so I stood in the back row, near the center, since I have some parts where just a few girls sang. We performed very nicely, I believe.

My math teacher told me I should be in a more advanced math class and that I needed a parent to request I be placed in a higher level class. I asked if he could do it, but he needs parental permission. I asked mom three times, and she said she would call the school, but hasn't yet. I can't catch her when she is sober so I think she forgets. I'm stuck in an easy math class when I should be in the advanced algebra and geometry class. My teacher said he wish he could help, but he needs to follow the rules. If only mom would take an interest in my life and school, it would be a huge relief. I wish I had another option. I could run away, but where would I go? Live on the streets? I would be vulnerable to creepy men. I don't have family to stay with, no friends. It feels like hell on earth with no end in sight. The black hole inside me seems to grow bigger with each bad event. I will disappear into nothingness soon.

SEPTEMBER 29, 1980

The harassment from Shena and Sam has become unbearable. Other kids join in the taunting. I decided to take matter in my own hands. I wrote on a slip of paper with my left hand (so it would look different than my usual writing) that I wanted to kill Shena so she better watch her back. I said I was going to stab her eyes out. I didn't sign it and slipped the paper through the vent opening in her locker. How will she know who it's from since she teases other people, too?

SEPTEMBER 30, 1980

I was totally busted with the death threat note. I was taken to the principal's office and I saw Shena in the office crying her eyes out and looking like she was frightened of my presence. Jeez. I wouldn't actually kill anyone. I told the principal that I just wanted her to leave me alone, to stop harassing me at my locker every day. The principal said this was a very serious crime, I could be arrested by the police and kicked out of school permanently! I had no idea. He said that since I've never been in trouble before, I'll be let off if I write a letter of apology to Shena, have my parents drive me to her house, and read the letter to her in front of both of our parents. The principal called mom at work to come and get me. Mom didn't say anything about it. She asked me why I did it and I explained. She said she had to tell Jim since both parents had to go to Shena's house. Jim wasn't very angry about it. He said we might as well get this over with and go to Shena's house this weekend to apologize. I am filled with terrible dread of going to Shena's house. I told my parents I was wrong and feel just terrible about scaring Shena. I felt empty inside.

OCTOBER 4, 1980

Today we went to Shena's nice, upscale home for me to grovel at her feet. I wrote my letter of apology and felt guilty about saying those cruel things, crying as I read the letter.

Shena's parents looked apprehensive when we first arrived, but mom and Jim apologized at least a dozen times then thrust me up front to say how sorry I felt about the entire ordeal. Shena sat huddled between her parents as if I were an axe murderer. They lived 20 miles from us so the drive there and back was long, silent and uncomfortable. Jim drove and told me to give him a beer. He brought a cooler in the backseat, so I handed him and mom one. They silently drove home, dropped me off, then went to the tavern to drink.

October 6, 1980 The principal moved my locker far away from Shena's, thankfully. I saw Shena and she looked at me shyly, did a little smile then ran off. Maybe it did frighten her. It stopped her from teasing me. Back to normal. No friends and alone.

OCTOBER 11, 1980

I have started my period today, before going to school, which was very inconvenient. Since mom had her uterus removed from cancer, she no longer has her period. However, she kept some maxi pads and tampons in case I needed them. I was suspicious of the tampon, and inserting it seemed impossible to contemplate, so I chose to go with the maxi pad, which felt like a diaper, and decided not to wear my white pants. I am so embarrassed. I should be excited, but it is more tedious than exciting. I wore a long shirt, which wasn't long enough to cover my butt, so I was self-conscious all day at school. I felt sure everyone would see the bulging maxi pad and went to the bathroom between every class to make sure there was no leakage. I saw a girl who had blood on the back of her pants from a horrible mishap, and I don't want that to happen to me. It felt like the longest day in my life and I wanted to go home.

To my utter disgust, mom felt it necessary to share with Jim that I am now officially a woman. If I was a snail, I'd go back in my shell and squish back to my room.

NOVEMBER 2, 1980

I feel almost like a normal person and went to the Sadie Hawkins dance at school, which is the dance where a girl has to invite a boy. Cold terror clenched a fist around my heart. Who would I call? What would I wear? Mom suggested asking Rick, the grandson of a woman my parents drink with at the Bean Bar & Grill.

I need to explain something here. Tubby, the owner and bartender of the Bean Tavern, and Jim got into a fight a few weeks ago. Jim probably owed him money, or maybe I called too often to ask when mom was coming home. I have the phone numbers memorized to the tavern and bar. Mom refused to give me details, except for the fact that Tubby banned Jim from the tavern. Mom, of course, put all of the blame on Tubby. He is a very nice man so I am guessing it is more Jim's fault. It seems it is not uncommon for bar fights to occur in town, and people migrate from the tavern to the bar and back again.

So now, my parents go to the bar where they met Wanda. She lives about a mile closer to town than we do, not far from our trailer. Wanda invited us over for a brief visit so I could meet her two grandsons. Rick is in the same grade as me and is rather cute, with strawberry blonde hair that is feathered. His brother, Tony, is three years older than Rick. Mom told me of a tragedy which occurred to the boys. She said that Wanda's son and daughter-in-law used to live in that trailer (it is extremely junky and barely livable, to be honest). When Rick was three and Tony six, their abusive, alcoholic father beat their mother severely before getting his shotgun and shooting her in the face in front of the children. Their father then turned the gun on himself and blew his own brains out. The kids were huddled in their bedroom for a while before the bodies were discovered. Since Wanda is quite old and doesn't work (very few people in Bean seem to work), she moved into the death trailer. The boys surely remember some of the nightmarish events, and making them live in the same trailer seems cruel. Obviously, the blood and brains were cleaned up. It makes me shiver to think about it. I'm so relieved Jim hates guns since he fought in Vietnam, and only has one antique rifle which was his grandfather's gun. It's very old, and is in the back of the closet behind the piles of pornographic magazines. There aren't any bullets in the gun or in our house at all. Jim has been drunk enough to kill mom before, but he keeps it to his fists. Jim doesn't use a weapon, except the belt on me.

Back to my first seventh grade dance. I invited Rick since he is one of the few boys that I know, and he said yes.

I was relieved, happy and surprised. I wore my purple flared skirt, my frilly cream colored poet's shirt and a brown pair of leather boots. It was so much fun. I haven't danced with a boy before. I did alright and figured it out fairly quickly. We also danced by ourselves to the fast songs, and some people I barely knew said that I danced really well. I didn't realize I danced so well. I did go to a disco once in California, and danced to *Saturday Night Fever* when I was younger and played the 8-track soundtrack to the movie. I don't know what happened to that 8-track. My parents probably sold it in the yard sale.

NOVEMBER 16, 1980

We finally got rid of Shasta. I hated her since Jim coddled and fed her from the dinner table. I asked him several times not to feed the dog from the table, yet he continued feeding her to spite me. Mom called the woman who sold us Shasta and she agreed to take her back. We wouldn't get our money back. I was thankful she wasn't dumped in the country, alone and afraid, like all the pets before. I didn't like Shasta, who peed on the carpet if you looked at her crossly, but I didn't want her abandoned. She wouldn't survive for long since she isn't the smartest or toughest dog. I'd rather have no dog than one that Jim treated like he loved more than me. The pet is supposed to be for me since I'm left home alone for most of the time.

NOVEMBER 20, 1980

Grandpa called, completely out of the blue, saying that he will pay for us to fly first class to Boston for Thanksgiving. This is mom's dad, who has only called about five times in my entire life, often forgets Christmas one year, only to send a card and $60 the next. I've never met him before, not since I was a year old. I long to meet the family I have never known. My godmother, Cathy, lives in Boston, too, and is mom's cousin. Mom has aunts, uncles, and cousins in Boston, which remain mysteriously vague and unknown to me. I have so much family, yet I know none of them. It makes me so sad. Jim visits his mother and siblings on a regular basis, several times a year. We have never visited mom's side of the family. Never. There are people in the world who might actually love me.

DECEMBER 5, 1980

We had a phenomenal adventure in Boston, where I was born. The airplane was beyond belief. It had a bar in first class that was located on an upper level via a small spiral staircase. The airplane was enormous. We sat in such luxury, it was beyond anything I've ever seen. Mom said grandpa must have made a lot of money from his seven weight loss clinics located throughout the Boston area. Since everyone wants to be so thin and disco glitter gorgeous, I imagine it is a lucrative business. It is difficult to believe that grandpa grew up a poor kid on the south side of town.

Grandpa's wife, Denise, has 5 children living with them, and two more who live somewhere else. None of them are his children, and each appeared to have a different father, because not one of them looked alike. I suspect Denise is the kind of woman who got pregnant in order to catch her man. She is beautiful and elegant, although rather cold and intolerant of anything she considers impolite behavior. I didn't warm to her, and she seemed strangely jealous of me, even though I am not close to grandpa, and he does not seem to love me.

Grandpa, Uncle John (mom's younger brother who is only 7 years older than me, quite tall and handsome) and Trent (Denise's son who has dark complexion, looking almost Hispanic) met us at the airport in grandpa's brand new Cadillac. Grandpa bragged about the adjustable climate control, heated leather seats, and smooth ride over potholes. He wore a gold pinky ring and a pin-striped suit. Grandpa is quite flashy, while Uncle John and Trent were subdued and submissive as grandpa corrected them on how they were sitting and acting.

A party was going full force at grandpa's exclusive mansion on a large, perfectly manicured lawn. The party was full of relatives I didn't know. They were friendly, although it was overwhelming for me to suddenly be in the midst of so many people after being alone for so long.

Gammy had heard from Uncle John that we were in Boston, so she was staying with her cousin and came to Uncle Theo's condominium to visit mom and me. It was an unexpected surprise to see her. I'm so glad she came up from

Miami. We had to keep her visit a secret because Denise would go through the roof with rage and grandpa would force her to leave if he found out. Such a bossy family!

Grandpa took us to the Museum of Natural History on the 4th day. We got there rather late and only had to see one glorious floor, the one with the dinosaurs, per my request. I didn't get to see the rest since we had a long drive back to grandpa's house. Only mom, Jim, grandpa and me went to the museum. Apparently, no one else was invited or allowed to join us. I could tell about the formal Thanksgiving dinner, but it was terribly uncomfortable since we had to dress in our finest, no child was allowed to speak, and Denise questioned me about getting too much food. Poor Rhonda was belittled, off to the side in the kitchen, for eating like a "pig", which was rather cruel to say on a holiday. All of the other children barely spoke, quickly cleaned up the table and put all the food away while the adults went into the den for cigars and high-end liquor. Jim acted as if he was accustomed to such luxury, and put on airs, so to speak, smoking his cigar and downing his expensive whiskey.

There was another party on our last night, and the family members and friends of grandpa attended, so we said our goodbyes and promised to talk on the phone.

We were taken to the airport in grandpa's leased Cadillac (he gets a new Cadillac every two years, leasing them so he never has to deal with repairs) with Uncle John and Trent in tow to carry the luggage. We flew first class back home to the Sea-Tac airport in the same type of airplane, with the spiral staircase leading up to the lounge a half floor up. Our car was in long-term parking, and we had a long drive home to Bean. Our car, rusty and rattling, cost as much as grandpa's Cadillac's tires. We drove home in silence as I played my fun hand-held video games uncle Theo gave me.

Finally home, we came into the dark trailer that was our home, isolated and lonely. Not even one light was left on for our return. It is such a completely polar opposite lifestyle than grandpa's. He didn't have love or affection for us, and seemed to like Jim best of the three of us. I can't say I like grandpa at all, and his wife is a deplorable viper. It was nice having such a wonderful adventure, though. I fear it will be our last for a long, long time.

DECEMBER 16, 1980

My parents got a new puppy, a cockapoo we named Cindy. I am hoping she will be like Asker, who was also a cockapoo. Cindy looks a bit more poodle than Asker. She seems sweet. I said I was lonely so my parents got me a pet. It wasn't exactly what I had in mind. It's better than being alone, I suppose.

DECEMBER 26, 1980

Another Christmas. It's just the three of us, which I find sad. It would be so enjoyable to have people come over for dinner, laughing, talking, eating, drinking. In Clarksville, I had friends to play with on Christmas day, showing each other our gifts, snacking on delicious left-overs. We have none of these things here, in Bean.

I quietly waited until my parents were ready for Christmas to begin. Surprisingly, I got an acoustic guitar and case, although I asked for an electric guitar and amp. I got a metallic, shiny shirt, small hoop earrings, a pocket camera (one that has zoom lens and built in flash) and an Atari game, *Missile Command.* Jim made a huge deal about getting mom diamond stud earrings. Jim says they are real diamonds but I doubt he would spend that much money on anything besides alcohol.

After a large breakfast, cooked by mom, some watching of tedious television, my parents dressed themselves and went to the Bean Tavern, which is open every day of the year. It seems they are welcomed back into the fold of the tavern folks. Tubby must have relented and graciously accepted their return. I tried to figure out how to play my guitar, and soon discovered that I needed a tuner, so my guitar was sadly out of tune. I wanted an electric guitar, but mom said it would be too loud. Too loud? We live in the country, with no neighbors for almost half a mile. It was too expensive, and mom believes that only boys can play electric guitars, girls should play acoustic guitars.

I sat home, alone, with Cindy, watching tv and being bored beyond belief. Mom called from the tavern, instructing me to start the ham, candied yams, mashed potatoes, homemade cheese sauce, broccoli and dinner rolls at the necessary times so it could all be ready for their return. I have cooked for years, so I easily prepared Christmas dinner. I waited for them to stumble in, was given no thanks for the dinner I prepared, and they ate it with no manners which disgusted me. Happy Christmas to all, and to all, and stupid night.

DECEMBER 27, 1980

The holiday season is so bleak, I feel broken and alone. Jim makes me so mad. He never asks me anything, he goes straight to upset. I went into my parent's bedroom to talk to mom, and Jim pointed his fat finger in my face, demanding me to leave their bedroom and never enter it again. It is supposed to be the holiday season, but it is only happy hour for them at the tavern.

They even occasionally rent pornography movies and put them in the VCR when they get home from drinking. I am trapped in the living room with moaning, and groaning, and my parents groping and tonguing each other on the couch, fondling, it's horrible. I tried to tough it out one time, but one woman used a bowling pin to have sex with another woman, so that was my limit. I go to my bedroom and put on my headphones to escape these horrors. I have this diary or I'd go crazy, but you can't help me. No one can.

DECEMBER 29, 1980

When I got up this morning for my birthday, mom already left for work and Jim was here since he didn't work today.

I opened my birthday presents. Altogether I got $63 this year, from grandpa, my godmother Cathy and some spare one dollar bills stuffed into my birthday card from my parents. I thought $8 in ones was rather strange. Mom came home early from work, taking me to the store to buy some things with my birthday money. I bought a pair of painter jeans, an iridescent shirt, and a blue wrap dress. Once we got back from shopping, Jim was waiting for mom to go to the bar. Mom made the usual macaroni and cheese and wiener wraps, my birthday favorite, before heading out the door. I didn't get a birthday cake since mom was so busy with work.

DECEMBER 30, 1980

I invited two girls from school to spend the night New Year's Eve, but they turned me down. They live 15 miles away, so the drive was probably the deal breaker. I tried.

CHAPTER 3

1981: AGE 12

JANUARY 9, 1981

The hostages in Iran never were released ad have been there for 433 days. The Iranians said they might kill the Americans, but also said they might let them go. I am hoping for the latter.

JANUARY 11, 1981

I got two aerobics outfits for my Aerobics class at school. It is a P.E. elective and is something I enjoy. Running track is definitely not my thing. I cough like I smoke cigarettes. In a way, I do, since both of my parents smoke inside the house and car and rarely open a window. Since mom purchased me two aerobics suits, Jim told her to make me clean the car inside and outside. I used Windex on the windows, dusted the console, and dumped the stinky ashtrays. I don't feel it is quite fair for me to work for clothes required for P.E.

JANUARY 16, 1981

There was a news break today saying the Iranian hostages will be released in a couple of days. The Iranian and United States governments are making agreements today. Something may be done by tomorrow. The news asked for us to continue to put a candle in the window until the hostages are returned. We stopped doing that a while ago. It's a fire hazard.

I don't return to school until January 25th because they are on the year round track system. I attend three weeks of school then get a week off. I had a little longer time off from the holidays. The reason the school system is doing the year round track system is because they are building another middle school and the schools are over-crowded. The year round track system allows for more students to attend school. I doubt if the teachers are too pleased about it. They never get a break.

I feel like my nightmares are becoming real. The other day while playing the organ in the extra room, I saw a faint shadow of an axe. I stopped playing, watched and listened, saw nothing more, so I started playing again. Again, I saw a shadow of the axe come down towards me on the wall but this time it was darker. I froze in terror and heard someone whispering to me. Then I saw the axe come down a third time, and this time, the shadow was so dark it looked realistic. I jumped up, ran to the door, threw it open and told my parents about it. They thought it was a bit odd but barely took any notice of me and went back to watching television.

JANUARY 19, 1981

The Iranian hostages are at the Iran Airport right now. They are finally coming home. I am so happy for them. They probably have families who miss and love them. It must have been terrifying not knowing if you'll live or die each day.

JANUARY 20, 1981

The President Elect, Ronald Reagan, and the President, Jimmy Carter, drove to the White House together. It is 8:30 am. At 9:00 am Ronald Regan will be the President of the United States. I have never seen a presidential inauguration before, so it is interesting to watch. News break: in a while the hostages are going to be in the air coming home. I guess they didn't make it out yesterday like the news predicted. We will know for sure in 15 minutes. Wait, the news reporter said the Iranian hostages HAVE lifted off in the airplane! The Iranians said they wouldn't release the hostages until President Carter was officially out of office. I have no idea why.

For the presidential inauguration, some guy gave a speech "Welcome to the history...". They sang America the

Beautiful. Some other guy gave a speech. A priest gave a prayer. Vice President Bush just swore in at 8:52 am PST. An old guy gave another speech. The band played God of Our Fathers. Ronald Regan was sworn in at 9:00 am PST. President Regan gave a boring speech.

The hostages are in the air. Yippee! Around 5:00 pm the hostages walked out of the airplane. They looked thin, but healthy and happy. They were held for 444 days in Iran as hostages. President Ronald Regan is the 40th President. He is also the first President that was divorced and remarried, the oldest President and the first actor. I am not sure that is completely the truth about being the first actor.

Here is the official report about the hostages: fifty-two American diplomats and citizens were held hostage for 444 days from November 4, 1979, to January 20, 1981 after a group of Iranian students belonging to the Muslim Student something, I couldn't write it down fast enough. They supported the Iranian Revolution then took over the U.S. Embassy in Tehran. It was the longest hostage crisis in recorded history.

JANUARY 21, 1981

We found out the Iranians students had beaten the hostages, put them in dark dungeons and left them there for weeks alone. Some people were in the dungeon as long as 400 days. The abductors pointed loaded guns to their heads and played Russian roulette, had frequent strip searches, fed them less and less over time, and many more terrible things. The hostages were told almost daily that they would be killed, and a guard told one man his mother had died, he could go to her funeral if he renounced the United States. The guards also put prisoners in front of execution firing squads to make them think that they were going to be killed. How horrible! No wonder the hostages looked so happy when they got off the airplane. I feel terrible for their suffering.

JANUARY 23, 1981

My parents actually took me out to dinner. We ate at the Moose Lodge for their fish and shrimp fry. I even drank 2 Shirley Temples. I wore my purple dress and beige blazer. It has been such a long time since we went to dinner together. Mom and Jim didn't go to the tavern tonight since they drank beer at the Lodge. A small slice of excitement in my usually uneventful world. The Moose Lodge was crowded with families and the elderly. It was so nice to hear people talking and laughing.

JANUARY 25, 1981

The Superbowl! But I didn't watch it. Philadelphia lost. I watched *Move Over, Darling*, a Doris Day, James Garner movie. It was quite funny.

JANUARY 30, 1981

I am having nightmares almost every night and wet the bed. It has gotten so bad I have to sleep with plastic bags under my sheets again. I don't know why I can't wake up and go to the bathroom like normal people. I wet the bed more nights than I don't. I usually do my own laundry since it is embarrassing telling mom about it. She doesn't know how much I do it.

I am becoming a great cook and made homemade macaroni and cheese again. Mom and Jim are still at the tavern. I called mom to see if she was going to eat dinner at home. No, they will stay there until 8:00 pm or 9:00 pm. When they come home, they struggle with the lock, stumble through the door, noisily locate the dinner plates I prepared for them, have a drink and cigarette while the food is in the microwave, devour their food like they are at a trough, put their dishes in the sink for tomorrow, close their bedroom door and go to bed.

I have to make my lunches for school. At this school, the kids prefer to bring their lunches and make fun of students who eat at the cafeteria, calling them "poor", whose parents can't afford food, which is the opposite of the school in California. No one really bothers me, I sit with one or two quiet students, while the cheerleaders and football players noisily occupy the middle tables, occasionally tripping some unfortunate student who has a lunch tray which goes splattering everywhere. A teacher always steps in and demands the offender to clean up the mess, and the cafeteria workers usually allow the student to get another lunch, unless the poor bullied student flees the lunch room.

Sometimes my parents eat at the tavern, which is so much easier for me when they do. I call the tavern every night to verify if I have to make their dinner or if they will eat at the tavern. Every once in a while, they will bring me fish and chips for dinner, even though it is a very late dinner and I am starving by that time. I've been playing my guitar almost every day. I'm getting better and got a John Denver song book.

School is not as I had hoped. I am learning the same things I have already learned at other schools. When I began 4th grade on the Air Force base, I was given an I.Q. test because I learned everything so quickly, without much studying. I am just below genius. They wanted to move me to fifth grade right away. I started school a year early in the Philippines so my mom said no. I wanted to go to the next grade level because school was boring. I begged mom to allow me to move ahead to fifth grade, but she refused. Mom said boys would take advantage of me. That is a strange thing to say.

Back to watching boring tv until I hear my parents drive up. I go to my bedroom and pretend I'm asleep so I don't see their embarrassingly drunken behavior. Goodnight, diary.

MARCH 30, 1981

President Reagan, a police officer, a Secret Service man, and Jim Brady have been shot. The president is in stable condition with one lung partially collapsed. The bullet went in the left side of his chest, just missed the heart. John Warner Hinkly, Jr. is the shooter. He is 22 years old and is from Evergreen, Colorado. Tim McCarthy, the Secret Service man, got shot in the stomach, which is serious, so he is not likely to survive. They were shot protecting the president.

I learned about the attempted assassination while at school, and when the principal made the announcement, some kids cheered. My teacher got quite angry and told them how terrible they were for cheering. I thought so, too, since we didn't know at the time if the president was going to survive.

The White House Press Secretary, Jim Brady, was shot above the right eye. He will certainly have brain damage and is still in unstable condition.

Dallas Deahanty, the police officer, was shot in the shoulder and neck area. He was alive at first but died at 5:15pm EST (2:15pm here, so he must have died at the scene, even though the reported stated he was alive initially). Mr. Deahanty was 40, married and had an 18 year old daughter and a 5 year old son. That is sad news.

The news reporter said John Hinkly, Jr. shot the president because of some infatuation he has with Jody Foster. I don't know what they are talking about, so Hinkly is most certainly insane.

Vice President Bush is talking on the news now. Apparently, it was a 22 caliber pistol which was used by Hinkly. There were 6 shots fired, and the president is back in surgery. Although the bullet did not hit his heart, the left lung partially collapsed. I didn't know a lung could partially collapse. I thought it either collapsed or didn't.

The shots were fired when the President was coming out of the Washington Hilton after he had given a speech. At 2:15pm, President Reagan walked out the front door, waving and smiling to reporters and spectators. First, he raised his right arm, then his left. He was beginning to turn around to answer a question from a reporter from Channel 4. That is when the 6 shots were fired. The Secret Service pushed the President into a car. I hope everyone survives the surgeries. Such a terrible thing to occur.

APRIL 20, 1981

Some things in my life are making it feel less bleak. Two things have been going on. I auditioned for the musical, *The Sound of Music*, and got the part of the second youngest daughter, Marta. A lot of people auditioned since it is a popular musical. I have been rehearsing three to four times a week after school, so I take the late bus home. I ride home with Rob, he is so cute. He practices football, even though his knee is wrapped up and he limps. I talk to him only a little bit since I'm so shy and can't think of a topic of conversation. My mind goes completely blank when I try to talk to him. For the late bus, they merge the two Bean buses into one bus home, instead of the two Bean buses in the morning. The late bus is driven by another woman who isn't Pearl. I don't see Rob in the morning because he rides the other bus.

The second thing of interest in my life is I started taking guitar lessons. Mom's tavern friend suggested a teacher in a small town near ours, so it is only 8 miles away. I have taken two guitar lessons in the last month. Mom drives me to the classes on Saturday morning, when she isn't working, before meeting Jim at the tavern. I learned some chords, was taught how to pluck and strum the guitar, and purchased a guitar chord book and another guitar book for beginners with folk songs. I really enjoy taking the guitar lessons.

APRIL 27, 1981

I can't believe it. After only three guitar lessons, Jim said it is too expensive and inconvenient for mom to drive me, so I can't go any more. I want to go to more lessons since practicing the guitar gives me something to do while I'm home alone. I learned the basics for acoustical guitar, but need more lessons to get past the simplest chords. I am so depressed.

MAY 24, 1981

Yesterday Jim and I drove to Mt. St. Helens to view the destruction and carnage which occurred a year ago. I was excited to go but got stuck going alone with Jim because mom wanted to stay home. I took my guitar so I played during the long drive and didn't have to look at or talk to Jim. I was hoping that he'd see my talent and suggest that

I take more guitar lessons. I brought it up, but was quickly shot down. Too expensive and inconvenient. That is difficult to believe.

The police didn't allow visitors to Mt. St. Helens until very recently. The mountain shows only slight activity, so it is deemed okay to visit the mountain now. Many of the mountain roads are still blocked with dried mud, houses, and other debris, or just completely gone. You can see where the top dome of the mountain was blown off. The trees down the mountain look like toothpicks knocked over, radiating from the point of the explosion. Nothing is green in the trees or ground. Everything is encased in thick, dark gray dust and mud. The mud settled twenty feet or more above the previous surface, so as we drove up the mountain, you can see only the roofs of houses sticking out of the mud, and occasionally a tall house with only the upper story window showing. Most homes are now located on the river bed, washed away from the top of the mountain to the base. A lot of the houses were mostly old, Victorian homes, so they weren't small. It is creepy seeing a house buried in mud up to its roof.

There was also ash and lava rocks further away from the mountain. There wasn't a lava eruption, but the explosion pushed out old lava rocks. I picked up a few lava rocks and collected a jar full of ash. I cleaned out an old peanut butter jar to fill up with ash. I thought the mountain would have ash everywhere but it didn't. Mostly mud, the ash was located further away from the mountain. It was about 50 miles from the mountain that we found the most ash. I know a large ash cloud engulfed cities far from the mountain, a hundred miles and more.

Jim stopped at a tavern on Spirit Lake, near the mountain, to have a beer. I was reminded of Harry Truman who thought this lake would protect him from a volcanic eruption. They've never found his body.

While Jim was in the bar and I was waiting in the car playing my guitar, looking at the mountain, he asked the bartender where we could get ash. That is how we found some. The bartender knew what he was talking about. It feels so gritty and heavier than dirt. But the ash seems lighter than dirt, too, because when you touch it, puffs of dust go everywhere. When I reopened the jar of ash, a small cloud of ash came out so I am not going to open it anymore until I find a nicer jar to put it in.

It was a fun excursion, except the part of being with Jim. We don't talk much which is weird, like he is a stranger. Mom was excited when we got back, saying we did a "father daughter outing." That made me sick. I hate when she forces me to do things alone with him. He scares me. When we got home, mom and Jim went to the tavern, as usual.

AUGUST 1, 1981

Today is rock history! At 12:01 am EST (9:01 am PST), MTV launched. It is musical television which has music videos of songs. They started with the words "Ladies and gentlemen, rock and roll," and began by using images of the first Columbia Space Shuttle launch countdown (which took place earlier this year) and the Apollo 11 countdown. Then, the MTV theme music played. I saw it all since it is a Saturday morning, and I don't have school! It wasn't very professional and had black screen quite often in between songs.

The first music video ever shown was The Buggles' *Video Killed the Radio Star*, followed by one of my favorite singers, Pat Benatar's *You Better Run*. It is so cool, that a girl who lives a mile from me, Gale, wanted to come over to watch it on our satellite dish. Her house doesn't have satellite, so I made a new friend because of MTV! I can't wait to go to school on Monday when everyone is talking about MTV. I will be one of the few people who saw the opening of the new video music scene. I'm so excited!

SEPTEMBER 5, 1981

A crazy thing happened last night. For the first time since moving to Bean, an enormous and frightening storm was unleashed on our lonely hill. I can usually sleep through anything, I mean, seriously, anything. Sumo wrestlers wearing steel-toed boots rolling on my bedroom floor wouldn't wake me. This storm did. The wind howled and reached near hurricane force, according to the news today. There was lightening and thunder, which is rare in Washington, and hail the size of softballs. The wind whipped and tore at our mobile home, which concerned me greatly, but it held out in the end. My bedroom has a large picture window to which my bed is pressed against so I can look at the stars at night. I witnessed the destruction from the comfort of my bed.

Mom heard the commotion and made her way to my bedroom, to make sure I was alright, which is a rarity these days. I told her to sit on my bed as we watched the whirling debris and blinding flashes of lightening. The hail was falling at a 45° angle due to the force of the wind, so it pummeled the front of the mobile home, not my bedroom window which faces south.

The wind pushed and pulled at the metal tool shed, bending walls and doors and making a horrendously loud sound. The metal doors bent in then out, as if the shed was breathing heavily. The quivering shed finally gave up one of the doors, which flew into the sky like Dorothy's house in The Wizard of Oz. Once the first door went, the second one quickly followed. The noise was deafening.

Mom said "oh, shit" about a hundred times while watching the destruction of our storage shed. The shed was secured with ropes tied to railroad spikes driven deep into the ground, so mom hoped it would withstand the attack. I must admit, I secretly hoped the shed would be destroyed. I got my wish.

The wind mercilessly attacked the shed, causing the floor to buckle and repeatedly lifted the shed so high we could see sky underneath, held to the earth only by the securing ropes. It was a bizarre sight, seeing the shed seemingly float in the air, even though it was filled with hundreds of pounds of tools, a work bench and riding lawn mower.

The strain on the ropes was enormous, and we saw the railroad spikes slowly rise higher and higher until they were released from the ground.

The shed hovered momentarily in the air, as if unsure what to do. The storm quickly decided, and with a great swirling wind, lifted the shed fifty feet in the air where it twirled like a ballet dancer before disappearing over the hill behind our home. It travelled hundreds of feet, finally crashing to the ground in the abandoned log mill. We couldn't see it land, but heard the screaming metal as it bounced around for a while. Everything within the shed was scattered for half a mile, some of which we still haven't located.

Jim didn't wake up during the entire storm since he was so intoxicated. Today, Jim vowed to replace the shed with a wooden one since there are pre-fabricated wooden sheds sold at the base exchange, so all he has to do is bolt it together. Most of his tools survived the onslaught, which surprised me. I found the toolbox fully intact at the base of our hill. Nature is an awe inspiring thing. Even though my parents were quite upset about the cheap metal shed, I found the entire event thrilling. There isn't much excitement in my life if a storm is the highlight of the year.

SEPTEMBER 6, 1981

A super frightening thing happened last night, more frightening than the storm. I decided to set up my pup tent in the front "yard" (more rocks than yard) since the back is all weeds as tall as me. I made a comfortable bed on a pile of blankets topped with my sleeping bag. Cindy camped with me, and before I went to sleep, I tied a triple knot on the tent door that I learned in Girl Scouts so no one could open the flap. If anyone attempted to open my tent door, the knots tighten. I am SO glad that I did! I woke up in the middle of the night to Cindy growling and barking and saw the silhouette of a man trying to untie the knots! He kept pulling at the strings and couldn't get in and began shaking the whole tent. I asked if it was mom, but there was no answer, only a pause, then more aggressive pulling at the tent flap. I suddenly felt so panicked that I couldn't breathe or yell. I was completely frozen in terror. Luckily, Cindy's barking woke up mom, so she opened the front door and called out to me, asking if I was okay. We have no street lights, so my tent was in complete darkness. I wasn't able to answer because I was so terrified I couldn't move. Mom came down to my tent and asked again if I was alright. The man ran off as she approached my tent. She saw his shadow, but couldn't see his face. I suddenly was able to move, so I shakily untied the knots, which wasn't easy because the man really tightened them from his tugging. I finally opened my tent door and told her what happened. I went back inside and slept in my bed.

We both think it was the brain damaged man who lives down the hill, whose father ran over his head. I never wrote about it, but one day when I came home from walking in the woods, I saw him standing on his bike seat, looking in my mom's bedroom window. I yelled at him and he got on his bike and pedaled through the woods. Mom had been undressing when he was watching her. Mom went to the police station downtown Bean and told them about it, but the police said not to worry. The policeman said that he had been caught peeping before but was harmless. We are not sure he is harmless, and believe it was he who tried to enter my tent. What was he planning to do to me? Since the police didn't do anything about his peeping, mom decided not to tell them about the attempted break-in to my pup tent. She also told me not to tell Jim.

Today, mom acts like nothing even happened. I will never camp out in our yard again.

SEPTEMBER 7, 1981

It is 4:00 am and I am watching the Jerry Lewis Marathon for Muscular Distrophy in my bedroom because I can't sleep, even though it is the weekend. I'm having my usual nightmares and woke up early, afraid to go back to sleep. The telethon goes on all weekend, day and night. The middle of the night, Jerry gets a bit sappy and sings melancholy songs. A girl in a wheelchair sang *Somewhere Over the Rainbow* with such a powerful voice, it amazed me.

I moved the old color tv from the spare bedroom to mine, which makes more sense. I have to use the rabbit ears since I can't use the satellite dish because it rotates when you change channels, so two different tvs can't watch different channels, only watch what the other person is watching on the other television. Yes, it is very complicated since the giant monstrosity rotates when channels are changed, searching the sky for unseen satellites orbiting the earth. Jim often watches Playboy Channel, which isn't really my thing, so I opted out of the satellite dish simultaneous television watching experience.

I can actually get some channels on my tv since we are on top of a hill. I can watch *Saturday Night Live*, even though it is usually rather silly. There is a hilarious skit by Eddie Murphy's doing his version of Mister Robinson's Neighborhood. His neighborhood is more like the one we stayed at in Tacoma. *Saturday Night Live* does have great bands performing, and since it is live, sometimes a swear word sneaks in. I saw Prince, Cheap Trick and Deborah Harry. It was so cool. Deborah Harry was the best because she had the f*ck you attitude. She is so beautiful. I wish I had an exciting life like she has.

SEPTEMBER 10, 1981

I've had terrible anxiety and fear because I started 8th grade today. No one seems to notice me, so I don't get picked on. A few of the older boys forced newbies to push pennies with their nose on the sidewalk in front of school. Other unfortunate boys got their heads flushed in the toilets. It's terrible. The teachers don't do anything to stop the harassment. I'm not picked on, but I feel sorry for those who are.

Today, on the news, scientists just discovered that leukemia may be a virus, not a disease, that begins in the body. This is the first step to finding a cure for the deadly disease. Scientists think that some people are more susceptible to leukemia than others. They now think it may not be hereditary.

SEPTEMBER 24, 1981

I can do good things sometimes. Today I gave my Mount Krakatoa presentation in science class, which terrified me so much I could barely speak. I was able to pull it off. Mt. Krakatoa was the largest volcanic eruption in recorded history, and occurred early in the morning of May 20, 1883. It was much bigger than Mt. St. Helens. Most of the island the volcano inhabited was destroyed and disappeared under the sea. Ash travelled around the world and altered the weather for quite some time. Huge tidal waves washed over the surrounding islands and were seen hundreds of miles away.

I created 4 boards showing the different stages of the eruption, with a cross section showing the eruption of lava. Mom gave me great suggestions, bought the materials with me, and assisted. We also built a paper maché volcano about a foot and a half tall that was cut in half and could be opened to show the interior of the volcano. It turned out so well, I was amazed! Mom hasn't assisted with my homework for years.

I wrote a corresponding paper about Mt. Krakatoa and pointed to the boards and model throughout the presentation. The teacher was so amazed that he asked to keep the boards and model forever to use for teaching in his class. I told him he could keep them. He said that it was the best report he has ever seen. Mom actually drove me to school on the day of the presentation, with the paper maché mountain and boards, so I got one morning when I didn't have to ride the bus. I definitely got an "A" on the Krakatoa project.

OCTOBER 3, 1981

I have been visiting Gail's house lately since her home is more stable than mine. Gail liked watching MTV at first, but after meeting my drunk parents, she hasn't been over since. Gail has so many good albums. She likes Van Halen, AC/DC, Pat Benatar, Ozzy Osbourne and others. We listen to music together and she shows me how to apply makeup. Gail is an artist with makeup, using purple and pink, blending the colors so they aren't garish. I made the mistake of leaving the makeup on when my parents got home from the tavern. Jim stumbled in, demanded dinner, and as I was getting their plates heated, he saw my face and said I looked like a whore. It was so shocking to be spoken to that way, and I know I didn't look like a prostitute. It was cruel and hateful. My mom didn't hear him say the comment. She was too busy eating.

Gail has done so much for her age. She's kissed boys, which is something I've never done. Gail told me a secret. When she was 9, she and Will, who is a grade ahead of us, actually did it! You know, sex. They used to have sex a lot, which I find disturbing at such a young age. The weird thing is Gail and Will look so much alike. I mean, Gail doesn't look like her mom, dad or sister, but she has the exact same toothy smile that Will does. You would think they were brother and sister looking at them, they look so much alike. I secretly wonder if her mom cheated on her husband. If Gail and Will are half-siblings, that would be so gross!

OCTOBER 13, 1981

This morning, I had a harrowing experience. At the bus stop, I was almost attacked by a pack of wild dogs. There has been a pack of abandoned dogs who banded together, searching for food. Most of them are quite large and mangy in appearance, poor beasts. I can only imagine one of my former pets living in the same terrible conditions.

My neighbor's dog, Taxi, almost always walks with me to the bus stop. I am the only one at the bus stop so I enjoy Taxi's company. While waiting for the bus, about 8 to 10 wild dogs came out of the woods, encircled me and began growling menacingly. I had no where to go. If I ran, I knew they would tear my apart. I stood still, trying to hold my ground when Taxi leapt in front of me, protecting me from the dogs' attack. Taxi boldly barked and snarled at the dogs ferociously. I was terrified they would kill Taxi. Just then, the school bus came over the hill and the stray dogs ran off into the woods, but poor Taxi was hit by the bus as it was coming to a stop. Luckily, it only stunned her, she was only bumped by the bus as Pearl slammed on her brakes. I waited until Taxi got up and ran back home before getting on the bus. I told Pearl about the pack of wild dogs and she said that it was lucky Taxi was there. Pearl said people have been complaining about those dogs killing their pets. Pearl said that she would tell her husband about it so he'll take care of the problem. He is a hunter, so I know what he will do. It is sad seeing former pets in such terrible condition.

NOVEMBER 6, 1981

I feel included, finally. I have been alone for so long here in Bean, no friends,, it's been tough. My self esteem has reached an all time low. Now, I have Gail as a friend, so my spirits have lifted a bit. I even smoked pot for the first, second and third time. The first time, Gail and I went to the Halloween football game and party at our junior high school. We ran into a friend of hers, then several more, and we all piled into a boy's car and they started smoking a joint. I asked to try it, but they wouldn't allow me at first. Finally Gail let me take a few tokes, although she felt guilty about introducing me to marijuana. She said that I probably wouldn't feel it the first time I smoked weed. She was right. I got a little dizzy but no other effects.

I wanted to try it again so I could get really high, and I did. Gail's friend, Paula, who I started hanging around with at school, got some good pot from her older sister. Paula and

I met up at Laura's bus stop, almost two miles toward town. Laura is another of Gail's friends, who regularly smokes pot with Paula before school. I have three new friends through connections with Gail's group of friends.

They are building a new junior high school, so our over-crowded school has two shifts, one starting at 5:30 am, and the second beginning at noon. We alternate shifts every three weeks. It is very difficult getting to the early shift since the bus picks us up at 4:30 am. The kids from Bean are currently on the second shift, so the school bus doesn't arrive until 10:45 am. It takes a little over an hour to get to school because of the lunchtime traffic close to school.

The three of us smoked weed before school at Laura's bus stop three days ago. I secretly walked the two miles since I didn't want my parents to know that I was going to another bus stop. Jim is still a part-time mail carrier, so I walked on the edge of the forest instead of the road, in case he drove by. I don't know his exact route, but he was working that day. Luckily, I didn't see him.

The second time I smoked weed, I did feel the effects. The first two hits did nothing, so I started feeling bummed out. On my third hit, I was just saying to Paula and Laura that I wasn't feeling anything, when suddenly it felt like space and time slowed almost to a stop. I got extremely dizzy and felt the world go slow-motion, all colors became vivid and all sounds became amplified. The song we heard at Laura's house before we left, *I'd Stop The World and Melt With You* started playing in my head. It was fabulous to finally escape the boredom of my life. While we were getting high, we hid in the bushes so Jim and Laura's parents wouldn't see us.

I bought some pot from Paula, and Laura showed me how to make a pipe from a toilet paper roll. I totally didn't understand where to cut the hole, and how to smoke with it, so Laura showed me after school.

So much for being bored at home now. I'm going to smoke some weed and blow the smoke out of my bedroom window. Laura told me to put a towel at the bottom of my bedroom door so no smoke escapes. I never would have thought of that. I burn candles, too, which helps make the pungent smell dissipate. I'm going to put on my headphones and listen to Van Halen's *Fair Warning* album that Gail and I bought from the record store in Tacoma last week. Her mom drove us there to buy albums. I get an allowance, so I can afford to buy albums, which are better than 8-track tapes. I have really good headphones, so I can't hear anything outside the music. I finally found something fun to do.

NOVEMBER 12, 1981

A new girl at the bus stop, Amber, just moved into the new trailer park they put at the end of the main gravel road. She has a younger brother and sister, who also waited for the bus, so I'm not alone anymore, which is kind of a bummer. I liked the privacy since I now have weed to smoke. I won't do it with those three nosy punks around. Her brother was friendly, but her sister is always looking at the ground, off to the side, looking suspicious of everything, and screaming "I'm a victim, hurt me!" by her body language. Something is wrong in her life. I'm sure of it.

Amber is extremely hyperactive, annoying and has been forcing her friendship on me. I have no choice. She never stops talking, which is rather annoying. We'll see how it goes.

NOVEMBER 15, 1981

Amber invited me over to her single wide trailer yesterday. It has three bedrooms, so she and her sister share a room. The bedrooms are very small, making our double wide look like a luxury home compared to Amber's. There are five people living in half the space we have. Amber's mom is as hyper as Amber and frequently forgets to pick Amber and me up from school. I have been staying late at school with Amber because she plays all different sports and doesn't want to go home alone. I have nothing else to do, so I stay after school and watch her practice volleyball. I told Amber we should just take the late bus home, but her mother keeps saying she'll pick us up from school, and Amber believes her. The other day, we had to wait over an hour after the bus left for her mom pick us up. She completely forgot until Amber called her at home from the payphone near school. I seriously don't understand why Amber won't ride the late bus home.

Amber's father is part Cherokee, which is of some interest, and explains Amber's chiseled nose. She is really quite stunning except for her nose. I'm just going to say it. Amber's dad is a super creep. He looks at me in a way that I don't like. He is a minister at a church in a small town about 10 miles away. Amber convinced me to attend church with her family this morning, and it was alright. I don't want to go to church, but it gives me something to do with other people. Nobody else around goes to church, as far as I can tell. The local tavern is their place of worship.

Amber brags about being born in San Diego, like it's such a magical, mystical city. I also hear frequent stories about Amber's cheerleader, best friend Chrissy, who lives in Longview, Washington. Amber's family moved to Bean from Longview.

Amber decided to join the choir with me at school, so I have a friend in there now. I begrudgingly call Amber my friend, yet she is more of a companion. Her constant chatter can get tiring.

I forgot to tell you, I am singing in a quartet at school called The Chantelles. We sing harmony a cappella. We won the talent show at school this year, just a couple of weeks ago. I got an award and a trophy that is kept at school forever. My teacher enrolled us in the Washington State singing competition which takes place near the end of the school year, in April 1982! We will sing *The Rose* by Bette Midler and some other song which hasn't been decided yet. The state has competitions for every grade level, so we'll be competing in the 8th grade section. I am so excited! I've never done anything like this before, being selected in the quartet when so many girls auditioned. My teacher picked me right away. I don't know why I didn't write about the choir stuff. It is cool, but getting high is more fun. I guess it just slipped my mind.

NOVEMBER 17, 1981

Today was one of the largest viewing audiences ever for *General Hospital* because Luke and Laura finally got married. I almost stopped watching during the stupid Ice Princess thing where Port Charles froze during the summer, Luke fled on his yacht to Mexico and Laura was secretly stowed onboard. With Rick Springfield on the show, it does add some interest. I like the song *Jessie's Girl.* Amber adores the show, so I invited her to watch the recorded show on our VCR after school. She eagerly accepted the invitation, so I have a friend who comes over every day after school, even if it is to use me for watching tv. She especially wanted to see the wedding of Luke and Laura. Even Elizabeth Taylor made an appearance, which mom got totally excited about, going on and on about growing up with Elizabeth Taylor movies, *National Velvet*, *A Place in the Sun*, and *Cat on a Hot Tin Roof.* I have seen a few of her movies, and she was incredibly gorgeous when she was younger. Mom doesn't care as much for Luke and Laura and tends to watch *All My Children* with me.

DECEMBER 3, 1981

Thanksgiving was the usual boring fiasco. I used to enjoy preparing and cooking the food with mom. It is tedious and unsatisfying now since Jim sits in his Lazy Boy, demanding beer. Thanksgiving is the only day of the year when the tavern is closed. It is open on Christmas but not Thanksgiving. Probably because Tubby likes his food too much. I don't blame him. He should close the tavern once in a while.

DECEMBER 13, 1981

Last night I really injured myself. I'm sure I needed stitches, but my parents were too drunk to take me and Jim said I didn't need any "goddam" stitches. I was at Amber's trailer playing Monopoly with her and her brother, Andy, when my mom called and told me to come home for dinner. I asked her why should I come home for dinner when they are never home for dinner. I was actually doing something with another human, which is rare, so it is very annoying to be interrupted for something as mundane as dinner with parents who are almost never home. Mom was drunk and told me not to talk back. It sounded like she was crying. Sigh. She cries at a drop of a hat when she's intoxicated. Jim wanted to have dinner together, so I was forced to go home before I got a "whoopin" for "upsetting" my mom. They are so selfish and don't understand my point of view at all.

It has been very cold and icy, so to get home faster, I decided to cut across the cow pasture. It is half the distance versus walking the gravel road which goes in a big "L" shape. The only problem is there is a bull who likes to charge everything that moves. I've cut through the field before, and had to run fast through that pasture because the bull does chase after me, snorting and stamping his hooves. The bull makes the ground shake because he is so big. The pasture is surrounded by a barbed wire fence. I started to climb over the fence carefully, my foot slipped on the icy wire when I had my leg part way over the fence. I fell to the ground on the pasture side and the barbed wire ripped a 4" gash in my leg, ripping my jeans. Blood was oozing out so fast that my jeans were soaking it up, making it hard to move my right leg. It was so cold outside that the bloody jeans froze to my leg.

I struggled to my feet, holding my injured leg, and began my journey home. I heard the bull's hoof stomp the ground before I could see anything in the dark. There are no street lights and it was foggy. I heard the bull grunt a few times and then started running towards me. It crossed my mind to climb back over the fence I just fell over, but was afraid there wasn't enough time. I decided to make a run for it. I was injured but ran as fast as I could toward home. Fear got me moving very quickly. The earth trembled under the weight of the running bull, so I knew he was close. I tried to fool the bull by running in a zigzag pattern. It worked. He stopped and tried to figure out what I was doing. I took that opportunity to get over the barbed wire fence, whether I was close to home or not. I made it, barely. The bull charged at me but didn't run into the fence. I was afraid that he would barrel through the fence to get at me, but he didn't. The top of the barbed wire has an electrified wire, which makes it even MORE difficult to climb the fence quickly. I'm not entirely sure, but I think I jumped the fence completely with one huge jump.

When I got home, I was going to remove my jeans and clean my wound, but as soon as I walked through the front door, Jim yelled at me demanding to know what I thought I was doing. I said that I was going to change my clothes, but he yelled at me to come to the dining room table instead. He wouldn't even let me go wash my hands for dinner. He said that if they are dirty, that is my problem. Jim glared at me so I went to the table and sat down. I didn't' even take off my coat. Mom was bringing out the food, stumbling the whole way in her toad green robe. She was so drunk. Seriously, we never eat at the table anymore. Jim got it into his stupid mind to do it one night. When he wants to do something, no one else has any say about it and we must obey. It makes me sick.

I was hiding my torn jeans and the blood, mostly because Jim would yell at me for ripping my jeans. He wouldn't care that I was hurt. I must have been pale and shaking all over because mom came over to me and asked if I was okay. I said that I was, but she saw blood on the arm of my coat. She asked where the blood came from, so I had to show her. Mom pried the jeans from the wound to look at it. It was frozen to my leg because of the blood. It's a bad gash about 4" long and appeared to be fairly deep. Mom asked Jim if I should go to the emergency room. He took one glance at it and grumbled that he didn't want to go to the hospital at that time of night and I would be fine. Mom told me to go and change for dinner, but Jim told me to stay at the table and eat as I was. I could clean up after I ate dinner. He is so cruel. By that time, my leg hurt so much, it was almost unbearable.

Once we were done, Jim actually made me help clean up the table before I could take care of my bleeding leg. Of course, he didn't help clean off the table and put the food away. He never does. Jim just sits there and barks orders. There was so much blood that my jeans were sticky with it from top to bottom. My wound kept bleeding throughout dinner, saturating my jeans.

I finally had the chance to escape to the bathroom, where I had to literally peel off my jeans. The pain made me dizzy, it was terrible, and mom forgot about it and didn't help me at all. The wound from the barbed wire is quite bad. It gapes open, and certainly needed stitches. I was getting the hydrogen peroxide out to clean the wound when mom knocked at the bathroom door. After finishing the dishes, I guess she decided that I was important. Mom cleaned my wound and made me walk out into the living room in my shorts and show Jim how bad it was. She said that I really needed stitches or it would scar. He said that it wasn't that bad and a scar would teach me to be more careful in the future. Then mom checked my medical documents to see when my last tetanus shot was given. It wasn't too long ago, so at least I won't get lock jaw.

I think that it cut my leg muscle a bit because it hurts to walk. Jim said it was my fault, as usual. Jim is the meanest man in the whole world. I HATE HIM! I HATE

HIM! I HATE HIM! I HATE HIM! I HATE HIM! I wish he was dead.

DECEMBER 18, 1981

Although I have made some friends, I still feel alone most of the time, and a little sad. I still have nightmares and wet the bed, at my age. It's embarrassing. Last night, I had a strange dream. I was in a playground after dark with a 7 year old girl. I wanted to go home, so I began walking away from the little girl when someone shot her with a machine gun. I ran to the girl and then I got shot. I didn't feel pain because it was so quick.

Suddenly, I was standing in front of a line of small buildings. I couldn't see the end of the buildings, they went on so far. There was grass and a side walk but there wasn't a street or car anywhere. Nobody was in sight. Nor were there any birds, insects or flowers. There wasn't even a breeze or trees. There was no sign of life except the grass and one woman who was walking down the sidewalk toward me.

I tried to speak to the woman but nothing came out. She looked at me, took my hand and led me into a building (one of the hundreds). It was very nice inside with a room filled with exotic animals in cages. It seemed strange that there wasn't a zoo smell.

The woman led me past the caged beasts and up a flight of stairs. There were hundreds of bedrooms with a person in each, young and old, living out their life in that room, not wandering out, staying isolated. The woman motioned for me to enter an empty room. I was terrified that I'd become trapped in the building like everyone else. I knew I would never escape the room. That's when I woke up. I feel like I won't ever leave Bean and be isolated forever.

DECEMBER 31, 1981

Tonight will be another stupid New Year's Eve all alone. I will watch tv because there is nothing else to do. Maybe there will be a scary movie. Amber and Gail are both out of town, so I am stuck in satellite tv land by myself. MTV and then the New York ball drop with Dick Clark. He was around when mom was a teenager, so he is old.

Christmas was okay, but after we ate our ham dinner at 2:00 pm, my parents went to the tavern. For my 13th birthday, nothing happened. I thought it would be special because I am a teenager now, but nothing. After the tavern tonight, my parents are going to a poker party at someone's house. I don't know where they will be. I think I'll get high now, play Space Invaders and listen to music for a while. Happy New Year.

CHAPTER 4

1982: AGE 13

JANUARY 2, 1982

I must have a black hole in me that attracts the strangest people. Something completely bizarre happened to me today. Mom and I went to the mall for the "after Christmas" sales and buy some clothes for my birthday. I love when we go to Nordstrom, especially to the The Plum (the junior department). I get modern, cutting edge clothes, but feel self-conscious when I wear them. I hate being like that. I wish I felt beautiful and positive. I used to dress up and didn't think anything about it, but now I am so self-conscious, mom constantly nags me about not getting too fat. I weigh 118 pounds and am 5'4" tall, so I don't think I'm fat. Mom picks at everything about my body, my feet are too flat, my toes are too long, my hips are too wide. The only part of my body mom says looks good are my calves. Gee, thanks, mom.

So, anyway, we also went to The Bon Marché, another great store, and that is where the creepy event occurred. We found bins full of wooden Christmas ornaments and were going through them feverishly. We found Dancer and Blitzen right away and were determined to find all of Santa's reindeer. It took about half an hour to find all the reindeer except for Rudolph. He was completely gone. Everyone wants Rudolph, apparently, but the rest of the deer can go to hell.

During our search for the reindeer, I had to use the bathroom. Mom kept looking for Rudolph as I made my way downstairs to the bathroom. On the way, I noticed a man, some pervert, following me. I was quite uncomfortable and walked as fast as I could to the bathroom. When I came out of the bathroom, he was still there and was staring at me. I practically ran up the escalator to where mom was searching for Rudolph. I told her about the man following me to the bathroom, so she went straight to customer service and told them about the creep. Security actually looked at their surveillance video by the bathrooms and we could clearly see the pervert following me. We sat in the manager's office while they were looking at the video. I felt guilty for causing such a problem.

The store manager sent the security guards out to apprehend the man. They escorted him out of the store and offered to walk us to our car. Mom told them we didn't need to be walked to the car. I would have felt better with security, but she didn't want to put them out (even though it's their job). I felt guilty, even though I didn't even do anything wrong. I hope that man won't hurt any girl. I attract the weirdos.

FEBRUARY 13, 1982

Here is some of my poetry from a school writing assignment:

> DISTANT HIGHWAYS
> The winding coast road
> Twists around enormous, jagged rocks;
> California roads snake around the coast,
> Taking a visitor to far away adventures.

APRIL 15, 1982

I went to the Washington State Choir Competition and we placed sixth in the state. It's good, I guess, but you don't get awards for sixth place. Mom never came to my choir practice and didn't show up for the state competition. I told her where it was located, not too far away, but she was busy with work. It was on a Thursday. Amber's mom didn't make it either, which isn't a surprise to anyone. That woman forgets what month she's in.

MAY 6, 1982

I have been seeing a lot of Amber lately, not really by choice, but because of convenience. She lives the closest. Amber invited me to go to church with her again. It gives me something to do.

Amber's father scares the crap out of me, though. He enjoys playing cruel jokes on people which the entire family finds strangely hysterical. Last Sunday, when we were leaving the church and I was trying getting into the truck, he started to drive away when I only had one leg in. I had a dress on and high heels while he and Amber were laughing at me because I had to hop in order not to fall out of the moving truck. He stopped the truck, pretending to let me in, and started driving again, three more times before I had to literally run and jump into the truck to get in. It wasn't funny and I told them. It really scared me because I could have fallen out and got injured on the gravel parking lot.

Another weird thing about Amber's father is the way he stares at me. I don't like it at all. He watches me for prolonged periods of time, which is not normal behavior, not with a 13 year old girl. I don't like going anywhere near him. Another strange thing is Amber's mom, sister, and brother drive separately to church in their own car which could easily fit us all, since it is a station wagon. I truly don't know why they take two different vehicles to church. Amber's dad will only ride in his truck and Amber likes going with him. I told Amber that next Sunday, I'd rather go with her mom and siblings in the station wagon instead. She got kind of mad about it. I don't know why she likes him at all he since he is so cruel. I would actually describe him as sadistic. I bet he'd like my parent's gross pornographic movies.

I still have a little homework to do. Not much since I almost always finish early. It is so easy in school. Too easy. I have learned everything they teach already. A lady here in Bean who works with mom at the hospital, pleaded with her to drive me to the school in Mesco, which is a much better quality school. I want to go to Mesco if it's better. Plus, it is only 8 miles away versus the 45 to 60 minutes it takes on the bus each way. A bus doesn't come here from Mesco, so mom doesn't want to drive me to school every day. I know why. Even though she works really early and gets off work at 3:30, she doesn't want to interrupt her stop to the Bean Tavern with Jim. She goes every day. I told mom she could go to the tavern after picking me up from school, but she won't do that. It's so frustrating! I want a better education, yet mom won't put out the minimal energy to take me to a much better school.

I did have a gross experience. I was walking down the hall on my way to choir when some boy in my grade came up to me and stuck his tongue in my mouth and forced a kiss on me. I have never kissed anyone before. I didn't like doing it that way for the first time. Plus, he had food in his mouth. I am about to gag right now thinking about the gross food in his mouth. It was horrible. No one saw, thank goodness. It wasn't right for him to do that to me.

JUNE 6, 1982

Gail invited me to a senior party in a cow field not too far from our houses. It was so much fun. Gail and I got there and someone had made mushroom tea. We were partying in the cow pasture and people were searching the cow patties for the right kind of mushrooms. I looked but couldn't find any. The shroom tea was so much fun. I could hear cows mooing nearby, and I talked to some boy whose dad owned the property, but I can't remember his name. I saw lights in the sky and thought it was an alien spaceship. The boy said it wasn't an alien spaceship, but a small airport. I was so surprised that there would be an airport in the middle of a field, but he told me his dad flies his own plane and there are small airports everywhere in the United States that we don't even know are there. It was still cool seeing the blinking lights from the low flying airplane when I was high on mushroom tea. I still like pretending they were aliens.

We didn't stay very late because Gail's mom picked us up. It was a super fun party. I don't know who anyone was since most are older than me and it was very dark in the cow pasture. It was the first time I took mushrooms. They are so much fun. I want to get more.

JUNE 23, 1982

I really love seeing Rob. He plays basketball and football and has a twin, Rick, but they are not identical. They look alike, especially from the back. It is hard to tell them apart from a distance, but their faces are different. He is so sweet, too. I enjoy going home on the late bus after my quartet practice so I can wait until he is done with football and ride home on the same bus.

Rob told me there is a path through the woods from my house to his. I've heard that from Laura, too. I want to find this shortcut. To go by road is about 5 miles to his house, but through the woods, it isn't more than a mile. Laura said she used to take the forest path to go and visit the Mabrey's house to see Ken, who sold weed. The Mabreys have lots of brothers, Rick and Rob being the youngest. Some are older and have moved away from Bean, lucky people.

JULY 11, 1982

I can't believe it. Amber was in my bedroom when I went to the bathroom. When I returned, she was reading my diary – you! She saw the part about her creepy dad and got mad at me. How dare she get mad at me when she is the one snooping. I told her that her dad is creepy. Amber went home angry, which was fine. She was going to spend the night, but if she is going to be like that, then she should go home.

I've been babysitting a lot, which is good weed money, and hopefully mushrooms to make tea, but I don't know how to make shroom tea. It's too dangerous to get the wrong mushrooms, so I won't try. I got my first babysitting job from people at the bar who drink with my parents. Mom recommends me. Now I get so many jobs because of positive referrals. The kids always ask for me because I do things with them like color and play games. When the kids go to bed, I always clean up the house and usually get extra money. It gets boring waiting until 2:00 am for parents to get home, so I clean. I tell them they don't have to pay me more.

There is a family who usually use Paula as their babysitter, and I'm the back up in case she's busy. The couple are nice and live in a small house in downtown Bean. I don't particularly like babysitting there because I think the kids, a brother and sister, do sexual things together. They have their own rooms but the boy always sneaks into the girl's room. They like to sleep together, which is fine, but I get the impression there is something else going on. It doesn't seem right, somehow, because they seem to be kissing and touching each other in inappropriate ways. I haven't told the parents. What could I say, anyway? I told Paula about it at school and said she has seen the same behavior but thinks it's innocent. There is something wrong with that family. On a good note, Paula said most of the parents around Bean either smoke weed or have cocaine because her older sister sells it to them. She told me of some of their stash locations. I haven't snooped before, but I will start to now.

Laura said she's going to take me to a head shop in Tacoma so I can get a glass pipe or bong. We hitchhike sometimes to Tacoma since Laura knows a lot of people that will get us high. We hitchhike together, and Laura has a switchblade she carries in her boot. Laura made me promise never to hitchhike alone since it can be dangerous. I told her I wouldn't.

I love listening to music while high. I leave my radio on to the classical station when I go to sleep, hoping it will prevent nightmares. Classical music is incredibly soothing and helps me to escape and relax. It doesn't seem to stop nightmares, though.

JULY 14, 1982

I went to see the Scorpions last night with my mom. I wanted to go with Gail, but her mom wouldn't let her go because we are going to see Iron Maiden in a few days. Mom listens to the Scorpions with me and loves the Blackout album. She bought some beer, Olde English 800 at my recommendation, since it is stronger. I drank 4 of them, and mom 2, one right after the other, catching a sweet buzz. We sat down for almost the entire show since mom is kind of old, but it was still fun. The Scorpions are incredible. They had a smoke machine and laser lights. Totally mind blowing. The show was at the Seattle King Dome. Mom purchased t-shirts for both of us with the tour dates on the back. It was pretty cool of my mom to go with me, and she turned her head away when the dude next to me offered me a joint. I totally did it, and mom didn't care a bit. My ears are ringing terribly today. I hope they heal in time for Iron Maiden!

JULY 17, 1982

I went to see Iron Maiden last night at the Seattle King Dome with Gail. Her mom drove us up there, dropped us off, visited some friends in Seattle then picked us up after the show. It was such a great concert! I bought a black Eddie t-shirt. That is the dead guy on all of their albums. We met up with Laura at the show and she snuck in a couple of joints in her afro. Her stepfather is white, and so is her mom, but her real father is Black. Laura is gorgeous and has skin the color of caramel. Laura seems to know so much about the world, about everything. She came across as intimidating when I first met her, because she is so intelligent and beautiful, but she turned out to be very nice. She's the girl who showed me how to make a toilet paper roll pipe and to smoke weed in my bedroom without getting caught.

The music was so loud that my ears are still ringing today! They had a light show which made me dizzy after we smoked a joint. Everyone smokes pot at the concerts. The air was heavy with pot smoke so it wasn't like we were going to get in trouble for lighting a joint. We were careful, though, and went up in the stands, to the top row, to smoke the joint. Laura went to smoke the other joint with another friend of hers.

AUGUST 13, 1982

I have been hanging out a lot with Laura. She is more intellectual than either Amber or Paula. We have some things in common, which floored me. When mom was driving Laura home the other night, Laura mentioned her dad did heroin, and that's how I found out my real father did heroin. Mom went on and on about the risks of heroin, about how he was jaundice once and really sick, stole our food and rent money, and took off for days without going to work or calling her. Laura agreed that heroin is a terrible drug and to never try it. Laura's mom left her dad in the 1969, like my mom, because of heroin. It is kind of a freaky coincidence.

Laura loaned me a book called, *Go Ask Alice*, which is a diary of a girl who becomes addicted to heroin and later dies from an overdose. Yikes. I am too frightened to stick a needle in my arm. I had rabies shots in the Philippines and that has put me off needles for life.

Laura is incredibly intelligent and mature for her 13 years. She has an old soul, so wise and calm, seeming to know so much about life. Laura has a strong sense of right and wrong, and even though she steals occasionally from cheerleaders and other preppy girls, she tells me not to steal from anyone who can't afford to replace the item. Laura steals for the challenge, taking a risk, and keeps the souvenirs of rings, bracelets, and a pair of shoes like trophies in the back of her closet.

Laura is best friends with Paula, who is the polar opposite of Laura since she is not intellectual. Paula also openly steals whenever she can, has sex with whomever, frequently skips school to drink and smoke weed, and is unashamed about doing things which are morally wrong. Laura has warned me not to follow Paula's example. I have to admit, I've skipped school with Paula a few times, and I get high with her before 4th period behind the shop building. That is the big weed and cigarette smoking area. I don't smoke cigarettes like my parents. Cigarettes are disgusting. None of my friends smoke cigarettes, just weed. Amber claims not to "do drugs", but she drinks alcohol, takes speed and doctor prescribed Ritalin. Those are drugs, so, whatever. Speed makes me feel physically ill. Once I felt so sick that I had to lay on the school bathroom floor, moaning in discomfort. Maybe speed is better for hyperactive people like Amber. I don't like speed at all.

AUGUST 21, 1982

My parents have been attending summer keg parties at different peoples barns who build bonfires in their field and invite all the people from the Bean Tavern and Bean Bar and Grill. Apparently, these barn keg parties are a thing which goes on every summer. I like that tradition. I enjoy going to these parties because I see so many kids from school. Also, it is really easy to sneak beer. Most of our parents will actually give us beer, even mom. So we don't even have to sneak it very much.

Rob rarely goes to the barn keg parties. I suspect he doesn't want to go to parties with his parents because his dad, who is a sweet teddy bear to me, will get into drunken fights. Rob's mom likes me a lot. They invite me over their house every time I see them. I get embarrassed, but I do go over there once in a while. I have snuck over to Rob's house after my parents go to bed. I located the secret deer trail, with the help of Gail who has partied at the Mabrey's house many times. It feels adventurous taking the deer path because it winds through a swamp and twists around so many times. Since I go at night and there are no street lights around, it is so dark you literally can't see your hand in front of your face. The moon can't penetrate the tree canopy, so I have to bring a flashlight. Once I forgot the flashlight, used only a lighter, and it took me almost an hour to find the Mabrey's house. It was scary out there in the woods alone in the dark. I won't travel without a flashlight again.

AUGUST 29, 1982

On an unpleasant, note, I will be starting 9th grade on August 31st. I was supposed to go to Heath Senior High School where they have grades 9 through 12, but due to overcrowding, the county is building two new junior high schools which will have grades 7 through 9 only. I think I mentioned before they were building Pinegrove, where I will attend school. I am relieved because I hear disturbing things about Heath High School. Heath High School is known to be the drug capital of Winder. Everyone says how easy it is to buy weed, hash, shrooms, acid, and LSD. That could be a good thing, however, I am craving an education, and it sounds like Heath is not the way to go.

I'm glad I don't have to go to Heath Junior High. Mr. Patrick is a dick who yelled at me during class time for talking, when I wasn't even talking. I tried to defend myself only to be called a liar in front of the entire class, so I told him he was stupid asshole. It just came out of my mouth. I wasn't planning to say anything to Mr. Patrick. I was sent to the principal's office for that one. After that, he had it in for me. If I turn around in my seat, he yells at me. He blames me for things I didn't do. Mr. Patrick the Dick blamed me for throwing a spit wad. I didn't do it. I wouldn't tell who threw the spit wad, so it just made him angrier. I still black out when I feel angry, so I say and do things I don't remember. I had him as a teacher in three of my classes, which was bad luck. Pinegrove will be transferring some teachers from Heath Junior High to Pinegrove. I am praying that Mr. Patrick the Dick won't be there. Please!

My parents don't know about the trouble I got into with Mr. Patrick last school year. The school sent letters to my parents, remarking about my poor behavior and attitude. Since I get home before my tavern drinking parents, I pick up the mail before them and open the school letters. I forged mom's signature then returned the copy back to the school's front office.

Once, Jim came home sick and got the mail before me. He saw only one of the school letters and got angry and gave me a horrible belt beating. I was supposed to pull down my pants but refused. I told Jim that I wouldn't pull down my pants. Jim grabbed and hit me with the belt everywhere. I fought him but he pushed me to the ground really hard and hit me wherever he could with the belt. Whenever he gets in a beating frenzy, I laugh at him. It makes him angrier, but I don't care. As he beats me, Jim yells at me how stupid, mean and whorish I am. I got hit in the face with the buckle that time which gave me a bruise. Jim immediately stopped beating me after striking me in the face and told me not to tell mom. It wouldn't matter if I told her, because whenever he gets angry and starts to hit me, she will goes to bed early and leave me alone with Jim.

Even though I am nervous about starting school, I am slightly enthusiastic to get back to classes where life isn't so horrible. Maybe school will be more intellectually challenging this time. It was so boring last year. I hardly learned anything new. I even asked my mom if I could go to the Catholic school in Tacoma. I saw in the newspaper how that Catholic school always scores top in science, math and music. Mom said private school is too expensive and asked why I wanted to go to a Catholic school. I told her for the education. I don't want to be a Catholic, but would love to go to a school where I could learn.

SEPTEMBER 11, 1982

I'm in choir again and plan on trying out for some upcoming musicals. For some reason, I really want to learn to play piano. I have been dropping hints to mom about buying a piano. Jim overheard my suggestion once and said he wouldn't spend that much money on something I probably wouldn't be good at or practice. I said that I would practice and he actually called me lazy. I am not lazy. He is lazy. I hate when he says such cruel comments.

SEPTEMBER 19, 1982

Last night, I stayed the night with Laura. She had an awesome plan to go to Tacoma and watch *The Rocky Horror Picture Show*. I said I would totally do it with her. My parents knew I was staying the night at her house. Laura told her parents that we were staying the night at my place. Double coverage. We walked to Bean, through town, and to the highway, which was about four miles from Laura's house. That is when we began hitchhiking. We would take a bus if one was available. There isn't public transportation within 14 miles of Bean.

Laura said it's best to hitchhike in pairs, so it is safer. We walked as we put out our thumbs. Two creepy men stopped but we declined their lecherous invitations. She said to wait for an old man, a fatherly type, to pick us up. She was right about women not stopping for us. Not a single woman stopped to give us a ride. Finally, an old man in a tractor trailer, without his load, stopped and gave us a ride. He told us we shouldn't hitchhike, and we obligingly said he was right. We needed a ride to the bus station that was south of Tacoma. He was a nice old man, lecturing us about accepting rides from strangers. Laura carries a switchblade knife in her boot, just in case.

We smoked a joint before getting on the Tacoma bus. There was a wooded area next to the bus stop, so it was easy to do. We took the bus to a sketchy part of Tacoma. It's in the same general area where my horrid grade school is located. Laura has been to the movie theater before, because she knew exactly where to walk.

The theater was frightening and rowdy. I didn't really want to go in, but Laura seemed comfortable with it. After we purchased tickets for the movie and entered into the chaos, people were jumping in their seats and yelling profanity at the screen. We didn't have to wait long for the movie. By lucky coincidence, the movie started almost immediately, to my great relief. The crowd was restless and seemed dangerous, although Laura appeared oblivious to any danger. We squeezed into two seats and the movie began.

Laura has seen *The Rocky Horror Picture Show* before and knew what to expect. I was in constant freak out mode and didn't really enjoy the movie. People were yelling, smoking, and jumping up and down. They also had squirt guns and other items prepared for the movie.

I don't remember much of the movie, being more concerned with the rowdy people. Laura, since she is Black, told me to just relax and enjoy it. I wasn't afraid because they were Black, but because the people were boisterous. My senses were overwhelmed. The movie finally ended and we took the bus back to the Bean Highway where we hitchhiked home. We didn't get many bites, so we walked most of the way. I probably walked twelve miles last night. It took forever to get a ride home. When we did, the man was twitchy and creepy. Laura had her knife ready, just in case. Nothing bad happened, but the man was definitely creepy, and I wouldn't want to be riding alone with him.

We were dropped off in Bean and walked the rest of the way to Laura's house, which was a mile and a half. Once we got there, she snuck into her bedroom window and asked me to go home so she wouldn't get in trouble. I walked home, the mile and a half, and snuck in through the front door. My parents were passed out so they never heard me enter the house. I snuck back to my bedroom and got ready for bed. I have a bathroom at my end of the trailer, so my parents never heard me, unless they were sober, which is never.

OCTOBER 3, 1982

Mom took me clothes shopping in Tacoma, which is always so much fun. We went to the mall and had our usual lunch in the Nordstrom cafe. We usually go to a movie after shopping and lunch. Recently, we saw *E.T.* (I cried) and *Porky's*. Mom thought *Porky's* was much funnier than it actually was, but I laughed because she bought us two big Old English 800 beers. *Porky's* is the kind of movie you had better drink or get high before seeing. Bathroom humor. This time, we saw *Poltergeist*, which was super scary. We loved it because we both love horror movies. I watch them while my parents are at the tavern. Gammy suggested we see the movie because the little girl apparently looks a lot like me at her age. I see similarities, except for the eye color, mine are hazel.

When my mom and I were at the mall, I asked her about my real father. Mom said that we all lived together as a hippy family for a short time and my real dad, Allen, worked in a coal mine for a little while to make money, since his father and grandfather did it before him. Allen didn't do it for long and apparently quit the coal mining job and started selling weed. Mom left Allen when a hippy couple had sex next to my crib. I didn't think it was too terrible since I was a newborn and didn't know the difference, but mom made it sound like they were child abusers.

Mom, Allen and I went to Woodstock, I also discovered. That is totally cool. Uncle Althan went, too, and hung out with his college friends so mom barely saw him. She brought bottled water with her because she heard rumors that there was going to be acid dropped in the public drinking water.

Mom finally left Allen for the last time when he took off to San Francisco to celebrate the Summer of Love, 1969. She moved in with Gammy and Uncle John in Miami. Gammy was getting a divorce from grandpa, not by choice. Gammy had a sister living in Miami, so that's why she moved there.

I sincerely hope some day I can meet my real father. Maybe he remarried and I have brothers and sisters. Maybe his family is loving and want me to join be a part of their lives. That would be nice.

OCTOBER 17, 1982

My life feels out of control. I do dangerous things because I don't care if I get hurt. Last night, I stayed at Laura's house again. We did our lie about Laura staying at my house while I told my parents I was at her house. I should have worn a warmer coat because hitchhiking up to Seattle was freezing! It took some time walking before we were picked up. We must have walked 8 miles before we saw someone who didn't look creepy.

We left early, around 1:00 pm, because it gets dark so early in autumn. It is a long bus ride from Winder to

Seattle. There was a band Laura wanted to see, the U-Men, who were playing at a dive bar she had been to before. I'm not sure how or why she was at a bar in Seattle, but Laura is full of secrets. I asked if we could get in, and she knew the bouncer, so it was cool. We brought the usual joints and Laura's flask filled with Southern Comfort, her favorite because it was Janice Joplin's favorite drink, and we could buy Cokes and mix it.

There was a weird man who pulled over for us, and seemed almost threatening us to get in his car. Laura pulled her knife and told him to fuck off. I was shocked. I'm not sure where she learned all of that hard living in the small town of Bean. I'm grateful she knows, because I was really frightened.

Finally, we found another old man truck driver, like before, who drove us to the Winder bus stop. I was very nervous about getting a ride from a trucker, even and old man, but Laura seemed cool about it. She said if anything happened, she'd stab him. Well, okay then. It never came to that. He lectured us about the dangers of hitchhiking, we agreed it was wrong, the usual drill. It is exciting doing something so dangerous. No one knew where we were, so if we disappeared, we were gone. Part of me just doesn't care. It's not like I have a normal home, so I kind of don't give a fuck.

We got to the bus stop and I fell asleep on the bus because it was hours to get to Seattle. Laura woke me up before the bus pulled into the station, so I was able to get acclimated to my surroundings. At least the bus was warm. Outside was freezing.

Laura knew where we were going, so I followed her through blocks of Seattle streets. It was getting late by then, almost 10:00 pm. It took us forever to get to Seattle. Laura said the show wouldn't start until after midnight, so we had a lot of time to kill. We smoked the joint in an alley, avoiding the homeless men who were whistling after us. We bought a Coke from a store and mixed some of the Southern Comfort in the can. We ended up drinking the entire contents of her flask, so by the time the show started, I was completely drunk, stoned, and stumbling. Laura knew everything: where to go, what to do, who to talk to, so I followed her lead.

As always with Laura, the night was hazy. I remember going into a dark, smelly bar and the bouncer letting us in. He scored us some beer, which was totally awesome. Laura seemed really friendly with the bouncer, I can't remember his name. It seemed like she had sex with him some time before because they talked in a private kind of way.

There were a couple of bands before the U-Men, so Laura and I stepped into the alley for another joint with the bouncer. He said he was taking his break. The alley smelled as bad as the bar: the nasty smell of urine and vomit. I kind of felt sick from the Southern Comfort, but didn't puke. That came later.

The band was awesome, what I remember of it. They were a rock band, not so much punk as I thought they would be. It was so cool. We were in middle school and going to a show in some dive bar in Seattle. Life doesn't get any better than that.

I have a fuzzy recollection of the rest of the evening. We took the bus to Tacoma and crashed at Paula's drug dealing sister's run down apartment. Her name is Kelly and she was having a party when we arrived. She was amped on something, and I was tired. Kelly is platinum blonde, wore black leather pants and a tight t-shirt. She has a lot of tattoos, which is cool. She scared the fuck out of me because she was interrogating Laura about me. Laura said that I was cool, so she finally let up. She didn't give us anything besides a joint, saying we were too young to do what she was doing, whatever that was.

When we woke up this morning, Kelly was passed out and no one was awake. Some people were sleeping on the floor, so Laura and I made our way back to the bus stop, and finally got to the road to Bean. The last and final leg took a while to get a ride. Laura didn't seem as concerned with the drivers since we were both hung over and tired. We got a ride with a young Army guy, who made me a bit nervous, but it turned out okay. He dropped us off in the town of Bean and then we walked the mile and a half to Laura's house, sneaking into her bedroom window. We slept for most of the day. I finally went home at dinner time and am writing in my journal. Mom asked if I had fun, and I said I did. I spent my baby sitting money on the show, but that's fine. There is nothing fun around Bean. I wish I lived in Seattle. There is so much going on there. I have no life here in Bean. Thank goodness I have Laura to take me on these adventures I would never experience without her. I don't know how she knows so many seedy people. It was a lot of fun.

NOVEMBER 1, 1982

I like hanging out with Laura because she is reckless like me. I invited Laura over last night for Halloween. Mom bought us a six pack of Schlitz Malt Liquor and Laura and we played quarters. That was a huge mistake. I need to practice quarter bouncing. I was horrible. When we ran out of beer, most of which I drank, we got a few drinks of whisky and Coke. My parents have some bottles of liquor in the cabinet and we snuck some. I have already drunk all those little airplane liquor bottles I bought as a kid for Barbie. I had 15 of them. I drank so much so quickly, I blacked out for hours. I have no memory of the rest of the night, only what I've been told. That is really, really uncool.

Since I am required to cook dinner, I completely forgot about starting the ham and mashed potatoes for my parents for when they got home. I should have done that before playing quarters and let them reheat the food. Laura told me that I got so drunk, I completely forgot how to cook. She didn't know what I was supposed to prepare, and tried to help as much as she could, but I was incoherent. Laura said that I went into my bedroom, opened up my umbrella and sat on the floor singing and laughing. I was too drunk to respond to her, so she walked home. I was in bed this morning, so I got there somehow.

Jim got really angry about not having dinner ready when they got home from the tavern. My parents didn't seem to care that I was drunk, because my mom bought us beer. My mom had to actually cook something for dinner. Not the ham, since it took too long to cook. How inconvenient of me. If I had cooked the dinner early and had it in the fridge, they wouldn't even been upset. It was the fact that I didn't have dinner ready and waiting for them after their night at the tavern which upset them.

I am so embarrassed that I acted like that in front of Laura. She wasn't nearly as drunk as me. So much for hanging out and watching a scary movie, like we originally planned.

NOVEMBER 16, 1982

I went to the Seattle Coliseum to see Judas Priest last night. It was the *Screaming For Vengeance* Tour. That album is so rad, I've memorized every song. Gail and I went to the show and mom drove us to Seattle. On the way, mom bought a 6 pack of Schlitz Malt Liquor beer. Gail and I each had 2½ beers and mom had one since she was driving. Gail and I were planning to get a ride home with her cousin who was also going to the show, so mom went home. The going home bit didn't turn out as planned. We ran into Will, who is the dude who had sex with Gail when she was like 9 years old, and also lives in Bean near us. It was actually more convenient since Gail's cousin lives in Tacoma, almost 20 miles away.

Gail snuck in two joints, one for each of us for the show. There aren't seats on the floor, so it is a huge pit filled with people, smoking joints, drinking alcohol. It was totally cool. Some guys gave us some whisky and Cokes. We both got pretty wasted. My ears are still ringing today.

During the concert, things got really crazy in the pit in front of the stage. Gail and I got trapped in the crowd. We were being pushed apart, so we decided to meet at a certain column on the east side if we got separated. We did get separated. It was so hot and people were pushing from every direction. I had a hard time staying on my feet because I was getting so dizzy from the smoke and the heat. Guys kept grabbing my ass but I could never see who was doing it.

I began fighting to get out of the crowd of people when an older man with red hair and a red beard grabbed onto me. He put his entire weight on me and kept begging me to help him. He was completely wasted and so much bigger than me that I felt panic at the idea of being dragged to the crowded floor. It was too dangerous to fall on the ground because the people were so packed in that you would get trampled for sure. Everyone was in a crazy frenzy. It was very frightening. Well, that man had a strong grip on my jacket so I finally pried his fingers off of me. I felt like I was drowning in a sea of people. I knew that I had to get away from him. I finally did, and pushed my way through the crowd to get fresh air. I was so dizzy, drunk and stoned and the heat was terrible. I knew that if I fainted I would be trampled to death in the crowd.

What is really scary is Gail called me early this morning because she got the newspaper delivered to her house. There was an article saying one man was trampled to death at the concert. I definitely didn't tell my parents about the trampling death and that I was stuck in the middle of it all. At Gail's house, I saw the newspaper with the picture of the man, it was that red headed guy with the beard. It was in black and white, but it was him. I swear it! I feel horrible and guilty. I couldn't lift him up because his legs didn't seem to work. But I still remember the pure terror in his eyes. It is like he knew that he would get trampled. Gail hid the newspaper from her parents so they didn't see that article, either. Our parents may ban us from any more shows if they heard about the death.

DECEMBER 5, 1982

I am no longer a virgin. Using the camping flashlight, I found the path right away and walked over to the Mabrey's house. Their dad bought a keg for some party the week before, so there was plenty of beer. The Mabrey's parents were still at the tavern since they stay until closing time most nights, the opposite of my parents.

Rob and Rick gave me beer and smoked some pot while we watched television, waiting until Saturday Night Live to come on. At about 11:30, we heard the rumbling of a Harley motorcycle and were told it was their older brother, Ken, who was in town for a couple of weeks before going back to California. When Ken arrived, Rob and Rick were happy to see their brother, and went outside to check out his new motorcycle. I didn't care much about the motorcycle, so I stayed in the house and watched Saturday Night Live which had the Smother's Brothers hosting the show. They are some old guys from Laugh, In a show my mom used to watch when she was my age. Laura Branigan was the musical number who had a hit Gloria. It wasn't a great show.

Rob, Rick and Ken came inside when Saturday Night Live was almost over, much to my relief since I think the show is generally stupid. Rob brought a joint to the couch and we smoke a few hits, then he said he wanted to show me something upstairs. We went into Rick's room and he showed me a new poster his brother bought. We started kissing and then it happened. It burned and hurt so much, sex wasn't very much fun. Gail said that is normal the first time.

We went back downstairs and Rob told me I should go back home before his parents came home. It was good timing since we heard the old truck pull up in the driveway. I left through the hole in the living room wall to the outside. The house isn't completely built. The hole is probably for a door in the future.

It was wonderful to have done "it" with Rob since I like him so much. I hope we start dating.

DECEMBER 9, 1982

It is sad to say, but Rob acts so shy around me now. I feel that way, too. I don't know what to say and neither does he. I wish we would date. I would like that very much. I hope he didn't use me for sex. Maybe someone else will love me. I hope so. I am sure I can find someone who will want to go out with me.

I don't have to worry about the pregnancy thing since I have been on birth control pill for two years now. As soon as I started my period, mom told me she didn't want me to get pregnant, so she took me to the Planned Parenthood office in Tacoma and got me on the pill. She didn't tell Jim of course. Mom told the nurse that she wanted me to be on the pill because it would regulate my period. That wasn't true at all. She just didn't want me to get pregnant like she did with me. I'm glad that I am on the pill. I don't have to worry about anything now.

CHAPTER 5

1983: AGE 14

JANUARY 3, 1983

I actually did something on New Year's Eve. The Mabreys had a huge party at their house. Their parents got us kids a pony keg. It was pretty crazy, especially since the bathroom upstairs has no door on it. Every time I had to pee, I did it as fast as possible before someone walked in. There was only one bathroom, for us to use.

Well, one time when I was upstairs going to the bathroom, Chris Jones walked in. He saw that I was using the bathroom and turned around. On my way out, he grabbed my hand and told me to wait. He is so cute. He is really big into the Motocross bicycle racing and sometimes gets in the Tacoma newspaper for winning races. Well, Chris led me into Ken's room and we started kissing, right on the same spot where I did it with Rob. Before I knew what was going on, Joe pushed me back, pulled off my pants and started having sex with me. It happened so fast that I didn't know it was happening at first. He is so cute, so I thought maybe he liked me. I was thinking, while it was happening, that I wished it was Rob instead. I love Rob so much.

When we got downstairs, Chris started talking to his football friends and completely ignored me. That cut like a knife. I knew I had been used. I tried to go up to him casually, but he had actually brought his girlfriend with him and went up to her and put his arm around her when he saw me approach. I didn't know he had a girlfriend or that she was even at the party. I felt so humiliated. It wasn't long after when Chris and his football friends left for another party. It was extremely depressing. I stayed a while longer, drinking and standing alone in the corner. I finally stumbled back home along the dark deer trail. I brought a little flashlight with me but still got turned around and did a loop back to Mabrey's house. It was like hell, returning to the scene of the humiliation. The trail to my trailer isn't very big and easy to miss. I hope Rob doesn't know what happened with Chris. I should have hung out with him since he doesn't have a girlfriend that I know of. I'm so terribly shy, I didn't know what to say. I feel so guilty and embarrassed about having sex with Chris.

JANUARY 31, 1983

I went over to Amber's trailer and watched the Superbowl. It was the Miami Dolphins against the Washington Redskins.

The Redskins beat the Dolphins 27–17 to win their first Super Bowl championship. The game was played in the Rose Bowl in Pasadena, California. Dan Marino is so hot, I was so hoping the Dolphins would win, especially since I used to live in Miami. The Dolphins didn't, but Dan Marino is still hot.

FEBRUARY 12, 1983

Rob asked me to come over last night so of course I did. I snuck out my large bedroom window as always, putting some pillows under the blankets to make it look like I was sleeping. My parents never check on me, but who knows when they might.

I snuck out around 10:15 pm when my parents were fast asleep. I was afraid of turning on the light to search for my shoes because mom got up three times to go to the bathroom. I couldn't find any shoes in my pigsty of a room, so I walked through the woods in my socks. I couldn't find a flashlight, either, but there was a full moon so I could see all right. What a mistake. It was so dark in the woods, I made the wrong turn three times. I didn't give up, though. I finally found my way through the trail and Rob was waiting for me. He asked me what took so long and I told him that I got lost three times. Rob saw that I had nothing on my feet except socks (and it was cold outside) and started laughing and asked why I wasn't wearing any shoes. I explained that I couldn't find them in my room, not a single pair, so I left without them. He started laughing.

Rob and I went upstairs so Rick wouldn't hear and we lay on the floor and made love a few times. It was so nice. Things were kind of crazy, though. Rob's parents came home and we didn't even hear them. Maybe because we were under a sleeping bag. We didn't use his bed because it squeaked. Anyway, Rob's mom, opened up the door suddenly and wanted to kiss Rob goodnight. She was very drunk and asked him why the hell was he sleeping on the floor. Rob laughed and said that he just felt like it. She just said "oh" and sat down on the bed to talk to him. I was hiding under the sleeping bag by her feet, hoping she wouldn't step on me and find out that I was there.

Mrs. Mabrey went on about how much she loved Rob, all of her boys and got sentimental and started crying. Rob was sweet to her and said that he loved her, too. I felt like I was intruding on a personal moment. Finally, she left, but she and Mr. Mabrey were awake and walking up and down the stairs, yelling at each other about one thing or another. Rob's bedroom is on the second floor and there is only one way down – the stairs. Rob said that he's dropped down from his bedroom window before, and it wasn't that bad of a fall.

I was completely freaked about jumping from a second story window, but Rob said that he would lower me down so I would be hanging from the window and then drop to the ground. The ground was pitch black because there were no lights outside and the full moon was on the other side of the house. Rob apologized to me for not walking me through the woods halfway like he usually does. I told him it was okay. Rob gave me a flashlight, so I wouldn't get lost again. It was very cold outside and I didn't bring a coat, either. Rob wanted me to put on a pair of his shoes, and I tried, but my feet kept slipping out. He gave me an extra pair of tube socks instead and told me to wear shoes next time. I laughed and said that I would.

Rob lowered me down and I dropped to the ground. I waved up at him and whispered goodbye. It was so sweet, really. I started walking through the car graveyard, illuminated by the full moon, when I felt something warm trickling down my arm. I looked down and saw blood dripping down my arm. I had fallen on some glass below his window and didn't realize that I had cut my arm. It ripped my shirt, too. I stopped and ripped a strip off of my old useless shirt and tied it around the wound. It didn't look like there was any glass in the wound, I think I just fell on the glass but it didn't break off in my arm.

It was surreal walking home in the full moon. I was so happy because Rob really does love me. I got home, changed into a new shirt, cleaned my wound and put a Band-Aid on it. I fell asleep thinking about Rob and smelled him on my shirt, which I was cuddling to my face. It was so beautiful.

FEBRUARY 28, 1983

I started Pinegrove Junior High School a couple of weeks ago. The first day the school bus drove up to the front door, someone the night before spray painted "666" on the front of the school in giant red numbers. There were two different reactions from kids; laughing until their sides hurt, or gasping in shock and horror. I gasped since the school was completely new, unused, untainted, so our first day was sullied.

I received a second shock. Mr. Patrick the Dick was hired as school principal. That was terrible news since he doesn't like me and seems to enjoy tormenting me. Unfortunately, he has been seeking me out for punishment. Mr. Patrick pesters me until I lose my temper and call him an asshole or tell him to fuck off. My mouth gets me in trouble. I can't help it. I black out from my anger and say and do things I typically know are wrong.

You won't be surprised that Mr. Patrick the Dick kicked me out of school today. My expulsion starts tomorrow, March 1 through March 4. I need to intercept the mail tomorrow before my parents get home to forge mom's signature. My parents don't have a clue what happens to me at school. I've been intercepting the mail for the past year and a half when my stupid Progress Reports started being sent for my parents to sign. Some classes are so dumb that I skip them. Then, the letters get sent home and I sign them and send the letters back. I am really good at forgery. I can replicate anyone's signature if I had to. Obviously, Jim doesn't deliver mail to our house. I would have been busted a long time ago.

I am only suspended for three days for "disrespect of a staff member and failure to follow directions." That was in Mr. Patrick the Dick's class. I came in as the bell was ringing, with about 5 other people, but he chose to make an example of me. It makes me so angry. Why does he always pick me out? This time, when he picked on me, he tried to make fun of me in front of the class, I told him that he needs to get a better toupee because the one he wears looks cheap. That got me suspended. I felt bad for saying something so personal to him. It just kind of blurted out. I would have rather said something not so personal. Or something about his teaching skills. Of course, the class laughed, but I did feel embarrassed for saying that. I didn't let Mr. Patrick see my guilt, though.

Since Jim is working part-time at unpredictable hours, I can't stay home, so what I typically do when I'm expelled from school is take my lunch and a book and go into the woods across from my bus stop and stay there all day. I bring my pipe so I can get high while I am there. That way, I can keep an eye on the mail, too. It is getting more difficult to get the mail now that Jim gets home early. He sometimes comes home after work and then goes to the bar. Other times, he will go straight to the bar from work at noon. It is hard to predict, so I must be extra careful. I don't know when a Progress Report from school might come in or some letter from a teacher. I've already intercepted dozens. Talk about trouble. I would get a belt beating for being kicked out of school. I must continue to be vigilant.

MARCH 5, 1983

I'm in year-round school, I think I've mentioned it before. The first thing I signed up for was yearbook staff. I am the resident artist. Can you believe that? I was asked to be the art director for the newspaper, too, after the teacher saw my drawings. Ms. Anderson the teacher said she is tired of using clip art for everything and wants me to draw some filler art. I was asked to draw something, so I drew the Pinegrove Pony mascot, which is a horse rearing up. I've done that genre before, so it was easy. Some kids suggested that I paint the horse mascot in the lobby but I'm afraid to do an entire mural. I don't know how to do anything that large. Neither did anyone else, so it probably won't happen.

Rob is on the newspaper staff as a sports reporter. If I had known, I would have joined the newspaper instead. We don't talk much. I think he likes me but he won't ask me out. I wish I was more brave and ask him out on a date.

MARCH 24, 1983

I feel absolutely terrible. I've hit such a low in my life. I got kicked out of school again. It was completely my own fault. It was for stealing a pair of Adidas tennis shoes. They are the real cool kind with the rubber lines on the toe, white with black stripes. I have been wanting those shoes for ever.

Rene in P.E. just got a pair and has been showing them off. I have been asking my mom to get me a pair for a while. Of course she won't take me to get them because she said I don't need new tennis shoes. Laura and I have P.E. at the same time. Our pathetic class was playing dodgeball. What a stupid fucking sport, if it even is a sport. It makes people pick out the weak, which is totally cruel. I don't see the point of it at all.

I stared at the ground so I wouldn't be picked for first round of dodgeball. I'm not the world's most coordinated person, so I'm usually one of the first to be hit. I wasn't selected for dodgeball, so Laura and I were sitting on the floor, watching the nerds get slammed with the ball. Laura whispered that I should quickly steal Rene's Adidas shoes when no one was looking. The coach wasn't looking at us, so I tried to blend in with the other kids who already were out of the game. I barely know Rene, yet she was stupid enough to put her shoes on top of her gym bag in the gym and not in her locker. I don't know why she didn't put them in the locker. Probably to show off to everyone that she got cool new shoes. The shoes were nearby, so I took a quick glance at them and they were my size.

Laura said that I should take them when we go outside to run around the track four times. She slid me her KZOK sweatshirt and said that I should put it on and pretend that it was mine. Then, when everyone was leaving, I would take off the sweatshirt at the last minute, fold it up, place it next to the shoes, and put them underneath the sweatshirt. I did it exactly as she said. No one saw me.

When we came back in from running after dodgeball, I grabbed the sweatshirt with the shoes hidden underneath and ran into the locker room. No one noticed me. We played dodgeball briefly again then the bell rang. I ran inside the locker room and got my things, putting the shoes with the sweatshirt wrapped around it in my backpack. That is when I heard the crying. Rene said that someone stole her shoes. I went over with the crowd of people to console her. I stayed for a few minutes then left. No one suspected me.

I wouldn't have gotten caught if I had listened to Laura. She told me not to wear the shoes for at least a month, put them away and not wear them. Well, I was stubborn and stupid and wore them after a week and thought it would be all right. Laura warned me right away that I shouldn't wear them to school, I should change into one of her pair of shoes (I went to her place to smoke weed before school). I was insistent that I would wear the stolen shoes since I scuffed them up a bit. What an idiot! The teachers were looking for those type of shoes. I didn't scuff them up enough and got caught. I felt really bad when the girl was crying in the principal's office and asked why did I do that to her. I said that my parents wouldn't buy me anything new. That was a lie. I just said that, I don't know why. Afterwards, I stuck to the story that my parents wouldn't ever buy me new clothes. Mr. Patrick actually had me strip searched by a female teacher after I was busted. Down to my bra and underwear. I don't know what he was looking for, but he probably just wanted to harass me some more.

Well, I had no other shoes to put on so I was walking around in my socks. That was so humiliating. I might as well have put a sign around my neck for everyone at the school saying, "I'm the thief! I'm the thief!" Isn't there a book with a similar theme? The Scarlett Letter, I think. Regardless, for theft, Mr. Patrick called my house directly. Jim was home. I couldn't believe my crappy luck. Why couldn't he have been at the bar? Then Mr. Patrick would have called mom. But, no, Jim came to pick me up from school. Mr. Patrick tried to have a discussion about me as I sat there, but Jim didn't say much. Mr. Patrick told me before Jim showed up that I may not get suspended if he had a satisfactory teacher-parent conference. I guess it wasn't satisfactory because I was expelled. Jim didn't say anything to me on the way home, as usual. He never speaks to me when we are alone unless he has to.

When we got home, I didn't get the belt beating like I thought. It surprised me. Instead, Jim dropped me off at home and went up to the tavern to meet mom. That is where he told her what happened. She had no idea. They came home a little earlier than usual, at 6:30 pm, to have a "discussion" with me. You know, I got the "why did you do it?" bullshit. I really wanted to scream that I get sick of them getting drunk every single day.

After the "discussion" from my drunk parents, Jim decides that my punishment for being expelled from school is to dig fence posts for our back acre. That sounded like an okay thing to me. Better than a belt beating. So, that is what I'll be doing tomorrow through April 6th.

MARCH 26, 1983

Oh, was I wrong. The fence posts are so difficult to dig. It took me an hour to dig one. The problem is all of the rocks we have in our soil. The yard is one big rock. I have blisters on my hands, even wearing gloves.

The good news is my parents didn't find out that I was kicked out of school before (when I hid in the woods). Mr. Patrick didn't mention it at all. I couldn't believe my luck!

APRIL 7, 1983

My humiliation continues. When I went to school today, Mr. Patrick took me into a private room where a female teacher did another strip search. I had to stand there in my bra and underwear while she went through all of my pockets. Unfortunately, I had my toilet paper roll pipe in my purse. She told me to get dressed and made a spectacle of showing the pipe to Mr. Patrick. His beady little eyes sparkled maliciously when he saw it. Mr Patrick nodded his head and said that the searching will continue indefinitely. Great. I didn't know they could or would do that.

APRIL 17, 1983

Last night, Amber and I went to see the *Evil Dead* movie. As always, the only ride we could get was Amber's mom. Amber had me sneak some whisky from my parent's bottle so we could mix it with our Cokes. I put some in a Tupperware container because I didn't know what else to put it in. I couldn't find a flask or bottle with a lid to put it in. It worked, even though it only gave us a little buzz.

The movie was scary. It freaked out Amber more than me, mostly because my parents took me to see horror movies since I was a toddler. I saw the *Exorcist* when I was 5 years old and *Rosemary's Baby* at some drive-in in Miami when I was 3, so I am well versed in the horror film genre.

Amber and I grabbed on to each other a few times, and were yelling at the screen when the girl wandered outside by herself. Why in the world would she do that? When Ash found the weapons in the shed, we cheered. The upgrade to the chainsaw was a wise choice. The movie was edge of our seat excitement. Ash is totally hot, even if he has a bit of a large chin. He was the cutest guy in the film by far.

After the film, when we went outside talking about our favorite parts of the movie, Amber's mom was actually waiting for us in the parking lot. That was more shocking than anything in the movie.

MARCH 6, 1983

Yesterday I went skiing with Amber! I have never been skiing before. Amber's flaky mom drove Amber, Andy and me to Snoqualmie Pass. That is the best skiing in our area. I always hate when Amber's mom drives because she talks all of the time and will look around at everyone and everything and not look at the road. She will often catch herself going off the road and will correct herself with jerks to the steering wheel. Even Amber doesn't like her mom's driving.

Amber had old ski pants that fit me, I wore my long underwear underneath, and she rented the skis. I wore my silver Moon Boots, which looked totally cool. I went on the bunny tow to learn to balance. Amber and Andy are much better skiers and went to the very top of the ski lift. Learning to stop was the hardest for me. That was the first thing that Amber taught me, how to do a snow plow. I kept falling on my ass the first four times but finally picked it up. It is harder than it looks.

Since it was my first time on skis, I fell quite a few times, got snow down my pants, soaking my shirt and long johns underneath. I started getting shivery cold, especially since I wasn't skiing much, only going around and around on the bunny tow. Amber convinced me, after she bugged the shit out of me, to go on the ski lift and go down a bigger slope. The ski lift is freaky frightening because you stand there and it comes up behind you and you sit down. A bar comes down, but there was enough room to slide out underneath the bar. Amber rocked the car, thinking it was hysterical or something. I wanted to smack her with a ski pole. It wasn't funny at all. I froze in terror and decided to get off at the first stop, not go all the way to the top.

After getting off that horrible ski lift, I was left alone on a rather steep slope, small by Amber's standards. I sat down in the snow and stared down at the dark grey of the clouds and snow, barely being able to see the safe bunny tow I grew so dependent upon. The snow plow was a life saver. Every time I got going fast, I'd snow plow. It took me forever to get to the safety of the bunny hill and flatness. I was exhausted.

We didn't bring a change of clothes so we had to use the dryers in the lodge laundry mat. Andy kept watch for people coming in as we stripped down to our underwear and bra. I put my coat over my bra and underwear while our clothes were drying.

With all of the craziness, I had a great time skiing. I was grateful when Amber insisted that she drive home since she has a driver's permit and needed the practice. It was much safer having Amber drive home. I wish my parents took me skiing. It makes me sad that we never do anything fun as a family.

MAY 28, 1983

I thought my life was bad. Laura just told me she's pregnant. Pregnant. I didn't even know she had a boyfriend. She was 13 when she got pregnant and is now 14, same age as me. She is only three months older than me. I've never known anyone who got pregnant in 9th grade! Laura is so smart, I am completely stunned by the news. It is impossible to say that I am excited since she is too young to have a child. She was on the pill, but it isn't always effective, apparently.

Laura acted strangely when I asked about the baby's father. She closed off completely and all she would tell me was that he is white. Okay. But who is he? I asked if she was raped, but Laura insists she wasn't. She said that he is much older (around 20, she thinks) and doesn't go to school anywhere and that certainly I don't know him. After much pestering, Laura finally told me a rather troubling and disturbing story of the other life she secretly leads.

Laura left the room and came back with two small bottles of vodka, Tang and a big plastic cup filled with ice. She mixed a strong drink which we shared while smoking weed from her toilet paper pipe. It crossed my mind that she shouldn't do this while pregnant. I wasn't going to say anything because I wanted to hear about her secret life.

After finishing the vodka Tang nasty drink, Laura apparently worked up the nerve to share her secret. Laura was quiet as she contemplated how to explain her situation. She paced the room a few times and I remained deadly silent. Laura pushed back some clothes in her closet and pulled out a fur coat hidden in the back and some sexy teddies. Laura said that she has been a topless dancer at a club in Tacoma. Ah, maybe that's where the baby's father comes in. As I fawned over her expensive clothes, Laura relaxed a little since I didn't react negatively against topless dancing. It's her life, plus she makes a lot of money in tips. I wouldn't go that route and was a bit surprised that she was an exotic dancer, wondering how she entered that life. We have hitchhiked to parties in Tacoma, which is very far away, so maybe she hitchhikes by herself and met someone seedy.

I thought the story would end there, but it didn't. Laura continued telling me that she also works as an escort for older men and sometimes has sex with them. The man who set up the escort service bought her the nice clothes and a fur coat. Laura said the men she sees are usually old and fat who just want someone pretty and young to go out with. In the rush to share her secret burden, Laura suggested that I should be a topless dancer with her. I wouldn't have to do escort and sex was not required. I'm thinking to myself that Laura is so tall and has a perfect body, slim hips and very large breasts. Of course she would get a lot of money in tips. I have a fat ass, so I was skeptical, but Laura guaranteed I would make money, too, because there are so many men who like different kinds of women. I was thinking about Jim going to topless bars in Tacoma and was suddenly horrified at the thought he could have seen Laura dancing. I didn't mention this to her. It was a bit too disturbing. Anyway, I thought you had to be 16 or 18 to work. We are 14 and she started dancing at 13. It all sounded sketchy to me. Laura said she got a fake ID so no one there knows her real name. The club pays in cash. I have to assume they don't offer medical benefits.

Laura excitedly told me her baby is due in October. She showed me a small lump which was the baby. It is hard to believe that she is actually pregnant. She seems excited and frightened at the same time, but her mom and step-father know and will support her, whatever decision she makes. Laura said she wants to keep the baby. I asked Laura if the father could be a client, and she said that it definitely wasn't one of her clients who got her pregnant because they usually wear condoms. I asked if the father was the man who runs the escort service and she didn't deny or confirm. Perhaps he is the father or she doesn't know and is embarrassed to tell me. Laura won't even tell me his first name. When I laughed and said it was silly, what harm could come from knowing his first name? Laura looked a bit frightened and made me promise never to try and find out his true identity because it could be dangerous. I said that perhaps she shouldn't work for him anymore if he is dangerous. Laura seemed a little surprised by my comment, thought for a moment, then said he wasn't dangerous to her, but he might be to me. That really freaked me out. She just won't tell me anything else and told me not to ask anymore. I backed off and told her everything was fine, I am still her friend.

After I left her house to walk home, I became worried about this mystery man. I am going to hide in the bushes across from her house and try and see the man when he picks her up for work. I want to know what kind of car he drives and what he looks like. I just don't like this at all. Laura could be so much more than a topless dancer, escort girl. Having a baby in the 9th grade sounds like a death sentence for her life. Well, technically, it will be 10th grade when the baby is born in October. Obviously, Laura won't be in school much longer. She told me she will go to an alternative school where she can get her degree. It is school for dropouts. I think that is the best thing to do. Laura is so smart. How could she let this happen? I know that she has a really high IQ. She could be so much more, but that life is gone. It is so sad.

MAY 30, 1983

Believe it or not, I am still being searched every day before school, although not stripped searched anymore. Mr. Patrick the dick and his silent female accomplice escort me into a small, windowless room and ransack my belongings, going through all of my pockets, looking for something to use against me. He even goes through my jeans pockets while I'm wearing them. What a pervert! Does he get excited from patting down my ass? It really makes me wonder. Why isn't the silent bitch doing it? While he was searching my pockets today, I laughed, sneered at him and quietly asked so only he could hear if he was enjoying himself. He quickly stopped the search and sent me to class late, with an excuse, of course. He purposely wants me to go to class late every day so everyone knows that I am being searched. They all know but I don't care. Amber or Paula sneak in my joints and Southern Comfort (with Coke from the machine) for lunch break.

JUNE 11, 1983

While sitting in the bushes across from Laura's trailer smoking weed, I finally got a glimpse at the skinny white man who picks up Laura for her topless dancing/escort job. She came out of her house wearing that fur coat and was really dressed up so she looked much older than 14. Obviously, Laura is still working since she really doesn't show her pregnancy yet. Only a slight belly, but Laura said that some men like that. Since she was wearing a dress and high heels, she probably was going on an escort date and not topless dancing. She wears naughty lacy teddies for that job.

The man wasn't attractive like I expected. He was skinny and rather scraggly looking and drove an old rusted Datsun. It didn't look like something a "pimp" would drive. I don't know if it is the baby's dad or not or even if he is her "pimp".

There was nothing else to see, so I made the slow walk back to my unexciting all brown, double wide trailer.

JUNE 12, 1983

Tonight I am going on my first official date, not counting the Sadie Hawkins dance in 7th grade where I asked Rick to go with me and we only held hands. At school, I got talked into going on a double date with Paula. She dates an 18 year old skanky janitor at our school who has a friend who is also a janitor. I reluctantly said yes. She didn't want to go on a date by herself (even though she's already had sex with him) so she convinced me to go with the other janitor at our school for a double date. He is 19 years old. My mom is grossly excited about my "first" date. Seriously, I am not excited at all. Paula promised me a quarter ounce of stink weed for joining her on this date. She better come through with the pot.

JUNE 13, 1983

Yuck! John drove up, rang the doorbell and handed me a single red rose. Mom said it was so romantic and rushed off to get a vase. John checked me out from head to toe and said how entranced he was with my beauty. Yuck. Mom made such an ordeal about it and took our picture.

What a horrible date it turned out to be. We ended up going nowhere except on a deserted road where we could "make out." Paula really likes her skanky janitor friend and they kissed forever. I kissed John a little bit, but I really didn't want to. Then, he kept trying to pull my jeans off. I flat out refused, constantly shoving his groping hands away. Before I knew what was happening, he stuck his dirty fingers into my vagina. I didn't like that at all and had to literally push him off. He finally made me really mad and demanded them to take me home. Paula complained the entire 15 miles home that I wasn't any fun. I just got sick of it. We didn't go to a movie or dinner or anything. I was told that we were going to dinner and a movie but it turned out to be a lie. On the way home, I was so angry at John because he wouldn't leave me alone. I told him that I am only 14 and it is statutory rape for him to touch me. John said he didn't realize that I was only 14. Well, duh! I'm in 9th grade, you freaking weirdo! The statutory rape scared him so much that he didn't even look at me the rest of the drive home. Paula is actually mad at me about the whole ordeal. She wanted to have sex with her skanky janitor. To add to the weirdness,

Amber was jealous that Paula and I were going on a double date and she wasn't invited. I felt like telling Amber to go on the date instead of me. She is a virgin, though, so John wouldn't have liked that one bit. Just like my first kiss, my first date was a complete disaster.

JULY 8, 1983

For the 4th of July I went camping with my parents. I was excited at first to be camping on a lake with paddle boat rentals. We never do fun things as a family. Family. It feels like a dirty word. I was given permission by the folks to bring a friend. I asked Paula since Amber drives me crazy.

Paula and I stayed in my pup tent right next to the camping trailer where my parents stayed. We wanted some privacy from my drunk parents. My parents invited their new best friends from the Bean Tavern, Sid and Betty, who camped in the spot next to us. For just three nights of camping, they brought 10 cases of beer for four people. I am not joking. Paula and I were so amazed at the mountain of beer stacked between their campers.

Paula and I stole five beers, but couldn't get any more since they were drinking the beer at an alarming rate. In fact, they were guzzling so fast I thought for sure they would notice five missing beers..

I have to tell you about Sid and Betty. Sid is almost full American Indian. He is very sensitive about being American Indian. It is almost like he is embarrassed. I don't know what he has to be embarrassed about. On all outward appearances, Sid is a handsome man, but inside he is an angry, hollow, black hole. Unfortunately for all of the drivers in Washington state, Sid is a State Trooper.

Since Sid knows all of the police in the area where he works, and openly brags about how he has gotten several DWI tickets thrown out. He says that he can drink and drive anywhere. Great. It makes me feel so safe and cozy inside.

Sid is also very violent and I have seen his quick temper when he thinks he has been slighted in any way. Sid gets in so many bar fights, he has to rotate his visitations to different taverns.

Like Sid, his wife Betty is a nice lady when sober, but is a daily consumer of alcohol like my mom. They have two daughters, Kimmy, who is about my age, and the other one is 7 years old, I forget her name. They are actually not Sid's biological children, but fathered by some other dude. Sid openly shows love and devotion to them as if they were his own, which is his only redeeming quality.

Kimmy doesn't hang out with her folks often, and is usually gone somewhere with her Army boyfriend out of town, so I rarely see her and she never wants to associate with me when she is around. Mom annoyingly tells me what a nice girl Kimmy is. What a sweet girl Kimmy is. How precious Kimmy is. My parents go over to Sid and Betty's trailer on the weekends without me because I'm usually not invited, and return, telling adorable stories about "the girls." How can my parents praise Kimmy when she has already dropped out of school middle school and is mostly living with an Army boyfriend?

The few times that I have been invited to Sid and Betty's trailer were during parties, and they always fight each other when they get drunk. Sid and Betty start yelling at each other, then swearing at each other, then Betty tells Sid to get the fuck out, then Sid drives away, spraying gravel all over the trailer, tires squealing on the asphalt when contact is made. It has happened the same way during the last three times I have been over there. Like clockwork.

Well, it's with this lovely couple we went camping at Lake Kapowsin. All weekend, my parents, Sid and Betty never did anything but sit at the campsite, drinking beer and eating half-cooked barbecue which they were too drunk to cook properly. They were always sitting there, smoking endless cartons of generic cigarettes, which was the main reason it was so difficult for Paula and me to steal beer. They never left the campsite except to use the nearby bathroom. Once they had enough to drink, the men openly pissed on nearby trees. Nice.

On the second day, Paula and I met a guy a few years older than us whose family brought a row boat to the lake. He invited us to join him. I told mom and she said that was fine since it was daytime and there were two of us. He was camping with his family, too, and was bored. He also smoked weed, so when we rowed out to the middle of the lake, we smoked it. We spent hours rowing around the perimeter of the lake.

When the sun began to set, the boy rowed us back to shore. I had a sinking feeling in my gut when I saw Sid standing on the bank of the lake, staring at us. My mom, Jim, and Betty were standing much further back. The boy asked if it was my dad and I told him it wasn't, only a friend of my parents. It was odd that Sid took an interest.

When we got to the dock, Paula and I got out while the guy tied the boat to the dock. Sid came running at us, grabbed Paula and me by our jackets, and flung us back towards where the others were standing. They didn't do anything but stare at Sid. Paula and I were in shock as to what was happening. I still don't know for sure, except while we were gone, Sid must have gotten it in his head that this boy was a rapist and murderer. Never mind my mom gave us permission to go and it was still daylight.

The boy looked rather nervous as he tied up his boat. As soon as he stepped on the dock, all hell broke loose. Sid ran up to the guy, grabbed him by the shirt and pushed him around, toward the water. I went over and asked what he was doing, since my parents weren't doing a damn thing. Sid shouted at me that it was none of my business. What? This guy did nothing wrong! He took us out his boat for a couple of hours. Big deal. Sid started interrogating the poor guy, asking why we were gone so long. The boy said that it was a row boat without an engine. That was the wrong thing to say. All Sid heard was "engine" and thought the boy said "injun", which was a derogatory slur against his ancestry. Ron began poking the boy's chest with his finger and went on a frightening rampage of violence, shouting in his face that his being an American Indian had nothing to do with the situation. I ran up to Sid and explained that he was talking about the boat not having an engine, he didn't say anything mean to him. Sid wouldn't listen to reason. Betty came up at that point and tried to drag Sid away. The poor kid was in shock and didn't know what to do. Finally, Betty got Sid away from the boy. As soon as that happened, the boy yelled "psycho" at Sid and ran off to his campsite. I yelled after him that I was sorry.

When we got back to camp, Sid lectured me about going out alone in a boat with a stranger. He kept interrupting me when I said my mom gave permission. Jim spoke up and told me to shut up when an adult was talking to me. Like Sid was even talking to me. He was yelling at me. For no reason. Mom didn't say a damn word. It was so disgusting.

Shortly afterwards, they all started drinking beer again and sitting by their fire. Paula and I really wanted some more beer but by then the coolers were literally right between Jim and Sid. I was determined to get at least two beers for us so I waited and hovered around the cooler until everyone was busy with the food situation. I quickly opened the cooler and grabbed four beers. Screw them. After the embarrassing situation they put me in I didn't care. I took the beer back to the tent where Paula and I hung out.

On the last day of camping, they actually ran out of beer. Yes, I know, how could that happen? They bought two more cases from the campground store. Oh, boy. So glad. I can't imagine Jim, Sid, mom or Betty being sober for a day. It may actually kill them.

What a nightmare!

JULY 15, 1983

I feel like I've been dropped into an Alfred Hitchcock film. I hope it isn't more like the film, Friday the 13th. While camping, I mistakenly told Paula about the man I saw at Laura's house. Paula talks about everything, so I am quite sure she is the one who told Laura about my spying. Now Laura won't talk to me.

The man in the old rusted Datsun has been following my school bus, twice. I know, I don't even have a driver's license or car yet, but I've seen the car several times now. When I was leaving school to get on the school bus, I saw it parked out on the street across from school. It was a good distance away, but since the car is orange with rust spots, it's fairly unique. There aren't many rusted out orange Datsuns around town. Laura doesn't attend our school anymore, she attends the alternative school which is only four or five miles from school. The skanky man could be watching me while Laura is in alternative school during the day. How could he have known that I saw him? Did Laura tell him? Could he really be dangerous? I am afraid to tell anyone about this. I have seen on the news reports of a murderer called the Green River Killer who places prostitutes' dead bodies in or near the Green River. There are a rash of missing prostitutes in an area that is near Laura's strip club. I don't know if Laura gets dates through the strip club or if she stands on the street. I don't know what to do and have nowhere to turn.

JULY 24, 1983

I saw that car again! I spotted it when mom and I were coming back from Tacoma Mall after shopping for clothes at Nordstrom. It is possible that he followed us there without me noticing. He was definitely behind us a few cars back all the way from Tacoma to Bean. Sure, it could be a coincidence. I don't know, that is an awful big coincidence. What could be so secretive that he would follow me? I don't even know his name and I never did write down the license plate number. This whole Laura thing is so bizarre. Last time I saw her, before the 4th of July weekend, Laura asked me again if I wanted to go into topless dancing or escort business.

JULY 31, 1983

I finally got a piano yesterday. I have been trying so hard to convince mom to get me one. I love the piano and feel like I have played it before in another life. I know that sounds weird. I can't read music but I have been aching for a piano. I wanted an electric guitar and then a saxophone before that, but mom laughed at my foolish requests.

The man at the piano store gave us a name of a great teacher. Her name is Ms. Wolcott and she has accepted me as a student. Her house is about 20 miles from our trailer but only 5 miles from school. I am so excited. It is an hour lesson once a week. Jim wasn't happy about that, but mom said that I would give up if I didn't have lessons. After much grumbling, he relented. They go to the tavern every day, including Christmas, and spend large quantities of money drinking and gambling, so what is $80 a month for me, their only child who is left alone and secluded with no hobbies and nothing to do but smoke weed and steal their alcohol?

AUGUST 19, 1983

It is difficult to believe that there is another exciting event in my lackluster life. I started piano lessons today. Mrs. Wolcott gave me a beginner's piano book with piano theory, illustrations of notes and their locations on the keyboard, and about 20 beginner songs. I am supposed to practice from 30 to 60 minutes daily. Once I learn the notes, I can read music! For now, I have two songs that I memorized. They are simple melodies and Mrs. Wolcott showed me how to change the key of the songs. I really loved the lesson because I have been wanting to play a musical instrument for ages. It gives me purpose in life. I don't feel as dark and empty as before.

SEPTEMBER 20, 1983

I started 10th grade two weeks ago. I'm now attending the dreaded Heath High School. It isn't that bad since I do drugs, therefore I am never in a shortage. The rumors were correct about it being the drug capital. There is a clear line between kids who get high and those who don't. It's like the school is split into two parts. Some people span both groups. They're able to interact with people who do and don't get high. I don't seem to be a bridge kind of person. I have friends but am lonely. I don't have any truly close friends. I seem unable to form real friendships, like there is something lacking in me. Amber seems to be the most available friend and I don't even really like her.

I have been sort of dating the drug dealer Mike for a few weeks now. We meet up secretly which is easy since he lives next to Heath Junior High School and I can take the late bus home. Mike is a nice dude, stays perpetually high like Jeff Spicoli from *Fast Times at Ridgemont High*. I could be compared to Stacy who has sex with someone to be popular, I guess. It's one of my favorite movies since it has the Go-Go's, Billy Squier and Oingo Boingo music. Amber called the girls "sluts" from the movie. She would since she is a virgin and loves telling everyone she's a virgin. The movie is a mostly accurate portrayal of our high school.

One of Mike's front teeth is missing and the other one is brownish, like it is damaged at the root. He lives with his father and brother and never sees his mother because she abandoned them ages ago. His father is hardly ever home so I go over to his house after school. Mom drove me out to his house four times during the summer. She dropped me off before running errands and picked me up a couple of hours later. She isn't making a big deal about it like she did for my first "date" with that horrible janitor.

I guess I see Mike because it is better than no one, plus I get free weed and hash. Paula says that I should date him openly. I am starting to have my doubts about seeing him. He is totally cool, we just don't have much in common. His bedroom has lots posters that glow under a purple fluorescent light. Mike also has the glow in the dark planets hanging from his ceiling. We were both voted "Most Shy" at the end of last year for the yearbook. He doesn't have many friends and is quiet at school like I am. I am not thrilled about being voted "Most Shy" after overhearing Renee at school. I was helping the newspaper staff, as resident artist, a couple of days before the "best in" votes came in. Renee, an orphan girl whose parents died, leaving her lots of money in asparagus farms, said being voted "Most Shy" is the worst one of all because being shy is like being a loser. Renee ended up winning "Most Popular" with my love, Rob Mabrey, and also, "Most Likely To Succeed". The second, "Most Likely To Succeed", is easy since she inherited a fortune. Once I found out I was voted "Most Shy" I couldn't bear to see any of the Newspaper Staff until the year was over. I was so humiliated since Rob was there during Renee's comment. To her credit, Renee blushed when she saw me, knowing she hurt my feelings.

Anyway, Mike and I had sex once. I let him fuck me because I felt sorry for him. As it was happening, I was thinking to myself this is a mercy fuck. I just let him the once. I think it was his first time because he was so embarrassed after having sex. Plus, his brother walked in on us while we were doing it, which was a double humiliation. I will break it off soon. It will hurt him more than me since I have absolutely no feelings for him, but it isn't fair to lead Mike on. I was trying to feel normal with a boyfriend, but this isn't who I want.

Piano lessons are going well, which is the only thing in my pitiful life that is. I am learning so quickly. Mrs. Wolcott often tells me how impressed she is with my progress. She loans me classical records of Bach and Mozart to listen to during the week. She told me to listen to classical music on the radio, too, to get acquainted with it, which I've been doing for a while to help me sleep at night.

I don't have anyone to listen to me play piano because Jim yells at me whenever I practice. He actually told me not to play until I get good. I don't think I am bad, I am still learning. Then, he'll yell at mom and say, "does she have to practice right now?" Jim told me to practice when he isn't there, which is most of the time, I was foolishly hoping my parents would be impressed with my playing after coming home from the tavern and eating the food I cooked for them. I'll practice after school from now on.

OCTOBER 8, 1983

Last night made me feel so low about myself. Sometimes I wish something really bad would happen to me so I wouldn't have to continue in this abysmal life. At school, while Ed and I were getting high behind the shop building (I'm taking the shop class, Small Gas Engines) and he said that his best friend, Ken Mabrey, was staying in a rental room in Tacoma and was having a party later that night. I was interested because I was hoping that Rob would be there since it is his older brother. I said, sure, I'll go to the party. Ed has his grandma's car and said we could drive to Tacoma after school. When I told Amber about it, and she wanted to crash the party. I asked Ed and he was totally up for more girls to go. Amber had volleyball practice after school, so Ed said he and I could get high at his grandma's trailer and come back and get Amber. Cool idea, sure. Ed's grandma was out of town visiting her sister so we had the trailer to ourselves. I don't find Ed attractive, so I put off his advances. He is cool, and we smoked hash from his massive bong. I got so high, it seemed like life was moving in slow motion.

We went back to school and picked up Amber, then drove to Ken's apartment in Tacoma. It was literally one room, someone's office with an old pull out sofa, small table with two chairs and a mini kitchen off a laundry mat. It was really a dump, to be honest. Ken had cases of beer, so I drank a lot, and so did Amber. I continued smoking weed, which turned out to be pot laced with LSD. No one told me until after I started tripping that I smoked LSD. Had I known, I wouldn't have drank so much beer.

Amber didn't smoke any pot, but she did drink a lot. She is a virgin and kept her chastity belt well on. I wish I had because Ed asked if I wanted to check out the laundry mat. He said he was going to lock up the laundry mat for the night so I joined him in the quest. There was no one left doing laundry, so he bolted the doors. Like most laundry mats, two walls were filled with windows. I couldn't see out of the fluorescent illumination of the laundry mat, so I don't know who might have been lurking around the dirty streets of Tacoma. I was passed the point of caring at that point. Ed brought a boom box with him and cranked up the rock station. I started dancing because I was a drunk idiot. Of course, Ed urged me on, and loving the attention, I kept dancing.

The night gets very fuzzy after that. I remember Amber dancing with me in the laundry mat for a while. We played quarters, at the insistence of Ed, and I kept losing since I could barely see the cup to bounce the quarter into. Needless to say, I drank a lot of beer shots. I blacked out for a bit and remember being naked from the waist down, sitting on top of a washing machine, legs spread, and Ed fucking my brains out. I don't remember how it happened, except that Amber came in yelling at me to stop being such a slut in front of the windows of the laundry mat. Her screams brought me back to some awareness, and I couldn't speak to tell her that I didn't plan on having sex with Ed. It was very embarrassing.

I don't remember anything else except waking up this morning with a killer headache and hangover. I puked somewhere because there were chunks of vomit encrusted in my hair. I called Amber to ask what happened. She said I threw up in the laundry room shortly after she yelled at me while Ed was fucking me. Ed drove us as far as the Bean

Highway, which is still 14 miles from home. Amber had to call her mom to pick us up at the bus station, where we were apparently waiting. I have no memory of this. Amber told me how disgusting I acted and what a slut I am. Great, thanks Amber. I didn't exactly do it willingly. I was so drunk and stupid, I didn't exactly give my permission. I may have been passed out when Ed had sex with me. Amber said that was no excuse and I was still a slut. It was a real bummer and made me feel even more guilty. I snuck in through my bedroom window, with Amber's help, so my parents never knew I was anywhere except hanging out at Amber's house. I washed my hair before mom saw me. I was still in my jeans and sweater from the night before, which had some spots of vomit and piss on them. I hope I peed my pants at home and not in at the laundry mat or in Amber's mom's car. I didn't have the nerve to ask. Since Amber didn't say anything about me peeing my pants, I must have done it in bed. I am a life long bedwetter, so that is nothing new to me.

I've tried to act normal today, for the short amount of time my parents were home. Thankfully, they left for the tavern at 1:00 pm, so I was able to lay on the couch and watch TV. I have been drinking water like crazy and took three aspirin. I really didn't want to have sex with Ed. I am so embarrassed. Rob never made it to the party, so he doesn't know about my stupid drunken mess. I hate myself sometimes. I am such a loser. Why did I have sex with Ed? Totally disgusting.

OCTOBER 21, 1983

Laura had her baby. Vanessa Ryder is her name. So, she didn't take the last name of the father, she took Laura's last name. I was hoping she would be named after her father so I would know the truth. I haven't seen the stringy haired weirdo follow me for a while now, so I think I'm in the clear.

Vanessa looks like an alien with a long head and body. She will be tall like Laura. I'm sure she will look cuter when she gets a little older. Newborn babies really aren't very cute.

DECEMBER 31, 1983

Christmas was the same as every fucking lame year. I got earrings, some clothes that I already picked out with my mom, some makeup and Impulse body spray. Jim said I will look like a whore with the purple eyeshadow. Great, thanks for your support.

We had the ham dinner at noon so my parents could go to the Bean Bar & Grill afterwards.

I got my learner's permit. I took driver's education in school and failed the class because I didn't make a complete and legal stop at the stop sign. My math teacher, who has a lisp, was the driver's ed teacher, and he got so mad at me he turned red and yelled at me that I needed to stop at the stop signs. I was so stressed, I didn't know what he meant. I found out afterwards that I was supposed to stop and let the car rock back. In my stress at being yelled at, I failed the class in school. However, I took the driving test at the DMV and passed, even with the snowy, icy roads. My parallel parking was good and I was careful to make a complete stop at all stop signs. I can't wait until I can drive my Mustang which has been sitting in the driveway. Well, not really a driveway. We don't have one. It is parked in our dumpy, rock infested yard.

CHAPTER 6

1984: Age 15

MARCH 4, 1984

Yesterday, I went skiing again with Amber and Andy at Snoqualmie Pass. It feels nice to be invited to do an activity with people. Unfortunately, Amber's mom drove us up there again, just like last year, since Amber still only has her learner's permit. And just like last year, she scared the crap out of me with her erratic driving. I was so afraid of hitting an icy patch and plummeting off a cliff, which is a real possibility in the foggy, dark mountains. At least some things don't change.

I convinced mom to buy me a ski suit this time. It is black with hot pink accents on my sides and is a one piece. I love it so much! It was on the sale rack at Nordstrom's and fit me perfectly. I didn't get as wet as last time since the ski suit is waterproof. It was so much fun.

I wish my parents would take me skiing and do fun things with me so I wouldn't be forced to go with Amber's creepy mom. My parents don't have any thoughts outside of the tavern. Beer and whisky is their main interest in life. It makes me sad to say that, but it's true.

MARCH 11, 1984

I spent last night at Gail's house which I haven't done for a while. She is so cool and likes to show me makeup tips. She uses eye shadow colors I never would imagine using, like purple, pink, yellow and white. Gail can do zig zag eye shadow designs that look so punk. It is a fun thing to do since we don't go out of the house with the heavy makeup. Jim would call me a whore if he saw the crazy eye designs Gail comes up with. I don't know where she gets the inspiration from, maybe Cosmopolitan magazine or Sixteen. I have a subscription to Sixteen Magazine, but not Cosmopolitan. My mom says that I am too young to read such crazy shit. I go over there sometimes because she lives about a mile away.

MARCH 15, 1984

I skipped school 4th period today, again, in order to go to Ed's friend's house for some pot. I agreed so I could get high which is better than school any day. His friend is nice enough, but barely stays in the room with me long enough to have any conversation. I have forgotten his name, and he has already graduated from high school and lives in the trailer park near my high school. I have been to his trailer before since it is next door to Ed's grandmother's trailer. I usually sit in the living room watching MTV while Ed and his unnamed friend drive somewhere else for pot. They won't take me because they think I'm a narc I guess. Sometimes they are gone a long time, leaving me with a few hits in the bong, and then immediately go back to the bedroom as soon as they get back. They are probably dividing up the drugs they purchased.

I really didn't want to have sex with Ed in that laundry mat in Tacoma a few months ago. I totally regret it. If I didn't get so drunk, I could coherently tell guys I don't want to have sex. I don't think I was conscious when he had sex with me, which isn't cool. It isn't the first time someone has had sex with me when I've been passed out and don't remember how it happened. I usually become aware of the situation as I'm told to get dressed. I start out playing quarters, my aim gets worse as I drink so I have to chug more, I black out, then some dude is throwing my clothes at me, telling me to get dressed so I can leave. I've had sex quite a few times. How many, I'm not sure since I have no memories of most of them. I want to be awake and consenting yet I want to get shit-faced so I can escape this hell called life. I'm on birth control pill so at least I won't get pregnant. It's my fault for getting so drunk at parties. That's what Amber always says. I feel so low about myself sometimes, I just want to cry.

MARCH 22, 1984

Last night I went to see the Scorpions in Seattle again with mom. It was weird going with mom, but Gail couldn't go because her family had plans out of town. Mom loves the Scorpions, which makes some sense since she actually went to Woodstock. I still can't believe she took me as a baby to Woodstock when I was six months old. Mom said it was miserable at Woodstock because she claims she never did drugs, it was swelteringly hot, heavy rain and extremely muddy. Mom said that the bathroom situation was almost dig a hole kind of deal: there was no food or water, so good thing she brought some water. I find it really difficult to believe that she never tried any drugs since my biological father did heroin and weed.

Mom and I put on our black Scorpion's t-shirt from the last tour. It has been a long time since we actually bonded. Like a repeat of the last concert, on the way to the show, mom stopped at a convenience store south of Tacoma and bought a six-pack of the strongest beer in the world, Olde English 800, and I drank 4 of them. It was the *Love at First Sting* tour. Mom wanted to sit in the stands instead of standing in the pit area, and that was fine with me since I always get so tired of standing and being pushed around by huge crowds.

We sat next to a group of four or five teenagers who were passing a massive Cheech and Chong style joint. My mom let me smoke some since we were at a concert, although she was really dramatic and said she would turn her head and "look the other way" while I did it. Still, it was totally awesome!

Later on, after the teenagers left, two other guys sat next to us and shared their joint with me. They were much older, around 18 or 20 years old, and were hitting on both of us. They thought we were sisters because we look similar and mom is actually fairly young and very pretty. Mom and I played along with the sister act for a bit until Scott starting talking about the Rolling Stones reunion tour. He had just gone to the show and was excited about it. Mom said she saw the Stones in concert, too. Scott asked if she had gone to the same show. She said, no, it wasn't that show but back in 1967. Scott and his friend's mouths dropped open and they just stared at us. That is when I said it was my mom, not my sister. They were totally shocked. She still looks pretty good and dressed in her denim jacket and jeans. After the shock wore off, Scott asked if he could take me out some time, even though he lived closer to Seattle. My mom agreed and so did I, even though it would officially be statutory rape since I'm under age. He was a nice guy and looked so much like a young Billy Joel, Italian with those large, pleading eyes. I have never gotten a date at a show before, let alone with my mom! Scott claims he will call me in a week or two. I look older than 15 and my mom looks younger than 34. It's nice to be noticed by a decent, polite guy. I was surprised mom approved since he was at least 18 and I am just 15.

My ears are still ringing this morning so I know it was a really awesome show. I wish mom would do more things with me. It is so rare for her to choose me over the tavern, which makes me really sad. I'll take what I can get. Of course, mom made me promise not to tell Jim she bought the beer, smoked weed, and talked to some guys. He's so jealous, he'd probably knock her around a bit. I said I wouldn't tell Jim anything.

MARCH 24, 1984

Last night I was unexpectedly awoken by a rapping on my bedroom window ("Nevermore") by Rick Sherman, with whom I previously went to the Sadie Hawkins dance. He said that I should come over to his trailer because his grandmother, Wanda was out of town. I got dressed and walked over there with him. He is a nice guy and I am always up for a party.

I have absolutely no idea why Rick came over after all this time. Anyway, we drank beer and kissed. It was really nice because I always liked him. We laid down on the couch and kissed some more. Then, we had sex. I wasn't expecting it, and I let him do it, even though I didn't really want to. He told me was a virgin and thought I was, so I felt sorry for him and fucked him. It was totally embarrassing because his older brother, Pete, came home when we were both naked under a crocheted blanket. Pete tactfully left the room while we dressed. We got up and drank a whole lot more, doing some shots and played quarters.

I didn't like the touchy feely thing Rick was doing, so I said it was time for me to stumble home. He offered to walk with me, but I told him I was fine to walk home since it was only a mile and a half. I started to go home but suddenly didn't feel like calling it a night. I knew roughly where Sam Johnson lived, in one of the trailers in a small trailer park. I don't know what time it was, but I knocked on the door very quietly, so I thought, and asked if Sam was there. If I was sober, I'd be embarrassed because it was the wrong trailer. They said it was too early in the morning and he didn't live there anyway. I went to another trailer and did the same thing. The next thing I knew, Sam drove up in his loud, rumbling Nova and said he would give me a ride home. Sam said that I had woken up the entire neighborhood and that a neighbor called up the Johnson household to tell them that some girl was looking for him. I guess I made a lot of noise. He thought that it was kind of funny and sweet. We parked at the end of a dead end road nearby, talked and started kissing. I didn't want to go home. We had sex in his car, which I wanted so much more than with Rick, but felt guilty while doing it since I just had sex with another dude less than an hour before. Sam drove me to the entrance to my road to drop me off (his car is so loud it rattles the windows). I walked home and snuck back in through my window, my parents never the wiser.

But, God, the next day, I felt so guilty. How could I have sex with two guys in the same night? What if they talk about it to each other? Could Sam smell Rick on me? I didn't think that Rick ever would talk about it, but Sam probably would tell everyone, which was a mistake. I don't want to hurt Rick's feelings since he is such a nice guy. I don't know why I have sex so frequently, with anyone who shows any interest in me. I start kissing a guy and then we move right into sex, well, except for that janitor, he totally grossed me out. I want a guy to like me, really like me, but casual sex doesn't seem to be the answer. I long for love and companionship, a friend I can trust. I want a boyfriend who will love me. I can't find a boyfriend. I have these cheap one off affairs. I don't want to have sex with every guy who kisses me. I get drunk, get high, lose my inhibitions and fuck anyone. Sometimes, when I black out, I don't know if I've had sex or not. There are plenty of guys around Bean who wouldn't hesitate to fuck a girl who is passed out. I hate myself for fucking so often. Why do I keep doing this?!

APRIL 12, 1984

Scott, from the Scorpions concert, has called me many times now. He asked to go out on a date, but then asked how old I was, my real age. Scott turned out to be 20 and since I am 15, that is a felony, or at least, statutory rape, even if I consent to sexual contact. That is a strange law, since rape is rarely prosecutable, and consensual sex, if the girl is under 18 in Washington, is considered rape. Scott thought that I was 18. He is cool about me being 15 and we have talked for hours on the phone. Scott said we should remain friends and that someday we can go out on a real date, when I turn 18. He is so intelligent to talk to, so maybe we'll keep in touch.

I had a very disheartening situation at school. I am bored stiff with school, since it is too easy for me. I am taking a creative writing class which has unleashed my inner muse. I spend time writing short stories for this class, doing the haiku and poems, and finally graduating to a short story. My teacher, Ms. Bitch Lawson, pulled me aside after class, my short story clutched in her hands. My first thought is she loved the story, so I perked up with anticipated pleasure. All hopes were quickly dashed when she accused me of plagiarism. I was in complete disbelief, I probably stood speechless for a short moment, before spitting back at her that it was my own writing, thank you very much. Ms. Lawson tried to use intimidation and asked where the original source for my story was located. I sarcastically said, in my head. I spent so much time on the story, editing it, re-reading several times, even tried to share with mom, who said she would read it when she wasn't drunk from the tavern.

Ms. Lawson pressured me for my source, saying she could expel me for plagiarism. I stuck to my story, no pun intended, since it was the truth: the story was my own. She accused me of being too young to experience so many ranges of emotions and relationships with men. Honestly, watching soap operas and fucking half of the boys from school has given me life experience. I wrote a story of unrequited love. She couldn't prove the plagiarism so there seemed no way I could be expelled from school. I left class in disappointment and deep depression. It cut me to the core. I really tried, for a change, on a school project (besides art, cooking and sewing, which were fun and easy for me), only to be accused of cheating. I may drink at school, smoke weed behind shop, skip classes, skip entire school days, get expelled for stealing, bad behavior, but I certainly didn't plagiarize.

When mom finally got home, intoxicated as always, I told her of Ms. Lawson's accusation, which infuriated mom. She asked for my short story, so I gave it to her and mom read it through on the spot. Mom said it was an incredible story, she believed me, and actually took my story to work with her and called Ms. Lawson from work. The next time I saw Ms. Lawson, she informed me she gave me an "A" for the story, but she would keep an eye on all of my work for the rest of the school year. Fuck that bitch. I found my niche in life, and she completely destroyed my initiative and ambition. It looks like her class will be the best to skip in the future.

MAY 14, 1984

I got caught skipping 4th period again, Ms. Lawson's creative writing class, which is when I get high behind the shop building. I got a suspension notice but no actual suspension. The letter just says that I will be expelled next time I skip 4th period. I'll just skip another class for a while, maybe 5th period, but that is math, and I love math, even if it is something I've previously learned. I haven't been caught smoking pot at school because I usually go off school property. I almost have been caught behind the shop building since the shop teacher tried to bust the cigarette smokers, but I haven't been caught yet. I don't smoke cigarettes, so the teacher doesn't seem to be looking for a joint. I am being really careful about it. Luckily, I caught this warning of suspension letter in the mail before Jim did. I didn't even know that it was being mailed out. A very close call. I was super lucky to have checked the mail before Jim.

I am doing my usual thing right now, listening to records with my awesome headphones. I do that every time my parents are home. I listen to Loverboy, Van Halen, Ozzy Osbourne, Motley Crüe, Iron Maiden, Led Zepplin, The Go-Go's, Pat Benetar, Ronnie James Dio, and Judas Priest. My headphones have saved my life because I feel like I am somewhere else. I listen and write in you, my diary. When I go to sleep, I leave the classical station on. It makes me feel more relaxed. I was hoping it would take away my terrible nightmares, but it really hasn't. It is reassuring to have the music on in the middle of the night when I wake up afraid. Amber makes fun of me listening to classical music.

I am smoking from my pipe right now and blowing the smoke into a pillow even though my parents are home. They are drunk and watching a porn video they rented. Disgusting. They won't be bothering me since they are probably fondling each other on the couch as I smoke, listen to music and write. Thank goodness I have weed to smoke or I'd go completely bat shit crazy. I feel so depressed. The black hole inside me gets bigger and smaller, depending on my parents. Right now, since they are watching porn, the black hole is really large and I feel vacant.

MAY 20, 1984

Yesterday, Amber and I went to see *Sixteen Candles* which was hilarious. Her mom drove us to the movie theater, to the closest one which is almost twenty miles away, and said she would pick us up afterwards. I was leery of such a promise, since Amber's mom tends to forget every commitment she makes. It isn't like we can walk home and Amber would never hitchhike like Laura and I do. I never told Amber about the hitchhiking because she would lecture me forever.

Before the show started, during previews, I told Amber I had to go to the bathroom. I went out the side door, propped it open slightly with a small stone, and smoked a joint. The movie theater has like two people working there since they only have one screen, so no one noticed that I slipped out the side door. I've done it before at the *Evil Dead* show with Amber. Laura taught me the trick. I easily snuck back in, went to the bathroom, washed my hands and sprayed Impulse "Always Alluring" on me to cover the weed reek. I sat back down next to Amber, ready to watch the movie, and the first thing she asked is if I got stoned. I thought I covered my tracks. She knew I sprayed on Impulse after getting high. She knows me better than I thought. Amber doesn't care if I get stoned, even though she doesn't get high. That's cool.

Sixteen Candles was totally awesome! It had good music and the funniest part was the foreign exchange student, Long Duk Dong. It was a parody of a typical, strange home life, with two parents and siblings. I can understand where the Molly Ringwald character was coming from; being ignored by her parents because of a more important wedding event for her older sister. I can imagine my parent's substitution would be the tavern and alcohol. I am not sixteen and am not a virgin, like the girl in the movie, and there will be no happy ending with my family suddenly caring for me. Still, I laughed my ass off.

After the movie, surprise! No car waiting for us. Amber called her mom from the telephone booth outside the movie theater and got no answer. It was dark and isolated, so while she tried to reach her mom, I lit up the roach. Thankfully, her mom showed up a half hour later. We guessed her mom heard the phone rang, realized she was supposed to pick us up, then left the house without answering the phone. At least she showed up. It got creepy standing in a dark parking lot by ourselves.

JUNE 8, 1984

My life has purpose for the first time in ages. Last night I had my first piano recital in front of an audience. The recital was held at Mrs. Wolcott's church with all of her students. I am so excited because my she made a special announcement to the crowd, that in her 20 plus years of teaching, she has never had a student learn as quickly as me. I was completely taken aback when she handed me a certificate saying I was the best performer of the evening. Normally, a student shouldn't even be ready for a recital so quickly. I am already reading music and in the 3rd level piano book in less than a year. I memorized Petite Gavotte and Czardas, the national dance of Hungary, for the recital. My parents actually came, both of them, and they were relatively sober. Can you believe it? I played really well, and I felt it. I did something extraordinary which my parents actually witnessed.

JUNE 13, 1984

Life is truly like a soap opera. *All My Children*, which Amber and I both watch, my life seems to be a pre-written script which I have yet to read. I am saddened, although not completely surprised, that on Monday, Amber's sister, Anna, had enough and went to her school counselor and spilled the beans about her father sexually abusing her since she was 5 years old. That is so horribly disgusting. I feel so sorry for Anna. Amber's dad always seemed like such a pervert, so it isn't shocking. Amber told me that she didn't know for sure about Anna, but her dad made her suck his penis a few times between the age of 4 and 6 years old. She never told anyone about her abuse before her sister came out about her sexual abuse. Amber's dad never did anything else to her after age 6. It looks like he moved on to the younger sister.

Amber's dad was arrested right after school, and they handcuffed his hands behind his fat back, which probably was painful due to his rotund physique. Amber said they all were in shock, yet Amber's mom defended her husband even while he was being handcuffed. She took the side of her husband over her daughter. Disgusting. Just hours after the police arrested him, Amber's mom drove all the way to the bank (15 miles away), withdrew money from their savings account, returned to the jail and bailed out her husband. No doubt she drained the family bank account to get him out of jail. It is such a shame. She should have left him there to rot.

When Amber's mom returned home with her hideous husband after bailing him out, Andy was livid. He loaded the family shotgun, pointed it in his father's face and told him to get out of the house before he was shot. Andy's dad wisely left and never returned. Andy is the sweetest boy in the whole world and I secretly love him, even though I am almost a year older than him. I really admire Andy since he comes from a similar broken and shitty background as me, yet he is so self-confident and stays sober and drug free. It is certain Andy didn't know about the sexual abuse of either of his sisters or he would have done something about it.

Amber told me her mom continued to defend her dad even when Andy pulled the gun on him. What is wrong with women who allow abuse to continue in the home while they pretend to live in a fantasy world? Why do some mothers look the other way and pretend bad things aren't happening? My own mom does the same thing every time Jim starts to hit me: she goes to their bedroom and shuts the door.

After Andy kicked out his dad, his mom left the house to stay with a relative for a few days. Her husband left town too quickly for her to join him. She just left Amber and Andy in the trailer by themselves. That is horrible! Anna was taken into state custody and has been placed in a foster home for now. Amber doesn't know where she is yet. The courts will let Amber and Andy know later. What an evil man.

JUNE 26, 1984

Anna was returned home once her mom returned from visiting her family. Now, all three siblings are together again, and Amber's mom is alone, penniless, and is too afraid to support her husband because of Andy's wrath. Amber's dad will certainly go to prison for a long time. Amber said she hasn't heard from her dad at all. Justice will catch up with him and he'll probably be repeatedly raped in prison. Karma is a fucking bitch.

Now, for my own soap opera of a life. Mom has flown out to Boston because she found out that her father is dying of lung cancer. He smoked when he was a young man, then quit 20 years ago, and now has terminal lung cancer. His wife, the wretched Denise from the Thanksgiving a few years ago, is a nurse, so she is looking after him at home. Grandpa's been with wife number four for a while now. Grandpa owns several weight loss clinics around the Boston and the Philadelphia areas, and Denise was a nurse at one of the clinics. Certainly, she quit her job once she landed the rich fish.

I wanted to go with my mom to Boston, especially since I'm not in school right now and I could be her support network. I heard Jim actually say that he didn't want to spend the extra money on airline tickets for me if it wasn't required. The amount of money he gambles and drinks away at the bar is far more expensive than an airline ticket. Jim actually has no heart. I believe if we looked in Jim's chest, he would be like the Grinch whose heart was two sizes too small.

Mom was sent on a reconnaissance mission to discover grandpa's exact medical condition, and whether he will linger for several months or die imminently. If it turns out to be the latter, I'll be allowed to go to fly to Boston and see my actual blood relatives. Have I mentioned how much I despise Jim? I wish he had end stage lung cancer instead.

I really want to see my grandpa for the second time in my life before he dies. I only met him recently at Thanksgiving when he paid for us to visit him, flying us out on first class. I am really at a loss as to why mom didn't take me with her. She lets Jim dominate her every movement. She should have stood her ground and brought me with her to Boston since she is the one who has a job and makes the money. She's not allowed to have her own checking account, so she doesn't have access to her own money.

JUNE 27, 1984

Mom called and told Jim that her father is in really bad condition. Jim didn't allow me to speak with her and picked up the phone on the first ring. I was in my bedroom, where I have my own phone, and was going to grab it when Jim beat me to the punch. He'd normally be at the tavern if mom was home. I quietly picked up the receiver, carefully covering the mouth piece so not to be detected, and listened in on their conversation. Mom is insisting that I fly out immediately. I'll be leaving tomorrow, thank goodness. She already bought tickets for me that will be waiting at the counter. I am excited and nervous about flying by myself for the first time in my life. It would have been easier to travel with mom. Jim complained about his huge inconvenience of driving me to the Sea-Tac Airport, named for the location between Seattle and Tacoma.

I have packed my large suitcase and small carry-on, because I am unsure how long I will be in Boston, so I am packing a variety of clothes, including my white, Playboy, one-piece swimsuit.

I packed too much, I'm sure, but one can never be sure. Mom and I shop at Nordstrom's, which has deliciously wonderful, stylish clothing. I have to look totally cool in the big city of Boston, getting out of this hick town, traveling on an airplane by myself, who knows who I'll meet. I packed Stephan King's *Pet Cemetery*, and *The Stand* to read on the plane and while I'm in Boston. I love Stephen King, and have read almost every book he has published, even though they usually give me nightmares. I love the horror genre.

I should be distraught for my dying grandfather, but since I don't actually know him, it doesn't affect me at all. I can only hope he leaves me, his only grandchild, a fortune when he dies. I highly doubt it since he has three ex-wives and too many step-children to count, not including mom and her two brothers. I can only dream of making a fortune so I can escape this dismal life in Bean.

JUNE 29, 1984

I am in Boston and I was greatly relieved that Jim didn't come into the airport with me. Mom made him promise to check me in, but he didn't, of course. He dropped my off at the Delta terminal and told me to ask the Sea-Tac Airport employees to assist me, since I am a minor. There were many helpful people at the airport who took me where I needed to go. I would rather go alone than have Jim browbeat me. I felt excited and adventurous. I wasn't first class this time, which wasn't an issue for me. Mom got me a window seat.

Mom picked me up at the airport in a brand new Cadillac, driven by grandpa's sixteen year old stepson, who I met previously, Trent. I was a bit overwhelmed by the entire experience, flying on a plane by myself, navigating through two airports, and seeing Trent again who was so incredibly gorgeous and only a half year older than me.

Trent took us on the tour of Boston, going through the posh neighborhoods, cruising around the outskirts of the city, delaying our arrival to his home. It was understandable since grandpa is deathly ill, lying in bed, high on morphine, with the smell of death and decay lingering in the perfectly manicured mansion. The grand house is on several acres within the Boston city limits, which I'm told is worth a fortune. With grandpa's six stepchildren, and multiple ex-wives, there won't be anything left for his one and only grandchild, who he has carelessly discarded and ignored for most of my life.

The only thing grandpa can do is lay in bed and watch Wimbledon, because he loves tennis. He played tennis weekly before his cancer struck him down. Grandpa liked to be in top physical form and brag to everyone about his physical prowess, that was until he got lung cancer and had a lung cut out of his body, leaving a large, hideous scar across his chest.

The first thing grandpa told me when I arrived in his lavish bedroom was to be careful around Trent, as he lifted a yellow arm and bony finger in Trent's direction. I told grandpa that he has been a gentleman to me. Grandpa told me to be careful of gentlemen and do not fall under Trent's manipulations. It was an odd thing to say. He had to be 25 years older than Denise. I took his comments with only a grain of salt.

Grandpa's bedroom was fully equipped with oxygen tanks, heart monitor, and large television with cable piped in to watch Wimbledon, starring Boris Becker, the 16 year old wunderkind who is only a year older than me, and same age as Trent. I hope Boris wins Wimbledon because he is so young. Grandpa is pulling for him since he is German, young, and beautiful, well actually, West German. The unnecessary Berlin Wall still lingers around, like a boil which needs to be lanced.

Denise is still a terrible tyrant. Mom unfortunately adores her and hangs on every word that skinny, cigarette smoking bitch says, worships the ground Denise walks on. I have seen her cruelty to her children, six of them in total although the eldest has fled the coop.

Denise doesn't trust me in the least, it is terribly obvious. I was using her bathroom (she has her own bedroom separate from grandpa's room, which appears well lived in so it was probably set up before grandpas cancer) because her brood were using all other bathrooms. Was she following me? I think that now. When I exited the bathroom, I noticed a pearl necklace sitting on her dresser. I picked it up and looked at it in the light just because I have never seen a pearl necklace before. Denise walked in and snatched it from me and told me to keep my filthy hands off her belongings. I told her that I was just looking at it since I've never seen pearls before and it was so beautiful. I was trying to be nice to her and asked if I could try it on, with her there. She told me "no" and locked it up in her wall safe. What a bitch. I wouldn't have stolen her precious necklace. She is terribly rude.

Back to Trent. He is very good looking so I make sure we do a lot together, in spite of grandpa's warnings. Trent has a classic 1970 black convertible VW Beetle. It is so cute! Really nice car because everything has been meticulously repaired and replaced, so it looks like it would in the original condition. Trent takes me driving in it and took me to the park where we passionately kissed. He is so sweet. We aren't related, he is the son of Denise, so it isn't incest.

JULY 3, 1984

Well, I have been laying outside in my gorgeous, white, Playboy bathing suit next to the greenhouse, showing off my midriff with the sheer, white mesh slashed diagonally across my midsection. Yes, grandpa's property has a greenhouse to grow lovely flowers for Denise. There is a koi pond with many lounging chairs surrounding it on an enormous patio. My tan is getting wicked, I have seen Trent watching me as he takes frequent breaks from his landscaping. He obviously finds me attractive, as I do him.

I have been staying up until 3:00 or 4:00 in the morning, usually hanging out in the basement watching television with one of Denise's children, who all seem to hate her. The basement is a mecca, a safe haven where Denise will not venture because it is unkept, smelly and informal. I stay up as late as possible, sleeping until 1:00 or 2:00 in the afternoon, because I don't want to see anyone dying, mom worshiping Denise, or any other bullshit which permeates this Colonial Revival nightmare. I am sleeping later and later every day, and have almost completely stopped eating. At first, Denise commented on my lovely figure, but when dinner time comes, she publicly ridicules me at the dinner table for shunning her fabulous cooking, as I notice how she eats only a few dainty bites throughout the evening. Denise cooks grandpa's favorite meals, preparing a special plate for him to pick at and vomit into a bucket next to his bed. Denise has selected me to be her whipping boy, and at meal times, I am told by Denise how ungrateful I am for not eating her wonderful cooking, or eating her fabulously good deli-quality ham sandwiches, ready for consumption in the refrigerator. She doesn't eat anything all day and smokes cigarettes in the kitchen, while grandpa is dying of lung cancer upstairs.

JULY 5, 1984

Things have been kind of crazy here in Boston. I almost got arrested three days ago. I went to a pre-fourth of July party with Rhoda, one of the older children who is 17, and got quite drunk, as usual. I did pace myself better than at home, but after several hours at the party, I ended up fairly wasted. They had joints passed around, too. A friend of Rhoda's, Todd, was making a beer run just before 3:00 am when sale of alcohol stopped, and asked me to go with him. I did because he is so funny, kind, and wasn't hitting on me. He is just a nice guy. Anyway, when he was going into the convenience store, some police were coming out and saw that he was obviously intoxicated. They frisked him and found a fake I.D. on him, which I had no idea he was also under age. The police knocked on my window, asked me to get out of the car and were going to arrest me for being an intoxicated minor, although we weren't being belligerent or anything. The police was were being so kind and courteous, that I was compelled to cooperate. I explained to the officer that I am from a small town, Bean, located in Washington state, and that I am only here in Boston temporarily because my grandpa is dying of cancer. I told him the street where grandpa lived and told the policeman that he could verify all of this, as his partner was handcuffing Todd to prepare him for the police station. I apologized to my police officer for being drunk as a minor and they ended up letting us both go after much talking amongst themselves. The house party was only a few blocks away and the police said that he would follow us there to make sure we got there safely. We did. Neither one of us got arrested or in trouble. Rhoda decided to go home after that. Well, we waited about a half an hour in case the police were still there and we both drank a gallon of water. It kind of ruined the party because they were almost out of beer and were relying on our beer run.

When we finally got home around 4:00 am in the morning, Rhoda asked if I wanted to sleep downstairs in the basement in a sleeping bag rolled and waiting for me. I said that I definitely did so I wouldn't wake mom. Strangely enough, mom was waiting for me to get home, although she knew that I went to a party with Rhoda. She asked me where I was going so I told her that I was going to sleep in the basement with Rhoda after watching some television. Mom freaked out for no apparent reason and demanded that I sleep in her room. I didn't know why she got so upset! I told her that I was just going to sleep downstairs, not drink or do anything else. That is when the bitch Denise came downstairs, belittled me, yelled at me and told me to get to my room, claiming I was waking the entire household. She likes to belittle people. She is very good at it.

While I was still on the stairs, Rhoda snuck off to the basement, mom admitted at 4:00 in the morning that she opened the mail that Amber sent to me and found a small bud (yes, marijuana) in there. It wasn't much, but Amber sent me some because she was being nice since my grandfather was dying of lung cancer. Why my mom opened my mail is another story, most likely, Denise's doing. I was so angry at her doing that and told her this. Mom is so brainwashed by Denise, she loves everything Denise does and wears, and tells me how beautiful Denise is, and how thin Denise is, but Denise is mean to the core. I was horrified and felt terrible for Rhoda, who tried to escape the chaos by going to the basement to watch tv and sleep. Denise stormed downstairs to lecture Rhoda about something or other, even though she gave her permission for me to go to the party with Rhoda. It was extremely embarrassing, to be honest. Once we got in the small bedroom with two twin beds we were sharing, mom passed out immediately. I laid there stewing about my ill treatment, why mom opened my mail, and why Denise was so upset about the party although she knew we were going there together. Denise probably made mom open my mail and wait for me until 4:00 am. Soon, mom was snoring softly as I laid in bed, confused and disturbed by the morning's events. I was tempted to go to the basement with Rhoda, and even tip-toed down there to see what Rhoda was doing. She was fast asleep on the couch, the television still on, so I went back upstairs so no one would get in trouble.

I might as well come clean and tell you that I have been having a fling with Trent. I love him so much. We had sex in his VW but he forgot to put on the emergency brake, and we noticed that we were moving while we were doing it! Trent scrambled over the seats and was finally able to put the emergency brake on in time before we hit anything. It was a close call. Trent didn't go to the party with Rhoda and I, because Denise wouldn't let him. He is her favorite child and always wants him around her for some reason. It is really twisted. I can tell that Trent can't stand her. Trent took me to see the fireworks and we parked and held hands while we watched them. It was so beautiful and romantic.

Uncle John took me over to see his apartment and even took me to see Pink Floyd laser light show, seated on enormous bean bags, while completely stoned to the maximum. Uncle John is only 7 years older than me and hates Denise, so he doesn't hang out at the house at all. Instead, Denise makes him watch over all of the weight loss businesses. Uncle John doesn't have much furniture besides a small love seat and his bed, but he has lots of bongs. He has one that is 3' tall. Uncle John said he felt guilty about smoking pot with me since I am so young, but I told him that I have been smoking for years. Plus, grandpa is dying and it is a relief to escape for a while. Not that I know grandpa at all. He just lays up there in bed and watches Wimbledon.

I have been over to Uncle Althan's condo a few times. Gammy, still desperately in love with grandpa, flew up to Boston to see grandpa before he dies. She's been staying at Althan's condo, and could stay with her family since his place is a cluttered nightmare, stuff piled floor to ceiling with pathways throughout the condo. It seems that habit runs in the family since my bedroom looks the same way, so it feels more homey than grandpa's perfect American dream home. Nothing is out of place there, nor can you touch anything for fear of awakening Denise's wrath.

It is wonderful to see Gammy, yet depressing since she wants to see her one and only love and no one will allow her, or even tell grandpa that she is there. He has no idea that she is fighting to see him, and I believe it should be grandpa's decision, not Denise's. I am completely on Gammy's side with this, Denise has no rights over grandpa. Gammy said she went to the house in a taxi, and Denise told her to get off the property or she'd call the police. Gammy tried to force her way in, but Denise slammed and locked the door.

Gammy drinks so much now, drinking bottle after bottle of vodka with a splash of tonic. She is so angry all of the time for not being allowed to see grandpa that it is sad to see her. Mom and Gammy aren't getting along too well right now since mom is practically worshipping Denise. Mom likes to give Gammy verbal jabs for no reason, for example, when Gammy told me that I have pretty feet, mom laughed at her and said that I have ugly feet and showed her my long toes. I was embarrassed and laughed, too, although I didn't feel like laughing. I hate when mom is so overtly cruel to me. To make matters worse, when I laughed about my long toes, Gammy misconstrued it and said that we were ganging up on her. Mom keeps throwing me in the middle, making me side with her but I don't want to be a part of her twisted behavior. Gammy stormed upstairs, taking her vodka tonics with her. I should have run after her, telling her that I wasn't laughing at her. I have no idea why I even laughed at my mom's comment. It was more of an automatic reaction. I am letting Gammy down. Not just me, but the whole family. I am a kid and keep quiet, because I don't know what to do.

JULY 6, 1984

Grandpa finally succumbed to his miserable illness. Uncle John and I went over to his apartment for a short time, so he could take a break from grandpa's suffering and Denise's hovering. Uncle John is much closer to grandpa than I am. We smoked some pot from the biggest bong of all, three feet tall, per my request. I had never smoked from a bong so large, so I chose it specifically.

I could see that uncle John is full of emotion that he doesn't know how to communicate. John doesn't talk much, and when he does, it is mostly small talk, around the other people. He did say he feels trapped and doesn't know what to do. I told him it is quite normal to feel that way.

After we got extremely stoned with some very fine pot, we finally decided to go back to the house, meaning grandpa's Colonial monstrosity. Neither of us wanted to go, and as soon as we walked in the door, Denise ran up to Uncle John, demanding where he had been because grandpa died and was asking for him. Uncle John and I left the house for only 45 minutes! Give him a break, bitch. Also, John has a telephone at home, she could have called him, unless the phone was cut off. That is a possibility.

Poor, guilt-ridden Uncle John ran up to see grandpa. I was following him up to the bedroom, too, when mom grabbed my arm with extreme malice and asked what I had been doing. She acts just like Denise now. I told her Uncle John and I were just talking, hanging out at his apartment. Mom kept asking me why I wasn't crying about grandpa's death and if I was stoned or on something else. She kept quizzing me and wouldn't let me go. I told her that John just needed to get out of the house and that was all. She never freaked out about me smoking pot before this visit. It is Denise's doing, I know it. And the third degree about me not crying was mean. I didn't have a chance to let it sink in before she was shaking me and asking me why I wasn't crying. I didn't even know the man. Why aren't you crying, since it was your father?

I went to see grandpa, but Denise made an ordeal about washing him clean before we could view him. Mom explained that people defecate when they die. That is a pleasant image. I waited patiently, next to a quiet Uncle John, while Denise washed and cleaned grandpa's body for the ceremonial viewing.

After viewing grandpa's corpse, mom surprisingly sprang upon me that we are leaving tomorrow, the day after grandpa died. Mom doesn't want to stay for the funeral so we are going home right away. We are not staying for his funeral, or his will reading, for that matter. It sounds like Denise's dealings to me. I'll miss Trent so much. That makes me sadder than anything. We promised to write to each other. I will miss him very much. Grandpa would turn over in his grave if he knew we had sex.

AUGUST 23, 1984

Back in boring Bean. Mom completely trusted Denise's account of the will reading. I strongly suspect that Denise strong-armed my mom, saying it would be best if she left Boston before the will was read. I told mom she was being duped. She took offense to the fact that Denise would dupe her. It seems obvious to me.

Uncle Althan got three weight loss clinics, Uncle John got two weight loss clinics, and Denise got one weight loss clinic, the mansion in the most expensive real estate in Boston, and most of his money, as far as we were told. Denise allowed no one except herself to be at the will reading, even though grandpa's three children had every right to attend the reading of the will, but were cowed by Denise.

Mom allegedly only received $20,000 in the will, and Denise conveniently gave the money to Uncle John to give to mom. I was extremely disheartened that grandpa didn't include me in his will. According to Denise, I wasn't in it at all. I am his only grandchild. That seems odd and kind of unbelievable. Well, Uncle John went to Amsterdam with his friend, flipping the bill, spending all of mom's $20,000 on hotels, drugs, air fare and food. I'm sure that John's friend was completely grateful. I know they sell cocaine there, in addition to hash bars, so a lot of the money went to drugs.

Denise made Uncle John call mom upon his return to repent for his selfishness. Mom said she forgave him when Denise was on the three-way line, but afterwards said she would never forgive Uncle John for spending her inheritance. I wondered why Denise gave John mom's money to begin with. She could have easily sent mom the money, but mom only blamed Uncle John, who is in his early twenties with no guidance instead of the real predator, Denise, who seemed to plan this all from the start. All in all, mom didn't receive a dime, which is terribly unfortunate since it may have saved us from this abysmal life with Jim.

It sounds like both my uncles plan on selling their weight loss centers to Denise, who offered them quick cash in place of their potentially prosperous businesses. Triple duped. All three of grandpa's children got completely taken by the big, red-headed bully, Denise. It would have been nice to receive something out of the horrible ordeal of watching my grandfather writhe in agony, vomit up his meals, and lay listlessly on the bed, pleading for death.

On a slightly more upbeat note, Amber's dad got sent to prison but was given only 8 years for repeatedly raping his daughter. I am relieved he is in prison because he is pure evil. I hope he gets raped 100 times a day in prison. Prisoners hate child molesters, so he will have his ass ripped open. Amber said that her dad got stripped of his ministry title, so he isn't a minister anymore. It came out in the trial, which Amber told me about.

No wonder poor Anna has always been so shy. All those years of him forcing himself upon her. And she was so young, too! Anna hardly ever spoke to anyone. She is apparently talking more and seems happier, but she has gained a lot of weight. Amber says that she must weigh 160 pounds now. Anna must have gained 50 pounds in the last few months. Poor girl. Stress does terrible things to the body and soul.

I've finally caught up with the piano assigned work. I have been going to my Thursday lessons again and am so glad that I have something positive to go to. Choir and piano make me so happy. Of course, I still can't play when Jim is home because he complains about the "racket" that I'm causing, when I'm trying to share my music with others, since it is depressing playing for myself.

AUGUST 26, 1984

Last night I stayed the night with Paula. We walked over to the park and two Tacoma boys, friends of Paula, met us there. Obviously they are older because they had beer, or else had fake I.D. She probably knows them through her drug-dealing sister.

The boys, I completely forget their names, took us for a ride into the woods behind Bean in their 4-wheel drive truck. It is a Ford Bronco, so it has back seats, not a flat bed. The dirt roads behind Bean are really part of the Army base that comes right up to Bean. There is no gate or fence around that part of the Army base, so it is really easy to sneak on. The Army has live ammunition and bombs in the woods back there, so we didn't go that far into the woods.

The bombs the Army plays with always shake our trailer, even from 10 miles away.

There is a secret clearing in the woods that Paula and I had been to before. We went with one of her many boyfriends after a party and got high there because the place is so isolated. There is a huge water drainage ditch made of concrete which is about four to five feet wide, and completely open on the top, except for two metal supports going across. It is filled with lots of rushing water that comes from underground on one side and returns underground on the other. It is very dangerous and it scares me because if you fell in, you'd be trapped in dark, dirty water underground. You'd die for sure. Strange it isn't protected to prevent accidents.

Paula started jumping back and forth over the deadly ditch. I was freaking out but the boys thought it was funny. It wasn't funny because Paula had to go way back and then jump over the gap which was as wide as a man is tall. If she fell in, she would be sucked under ground and we wouldn't be able to save her since the water was going too fast. Paula kept doing it although I begged her to stop. Paula called me a pussy for not jumping over it. I was terrified. She and the two boys started walking around me and pointed their fingers in my face calling me names for not jumping the small gorge, although only Paula had done the stupid act. To be honest, it freaked me out that Paula joined with the boys in the taunting. I finally relented and jumped the raging gully. I said I would do it only once. I got way back and ran as fast as I could and jumped high into the air. I made it to the other side, but barely. That was it for me.

The boys were impressed and got me high after that, holding out with the weed until I completed the dangerous feat. I drank more beer fairly quickly after the culvert jumping ordeal. Strangely enough, the boys never did jump the ditch. Who's are the real pussies, Paula?

We were hanging out in the clearing, away from the rushing water, for about an hour when an Army jeep drove up next to us. We hid the beer and pot since it was the Military Police. One of the men said that he knew we were drinking and he wasn't there to arrest us. He said that we had to leave the area right away because it was dangerous. Paula asked why it was dangerous, although the rushing culvert of water was dangerous enough for anyone. At first, the MP didn't want to say anything and kept looking at each other. I asked if it was because of the ditch. He said that the ditch was dangerous, but there was something worse. We wanted to know what it was! Finally he said that they had found two bodies at that very spot! Just within the last few months, two separate females around 16 (my age!) were found naked and decapitated. They never found their heads. I asked if the murderer could have thrown the heads down the ditch. The Military Police said they had already checked the other end and there were no heads. The heads were taken somewhere else. He said that since the girls were our age, we had to promise never to come back again. I promised right away. Paula, being the stupid girl she is, just laughed and laughed. I told her to promise, too. She said she promised, but I didn't believe her. It scared the freaking shit out of me because there are so many serial killers here in the Pacific

Northwest, and the military is a magnet for murderers since they can kill for their government without raising an eyebrow. I asked the police why it hadn't been in the news. I haven't seen any murders in the area and none of us had ever heard anything about this. The police looked at each other and then said that it was a military case. But, I said, it was dangerous not to know about it since people often come to that spot to party. Paula and I had been there before. He agreed but said it wasn't up to him to tell the press. The military keep their secrets. The MP said they don't know the identity of either girl and they are probably from Tacoma and not Bean since we didn't know of any missing teenage girls. We went back to Paula's house which was only ten minutes away. That means the killer comes right up to the town of Bean. Some crazy Army man was loose and no one will ever know about it. It made me wonder how many other murders aren't on the news.

SEPTEMBER 6, 1984

My mom actually did something surprising and unpredictable, which is completely out of character. She signed us both up for weekly tennis lessons in Winder. I have piano lessons on Thursdays, and now tennis lessons after school on Tuesdays. Now I have two days a week where I don't have to sit home alone or with chatty Amber, mooching my MTV and satellite dish, which gets every premium channel on the planet. Mom took me to a sporting good store after piano lessons yesterday, while we were in town and bought us both good tennis rackets. Today we started our first tennis lesson. It was really enjoyable, and I am guessing she was inspired by grandpa's love of tennis while he was dying in Boston. I'm appreciative, wherever this inspiration came from. I am catching on very quickly, which is unusual for me since I can barely catch a baseball. The instructor, Neil, is incredibly gorgeous in a preppy sort of way, and I could have him hand-over-hand train me every day of my life. My heart beats faster when he puts his hands over mine, correcting my grip and racket direction. Neil commented to mom that my serve is impressive already, that I exude a great deal of power and authority. A lot of pent up anger, I am assuming. I don't really require two hands to swing since I work out and am so strong. I do the Jane Fonda aerobics almost every day.

As for my tennis swing, I've always been very strong for my size, as if my coal mining ancestors have somehow enhanced my strength through inherited genes. Neil suggested I use two hands for more control when returning the ball backhanded since that is my weakest point. After only one lesson, I'm completely hooked on tennis. Lessons will be going on a month by month basis, because mom was probably told by Jim not to commit to anything long term. Not since our ice skating experience, when Jim was still living in California, has mom done anything so extreme as signing up for a class together. I hope it continues indefinitely, because I really love tennis. It's nice beginning 11th grade with a gift – tennis!

SEPTEMBER 13, 1984

During today's tennis lesson, an attractively preppy young man came up to me from the advanced tennis class and excitedly informed me that we went to high school together, although he is a grade ahead of me. I was completely clueless who he was since we don't hang in the same circles; me the stoner circle, he the preppy one. Honestly, I didn't know him at all yet he recognized me. His name is Ty. I hope he hasn't heard terrible things about me. Perhaps that is why he was so excited to see me, because he heard I was an easy lay. Ty asked if I wanted to go out on a date this Saturday night, which completely shocked me into speechlessness. I said yes once I came back down to earth since he seems like a normal, kind and considerate person.

There is a bit of a conflict. My parents and I are going over to a wedding party in the early afternoon. We don't get many Bean parties a year, so it is best to attend the ones that come up since all the Bean kids are there with their drunk parents. Of course, my beloved Rob will be there. Since Rob and I don't seem destined to go steady, I am looking forward to my date with tennis Ty.

SEPTEMBER 16, 1984

Yesterday was a horrible and humiliating experience. Ray and Rita's party was fun and entertaining since everyone was there, the Mabreys and other kids from Bean. My parents let me get beer from the keg, as did the rest of the kids. Paula didn't want to go to the party since her dad was marrying a topless dancer and Amber wasn't invited. The kids from school were drinking in the barn and talking. There was badminton set up, rock music blaring through two large speakers, and multiple groupings of chairs set up throughout the property around the single wide trailer.

I was having a great time, talking to the Mabrey twins and other boys from Bean in the barn, drinking my fill from the keg, which was available to all. A little too available since I never know when to slow down. If alcohol is available, I drink, no questions asked. It is always my downfall. Boys usually bring me drinks, out of politeness, I suppose.

The party was going well, we were talking in the barn, when a ruckus burst out. We were wondering what was happening, so we made our way to the center of the adult party, which was outside, near the trailer. It turned crazy, because Rita had taken off all of her clothes, not stopping at her undies, and was doing a table dance, on a foldable table that sagged under the weight. Ray was yelling at Rita to stop acting like a tramp and get her clothes on. Rita flat out refused. Ray lunged at Rita, on their wedding night, slapped her across the face and started yelling at all of the men who were watching Rita. Mom tried to herd me to the truck so I couldn't see the mayhem. I really wanted to stay and watch the unfolding drama, worthy of any soap opera. Ray became so enraged that he grabbed his gun and starting chasing off all of the men who were gawking at his wife's tits. Mom, Jim and I went home immediately. I am not sure that Ray and Rita's marriage will last since it couldn't even survive the wedding night. I didn't have time to say goodbye to Rob since mom was pushing me toward the truck.

Once we got home, my parents grabbed a couple of beers and watched trashy tv. I called Ty, just like we had arranged. I was fairly drunk, which was my misfortune. Jim forgot that I was going on a date until Ty drove all the way out to our trailer and I was just about to go with him to see a movie when Jim wouldn't let me go. Jim said that I was too drunk. I still can't believe it. Jim never gives a shit what I do, but suddenly cares when a nice boy drives 15 miles to take me to a movie 15 miles back the way he drove. Jim knew that I had the date and he is the one who let me drink the beer. Since when has Jim become a caring father?! Ty was a little freaked out by Jim, I could tell. I was extremely embarrassed because Jim was yelling at Ty to "get the hell out of here!" It would have been nice to tell Ty before driving all the way from Winder.

I hope Ty will call me back, but I sincerely doubt it. I'll never have a chance at a normal life. Today is Jim's birthday so I am supposed to say happy birthday and all that loving shit when I wish he was dead.

SEPTEMBER 23, 1984

When mom and I went to the army base to go grocery shopping, we discovered they built a new gate on the Bean side. The army base has finally built a fence around their property on the Bean entrance and put in an armed gate. I never told my mom about the dead bodies out there but I knew that the fence was put up because of the murders. Mom would have asked what I was doing out there so I thought it best not to tell her.

It is too much of a coincidence! The area with the ditch, where Paula made me jump across the rushing water, where Bean teenagers go to party, is completely inaccessible now. Mom was upset at the inconvenience, although she has a gate pass, so I don't know what inconvenience it is to her. I am actually relieved that they put up the 12 foot fence with barbed wire around that area. The murderer can't come into Bean without going through the gate. Since the Military Police stop everyone at the gates and take a really good look at every face that comes through, the murderer will be less likely to come that way. I'll never know if the murderer was caught or not since the military is so secretive. Nothing on the news was ever reported about headless girls' bodies found outside of Bean on the army base.

OCTOBER 19, 1984

Ty never called me back. He was frightened off by Jim, I expect. I saw Ty at school and at tennis practice, the last time we went, he tried to avoid me, said that he was sorry we didn't go on a date, then ran off so quickly I didn't have a chance to respond. By coincidence, perhaps, mom and I haven't gone to a tennis lesson for two weeks. I think she was pressured by Jim to stop spending money on fun with me. He really is an evil troll.

Another soap opera event has taken place; Lee Simm's attempted murder. He is a bar buddy of my parents' and we have gone to some parties on his property before. Lee is nice enough, but very moody. I've heard stories about how was tortured for years in Vietnam. Lee was in the Army, captured by the Vietcong, and tortured by being put in a pit, beaten, starved, and other atrocities that he won't discuss. It is really quite sad because he will suddenly freak out and thinks that he is in a dark hole in Vietnam, about to get bamboo slivers stuck under his fingernails. Mom says that whenever he gets that way, no one can calm him down. Other times, Lee will just hunch over his beer and not talk to anyone. He has always been very nice to me. People in the bar try and help him out, especially when he gets confused as to where he is. They'll drive him home and do nice things like that.

Lee has two older step-sons from a previous marriage. They are a few years older than me. I think Brad is 21 and Jess is 18, both of whom I met last year at Roy's party. The boys are creepy, that's for sure. For some reason, Roy's ex-wife absolutely hates him so much, that over the years, she slashed his car tires and vandalized his house. Also, she sends her sons over to do the dirty work. I think it is because she isn't getting the alimony payments or something stupid like that. It isn't like Lee is rich. He is on Medical Disability through the Army due to his mental instability. She should feel sorry for him, not harass him.

Just last week, when Lee was coming out of the Bean Tavern, one of his ex-wife's sons (the police aren't sure which one did it and Lee can't remember since he was drunk) shot him with a small caliber gun 6 times. All of the shots were aimed at his private parts, so most of the wounds were in the thigh and pelvis, although one bullet shot off the end of his penis. He is still in critical condition, but they think he will live since it was a small caliber gun. Lee lost a lot of blood before getting into surgery but he is tough. What a vengeful, manipulative woman.

Both of her sons can't be found for questioning by the police but as police are searching for them, I received a letter from the younger one, Jess, just yesterday. This is a creepy story. Last year, when I was 15 and went to that party at Lee's trailer with my parents, Roy's stepson, Jess, dropped by for some free beer. He was 17 or 18 then. Roy wanted him to leave, but he stayed there for a while and was hitting on me. He asked me out then but I told him no. He had a Trans Am which he thinks instantly made him cool. I didn't like him in the least. To make matters worse, when I told mom what had happened at the party, she said that I should go out with him. I couldn't believe it. He is out of high school and I am in high school and mom thinks it is okay to date him. Plus, he was really weird. I don't know what it is about him, but he scares me. You know, that gut instinct.

Off and on since last year Jess has written me letters and called a few times asking me to go out with him. I got trapped talking to him on the phone once and told him that I don't want to go out with him, ever. Now, just days after either he or his brother (or both) attempted to murder Lee, I received a letter from Jess saying how much he likes me and that he would do anything for me. Mom didn't even seem shocked by it. The only thing she said was that I shouldn't go out with him and that she had a bad feeling about him. Well, no kidding! I've been saying that from the beginning, when she said I should date him last year. She never said anything bad about Jess before. Just what I need, a psycho trying to contact me while he is running from the police for attempted murder.

OCTOBER 23, 1984

Last weekend, my parents and Sid and Betty got kicked out of the Bean Tavern again. I have only found out things from eavesdropping on phone calls that have been bombarding the house this week. Apparently, Jim and Sid got into an actual fist fight. Usually they just fight other people, but this time they attacked each other. Not really a surprise since Sid is like a loaded pistol with the safety off. After that incident, there have been harassing phone calls from Sid and Betty separately on a daily basis. I picked up the phone in my room to listen in to the conversation. It wasn't really a conversation, but Betty calling mom a fucking bitch and she said that Jim was nothing but a fucking drunk. Another time, it was Sid yelling at mom to speak to Jim. Jim said he wouldn't talk to Sid so Sid called Jim a fucking pussy and then mom hung up. My parents have been going back to the Bean Bar & Grill and Sid and Betty have been going to the McKenna Lounge. They all have their rotating watering holes. The phone calls don't start until 9:00 pm when they know my parents are home since they pass out in bed by 9:30 pm every night. I guess drinking for 5 or 6 hours straight makes you tired.

I tried asking mom what was going on but she said that it wasn't any of my business. The usual answer. She acts just like Jim now, so it shouldn't be a surprise. I wish I had normal parents, people who wanted to spend time with me without being drunk every day. People who would take me to the zoo or the park or fishing or to Seattle for the day. They won't do anything that doesn't involve drinking and smoking. They never reprimand me about drinking. They know better. But Jim hates me smoking pot. He thinks it is the most evil drug in existence. He is such a hypocrite. He drinks daily, gets violent and I smoke pot and listen to music. That is so evil of me.

NOVEMBER 1, 1984

Amber's "best friend" Chrissy, is spending the week at her trailer. Amber always talks about how wonderful Chrissy is, referring to her in every conversation as "my best friend, Chrissy" and lectures me about how Chrissy will always be there to help her through family emotional problems. Whatever. Like I haven't? Unfortunately, I'm no one's best friend since I moved too many times when I was younger.

Well, I did have Diane as a best friend for two years. It is too late for me. I am too old to get a best friend. That is so depressing. I wish I had a best friend. Laura says that Paula is her best friend, so I don't have them, either. I have you, my little diary.

NOVEMBER 17, 1984

I went camping with Paula last night. It was a spur of the moment decision made on Friday night. I was bored, Paula pleaded with me, so why not? A semi-boyfriend of Paula's (more of a fuck friend) invited her and a friend (me) to go camping on Mt. Rainier. It is a bit late in the year to camp on Mt. Rainier since the snow will be deep, but it is better than staying in Bean. I called mom at the Bean Tavern and made it sound like I was going camping with Paula and her mom at a nearby lake. Mom put down the phone and talked to Jim and they agreed to allow me to go camping. I packed my sleeping bag, long johns, and pillow and Paula and her sex partner, Eric, picked me up. I have no idea where she meets these boys because they don't go to our school and I suspect they already graduated from high school.

We drove for hours up to a very remote campsite on Mt. Rainier. It wasn't in a park at all but in a secluded part of the forest. There were two tents and a second guy was already waiting for us. The other boy, Daniel, was a skinny, unattractive boy whose left arm was in a cast. I felt instantly trapped at my impetuousness.

Paula almost immediately started to cuddle up with Eric while the one armed freak, who wanted to show off his manhood, started chopping down trees for firewood with one arm. Daniel kept bragging about how tough he was to cut down a tree with one arm. It was completely unnecessary. He was obviously highly intoxicated and wandered around in the dark with an axe, which was unnerving. I huddled close to the fire and as far away from him as physically possible.

Daniel added wood to the fire so we all sat by the fire to get warm, except him, since he was busy felling trees with his one good arm. It was bitterly cold and it became quickly apparent that I didn't bring enough clothes. I put layer after layer on and was still cold, even with gloves and a scarf. We drank a beer and then Paula and Eric went into a tent for the night. I was appalled! I was left with the weirdo, who kept trying to sit very close to me. He made numerous attempts to put his uninjured arm around me which I quickly removed each time. Weirdo tried to kiss me so I left the fire and went into the tent alone. He followed me in there (it was his tent and I was told not to bring my own). I explained that I didn't want a relationship, that I would be friends with him. I said that we could both sleep in the tent if he would stop touching me. He assured me he would stop.

I got in my sleeping bag and piled all of my clothes on top of me for warmth. I closed my eyes to go to sleep when I felt creepy boy lay down next to me and put his arm around me and start kissing the back of my neck. I became instantly angry. I specifically told him at least six times to leave me alone, in a nice way. By myself in a small tent with creep, I stopped being nice. I told him to stay the fuck away from me and not to ever touch me again. I got up to sleep by the fire when creep told me to go back to the tent and then left in a huff. Then, Daniel picked up the axe, and to my horror, started chopping wood right next to the tent. It was like a horror movie because I could see his silhouette with the axe. It was as if he was threatening me. I had a difficult time falling asleep. Not only was I freezing, but we were miles away from humanity and Paula wouldn't come out of Eric's tent in order to sleep with me. I was afraid of Daniel and what he might do. He was aggressive and angry with me, I didn't dare leave the tent. I huddled in the corner for hours before I finally fell asleep.

When I awoke, Daniel was not in the tent, thank God. He had slept by the fire and had kept it going all night. What a loser. I asked Eric to take me back home immediately. I didn't want to stay Saturday night, too. Paula kept begging me to stay, but I refused. Eric and Paula drove me home and then returned to their secluded campsite.

When I returned home, mom said that she couldn't remember if I was camping one night or two and was surprised to see me home so early on Saturday morning. I told her it was for one night. I didn't tell her the truth. Like it mattered. I do so much that she doesn't know about, mom doesn't care or even remember anything since she drinks herself into oblivion every night. It was frightening to think that I may have been with a murderer in an isolated location. Daniel was very scary. I don't care if Paula is mad at me or not. It was a horrible situation and I am glad to be back home, although I never thought I would hear myself say that.

DECEMBER 4, 1984

Tonight I had my second piano recital. I memorized By The Sea and The Hungarian Rhapsody. This recital was only for the advanced students so I was surprised when Mrs. Wolcott asked me to play. Mrs. Wolcott told everyone that I have only been playing since August of last year but I am already in the advanced books. I wasn't expecting that at all. On top of that, Mrs. Wolcott gave me a certificate for being her fastest learning student and I got a standing ovation from everyone. It makes me want to cry right now. I was embarrassed but happy. I love the piano so much. I don't know what I would do without it.

DECEMBER 30, 1984

Same old thing at Christmas. We had an early dinner and my parents went to the bar. I turned 16 though. That is so exciting! I already got my driver's license on my birthday. I am glad they were open. I passed the test the first time, too.

I got a surprise for my 16th birthday. I thought that I would get a party, but this was a real party. Mom bought a pony keg of Michelob Light beer and it was taken over to Frank's trailer (Amber's mom's boyfriend). There weren't a lot of people I knew who were made it to the party, mostly Amber's friends from Longview, Chrissy and her male friends. Gail, Paula and Laura couldn't make it because it fell between Christmas and New Years Eve, so they had family plans. It was all right, though. Frank was watching some college football game.

We'll never finish that much beer. I told Frank to have as much as he wanted, which he was happy for because it was over the college football bowl games and he would have beer for it. Frank gave me a bag of some really good weed. That was nice of him. That keg is still over there, almost full. I was afraid to drink too much and make another ass of myself. Amber drank quite a bit. That's good. I just stayed the night at Amber's trailer that night instead of coming home. My parents were at the Bean Tavern anyway.

Amber's mom doesn't live in the same trailer with Amber and Andy. Amber's sister is staying with her grandfather over the holidays. Amber's mom moved in with Frank while Amber and Andy live alone in their old trailer. I stay the night with Amber as often as I can since there is no adult supervision.

Amber wants to go to some party in Longview that her friend, Chris is having. I guess I'll go. I told her to help pay for the gas.

CHAPTER 7

1985: AGE 16

JANUARY 1, 1985

Last night was terrible! What an ordeal. Just days after turning 16! Amber and I drove my Mustang to the Longview party that was a friend of Amber's "best friend" Chrissy. The party was dreadfully boring since everyone knew each other except for me. We ended up staying there for hours drinking. Just before midnight, Chrissy's boyfriends wanted to go cruising in their cars on the Longview strip. How stupid! I hate doing that even though Amber loves it. It is so 1950's. What fun is it driving up and down the same road, yelling at people? I definitely didn't want to go, although I didn't really want to head home either. Neither did Amber. There is nothing in Bean. There were police on the Longview strip which prevented cruising, thank goodness, so we went back to the house party.

Amber decided that she wanted to go to Gig Harbor to visit her massively self-centered boyfriend, Dale. He's rich and has a jacuzzi. I've been to his house before. I didn't want to drive all that way since it was getting late and we had been drinking. Plus, I didn't have enough money for gas. Amber decided to hit up everyone at the party for their spare change. Talk about embarrassing. She scraped together a few dollars in change so I had no more excuses for not going to Gig Harbor.

Dale's actually lives with his father in Gig Harbor. His mother has a nice house outside of Tacoma. Amber wanted to surprise Dale. I didn't know if that was a good idea, just to drop by someone's house whom she barely knows that late at night. I was thinking to myself that he may even have a date there. That would be okay because he is such a mean jerk, Amber needs to find that out. Dale regularly embarrasses Amber, puts her down and brags about how much money his family has.

We got some gas with the change retrieved from the party and drove out to Gig Harbor. I was pretty drunk and getting sleepy and Amber said that we could stay at Dale's father's house (even though she hasn't even met the man yet!) We were going across the Tacoma Narrows Bridge (it's the famous one that started rolling from the wind and threw cars off back in the 1930's) when I saw the dreaded blue lights in my rear view mirror. Actually, I didn't see them at first because I was trashed but Amber told me about them. I pulled over once we got across the bridge. I know I wasn't speeding.

The police had me get out of car and do that alphabet backwards, then walk heel to toe on a line. I failed both badly. The alphabet backwards was really difficult. I had to sing the alphabet and kept restarting. After locking up the car, the police arrested me for a DWI. (driving while intoxicated) and put me in the back of their patrol car with handcuffs behind my back. I didn't like the handcuffs behind my back so I slipped my hands under my butt and was able to get the cuffs to the front. The police didn't like that but I told them it hurt behind my back. They said okay just as I threw up all over the back seat and through the metal screen into the front seat! I don't remember much after that, just some hazy parts. But Amber said that the police were really upset and it got on them.

Once we got to the police station, I remember the bit about the police asking me for my home phone number to call my parents. I gave it to them because I didn't think they would be home yet since it was just after midnight on New Year's Eve. As it turned out, they weren't home. The police asked where they may be. I said that they are at the Bean Tavern and go every day. I remember they looked sad about that to each other. I know the Bean Tavern and the Bean Bar and Grill numbers by heart, so I told him. They thought this was sad, too. I said they would be at the Bean Tavern because my parents were recently kicked out of the Bean Bar and Grill for something, they won't tell me what it was. Probably a fight. It could have been my mom or Jim who fought. My mom has been in some fights in Bean lately.

Anyway, the police got a hold of my parents at the Bean Tavern and asked them if they were okay to drive out there. They said they were. Ugh! How horrible! I was hoping to at least stay the night in the jail so I wouldn't have to go home.

I took the breathalyzer and they had to do it twice because my blood alcohol level was so high and they couldn't believe it. It was .20. They said that I should be unconscious or dead at my age and weight. I have been drinking for years, so they don't know how much I can drink. They were discussing whether they should take me to the hospital or not. They didn't because I seemed like I wasn't going to die.

I don't remember the rest of it because I was so sleepy. On the ticket, however, there was something really strange. The police said that they stopped when I was trying to change a flat tire. I know for a fact that I wasn't changing a flat tire. I wonder why they said that? One of my parents drove home my car and didn't mention a tire being changed, either. Maybe they pulled me over illegally and changed the facts around. It is very strange, Amber and I talked about it today.

My parents actually haven't said anything about the DWI. Nothing. It is like it didn't happen. The ticket had a court date, a hearing, in a couple of weeks. I am sure I'll get in trouble then. Time to go now. Bye!

JANUARY 14, 1985

Mom and I went to the DWI. hearing. The judge said that since this is my first arrest and offense, I should get a lawyer before submitting a plea. I am clueless in the way of the law. Tubby, the guy who owns the Bean Tavern, kept telling Jim that I should get a lawyer and Jim said "no". Tubby said that he had a good lawyer who got him out of two DWIs. It looks like I'll be getting my first lawyer.

JANUARY 21, 1985

Jim sold my 1968 Mustang to pay for the lawyer. He didn't even give me warning. He just sold it. Jim is the one who taught me how to drink and drive. I mean literally. Jim showed me when I was 15 how to keep your beer down between your legs so no one sees it and take sips only when there aren't any cars around. He drinks and drives all of the time. He barely does anything without a stupid beer in his hand.

So now, he sold me car without even discussing it with me. He doesn't know the meaning of discussions. The lawyer said that he was pretty worried that I had a .20 at age 16. The handsome young lawyer said that even in his years of DWI. experience, he rarely has seen a level that high while a person is conscious, let alone a 16 year old. I didn't know I was unique.

What is worse, Jim cancelled my piano lessons. He said that I didn't deserve them and needed to save money. That was heart wrenching. It's the only good thing I had in my miserable life. Save money, save money. This lawyer is expensive, I guess. He is really good looking, though. He isn't very old. He'll be there talking for me at the next court date. He told me that whatever I do, don't say a word unless I am specifically asked a question. He said that I should look guilty, sad and scared. He said that the judge and prosecuting attorney may say mean things to me but I should not get angry. If anything, he said I should cry. He told me to agree with everything they say to me and be humble. Well, I used to act in plays. I still act, really, so that won't be a problem. I don't know when the next court date will be. The lawyer will handle it. He has another big case so he will try and postpone my court date as long as possible.

FEBRUARY 9, 1985

Yesterday, at school, was severely depressing. Ty, a boy from my school, died in a car crash, with a high blood alcohol level and speeding. Paula was incredibly upset, probably because she had sex with Ty. I don't know if you remember, diary, but Ty asked me out on a disastrous date that never happened when I was taking tennis lessons. Jim refused to let me go on the date. Could I have been in the car when he died? Maybe. I didn't actually know him, so I didn't cry like Paula did during the school assembly, when the principal preached about the D.A.R.E. and the dangers of alcohol, we should ban together to heal from our pain, go through rehabilitation if we are addicted to alcohol. It was such a boring bullshit speech. My parents need it the most, but they would never consent to treatment. I feel terrible that Ty died at such a young age. I know drinking and speeding are a very bad combination. I know that drinking and driving was horrible for me. I don't speed, so I thought I'd be alright.

MARCH 18, 1985

I got my first long term suspension from school. This time for 10 days. I got caught being publicly intoxicated at school. Amber and I procured rum from my house, at her suggestion, bought Coke from the machine at school and drank it at lunch. We went to our class and the teacher smelled it on us. That is Amber's first time getting caught so she didn't get in as much trouble as I did. I only brought the rum at her insistence. Drinking during the day is not my thing. I'd much rather smoke weed.

I retrieved the letter from the mailbox, but I am a bit worried about this one. The letter says that a parent should call Mr. Morrison, school principal, upon receiving the letter. That isn't going to happen. Also, he wrote that the "suspension will be reduced to 2 days in school suspension upon assurance that Leigh will be receiving treatment. Verification of treatment is necessary on or before April 22, 1985, or suspension of 10 days will be placed back in force." Whoever wrote the letter did a lot of underlining, which I won't repeat here. I guess it will be 10 days out of school. It starts today and will be completed on April 11, 1985. Luckily, when they called my house the day I got caught at school, no one was home. Mr. Morrison asked if I knew where they could be reached, and I said no. That wasn't true, they were at the Bean Bar and Grill (their new hangout again). I have the number memorized, but I am not stupid enough to tell the principal of my school the number. On another stroke of luck, Amber's mom was home and did pick up Amber. Mr. Morrison said that I could go home with them. Amber got suspended 3 days. Her mom wasn't too upset. Lucky for Amber.

On a good note, my mom started my piano lessons again. Mom convinced Jim that a positive hobby will be better than none at all. Good point. Luckily, she persuaded Jim, so I'm hugely relieved to be receiving piano lessons again.

MARCH 25, 1985

My first court hearing was today. I am actually kind of pleased with the results. The court ordered me to go to an alcohol rehab within 6 months. Not just a treatment center, but an in-house 30 days type of center. They said that if I complied, then they would not put the DWI on my record. The judge left it open until they receive proof of my being in rehab. Mom was there and the judge asked her if she would comply. She said yes. Jim never showed up for either court date. Nor did he ever go to see the lawyer.

I am excited about getting out of the house for 30 days! Getting away from my parents! I am so happy! It couldn't have been better. I am actually looking forward to this. It's almost like a vacation.

APRIL 12, 1985

It is all settled. Mom and I went to see the lawyer with the sentencing details and to finalize the treatment program. Ironically, mom had me drop her off at the Bean Tavern to tell Jim this information and let me drive home without a license. It will be restored after treatment. I wasn't going to argue. I will be going to St. Joseph's Hospital alcohol rehabilitation in Vancouver, Washington, during the month of July. Apparently, the Air Force medical doesn't cover rehabilitation and it will be $1600! It is so expensive because it's one of the best treatment centers around and it is right across the Columbia river from Portland, Oregon.

They don't have a teenage rehab yet, they are actually building it now since there is more of a need for it, so I'll be going to the adult rehab center.

Jim is livid about this enforced rehab, but his own mother thinks it is a great idea. His mother, Margaret, married a recovering alcoholic who hasn't touched a drink for their entire marriage, unlike her first husband, Jim's father who beat her and the 9 children. Grandma Johnson told Jim that he had better send me to the rehab and not complain about it. She is the only one who can put him in his place. It is hilarious.

Paula and her mom are really happy about this. It seems like everyone is happy about this except for Jim and mom. They look like grim death every time it is mentioned. I am really excited. I can't wait to go there.

APRIL 15, 1985

I got in trouble at home for "mouthing off" again. It is getting so bad at home, July feels like a lifetime away. My parents let me go camping in the woods with two guys I don't even know with Paula, but won't let me go hang out with Amber. Jim keeps saying that she is a bad influence. That is the stupidest thing I've ever heard. Amber does drink, but she doesn't smoke pot. It makes her vomit. I told Jim that it was stupid and inconsistent on his part. That is when all hell broke loose.

Jim slapped me across the face so I slapped him back. He punched me in the chest, which knocked me to the ground, so I got up, laughed in his face, and punched him in the chest. I was determined to do everything he was doing to me, right back. Finally, after being hit to the ground a few times, I got dizzy so I ran into my room and locked the door. I put my dresser in front of it and called up Gail, telling her that I had to get out of the house. She told me to come over. I opened my bedroom window and took off. I had a bloody nose. I changed my mind halfway walking to Gail's house and went to Amber's trailer instead. They don't have a phone there and her mom doesn't live there anymore. It is just Amber and Andy. It'll be less hectic. Plus, I wanted my parents to be worried where I was at. They don't know where Amber's trailer is located.

I stayed the weekend there and finally went over to Frank's trailer to use the phone and call mom. I told her that I was going to stay where I was at for a while. She cried and begged me to come home, but I refused. I knew they weren't going to do shit about it because Jim would never call the police. I think I'll stay here in Amber's trailer for a few weeks. Maybe it will teach Jim a lesson. I doubt if he even cares. I am sure he thinks it is all my fault. He never admits he is wrong. He is always saying how horrible of a child I am, or how much of a slut I am, or how stupid I am, shit like that. He won't look in the mirror and say, "I am drunk every day of my life. Maybe it is my fault." Nor will my mom. She just does whatever Jim tells her to do. I've tried to convince her to leave him but she won't. She almost did once, but Jim told her how stupid she was being and that was the end of it. Neither one deserves to be a parent. If there was a parent test, they would have failed it. "Sorry, no child for you. Next, please."

APRIL 18, 1985

I skipped 4th period again and got caught yesterday. The principal asked me why I do what I do. I asked him if he really wanted the truth. He said he did, so I showed him the dark, purple bruises on my arms. The one on my face faded, but the ones on my arms were still vivid. Well, Mr. Rich looked at them while I told him how my step-dad hits me with his belt, slaps me in the face, grabs my wrists and twists them, hurting me. You know what he did? He called my house right in front of me. Jim apparently answered the phone, and Mr. Rich proceeded to tell him exactly, word for word, what I just told him. I couldn't believe it! Mr. Rich thought that I was lying or deserved to be treated like a stray dog. To make matters worst, he asked that Jim pick me up from school early and take me home! The idea terrified me, and I told Mr. Rich how scared I was. He pushed me out of his office, told me to wait in the outer office, and closed his door.

I sat there thinking that I should make a run for it right then. I started thinking that if Jim hits me again, I will get him in trouble once and for all. Well, Jim got there pretty fast, he must have been speeding. He came in and the principal shook hands with the bastard. Jim thanked him for informing him about the lies I had been telling at school. Lies! They weren't lies! I felt so betrayed. I really was scared. In the end, I didn't have to be afraid. Jim didn't speak one word to me on the 30 minute drive home. He just dropped me off at the trailer and drove right to the Bean Tavern. I left home right away and went back over to Amber's trailer to stay.

Oh, yeah, about those bruises. Something else weird happened. The really quiet, nerdy kid in my science class saw the bruises and went ballistic! He was so angry that he wanted to kill my step-dad. I said that I didn't want to kill him, but Sean said that he would kill him for me for free. I told Sean that no one deserves to be murdered. I asked him to promise me that he would never hurt my parents. I said they are bad, but I don't want them dead. I don't want to kill anyone. Plus, he would get caught and then I would get in trouble for something I didn't even want done. I have to slowly distance myself from Sean now. He seemed too excited to kill someone. That isn't normal.

APRIL 30, 1985

Yesterday was Senior Skip Day. It is an unofficial day off, although I am not a senior so I am not allowed the day off. Some guy had a party at his parent's single wide trailer. I went with Laura who decided she needed time away from her baby. I was determined not to get too trashed. I did pretty well. But everyone else didn't. The poor guy who threw the party was so terribly mistreated. For the first couple of hours, the party went along well. I was inside getting high when the disaster started.

Laura, me and a guy were smoking a joint when we started hearing some guys scream the words to the song on the radio. Okay, slightly annoying. They began to jump in unison, then purposefully swayed back and forth in order to shake the trailer. It was only a single wide, and it didn't take long before a hole opened up in the floor. The crowd turned ferrel. I've only seen that behavior at metal concerts, not someone's home. Some guy picked up a heavy object and began pounding holes in the wall while another ripped up the carpet and flooring. Laura and I went out the back door very quickly. It was bad news. We could see the trailer shaking from side to side, heard breaking glass and furniture being flipped over and thrown through windows. The guy throwing the party actually lived in that house. His parents were kind enough to allow a party. The house was demolished. We heard the police were called after we left but no one was caught. Everyone fled the premises. The kid's parents must have been horrified to see their home, all of their belongings, utterly destroyed.

Laura and I went back a couple of days later to check out the damage. There was police tape on the doors. The trailer was deemed unsafe and was set to be demolished. We were horrified! Laura and I walked back home in silence.

MAY 6, 1985

I decided to move back home because mom was giving me such a guilt trip. She cried over the phone and said how unfair this was to her. She also used piano lessons as bribery. I can continue them if I move back home.

I got expelled again. This time, for 0 to 5 days, depending on if there is a parent-teacher conference or not. Doubtful! Especially since I intercepted the letter. I guess it will be for 5 days, then.

I got kicked out for chronic truancy this time. I don't know why I skip school so much. I don't seem to fit in anywhere so I chose to avoid it, I guess. The letter stated that "A parent conference is required before Leigh can be readmitted to school. Please contact Mr. Rich to arrange an appointment. The suspension may be reduced after conference." He scheduled the conference for May 7th at 9:00 am.

The letter also says that I can return to school on May 14th. I am just going to go back to school on May 14th. Who knows, maybe Paula will want to skip with me while I'm kicked out of school.

Most of the time, I was skipping with Amber. She likes to go to the mall during the day and hang out. I think going to the mall just to hang out is a strange way to pass the time. I'm not sure whey Amber loves to be a mall rat. Sometimes we go to the lake in Winder. We usually sneak some beer or alcohol and I bring my pipe to smoke my pot. I have gotten people to buy me beer at convenience stores. Amber always makes me do it because she's afraid to get caught. I stand in front of the store with money and ask any man who looks like he may be willing to buy a six pack for me because I "lost my I.D." It takes a lot of asking but it does eventually pay off. Bingo. There was a man about mom's age, not handsome and overweight, and he asked me what I'd do for him if he purchased the beer (with my money). My skin crawled. I'm not that desperate. I told him, "I'll give you money for the beer and you can take one" which worked like a charm. I hid the 5 pack in the bushes and hit up another middle aged man who looked like he fell on hard times. He almost got violent when I asked for a six pack, holding out my money. Another man behind him grabbed my five dollar bill and said he'd buy a six pack of beer for me. Eleven beers scored at the convenience store. Amber waited at the lake where I carried the booty and we proceeded to drink the beer.

Speaking of trouble and detention, I saw a good movie, *The Breakfast Club*. I wish I could meet cool people in detention. Instead, detention is a living hell where you have to write reports about the history of soccer and basketball. Like I fucking care about the history of basketball.

MAY 13, 1985

My luck didn't hold out. Mr. Rich randomly called my house and Jim happened to be home that day and got the call. That was on May 8. I left the house in the morning like I was going to school, hid in the woods near the bus stop, behind the mailboxes, got the mail, then waited for the other kids to get off the bus so I could walk home.

On May 8th, when I got home "after" school, Jim was furious. He grabbed me, shook me and asked where I had been all day. He said that he got a phone call from the principal's office saying that I had been kicked out long term. I told him it wasn't any of his business, since I didn't like the way he was being so rough with me. When he gets abusive like that, I tend to act tough, not cry or look scared, and give it right back. That never goes over very well. He slapped me hard and I fell against the living room side table, knocking over the lamp. I jumped up and slapped him back. Then Jim punched me in the shoulder. I am not sure how many punches and slaps there were to my face and head, but I got dizzy and my nose started bleeding, again. He then took off his belt and beat me wherever he could while I was laying on the ground. I couldn't get up that time. I tried, but he kept kicking me and pushing me back to the ground.

After that was over, Jim went into the kitchen and got a beer. I took the opportunity to quietly jump out my bedroom window and started running to Paula's house, still feeling kind of dazed. I decided not to go to Amber's trailer because my parents found out where it was located, so it wouldn't be safe.

Jim drove after me, looking for me, and finally found me when I was in downtown Bean. He tried to force me into his truck, but since people could see him, he decided not to use force and drove away. As I was standing there, I thought I should walk right into the police station and tell them what happened. Then I remembered what the school principal did to me when I told him. He called Jim to pick me up from school and told him everything that I told the principal in confidence. Well, the police might do the same thing and call Jim and force me to go home. I decided not to go to the police.

When I got to Paula's house, her mom, Ruth, helped me right away. She said that I could live with them. I was hugely relieved. She even called my parents and made them pay for room and board! They had no choice because Ruth is really tough and used to run with the Hell's Angels. So now, I stay in Paula's step-sister's room because her room is only used one weekend a month for visitation. I can't believe it!

I start back to school tomorrow. I will be so much happier now. Although, Paula likes to skip school, so it will be really tempting to ditch school and hang out somewhere more fun. Ruth warned us not to skip school, or she wouldn't allow me to live under her roof if I didn't follow her rules. It was fair. I hope my resolve holds out.

Mom called Paula's house to talk to me and cried hysterically on the phone, begging me to come home. I told her I wouldn't because they are never home, make me clean and cook for them, and they act like they don't want me around.

I was able to get my stuff when my parents weren't home. I didn't want to be anywhere near them. Ruth had agreed with that and drove out to the trailer and I got most of my clothes and you, my little diary.

MAY 24, 1985

Ruth handed me the phone because there was serious news from Jim. Not the person I wanted to talk to. He said it was urgent. Was it mom? Gammy is terminally ill with cancer. I felt as if the earth would swallow me. Mom already flew out to Tallahassee where Gammy was in the hospital, not doing well at all. She moved to Tallahassee from Miami a couple of years ago. Like with grandpa, mom purchased an airline ticket for me the next day to see Gammy before she died. It was so painful. I quickly packed and waited for Jim to drive me to Sea-Tac airport. Not a word was spoken as I was dropped off in front of the Delta booth. Off I went, sadly, to my airplane.

I flew into Tallahassee where Uncle John and his friend, Kyle, greeted me. We went straight to a restaurant and met mom. The four of us ate, Kyle being exceedingly hungry with his order of two hamburgers. Mom told me to be prepared. Gammy doesn't want to live anymore, she has given up and won't speak to anyone. She wanted to die because she missed grandpa. We went to the hospital after our meal and Gammy had her back to the door. I purchased a small teddy bear in the hospital store to give to her, but Gammy told me to go away. I walked in, put the teddy bear next to her back, kissed her cheek, and left. I turned around to see if she took the bear. No movement. No recognition, no Gammy. She died just days after my arrival.

The night that Grammy died, we all went to a bar where they served me drinks. I am 16 but the drinking age is 19 in Florida, and since I was in the company of so many adults, no one seemed to care when I ordered alcoholic drinks. I didn't know what to order, so I asked Kyle, as an excuse to talk to such an unbelievably handsome man. Kyle started me out with a strawberry daiquiri, followed by a tequila sunrise, then a sex on the beach, and for the grand finale, a round of kamikazes for everyone. I usually drink beer, so the hard alcohol really did a number on my. After the kamikaze, I completely blacked out and don't remember coming home. I was too embarrassed to ask anyone what happened and no one seemed to care because they were depressed. It appears that I didn't throw up (at least on myself) and didn't piss my pants like I usually do when I pass out. A few days later, Uncle John implied that I did throw up, so I must have done that outside somewhere. I don't remember.

John's high school friends, Kyle and John, were always around at the trailer where John and Gammy lived. They were so friendly and kind. We all went down to mom's cousin's house on the water. They a really cool flat bottom boat with a covered seating area. Mom's cousin, Stacy, passed around a joint to Uncle John and his friends. I popped in the middle to get in on the action.

After visiting Stacy's house, it was decided to go out on the boat for the evening. I didn't have a swimsuit so Stacy lent me a spare bikini she no longer could wear. It was exhilarating, coasting through the waterways, spotting alligators and exotic birds, drinking beer and relaxing. The boat docked for a bathroom break and to buy more fuel for the boat. Kyle said we should jump in the water. I was terrified of the alligators, but Kyle said it would be alright for a few minutes. I took off my over-sized shirt, exposing my bikini, which Kyle couldn't take his eyes off. I went down the boat's ladder into the water. Everyone else went up to the store, leaving Kyle and me alone. We swam to the outside of the boat, away from the store, and Kyle kissed me! He said he probably shouldn't have done that, but I thought she should, so I kissed him back. Kyle felt my breasts and ass, his hands all over my body. We heard someone walking on the dock, so we swam back to the boat's ladder and climbed in. I grabbed my t-shirt and got dressed, feeling self-conscious in the exposed bikini. I don't think I'm fat, but mom always picks at my body, saying I could always be thinner and warning me against the horrors of becoming over weight.

I was only gone a week but it felt like an eternity. I miss Gammy and wished she would have talked to me before she died. She didn't even look at me, and I know she loved me deeply. She was already gone before her body gave up.

When she died, I was at the trailer with Uncle Althan while mom and Uncle John were at the hospital. Althan received the dreaded phone call that Gammy died. During the time he was on the phone, the fan in Gammy's bedroom turned on by itself. That was really strange. Althan and I both saw it and it sent shivers down my spine.

It was amazing to see how much alcohol Gammy had in that trailer. There were bottles stashed everywhere. I even managed to sneak out an entire bottle of rum and put it in my luggage. I haven't gone to alcohol rehab, yet. The bottle is still sealed. I'll wait and give it to Amber as a gift since she loves Rum.

JUNE 2, 1985

I made a terrible mistake at Ruth's house, I could kick myself. Paula and I skipped school a few times and Ruth found out about it and was forced to evict me. She warned me not to skip school and I did it only because Paula pleaded to do it. God, now I have to live at home again. What an idiot I am! I didn't even plan to skip school, but Paula kept saying we should steal some alcohol from the Bean Bar and Grill and go over to her skanky ex-boyfriend's trailer. She has sex with him a lot because he sells pot, but he is extremely unattractive and much older. I know he's already graduated high school.

I am the one who actually stole the rum bottle. Paula and I hid from the bus at the last minute, even though I tried to convince her to go to school, which is highly unusual for me. After the bus departed, it was early still morning, so we walked behind the buildings to get a layout of the Bean Bar & Grill. There are two doors: one for the restaurant located in the front, and one on the side, entering into a small room before going into the bar itself. We soon discovered during the morning hours, the Bean Bar and Grill had propped open their side door for alcohol delivery. Well, there was a window of opportunity when the alcohol truck pulled away and the bartender took the till to the restaurant to get some money. Paula didn't want to do it, but it was her idea. She told me to go. I crept into the bar and stole a bottle of rum. We snuck out the side door and were never caught! I don't even know if they realized a bottle was ever missing because I took one from the back, not the obvious one from the front.

We went over to the gross guy's house, Paula pounding on the door to wake him up. We needed a mixer for the rum. As soon as we went in the house, the guy pulled Paula into the bedroom, closed the door, and they had sex. I went into the living room, rum in hand, and noticed another guy waking up on the couch. I think these were the two guys we went to the reservoir with, when the M.P.s asked us to leave. I still don't know or care what their names are. It was uncomfortable waiting for Paula while this other guy tried hitting on me. I said I wasn't interested and asked if he had any Coke to mix with the Rum. I told him how I stole the bottle from the bar and he laughed, saying it was the most awesome story he's heard. They didn't have Coke, but there were a few cans of Sprite. I said we could give that a try, so we mixed some drinks, incredibly too strong, and drank in the living room, waiting for Paula and her pet to exit the bedroom.

Next, Paula decided we should head over to Mike's house since he was kicked out of school now. Mike is the preacher's son. His parents got divorced because his father, the preacher, was caught having an affair with the woman I use to baby-sit for. I saw him around her house sometimes but had no idea. I thought that she was just really religious. Now, Mike pretty much lives by himself because his mom works two jobs to pay bills. She is a waitress and she doesn't get much money. Mike is incredible at playing drums, which he demonstrated to Paula and me while we cheered him on. He was really good, I was amazed. We shared the rum with Mike who had some Coke and Mike rolled a couple of joints. It was much more fun staying at Mike's house since he isn't after anything, he is a quiet, genuinely nice person.

We tried to sober up a bit and get the pot smell off before heading to Paula's house after the school bus arrived. As soon as we walked up to her house, Ruth was standing outside. We knew we were in for the shit. Ruth got a phone call from the principal saying that Paula was out of school. I never saw Ruth so angry, she got in my face, telling me she trusted me and I let her down. I felt horrible beyond belief. Ruth told me to pack my things and go home. There was no changing her mind since we were caught skipping before. That was the final straw. I packed, put the rest of the rum in my backpack, and walked home. Ruth said she'd drive me, but I preferred to walk the 2 1/2 miles. She called my parents so they knew to expect me. I didn't have to walk all of the way home because Jim came and picked me up halfway. He didn't seem happy, sad, angry, nothing. Business as usual.

JUNE 5, 1985

Everything that has ever happened to me in the past is nothing compared with what just happened. I am a nervous wreck, sick to my stomach, and feel that black hole inside me swallowing me alive. I don't even know how to begin. I am caught in a living hell. Last weekend, Saturday night, there was a senior party at someone's house. Oh, God, how can I be so stupid!

I went to the party with Laura who needed a break from her baby. Mom drove us there since I don't have a car or license anymore. The person having the party set up a bunch of tents so no one would have to drive home. We were going to stay the night if we had to. Mom knew about the tents because we told her. She later forgot.

At the party, I started playing quarters with the boys and got talked into doing the beer bong which is a funnel at the end of a long tube, sending beer into my mouth at an alarming speed. I started getting so drunk but was having a good time like everyone else. As the sun was setting, Laura was ready to leave. She wanted me to go home with her but I refused to leave. I was having too much fun, enjoyed being the center of attention, and wouldn't budge. That was the biggest mistake of my life.

I stayed at the party alone, but knew everyone there. Later on, I don't know when, Sam Johnson and I went to his car and made out. One thing lead to another and we had sex. While we were having sex some guys banged really loudly on the car roof and on the doors. I was horrified that we were being watched. We stopped because he didn't like it either. I don't know who was out there. It was so dark and they ran off yelling into the night.

John and I went back and played some more quarters. I blacked out for a while and then I remember vomiting in the bushes. Not on myself, for a change. Someone, I don't know who, made the suggestion, said that I should lay down in a tent. Being strangely naive to predatory behavior, especially when I was more intoxicated than my DWI, I went to a tent and took off my shoes and laid down on one of the many sleeping bags. I still can't believe it. I feel so humiliated writing this down. I must.

I woke up and realized that Ed was having sex with me. There were two other guys from the football team, one holding each one of my arms and laughing at me. They jeered and pointed at me and laughed. I was so intoxicated, groggy, and confused, I tried to get away but couldn't move.

I felt so sick. All three of them took turns. I thought Ed was my friend. We had hung out before without sex. I can't go on. Hold on.

Okay, after that, I passed out again. I have no idea how many other guys took advantage of me. My next memory was of Sam trying to pull me out of his car and dragging me to my doorstep. The sun was just coming up. John parked down the dirt road so no one could hear his car loud car. He left me on the porch and drove away.

Mom opened the door and I came in. She and Jim were sitting awake waiting for me. She knew where I was the entire time since she drove me to the fucking party! She also said that I could spend the night in the tent if I had to. I guess Jim had changed his mind. As soon as I got in, Jim asked me where my shoes were. I didn't know they were gone. I had taken them off when I went into the tent originally to sleep. I couldn't get that information out. I could barely speak, from the alcohol, from humiliation, from anger. Mom just waved her hand and told me to go to bed, I wasn't any use to anyone in my state.

The next day, mom laughed about how drunk I was and said that they were worried (yeah, right!) and how hilarious it was that some boy drove me home and parked down the street. Yeah, funny. They don't even know what happened. Jim said that he was grounding me for 2 weeks. For what, leaving my shoes at the party? They gave permission for me to attend the senior party. I didn't care about the grounding at that point. I couldn't tell the truth because Jim would blame me. I gave permission to have sex with John, sure, but not the rest. Not that Jim would care. I got in trouble coming home late from a party, overly intoxicated and missing my footwear. It was so emotionally painful, I didn't argue at the injustice of it all.

Yesterday morning, on the bus, John threw my Adidas shoes at me. I couldn't look at anyone. He said that he wasn't able to wash all the cum off of them. His friend, Tony, who was staying the night and was riding our bus that day, laughed so hard and kept saying mean things to me all the way on the 45 minute bus ride to school. He kept making oinking sounds because of my nose and saying that my nose looked like a pig. He said that sluts have pig noses. The cruelest of comments spewed from Tony's mouth, someone who never rides our bus, taunting me, belittling me, when he doesn't even know me. John didn't laugh much at the jokes. Rick Sherman didn't laugh at all. I am glad that other people didn't. But I couldn't look at anyone. I kept looking outside or down at the ground and continuously crying as quietly and discreetly as possible so no one would hear me. Had I known about the day to come, I would have not gotten on the bus. The taunting by Tony was only the beginning of a day of horror.

When I arrived to school, entered the doors, and was walking to my locker, I was taunted by calls of "slut" and "whore" the entire walk. I couldn't look up from the floor. Amber wouldn't walk beside me because she said that I deserved it. That hurt so much. I told her that I didn't want to have sex with the guys from the football team, but she said that it was my fault. It made me feel so sick.

Through class, I got the same taunting, whenever the teacher wasn't looking. People threw spit balls at me. I would have sat at the back of the room if we didn't have assigned seating in each class.

Science was worse. Two of the three guys, Mike and Jim, the stupid football players who did that, sat right behind me. Literally. Mike kept whispering horrible things to me. Calling me a slut and said that I would have sex with the whole football team if I had the chance. The teacher didn't hear any of the verbal attacks or he would have stopped it. I just looked at the ground and withdrew inside. What else could I do. I felt so numb.

For lunch, I sat alone in the cafeteria barely eating. Debbie, this girl I shared my locker with in 7th grade and who use to wear a back brace but I never teased her, said really loudly that "Leigh had a gang bang, gang bang, gang bang." She kept chanting it and other started to chant it, too.

There are only a few more weeks left of school, but I can't do it. Laura was the only person who was civil to me. She told me that what happened is rape, nothing less. She is the only one who told me that sex with someone, even while they are intoxicated, is rape if permission wasn't given. They were holding my arms down, I remember that part. I've had sex with so many guys, I don't intend to, but get absurdly intoxicated and want someone to care about me, to love me, so I have the sex only to be ignored and treated like dirt afterwards. It is such a viscous cycle.

It hurts so much. Laura said that I should go to the alternative school she does, for people who drop out. I agreed and didn't go back to school again. I told mom that I was failing out of school and wouldn't pass the 11th grade, so I might as well stop going and begin the alternative next school year. It wasn't a complete lie, because of my skipping, I was failing out. I guess she believed me. She never said anything about it. They don't know what happened at that party.

That one day of living hell was enough. It made me want to drop dead. I still don't want to look anyone in the eye. Amber ignores me because she says it's my fault and I deserve it. Do I deserve this? Everyone just believed the story that I willingly did this grotesque gang bang. It isn't true. I didn't say anything to anyone all day at school. Nothing. I just pretended that I was a different person, someone who couldn't feel pain. But that didn't help. I still felt pain. But I still feel like I am in some twisted dream. Everything is slow motion and unimportant. I feel so low.

JULY 8, 1985

I'm at St. Joseph's Hospital in the drug and alcohol rehabilitation unit. It is great to be away from that living hell. I feel reborn. There are so many different people here, from prostitutes to rich guys who got in DWIs. There are about 16 teenagers and about 50 adults. The teenagers are in the same group as the adults. I appear to be the youngest of all people seeking treatment. I share a nice room with a girl about a year older than me, but she'll be leaving in a few days to I'll have my own room. It has a calm aura about it and so many people who seem to care about me and the state of my home life.

There are group and individual psychological sessions every day. In the group classes, filled mostly with adults, I hear stories about people addicted to heroin, cocaine, and alcohol. It's a treatment center for all types of drug addictions. There is a prostitute who loves Sting here who is nearing the end of her treatment. She seems to be in a good place, and I never would have known she was a prostitute. Like Laura, she is intelligent, kind, and got caught up in the drug scene.

I have to stay on the hospital floor, no elevators unless accompanied by a staff member. Some people try to escape. There are very few rules except you must attend the meetings. There is a relaxing reading room and another tv room. The food is really good, too, and they have soda dispensers in each kitchen with some snacks in the refrigerator whenever we want it, day or night.

JULY 12, 1985

I am finally allowed my radio and cassettes in my room, to be played at a very low level. I ended up getting another roommate, although I didn't want one. Another girl who is my age, 16. She is very withdrawn and is hard to talk to.

She wants to sleep all day and hates it here. I told her it is a relaxing and liberating place to be, she shouldn't hate it. She didn't seem to want to listen, just laid in bed, turned toward the wall. I did the best I could to help socialize. She doesn't want to talk to anyone.

During one of my individual sessions last week, the psychiatrist said that he wanted to sit down with my parents and me for a private session. I was going to be allowed to say anything I want about their drinking. I couldn't believe it! I could say anything at all and not get hit for it! That was an opportunity of a lifetime. Of course I want to do the family session.

At the beginning of the family session, I couldn't say what I felt inside so I just told my parents where that bottle of rum was in my bedroom, the one that I took from Gammy's trailer. Suddenly, I opened up like a bursting dam, getting all of my feelings off my plate and handing it to my parents. It didn't go well. I explained how it hurt me that they went to the tavern every day, got drunk and rarely spoke to me other than yelling fits. I said their behavior was embarrassing and that we never do anything together except go on their drinking camping trips with their friends. Mom kept crying and not saying anything, and when the doctor suggested that we continue family therapy in the future, there was a lot of pain which needed to be addressed. Especially since I'm still a minor who'd be going back to the same living environment after leaving the happiness of the hospital.

Jim went completely insane with anger and refused family therapy. Jim yelled and swore at the doctor and told him to mind his own goddam business. Jim used the twisted reasoning that I was the one who needed help, not him. The doctor looked at me because I was cringing (my usual reaction when I expected to get hit) and then told Jim and my mom that they obviously are in need of help, too. Jim said that he wasn't going to take this shit since it was me who had the problem. He got up, grabbed my sobbing mom and left before the session was over. I warned the doctor that would happen, but he needed to try anyway. The doctor said he was sorry that my parents wouldn't be more open minded about recovery and said that he would try a few more times. I thanked him for it but knew it was hopeless.

JULY 16, 1985

I met a nice guy named Barry in here. He just left and lives in Portland and said that he wanted to go on a date with me when I get out. He is 23 years old, 7 years older than me. This was his 6th or 7th DUI. They call them Drinking Under the Influence (DUI) now. That is a lot of drinking and driving. We aren't allowed to have relationships in the hospital, so I stuck to the rules. Barry may be my way of getting out of Bean. Maybe he'll be the one who loves and cares for me.

I am ashamed that I got two people kicked out recently. I didn't mean to, but these two teenagers kept having sex everywhere. In the elevator, in other people's rooms, in bathrooms, wherever and whenever. I drew the line when they were in my room. During the next group session, when the doctor asked if anyone had anything to say, I said that I did and told all about it. They both were in the room and the guy got so mad at me that people had to hold him back. He lunged at me like he was going to hit me. I said that I wouldn't have cared if they didn't do it everywhere. They both ended up getting kicked out. He was told to leave immediately because he tried to attack me and the girl was being a real bitch and telling people off so they asked her to leave, too. I didn't want them to be kicked out. If they would have been all right about it then they wouldn't have been kicked out. The doctors don't want people having relationships while they are there so they aren't distracted from rehabilitation.

There is still a huge part of me that doesn't want to quit drinking. If I am careful, I should be okay. They say that I can't ever go back to drinking or smoking pot, that all vices will lead back to addiction. I go with the program and say what they want to hear. Another patient, an adult, suggested staying away from Barry, he'd be no good for me, my sobriety, or sanity. He didn't think Barry could change after so many times in treatment. One more DUI and Barry will go to jail for five years. The only thing I don't want to do is return home.

JULY 21, 1985

I get a lot of visitors here, which was not expected after being alone for so many years. Grandma Johnson has come every weekend even though it is a 6 hour drive each way! They come in their camper. Of course mom and Jim come, but they don't do the private sessions with me. Also, Paula writes me almost every day. I get so many letters from her.

My wisdom teeth are starting to cause me pain. One of the nurses looked in my mouth and saw the tip of a wisdom tooth. She said that my mouth was too crowded and that I should get my wisdom teeth removed as soon as I leave the hospital. Mom is making an appointment for surgery since it is covered still under the Air Force dependent medical. I have insurance through age 18 or 23 if I am in college. Jim would never pay for college, that option has never been on the table and my parents have always tried to be rid of me, both physically and financially. The one time I mentioned college, mom started going on and on about how her father wouldn't pay for a woman to go to college, it was unnecessary. I tried to explain to mom just because her dad wouldn't pay for college doesn't mean she can't. Mom went quiet and college talk was dropped forever.

JULY 26, 1985

I only have a week left here at rehab. The more I see what my parents are really like, the less I ever want to be under their roof again. I must find somewhere else to live, and Paula's mom made it clear she doesn't want me staying with her anymore. I don't know what to do right now, but I'll figure it out. I have been living a life of bliss here, talking about my feelings, sharing my experiences with others who actually care and give suggestions. Listening to other people's stories, bonding on some spiritual level. I believe there might be a God, which we are supposed to seek, a higher power, to whom we give our pain, grief, and receive healing and guidance. I wish that were true.

During my phone calls home, mom does nothing but cry and act indecisive about everything. There are times she vows to drink less, pick up tennis, go ice skating together, then other times she forgets about those promises and says I'm trying to wreck her marriage. Sigh. Mom doesn't understand they are to blame in most of my problems. I need a role model, direction, help with school, support my piano practice. Mom acts guilty but won't say anything to me, no apology or anything. Once, I specifically asked for an apology, yet she turned it around, blaming me for all of my problems, saying that I was a terrible child. Jim will never apologize and claims he doesn't have a problem with alcohol. Jim has been drinking every day of my life, every single day I can remember, he has been drinking. Every car trip there's the cooler full of beer, since I was little, I opened his beer and handed it to him while he was driving. Every time we have gone camping, my parents bring cases of beer with them. Even on holidays he doesn't take a day off. I just wish they would admit they have major parental issues. That would make me feel so much better. Then we could move forward and be a family. We have nothing resembling a family. I don't know what to do. I feel a welling sense of panic and dread.

AUGUST 7, 1985

I am back living with my parents. Nothing has changed. My piano lessons have been cancelled in order to save money from the expensive rehab hospital I was in for a month. They still go to the bar every day straight after work, around 3:30 pm until 8:00 pm or 9:00 pm. Mom's been getting more intoxicated than usual. Jim seems the same. He has drunk so much in his life he doesn't know what sober feels like. Mom acts foolish and embarrassing, cries over the most minuscule shit, misunderstands what I try to tell her then gets angry with me. The next minute she'll be overly sentimental about the good old days, if there were any, and wants to hug me. I don't like the way she acts. The way mom clings to me, crying, I gently push her away. The she calls me an ungrateful daughter, I am the reason for all the trouble in their lives, and starts crying again. Every time she cries, Jim feels this overprotective need to rectify the situation. In his eyes, I am the cause of the pain, I made mom cry because of my actions. I really wish I hadn't told my parents about that bottle of rum in my closet. I didn't tell about the weed in the outlet. It is the perfect hiding place. I unscrewed the outlet cover from behind my bed, stuck my baggy in there, and replaced the cover. The pot is dry and not the greatest, but I'm so tempted to smoke some.

I entered into a talent contest at Heath High School with Paula and Amber. I know, I am not even a student there anymore, but Paula begged me to join her because was doing She-Bop by Cindy Lauper and wanted Amber and me to be her back up singers. I dressed up like Madonna, layered, ripped shirts, denim shorts with lacy tights, black boots, bracelets, dangly earrings, rings and a lot of gel in my hair. It was a lot of fun practicing and performing. We got 3rd place. It was strange going back to school again. Some boys playing Morris Day and The Time lip sink won first prize for singing Wild and Loose, the one that starts off with "What time is it?" from the movie *Purple Rain*. They were excellent, so all the students were jumping and cheering for them, even me. It was hilarious seeing those geeky white boys pretending to be really hip. Two people told me that I should have done Madonna since I looked so much like her. If I was in school, maybe.

I get my wisdom teeth pulled next week, on a Friday. Barry called me, wanting to meet up and decided to rent a cabin on a lake where we will stay while I recuperate. I will be drugged and sleeping, so it would be a waste of money. I tried to reason with him to cancel the cabin until I was well. He insisted on taking care of me. Better than being at home with the drunkards. My parents never met Barry. It makes me sad that they don't object to me staying over night with a grown man in his twenties. I want mom to say, "no, I'll take care of you while you recover." It's not happening. I might as well go see Barry. It gets me away from my depressing life.

AUGUST 19, 1985

I got my wisdom teeth removed, all four at once. I was completely put under so that part was enjoyable. I didn't know that taking the birth control pill was going to cause such a problem with healing. The doctor never asked if I was on the pill because of my age. I had lots of bleeding from my mouth wounds over the weekend with Barry, so much that I saturated all of the gauze I was given and had to use paper towels. I wanted to go home early to see a doctor, but Barry didn't want to waste the money on the cabin.

I was in bed the entire time and began running a fever. I felt achy and shivery all over. Still, Barry wouldn't take me home early. I couldn't eat and felt like vomiting for most of the time. I kept taking the pain pills the doctor gave me which helped me sleep. Even though I was in so much pain, Barry insisted on having sex with me. I relented just to get him to leave me alone. He is so pushy. Staying at the cabin with him was such a mistake.

I went back to the doctor yesterday and he said that I have dry socket in each hole. The clots won't stay in place because the pill is a blood thinner, which is something I didn't know. I could have died, under drastic circumstances. A clot could have gone to my heart.

My fever was due to food being trapped in the holes which got infected. That is why I was feeling so badly over the weekend. The nurse used a q-tip to gently scrape each hole, removing all blood and food product. It was a painful experience. Since I'm on the pill, I'll have to clean the holes myself at home. I opted to eat only tomato soup and rinsed with salt water. It hurt too much to clean the wounds. I don't know about Barry, he seems rather self-centered and unhelpful. I feel he is my only way out of Bean, as terrible as that sounds. I need to get out of the house one way or another or I'll never survive.

AUGUST 29, 1985

I started healing much faster this week since I've been keeping my wounds clean and dry. My wisdom teeth holes are finally starting to grow tissue over them. It is still pretty gross to eat though. Food gets caught in it and we had to buy a Water Pik to clean it out every day. I hate that part. It feels so strange and smells terrible.

I started a part-time job at Paolo's Pizza in Longview while I'm taking the G.E.D. courses in Winder, the same school Laura is attending for her G.E.D. It is so much more pleasant sitting on bean bags, working in small groups to learn. I absolutely love going to the G.E.D. school. Had I known about it before, I would have transferred sooner.

It is a long drive to Paolo's Pizza. I started on stocking the salad bar before I work my way up to the kitchen, then cashier. They are giving me a little more time to recuperate after my wisdom teeth experience, keeping my hours low for now. It is very kind of them. Since I have my driver's license back, my parents bought me a beat up old Volkswagen Super Beetle for work. The heater barely works so it will get cold in the winter. I'll have to bundle up. The car didn't cost very much, obviously, and, no, Jim will not get the heater fixed since the heat works a little.

No one wants me to baby-sit for them anymore because I was in alcohol rehab. I am sure that is why. I never drank or did any drugs when I was baby-sitting, not even smoking pot. I was tempted a few times, but didn't in case there was an emergency with a child and I had to use CPR or Heimlich maneuver.

Jim is making me pay for rent to stay at home now even though I am still only 16. He is charging me $100 a month since I am not in high school, even though I am at the alternative school working towards my G.E.D. On top of that, I have to pay for my own high school courses at that alternative high school. Jim doesn't see that as being the same as high school. He is so mean. I want to get out of this town so badly. I have been visiting Barry in Portland on the weekends. He still lives with his parents although he is 23 years old. It is better than here.

SEPTEMBER 3, 1985

Life has slipped back into the bleakness and I have that black hole inside me. Even so, alternative school is going so well. There aren't classes but our work is assigned at our own pace. There are a few teachers who offer group discussions, then we do our homework as the teacher helps, as needed.

There are a lot of delinquents here, and everyone is really nice because they want their high school degree. It is set up like a living room, with couches and comfy old arm chairs and a fireplace. It is in an old house with some additions to it. It makes me much happier, although Amber and Paula are still mad at me for not attending high school with them. I just couldn't ever go back to where everyone in the school knows about the rape and act as if I am at fault. Here, they don't know anything about me.

Last weekend, when I went to visit Barry, his dad took me up in his airplane. He has a two seater prop plane and goes out of town all of the time on weekends (with his girlfriend, I'm told). It was so much fun. Mr. Peterson did a loop, which I definitely did not like. He only did one because I said that I didn't like it. He flew in large arcs, but I didn't like that either. It felt like I was going to fall out of the plane, although it has an enclosed cabin. It made my head feel strange. It was a great experience, but I think that is the first and last time I go up in the plane.

Barry told me that his dad often goes on weekend excursions with Cliff Robertson. An old guy from TV and movies. He is in some telephone commercial now for a phone company, I believe. Although he lives in Los Angelos, he has a cabin somewhere in Oregon so Mr. Peterson will pick up Cliff Robertson in his plane and they go stay in the cabin. Barry doesn't even know where the cabin is because Mr. Peterson is so secretive. His wife doesn't even know where he is most of the time. Maybe I'll meet Cliff Robertson some time.

Barry is clingy, pushy, and doesn't treat me well over all. I don't love him like I did with Rob. I would much rather be with Rob, but we don't talk at all anymore. I can either live at home in a dark situation, or move towards Barry, who is less dark. I don't know what to do and don't have anyone to talk to about it. Paula thinks any boyfriend is cool and doesn't ask about what it is really like. I will continue on.

SEPTEMBER 13, 1985

Something really scary happened last night. I came home from Paolo's Pizza at around 9:00 pm. The front porch light was off and the house was completely dark when I pulled up. I sensed something wasn't right. I kept my car unlocked and left my purse in there and walked quietly up to the front door. When I got up on the front porch I could see that the door was open about two inches and that someone had kicked in the door. I was about to push open the door when I saw someone move inside. I was terrified so I ran as fast as I could to my car and drove to the Bean Tavern. I ran to the tavern door and yelled inside for my parents. My mom finally came out and I told her what had happened. They called the police.

By the time we all got to the house, the police were going through and dusting for finger prints and looking around. There was our butcher knife on the floor right by the front door! The police thinks that the burglar had the knife in his hand and was hiding behind the front door when I almost came inside. It is lucky that I didn't come in. He may have stabbed me with it. Or more of a hacking since it was a big butcher knife. That is very frightening.

The worst part of the whole thing was my bedroom. The rest of the house was ransacked, things stolen, but my room was utterly destroyed. Everything purposely broken. Every piece of furniture overturned and scratched with a knife. My underwear were stolen, too. Some of my clothes, but it was the destruction that was so horrible. They took Gammy's wedding ring, the one that was engraved from grandpa. They didn't take her engagement ring because I had worn it a few days ago and dropped it inside of a candle holder by my bed instead of putting it in the jewelry box. That is a lucky break. But it makes me sad about her wedding ring. I really wanted that when I get married.

The police think it was someone I know from school. Someone who may have a grudge against me. I couldn't think of anyone who would have a grudge against me, but who can tell. The police mentioned Sam and Rick because both have been caught burglarizing the area. I have had sex with both of them, so they both could have a motive. I said that it could be, but I didn't see anyone. I didn't even see a vehicle around. They could have parked in the back yard, though, because Jim put in a big gate which he leaves open all of the time. So, the burglars could have parked in the back yard and I wouldn't have seen them.

Things at home are just as bad as they used to be. My parents drink every day and come home and demand dinner and Jim will change the tv channel as soon as he comes home even if I am watching a movie. Mom still gets overly sentimental and weepy. It is discouraging. I have been talking to Paula, and her mom will let me live there again as long as I continue those high school classes, the alternative program. I will do it. I just don't know how to tell my parents. I think I should just pack and go over there and run away. Or else Jim might get violent.

SEPTEMBER 20, 1985

I finally moved out of the house again and am living with Paula's family again. I used the excuse that I can't be around them drinking every day when I am sober. I just can't take their drunkenness anymore.

Ruth lets me live there again since I don't drink or smoke pot anymore. Paula has stopped, too. I seemed to have inspired her. I have a Volkswagen Beetle, and old beat-up red one, that I use to drive to the alternative school.

I feel so much happier here. Paula's very quiet but very good-looking older brother, Ray Jr., who still lives at home, has set me up with a date with a friend of his in a couple of weeks. Ray's friend knows me from high school. He just graduated. I don't know who he is but we are going to a drive-in movie in Winder. I like drive-ins but not really for the first date. The boy's name is Scott. He was really insistent on going to the drive-in. I guess I'll give it a shot.

OCTOBER 21, 1985

The date with Scott a few weekends ago was a complete nightmare. My self esteem has plummeted again. The movie playing at the drive-in was some super bloody Chuck Norris film. It was so gruesome that it made me feel dizzy. Scott kept trying to put the moves on me right away. I didn't like that at all and pushed him away. He wouldn't even talk at first, it was straight to feeling me up. I asked to be driven home early. I didn't want to wait until the movie was over because I hated the movie. It was so violent.

Scott asked me to come by his apartment but said that he didn't have a key to get in and I would have to go in through the bathroom window to unlock the front door. At first I said I would. But as I started to think about it, the whole thing sounded suspicious. I then asked to be taken home. Scott got really upset and said that I wasn't anything like what he had heard. I was devastated when he said that. I imagine it was that horrible rumor that I willingly had a gang bang that interested him. All he wanted was sex. To make matters worse, the next day I was constantly teased by Paula, Ray and Ruth because they were told that I had sex with Scott. Scott called up Ray afterwards and made up this story about how we went back to his apartment and had hours of sex instead of going to the movie. It hurts that Paula and her mom don't believe me. Even Ray, who never used to talk to me, now only laughs and makes sexual references about Scott to me. I can't stand the teasing. It really hurts.

The other weekends I have been going down to Portland still to visit Barry. I stayed home last weekend because of the stupid date. Barry is getting more serious, although I like him all right. He has 6 DUI's now and is serving his jail time from the last one. I have been visiting him in jail because he really wants me to. Barry doesn't have to serve as much jail time because he went to the treatment center. He only has to be in jail for 30 days. He is really lucky. He could have been sent to prison for 10 years. I stay with his weird parents. His mother is so pushy about getting married. Jeez, I've never seen a mother want to marry off her son so quickly. It is kind of creepy, really. I don't know why I go down there. I guess to get out of Bean and to go to a real city, Portland. It gives me something to sort of look forward to. Barry is talking about living together after he gets out of jail. I don't know. I have that alternative school until next June. Plus, right now, I am still 16. I don't know what to do.

My mom keeps trying to bribe me to move back home. I don't want to at all. They drink just as much and Jim won't even admit that he is a bad parent. Neither will she. I know I have done bad things. I did them more out of boredom than anything else. I don't ever want to move back there. I would rather move in with Barry before moving back home. I know I'll have to go back for Thanksgiving, because my mom cries on the phone all of the time for me to come home. She gets drunk and then calls me and cries and talks about how she will start doing things with me again. I don't believe it, because after I went to the drug and alcohol rehab, nothing changed at all. So why would it change now? I just want to escape from my life.

Laura isn't even in my alternative school anymore because she worked extra hard and earned her diploma a year early so she can take care of her baby, Vanessa. Laura is 16, too, and has been working still with that weird man as a stripper and a call girl, although she says that there is no sex involved. I don't believe that for a minute. Especially when she has already told me that she has had sex with clients sometimes. I mean, why would men want to pay money for her just to go to dinner with them? I can't imagine that men would pay without getting something in return. Plus, I am afraid that it may have been a client who got Laura pregnant when she was 13. She looks older, so I am sure that he would drop dead if he knew she was only 13 at the time.

DECEMBER 13, 1985

I am still living with Paula, still working at Paolo's Pizza, and still going down to visit Barry on the weekends. However, last weekend, something did change. Barry has been out of jail for a couple of months now and got a full-time job at Security One warehouse where his brother and high school friends work. He asked me to marry him. I don't have a ring yet, but I accepted. I mean, what else is there to do? Barry's mother is handling all of the wedding plans. She is so overboard with it. May 17, 1986 is the date set. I'll be 17, but in Oregon, as long as I am emancipated from my parents, I can get married. I can either get their signature to get married or get emancipated. If I go to court and do that, then I can legally work like an adult. I can work full-time then. I plan on doing it. I don't know how to do it. I'll find out later.

Barry has been really pressuring me to move in with him before that date. It looks like I won't be finishing the alternative school, but he assured me that I can get a G.E.D. at the community college in Portland. I guess I'll do that. He wants me to move in by Christmas. Barry has already rented an apartment, the old one where his brother used to live. Leslie doesn't live there anymore because his ex-girlfriend, Clara, kicked him out and moved to another apartment in the same complex. Also, since Leslie was so physically abusive to her, Clara filed a restraining order to keep him away from her. Now Leslie wants us to live in the same apartment complex so he can come over and spy on Clara. I am sure that is what he is thinking. He isn't supposed to come to the apartment complex because of a restraining order. It is kind of sneaky, if you ask me.

I don't really want to get married to Barry. I don't love him. He just is a better alternative to living in Bean. I feel so bleak about my future. I am unsure what to do and have no one to ask.

CHAPTER 8

1986: AGE 17

JANUARY 3, 1986

I am living in Portland. I moved in with Barry's new apartment on December 20th, when I was still 16. It's a one bedroom and quite roomy, although the location is a bit odd, being located directly under the interstate and fairly close to some strip clubs. There are wild blackberries growing under the interstate, which I picked and made a homemade blackberry pie out of sheer boredom. I rinsed the berries very well since they are most likely covered with filth. It wasn't the prettiest pie in the world, but tasted very good. I followed my cookbook's pie crust recipe to the letter, which helped tremendously. My pie doesn't look like the picture in the cookbook. Not yet.

Barry borrowed his brother's pick-up truck which has a small bed, and I was only able to fit my double mattress set and a few boxes. My bedroom furniture and piano definitely won't be transportable with just Barry and I since those items are too heavy for the two of us. Barry is tall and skinny, with curly dark hair and blue eyes. That way, you can imagine what he looks like. His face isn't very attractive.

I had Christmas in our new apartment which was not what I intended. Barry's mom was really weird and insisted that she see how well I could cook Christmas dinner. She came by herself. Barry's dad openly keeps a mistress, which I don't completely blame him since Mrs. Peterson is robust and highly unattractive. It gets even stranger since Barry's mom was determined that I should cook a chicken. Who cooks chicken on Christmas? Plus, Barry's mom said that she would go grocery shopping for me and bring it by on Christmas Eve. Well, she did. She brought over a dead chicken! It still had it's feathers in it! Who plucks their own chicken in Portland? We don't even do that in Bean. I told her that I wasn't going to cook that chicken since I don't pluck feathers, not when the grocery store has chicken pre-plucked. His mom tried to force me to cook it but after she left, I threw it away in the dumpster and went out and bought a ham. I made a wonderful ham, yams, mashed potatoes and homemade rolls with homemade blackberry pie and ice cream for dessert. Barry was not happy, but I told him that I was the one cooking and there wasn't any way in hell that I am plucking and gutting a stupid chicken for Christmas. I still think his mom is just testing me or something. It is a strange test. I mean, where do you even get a live chicken? She probably wrung its neck herself. Maybe I'm shifting into a stranger family than I originally anticipated.

One weekend, when I was visiting and staying with Barry's parents (when Barry still lived at home), his mom asked me to do the dishes. I gladly did them. I washed them well, I know I did. Anyway, when Leslie went to drink his water at the dinner table, he made a huge ordeal about how there was milk mixed in with it. Barry's mother actually blamed it on me. She said, "well, Leigh washed the dishes. I just filled it with water after she had washed and dried." I told her right there that I had washed the dishes quite well and there was definitely no milk residue left over in the glass. I used the glass scrubber specifically. The family teased me about it all through dinner. I knew that his mother did it on purpose. The strange thing is, they all seemed to know it too but still made fun of me. That family is so twisted.

During dinner, the phone rang and everyone just stopped and stared at each other like it was an alien sound or something. It was odd. Then, when it rang about 8 times, Barry's dad finally picked up the phone. No one else would answer it. It was obviously his mistress calling, because he said that he had a personal call and asked if someone could hang up the phone once he got on the phone in the bedroom. Barry's mom covered the mouthpiece of the phone and listened. I heard his dad yell from the back room to hang up the phone. He had to yell it twice before the bitty pretended to hang up the phone, only to put her finger on the receiver and listened to the call. Confront your husband if he is obviously having an affair! Tell him not to have his mistress call him at home! Everyone obviously knows he is having an affair but they all act like he isn't. That is seriously twisted. Apparently, this affair has been going on for at least 10 years, too. Not that I blame him, Barry's mom is so fat, wears the frumpiest clothes, loves pink, lace, doilies, and has dozens of ceramic Hallmark Precious Moments figurines.

Another weekend, when I was visiting, Barry was insistent that we have sex upstairs in his brother's old room. We never had gone in there before. When we came downstairs, his mom said not to have sex up there anymore because they could hear it. I was so embarrassed! His parents talked about it like it was a tv that was too loud. I have a feeling that Barry did that on purpose. Don't ask me why, but I do. I feel that the family has these little jokes that they pull on me, twisted things to see my reaction.

On still another weekend, when Barry had to do some community service trash pickup on Saturday, Leslie said that he would hang out with me. He acted really hyper and then got out his 12 string guitar and asked me to drive him to pawn it for some beer. He said that he would share it with me. I told him not to pawn his guitar for some beer. That is stupid! Then Leslie told me about this game he plays. He pawns the guitar, buys his beer, then talks about how he had to pawn the guitar for the electric bill in front of his mom, then she will give him the money to get the guitar back. He said that he has done it 4 times already, although he sometimes says it is his phone bill or something different. I couldn't believe it! I really didn't want to be part of his ludicrous scheme, but Leslie finally talked me into driving him up to the pawn shop and then to the 7-11 for beer. He can't drive because he has no license since he also has 5

DUIs. Leslie has his own apartment even though he hangs out at his parents' house and works at the same place Barry does, Security One warehouse. Leslie mooches rides from his mom and other people. When Leslie bought the six pack after pawning his guitar, didn't get much money. I refused to drink any beer. I mean, I am still "dry" from rehab, so he really shouldn't have asked me. Plus, I didn't want to be part of his bizarre user scheme. Leslie was fine because it meant more beer for him. It is such a strange family.

For New Year's Eve, Barry invited his strange security guard friend, Ed, who talks about being a cop so he can kick some ass. Okay, that is definitely creepy. Ed's girlfriend, Nancy, was actually a normal, kind person. She seemed way out of Ed's league. Perhaps that is similar to me and Barry.

Ed and Nancy brought Cold Duck with them. That stuff is so gross. The more he drank, the more Ed twirled his nightstick, attached on his belt. Ed had hand cuffs, a knife, and a badge which made him look like a police officer. If he pulled me over, I would think he's a cop. Barry explained that Ed has tested to be a policeman three times and failed each time. I'm thinking it is a psych test he's failing because there's a lightbulb in the attic that isn't turned on.

The night consisted of Ed telling stories about his department store security guard antics. He caught some shoplifters and threw them to the ground with his karate moves and explained how he put the cuffs on them. He always talks about how he wants to get in a life or death struggle with a criminal so he can show who is "boss". Ed gives me the creeps. Ed is only about 5'6" tall and can't weigh more than 120 pounds. He is so small! But he has a very mean temper. Plus, he has his weapons on him at all time. It wasn't a very fun evening. I ended up drinking the Cold Duck, because, hey, why not. I got so drunk I blacked out and can't remember when Ed and Nancy left. I vomited in the toilet, or someone did, because some Cold Duck was splattered on the tile behind the toilet. I woke up asleep in my clothes on the living room floor. Barry didn't seem to care that I drank or passed out on the floor. So much for staying off alcohol.

JANUARY 20, 1986

Thank goodness I wouldn't let Barry's mom have her way. She wants me to marry Barry on February 14th for Valentine's Day. I am trying to put it off as long as possible by selecting a random date, May 17th, which was as close as I could get to Mt. St. Helen's May 18th anniversary. May 17th is a Saturday. Dear God in heaven, this week, Barry's mom is going to print the invitations, order the flowers, and is trying to get me to buy a dress. She is so pushy about this wedding business.

The other weekend, when Barry's sister, Joanne, had a dinner party at her house, she took me aside and said that I shouldn't marry Barry. I asked her why not but she wouldn't tell me any details. She just said that I shouldn't marry him. I must get out of this relationship. That was unusual. I wonder what he did before. I don't like the sound of it. I will heed her advice and pry myself away from Barry, one way or another.

FEBRUARY 3, 1986

I have been working at Paolo's pizza in Portland. I transferred from my old job to the Portland location when I moved down here. I am also getting my G.E.D. so I can find a full-time job. I need to escape from this relationship. I am trying to finalize everything as soon as possible. The G.E.D. program is only 6 weeks and then there will be an exam. I am already 4 weeks into it. It is going well. Barry actually didn't want me to get my G.E.D. I think he wants to keep me down. I won't let him. I'll show him.

Leslie's new girlfriend told me about how her job would hire me if I had my G.E.D. She is a nursing assistant at a nursing home right across the street from Paolo's Pizza, so she has been coming over for lunch and talking to me about it. I would make $9,500 a year starting out. That is much more than I make now with minimum wage, although it isn't much over minimum wage at the nursing home. Karen told me that I must finish a 6 week program to get my certified nursing assistant. They offer the course at Portland Community College, too. That is where I am getting my G.E.D. I must pass that test so I can immediately enroll in the C.N.A. program. The nursing home will pay my tuition since they have a shortage of nursing assistants. I am doing this all kind of secretly. I mean, Barry knows about it but doesn't know that I am doing this so I can live on my own. I have a tight schedule now. Barry's mom even forced me to get a wedding dress already. I did because I wanted to get her off of my back. My mom actually paid for it. I can return it later. I've left it in the plastic. I can't tell mom about my scheme because she believes if I promised marriage, I should go through with it. Mom doesn't see the big picture and the fact that I can earn enough money to pay rent in my current apartment. That is the plan: stay in the apartment and kick Barry out. He can go back home to live. Since he doesn't have a driver's license, I have to drive him everywhere. Luckily, one of his friends picks him up and takes him to work most days. He'll be okay.

FEBRUARY 12, 1986

Do you remember when I told you about Lee Sims getting shot by his step sons back in October of 1984 in Bean? Most of the bullets penetrated his pelvic region, with one taking off part of Lee's penis. Well, just last week, Lee's car went over a cliff! The police are very suspicious because he brakes were not working. They think that someone drained the brake fluid. It had been icy when Lee drove to eastern Washington to visit his family. It happened when he was crossing the mountains and went right over a cliff. Luckily, they have arrested both sons and Lee's ex-wife on suspicion of murder. I don't know if they have enough evidence, but I sure hope they get prison time. Crazy.

Things are just miserable here living with Barry. He is so jealous and made me sell my car in order to buy a Pontiac Firebird he wanted. My Volkswagen Beetle was having issues anyway. Barry just had his friend paint it bright yellow, too. He wanted to chop the top but I wouldn't let him. One time, when driving home to visit my parents, the CV joint broke and my car skidded into a ditch. There was no warning at all. I had to walk miles to a pay phone. When Jim arrived with his truck to tow the car to their house, he kept telling me how the accident was my fault. I asked him how it was my fault and Jim said it was because I dump the clutch. When the Bean mechanic fixed the car, I asked him if the CV joint broke because of me and he told me definitely not. The mechanic said that Super Beetles all have CV joint problems because there is something wrong with the axle. Jim walked off when I asked the question so he never heard the answer. What an asshole!

Anyway, I have been working full-time as a nursing assistant finally. They let me go through training while they hired me at the nursing home. The manager at Paolo's Pizza suggested I deliver pizzas in the evenings. He said I can do it whenever I need the money and don't have to be on regular hours since they can always use a reliable pizza delivery person.

Barry especially hates me being friends with Clara, his brother, Leslie's, ex-girlfriend. She lives in the same apartment complex that we do and has parties all of the time. Barry doesn't want me to start drinking again. It's like he does't count New Year's Eve and the Cold Duck drinking. Clara supplies me with weed, which is a huge relief. Clara knows Barry and is emotionally supporting me to dump his skinny ass. Clara thinks I'm clever for the planning I've been doing to carry off the break-up and afford to continue living in my apartment.

Once, when Barry tried to choke me while pinned against the wall, I just lost it. I blacked out from anger and beat the crap out of him. I don't remember doing it and it really scared him when it happened, as well it should. I haven't even been drinking when I black out. The anger black outs have happened 3 times so far while living with Barry in Portland. Barry either hits me or slams me against the wall and I go crazy. The next thing I remember is him holding my hands and looking scared. I don't feel bad about it, though, since he tries to hurt me over stupid things that are only in his twisted imagination of his jealous mind. He thinks I am seeing someone else, which I am not! I can't even keep any friends. I invited a girl over from work over one night. When Barry got home, he got so angry and yelled at me right in front of her that I should have called him first to get permission. Yeah, right. He calmed down but seemed to know this girl from somewhere. They both said they didn't know each other, but I could see it was not true. They definitely knew each other. I went to the bathroom to escape from Barry, and when I came back out, Andrea was gone. He said something mean to her because she avoided me after that and wouldn't return my calls. I don't know what he said, but it really scared her. Maybe he threatened to kill her. Afterwards, Barry said that he did know Andrea and that she was a real slut. I was thinking to myself that they probably slept together at some point and he didn't want me around her. Like I care!

I go over to Clara's apartment every opportunity I can. When Barry is at work, of course. I get home an hour and a half before he does. Clara suggested that I should have the landlord change the locks and then kick him out. I'll have to get my nerve up. I'm getting close. Only Clara knows about my schemes.

MARCH 14, 1986

I have been saving every penny I can to put a down payment on the apartment in which I currently live. The apartment is in Barry's name, and after talking to the very helpful land lady, she suggested I save up the $250 downpayment so she can evict Barry and put the apartment in my name. Due to his abusive nature, she said she has the right to evict him immediately once I have the money. Her husband is a police officer and will come over on the day of the eviction, to make sure there are no problems. Barry doesn't know it's coming. All of the furniture is mine, and the couch is a second hand one she gave me. Barry only needs to pack his clothes and a few other belongings. I still don't have my bedroom furniture and piano down here, so I don't have a lot, either.

I am going to start doing the final switch. I have enough money now, and with the apartment manager and Clara on my side, I will be able to succeed. Barry is just plain scary now. We have both started drinking for a couple of months now. He started first and then got me to drink. We have been getting into violent fights lately. Barry illegally drove home from his parent's house, prying the keys from my hands. His parents did nothing. I told him if he gets arrested again, it will be prison. That incident made me so mad that I took the keys out of the ignition while he was driving then jumped out of the moving car and ran into the darkness. I didn't know where I was running to, but just kept running. I was miles from the apartment. I tried to hide from Barry, but he caught up with me on foot. I didn't hear him and he jumped out of the bushes and scared me. He knows not to hit me or I'll hit him back, so he grabbed me really hard and pushed me around. He'll throw me into walls and then cry afterwards. I hate him now.

One night, when Barry invited his creepy police want-to-be friend, Ed, over again. Ed brought his Cold Duck with him but not his girlfriend. I was so depressed I just drank and drank. I blacked out and woke up on the bed with purple vomit all over the front of me. I also pissed my jeans. Barry was on the couch. It was okay because Barry said that he blacked out, too. I just wanted to escape life, so I drank. I have been smoking pot that Clara gives me once in a while. She deals cocaine but never lets me purchase any. Clara will give me an occasional line or two, but won't sell me any. Instead, she gave me a quarter ounce of pot for free. That is fine with me. She makes a lot of money from selling cocaine. She acts like a big sister and tries to protect me. I couldn't get through this without Clara. She knows exactly what I need to do to get rid of Barry. She is very devious, in a good way.

Clara recently went through an ordeal. I was at Barry's parent's house last week and heard on his dad's police scanner there was going to be a drug bust at Pacific Avenue, just off of Martin Luther King, Jr. Blvd! That is where I live, so I knew immediately the drug bust would be at Clara's apartment. There weren't many apartments at the complex and I didn't know anyone else who sold drugs there. Luckily, Barry was in the other room with his dad and neither of them heard it. It was like fate that I should overhear. When we got home, I made up an excuse to borrow some margarine for cooking something from Clara (after I threw ours away) and told Clara about what I heard on the police scanner. It was on a Thursday night and they said the bust would be over the weekend. Clara believed me right away. She said that she noticed a car parked on the street which wasn't there before (I guess she kept an eye on who parks around there). Clara decided to stay at her cousin's house that weekend. She packed up and left that night. Clara has been so helpful with my planned escape from Barry that I am glad that I could help her. I kept an eye out that weekend for a drug bust. All I saw were a couple of guys knocking at her door on Saturday night. Maybe they were undercover policemen who were going to pretend to buy some cocaine. They walked around to every window to try and see in but Clara closed all of the curtains. There were no lights on, her car was gone, and her apartment was deadly quiet. Since Clara had parties every weekend, the men knew she wasn't home. I am sure they weren't happy to find an empty nest.

Oh, I didn't tell you. After Joanne told me not to marry Barry, I have been snooping through his old love letters and things. There is one girl from high school who he seems to be obsessed over. The letter begs her to get back with him or he'll kill himself. There are a dozen letters along the same line to her that she obviously returned to him. They are flat out frightening. Barry says in the letter how he follows her and is jealous when she is with anyone else. He then describes how he wants to have sex with her, in great detail! The most recent letter is dated only days before I met Barry in the alcohol rehab center. That means he was probably following her while seeing me. That may be the secret that Joanne has been keeping. I bet this girl has called the police on him since she has sent his letters back and since Barry admits to following her everywhere in the letters. Following her is not friendly, it is stalking. I can imagine him doing it. Especially since his brother, Leslie, was so abusive to Clara and stalked her day and night, trying to break into her apartment a few times. Once, Leslie grabbed Clara and tried to rape her, but she kneed him in the balls and ran off. Craziness runs in that family. I stole one of the Barry letters to show Clara. She'll be interested. He shouldn't miss one letter.

MARCH 20, 1986

I finally did it! I switched the apartment lease over to my name starting March 16, the day I evicted Barry from the premises. I packed his belonging while he was at work and left them stacked outside the door so there was no reason for him to come inside. The landlady was the one who suggested I pre-pack for him and leave his belongings outside. Great idea, no fights, no confrontation. Of course, I told her that I am 18, which I am not. Legally, I am not emancipated so I can't rent an apartment. The rental manager required a copy of my birth certificate, so I altered a copy to say December 29, 1966 instead of 1968. The number eight looked kind of like a six so I went with that date. I feel kind of guilty doing that, but it is the only way, unless I want to move back with my parents, which I would rather live with Barry than live with my parents.

The landlord changed the locks on March 16, first thing in the morning after Barry left for work. I have since gotten my electric service. They required me to set up a new account, I couldn't just switch it over. Same with the phone. That is okay because Barry won't know my new phone number. I am staying unlisted. There was a lot I had to do to switch all utilities over to my name, but I didn't let that stop me from doing it.

Barry comes by every night after work, mostly driving himself over here in Leslie's unused car illegally since he has no driver's license for 5 years. I am stuck with that stupid noisy Firebird since Barry sold my VW to pay for it. I haven't let him in after the original kick out. That was tricky because of Barry's erratic behavior. I said I wanted to postpone the wedding indefinitely and to try and live on my own for a while. I told Barry that I would never see him again if he didn't cooperate. That was a lie. I did it so he wouldn't fight me as much and do God knows what else. Since he is drinking, he is highly unpredictable. I didn't want him to hold me at gunpoint or something terrible like that. Barry left with all his things, which I made sure there was nothing of his left behind so there would be no excuse for him to return.

Now, Barry gets drunk and bangs at the door and even tried kicking it in once. I have called the police twice already. Plus, the neighbors have called, too, because of the racket. I get so angry and scared when Barry does that, I can do nothing but scream at the top of my lungs until my voice gives out. I can't speak or anything. I don't mean to do that, but I just feel hysterical. At least the neighbors will hear and call the police. I don't know if Barry has a weapon or not. Nothing would surprise me when he is drunk. He could easily get a gun from Ed. Ed would even help him kill me, I'm sure.

I still have that stupid wedding dress, though. It is too late to return it and my mom doesn't want it. I told Barry to take it to his mom so she can sell it, but he won't. He wants me to keep it. I'm never going to get married to him in the future. Clara says that I should just take it to a boutique which buys used clothes to get rid of it. At least I'll get a few dollars out of it. I think I will.

Being a certified nursing assistant is an extremely difficult job. The nursing home is so understaffed, I barely have time to care for the patients. I about twenty patients to care for which I have to bathe and dress, help feed, assist to the bathroom, take their temperature, pulse and blood pressure. I don't have time to do anything but see them a few minutes out of the day. I hate leaving them in urine soaked linens, but there is nothing I can do. I am working as fast as I can but am given 20 patients to look after. I was told it gets worse. Eventually, once I am done with the training period, they give entire wings to just one CNA. Those poor old people! Not all of them are elderly, though, which is worse. Some are in their 40s and have MS or MD and there are a couple of teenagers who had car accidents and are brain dead. Some elderly have Alzheimer's and have to be restrained, which I hate because sometimes they are lucid. One time, I was taking away the food tray from a lady and washing her face with a washcloth when she suddenly hit me and called me horrible names. That is from the Alzheimer's Disease, it isn't her fault. I am supposed to restrain her wrists and ankles but I didn't have the heart to. It is so cruel to be restrained all day and night.

I will work there for more experience and then go to the agency. That is what most people do. The agency sends out CNAs to different nursing homes around Portland to fill in. They get paid $9 an hour to start! If I work swing shift, it goes up to $12 an hour, and graveyard, $15 an hour. That is almost double what I get paid now.

As for Clara, some good things have happened to her. She has been dating a sweet guy, Mike, from the office where she works. She told him everything about the "almost" drug bust and he told her that he always wanted her to stop doing cocaine. He actually asked her to move in with him which she did immediately. Mike has a house on the west side of town. He does smoke pot and drinks Budweiser, but doesn't do any other drugs. He likes to fish and go camping and is very kind. I will be visiting Clara soon, when she gets settled in. I haven't met Mike yet, but I am looking forward to it. I am very happy for her. I hope it works out. I certainly miss having her as a neighbor. It won't be the same without her.

APRIL 14, 1986

Todd, the owner's son from Barry's job, Security one, used to buy cocaine from Clara. He stopped by her place just before she moved. I think she sold him the rest of her stash. I went over to Clara's apartment and he recognized me. We talked for a while and he wanted to be sure Barry and I are broken up for good. I said we were. Todd asked me to go to the go-carts with him and I said yes. He is a bit chubby but has a handsome face. He likes to tell the story about how he was adopted. I'm not really sure why people seem to think that's a big deal, but whatever. I've never been in a go-cart before. I'm so excited!

APRIL 21, 1986

Todd took me to the go-carts and I had to get my "driver's license there. Todd already has one. They took my picture and made it look like a real driver's license. It was so much fun even though Todd kept trying to run me off the road. I told him to stop but he wouldn't. I drove as fast as I could to keep away from him. There are bales of hay around the track and I wore a helmet so I'm sure I'd be fine if I did crash, which I'm proud to say that I did not. We did cocaine and went to his house and played pool in the basement. His parents were out of town. He wouldn't let me see the rest of the house, only the basement. It's kind of strange. There is a huge tv and couch, so the basement is as big as an apartment. I had a fun evening.

MAY 12, 1986

Todd and I have been hanging out together recently, usually in his basement playing pool and watching movies on his VCR. He has a ton a movies to choose from and frequently rents them. Last night was just creepy. I don't want to see Todd any more after his bizarre behavior. I had $10 in my purse for groceries and gas for my car. Todd saw the $10 because it fell out of my purse when I was getting my lipstick. I thought it was no big deal. We got to Todd's basement and he put down four lines of cocaine. He did two then asked me to watch *Faces of Death* with him if I wanted to do the coke. He had the movie in the VCR and started playing it and animals were being tortured! I couldn't watch it and told him to turn it off, that I'd rather watch another movie. Todd kept playing the movie so I went into the other room and played pool by myself. I could hear the horrible animal death torture sounds since it was turned up so loudly. Todd paused the movie and came in to me to offer coke. I said yes and asked again to watch another movie. Todd then said I had to pay him $10 to do coke. I told him it was stupid but finally agreed and got my purse. When I opened it, my $10 was gone! I told him he stole it, to which he only smiled and said he didn't. Since he took my $10, I should have the lines of coke. He snorted them and went back to that evil movie. I told him I wanted to go home. Todd said he would take me after the movie was over. He actually laughed at parts when animals were brutalized. I can't write it down, it's too horrible.

As we were driving home, I told Todd I knew I had $10 in my purse and he had to taken it from me. I explained the money was for food and gas for my car, but he wasn't moved in the slightest. As soon as I arrived back home, I ran inside and locked the door. I told Clara about it and she called him. Of course, Todd lied to her about it. She was so angry, she told Todd to go somewhere else to buy coke. Clara is so good to me. She always looks out for me. I feel safe again.

JULY 5, 1986

I walked around Portland today during the Waterfront Blues Festival. I didn't have anyone to go with because Clara never wants to do anything outside of her house, so I went by myself. It was such a beautiful day today. People were water-skiing and doing jumps and pyramids. It didn't cost anything to go to the park and listen to music. It was nice but pretty lonely and kind of embarrassing by myself. I wish I had some close friends. I don't know how to make friends. I don't know how to do small talk and people treat me like I'm invisible and never invite me over to their place.

Something really strange did happen. I ran into Scott from the Scorpions concert. He and his same friend were down from Tacoma (that's where he lives now) and were just leaving when we saw each other. We talked for a little while but Scott's friend (I can't ever remember his name) was really drunk and tired and wanted to go home. They had a long drive ahead of them so I said goodbye. Since I am living on my own now, Scott wants to come down and visit me in a few weeks. That will be fun. I gave him my new phone number. I hope he calls so we can set up plans. He is such a sweet guy, I can't believe I saw him again so randomly. He has the biggest eyes I have ever seen. I am so excited. I'll keep you updated.

JULY 27, 1986

I am a living example of a complete loser. My picture can be found in the Encyclopedia Britannica under imbecile. I talked to Scott, and he agreed to drive down to my apartment last Saturday, then we'd decide what to do once he got here. Clara gave me the recipe for a killer homemade Kahlúa with a vodka base, coffee, brown sugar, and a few other items. I made a batch a week early so it could steep and get the full flavor. I was saving it for Scott. I was waiting around for Scott when he called me in the early afternoon and said that he was going to be a little late because he had to fill in at work for someone. I told him that was fine. I should have just waited, but no, I wanted to sample the Kahlúa. It tasted so good with milk, it was incredible. As time went on, I got nervous, so my drink strength and quantity gradually increased. Clara gave me a few lines of cocaine to do, so instead of saving it for Scott, I went all out and did two of the 4 or 5 lines. I was listening to loud music, dancing, and doing lines of cocaine once in a while in the back room, so I left the front door unlocked in case I didn't hear Scott knock. I thought the coke would keep me going, but the alcohol got the better of me. I ended up drinking over half of the Kahlúa, which is over half a 1.75 liter vodka! I haven't drunk that much vodka in a long time. I completely blacked out. I only know what happened from what Scott told me on the phone today. I am embarrassed to even write it down!

Scott said that when he got to my apartment he knocked and knocked but got no answer. He arrived around 8:00 pm. He could hear loud music so he finally tried the doorknob. It was still unlocked, so he came in. He said that I was passed out on my bed with vomit all over me and the bed and he couldn't wake me up no matter how hard he tried. Scott didn't want to stay there so he drove all the way back home. He told me that I shouldn't have left my door open because anything could happen to me. He ended up making me feel really guilty because he was worried about something bad happening to me. When I finally woke up today, I not only had vomit all in my hair and on the bed, but I had peed my pants several times so they were soaking wet past my knees. I hope Scott didn't see that, too.

I am so hung over today and depressed because Scott will probably never come visit me again. Why would he? What a loser I am. I am always embarrassing myself. I had to do so much laundry, too. Not only my clothes but my sheets and comforter. It all soaked down through the comforter and through the sheets. I had to tell Clara what happened because she called wanting to know how things went. I just told her that I was passed out, I didn't tell her about the vomit and jeans pissing. What an idiot I am. I hate myself when I do stupid things. I am going to try and eat something now. Bye.

OCTOBER 14, 1986

I did something I'm ashamed about. I pawned my guitar and case. I don't play it very much, but sometimes. I like the piano more but I don't have it here so I play the guitar. I almost couldn't pay rent so I pawned it. I am having a hard time keeping up with my bills. I barely pay them every month and I often pay them late, except for rent. I have paid rent late twice, but the landlady is so nice and tells me that she will get in trouble for not charging me late fees, that I try very hard to pay rent on time. I can't get kicked out. Where would I go? I don't think I'll ever be able to get my guitar back because I'll need all the money I have just to pay bills. My electricity is in danger of being cut off, it is over due. It could be shut off at any minute. It is so depressing. I need to go back to delivering pizzas at night to make extra money. Either that, or try and get on with a nursing agency so I can get paid more money. I'll do something positive for the new year. I am not very responsible with money. I should pay bills first, then spend money on drugs and alcohol.

DECEMBER 25, 1986

Merry Christmas! I refused to visit my parents, so I chose to stay in my apartment by myself for Christmas. I purchased a small tree, went to K-Mart and bought lights and three boxes of ornaments. I need to get a star next year. It doesn't look right without the star. I'm sitting on the couch, smoking some weed, and staring at the beautiful lights. Clara is spending her first Christmas with Mike, so I didn't want to intrude. I didn't tell her I was staying alone. I'm okay with that. I have been delivering pizzas a few nights a week for extra money. It isn't much and people don't tip for shit. The restaurant pays extra for gas, so I write down my mileage before work and after my last delivery. I'm so happy not to be home alone at my parent's house when they go to the tavern. If I'm going to be alone, I want it my way. I'm almost 18. I'll be an adult. I'll be able to vote. Sweet dreams.

CHAPTER 9

1987: AGE 18

FEBRUARY 21, 1987

Something positive in my unstable life. I started working for a nursing staffing agency last week. I get paid $3 more per hour, which is incredible. I couldn't take it anymore at the nursing home where I was at because there were too many patients and I had no time to take care of them. One of the ladies there was a classical pianist who had such severe arthritis, she went completely insane and was placed in a nursing home. She was only in her 40's and her friends said the classical music station must be played all day and night. The poor woman cried all of the time. Literally, all of the time. I was feeding her peas when she inhaled one and stopped breathing. I have CPR training for the job, so I didn't panic, went behind her, found the right location on her diaphragm, pushed my fist up and out the pea flew, all the way across the room. I was proud of myself until she started crying even louder than before. I apologized for saving her life. I didn't know what she wanted. I took her food and went to the next patient.

I'll also miss Walter, the old Jewish man at the hospital. He had been in a concentration camp because I saw the tattooed number on his arm. I didn't dare inquire about it because he was already very sensitive. Walter had both legs amputated just above the knee because of diabetes. He is so kind and sweet. He tells me how beautiful I am and asks how I am doing. He is so grandfatherly, at least a grandfather I would like to have. His family pays for a private room, so he gets better care than most. They visit him every month. I think Walter has flashbacks sometimes. He suddenly starts tossing and turning, yelling and crying. He seems to relive some atrocity that happened to him as a child. He tells invisible people to stay away from him and speaks in German during those times so I don't know what he is saying. I can tell he is afraid of someone because he puts his hands over his face as if he is shielding himself from a blow. He will cringe and cower in his chair or in his bed. It makes me cry to see him like that. The only thing the nurse can do is sedate him. The next day, Walter will be normal again and doesn't seem to remember what happened. I will miss him the most.

I can select which shift I choose to work at the new job. I am doing the 3:00 pm to midnight shift because it is perfect. I can sleep in and get paid $1 more per hour. I can also do the dreaded midnight shift, 12:00 am to 9:00 am for even more money, but it's too rough. I feel like a vampire, never seeing daylight. I am called to fill in at different nursing homes around the city, wherever there is a shortage, which is everywhere. Some of the homes are filthy and horrible. I have to keep my mind off the circumstances or I'd be an emotional wreck.

The staffing agency offered me a cushy job looking after a home bound lady who has cancer. It is the graveyard shift, though. All I have to do is stay awake and be nearby in case she needs anything in the middle of the night. Something to drink or medication for the pain. The only problem I have is that I don't want to be around a cancer patient after grandpa and Gammy. It would pay more, though, and all I would have to do is read all night. I may do it.

MARCH 5, 1987

I did take that cancer patient, and it was very difficult emotionally. She was a really nice lady but the situation reminded me of Gammy and grandpa so much. I already screwed up and lost that job. I am kind of relieved, actually. I did something that I have never done. I went out with one of Barry's high school friends who used to buy cocaine from Clara. I met Dale before and he knew that I lived in the corner apartment, so he came by my place and asked if I knew anyone who sold coke since Clara moved away. I said that I didn't and he asked me out on a date after asking me five times if Barry and I are really separated. I assured him we were. Everyone asks that question about Barry, so he must be a psycho.

Dale must have found some cocaine because when we went on our date a couple of nights ago, hours before going to my cancer patient graveyard job at midnight, he brought some coke with him. We did the coke and drove around being crazy, doing nothing in particular. We'd stop by the river and just yelled. Then we parked on a hill overlooking Portland and enjoyed the view. It was getting dangerously close for me to be at work. Dale jokingly said he would never return me to my car. I asked him to please take me home, but my heart wasn't in it. I finally called the agency from a pay phone to find a sub for me, saying I was really sick and couldn't make it. The next day, the husband of the cancer patient was so upset with me that he told the agency he never wanted to see me again. It hurt, to be honest. I really let the cancer patient down, so I feel horrible about the situation. I got a warning from the agency and went back to swing shift. It is easier than graveyard.

Dale and I ended up kind of having sex later that night, or morning, technically. I wasn't even attracted to him, but as the night wore on, and we did more coke, he became more attractive. Dale said he wanted to have sex but he had a medical condition which was extremely embarrassing for him. I assured him nothing would upset me, I certainly would not make fun of any abnormality. Dale was so self-conscious it was difficult getting the truth out of him. Dale was afraid that I'd make fun of him like other women because he has a small penis. I told him that I wouldn't make fun of him. I couldn't imagine that such a tall man could have a small penis. He really did. It was only 2 or 3 inches when it was hard. I felt so bad for him, but told him that it wasn't a problem.

I never was attracted to him, small penis or not, and didn't want to date him. I told him we shouldn't go out again. Dale misunderstood and thought I didn't want to see him because of his dick. For goodness sake, it had nothing to do with that. He was a neurotic odd duck, and I just wasn't attracted to him. Plus, he pressured me to miss work, and I was a bit upset about that. Dale keeps calling me and asking if I hate his penis. Fuck! I finally told him that he should be careful in case Barry is watching me or he'll get beat up. That scared Dale off completely. I haven't heard from him again.

MARCH 20, 1987

Yet another one of Barry's high school friends, David, whom I have only met once, came over to my apartment to warn me that Barry has been following me everywhere. When I go to Paolo's Pizza to work at night and come home, he has been following me. David, who is extremely hot, told me that his ex-girlfriend, Katie, had a roommate who just moved out and needs a new roommate for April. He has a truck and told me that he will help me move. That freaked me out so much that I am going to listen to him. David said that he has been friends with Barry since grade school, but is afraid that he will do something very bad to me.

I went and talked to the landlady again and told her what David said to me. She agreed that I should move out and that she will allow me to break my lease. However, the deposit will be kept by them. I said that wasn't a problem. She was so nice! The landlady said that she would even give me a good reference if I needed it. I can't believe she was so kind about all of this. I was worried that I wouldn't be able to break my lease.

I'll be moving in a week and half. David has already asked one of his other friends, another David, to take Barry fishing on the weekend that I'll be moving. Barry agreed to go fishing. He'll be safely out of the way while I move. David said that he will never tell Barry where I am living. I completely believe him since he came to me out of the blue to warn me about Barry. I am so amazed that some people can be so nice.

I'll be closer to Clara's house, although I haven't been there yet. I was planning to go over there soon, but after hearing about how Barry is following me, I was afraid Leslie would find out where she lives. I will visit her after I move in with Katie to be safe. The stalker brothers. What a mess.

It will also get me away from Pete from work, since he knows where I live. This is yet another ordeal. Pete is another CNA at a nursing home where I have become a regular. Pete and I use to smoke a joint every day after work for a couple of weeks. His house was only a few blocks from the nursing home. He seemed nice so I thought it would be good to make a new friend. Boy, was I wrong! He has a house by himself, I guess he inherited it when his mother died. At any rate, one day, after work, Pete got really quiet and said that he wanted to tell me a secret. I said, sure, why not? The secret was horrible! He said that he has been having sex with comatose patients for years! He told me that they really like it, it gives them pleasure even when they are in a coma or semi-coma. I didn't know what to say to that. I was shocked. Pete could see that I didn't approve of what he was doing and suddenly turned threatening. Pete screamed in my face that it was for their own good and began throwing things angrily around the room. Then, he pretended to hit me but stopped inches from my face and put his face really close to mine and told me that if I ever told anyone what he just told me he would kill me. Pete said that he knew it would be me who turned him in since he never told anyone else. He also reminded me that he knew where I lived. How can these things keep happening? I am such a bad judge of character. I thought that he was nice. We were just friends, but I had no idea that he was a complete psycho!

MARCH 28, 1987

A sultry sex scandal has rocked Christianity. The tv evangelist, Jim Bakker, drugged and raped Jessica Hahn, who was church secretary. It doesn't sound like any of the sex was consensual. Jim Bakker, the creep that he is, went on tv with his wife, crying his eyes out, saying how sorry he was about his actions. That man makes millions of dollars and will continue to make a fortune, even after his real character comes out in the press. Playboy offered Jessica Hahn a lot of money to be their centerfold and she apparently said she would tell her story, and pose in the nude. I really have no opinion one way or the other about Jessica posing nude for Playboy. She was raped by Jim, so I don't blame her for making money out of the ordeal. Posing nude isn't a crime. We're born naked, so I'm not sure why nudity is looked on with shame.

APRIL 4, 1987

I am living with Katie O'Reilly now! David and his friends helped move in everything. We don't have a lot in common, but she is nice. She is 5 years older than me. The apartment complex is so huge. There are two swimming pools here and a weight room. We live in a two-story townhouse with the bedrooms upstairs. It is closer to downtown, right over on the edge of a really nice neighborhood, with the biggest houses that I have ever seen. It is so beautiful to go walking around there, especially by Woodstock College. Everyone calls it the "hippy" school because it is a private college of arts and music and the students still dress like hippies. I wish I could go to school there for music. That would be a dream. It is too expensive for me, though. My bills won't be so bad with a roommate. I'd rather live alone, but this will work out well.

I got a transfer to another hospital to get away from that freak, Pete. He would often threaten me while I was at work and would pretend to hit me whenever no one was around. Really scary guy. I did tell a nurse to watch Pete. I didn't tell her why, nor did I inform her about his threats, but I said to just watch him. I did what I could.

Already, I met another psycho! Well, at this new nursing home, I met a really good looking guy, Tyler, who is a janitor at the nursing home. I won't hold it against anyone for being a janitor, so I said I would go out with him. I drove to his house and was totally shocked to see that he lived in a 3 bedroom house with a big front and back yard. Although he drove an old beat-up Honda, he had a black Corvette in his carport. Just like Pete, he inherited his house. That was kind of creepy. I knew he couldn't afford a house and car like that on a janitor's salary. I should have suspected something then.

Anyway, when we went to the movie, we took the Honda. I asked if I could have a ride in the Corvette but he said that he wouldn't let any woman in his car. He wouldn't even let me go up and look at it. Tyler got really defensive and refused to drive the Corvette to the movie theater.

I put that incident out of my mind because the dinner and movie were wonderful. Tyler was a complete gentleman and was interesting and funny. I went over to his house a few more times later in the week to watch movies. Tyler had a huge Rottweiler the first time I met him. He kept the dog in the back yard because it was enormous. Tyler said that he kept his dog mean to be a guard dog. The third time I went over to his house, Tyler's dog wasn't there. I asked him about his dog. Previously, Tyler would talk about his dog like it was his best friend. I wasn't allowed to pet the dog either, just like I couldn't touch his Corvette, which was strange. Then Tyler said casually, "oh, the neighbor shot him." I was shocked and asked him if he called the police. He said that he hadn't because he couldn't prove it. Then Tyler kept trying to change the subject. My instinct told me that he was lying. If he loved that dog so much, wouldn't he do anything to get the murderer in trouble? Unless he killed his own dog. I watched the movie we started, biding my time until it was over and I could casually go home. I started getting scared. During the movie, Tyler kept trying to kiss me. I didn't feel like it but he forced himself on me. Tyler grabbed me and threw me on the bed. He pinned me down with his knees while he undressed me. I didn't want to have sex but decided to just let him do it. He is a big man. Anyway, he held my hands together above my head and had extremely rough sex. I mean, rough. It hurt, he thrust so hard. His hipbones bruised by thighs pretty badly. I couldn't move at all. Afterwards, I acted like nothing was wrong, got dressed as quickly as I could without raising suspicion, and got out of there.

I have a really bad feeling about him. I am certain that he killed his dog. Plus, with Tyler's anger over his Corvette, not letting me even touch it, was strange. Tyler really got angry whenever I asked for a ride in it. On top of that, the rough sex that I didn't want to have frightened me. I had a feeling that he has hurt someone before. I wouldn't be a bit surprised if he had murdered someone. He seemed like a serial killer. He was so nice, too. Luckily, I am no longer working at his nursing home. I worked there only 2 days. Katie has been telling him that I am not home whenever he calls. I never want to see him again. He scares me.

I didn't mention, but one of the guys who helped me move, Jeffrey, yet another high school friend of Barry's, asked me out. He has a red Corvette but still lives at home. He has such blue eyes and is so handsome. But like Tyler, he won't let me ride in his Corvette. He will drive his Honda instead. Katie doesn't like him at all, especially since we never actually go on dates but stay in his bedroom. Jeffrey is super paranoid about Barry finding out so I have to park around the corner since his parents' home is literally across the street from Barry's. Jeffrey is so good looking, though.

APRIL 28, 1987

Last Saturday, I severely hurt myself while transferring a patient at work.

I went like this: I was working at a nursing home where all their employees quit at one time so they needed temps quickly. There were only 4 of us for the entire floor, meaning each of us got a whole wing. I hate that job. It is extremely cruel to treat people worse than a stray dog, leave them in their feces, urine, hungry, sore, lonely. Being a certified nursing assistant has to be one of the lowest jobs on the planet. I get run so thin that I only have time to see each patient only once daily. That means I can't change their sheets, clean them, turn them, feed them, take them to the bathroom. It is so stressful and painful to view the suffering every single day. I don't want people to be in places like that. The people in the shit hole homes don't get visitors, their families leave them and forget them. Usually visitors come once or twice a year on some minor holiday. Never Christmas, always Veteran's Day or something. Only in the hospitals where most of the patients are Black are there any visitors. Blacks support their family, visit their elderly weekly. Whites visit twice a year. It's despicable.

Back to my story about working an entire wing. Luckily, there were some patients on my wing who could do some things for themselves. This very large woman wanted to be transferred to her wheelchair. I told her that I needed help transferring her. I went looking for someone but there wasn't anyone around. I specifically asked the woman if she could stand at all. Not walk, but just take some of the weight. She told me she could stand just fine. Ha! I did the correct transfer when this woman starts flailing her arms and tipping over in the opposite direction. I couldn't just let an old woman hit the ground, she could break a hip, so I grabbed onto her arm to ease her down. When I did, I felt something kind of burn in my shoulder. My arm went weak and I told the nurse exactly what happened. They didn't blame me and said that I should go home and rest. I didn't think it was that bad and said that I could still work, but they still sent me home.

Now today, that shoulder muscle got so weak that I can't lift a pen. I went to Katie's boss, a chiropractor. He works with injuries, so Katie suggested I see him immediately. It turns out that I tore my trapezius muscle almost all of the way through as well as some other ligaments in my shoulder. Dr. Cohen used little electrodes which made the muscle twitch a little bit. Also, some heat treatments with a magnetic devise. I don't know what it is, but they put on Mineral Ice, it is warm, and vibrates the muscle. The doctor suggested that I continue the treatment in order to increase blood circulation to the injured tissue and encourage regrowth and regeneration of the damaged muscle without leaving too much scar tissue.

My right trapezius is emitting so much heat and feels like it really needs to be rubbed, but when Katie touched it, the pain was so excruciating that she could only put soft, circular touches on it, not even a massage. I can't use my right arm at all, it is too weak to do much. Plus, it makes me tired all of the time. I have to keep taking lots of ibuprofen every day for the swelling. It keeps most of the pain away, but it hurts to lay down and sometimes it has muscle spasms that are terribly painful. I am getting tired now, so I am going to bed. Good night.

MAY 12, 1987

I have been secretly seeing Jeffrey, strangely, at his house which is across the street from Barry's parents. Jeffrey is so gorgeous, I melt looking at him, but Katie can't stand him, she said he is a strange duck. That is probably true. I am hoping to lure him out into the real world, but I haven't yet.

I have gone over to Jeffery's house 6 times now. But we never go out, we just sneak into his bedroom and have sex. Katie keeps telling me that I should get rid of him, that she never liked Jeffery. She might be right since he will never take me to dinner or a movie. I just want someone to be into me, to care and love me. I want to have a boyfriend. I don't know how to get one.

Katie has been helping me with my resume and trying to encourage me to get an office job instead of going back to nursing homes. The nursing agency wasn't happy that I was forced to go on Workman's Compensation. It wasn't by choice, but necessity. It's the law: I got injured at work so I had to go on Workman's Comp. There is one nurse at the agency who is like satan's sister and got angry about me signing the paperwork so I got paid retroactively from the Monday after my injury. Of course, if I get a job with another company, the Workman's Comp will be canceled, but I don't mind. Dr. Cohen said that the Workman's Comp will still pay for my medical treatments but will drop the income payments if I find other employment. Why do I feel guilty for being on Workman's Comp? Is it society browbeating me? I have been working hard and the accident wasn't my fault. I feel guilty about everything, so what's new.

Katie got David to borrow his dad's van and we went to Bean and got my piano. I have been talking about it for a while, I guess, and Katie had David invited two friends to come with us. We stayed at my parents house. Of course, they all said how nice my parents are. Everyone says that. My parents act sweet to visitors but not to me. Katie knows how they really are. It was so nice of Katie and David to get my piano. She actually likes to hear me play the piano and requests me to play. I have never had anyone do that before. It is so pleasant. The piano fits perfectly against the wall in the living room. It is a small wall under the stairs where nothing else fit. It is funny that the piano fits so perfectly.

Katie has been teaching me some basic 10-key skills and bookkeeping, bringing home some of her work to show me. I have just started calling ads in the newspaper about jobs. I feel bad lying about not having office experience, but Katie said that it is easy to do, the filing and stuff, and that I'll learn quickly. Also, she said that I need experience to get hired but if no one hires me, I can't get experience, so I may as well lie about it. I added on my resume a job at a veterinary's office as an assistant, saying that I did filing, answered phones, and did some basic bookkeeping. I hope I find something. I am not going to tell them about my injury. I can work well enough without telling them. They may think poorly about me if I tell them I'm on Workman's Comp.

It's nice having someone be a friend like Katie. I can't seem to get close to her, though. I don't know how to open up to people. We don't do things together like friends, which is sad. I have been seeing Clara, so that's something. She's a friend I can connect with. The only one, it seems. Maybe she is broken inside, too. I think we have a lot in common with our background, home life.

MAY 18, 1987

I actually got a bookkeeping job already. It is for the Typewriter and Computer Repair Company. I told them that I only did minor bookkeeping but they said they will train me. I won't get paid as much as the agency, but it will be a stable day job. I am scared, but excited. I started today. I have so much to learn at work. I must really pay attention. I took notes on everything. They probably think I have no memory or something.

I have been seeing Jim, yet another high school friend of Barry's. He's been like the tenth person who went to school with Barry. I'm in a large city, but the neighborhoods are close by and people seem to know each other. Jim works at the ice skating rink where I've been going for months. He is so sweet, but does the same thing as Jeffery; only wants to stay at his house and have sex. We play pool in his basement, but never go out. I like him so much, though. He is so gentle and kind. I wish we would go on real dates.

MAY 30, 1987

Katie had a Mike Tyson party tonight and invited her many male friends. I am not really a boxing fan. Mike Tyson is unbeatable, and some people placed bets at our apartment on the outcome. Katie ordered pizza, bought beer and wine coolers, so it was a fun event. We all watched as Mike Tyson beat Pinklon Thomas by TKO in the sixth round. The fight was billed as the "Hard Road to Glory". I don't understand how each fight seems to be for some sort of championship. There are more fights scheduled in the year. Katie was enthusiastic about the fight. I can't tell whether she likes it or is flirting with her male friends. Maybe a little of both. I enjoyed it since we had a party at our house. Mike Tyson is the most popular fighter since Mohammad Ali.

JUNE 10, 1987

Political scandals abound. Gary Hart, who was running for president, got caught in a sexy photo with Donna Rice, a girl he was having an affair with for while. They were seated on a boat, named Monkey Business, with Donna in Gary's lap. It's all over the news and tabloids. It's such a bad scandal that Gary Hart will probably have to drop out of the presidential race. Apparently, Playboy offered Donna a lot of money to pose as their centerfold. She said she'd do an interview but no nude photos. Playboy will probably not be interested without pictures. There have been a lot of sex scandals this year.

JUNE 21, 1987

Katie's boyfriend, Larry, has called a couple of times trying to get a hold of Katie. It is Father's Day, so she is celebrating it with David's dad since he has brain cancer. She has known him for a long time since Katie and David dated for years. I am here alone because I don't want to celebrate Father's Day. My stepfather, Jim, doesn't deserve the title of father.

Katie's dad lives in San Francisco so she can't be with him. Larry is a Jehovah's Witness so he doesn't celebrate Fathers Day. It's odd Katie being with a Jehovah's Witness when she is Catholic. When two strict religions come together, look out. I don't believe Katie loves Larry, but he's handsome, a bit younger and naive. Katie has him wrapped around her skinny little finger. Katie is the thinnest person I've ever known. She barely eats because her sister is incredibly obese so Katie doesn't want to end up like her sister.

Mom called and forced Jim on the phone. He thanked me for the card, which mom bought for him, but when I started telling him about my car problems, he cut me off, saying that his back hurt. I know it did, but it was rude. He always blames me for any car troubles. I have had so many really cheap and bad cars, I can't afford a good one. The problems aren't my fault. I sold that Firebird and got a 1974 Mustang. You know, the ugly kind that looks like a Pinto. It is such a junker! It was all I could afford. It is baby blue.

David said something kind of offensive. He told Katie to put on jeans because she is the only girl he knows that looks good in tight jeans. So she did, of course. What am I, chopped liver?! I think I am. I have to lose weight. I weigh 140. Way too much! I think, because of my shoulder injury and lack of exercise, I gained 20 pounds in a few weeks. That is not a healthy thing to do. A couple of months ago, I weighed 120. How shitty. You will help me, little diary. I will write all the food I eat in you. I have to lose weight so people like me.

I've been having vivid, bloody, violent nightmares which I'll start writing down in you, diary. I had one last night that went like this. I was in Nevada, in the desert with Clara, Mike, Lori and Dean. The were on their honeymoon, all four of them. They had a double wedding. (Lori and Dean are friends of Clara and Mike. Lori was a friend of Clara's who met Mike's friend, Dean, and they moved in together.)

I heard something in the bushes. I went over to investigate and saw to my horror that a boy with his arms hacked halfway off was lying there, moaning and thrashing in the bushes. His eyes had been burned out with cigarettes, it was horrible. The boy wore a shabby blue sweatshirt and blue jeans. A pair of mangled eyeglasses covered the burned and gaping holes that used to be his eyes. The glasses were twisted like they were stepped on and placed carefully back over his eyes.

The boy was still alive! I was horrified and wanted to help him in some way. I realized the person who did this atrocious act was probably lurking nearby. The boy thrashed and twitched, not knowing I was standing near him since he had been blinded. I wanted to kill him to relieve him of his suffering. I didn't have the courage. I ran from the hideous scene, leaving the poor boy to his fate.

I am tired now. I will go to sleep and hope to have sweet dreams. Until tomorrow, se la vie.

JUNE 22, 1987

I am going to sleep soon. Today at work I learned so much my head is spinning. They are two months behind in bookkeeping because Kim's computer has ironically been down. Since the company repairs computers, it seems like it should have been taken care of by now.

I just started with April's bookkeeping. There is so much work to do, but the lady who is training me, Teresa, is so nice. She wears really thick glasses and is kind of geeky, but is so sweet and patient. I am glad I have someone so nice training me. I think it will work out all right. Teresa gave me an ironing board and some kitchen supplies since she just moved in with her boyfriend. He is also a geek and has an Edsel. That is an old type of car which has been made fun of due to it being a piece of junk. He fixed up the Edsel so it runs well and likes to show it off. He is very nice, too. They seem so perfect for each other.

I watched *Reckless* with Daryl Hanna. She is gorgeous. It was a sweet love/hate story. They fell in love. I wish I would. I am so lonely. I long to meet someone who will love me. I know I will someday, but that is so far away. I felt like this 5 months ago, then I lost weight and picked up four or five guys at once. I was fighting them off. Jim, the ice skater, said how hot I am now and how much better I look now that I lost weight. He went on about it so much that it made me mad. I told him I was the same person as before. I haven't seen him much lately. It is for the best.

Speaking of losing excessive baggage, I did very well today. You should be proud of me!

BREAKFAST

- 1 bowl of cereal (220 calories)
- 1 cup skim milk (120 calories)
- with banana (120 calories)

LUNCH

- Steamed veggies (80 calories)
- 1 muffin (120 calories)

DINNER

- 5 crackers (100 calories)
- with peanut butter (110 calories)
- 1 muffin (120 calories)

Well, I guess I ate a little too much. 990 calories, approximately. I worked out a lot to make up for the food. I rode the bicycle at the gym for 20 minutes, then did arm, leg and stomach exercises. Dr. Cohen says it is alright to exercise again.

I took speed this morning. What a druggie. No, just kidding. It helps me to lose weight. I will. I am going to wait until Friday to weigh myself. Speed used to make me feel sick to my stomach but doesn't anymore.

Life's path is never a straight route. There are many twists and turns which try to deceive you. I seem to take the wrong turn so often, only to retrace my steps to find the right path. It can be a weary game. I must rest now.

JUNE 24, 1987

Good evening, young friends. Yes, it is nighttime again. 10:38 pm to be exact. It is a hot, balmy night, with a gentle breeze which caresses my half naked body. An old Led Zeppelin song is softly singing to me on the radio. It was in the 90's today and tomorrow they anticipate a "heat wave" to hit through the week. Isn't that great?!

I went swimming today at one of the apartment complex's pools. I really should make use of them since they are open for most of the year. I'm not brave enough to go alone, I suppose. Today, I met Lori and Dean at the pool closer to their apartment. This complex is enormous, like a city unto itself. I like the other pool better because there is more room to swim and less people. After cooling off in the pool, I went back to their place and had one beer. I was careful not to drink too much and made a point of only having one beer, although I was offered more. I don't want to lose control and black out, especially when I'm making friends. Afterwards, I went to a tanning salon to get a bit more color, to make it appear I spent the entire day in the pool.

I am almost caught up at work with the backdated bookkeeping which is being done in physical books instead of the computer which it was previously. It seems the information was lost, although we had a book version which was done hastily and sloppily, so I'm merging several books into one large bookkeeping binder. When I started May 18th they were still "in" April, well the paperwork was. While I was being trained we got more behind. But now I am almost caught up because I'm picking up speed, learning how to keep books and can do ten key by touch after all my practice. I use a large calculator which prints out the math tallies. I tear off the paper and staple it to the back of the corresponding bookkeeping page as an extra way to keep the books balanced. It's a way for my superiors to look over my calculations to make sure I'm doing it correctly.

I have to reposition my body, just a second. Oh, there, I'm comfortable now. I ache all over from doing so many aerobics classes and weight training. It's great, though! I did laps in the pool today, too. Tomorrow I am going to the park to see Crazy Eights at Blue Lake. Me, Katie and some of her friends are going to bring vodka and orange juice. I'm looking forward to our picnic in the park while listening to live music. Katie has a large blanket and cooler ready for tomorrow's events.

I am so lonely. I wish I would find someone who is a sweetheart and good looking. Like Matt at work. I think I really like him. I have felt like this before, though. We'll see how it goes. I'm doing the sly approach. Should I ask him out? He only works summers at the company I work for because he attends college full time at the University of Oregon and is related to the owner, my boss. Matt is 21 years old and has an identical twin brother, Mike. Matt is more of a yuppy while Mike rides a motorcycle and wears a black leather jacket. It's a difficult choice, but I kind of like the preppy look so I'm leaning more towards Matt.

My 1974 Mustang has already broken down with transmission problems, so I bought another VW Beetle for $250. It is so old but I hope it runs for a while. I'm wandering off the path again, just like in life. I should get some sleep, working two jobs is taking its toll, especially since my shoulder injury is still in rather poor condition. Time to rest my tired muscles. Good night!

JUNE 25, 1987

A day that started with such beauty and promise has ended in tragedy and pain. Katie and I and two of her friends went to that Crazy Eights show in the park, put down our blanket about twenty feet from the lake, underneath some trees, since the days have been so hot. There was another band playing when we arrived.

We started drinking our wine coolers, since Katie bought them instead of vodka and orange juice, and we sat on the blanket, talked and listened to the band. One of Katie's friends is a Grateful Dead fan who travels around the country, following the band. She's seen them eleven times now and plans on going to another show next week. She asked if I wanted to go. Of course I did, but I have a job I really need to keep, thank you anyway.

We were starting to get buzzed and were there about an hour and a half when a man by the lake started screaming in a pitch which was unnatural for a man to yell. The scream was guttural and turned my blood cold. We weren't far from the lake so we got up and ran over. The sobbing man was pulling out what looked like a 3 year old boy from the lake. He was so blue, his lips were blue, he looked like he had been in the lake a while. It was horrible. People were yelling for his parents, who weren't around. I was stunned.

Someone started CPR on the boy, which I was really glad about. I know CPR but I was frozen in place. The CPR would never help. He had been dead too long. The man who screamed scanned the crowd, asking for the boy's parents. We all looked at each other and no one stepped up. This made him very angry, so he started going through the park asking who was missing a 3 year old boy. The crowd parted before him, it was a strange and terrible scene. He finally found the parents on the other side of the park and screamed in their faces that their son was dead. They seemed pretty out of it. Like they dropped acid or something. They didn't really get it that their son was gone, permanently. Some people were holding the angry man back so he wouldn't attack the parents. Katie and the rest of us decided to leave. It was too much. We hurriedly packed our things and ran to the car.

On the way home, Katie was crying the entire time. I felt so sad and devastated but couldn't cry. Katie must think I'm a monster since I didn't cry. When we got home she went straight to her room, slammed the door, and called David, her ex-boyfriend. I was left there by myself with no one to talk to but you, my little friend. I feel so sad. It made me think of my cousin Jack. He was 3 when he died in that fire. The shock of the event left me listless and strangely unemotional. I wanted to talk to Katie, but she was crying to David, telling him all of the details, the bloated, blue body of a toddler, an image which is burned in my memory. It will be something I'll never forget. I'm crying on the inside. I feel unable to show my feelings. What is wrong with me?

JUNE 27, 1987

I did it again. I made such a fool of myself. Last night was Clara's wedding reception. She rented an RV and hooked it up in a camp spot so it'd have a refrigerator and toilet. Some people built a fire, even though it was hot. It was a lot of fun, but I got extremely shit-faced. I am completely embarrassed and humiliated today. I wish I had a dollar for each time I wrote that sentence down in you, diary. I wasn't drinking at first because I was afraid to lose control, and then Clara kept pushing beer on me. They had a keg and needed it gone. I started drinking and having fun, but it didn't take me long to get fuzzy. I don't remember hardly anything after my fourth beer, but apparently, I passed out in the corner and vomited on myself later on. I am so humiliated! Clara told me she was mad at her cousin because he came over to me when I was passed out and made a big deal about asking me for a dance. Everyone laughed but Clara said she told him to shut the fuck up. That was sweet of Clara to defend my honor. Clara had Dean drove me home since we live in the same apartment complex. I kind of remember that because I was hitting on Dean. Lori was there, too, she said. They weren't mad at me for trying to hit on Dean. Lori told me it was okay, she has been there before and she wasn't mad or upset in the least. Lori is so sweet. She isn't very smart, but it doesn't matter. She is so kind-hearted. Man, that is the last time I pass out in front of people. And vomit on myself. I mean it. I didn't eat yesterday. That is what did it to me.

Well, anyway, that is all behind me now (thank God!). Today, Lori, Dean, Clara, Mike and I went to lunch at a Mexican restaurant. My first real Mexican food. I don't really like it because it is very spicy. It upset my stomach. Later, we went swimming (after we picked up my car from the place of the party).

To change the subject, Larry and Katie haven't been getting along very well. They just got into another heated argument on the phone. Whew! What a doozy! He is overly possessive of her and needs to loosen his grip on her or he'll lose Katie. He can't comprehend her wanting to do her homework and laundry by herself. He is a great guy except for the extreme neediness, which I can relate. I can't get a man interested in my mind, only my body. I shouldn't have sex so early in a relationship. It probably gives the wrong impression. Guys want sex but don't want a girlfriend who gives sex too quickly or easily. It's all so confusing.

AUGUST 1, 1987

Katie had another Mike Tyson party for the fight tonight. This time, I invited Matt, and he accepted. The apartment was pretty crowded, and we ordered pizza and Katie stocked up on beer. Mostly Michelob Light and Fosters. People got there early so it was animated. Two guys started wrestling in the living room before the fight. It was random and everyone picked up their beers so they wouldn't get spilled on our white carpet. We don't have much furniture, so there is room to wrestle.

Tyson won yet another fight. He defeated Tony Tucker and was recognized as champion by several boxing organizations. I like watching Seattle Seahawk games, and know football better than boxing. The Seahawks don't win many games. I watch them, but I can't have Seahawk parties for a while. I'm so glad Matt came over and enjoyed himself. It made me feel good having someone there for me and not Katie.

AUGUST 13, 1987

At work today, I talked to Matt for 45 minutes. I planned to meet him and a few of his friends at Dakota's, a swank nightclub. Katie went with me to meet some of her friends from work. She went in first, then I walked in and showed them my ID. No deal. They wouldn't let me in to the bar. It is 21+ only. Katie wasn't going to leave on my account and I could see Matt talking to some people, a couple of girls who were hanging on his every word. I stood outside for quite a while, staring sadly in the window, watching everyone have a good time. I eventually had to go home. I slowly walked back to my car. No one came out of the bar to tell me they were sorry I couldn't come inside. No one cared.

Now, I am here alone in my room, thinking. It is probably better I didn't get in, I'd probably drink too much and make a fool of myself as always.

I talked to Amber again today. She ended up marrying Greg and now she is pregnant and overdue by 8 days. She is so big now. I can't wait to see her baby. I went to her baby shower a few weeks ago and got the responsible job of writing down the gifts and who they were from for thank you cards. Glad I could be of some assistance

I wish I could see Matt. I long for the times when I can see him. I miss him so much when I don't see him. I even dream about him and always think about him. Am I in love? Does he like me more than a friend? He does seem to enjoy talking to me. We have sat and talked for hours more than once and I love to be with him. He is so easy to get along with. I have never felt like this before. What will I do when he goes back to school in Corvallis?

AUGUST 15, 1987

Good morning. I woke up at 7:00 am on a Sunday morning. What a crime. I had a lot of fun yesterday. It makes up for my deathly boring Friday night.

Katie wanted to go to the "Bite" of Portland, so I was easily talked into tagging along. We left for the "Bite" at 2:30 pm. and bought a six pack of Henry's Dark, which I drank four. Katie and I walked around the Saturday Market, ate a Gyro, watched the water-skiers do pyramids and make jumps. They must do that for every event in Portland. I saw them before. There were two stages set up for music; one with Country music and the other with good old fashioned Rock 'n Roll.

We saw a few people we knew and a lot of super high people I did not know. Men flocked to Katie and spoke to me as a side gesture. I know she is beautiful, blond, thin as a bean pole, everything my mom loves in a person. The best person we ran into was Richard, a friend of Katie's who is intensely into the stock market and follows investments and talks about being on Wall Street some day. Richard is highly intelligent and seems to be a mathematician since he worked out stock percentages in his head. Of course, Richard is incredibly handsome, so much that he could be a model. He is a pale skinned Black and has bone structure like a classical statue. He was waiting for his ex-girlfriend, Tami, who Katie is very good friends with. We all walked around waiting for Tami but she never showed. I saw Mike there (Matt's twin brother) but he didn't see me.

We left at 7:15 pm, so I actually had a social engagement for hours. As we were driving home, we passed Chris (another male friend of Katie's). He turned his car around and came over to our apartment. He knew about a party near the Dog Racing Tracks. Larry came over and we all went to the party, which was a blast. I had three beers and Larry seemed to be a hit with the high school crowd, most of whom he went to high school with. I said he was young, he is probably my age.

We left the party between 10:00 pm and 10:30 pm and Chris talked us into going to the Dog Racing Track. Chris placed a bet with my money (since I was too shy to do it) but I lost. Chris and I split a large beer and Katie bought some popcorn so I wouldn't get too messed up. It was fun at the Dog Track.

We left the Dog Track around 11:30 pm and went to the Hospital Pub and watched Arm (Chris's brother) play in his band. He is pretty good. The band sounds kind of like R.E.M. It was so easy to get in. They didn't even look at me twice about my age since the bar was really laid back and easy going. People were coming in and out, getting high, going to meet people. I was drunk enough not to worry about getting carded. I was out of money so I couldn't buy any more beer, which was fine with me. I was feeling no pain.

We left the Hospital Pub some time around 1:00 am and came back home. Chris was really cool with me but wasn't into me. That's okay. It was a rare day when people actually talk to me, like Chris, who asked me what I thought about the band, made me feel like part of the human race. It was the best day ever.

Then, like an idiot, I woke up at 7:00 am this morning. Don't ask me why, either.

Oh, by the way, I've lost a total of 12 pounds! I am at 130 again. Up and down like a roller coaster. I want to get to 125 by next weekend for that picnic at my parent's house.

I would like to ask Matt to go with me. I'll try and work up the nerve to ask him.

AUGUST 17, 1987

A flashback to Bean. That whole Lee Simms murder seems to be wrapped up now. Although everyone knows that his ex-wife hired her sons to kill Lee, they refused to turn her in. The police had to release her and Jim, too, because the older brother, Brad, claimed to have done it all on his own. That isn't true. I am sure all three were involved. I really do. Those two freakish brothers did everything together. That is too bad. Brad got 20 years to life. Not long enough, in my opinion.

AUGUST 19, 1987

I finally got up the nerve to ask Matt to go with me to my parent's picnic. He said yes, he'll go with me. Can you believe it? I like being with him, especially for the whole weekend. He seems excited, too. I can't wait for the weekend! He has friends nearby so we'll spend a night there before coming home.

Amber still hasn't had her baby. I have been a nervous wreck for the last few days. The doctor was going to induce labor today, but decided to wait until Tuesday. I talked to her this morning. She said that she had gone into labor last night and walked around hoping that she would have the baby, but no luck.

Maybe she'll have it this weekend. Hopefully, so they won't have to put an IV in her arm to induce labor. How awful! That poor girl. She said that she has been so tired. She is two weeks overdue. She really does look enormous.

Well, I'm kind of tired after going to aerobics today. It is 10:30 pm. I didn't realize it was that late. Even though 10:30 pm isn't late, but on a work night it is. See ya!

AUGUST 20, 1987

Yes, here I am again. It is 10:27 pm on a Thursday night. Tomorrow is what I've been waiting for! I am leaving a day early with Matt to go up to my parents for the weekend. We are taking his car (it's safer – at least his axle won't fall off) and are staying at his friend's house to p-a-r-t-y. I am painting my toenails and fingernails a salmon color. I am listening to Heart on the radio.

I kind of pigged out so I puked it back up. It's okay, really. I ate plenty to sustain this existence called life.

All I can ever think about is Matt. We talk on the phone for 45 minutes at a time. He likes me, I know he does. He can't help himself (ha! ha!). I wonder if it is real or is he going to try to use me? Oh, stop thinking those thoughts. Please like me for me. He has to, I haven't even kissed him the entire time I've known him. I plan to kiss him, just once, this weekend. That is my goal. Yes, just once.

Oh, please. I like him so. Is it, dare I say, love? I am afraid, little diary. He is a truly good, normal man.

AUGUST 23, 1987

I'm back and I had a fabulous time. A worthy weekend adventure, plus I brought a nice, handsome, man with me to my parents' house, kind of a show-off move on my part.

We drove up in Matt's car on Friday (I wore that cream color dress) and stopped at his college roommate's house since he was still on college break. His name is Kurt, he drives a Honda motorcycle, he is funny, gentle, and friendly, and you could tell that he is a college football player.

Matt bought a pint of Jack Daniels and a pint of Yukon Jack's to bring to Kurt's house. The intension was to stay the night there, so drinking was on the table. Matt and I worked on that Yukon and Coke and finished the bottle, which isn't saying too much since it was only a pint. I am certain it was a good thing for me. Kurt finished his pint, too.

With perfect timing, Mike's sister, Molly, showed up with a few stoner friends. They were around my age, some a bit younger. They didn't want to hang with the big brother and went into Molly's room.

As I mentioned, Kurt has a motorcycle and we went outside to look at it. Matt drove up and down the street by himself. I think he is learning how to drive a motorcycle because he didn't want me on the bike with him. Kurt offered to give me a ride. At first I only wanted Matt to drive, but since he refused, I decided to live a little. I'm not used to getting on motorcycles and touched my calf to the tailpipe which burned me fairly well. My legs were exposed since I had on a sun dress. Kurt asked if it was okay, and we cleaned it up after we went for a ride. Wow! I loved the ride. We must have been going 85 mph on the country roads as I held on tightly to Kurt. The telephone poles flew by like toothpicks being tossed aside. It was so dark on the country roads, the only light coming from the motorcycle headlight, the moon and stars. It was gorgeous. It felt like flying.

We returned to Kurt's house and scrounged up some more to drink. Molly was sitting next to Matt on the couch when we returned. Molly asked Matt if he'd give her a ride on the motorcycle and he said yes! I was mortified! I pleaded with him to give me a ride and he refused. That hurt me deeply. I felt jealous, too.

Kurt could tell that I was angry, so he mixed me a drink and started talking to me about how I met Matt and about my job and my parents' party. He was great company, so I didn't feel too badly about it. I think Kurt is equally as handsome as Matt, if not more. His body is perfect.

Later that evening, after the stoners and Molly left for some party, Matt and I sat on the couch and Kurt sat over in the chair. It was getting late so Kurt soon went into his room and crashed. Matt and I sat there while I rubbed his hands with lotion. We turned off the TV and kissed a little then fell asleep together until he got up around 5:30

am and went into the bedroom because we were squashed. He covered me up and I fell back asleep.

It was kind of sweet. I wish it would have happened when we weren't drunk. Did he do it because he wanted to or because he had been drinking? I do hope it was the former and not the latter.

We both woke up at 9:00 am, ate breakfast at a Waffle House and went to my parent's house. We got there at 1:40 pm. There were a few people and it was really dead. Matt and I played darts which was fun, at least. We can communicate, it seems. We have a good friendship which is a good beginning to any relationship. Maybe that's the whole point with Matt. He might like me but doesn't want to rush things.

When we first arrived, Reggie, my parents' miniature Manchester Terrier, got angry with me for bringing a Matt. Reggie really likes me when I visit and gets so excited to see me. When he saw Matt with me, Reggie shunned me for hours. We set up the chairs in a circle, so Reggie took his squeaky toy to everyone in the room except for me. He even took it to Matt. It was hilarious seeing a little dog get so jealous. He is a very smart dog, though.

After a while, more people showed up and it got a little more exciting. We started up the volleyball game. It was the first real party my parents ever had, and I wasn't even living at home anymore. Why didn't my parents buy the darts and volleyball net when I lived at home? They bought them just for the party. That really hurt.

I am going to keep this short because it is 1:10 am and I have to work in the morning. Basically, Matt and I drank and slept in separate rooms, although mom said we could share a room. That was a little embarrassing. Matt doesn't seem to remember kissing on the couch before falling asleep at Kurt's house. Maybe he does, and is trying to forget. Maybe Matt has a girlfriend and I'm only a friend to him. I should take what I can get, even if it is painful not to be loved. I tend to rush into things too quickly, so I should be happy with what we have.

SEPTEMBER 10, 1987

I am listening to a song called *Love Hurts* which is appropriate under the circumstances. Matt came over tonight and we rented a VCR since I don't have one and *Beverly Hills Cop*. Matt bought a four pack of wine coolers. Sure, it was great. But when he went to leave, I hugged him because he is going to California and then off to college. What a hug. Ha! He barely hugged me back. That should sum up the whole relationship right there. He only wants to be friends and I practically threw myself at him, which is embarrassing. I probably scared him off for the future.

I have to seriously go on a diet! I have to do something. I could do it by Christmas when I see Matt again! Listen to me. I am still talking about Matt.

You know, I'm kind of buzzed. I had a couple of coolers and bought some weed from a guy at work, Aaron.

I didn't smoke around Matt since he doesn't strike me as a marijuana smoker. I can smoke it now, in my room. I feel so at peace with you, diary. I can tell you anything.

SEPTEMBER 15, 1987

I can't seem to find a normal life. I feel like I'm on the outside looking in, can't connect to people. I'm so broken. I was arrested earlier today. Over the past few months, I have been shoplifting for reasons I am not sure about. I feel obsessed with planning and carrying out the theft of some really nice, and not so nice, clothes. I should have known that Nordstroms would be the most diligent against shoplifting since they have video cameras everywhere. I know they must have cameras in the dressing room since I was caught, which is completely illegal on their part. I asked security point blank if they had cameras in the dressing room and they didn't answer me.

I feel like I lead a double life. Katie noticed the new clothes. She thinks I'm spending bill money on clothes which isn't the case since I've been stealing them. I can't exactly tell her that, now can I?

The thing was, I had a bad intuition that I was going to be caught but I stole that dress anyway. I should listen to my intuition because it is always right. Now I have to go to court, pay a fine, and possibly have Theft II on my record. Worst of all, I had to sign a paper saying that I could never go into a Nordstroms again as long as I live or they will charge me with a misdemeanor!

I can't believe that I've been arrested twice in my lifetime! The first was for the DUI when I was 16 which was expunged from my record since I went to a treatment center. The courts won't know that I have a previous arrest, thank goodness. I feel guilty for stealing all of those clothes, but it's like I couldn't stop myself. I know it is wrong, but did it anyway. What's wrong with me?

I'll go downstairs and watch *Whose The Boss*, *Growing Pains*, and my favorite, *Moonlighting*, and try and act normal. I can't bear to stay in my bedroom every night. Tuesday has good shows on tv. I can at least enjoy something in life. The only other day I like is Thursday night when *The Cosby Show* is on.

Thank God I have you to confide in or I may go crazy. Goodbye for now, but not for long; I have an eternal need, to belong.

SEPTEMBER 22, 1987

You are reading the diary of a madman. I think my mind will burst sometimes. I feel like I am going crazy and don't know why. I feel like I am going to jump out of my skin. I pretend to be normal and come across as a kind of zombie instead. Most of the time, I don't talk because I don't know what to say, how to start a conversation, or keep a conversation going. I sit like a lump of clay. I'm not animated and fun like Katie. Mom comes down and goes to dinner with me once in a while. I take her to the nicest restaurants in town, something different, not a chain. You should have heard mom talk about how perfect Katie looks. She has the perfect body (no boobs, though), she has the best thick, blond hair, she is vivacious and fun to be around. Mom talks about Katie so much I try and find times she's out of town to invite mom over. It hurts me so much that I don't get complements about anything. I did cut my own hair to save money, and it turned out so well, Katie mentioned it to mom. She can probably tell mom isn't very kind towards me.

I will lose weight. You will help me. I will write down everything I eat or drink and what time. I shall carry you to my death bed. Mom would say nice things about me if I was thinner. My weight goes up and down a lot. I spiral between 120 and 145. 25 pound of yo-yo dieting is seriously wrong. Curse my fatness! I like food too much to stop eating.

Katie has a new boyfriend, Troy, a Greek god, so she'll be up in her room or at his place now. It is pretty serious. He is a great guy, of course. Incredibly handsome, intelligent, charming, easy going, and energetic. If only I could do the same.

I went to court on Monday, which was just yesterday. It is hard to believe. It feels like a lifetime ago. I was told to get a court appointed lawyer. The judge suggested that I get one because Theft II can get up to one year in jail and/or $2,500 fine. I am scared shitless. I was such a fool. All for what? Nordstrom's has already fined me $260. I'll have more fines and I'm always broke.

My head is swimming because I start college tomorrow and Thursday night. My other life. I lead so many different lives that don't seem to merge into one. I'm taking Introduction to Business and Computers in Business. Impressive, huh? I thought you would like that. The classes are at Portland Community College. At least I am spending my money on something good for a change.

My car situation is disastrous. I have two cars, both of which don't run. My parents are going to get me another one that actually runs. I'll believe it when I see it. I will give them my second Volkswagen Beetle that is broken down and the Mercury Capri, which is going under fast. I just got it, too. It's the one my parents bought for me for $400. The blue beast rattles, knocks, sputters and screeches. The gas gauge doesn't work and it won't go over 45 mph. The mechanic who has repaired it three times in two months told me the Mercury Capri is the biggest lemon in the history of cars. He jokingly called it the Crappy. I would laugh if it was funny. My nerves are frayed from driving in an unsafe vehicle.

On top of all the other things going on, I called an eating disorder place. I may have messed up because she keeps calling now since I left my name and number on Friday after I scarfed down a whole bag of animal cookies. I love those stupid things. Why? I hate my fat, ugly body! What a fat ugly slob! No wonder I have no boyfriends. Starve! Feel some real hunger pains. Do it now! You don't want to look like a fat pig, do you? You should look thin. Now do it.

SEPTEMBER 23, 1987

The first day of school was tonight at 6:00 pm to 10:00 pm. Mr. David is the instructor and he is incredibly intelligent and knowledgable about running a small business. I couldn't afford to get my book yet since it cost $33.16! My God! How expensive!

My brain is a sponge, a dry sponge that seeks liquids to absorb, knowledge, education, so my brain can swell and emit an intellectual aura to everyone who meets me. I want to be the smart girl, the one people ask questions when they need to find the answer to anything and everything.

I stayed behind and talked to Mr. David, since he is interested in his students. He suggested I take psychology next semester. He is also really into arts and music and said maybe that is what I should do, try different fields to see where my expertise lies. Oh yeah, I start back to my second job this weekend to help pay for my bills. I'm working at Paolo's Pizza in the kitchen until I get a reliable car to do deliveries again. I may be working register, which is what I'd prefer, although I enjoy making pizzas in the stone ovens.

Busy bee, I am. I work full time, go to school two nights a week and work weekends. I will go to aerobics Monday and Tuesday and work out Saturday. That is all I have time for. I like being busy. It keeps me out of trouble.

I had a strange dream. The whole company I work for went to Florida on vacation and rented our own jet. Mom was tagging along with us. So was Matt. I went up to

Matt to say hi to him and then he left to talk to someone else. I tried approaching him again a few times but he kept doing the same thing, acting the whole time like he didn't see me.

Our jet stopped in the Atlanta Airport. Matt got off the jet to look around. I went to follow him, but lost him the crowd. I realized that he was playing a trick on me. He was back on the plane - I could see him through the window. He just watched me from the plane as I struggled to return.

To my dismay, the jet started to take off without me. I ran as fast as my feet would take me to catch up to the plane, waving my hands wildly in the air, hoping someone on the plane would see me. It was too late. The jet was flying. I still tried to catch up to the jet and I started to fly. You know, those crazy dreams where you fly but it seems more dangerous than enjoyable.

I flew after the jet for a little while before I crashed into some family's back yard. While I was on the ground, trying to fly again, bees started chasing me so I swatted them away. I was able to fly again and tried to slip through some tangled telephone wires. I misjudged the distance and got ensnared in the wires, unable to fly or break free. In the distance I could see the plane flying away to Florida.

SEPTEMBER 26, 1987

Yesterday, Ted Kennedy and a young blonde woman were caught having sex in a restaurant. It isn't known whether it was consensual or not. Apparently, Ted Kennedy has accosted women in restaurants in the past, throwing down waitresses and rubbing his penis against their crotch. Whatever happened in the restaurant, Ted Kennedy leaves a sad legacy of the Kennedy family.

SEPTEMBER 27, 1987

I feel like a dismal loser. I did yet another idiotic act. I went to a party at Cindy's house from work. She's the saleswoman. I still work at the typewriter and computer repair place, owned by Matt's dad and uncle. Well, Cindy had a barbecue and beer party. Matt was going to drive up from Corvallis for the party and stay with his dad.

Well, what do you think happened? I became overly anxious and nervous about being in a crowd of people. I knew everyone at the party but I never feel like I fit in. I can never think of anything to say so I must come across as being really stupid. I starting drinking beer. And drinking. I don't know how much I drank. I blacked out just after Matt showed up. I was very drunk, I know I must have been, when Matt showed up at the party. He said hi to everyone except for me. He snuck out pretty quickly. I think he had a girl with him. I was devastated so I drank more. My memory is hazy.

I woke up in a strange bed this morning. It was the Cindy's extra bedroom from work, the one who had the party. She let me stay there. She said that I got sick in the back yard in front of everyone! She was very sweet, saying that it happens to everyone in their lifetime, so I shouldn't worry about it. I did worry about it. I do it so often, it frightens me.

To make matters worse, I slept in my clothes and pissed my jeans. It got the bedspread a little wet. I was horrified. I tied my sweatshirt around my waist and hoped they wouldn't notice the wet spot inside my thighs. I kept my legs tightly closed. Cindy asked if she could cook me breakfast. I couldn't believe she was being so nice to me. Almost everyone else wouldn't be so nice. Most people are mean about those kind of things, making fun of you and laughing at you when they are around other people. I thanked her and said that I had to go home now. I didn't want her to see the wet stain.

I got in my car and came straight to my room. I have been in here all day. I am so ashamed and hate myself so much. I made a complete fool of myself in front of people I work with. On top of that, Matt saw me drunk and ran away from me as fast as possible. It hurts so much. Why can't I be normal? Why do I always have to mess things up? Physically I feel horrible, such a hangover. I still feel really sick and dizzy. I must have drank a lot and didn't eat the barbecue. I will try and get some sleep. The loser is signing off.

OCTOBER 5, 1987

A crazy thing happened to me today. I was going to work as usual when a car pulled up beside me and someone started yelling at me and honking their horn. It freaked me out so much that I was afraid to even look at them. Finally, I had to look. It was a man and a woman telling me something about my gas tank and that I should pull over. I thought that maybe it was a trick but they kept honking and said that there was a hose sticking out of my gas tank. Now that could be true because someone keeps stealing gas from my car. I think it is that idiot Barry messing with me.

I pulled over and went around to the gas tank and sure enough, there was 3' of cut garden hose sticking out of my gas tank! Someone was obviously siphoning gas out of my tank when they were almost discovered. I didn't go anywhere all weekend so it could have been any day. Since the tank is on the passenger side, I didn't notice it when I got into my car.

I hope it wasn't Barry who has been syphoning my gas, because that would mean he found out where I live. David, Katie's ex-boyfriend and high school friend of Barry, told me that he was talking in an obsessed manner about me again and that I should be careful. David said that Barry hired a private investigator and now he thinks Barry has been following me. That might explain the keying someone did to my car a while back. Like it matters since it is an old Mercury Capri on its last legs, or should I say, wheels. I mean, the gas gauge doesn't even work, so I keep running out of gas. Especially when that bastard keeps siphoning my gas! My gas gauge always says "empty" even when it isn't, so it is really difficult to know for sure. I can't afford to keep putting gas in my car only to have it stolen.

Twice, I ran out of gas on the way to work. Both times, it was in the dead center of a bridge. Both times, there was a man in a large truck behind me who pushed my car while I kept it in neutral over the bridge so I wouldn't be the cause of an accident. There is no shoulder on the bridge. Both times I had to walk to a gas station with my gas can. Hugely embarrassing. Once, a police car drove slowly by me as I was walking the two miles, and then kept on driving. I waved at him, hoping for a lift, but he completely ignored me, even though we made eye contact. I thought police were there to help citizens. What if a serial killer drove by and abducted me?

OCTOBER 11, 1987

Oh, boy, I've done it this time. Katie is so mad at me she won't speak to me at all.

Last night, Saturday, David came over to hang out with Katie and me. Mostly with Katie, I'm a second choice. The three of us watched some crappy movie on tv and drank lots of beer. Since Saturday nights are terrible on tv, David and Katie went upstairs to talk for a while. Katie is still going out with Troy, but she is still very close to David, her first boyfriend. I don't know the details as to why they broke up. I'm guessing David cheated on her since he made out with me the first night we met at my old apartment.

Katie says she is still a virgin, which shocks me tremendously since she has boys spend the night so frequently.

She was raised Catholic and will kiss, cuddle, and maybe oral sex, but no intercourse. Shocking. Katie isn't embarrassed to walk around naked at any given time. She doesn't need to wear a bra since her breasts are small, and often only wears a pair of white, lacy underwear. Katie is currently starving herself to fit into her cat suit for Halloween. Fit into a skin tight suit? Are you kidding? Where is the fat? Katie says her butt is too large. Boys seem to think otherwise since David said she had the best ass in a pair of jeans.

Well, I kept drinking and watching dull tv down in the living room by myself. An hour or so later, Katie and David came downstairs again and sat on the couch. Katie was drunk by her standards and very sleepy. I was sitting on David's left side and Katie was on his right side. Katie put her head in David's lap and fell asleep.

After Katie fell asleep, David and I began to talk. Small talk, nothing important, when he off and kissed me! We started kissing, which was extremely stupid since Katie was asleep on his lap. Katie woke up and caught us and yelled at both of us. I felt so low, it was awful. There was no getting a word in with Katie, she was on a tirade, yelling half the time about how I betrayed her, and the other half at David asking how could he when they were just kissing upstairs. Uh, oh. I didn't know that part. Not at all. Katie was so angry, she started hitting David over and over again, really laying it out. She is about 105 pounds so David just put his hands up, not striking back. He was trying to calm her down by saying I didn't mean anything to him.

That's when I ran out of the house, actually wearing her other boyfriend, Larry's, shirt. I borrowed it from him a couple of months ago, when Katie and Larry were dating. It was a cold night with a steady rain, and I didn't get a coat. I was so depressed and hated myself I just kept walking and walking in the rain. I walked to a park and sat on a swing for a long time. I withdrew into myself, making everything around me fade out until it is dark and quiet inside.

After sitting there in the park for hours in the dark, soaking wet, freezing cold, numb down to the bone, not caring if someone murdered me, I finally came home and Katie was still awake in her bedroom. She glared at me and closed her bedroom door. She hasn't talked to me yet. She left the apartment today. I feel like such a tramp. I'm so sorry, Katie. She'll never believe me, but I'll tell her again when she gets home tonight. If she comes home, that is.

OCTOBER 24, 1987

This year has been a rocky one. I had an experience today which will never leave my memory. It started out to be a good day. I decided to go to the mall to do a little underwear shopping and pay on my Meier & Frank bill. Katie asked if she could go shopping with me. I was stunned then elated. She is finally talking to me again, so I told her, yes, we can go to the mall together. We've never gone shopping together before.

I was driving to the mall and we were almost there, crossing over the I-5 overpass. We saw cars stopped in the road and it looked like part of the overpass railing was gone. Katie told me to pull over, so I pulled over and parked the car. We both ran over to the edge and saw a terrible accident. A truck with one of those campers on the back went over the edge, through the railing. The man must not had on his seat belt because he was laying on the highway twitching. His arms and legs were all in unnatural positions. It looked like they all were broken. His head was on its right side. His skull had been crushed.

While we watched, we could see the puddle of blood getting bigger and bigger. I just stared at him as his body still twitched violently.

The fire truck got there pretty fast on the I-5 part (we were on the overpass). We watched as the fireman went up to the man on the pavement. The fireman felt for a pulse but the man was obviously dead. The fireman turned the man over and that is when I saw the skull open, exposing his brain. The man's face was completely gone.

I started feeling dizzy, especially when the other fireman crawled into the upside down truck cab to see if there was anyone else in there. As the fireman got back out, I heard him say there was nothing left of the other person. She or he had been crushed between the camper and the pavement. The other person was still in the passenger seat, but the camper came through the truck's back window and slammed the other person into the pavement. The person was almost liquefied.

Katie started fainting, and I felt like fainting, but I helped her to the car and we drove back home. It seemed like slow motion getting home. It is hard to remember that part.

When we got home, Katie called Troy and they went up to her room to talk. She closed the door. I have no one to talk to except you, diary. I don't know how to process what I saw. It was a horror film in real life. I've never seen a person without a face. His body was so broken, limbs in all directions. It makes me feel sick. This is the second brutal death I've seen this year. The first was the drowned, bloated, blue boy. I feel really tired all of a sudden, even though it is only 6:30 pm. I am going to sleep now.

OCTOBER 27, 1987

I am having difficulty sleeping because my nightmares are horrifying. I can't remember them all, just the most recent one. I was walking along the railroad tracks by myself in my pajamas, wondering why I was there. I felt someone watching me, so I turned around and a man was watching me from the shadows. He frightened me so much I started to run. I was in my bare feet and there was glass on the ground, so my feet got cut and were bleeding. I kept running. I heard a woman's voice calling for help, so I followed her voice. She was behind a train car, next to the river. I got up close to her and saw that she had no head. Her body was nude and there were stab wounds on her body and her head had been cut off. The head was not near the body, I couldn't find it. I was searching for her head when I woke up.

NOVEMBER 5, 1987

Katie went to a Halloween party dressed as Cat Woman and I stayed home alone. I wasn't invited. I asked Katie to buy me some wine coolers before she left, which she did. I couldn't watch a horror movie, like I usually do, since the horrific accident. My nightmares are every night. I can't remember most of them. There is always a lot of blood.

On a more positive note, I guess, the Playboy of Jessica Hahn came out and people went absolutely crazy. Katie stood in line to get one so she could read the sordid details of how Jim Bakker and another preacher drugged and raped Jessica. The press was out of control, people stood in lines for hours to buy a Playboy. They sold out in record number. I think they will have to print more. There's talk in the press that she'll pose for December's Playboy centerfold, too. Hugh Hefner is making a fortune off the scandals of famous people. I'm fine with Jessica making money from her rape. The crying and pleading of Jim and Tammy Bakker make me absolutely sick. He is making more money than ever before with his misdeeds. So many people forgive him and call Jessica a liar. We live in a grotesque world.

NOVEMBER 19, 1987

"Good Evening" as Alfred Hitchcock would say. I met another boy in one of my college classes. His name is Timothy. He actually like me! Tim said that I was really pretty and gave me a big hug. He going to escort me to Patty's wedding, a Catholic girl friend of Katie's. I hope I didn't make the wrong decision in going on a first date to a Catholic wedding. I stressed the point to him, and Tim said it was fine.

Tim is about 6'3" and plays as a tight end in football. Whew! Nice looking specimen of a man. One bad thing is he said that he is moving to Salem soon. Shit.

Tim has a serious hand injury from work. Poor Tim. It didn't really bother me when he showed me his hand. After seeing a man without a face, an injured hand is minimal. Three of his fingers were cut off from a radial saw. It was a clean cut so he took his fingers to the hospital and had them sewn back on. Luckily, the fingers adhered and weren't rejected. He can move them slightly, but not with much control and no feeling. It's his left hand and he is right handed so it could be worse. Tim is totally fine with it, which is great. I didn't even know that you could sew fingers back on. The trick is putting them on ice right away.

Tim came over to the apartment and met Katie and asked me to play the piano. I did since it is a rare request. I'm going to wear my purple sweater dress to the wedding.

NOVEMBER 23, 1987

My Mercury Capri finally died for good. It broke down on the Ross Island Bridge again! In the same place I ran out of gas. Someone pushed me off the bridge yet again with their bumper. What a terrible coincidence. It was kind of creepy, actually. I had my well worn 2 miles trek to the gas station. I called AAA to have them tow my car again. I've had my cars towed twenty times in a year, so AAA suspended my service. That was something I didn't know. I've been so dependent on AAA saving me from precarious situations. It's a sad day when AAA won't even help me. I got my money's worth for the annual fee. That's why they dropped me, no doubt, because I wasn't giving them a profit.

Jim felt so guilty about purchasing the Mercury Capri, that he came down to Portland and bought me another car. I got a 1980 Plymouth Champ, which I've never heard of in my life. I'm highly suspicious of its reliability since there aren't a plethora on the roads.

To our great disappointment, the clutch went out on it right away. Along with a few other problems. All repairs came to $458.14 because it is a front wheel drive and more expensive (they said it is an import, too). The Capri is still sitting in the parking lot that needs to be gotten rid of. No one would take it as a trade-in. Sell it for parts, perhaps. I'll probably have to give it away for parts in order to pay for the towing since I don't have AAA anymore. That's my best bet.

Tim and I enjoyed our date, although the long Catholic wedding was a bit of a downer. Since he is moving away, I feel reticent to become attached to him and haven't returned his calls. I'm sure he understands. It will be too painful to lose someone I like to a city so far away.

DECEMBER 5, 1987

I've been hanging out at Clara's house a lot. She never wants to come over, so I drive to her house, which isn't far from here. We usually sit in the basement, smoke weed, watch tv until her husband comes home. I hang out with him, too. He isn't a very exciting person and just sits there watching basketball games. While Clara and I were listening to the radio, KMJK, she mentioned she knew the DJ, Curtis Sanchez, because they did cocaine together. She suggested I call in to win tickets whenever they give them away. You can't win unless you play.

Last weekend I met Curtis from KMJK. I called up on Friday night to request *Satisfaction* by the Rolling Stones. He ended up playing the recording of my voice back on the air and kicked off the half hour show with my song.

I called Curtis again to thank him for the song request, so we began talking as he played more of my requests. It turns out he used to live here at the same apartments as me but moved out this summer. He invited me to the station, and me, with nothing else to do at 10:30 pm on a Friday night, took him up on it.

The radio station is located on Barbur Street, and Curtis gave me the private phone number to call when I got to the building (there is a pay-phone at the front of the building). I called him and Curtis came down and unlocked the front door. He only about 5'4" (I'm 5'5") and looks Latin. It turns out he is Filipino, and since I lived in the

Philippines, I shared my stories with him. We talked for a while in between air time. He is very interesting, intelligent and a nice guy. I stayed until the next DJ came in for his shift. Almost all the music is on cd. There must be thousands of cds, every album and song I can think of. They hardly use records anymore. I don't even own a cd yet. They have only been around for a few years and are expensive. Well, the cd player is really expensive.

While I was looking at the cds, a friend of his called and invited Curtis to his birthday party that night. Curtis asked if I wanted to go. Of course! I knew where he worked and his name, so I'd be safe, right? Not that anyone knew where I went to that night, or even cared.

The party was out in Beaverton and it was a wild cocaine party, the stuff of legend. Johnny Limbo and the Lugnuts showed up after their gig. A bunch of groupie girls followed him in. There were local Portland musicians and other DJs at the party. I went into the garage to fill up my beer since that is where the keg was kept. As I was pouring my beer, a boy asked if I had ever posed in Playboy Magazine. I thought it was a line, for sure. I told him it wasn't the best pick up line ever used. He ran over to the wall, grabbed a Playboy calendar, and showed me September. Wow, it did look a lot like me. The boy said I should just say it is me, but I didn't. I went back inside and looked for Curtis. He was doing some lines and asked me to join him, which I did.

It was a lot of fun. After the party, we went over to Curtis' apartment since it was close by. We watched *The House* on HBO and kind of slept. I wasn't too tired because of the coke. I slept in his bed with him but nothing happened what so ever. I swear. He is too old, 32 this December 1st, and has a kid, too. Curtis did try to kiss me, but wasn't very pushy.

Oh, yeah. I forgot to tell you about the theft court case. Well, I did get a court appointed lawyer who didn't cost much because he is based on a sliding scale of my income. I am glad I got a lawyer as suggested because he made it so I didn't have to go to court. We met with the judge and a woman from Nordstrom's and they all discussed it. I never had a conviction of anything before, so they decided to give me a break. It would not go on my record at all. The judge said that he was attaching a note to my file saying if I got in trouble for shoplifting again I would be charged next time. I won't do that ever again. That was too close. I could have gone to prison and had a felony on my record. I gave my innocent, I'm sorry, eyes through their entire conversation in the judge's quarters. Thank goodness I did. I really felt bad, so it wasn't an act.

I have barely slept for a couple of days so I'm exhausted! Good night, or morning. I'm mixed up. Cocaine will do that every time. I hear coke can be dangerous to do, so I really should be more careful.

DECEMBER 13, 1987

Bad things just keep happening. I went up to the mall to do a little Christmas shopping. I was on my way back home, and traffic was heavy and slow, especially since there was freezing rain. As I was sitting at a light, I saw the prostitutes standing out there in the cold. Some of them were wearing hardly anything, even in the cold. I feel sad that their life took such a wrong turn to end up on a street corner, selling sex for money or drugs. I am sure they didn't want to become prostitutes, bad things happened to them, too.

I was driving in the middle lane and was coming to a light when I kind of blacked out. I was hit by a Suburban truck from the right side. He was trying to make an illegal left turn from the right lane. He drove away without stopping. My Plymouth Champ is small and smashed like a tin can. I had my seat belt on but it broke and I flew into the left window, breaking the glass with my skull. I really didn't know what was going on. I think I kept saying, "I had my seat belt on. I really did." That is all I really remember of it. Except for a moment just before the ambulance got there. The accident happened in front of the homeless shelter. A very nice man ran up and stroked my hair and told me it would be all right before the ambulance got there. He looked homeless, his clothes were shabby and his hair greasy but he was so kind. I am so glad he was there.

When the sirens got close, the man ran off. I asked him not to go, but he said he had to. I don't remember much until Katie picked me up from the hospital later that night. The doctors said that I got a concussion and Katie should wake me up a few times through the night. This happened two days ago. I had car insurance this time. I am so glad. I can't always afford to pay for car insurance, but recently caught up with my bills after working delivering pizzas. At least that part was good luck.

But the awful thing is that my shoulder is really hurting again. I'm going to see Dr. Cohen again to see how badly the trapezius muscle was re-injured. My neck sure hurts. I know my car is totaled.

DECEMBER 20, 1987

It turned out that I was more injured than I thought. The accident re-tore that same trapezius muscle. I have to start over with all the hot treatments, the little electrical currents, and physical therapy. The pain is really bad again. I was just able to write, but I can't again. I can't hold up my arm. Dr. Cohen said that I should try and get some time off from work to rest. I'm worried about asking them. Wish me luck!

DECEMBER 24, 1987

I can't believe this! I am so tired of life beating the crap out of me. Yesterday, on Wednesday, I went to ask for some time off because of my should injury. I told them my doctor said I should rest to help it heal faster. They told me that I could take time off. I went home yesterday feeling relieved. But when I went in to work this morning, it was only going to be a half day, I was told right away to come into the office with Mr. Harrison. He closed the door so I knew it wasn't good. I sat there in shock as he told me that they were laying me off. They were only laying me off, of course, and no one else. I couldn't help crying, I don't have any money saved. I was so scared and asked if I could just stay around a couple of weeks to find something else. Mr. Harrison said that he couldn't because of tax reasons for the new year, or something like that. They had already packed my belonging to take home. The other women in the office looked really sad. I think I was laid off because of my injury. It had to be. I worked really hard every day. I just asked for time off yesterday, that was it. I shouldn't have. Now I have no job and no money for Christmas! Not that I ever could afford presents, but what about bills? I couldn't help telling Katie about this because I was crying so hard when I got home from work. I just feel like crying all of the time. I wasn't planning on telling her. It may scare her.

I am feeling very sleepy again. It's a horrible Christmas. Katie left to San Francisco to visit her dad. I'll be here by myself. I'm never going to my parents' house for Christmas again. I'm going to sleep now.

CHAPTER 10

1988: AGE 19

JANUARY 5, 1988

My isolated life was lightened a bit. Something fun happened after the dismal Christmas without a job, tree, friends, or family. Katie's cousins drove up from Los Angeles for 12 or 14 hours straight and showed up at our door unexpectedly and late on December 30th. I was already in bed and so was Katie. It was really early in the morning, like 3:00 am. The only thing I remember about it was two very tall guys coming into my room, which was an embarrassing disaster zone. I had a path from the door to my bed, and they sat down on my bed, which had piles of clothes two feet thick being used as blankets. They told me that they were Katie's cousins and were trying to get me out of bed. They tried to lift me up and pull me out of bed. I kept yelling at them to leave me alone. I think they were kind of drunk. Katie finally came in there and yelled at them, saying that she had to work the next day. I didn't. Oh, lucky me. They left me alone, finally. I'm glad because I had wet the bed the night before and was sleeping on the other side of the bed. I didn't want them to sit on a wet area. I don't want my humiliation known to everyone.

The next day, her cousins told us their scheme. They came up to visit Katie in Portland so they could go over the pass to their cousins house in La Grande in eastern Oregon. They have a farm there with horses and wanted us to go with them. There is a guest trailer on the property so there are plenty of places to sleep. Katie's cousins from Los Angelos, James and Brian Gallagher, wanted to bring Katie's friend, Richard, too.

Katie called up Richard and he wanted to go. He came over packed and then we were figuring out whose car to drive. Katie's Datsun was too small, James and Brian's car, the same Datsun as Katie's was also too small, and Richard's had a Carmen Ghia, two-seater. I happened to have a 4 door Chevy Cavalier rental car that my insurance was paying for. It seemed like we were meant to go. However, we didn't have any chains and there wouldn't be any auto store open on New Year's Eve. You had to have chains on your tires to go over the pass at that time of year.

Katie tried calling around to see if anyone had any chains. No one did. She then called to see if Fred Meyer's was open. It wasn't. Well, we all decided to go on with the plan anyway.

James drove the first leg of the journey but started getting tired because they didn't get much sleep the night before. He and his brother went in the back seat to sleep. Katie was tired, too, because she didn't get much sleep either. So, I was driving and Richard was next to me in the passenger seat. It was very dark and lightly snowing. There were really low clouds in the mountains. We didn't have any chains on, but we seemed to be doing all right on the packed snow.

I have to say, I have never been more frightened in my life. There was a part that had no guard rail and the road kept getting more winding. The drop offs were getting much more deadly. We had to keep moving or we might get stuck. Richard and I were so tense. Just when we thought nothing could get any worse, we passed a sign that said "Dead Man's Curve Ahead." Richard and I looked at each other with shock. We could barely breathe. We were both very quiet. Finally, after what seemed like sixteen hours, we got to the other side of the mountains. The boys and Katie were just starting to wake up again for New Year's Eve when Richard and I were very frazzled. They missed the entire scary part of the drive.

We drove straight to the little Pub in La Grande where the O'Reilly and Gallagher families would be. Even though James was my age the bar let him in because they knew him all their life. They wouldn't let me into the bar all night. I had to stand outside by myself. I tried to look fine with that but went off to cry. James brought out his beer and shared it with me while we talked for hours and looked at the beautiful clear, cold night. Everything was white from snow and the moon was so large, you could see the river down below and fields of snow.

It was fun with James there. We are both 18 and he is in college at UCLA. He is a Freshman there. I didn't think he was very cute at first because he has red hair. I kind of ignored him. But then, I saw that he is very good looking. Plus, he is very tall. He is 6'3" and his brother is 6'4". James is a real sweetie, too.

After the bar and after the New Year's celebrations, a bunch of people apologized for not letting me into the bar, but said they were glad James shared his beer with me. They wanted him to. I felt better after that. I didn't feel so left out.

The younger people went to the trailer to hang out and the older people went to the house. I never did see the house. We spent all of our time at the trailer because the horses were out there.

The next day, we went out to ride horses. Not everyone wanted to go because of college football games, but I definitely wanted to ride a horse. They found a very old and gentle horse for me. That is what I asked for. I have ridden horses, but the last time was when I was 10, so it has been a long time.

It is so beautiful out there. The sky was so blue and the snow was getting really deep in eastern Oregon. There was the Snake River nearby, and lots of creeks. We rode the horses slowly over the property. We were crossing a stream when my horse slipped on the rocks and fell on its right side! My leg was under the horse, but the horse wasn't putting his weight on me. I thought there was something wrong with the horse because he wasn't moving. There wasn't, he was waiting for me to move clear before getting up. The horse turned out to be just fine. My shoulder hurt a little more after that, plus I had big bruises all down my right leg from hitting the icy rocks in the river. We rode back to drop me off at the trailer. I didn't feel like riding anymore because my leg hurt. It was okay at the trailer, because some guys were watching the games. I wanted to be riding a horse still. It was so depressing!

I sat at the trailer for hours with one guy until well past night fall. I wondered where everyone went because no one came to get me. Apparently, they all met at the house and had a get together. I was stuck in the trailer. I didn't know. There wasn't a phone in the trailer, so they couldn't call. No one wanted to drive back and get me. That made me sad.

Later that night, in the middle of the night when everyone was asleep I got up to go to the bathroom. While I was pulling my pajamas back on, I could see a guy come into the bathroom. It was Brian. He sat me back down on the toilet and started kissing me. I was really surprised and kissed back. Then I realized this was strange, so I told him I was leaving. He grabbed me and forced me back down. I told him I was serious, but kept kissing him. That was stupid. Anyway, during one free moment, I jumped up and left the bathroom. I know that Brian has a girlfriend so he wouldn't be serious about me. He is quite attractive, but his girlfriend was a friend of Katie's who lives in Portland. That would be a bad situation.

We came back home the next day, me driving the entire way because I was sick to death of being ignored and wanted to ignore everyone else. People kept offering to drive but I refused. James wanted to stay with Katie and I because Brian was going to stay with his girlfriend in Portland. I don't have any job so I will be around the apartment. Plus, I have to rest my shoulder a little longer. I will start looking for a job next week.

That was a lot to write about! My hand is tired and my shoulder hurts. It is time to go to sleep. I am excited about hanging out with James this week. It should be fun.

JANUARY 16, 1988

James and I are getting along so well. We do everything together, making meals, watching tv, looking in the paper for jobs. He's not getting a job, just me. I'm still waiting for the lawsuit to go through. I didn't mention, but the hit and run driver in the Suburban was found by a lawyer friend of Dr. Cohen's who is going to sue for cost of my car plus suffering. I didn't want to sue for much more than necessary, to the lawyer's dismay. He gave me a special 20% rate instead of his usual 40% fee. That was weeks ago, so we're waiting for the lawyer and insurance company to come to an agreement and write me a check. Katie doesn't seem to believe that I'll ever get paid and I'm behind in all of my bills. I'm a real financial burden, especially with James here with so little money. Katie gets angrier by the day, especially when she heard us having sex one night. I new my neighbor didn't care since he is a pimp who asked if I would work for him. After that embarrassment, James and I had sex when Katie was at work, and once at the botanical garden parking lot, in my car. We fogged up the windows completely which made us both laugh so hard. It was like a movie scene.

I feel so comfortable with James, it will be sad when he leaves for college. He says he lives in a one bedroom apartment with three other people, and they all put up ropes with blankets as walls. I wanted to visit, but he said it's too crowded. That made me sad. I'd love to drive to Los Angelos. Wouldn't it be great to attend UCLA? I can only dream. James is barely getting by in college since his brother, Brian, lives with him and also attends UCLA. Brian's big breasted girlfriend also lives in the one bedroom apartment, so it's a tight squeeze. I wonder who the fourth person is? Could it be James' girlfriend? I can't even imagine that. I asked James if it was his girlfriend, and he said no, but it is a girl. I'm heartbroken until James takes me in his arms and talks sweetly to me. He is so charming. I melt like butter in his arms.

JANUARY 22, 1988

No luck finding a job, although, I admit I haven't been looking very hard since I'm waiting for my settlement from the car accident. It should be enough to keep me home and healing for a month or two. James being here all of the time is making it more difficult. I have been doing physical therapy twice a week on my shoulder and neck. It is so painful, especially afterwards when it is inflamed and sore. I still see the chiropractor, Dr. Cohen.

James and I hang out all day, until he leaves to go back to UCLA. I'll miss him once he's gone. Speaking of gone, he's flat broke now. He's gone through all of his money so we have been eating very light, like splitting a box of macaroni and cheese. We were out of milk so James thought we couldn't make the mac and cheese, but I showed him a trick. You add more margarine to make up for the milk and it works just fine. You really don't need the milk, or not very much. When you don't have any, you learn to improvise. It doesn't work well with cereal, so we'll have to get some milk. Maybe Katie will buy some. She isn't happy about us both sitting at home while she is working. I have money coming. She doesn't seem to believe me. I got the lawyer through Dr. Cohen, he is a friend doing a favor and helping me out with the hit and run. The Workman's Comp is paying for the doctor's appointments still since I was still receiving treatment from the patient transfer accident when I was working as a Certified Nursing Assistant. My life is so complicated right now even though I'm barely doing anything. I updated my resume on Katie's word processor and printed a few copies on some nicer paper for when I go on job interviews. I'll be ready when the time is right.

FEBRUARY 7, 1988

I finally got my settlement from the car accident, $3,700. The hit and run totaled my Plymouth Champ, which didn't have a very high blue book value. Most of the money is for personal injury, which is legitimate. Katie didn't think I'd ever get that money so she decided to find a place to live by herself March 1. Katie said she wouldn't have given notice on this apartment if she knew I'd be getting money. I told her so many times, she just didn't believe me. Now I'll have to find a place to live. I'll have to find a place to stay quickly. At least I have this money for deposits. I am starting to get really worried what I should do.

I loaned James $125 of it since he spent his school money while he was here. I hope he pays it back. James needed the money to return to UCLA. I really love him. We got along so well, it was sad when he had to go back to school for enrollment. We spent every day together. I drove along side him until he got onto I-5. James asked me to see him off. I'm still driving the rental car which I'll have to return now that the settlement has gone through. I need a vehicle very quickly! I'm not going to ask Jim to help since all of his choices have been lemons. He isn't trying to help me. He's only buying the cheapest car he can find.

I want to go down to Los Angeles with James. He just left and I miss him already. He said that he will really miss me, too. My heart is broken.

FEBRUARY 20, 1988

I really cut it close. I caught up with my current bills and had enough to move into a place of my own. I found a place to live which is right across the bridge from downtown. I have a great apartment in an old historic house in the front parlor. It has been restored and has beautiful dark wood and tall ceilings. There is a niche for the bed, not really a bedroom. It looks like a closet but when you open the two accordion doors you can see where a double bed fits perfectly, so I can close the doors to hide the bed. It is in the living room, so I can lay in bed and watch TV. I paid movers to get my furniture over here. I packed the boxes and they moved them. It was easier than trying to find someone to help move. I hate moving, plus I have a piano. The piano was small enough not to cost extra. Lucky me.

The windows are huge and the bathroom is so cute with a window way up at the top so no one can look in. They have a washer and dryer in the basement. This place is so beautiful. It includes rent, water, and all utilities for only $280 a month. What a deal. I got so lucky. I got a bike so I can bicycle to work downtown. I got employment with a temp agency, doing secretarial stuff. It is a job at least. I am actually working as their receptionist. I don't like answering phones, but it's better than nothing.

Maybe this will be a start of a good life. I hope so. I see Clara and Lori quite a bit, but they are 7 years older than I am. I don't have any friends my age. I don't mind, as long as I have some friends. I was able to get a fake ID with Katie's old driver's license before we moved apart. It was time for her license to expire, so I went in her place and got a new one with my picture. I don't look anything like Katie, so it was a lucky break for me to score with a fake ID. Katie then said she lost hers, went in and got her driver's license.

It worked, just like she said. I can buy alcohol now. I bought some wine coolers to celebrate.

FEBRUARY 23, 1988

I looked at a Suzuki Samurai and took it on a test drive. I really liked it but when they ran my credit, it wasn't good enough without a co-signer. My credit isn't too bad. I have the one store credit card which is a bit high and close to the limit. The salesman said to find a used car or something less expensive. He was really cute and asked me on a date. He ended up coming over with his VCR and we watched *Beverly Hills Cop*. I don't know if I'll see Bob again since his date consisted of staying in my apartment. I'm not asking for much, but a dinner and a movie out would have been nice. I think I'll hold out for someone else. I miss James terribly, and he rarely calls anymore. He's losing interest in me now that I am far away. I said I'd visit, but he doesn't want me to do that, even in a new vehicle. He probably has a girlfriend down there. It breaks my heart.

FEBRUARY 25, 1988

My luck might be changing for the good. I have a bit more self confidence since finding this great apartment. I purchased a slightly used Toyota pickup today. I wasn't searching for a truck, it happened to be a test model with some mileage and the salesman suggested it to me since Toyotas are great vehicles. It's white with a black bumper and has a sliding window to the truck bed. It has under one thousand miles so it will last a long time. Finally, I have a vehicle which won't break down and need AAA once a week. It is only a four cylinder so the gas mileage is really good. It's super light because it's a small truck, not a 4 wheel drive. It has a cassette player, too!

MARCH 15, 1988

I am so incredibly depressed. James doesn't want me to visit him down at UCLA. We talk less and less. I am sure he has a girlfriend down there. Plus, his brother, Brian said bad things about me to everyone. Brian said that we had sex in the bathroom that night after New Year's Eve in eastern Washington. I did kiss him, but we didn't have sex. I swear it! Plus, James and I didn't go out until after that time, so what is the problem?! James says that he heard us having sex in the bathroom. That is a complete lie! Why do men lie about having sex when they don't have it? Don't they realize how much harm that does to a girl's reputation? It has crushed me completely.

I was wanting to move to Los Angeles to be close to James but he doesn't want that. He won't visit me and won't let me visit him. It really breaks my heart because I love him so much. We really worked well together. I feel others are talking him out of seeing me.

He never paid me back that money. I only asked him once so I wouldn't make him mad. I wish he would pay me back. I really don't have much money. I am working part-time again at Paolo's Pizza as a delivery person. It pays all right since I get gas money. I work some week nights and weekends. It makes me kind of tired to work 2 jobs. I wish I could take another college course. I never could pay for the Psychology class that Mr. David recommended to me. That would have been interesting. I enjoy learning new things.

My main job has been working for that office temp company. They sent me over to Atlantic & Pacific Freightways Inc, in south Vancouver, Washington. It has been working out great there. I am doing the microfilm editing. I work in a dark closet, which I like, but they want to hire me permanently and move me to a bookkeeping job. I like working in that dark room, but they think I can do better. The problem is, I don't know if I can be hired there directly or if the temp agency, who originally sent me there, will try and make them pay for me. The manager at A&P Freightways says that his boss won't approve paying money to the agency. I told him I will give my 2 week notice to the agency then get hired there. The agency didn't get me the job, I was filling in for the microfilm when a permanent job opened up. It isn't like they sent me to a job interview. I hope it all works out.

MAY 6, 1988

I live my life alone almost all of the time. It's sad not having close friends. Clara won't ever leave her house, I have to go see her. All we do is watch tv and smoke pot. I want friends to do things with. I don't even know how to do that. So, I did something spontaneous and bought a Bruce Springsteen ticket through the radio station for $60. The show is sold out and even though I am not a huge Springsteen fan, he is suppose to be a living legend, so I thought that I should see him. Curtis Sanchez, the DJ who I befriended, talked me into it, even though he isn't going. The ticket includes a bus ride up to the Tacoma Dome and back again (I drive my car to a pick-up point that is in the mall parking lot). There was also a party before the show at a nearby bar for people who got their tickets through the radio station. It was kind of sad going by myself, but adventurous, too. I was hoping that there would be beer on the bus, but people brought their own and weren't sharing, even though people brought coolers full of beer. I should have tried to buy some. Katie took back her fake I.D., so I have no way of buying beer now. I guess I could've had Clara buy some beer for me. During the ride up, I sure wished that I had bought some beer since everyone was having such a great time on the bus.

The bar party turned out to be disappointing, too, because there was no open bar. You had to buy your own drinks. I was broke and had no fake I.D. so I was totally out of luck. I tried talking to some people but they blew me off and didn't want a girl latching on to them, I guess. No one was very friendly. I started to get really depressed until I ran into Scott at the bar. He wasn't going to the Springsteen concert, although he wanted to. That is the same Scott who I met at the Scorpions concert with my mom. He bought me a few drinks, whisky and Coke so it would be stronger, and I could get drunk faster before the show. I was embarrassed at first seeing Scott because of that previous drunken incident at my place when I passed out and never saw him, but Scott didn't seem to hold any grudges against me. He said that maybe he'll call me. He didn't seem too sure of it since he has a girlfriend now. We didn't hang out very long while I was at the bar because his girlfriend was there and he didn't want to invite me over and kept coming back and buying me a drink and then leaving again. I would have rather him stay and talk to me, but I guess that is how it goes. I hope he wasn't embarrassed of me since he didn't invite me over to where his girlfriend and other friends were. That was depressing, too. I felt so alone.

The concert was really good, though. Much better than I expected. Springsteen had the E Street Band with him so he had Clarence Clemons play his saxophone. The band made the show so much better because it was kind of like the blues. The show lasted a long time with a couple of encores. Springsteen even played some classic songs by the Beatles and a couple of songs from the 1950's. I was surprised that the show was so good. I can understand why some people are totally obsessed with seeing Bruce Springsteen as often as possible, like that guy from my office who travels almost every year to see Springsteen, even if the show is hundreds of miles away.

I was afraid I'd miss the bus back to Portland, so I walked around to find the bus a little early. I was pretty drunk from the whisky and Cokes and was getting tired. I found the sign for the bus and finished listening to the concert by the exit door. When I got on the bus, everyone was so tired and drunk, almost everyone went to sleep. I was afraid to sleep on the bus in case I peed my pants or something embarrassing. I didn't sleep very much but was exhausted.

I had to go to work today so I didn't feel that great. I am going to go to bed now. See you!

MAY 13, 1988

I think Barry has found out where I live. He must have hired a detective again. There was a robbery in the attic where I live and the only things stolen were mine. When I moved in, the landlord said that I could put some of my extra boxes (Christmas decorations and high school yearbooks, that sort of stuff) in the attic. He did warn me that it wouldn't be locked and it wasn't necessarily a safe place to keep items, but since the front door is always locked, it should be okay. Well, he was right, it wasn't safe. The landlord has been renovating the rooms upstairs, making two more apartments similar to mine. He built a bathroom and kitchen in each unit but is keeping as much of the original wood as possible.

During repairs, he had workers come in and out of the house. The landlord actually notified me of the workers and said that the attic may not be protected at all times, but there was nothing of value so I didn't worry about it. Just a few days ago, I went upstairs to try and find a photo album and that is when I noticed the burglary. Only my boxes were opened, nothing else seemed to be pillaged. The items missing were my fishing pole, tackle box, black bucket sheep skin covers, my Talent Contest first place trophy (and only trophy I ever received) from the junior high school singing quartet, my favorite ratty stuffed animal Aphrodite the camel, a small black and white tv, and Barry's old love letter to that girl that I took when we were living together. I should have put it back, I just forgot about it. Apparently, he didn't forget about that one stupid letter. I know it had to be Barry because who else would steal an old love letter, my beloved stuffed animal, and my only trophy? He took the other things just to make it look like a burglary. I am positive. I called the police and they came by, took a statement, and told me they couldn't do anything. They didn't dust for prints. I did tell the policeman about Barry and how I thought it was him. However, the policeman said that since there were workers in and out of the house recently, it could be anyone. Yeah, right. Highly doubtful.

I have to admit, it really scares me that he is still watching me. I don't know how many times he has been following me, but I don't like it. I never see Katie or David or any of Barry's old friends anymore. Katie thinks I'm too weird, and the other guys don't want to see me anymore because I was just sex to them. I was stupid to think that there was a relationship with any of them. I see Clara and Lori most of all. I do wish that I had some other friends. I just can't keep any friends. I don't know how to make them. I have tried a few times, especially when I was at the temp agency. I met lots of people.

I met a girl, Kim, who is nice. We have done things together, gone to Seaside and had dinner. She has a baby from a rape. She is a very religious girl and has a very religious boyfriend. But Kim is so shy and withdrawn. Yeah, I know, like I'm not. However, she was raped twice within a year. Both by complete strangers. The first time was a man who pulled her off the street and raped her in the bushes. The second time (only months later), was a plumber who came by to fix her sink. By some strange coincidence, a plumber came up to her house and she let him in. It turned out that he wasn't with the company that she called. They claimed not know who this man was, but she is sure they are covering up for him. He may have been a freelancer for their company or something Kim said, because the police didn't find a man fitting his description at the plumbing business. Kim became pregnant from this second rape, unfortunately. She was a virgin for the first rape. That is the worse thing that I have ever heard. You can tell that she has been victimized because she doesn't look people in the eye, she looks at her feet.

Kim keeps pressuring me to join her church. I went once to get her to leave me alone but it was a day when they had that wafer thing, even though it was supposed to be a modern church. I don't like being pressured by her and her boyfriend to attend church. I don't want to go. Plus, it is so depressing hanging out with Kim because she talks about the rapes quite often, especially since she has a child by the rapist. One thing about Kim is that she has the bluest eyes that I have ever seen. They are so vivid and clear and beautiful, it is incredible. She is a very kind person. We just don't have much in common. Her little girl is so cute and has the same blue eyes. Kim does love her baby very much. I don't really want to do things with her any more. She is too church oriented. We'll see.

JUNE 10, 1988

I'm tired of living in loneliness. I've decided to move to Florida and live with my Uncle John, make a clean, fresh start to my life. I called James and said that I could still move down to Los Angelos instead of Tallahassee, but he said that Tallahassee would be better for me. That is pretty obvious he doesn't want me near him. James talked about how we would both be competing for the warmer climate now. I asked again about the money he owed me, and James told me to meet him at the pizza place near his family's house in eastern Oregon. He gave me some vague directions, but I called information and got the address. James said that he would meet me at the restaurant to see me one last time and pay me the money that he owed me. My heart leapt into my throat from the thrill of seeing him again. We scheduled a day and time, so I was sure to be there.

I arrived at Shakey's Pizza slightly before the time we were supposed to meet. I ordered a diet Coke and waited, and waited. I played some Pac-man and waited. James was over an hour and a half late, so I began to get suspicious. I was afraid he wouldn't show up and it happened. I drove the few blocks over to his family's house, because I remembered how we walked from that house to Shakey's Pizza before. I drove up and down each block until I found the house. I was sure it was the right one. The lights were off and no cars were in the driveway. My heart sank yet again. I knocked on the door for at least ten minutes. I know how desperate that sounds. I was aware of my great humiliation. The money wasn't what was bothering me, it was being purposely avoided by James.

I went back to my truck, found a piece of paper and pencil and wrote a heartfelt note to James, telling him how much I loved him and how sorry I was that I missed him. I even humbled myself by saying that he may have forgotten the day and time, but I know I was only fooling myself. He never meant to meet up with me. He was probably surprised when I actually found their home and left a note. I asked him to call me in a week at John's house. I wrote down the phone number. I doubt if he will call me. I sat in my truck for another half hour or more, I even drove by Shakey's Pizza again, but he still wasn't there. I finally left. I secretly wanted James to say, "don't go, please move in with me in Los Angelos." I would have done it in a heartbeat. I never got his address, so I couldn't drive down there and look for him. James could live anywhere. I knew then that he doesn't love me, Brian tainted his mind with lies about me. I wish I would have slapped the shit out of Brian and went straight to James instead of lingering in the bathroom, kissing Brian because I felt that I had to, but did not have sex with him.

He tried to force me, but I got away. I wish I could go back to that night and change everything.

JUNE 12, 1988

I am going to drive across country tomorrow morning. I am going with Keelie Megan Maskrey, my little black fluffy kitten. I got her a couple of months ago from the Vancouver Humane Society. They had one black kitten left. I wanted that kitten and there was a little kid who wanted her, too. I said I would pay for her right away. It was $25. That included all of her shots and a discount when I get her spayed.

I sold all my furniture and kept only my bed and my scrap books and stuff. I had to sell my bike to get as much money as possible. I even had to sell my piano, which was the hardest thing to do. I rented a small U-Haul trailer and have a little over $300 left to travel across country. It will be very tight, because I have to pay for the motel out of this money. I don't have any credit cards because my credit history is so bad. Plus, I can't really afford one.

I am going to stay in Motel 6 all the way across America. I will spend the first night in Salt Lake City, Utah, which is the longest part of the trip at over 800 miles. The second night Denver, Colorado. The third night I will stay in Kansas City, Missouri. The fourth night Nashville, Tennessee so I can visit Graceland. The fifth night I will be in Tallahassee. Me and Keelie driving across the United States.

Since I have AAA again, I had them do a TripTik for me. They gave me lots of maps. I am going to go along the old highways, the way that truckers go because the roads don't go through many towns. I am not driving on any freeways if I can help it. I want to see the country and have less traffic. That will be so beautiful.

I learned to change the air filter on my Toyota truck and tried to change the oil, but messed up because I wasn't strong enough to unscrew a bolt. Then when I did, I got oil all over my face. Last time I try that. Luckily, Mike changed the oil for me. That was embarrassing.

Tonight I am staying with Clara and Mike in Portland before leaving on my big adventure. Keelie is pretty freaked out and hissed at Clara. I think she is just scared. She is a nice kitten. So cute, too.

There are so many people I haven't even told that I'm moving. I really don't have many friends, just people I know. I figure they won't notice the difference. I hate saying good-byes because I had to do it as a child. We moved so much, now I want to move. I want to be where it is warm and sunny and swim in the Gulf of Mexico. I am so excited!

I did something impulsive two nights ago. I was given some crank by a drug dealer lady I know when she was out of weed. Well, I called up Larry, Katie's ex, for some reason, and asked if he wanted to hang out. He said yes. I went over there and his friend, Paul, who Katie said has always liked me, was there. Larry didn't like doing crank, he liked coke better (who doesn't) and went over to a girl's house. I was left with his roommate, Paul. We talked for hours and stayed up so late. He really is a nice guy. He is one year younger than me. We made love and then I left, telling him I would visit him at work before I left town. Yesterday, I went to his work (a men's clothing store) and Paul was really bummed out. He didn't think that I was really moving to Tallahassee so soon. He thought that I was just talking. Then, Paul got really cold and I said good-bye. I feel really bad about it because he did like me after all. I don't know why I blew him off before. I don't think he has had sex often and he took it as being more of a relationship. What an idiot I am. I could have had a boyfriend the whole time. I've been used for sex so many times, I know it hurts. I wish I didn't do that.

I had better try and sleep. It is very difficult since I am so excited. I leave at 7:00 am. My friend, Aaron, who use to work at the typewriter and computer repair shop, is coming by at 6:30 am to hopefully bring me some pot for the trip. I will miss Portland though. I cried when I left downtown yesterday. It is such a beautiful city on the river. I really do love this city.

Well, good night. I must try and sleep.

Amendment: Something really weird happened this morning. I woke up around 4:00 am with a feeling of dread. I don't know what it was, but I felt like something was wrong. I ran outside in my pajamas to check on my truck and trailer and saw the driver's side door open (on the opposite side of the truck). I saw a dark figure crouched down. I was so scared of losing everything that I ran over to the burglar and told him to get away from my truck. Luckily, he ran off and didn't have a gun. I went over to the driver's side and I could still smell the sweat from the burglar. The steering column had been removed, well, the plastic part, and the wires were exposed and ready to hot-wire. Not that I know how to hot-wire a car. Anyway, the burglar also left his lock picking tools on the seat. I took them inside and can't sleep now so I got ready for my drive.

That was so close. I almost was completely devastated. I don't have car insurance on my truck or U-Haul. If he took the truck with the trailer attached, I would have nothing left, completely destitute. I don't know what I would have done. I never want to move in with my drunken parents again. A very close call. It was strange how I was psychic about the theft. Just seconds to spare. Whew!

Aaron came by early but had no pot. That was kind of a downer. He wanted the theft tools, so I gave them to him. Why not? I'm not going to steal a car. I don't think he would either, but who knows. Time to go!

JUNE 13, 1988

I saw so many beautiful sights into Salt Lake city. The city was like a dream when I arrived, although it was the longest leg of my journey at 758 miles! I was exhausted mentally and physically. There weren't many other cities to stay and I thought that distance would be fine. It wasn't. It was horrible.

When I finally arrived in the Mormon city, the sun was setting and the sky was a wonderful orange and pink.

I could see water evaporating from the lake into the sky. It was amazingly gorgeous! A beautiful haze hung over the city. It was one of the most perfect places that I have ever seen. There were white houses with white picket fences everywhere, with perfectly square parcels of land with the greenest grass I've ever seen.

It turned out that Salt Lake City was having a Mormon celebration. I stayed right across from the Mormon Tabernacle and they had music and rang their bells well into the night. A guy about my age knocked on my motel door. I was very cautious when I opened it. He asked if I wanted to come out and dance and watch the fireworks. I was so exhausted I just couldn't. I was sick to my stomach I was so tired. It was nice of him, though.

When I left the city, the east side was as ugly as the west was beautiful. The southeast side of Salt Lake city had these ugly mines, dirt piles everywhere, machinery, and just ugliness. It was kind of a let down after the beauty of the city.

I used the AAA TripTik, which worked like a charm. County roads the whole way. The country is so gorgeous, I wish I had a camera to take pictures. It's like a dream. I brought only V-8 juice, bananas and water so I'm starving. I got some chips from the vending machine at the Motel 6. It's clean, and I snuck in Keelie in her kitty litter box which has the cover. She was so excited to be out of the hot truck she bounced back and forth between the two beds. It was adorable. I got her food and fresh water, which she finally ate and drank. I was a bit worried because Keelie didn't eat or drink water the entire drive. I tried giving her water from my cup.

Keelie wears an elastic collar and I bought a red suede leash which I can attach to the stick shift when I run in to pay for gas or use the bathroom. I am driving such a rural route with the truckers, there are hardly any towns so I am sure to fill up with gas at each town. I don't have much money, only $300 to start. $19 for Motel 6, and gas is a bit expensive. I'm not buying food to save money. I buy bags of ice and drink the melted water, it's so hot with the drought. The Toyota doesn't have air conditioning, so I roll down the windows and open the back sliding windows to get air circulation. It works since I drive in my bikini top and cut off shorts. The truckers honk at me when they pass. I drive between the truckers to stay away from police. I can speed with them.

JUNE 14, 1988

On the second day of my travel, a scary thing happened. Keelie got really hot in the Midwest but wouldn't drink anymore. She stopped eating, too. I was getting really worried.

When we were driving through Kansas, I checked Keelie and she was as limp as a doll. I thought that she was dead. She didn't move at all in my hand. I didn't even pull over (no car was within sight for miles in the flatlands), grabbed Keelie and dunked her right in my glass of ice water. I put her in up to her head. She woke up then. She started drinking the water finally.

After that, while we were in the midwest, I kept Keelie cool by dunking her in the water once in a while. She was happy about that. She started purring. She was too hot. It is the only time that a cat liked to be put in water. I had to get another cup out of the back since my drinking cup was now full of cat hair! I almost lost little Keelie. I am so happy that I didn't.

Another thing happened in Kansas City. I couldn't find the Motel 6. I stopped and got directions, but the person who answered gave really vague directions. I drove around and around in the city. I kept going over this stupid toll bridge. I don't know how I did it. I ended up going over it 3 times.

I was so tired that I stopped at another motel. They were booked up. They told me that all hotels would be booked up because Bruce Springsteen was in town. It was a sold out show and nothing was available. Great. Probably part of the same tour I went to in Tacoma. I was exhausted and started crying. I decided to continue on my journey out of Kansas City. I ended up taking the wrong County Road, so I pulled over again and looked at the map. Luckily, I wasn't very far off course. I got back on the highway that I was supposed to be on and stopped at the first hotel or motel I saw. When I went inside, it was some kind of adult hotel. You have to be 21 to get in. Plus, it was very expensive at $100 a night! I could never afford that, anyway. I asked if there was a Motel 6 nearby and he said there was if I keep going East on the highway.

Eventually I found a Motel 6 not far from that strange adult hotel. The next morning, I noticed the wire connecting my tail lights to the trailer tail lights was completely frayed through. It had been dragging on the ground and I have been driving for I don't know how long without any tail lights, brake lights, turn signals, nothing for the trailer. That is very dangerous! I couldn't do anything about then, so I took my chances. I was worried though because I didn't pay for my car insurance so I wasn't even insured.

I hadn't seen very much on the way to Kansas City except for a couple weird attractions. Like the world's largest ball of yarn or conjoined calves in jars. It is rather strange. Another night, counting every dollar. It will be close. Gas is the most expensive. I stopped speeding to save gas, hence, money. It should help. Plus my trailer has no tail lights! If I see a U-Haul rental office, I'll ask for some help. I'm sure I'll see one soon. I think the heat is making me tired. It's strange that driving can make you so sleepy. It feels like I ran all the way to Kansas City, as tired as I feel. Keelie and I are going to sleep now.

JUNE 15, 1988

The mountainous route to Denver was the shortest drive of the trip. It was still early in the evening and I had time to drive around the city for a bit before checking in to the Motel 6. I didn't have money to go anywhere, so I decided to relax in the motel room with Keelie for the evening. I splurged on a bag of Cheetos from the vending machine. I still am stocked with V-8 and water.

I passed by a U-Haul store, stopped, and they fixed my shorted out wire. I now have brake lights and turn signals on the U-Haul trailer. They fixed the wire for free. I was hugely relieved. I don't have to worry about someone rear ending me at night or getting a ticket from a cop.

JUNE 16, 1988

Nashville was a complete disaster! I thought Graceland was in Nashville but only the Grand Old Opry makes its home in Nashville. The lady at the Motel 6 laughed her ass off and said that everyone knows that Graceland is in Memphis. Had I known, I would have gone to Memphis. Now it's too far out of my way and I'll run out of gas money. I don't want to go to some country music venue. I am so disappointed. Early to bed for Keelie and me.

It was a hot drive in the south. I don't have air conditioning and the air is heavy with moisture from the frequent heavy rain showers. There have been some downpours that make visibility to the end of my hood. I've been drinking a lot of water.

I had an encounter with an asshole in Illinois. It was a small town, the type with one flashing yellow light. I stopped at the only gas station. I had gotten traveler's checks for the trip, so I went inside to pay with one. The hick said he never saw one before and wanted real money. I had to explain to him five times that it is real money. I got them through AAA so if my money is stolen, it's insured and will be reimbursed. As I was arguing with him, a man came in and calmly told me that I had a cat hanging out of my window. I ran outside and poor Keelie was hanging from her leash attached to the stick shift. She was still as could be and slowly twirling. Luckily, her collar was elastic so there was no harm.

The man who argued about the traveler's checks said that I was in bad need of new tires. I'm not a complete idiot and had enough cars to know when something is wrong. I asked him to show me the bare tires. I know if you put a penny in the tread and can see Lincoln's head, you're okay. Well, I pulled out a penny and showed the jerk that my tires were new and in perfect condition. I told him he should be ashamed to try and rip me off. The other man who told me about my twirling cat laughed at my comments. I said I didn't have time to argue about the traveler's checks and was leaving. Goodbye small town in Illinois.

In Kansas, I saw an actual roadrunner! I "meeped" at him as he ran along the road next to me. I slowed down to see the beautiful bird up close. He was a fast little runner. Look out! The coyote's after you!

JUNE 17, 1988

I'm in Florida! What a trip. I only had less than $20 left by the time I got to Tallahassee. That is cutting it very close.

I tell you, I never saw a police officer until I got to Georgia. From Georgia through to Tallahassee I counted 14 of them! Plus, it was pouring down rain the entire time through Georgia to Tallahassee. It started raining almost as soon as I crossed the state line.

It was exciting hearing the crickets singing so loudly. We don't have that in Washington state, not like in the South.

By the time I got to Tallahassee, I was so tired. But Uncle John had his friends over for a little party celebrating my arrival. Kyle was there (his good looking friend I had met before), Sam, Kyle's girlfriend, Jan and her friend Paige, Paige's boyfriend Keith and his brother George (I think George is a little slow). They helped me bring in the boxes. Everyone helped so it didn't take long. I was thankful for that.

The trailer park has really become a dump. Complete white trash live there now, not the sweet retirement community it once was. There are raggedy children running around barefoot everywhere, dogs not on leashes, and abandoned cars in most of the yards. Hardly anyone keeps up their yard or cuts their grass. It wasn't like that when Gammy bought her single wide trailer, it was a retirement community. Not anymore. I was really taken aback by the condition of the trailer and the white trash neighbors. It will be cheap to stay with John, though. It is nice to have someplace to live.

I really need to find a job soon. My truck payment is a month past due. I have only $20.

AUGUST 12, 1988

I finally got a job. My truck is 3 months past due, which is terrible because I feel such guilt. I really want to pay it, I just don't have any money. Neither does John. He barely makes ends meet himself.

Kyle used a connection of his mom's to get me a bookkeeping job and microfilm processor. I have had experience in both areas so it is perfect. The company is McKenzie Tank Lines, Inc. I started a few days ago. Another trucking company. That was the last job I had before moving to Tallahassee. My boss asked for a urine test, two weeks after being hired. I smoked pot last weekend with John and Kyle, plus I did some cocaine. I am sure the coke is out of my system, but the pot probably isn't. I only have 2 days until they test me. I am really terrified the test will come back negative. I was told that poppy seed muffins can altar the readings. I don't know if that is true. I will drink a lot of water. I should have been more responsible and not smoked pot. I knew the drug test was coming up.

The job is good, though. I really hope I can keep it with the upcoming drug test. One thing really strange happened. A woman at work gave me a piece of candy. Someone in the office who I didn't know, but I had seen her around. I accepted it. Within minutes of it, I was so sick I barely made it to the toilet in time. I began sweating heavily and dry heaving. I was so weak and sick that I couldn't stand. I could only crawl. I was hoping that someone would come into the bathroom soon.

Finally someone came into the rest room looking for me. I was on the floor, still dry heaving. She told me to go home. I had to be assisted to my truck. On the way home, I was so dizzy and sick that I had to throw up out the door of my truck. I hadn't eaten anything that day. It had to be the candy.

I asked around work about the candy, where they got it, but the woman who gave it to me said that she bought it at the convenience store a block away and she had some and she never got sick. I was very suspicious about the whole situation. I know that the person before me was fired. Could it have been a revenge poisoning by that woman? I was fine the next day.

I won't get my first paycheck for weeks, so I called my parents and asked if they could loan me $350 to pay for 2 of the 3 months for the back due payments on my truck. Mom said that she didn't have the money and made me ask Jim myself. I told him that my truck was going to be repossessed if I didn't make the payments. I explained that I got a job and the paycheck will come in a few weeks. I said that I could start paying them back when I got regular income. Jim said he wouldn't help me. I was devastated. I asked him why he wouldn't help. I couldn't stop crying. I finally have a vehicle that is dependable, I really have to try and keep it, especially since I live way out in Perry, Florida, which is outside of Tallahassee. Jim said that he wanted to teach me a lesson. I was so disgusted. I said that if I didn't have a car I couldn't get to work. There is no public transportation in the country. He just didn't care. He is so cold and heartless.

I will get my nerve up to call the loan company and see if I can work out a deal. They don't know where I live right now. I haven't received any mail from them and didn't put in a forwarding address. I am not trying to dodge them and I want to tell them the truth. I am scared to call. They may not let me make arrangements and take the truck. Then where would I be?

On a good note, Kyle has been spending a lot of time over at our trailer. He'll spend the night on the couch and sneak back into my room and we make love. He is so incredibly handsome and drives me crazy. Maybe he'll leave Jan. Of course his mom and dad love Jan, his high school sweetheart. Jan seems to sense something because she and Paige stopped being nice to me and talk about me so I can hear them. It is such petty behavior.

Kyle's family owns a country clothing and boot store in Tallahassee. He runs the store now that his father is semi-retired. I go by and visit Kyle at work quite often since it's on my way home from work. I love hanging out with him and talking. I got him a Carl Sagan book for his birthday because he mentioned that he was interested in him. Kyle seemed to really like it. Of course, I can't stop by now very often now that I work full-time and Jan is often at the store after she gets off work, so we had to put an end to that rendezvous. That's kind of sad.

That girl, Kim, from Portland tracked me down. She is the girl with the very blue eyes and really religious. She has left a few messages with my other roommate, Sam, and on the answering machine. How in the world did she find out where I moved? I have no idea since the phone isn't in Uncle John's name. It is so weird. I haven't had the heart to call her back. I don't know why, I just don't want to call her. I probably will never see her again and I didn't say goodbye to her so she might be mad at me. It gets too painful to always say goodbye. Sam says I should call her since she sounds nice. I am not so sure.

Wish me luck on the drug test!

SEPTEMBER 4, 1988

I failed the drug test after almost a month of positive work experience. Kyle is furious since he got me the job through his mom's friend. I knew the drug test was coming and shouldn't have gotten high. The manager was sorry to see me go since I had been working very hard and doing a great job.

On top of that, I tried to do the honest thing and called the loan people on my Toyota truck. I told them I was going to get a paycheck in a couple of weeks (this was before I found out about the drug test result) and wasn't purposely stealing the truck. I begged for them to let me pay extra each month to catch everything up. The man I talked to said that should be fine, but he had to talk to his manager. Then, he asked me for my current address. I hesitated, but gave it to him. What a mistake! The next morning, a man came to repossess the truck! I ran out there, thinking perhaps it was a thief. The man stopped quite a distance from me. He asked me to stop running and to stand still and asked me if I was armed. Of course I wasn't. I know it is a white trash neighborhood, but I would never hurt anyone.

He let me approach the truck as he got out his gun. He told me that I could clear out the truck before he took it. I didn't want to, because I wanted to get the truck back. I took a few things and grabbed the miniature baseball bat that James gave me. I didn't even think about that as being a weapon, but as soon as I got it, the repo man jumped backwards and pointed his gun at me. It really freaked me out. I said that I wasn't going to hit him. Just take the truck and leave. It was horrible.

When I did get paid at my former employer (I did, after all, have almost a full month of full-time employment) I had a couple hundred dollars left over after catching up with John's bills (not enough to get my truck out of hock). I had to let my truck go and bought this crappy baby blue Pinto from one of George's friends. I was warned that it wasn't very good. It didn't have power steering, the brakes didn't work too well, and it burned a lot of oil. It was all I could afford.

He told me it burned some oil. Ha! It goes through a quart a day. Every time I drive the car, it burns up a quart of oil, spewing black smoke behind me. I feel terrible for the environment and ozone. More guilt. What can I do? I am searching for a job. I can't really go to a temp agency because my transportation isn't dependable enough.

I have to buy oil by the case now. I went into the auto parts store and grabbed an entire case of oil. The man behind the counter laughed and asked me if I was a mechanic. I answered no and told him about my Pinto. He looked like he felt sorry for me. I was humiliated and very embarrassed. I quickly paid for the mass amount of oil and got out of there. If only I still had my truck, I wouldn't have a problem like this. The Pinto won't last forever. It is barely driving now. I feel so useless. I just can't ever do anything right. Every time I try something, I fail. I am so tired of this.

SEPTEMBER 6, 1988

Uncle John pressured me into getting a temp position. I will do office work when it comes available. I went in to their office yesterday and filled out my application. I already got a job. What excellent luck, too. The job is just a few miles from our trailer. It is across from Lake Jackson. I won't have to drive far in my Pinto. The job is very boring. I have to assign a microfilm number and folder for old documents. Not very intellectual. There is another girl about my age who is also a temp. She talks a lot. I feel guilty talking so much during work hours. I need to do my job. She doesn't care at all about her job. Her name is Liz. She wears a black mini-skirt to work and talks about her boyfriend who is a guitarist in a band. Liz has already asked me to go listen to his band. That will be cool. I told her I would.

SEPTEMBER 11, 1988

Wow. What a crazy two nights. Earlier in the week, while at work, Liz asked if I wanted to smoke some weed at lunch time. I told her it wasn't appropriate at work, but she said how good the quality of the weed is the best, so I caved in. We drove to a nearby park, sat in the car and smoked a joint.

Liz easily talked me into seeing her boyfriend's band at some bar, I can't remember the name. She said that she would drive if I drove over to her apartment. I did just that. We smoked a lot of pot and drank beer before the show. I wore my black mini-skirt, and so did Liz.

We stayed at the bar until closing. I wanted to go home earlier, but Liz bought me some beer, then more beer, so I drank it. The more I drank, the more fun I was having. I danced at the front of the stage with Liz and a strange blond-haired boy, a friend of Liz's boyfriend. I think his name is Kyle, or Kurt. Yeah, Kurt. His hair was a little longer than most, and cut like Kurt Cobain. Liz said it was the guy from Nirvana. I don't know what the dude from Nirvana looks like, but I guess Kurt is trying to be him. She warned me that he is psycho and her boyfriend doesn't really like him but hangs around because he always has weed. Kurt danced next to me, but I was looking at the hot guitarist from the band (not Liz's boyfriend, but another guitarist). His name is Jay. Kurt kept forcing his way between me and Jay, but Jay told him to get lost.

I don't know how it happened, but I have some fleeting memories of having sex with Jay and the next thing I can remember is waking up wearing men's underwear. I had put his on by mistake. I couldn't find my underwear, but there were other people in the apartment. One of which was Kurt, who didn't actually live with Jay, but came over. I thought it was kind of strange.

I was without transportation so I wanted to hang out. Jay told me not to get mad, but he has a girlfriend. This girlfriend will be coming over for the party he was having that night and asked that I be cool about it. I was still trying to get my bearings and remember how I got there when I am told, basically, don't touch me. Jay then said that I could hang out and stay for the party, but if I told his girlfriend then I'd have to go home. I agreed. I wasn't sure what to do. I didn't have a ride right away so I decided to stay all day until the party. Maybe some drugs and alcohol will come my way. What the fuck, it is better than being alone.

Kurt offered me a ride home but I wanted to stay for the party, and if I went home, I probably wouldn't find this place again. For the entire day, I sat on the couch and stared at the television as people came and went. Kurt sat next to me and tried to put his arm around me, but I asked him not to do that. Kurt said that it was shitty what Jay did to me. Yeah. I didn't want to talk about it.

Finally, the party started and Kurt made shroom tea but wouldn't give me any. He said that it was too dangerous. Whatever. I've had it a few times. I kept trying to get some and he gave me a tiny cup with some in it. It made me angry the way that Kurt was trying to manipulate everything I did, everything I drank and didn't want me to smoke weed. He was the one with the drugs and was sharing it with everyone else, but was trying to "protect" me, he said. I snuck some more shroom tea, which made the night magical.

I still sat on the couch for most of the night. Jay was talking to Kurt about me. I pretended to watch television but I heard them. Jay asked if I was going to be cool about his girlfriend and not freak out or anything. Kurt said he would keep an eye on me. Gee, thanks. I stayed at the party almost for spite. When Jay's girlfriend finally showed up, she was hugging on him. I couldn't look. I saw Jay look my way a few times, worried that I would do something crazy. I didn't. A promise is a promise. I guess that is why they wouldn't give me much to drink or smoke. I felt humiliated. I was just some slut. I had some stupid idea that Jay would tell his girlfriend to go home, that he wanted to hang with me instead. What was I thinking? That never was going to happen. I can convince myself, I can fool myself to believe that people care about me more than they do. I was an object, a thing, not a possible girlfriend. Jay spoke to me throughout the night and was nice enough, so I couldn't get really mad. I didn't talk much that night. I was a dark shadow on the couch.

Finally Liz showed up. She didn't live very far away and I asked if she would drive me to my car, which was still at her apartment. She agreed. I didn't talk much to her, either. Later today, Liz called to ask why I slept with Kurt since he is really creepy. I told her, no, it was Jay. She thought that was cool. I told her Kurt kept sitting next to me and hitting on me but I wasn't interested in him. Kurt talked about me with Liz after I left as if he and I were going to see each other. What a liar. I don't know why he said I was his girlfriend to people. That is really strange.

I don't know how to feel about this weekend. I had fun some of the time. Now I feel like I was seen as some sort of hanger-on, another loser like Kurt. What a stupid freak I am. I stayed at that apartment all day for some stupid party at night. I barely spoke to anyone, felt rejected and depressed but wouldn't leave. Jay is a nice person and really good looking but he isn't interested in me. I have to forget about him. I don't think I'll see the band play again. I'll just be that loser girl who gets too drunk.

OCTOBER 9, 1988

The last two weekends I went to the same bar where Jay's band played. I haven't seen him. I told John that I was going to Liz's apartment. I haven't spoken to her since the party. I don't know what I am really looking for at this bar. I sat at the end of the bar, in the darkest place and tried to order a drink. I wasn't carded so I bought another two drinks from the same bartender. He was kind of cute. I didn't have much money so I couldn't drink much. The bartender's name was Brian and asked if I wanted to wait until he got off at closing and do something. I didn't have anywhere to go or any money to do it with so I had to say no, but that I wanted to stay. I said that I felt a bit drunk and was afraid to drive home (actually, I barely had a buzz by 1:00 am). Brian said that he would drive me home, even though I lived in Perry. The bar he worked at was on the west side of town, so it wasn't too far, but probably 6 or 7 miles one way. I waited and waited, getting more sober as time went on. Was this a good idea? What am I doing?

Finally, at 2:15 am, Brian drove me home, leaving my blue Pinto stranded in the darkness. He said it really was far in the country, and didn't realize it would be such a long drive. I explained to him that I lived with my uncle in a dumpy trailer and it would be too awkward for him to come in (Kyle would probably be sleeping on the couch anyway).

We finally got to the trailer and Brian looked around a bit nervously. I had already given him my phone number. Maybe I shouldn't have let him see the dump I live in. I didn't even think about the Pinto and living in a trailer park full of white trash. I hope he calls, but I didn't get his number. Brian seemed so nice, too, wanted to go on a real date. He saw the dump where I call home and was freaked out by it, I know he was. I saw it in his face. What a fuck-up! And my car is still at the bar! John drove me to get it in the morning. He was cool with that. I hope Brian calls me.

OCTOBER 17, 1988

I was shocked and amazed that Brian called me last Thursday and asked me to dinner. I said I could meet him somewhere, but he said he would pick me up. That was so sweet of him. We went to dinner at Barnacle Bill's, a seafood place that was very casual but had great seafood. Through dinner, I was mostly quiet. Talking is the part that gets me every time. I don't know how to keep a conversation going. I can never think of anything to say. Whenever Brian asked me a question, I answered quickly instead of taking the time to really talk to him. We didn't drink there, or at least I didn't drink at the restaurant because Brian knew that I was underage and didn't want anyone getting in trouble for serving a minor.

After a mostly silent dinner (on my part because I never know how to do small talk), we went to Brian's apartment where he made some delicious cocktails. There were some vodka drinks that were very good. We did a bit of kissing, he seemed to be old-fashioned and wanted to take it slowly. That was fine. I just wish I wasn't so damn boring. I drank the drinks a bit too fast and Brian wouldn't make any more for a while. We had a good time listening to music, but I feel like I have absolutely no personality without alcohol. I am bland and feel separated from my body, no emotion or excitement, no feelings. I am always hoping that sex will lead to a relationship, but I am afraid I have it backward.

Well, Brian and I didn't have sex, but he let me sleep in his bed while he slept on the couch. He asked if that was alright since he had too much to drink to drive 14 miles one way. That was fine. I was hoping he'd sleep with me, but he didn't. If I could learn to do small talk, I would have friends and boyfriends. People get bored with me, thinking that I am a flat, featureless creature with no emotion and don't want to see me anymore. I have so much inside me, I don't know how to let it out. It only comes out with alcohol, but I drink too much too fast and do things I regret, or worst still, I black out and don't remember what I've done and who I have been with.

Brian drove me back home the next morning and was still being nice to me. I think it is an illusion. I don't have his number still. Brian said he would call me.

OCTOBER 21, 1988

I went to Brian's bar since I haven't heard from him. I waited a while because I didn't see him. They wouldn't serve me so I had a diet Coke. Finally Brian came by, carrying a case of bottles, restocking the bars. He said that he was busy that night and he would call me soon. Brian said he didn't have time to hang out with me. He did seem busy, but I'm not sure. I convinced him for one drink, which I got, but he said that would be it or he might get in trouble.

I drank that one drink and waited, hoping Brian would stay and talk to me. He came by, smiled and said hello, but he was still too busy, so I left. I should have said goodbye. I usually forget to say goodbye to people. My way is sneaking out when no one is looking. I have said too many goodbyes in my lifetime, I don't want to do it again. That is why I couldn't talk to Kim. I don't want that fading long-distance friendship, where the letters come less frequently until it fizzles away. It is best this way. Less pain to secretly leave. Brian probably won't call me again. I looked desperate. I'll just have to wait and see. I won't go to his bar anymore unless he calls me. I never saw Jay or that freak Kurt there again. I was relieved. I didn't want Brian seeing me with them.

I didn't mention that Kurt happened to run into me at Winn Dixie. I found that difficult to believe since he lived on the other side of town and my Winn Dixie would be out of his way. He followed me around while I did some grocery shopping. He offered to carry my groceries to my car, but I respectfully declined, saying I had to go. Kurt stood there watching me as I drove away. I don't know what type of car he drives. I've never seen him with a car. Did he take the bus all the way to run into me? I think he's stalking me since I've run into him more than once. I hope he is harmless.

OCTOBER 30, 1988

I finally got a permanent job after scouring the want-ads every Sunday. I work for Employee Benefits Management as a customer service representative on an 800 number. I answer questions about people's tax-free insurance benefits. There is so much to learn, I've been reading through insurance plans when I'm not on the phone. I am still in their formal training program so I am not on the phone all day yet. I answer calls for one to two hours a day, in order to get a handle on the job and the type of questions thrown at me. It is an incredible opportunity with a lot of young people who go to college during the day and work part-time at night in customer service. The phones are open 7:00 am to 11:00 pm and the boss is very flexible with hours since they need people throughout the day and evening. My boss is actually the daughter of one of the owner's of the company. Her name is Sylvia is fairly young and inexperienced as a supervisor, which she readily admits. I feel quite comfortable with her and am thrilled to have a flexible job with people my age. Since they are a benefits management company for school districts throughout the state of Florida, I am receiving excellent benefits with a matching 401k savings plan. My head is spinning. So much to learn. Also, no drug testing. What a relief.

I am keeping my fingers crossed that my oil-burning Pinto keeps going. Luckily, the company is on the side of town where I live, even though it is ten or eleven miles away. My uncle and I live in a trailer court smack in the middle of nowhere. Country. Nights so black outside you can't see your hand in front of your face if the moon isn't out. Crickets and bullfrogs blaring in hi-fidelity all night. It is soothing to me, somehow, even though the noise of nature is quite loud. It takes away from the stress of debts and car problems.

The company is having a Halloween costume party at the boss' house tomorrow night, to which I am invited. I am so excited! I still have my French maid costume, with the short black dress, frilly white apron, white doily for my head, long white gloves, fishnet stockings, and the feather duster I had from Portland. That should make a statement. I've been jogging in this white trash neighborhood and am in pretty good shape. I am supposed to bring some side dish, and after racking my brain for what to make, I decided on my homemade macaroni and cheese. That is the best thing I can cook, other than clam chowder. I am a little worried about keeping it warm enough to still taste good. I can use their microwave to heat it up. I can't wait!

I was hoping Brian would call so I could invite him to the party, but I never heard from him. I know I bored him to death, like most of the people I meet. I freeze up and don't know what to talk about, and end up sitting there quietly until I get bold enough to kiss the guy because I don't know how else to make men like me. My junior prom in high school was a silent nightmare. My friends were talking away, laughing, having fun while I sat in the car, looking beautiful in my black and white evening gown, but too scared to say a word. When I do speak, it is usually too soft for anyone to hear, so they talk right over me, like an invisible steam roller pressing me back down into shy despair. What a horrible bore I was! I didn't even dance with Maria in front of the headlights with her. She kept calling me out from the car to dance, but I sat in the front seat like a mannequin, afraid to move or speak, and too frightened to dance in front of everyone. I really needed to be taught how to communicate with people by my parents, but they left me alone so often that I never quite learned the art of small talk. Or any talk, for that matter, unless it hits upon something I'm interested about. Other than that, dull as dishwater dingbat. I hate myself for being so shy and terrified around people.

On another depressing down note, the girlfriends of Kyle and Todd are treating me like a leper. I've been told I flirt with men. Jan and Paige stopped coming to the trailer to visit. I believe they've told their boyfriends not to come over anymore because we get less visits. I can tell by Jan and Paige's looks that they can't stand me and talk very poorly about me, whispering and giggling across the room, quick glances at me and back to their whispers and giggling. It is as obvious I have become an outcast. That was not my intension when I first arrived here. I truly wanted friends. I fucked it up by continuing to have sex with Kyle late at night when everyone else is asleep. Kyle quietly creeps into my room and silently makes love to me, covering my mouth when I reach a climax so no one else will hear. I suppose Jan has her suspicions, but no real proof other than Kyle wanting to spend the night at the trailer. They are engaged but I've always secretly hoped he would leave Jan for me.

It really turned ugly after a humiliatingly stupid incident just after I lost my McKenzie Trucking job. I am so embarrassed still, that I am having a difficult time writing down the evening's events. There was a bonfire party on the property of Paige's parents. They had a keg of beer and plenty of food for the taking. Of course, like the idiot I am, I don't eat much around people because I don't want to get fat. On top of that, I drink faster when I'm in a crowd since I am so painfully shy. My plan was, as always, to relax with a few drinks then coast the rest of the night with witty conversation and popularity. Like that has ever happened. In my mind I see it could happen but it never does.

Well, I relaxed a bit too much. I probably should eat food when I drink alcohol, because I starved myself all that day to look thin. I blacked out, again, and only remember the first couple of hours. After that, I was an embarrassing mess. John told me all about how I hung on Kyle and Todd, making Jan and Paige quite upset with me. I was horrified to hear that Paige asked John to take me home, that I wasn't welcome at their party. John must have told me to leave the group because he didn't take me home. After some time, I crawled into what I thought was John's truck. It turned out to be Todd's truck (they both are blue). Todd noticed someone in his truck (me) and came over to open the passenger door. With perfect timing, as he opened the door, I spewed vomit right between his legs, onto the ground. Todd was able to jump back out of the way of my vomit before any of it got on him. By dumb luck I didn't throw up in Todd's truck. John said Todd carried me to his truck and laid me down. I was so humiliated while John recounted the story, I wanted to shrink into the cracks of the sofa. I can't believe Todd was able to carry me! I weigh too much and must have been so heavy. I only remember waking up in the trailer, in my bed, with dried vomit on my shirt. I knew something terrible had happened – again.

Why do I keep repeating the same horrid cycle? During my drunkenness, I drive people away from me by acting like the party drunk. Now, Paige and Jan make a point of shunning me. I know it is my fault, though. I really hate myself when I act stupid and embarrassing. I really hate blacking out because it scares me so much. Sometimes I actually drive home and think to myself I could have killed someone, run over a pedestrian so easily and I wouldn't remember. After every blackout, I always discover that I have made a complete fool of myself in front of everyone. I kiss and hang on guys, even if their girlfriends are around. I hate myself when I act like a tramp.

I definitely won't be drinking much at the Halloween party tomorrow night. One drink and some food. I just got the job which will save me from utter destitution, I don't need to show everyone how much of an idiot I am.

Well, I am going to bed now. Only John's male friends like me now. What a loser.

NOVEMBER 1, 1988

The party at the C.E.O.'s house was extraordinary. It was the home of Sylvia's dad, my supervisor. She grew up in that house. The home is gorgeous, very expensive with a pool out back that was unused for the party since it was too cold. I haven't seen many rich homes on the inside. I was in awe of the beauty of it all; dim and shadowy lighting, new furniture without crocheted blankets strewn over the back, works of art hung on the wall instead of neon beer signs, shiny wood floors without matted and stained carpet. The lovely surroundings made me want to act better, stand up straighter, be delicate and refined. I successfully sipped on one glass of champagne for a long time and didn't get drunk. I daintily nibbled on the artistically displayed appetizers and side dishes. My macaroni and cheese was a poor choice. It looked so soggy, limp, grotesque next to the little rolled meats and cheeses, delicious salads, shrimp cocktails and Swedish meatballs. I heated the mac and cheese in the microwave, considered hiding it but Sylvia saw I had a dish and wanted to assist. After that, the drab macaroni and cheese grew shriveled, cold and lifeless throughout the evening.

I dressed up in my French maid costume as planned and my roommate, Sam, said "damn!" I took that to be a good thing. The party was a very long drive, so I hoped my car would make it. Sam told me about a county road which cuts through a dense forest owned by the television station and shaved at least five miles off my drive. The county road was a bit tricky to find since street lights are nonexistent out in the country. It was a dark and lonely highway, with no towns, no houses, nothing but untouched forest. I crossed my fingers and hoped I was going the right direction because my car burned oil like a son of a bitch. I added another pint of oil before leaving to be safe and began my adventure. That was my last quart of oil and I didn't have the money to purchase another one at the convenience store up the street. When I say the Pinto burns oil, it really burns oil. I can almost picture in my mind squirrels, rabbits and deer dropping dead behind me.

It made it safely to the party and I parked as far away from the other new shiny cars as possible. The macaroni and cheese was a nightmare, and later in the night, when I was actually eating food, I heard Sylvia's fiancé say, "Look at this shit! What is it?! Macaroni and cheese? Who would be stupid enough to bring that to a party?" I was two people behind him in line and turned bright red, I'm sure, because I could feel my cheeks flushing hot. He proceeded to stick spoons in the macaroni and cheese, to demonstrate how thick it had become. Sylvia quietly shushed him, and he finally stopped his teasing. I was secretly heartbroken. It was a stupid thing to bring. It tastes good when it is warm, but not when it gets cold. I should have known better. I don't get invited to too many parties, especially nice ones without a keg, to know what sort of food to bring. Not homemade macaroni and cheese ever again.

I was so embarrassed about my food that I couldn't stay at the party much longer after that. I snuck out quietly like a thief without saying goodbye to anyone. I should have said thank you to Sylvia or her dad. I do feel guilty about that, too. I didn't really talk to anyone beside a few brief encounters and the person would quickly excuse themselves and I was left standing alone in my painful stilettos. I am so shy, too shy to start a conversation with anyone. I had to be careful removing my macaroni and cheese so everyone wouldn't know it was mine. I quickly retrieved the casserole dish and tried to hide it under my purse and got out of there as quickly as possible. I didn't drink much, but still managed to make an idiot of myself. Not very uplifting, although I was grateful to be invited to the party. I glanced back at the large picture window and saw the normal people carrying on conversations as easily as breathing. I headed back to my other embarrassment, the baby blue rusty old Pinto.

After leaving the warmth of the house, I drove slowly so not to miss the county road which would get me home faster. I found the road and was far enough along to be in the forest, without a light to be seen, when the engine froze and died. I didn't have more oil for the trip home. If only I added a quart of oil for the return trip, my car wouldn't have left me abandoned on an old forsaken highway that few people knew of its existence. I coasted the car as far as possible in neutral, until I came upon a small hill which brought me to a complete stop. I was able to put the car in neutral and roll back, turning onto the side of the road instead of being in the road.

I was still about 15 miles from home. I have AAA, so I could get a tow, but there was no phone with which to make the call. Plus, they would only tow for five miles and charge me for anything after five. That could get expensive at fifteen miles. I felt a little panicked when I looked around at my surroundings, my prospects. I could walk back to the party but that was at least 5 miles the other way, into the darkness,. It was cold enough to require a coat, which I did not bring with me. Walking any distance in stilettos was out of the question so I tried walking toward home barefoot, but there was so much gravel on the road, hurting my feet. I started walking in the grass next to the road but saw a broken beer bottle. I could step on something unseen. I was wearing a French maid costume, no coat or blanket with which to cover myself, so I started to become even more terrified. After my near abduction as a child, I am quite skittish when left in a vulnerable situation (except when I'm drunk, apparently). Even if I found a house with a phone to use, I was broken down late at night in the middle of nowhere. How could I ever explain to the towing company where I was located? I am not familiar with that area so there were no points of reference to describe my location. I was in the middle of a forest.

I was cold and decided to go back to the car to think things over. A car came up behind me which completely freaked me out. The locks on the car don't work and I had no weapon. I put on my right turn signal and wave the person around. Thankfully, they drove quickly by without seeing a single female in fishnet stockings.

I saw some headlights coming up ahead and got frightened all over again. I got out of the car on the passenger side so the driver wouldn't see me, walked through the ditch and was going to hide behind a tree when I saw an eight foot high electrified fence. The trees would provide me no safety since I couldn't reach them. I crouched low in the cold, wet ditch. I didn't want to be near the car because someone may get out of their car and walk around the Pinto. I had to be far enough away so no one would see me. I took off the white doily, gloves and apron so I was completely in black. I laid down flat in the ditch, praying no one would see me.

As predicted, a man did stop, get out and walked around the Pinto (I left my hazard lights on). There are absolutely no street lights out there but the moon was full and bright and I prayed that he wouldn't see me. I stayed completely still. After a few minutes, he drove away. Maybe he was a nice man, trying to help, or maybe he was a cruel person taking advantage of a bad situation. Out there, no one would see me abducted, there was no place to run.

I hid in the ditch twice more as cars passed by. There was one woman that I saw too late. I got up and waved at her but she didn't see me in her rear view mirror because it was dark and I was wearing black.

I prayed very hard as I shivered in the ditch. I prayed for some help, something safe because all I wanted at that point was to get back to the trailer and cuddle up with my cat, Keelie.

Not much time passed before another truck was approaching from the direction of my home, so he was going the wrong way. By a chance of luck (I have it sometimes) I could see it was a tow truck. His truck even had the AAA logo on it so I knew he was legitimate. I gathered up all of my courage and stood up from the ditch and waved the driver down, asking myself if I made the right choice. He saw me, so I had to follow what fate had in store for me. The guy lived on the other side of the highway where there were houses and he was coming home after a tow. My heart fluttered in my chest. Excitement at getting what I prayed for but scared it could be a horrible end to my life. As he looked at my appearance, a muddy French maid by that time, he asked where I lived, I told him the trailer park where I lived and he gave a whistle and said he was just going home after a long day. He could certainly see the dejection and fear on my face, so he said his wife wouldn't want a girl to be stuck in a situation like that one, so I had better hop into the truck. He even had a jacket I could lay over myself since I was shivering from the cold from laying in the ditch. Better still, he knew a shortcut to my house and said that he would tow me home. I couldn't believe my luck. I was so happy I felt like crying. I got a little lecture about driving out there in the middle of nowhere in an old beat up car, but it was a kindly lecture. My prayers were answered! Help arrived not long after I prayed with all of my strength to God. I would have been so screwed if he hadn't driven by. Honestly, there isn't even a gas station because it is forest owned by a news station, the tow truck driver told me (which is what Sam mentioned, too).

We got home so much quicker than the route I was going. The driver told me it was 7 miles. It was 2 miles over what AAA would cover. However, since I had such a harrowing experience, he wrote it up as 5 miles so AAA would cover the cost (he saw the dump of a trailer I lived in). I thanked him like a hundred times, and he said it was no problem. His wife would understand. It lifted my spirits to meet such a kindly person, a helpful individual in the time of need. I usually attract the psychos and weirdos. God or someone surely answered my prayers that night. I couldn't have been luckier.

We brought the Pinto to the trailer since I told him my roommate is a mechanic and would look at it. It was late by the time I got home, John and Sam were already asleep. I tiptoed into my bedroom, got into my pajamas and cuddled up with Keelie. I had never been happier to see that run down trailer.

As I suspected, once I put in some oil this morning, the Pinto started right up again. John and Sam were at work when I awoke so they knew nothing of my experience. I don't plan on telling them. Boy, it is getting expensive putting a quart of oil in that thing almost every day. Plus, people laugh and stare at me in my smoking car. If only I didn't screw up with my truck, letting it get repossessed, or calling the creditors to tell them where the truck was located, believing their lies of letting me keep it. I wish my parents would have loaned me the money to make the payments on my truck. I was two months, going on three months behind. I am so destitute, just barely paying for gas, oil, and my portion of the utilities (which is hardly anything since Sam works for the cable company and we get cable illegally). On the bright side, I have a job again and I got home safely from a situation that could have turned deadly. Thank God!

DECEMBER 25, 1988

I am alone in the run down trailer because Uncle John went to Kyle's family's house for Christmas and I wasn't invited. Sam went to visit his own family, has a girlfriend, so I wasn't invited there, either. I watched tv with Keelie, staring at our table top silver Christmas tree that Gammy used to put out. It was pitiful. No presents, nothing to open. Me alone, again, on Christmas. I'm sure my birthday will be dismal. Thankfully, John left me weed to smoke. I got super high and drank some beer. The trailer heat doesn't work so I piled on the blankets. It's a chilly winter this year, apparently. It comes in cycles. Some years it's warm, while others are bitterly cold. There is a Joe Bob Briggs movie on, which is hilarious. He does a boob count for every bad movie he riffs. I got lucky! There's something on tv.

CHAPTER 11

1989: AGE 20

JANUARY 3, 1989

So much has happened in the last week, mostly bad, as usual. There are two girls from Benefits Management Company who are both from Panama. They share an apartment near work and both went home for Christmas since they are typical college students. Monica McGreggor, from work, and I were given the keys to the girls' apartment to look after their cat. We both had their key and I was told that I could drive their car while they were away if I needed to and could stay at their apartment. I didn't want to drive their car unless I had to because I was afraid of doing something stupid.

For my 20th birthday (December 29), I met Monica and Miguel at a house party where a band was playing. Monica was invited because she works part-time at the Florida State University ticket office.

I wasn't very familiar with college campus, but I found it. We were upstairs at the party drinking massive amounts of alcohol. They had a keg and sold each drink for a dollar. I wasn't carded since it was someone's house.

Monica started getting completely trashed so she and Miguel were going to leave. Miguel kept trying to get me to go home with them and leave my car there. I wanted to stay and drink more. There was no way I was going to go home yet. I really should have. Miguel almost dragged me out of there, and Monica even said that I shouldn't stay any longer. But I did anyway. They left and I was at a party where I didn't know anyone. Then I saw that creepy guy, Kurt from months ago coming up the stairs. He was alone but seemed to be looking for someone. I didn't want it to be me, so I hid behind a group of people and ducked down the stairs and left.

I drank too much so I was going to drive to the girls' apartment which wasn't very far away. When I left the parking lot, I was really turned around and didn't know where I was in relation to the apartment. I just started driving. I was still driving my Pinto, there was a sharp curve and my steering doesn't work very well. It has no power steering. I tried to slam on the brakes, but my brakes didn't work at all. They have been getting worse lately. I went through a chain link fence and blacked out. I think I hit my head, but I don't know for sure what happened. One minute I was trying to turn a corner and the next I was waking up to a police woman pulling me out of my car. The police shouted at me to lean against the car as they searched me. She asked me where my crack was. You know, crack cocaine! I don't smoke crack. I told her that but she didn't believe me because I was in a crack neighborhood. I told her that I was at a house party but didn't know where (which was true) but again, she didn't believe me.

The police impounded the Pinto and took me into the police station and booked me for DUI and destruction of public property (the chain link fence was ripped down where my car plowed into it). That's one way to get rid of that shitty Pinto.

I took the breathalyzer at the police station and it was really high at 0.19. Just so you know, 0.06 is the legal limit. I didn't know what to do, I certainly didn't want to call Uncle John, so I stayed the night there in a private cell. When they woke me up to go, I got my beat up Pinto and left. I didn't tell them that the brakes barely worked. I just wanted to go home. I kept it quiet from everyone. I didn't want anyone to know about it. Only you know about it.

That wasn't the last of it. On December 31, Monica, her boyfriend Miguel and I met at Roosters for dinner and drinks, even though drinking age in Florida is now 21. I drove Leslie's car since my Pinto's brakes were in terrible condition.

Of course, I couldn't afford dinner, so I spent what little money I had on drinks. I am always broke. I don't manage money very well. We were there watching a college football game at Roosters. No team that I was interested in. I don't watch college football.

While I was there, I started dancing with this guy name Guy. What a stupid name. I know, he can't help it. I don't know what I was thinking, he was so much older and wasn't good looking. Also, he was really weird. Miguel told me not to hang out with him but I did anyway, especially since Guy was buying the drinks.

Monica and Miguel decided to go back to the girls' apartment since it was closer than Monica's apartment. They tried to get me to leave, but I demanded to stay, again. Miguel told me that Guy was very strange and didn't trust him. I laughed at Miguel. I really didn't care if he was weird, I just wanted to have someone, you know?

Later on, Guy said that we should go. I told him about the apartment I was looking after and we could stay there since it was nearby. He asked to drive, but I said no because it wasn't my car.

I was driving back the short distance to the apartment when there was a road block on the street on which they lived. There was no other way to get to the apartment. I definitely wasn't going to take Guy home to the trailer. There had been an accident at that intersection and they were still clearing it up. I drove past the road block then turned around. I stopped and asked a police if I could get by because I lived a block away. The police said no, so I drove through the road block anyway and went toward the apartment. Well, the police stopped me immediately when a police car blocked my path. I told them that I lived right up there. The police then told me to get out of the car. I did the roadside sobriety test but failed (I didn't think that I had failed).

The police arrested me for DUI and Guy followed me to the police station. The breathalyzer was .17 this time. I didn't tell them about the DUI on December 29th. They didn't have it in their system yet. Guy convinced the police to let me go and he would drive me home. They decided to release me and Guy drove back to the apartment. The accident was cleared up by then so there was no roadblock anymore.

Guy stayed the night, and when I awoke, I realized what had happened. I looked at Guy and he was really creepy looking. He must be 35 years old! What was I thinking? He was nice to get me out of jail, but there was something strange about him that I can't describe. You know, when you get a feeling that someone may be capable of killing someone and you feel uneasy? That was what he was like.

I told Guy not to tell Monica and Miguel about the arrest. We watched some football game, then I took him to Rooster's to get his car and I went back to the trailer. I felt physically ill and also mentally beaten up. I have just gotten 2 DUIs and I will get in a lot of trouble. I am so scared. It is another case of me fucking things up. How can I continue to be so stupid?! When will I ever learn? Why do I have to drink until I black out? I can't ever stop. Only if I prepare myself mentally beforehand can I drink a "normal" amount. I really hate the way I am. Plus, I could have crashed Leslie's car. I didn't drive it after that. I don't want to tell anyone about this. It is bad enough without being lectured. I have already kept it hidden, so I think I still can. Only time will tell. I feel guilty for driving while I'm drunk. I could have really hurt someone being as drunk as I usually get. I need to stop driving after drinking or don't drink so much. So much guilt and shame. Only you, my diary, knows about the terrible situation I am in.

FEBRUARY 16, 1989

I finally bought another junker car. This time it is a $300 Honda Civic. It isn't any better than the Pinto, except for the name; it is less embarrassing saying that I have a Honda than a Pinto. People laugh at Pintos. It is one of those old, small Civics, the really rounded ones. It is white. It is stained with exhaust fumes, scratches and dents. It doesn't burn quite as much oil as the Pinto.

FEBRUARY 23, 1989

I was terrified going to my court date alone. I dressed professionally and looked as dejected as I felt. Guilty is how I feel. The court ordered me to go for regular urine tests and go on Antabuse until my actual court date. That Antabuse tastes terrible. I haven't tried to drink since it is supposed to make you feel really sick and vomit. It was strange, but when I went for my weekly urine test in the trailer next to the jail, when I came out of the trailer, crazy Kurt was just hanging out in the parking lot. I asked him if he had urine testing, too. He said he did and wanted me to wait. I had to go to work. Kurt keeps popping up places that I go, the grocery store, house party, and now here. It seems a strange coincidence. I don't ever run into the boy, Jay, who I had sex with, or anyone else I know. Just him. It seems far-fetched, but is he following me? Kurt keeps asking me to go out with him, I say no thank you and try to leave as quickly as possible. He doesn't have a car and he asked me to drive him home after his urine test. I said that I would wait for him after he pestered me about it, but drove off as quickly as possible once he went in the trailer doing the urine test, if he was even really doing it.

On a positive note, I now live with Monica, from Benefits Management Company. She works in customer service, too, and is so much fun. Last time I stayed over at her apartment, we got shit faced, she asked if I wanted to get an apartment with her. That would be fabulous, especially to get out of my dumpy trailer with the big hole in the hallway leading outside, covered up only with carpet.

MARCH 3, 1989

Monica and I moved into a two bedroom in the same apartment complex that she already lives. That way, there wasn't a deposit. Well, there was a $200 deposit for me since I have a cat. Luckily, Monica loves cats, but she does have a parakeet in a cage.

MARCH 27, 1989

I had a great Easter for a change. Monica celebrates Easter, so she bought two dozen eggs and Pez to decorate Easter eggs.

She went out and picked a palm, too, since she's Catholic. Monica bought two dozen shrimp, boiled them and made German potato salad. Keri, her cousin from Illinois, came for a visit. Keri is a lot of fun and brought weed with her. I made a toilet paper roll pipe since no one had a pipe or wrapping papers and Keri and I got really high. Monica didn't smoke as much as Keri and I did. She didn't want to get too fucked up over Easter since she was raised Irish Catholic.

We had a lot of fun decorating Easter eggs. It was so nice having real friends to hang out with. Keri is two years younger than me and is really cool. Her parents are well off, Keri's dad is Monica's mom's brother. Keri's dad has oil wells and Keri gets just about everything she wants, but she isn't selfish. Keri is sweet and is thinking about moving in with us. That would be so much fun. I hope she does!

I didn't get drunk on Easter and smoked more weed instead. We had a little bit of rum and Coca-Cola. I didn't drink much since I might get sick from the Antabuse. Since Monica mostly abstained, we followed suit. It was the best time. It made me forget about my upcoming court case. That is a complete nightmare, which is literally giving me nightmares every night. I have gory, bloody nightmares full of death. No one knows about my two DUIs and I'm keeping it that way. I suppose Kurt knows since he's stalking me.

MAY 4, 1989

This afternoon, I saw the Atlantis Space Shuttle launched! I was watching ESPN when the shuttle countdown started, so

I turned the tv to face the back porch where I ran outside to try and see the event. It was exciting to hear the countdown and seeing the space shuttle in the sky just a moment later. At first it looked like a fire ball rising up from the tree-lined horizon. When ESPN said that the rocket and booster separated, I actually saw a line of smoke circle back down towards the ground. I watched as the shuttle faded out of sight. The faint trail of smoke ducked behind the misty line of trees.

I went and laid out by the pool after that since the apartment overlooks the pool and I could see that no one else was out there. It was so relaxing after that near death ordeal last Tuesday night.

I was at work by myself in the customer service department since I work nights now while I go to Tallahassee Community College during the day. At first, I felt a little nauseous. The Antabuse I'm required by court to take often makes me feel queasy. I have to take the Antabuse until me hearing.

Around 8:30 pm my heart started beating so hard that I could actually feel in throbbing throughout my entire body. I got up to go to the front door, to get some fresh air, but I became dizzy and couldn't stand. I fell to the floor and couldn't get up, the pain in my chest was so severe. I crawled to the phone and called Keri, my friend and new roommate, to come and take me to the hospital. My other roommate, Monica, took the phone from Keri and asked what was wrong. I could barely speak, my breath was so shallow. I whispered that my chest hurt. Monica told me to stay put and she would call Selene and Leslie, two girls from work who lived only a mile away. They live in the same apartment I was trying to get to during both DUIs. Selene had a key to unlock the front door and Monica didn't. I couldn't get to the door to unlock it, as much as I tried. I was going to pass out if I stood up and didn't have the strength to pull myself up.

Leslie and Selene got to the office and unlocked the door. I was still on the floor. They came running up to me and tried to get me up into a chair. It was so painful, I felt like passing out. Just then, Keri pulled up and they all helped me into her car so she could take me to the hospital.

Keri drove like a banshee to the emergency room. Since I couldn't walk, someone came out with a wheelchair. The nurse then had me get my insurance card. I was in such pain and my arms were numb that I couldn't get the identification out of my purse. Keri got them out for me. The nurse handed me a bunch of forms to fill out. I couldn't even hold the forms, let alone fill them out. Keri told them that I had to be taken in right away. The nurse said I had to wait.

Once the forms were filled out, the nurse said that I had to sign them. She put a pen in my hand but I kept dropping it. I couldn't write so the nurse held my hand and helped me sign my name. She said that we had to wait some more.

I started losing consciousness and slid down in my wheelchair. That is when Keri lost it and started screaming at the nurse to take me back now. They finally did.

It turned out that I had a reaction between my asthma medication and the Antabuse that I was taking. It made my potassium level drop drastically in my heart, so I would have had a heart attack if my heart was weaker.

It hurt so much, I can't describe the pain. I don't want to ever have a heart attack. My hands were numb, my arms tingled. I could only whisper to the nurse what medication I was on. The doctor came in and started grilling me, asking me what street drugs I had taken. I hadn't taken any, but he didn't believe me. He started searching my clothes to find some clue, but there was nothing. The doctor became very mean to me and told me that he knew that I was lying. I wasn't. He started examining me very roughly and rudely. I had terrible abdominal cramps so he did a very painful and rough gynecological exam without closing the curtains. The nurse finally closed them and held my hand. I could tell that she didn't approve of the doctor's behavior.

He said that I was fine in my abdomen. The nurse drew blood for testing, to see what was wrong. They soon found out that my potassium level was dangerously low and I was having a heart attack. I didn't have one completely because my heart was strong enough, but it was very close. The doctor said there were no street drugs in my system, but he didn't apologize. He barely looked at me after that, the nurse did most of the work.

The nurse stuck an inch long plastic tube the size of a drinking straw into the left artery of my arm to administer potassium by large quantities. That tube was as painful as my heart. It was constant agony but they couldn't do anything for the pain. The tube was so large that it seemed that I was going to die from the pain.

The nurse hooked me up to a heart monitor and placed me by the nurse's station. Almost the entire time, the pain was so great that I wanted to pass out. The nurse would keep waking me up, saying that I couldn't sleep. I pleaded with her to let me sleep because the pain was too great. They still wouldn't let me. I guess they were afraid I would die. There were several people watching me at all times and they even brought out a cardiac machine.

Out of the blue, I started vomiting so much that it hurt. I had been given two bags of potassium and fluids. I kept dry heaving while they were putting the potassium into my artery. Finally the nurse gave me some Dramamine directly into my left arm artery tube for the nausea. It burned and caused excruciating pain up my arm.

I started feeling very dizzy and could hardly keep awake. I started dry heaving again. It wouldn't stop so the nurse shot two more whole vials of Dramamine into my arm. After another 15 minutes of dry heaving, I started to feel better. I stopped the dry heaving after that.

I was at the hospital from 9:20 pm until 8:00 am the next morning, with that tube in my arm almost the entire time. It was the worst pain I have ever experienced. I really thought that I was going to die.

As for the DUI stuff, I went to a hearing a few days ago and the court rescheduled a new hearing for May because they realized that I had two DUIs, back to back, and are going to reset the dates and do them both at one time. I didn't want to tell the police that I had just gotten a DUI days before my last one. I was hoping one of them would get lost in the shuffle. I guess not.

Since I can't afford an attorney, I received a court appointed one, Mr. Johnson. Feeling of déjà vu from the time I was arrested for theft in Portland. My court appointed attorney is really young and just graduated from college. He has a wife and met with me at his home office. His wife was really nice and gave me some juice since I don't drink coffee. I'm one of his first cases and he is concerned that he won't be able to help me. I explained that I have no money for an attorney, so he became committed to my cause.

Mr. Johnson is kind of worried about this case because he hasn't tried a DUI case yet. Luckily, they didn't know about the DUI I got when I was 16 years old in Washington State. It was "written off" my record because I went to that 30 day rehabilitation treatment center.

Well, two DUIs are really bad. Not only the fines, but the real possibility of jail time. I am really scared now. I am afraid that I'll lose my job and everything will be ruined. Mr. Johnson said that he will do everything he can to have me keep my job so I'll be able to pay all of the fines plus the damage to the fence. He can't be sure how it will turn out because it is his first DUI case. He even asked if I wanted to get another court appointed attorney. I said no, that's all right. He is nice, considerate, so I'll keep him. I deserve all the bad things I get anyway. I just don't want to lose my job and have everyone find out about this. No one knows about this court shit and I don't want anyone to ever know.

Oh, I almost forgot, but when I went to the hearing for the court rescheduling, Kurt was sitting in the back row of the courthouse. He was sitting next to the door so I had to pass him on the way out. I didn't notice him before. He motioned for me to sit next to him so I did for a short time, until my turn with the judge came up. I asked him quietly if he was there for a ticket. Kurt said that he wasn't. Then why was he in a courthouse? Kurt just shrugged his shoulders and asked for a ride home. I said I wouldn't give him a ride and I got up and moved closer to the front of the courtroom to get away from that freak. Kurt was waiting for me when I left. He was standing by my car. I asked him where he needed to go and it wasn't far so I told him to get in. Now I am starting to get the feeling Kurt is following me. Why else would he be in that courtroom at that time when he didn't have any tickets. It makes me wonder if he ever really had that urine test at the trailer when he showed up. I really don't need extra stress on top of everything else I am going through. Kurt said he is a good listener and that I should call him. I don't think so. He looks normal and attractive but there is something frightening about him underneath. I don't know what it is, but he makes my skin crawl.

So, apart from some freak, no one knows about this living hell that I am enduring. It makes me so sick all of the time. My stomach ulcers are back and I need lots of sleeping pills to fall asleep at night. I feel so trapped. The feeling of a black hole inside is eating me alive.

MAY 16, 1989

Bad news. Like that is a surprise. My Honda Civic just blew up. Not really blowing up, but there was a pop and the engine started burning black smoke. I pulled over and only just averted a car fire. My car was still smoking as I walked away. I took everything in it with me because I won't be able to afford to get it towed. Why should I tow it? To fix it? That would cost more than the $300 it cost me to buy it. I am taking the bus now.

Mom called to tell me that Sid and Betty's oldest daughter, Kimmy, finally married her Army boyfriend she has been living with since she was 15. Big deal. Like I care. Then, mom went on and on about how sweet Kimmy is and that she is pregnant (I guess that is why they got married) and her husband has been transferred to Pensacola. There is a small Army base around there somewhere. I don't know the name of it. Mom talked for ten minutes about how sweet and good Betty's daughter is and she will miss her so much. Of course, mom went on about how thin she is. That is always important to her. After her long loving conversation about bitch girl was over, I asked mom if she expected me to go and visit her since Pensacola isn't too far from Tallahassee. Mom said that would be nice. I reminded her that I have only met her once and we aren't friends. I get tired of hearing about the wonderful people. At least I got my G.E.D. which is more than you can say about Kimmy.

MAY 21, 1989

I have been having some fun before I am sentenced for my idiotic two DUIs. Monica's boyfriend, Miguel, is a windsurfer and has taken us to Alligator Point the last two weekends and teaching us how to windsurf. It is very difficult, so much harder than it looks. Miguel wears a Speedo and Monica and I giggle over it, although he is in good shape.

Yesterday, while Miguel was out in the gulf, a storm was coming in. I mean, a really terrible storm that looked like a tornado coming across the water. Lightening was flashing and the sky darkened as if it was suddenly night time. A funnel of water was darting around out there and Miguel seemed to be surfing all around it. Monica and Keri screamed at him but there was no way he could hear us. The wind picked up to a frightening level. We gathered all of our picnic gear and got under the concrete picnic table. We were so scared, especially since Miguel was out there in the water. The trees were whipping around, laying almost flat. The storm was small and localized, I think it's called a downburst, and it was fierce.

The storm passed fairly quickly and the sun came out again as if nothing happened. Monica, Keri and I were shaken because it was so windy and the lightening was right on top of us. For a minute we couldn't see Miguel. All three of us yelled for him at the top of our voices. Finally, we saw his sail and he made his way to shore where he was promptly yelled at by both Keri and Monica. Miguel said that he was safer out there because he could avoid the storm since it was concentrated in a funnel. I guess that makes sense, but Monica wasn't happy. She was crying and Miguel thought it was sweet she cared so much. Well, of course. Miguel is a great person and always tells me that I can do better with my life, I shouldn't drink and act so crazy. I should listen to him, I know. I can't. I can't stop myself. It sounds simple, but it isn't. It is as if there is a monster living inside me which makes me do things that I don't want to do.

When we were driving back home, I saw my Honda Civic still abandoned by the side of the road. It had stickers all over it for tickets. I never registered it, so they won't be able to track it to me. Haul it away! I don't want it. I feel guilty. Like I did this huge littering or something. I feel guilty quite a bit because I usually fuck something up.

MAY 31, 1989

Keri and I travelled to Pensacola to visit her cousin, Matt Kennedy. Keri's aunt lives in Pensacola, too. She's Monica's mom's sister, Irene. Keri and I tried to get Monica to come with us to Pensacola, and she really wanted to, but she had to work her shift at Florida State University ticket office, her part-time job. There was some event going on for Memorial Day and most of the other employees are students who were out of town.

When we went to the beach with Matt and his German Shepherd with hip dysplasia, which is a dreadful disease. Matt is being selfish to keep the poor beast alive, the dog is obviously in a great deal of pain and whimpers almost all of the time. Matt drew "Monica" in the sand and Keri took a picture of it since they have always been really close cousins.

We listened to Irish music, my Irish cd's actually, danced and drank. Matt and his friend, a Hawaiian looking guy named Sean, Keri and I went to the beach at night. Sean has grown up with Matt and has been in love with Keri since she was a little girl. Keri is unquestionably unforgettable with black curly hair and large, luminous blue eyes.

That night at the beach was a bit strange. Keri and Sean were walking ahead of us, drinking their daiquiris, and Matt and I were walking behind them. Matt kept slowing me down. Matt is a gorgeous boy. He has pitch black hair and blue eyes and people often think that he and Keri are brother and sister. They actually do look a lot alike.

The beach was dark and the dunes were sugar white so the light from the moon was all we had. Matt and I were behind a sand dune when he threw me to the ground, quite literally, and pulled off my underwear. I was taken by surprise since he didn't show any interest in me before. I was on my period so he grabbed the tampon and threw it in the bushes. He did this all so fast I didn't know what was happening. Matt had already inserted his penis and was on top of me having sex. He put his hand over my mouth. I was drunk and confused but didn't make any sound. Matt was done quickly and threw my panties back at me to put them on. It was all kind of humiliating. Of course, Matt told Keri later that night that we had sex. I guess that is what you can call it. I am not so sure. I didn't have a say in the matter.

The next night, I was sleeping in the same room with Keri when Matt got into the sleeping bag with me. He wanted to have sex with me. I told him no, not a chance. He pleaded with me, but I wouldn't let in. I said we weren't going to have sex again, especially next to Keri. Finally he relented and just laid down next to me, putting his arm around me. Apparently, he called Monica, too, and said that he had sex with me the first night but I was alright after all. Monica told me this and I was shocked. She asked, in front of Miguel, if he was good in bed. I didn't know what to say since it happened so fast and it wasn't consensual. Monica went on to say that Matt used women all of the time and treated them like dogs, or worse than dogs, and for him to say that I am "okay" was a compliment. Monica said that I must have made an impression on him. What, by saying "no"? I guess so. I didn't feel comfortable telling Monica that I was raped. I believe I was since he pushed me down without even a kiss or a word. Monica and Keri keep teasing me about it. Miguel could tell something was amiss because he told them to stop pestering me. I'm glad he did because I wanted it to go away. I guess I should have told her the truth, but I didn't want to come between cousins. I kept silent, but I don't feel good about it. I won't ever consent to have sex with him, no matter how good looking he is.

Well, I am going to sleep now. I have a science class at Tallahassee Community College in the morning and after that, work at Benefits Management Company. Good night.

JUNE 6, 1989

Last Friday, I got yet another vehicle. Matt Johnson, from work who is getting married, has been trying to sell his baby blue Chevrolet Chevette and convinced me to buy it. He asked for $600. I gave him $250 from my paycheck as a down payment. I was excited, at first, because Matt told me the Chevette (which looks alarmingly like a Pinto) has air conditioning. What a relief, so I thought. Well, as it turns out, it does have air conditioning, but every time I use it, the car overheats and stalls. I can't use it at all. The car keeps overheating. I have been ripped off completely. I don't think I'll be paying the rest of the $600. What a lying fuck Matt is. We'll see how long car thing lasts.

The out of town representatives from Benefits Management came into town. I adore Martin Fourneir from Baton Rouge. Everyone went to get drinks at the bar. I have discovered that I can drink a couple of drinks without getting sick on Antabuse. At the bar, I was flirting with Martin and he invited me over to his hotel room, secretly, of course. He said I should leave first and wait in my car at the hotel until the coast is clear. I did just as he said, and Martin waved me into his room, quickly. We made love three times before I went home. It was heavenly. He is so good in bed, it drives me crazy. He's married and has a college mistress, so no chance of hooking up with him. Too bad. He'd cheat. Those kind of men always do, but I still really like him.

JUNE 12, 1989

As expected, it turned out badly with my hearing. I went to the court date of doom for those two DUIs. The prosecuting attorney had such a hatred for me, yelling and belittling me every chance he had, thinking I was a pampered Florida State University sorority girl. My lawyer said that I should not request a trial by jury because if I get a M.A.D.D. mother on the jury, they will probably give me the maximum, which is 5 years in jail. So, I decided to have a judge decide what the verdict would be. The prosecuting attorney wanted me to go to jail for six months straight. I broke down crying and said that I would lose my job. He yelled at me and said that he didn't care since I didn't care about the laws. I said that I wouldn't be able to pay the fines if I lost my job. I don't have family to help me out. It is just me. Luckily, the judge agreed. He sentenced me to a thirty days in jail to be served every night at 7:00 pm through 7:00 am on the weekdays, and on weekends, I will go in at 7:00 pm on Friday and stay through 6:00 pm Sunday. I will have one night a week at home, Sunday.

I told Monica and Keri that I was working another job near Perry and that I would be spending the nights and weekends at the trailer. Monica is spending most of her time with Miguel, and Keri went home to Illinois for a couple of months to be with her family. She hasn't decided if she is moving to Tallahassee permanently or not. There won't be too many questions.

I start jail time tomorrow night. I am so scared! The bus doesn't go from my apartment to the jail, so I'll have to drive and park far away. I am so frightened that they will find out that I drive to jail. They took away my license for 5 years. I'll never be able to get car insurance now. I technically can if I pay a small fortune. Since I have fines and court costs, there won't be any extra money left for car insurance.

AUGUST 2, 1989

I am barely getting by anymore. I am so depressed all of the time. The jail is a living hell. The police sadistically enjoy to humiliate every inmate.

I also had a cervical cyst frozen off by a very cruel gynecologist. Everything happened at the same time. The doctor was so hateful and rough with me, I just didn't understand it. He didn't say it was a venereal disease, he said it was a cyst. But he was so rough he bruised my thighs, just like that cruel doctor in the emergency room who thought I was on crack. I had to go to jail the next day after the surgery so I asked the doctor if he would write me a note to get out of the first few days of jail. He said no. Maybe that is why he was so mean to me. It bled for days and I had to wear maxi-pads, not tampons. I drove an hour and a half to St. George beach just to sit there for hours, breathing in the salt air. It is the only place which makes me feel peaceful.

When I arrive to jail each time, they strip search and spray me down with anti-lice spray. Almost all of the employees treat the inmates like subhumans. Sometimes, they keep me in a holding cell before sending me back to my cot just so drunk men can sexually harass me. The holding cell has both men and women, and the men act lewd and repulsive, saying things I don't want to hear.

I learned right away that I needed some drugs to survive in there. I decided to sneak in sleeping pills. I figured out a way, too, although I am terrified every time I do it. I take a maxi pad (which I had to wear at first because of my surgery) and cut a sliver of it open underneath the side which affixes to my panties and insert 10 sleeping pills. I can't sleep with less than 10 sleeping pills now. Any more pills are too bulky and might be seen. Since I stopped spotting, I smear a little ketchup on top to look like blood. None of the female police want to touch my maxi pad, so they have never discovered my secret. Yet.

Getting the pills out is tricky. The jail is entirely open, a large rectangle with toilets and showers along the wall opposite a giant fan. There is no air conditioning. It's a miserable, sticky, sweaty place. There is no hiding when you're on the toilet. Everyone can see.

I sit on the toilet and put my head down like I'm taking a crap or something. I take off my maxi pad, like I am wrapping it up in toilet paper and throwing it in the trash. Well, while I am wrapping it up, I casually look around to make sure no one is watching, remove the pills then finish wrapping up the maxi pad. I threw away the pad and went to sit on my cot. You can't lay down until after dinner and cleanup. I have to be careful taking the sleeping pills, so I have to take them all at once or it would look suspicious. I cough, put my hand to my mouth, and in go ten sleeping pills. I go to the water fountain and wash them down. No one has discovered my secret. I am able to stay mentally numb, at least, while I'm there. Ten sleeping pills make me drowsy and allow me to break from reality.

The guards won't let me keep my book to read (just to be mean, because other people have their own books), so I have to read their stupid books and magazines. Weekends are difficult since there is so much more time to spend in jail. Last Friday night, I took the chance and put in 20 sleeping pills. I keep my maxi pad on so I can retrieve the pills when I'm ready.

Since the bathroom is completely open to the room, I don't ever shower. It is so embarrassing taking a crap, so I stopped eating so I wouldn't go. Even going pee is embarrassing.

The male police come in without announcing themselves. Women are showering or going to the bathroom, but the police do it to humiliate us.

There are about 100 cots in a large, rectilinear room. There are no open windows and we can't go outside except once on Sunday for a short period of time. I have never sweated so much in my life. I really miss air conditioning.

About 90 percent of the inmates are Black women, and the first night I was there, a woman tried to intimidate me into giving her my clothes that I was wearing. I said that I didn't have any other clothes but she said she would give me hers. I decided to act kind of tough and said, "no fucking way!" and walked off. It worked. She left me alone.

I listen to people talking, and most people are in there for writing bad checks. Usually for small amounts, too. I have accidentally written back checks and have barely paid them in time before being sent to court. Thank God I have kept up on them. I don't want to go to jail for that, too. I've had so many bounced checks. Almost all are on accident because I am always so broke.

My duty in there is mopping the floors every morning. They wake us up at 5:00 am to clean before breakfast. The food is horrible. The eggs are always under cooked and slimy and the grits have no butter or cheese, just plain. Everything on the food tray is repulsive.

Because of the heat, there were lots of palmetto roaches crawling around. Once, a woman woke up in the middle of the night screaming because a big roach fell from the ceiling onto her face. She could see it because they never turn out all of the lights.

I can hear some women having sex in there. I close my eyes and try to ignore it and hope that no one will try it with me.

I don't talk to anyone so no one talks to me. I don't make eye contact with anyone so they don't say anything to me. I started wearing my crappiest clothes so no one would try and take them off me again.

Every minute is a living hell. I cannot even describe the feeling of captivity when you can see freedom outside the fence on Sundays. They have razor wire, and I imagine myself breaking out of there. I wouldn't do it, because I'd have more jail time or be shot, but I like to pretend. I've made up these elaborate escapes in my mind. I never want to go back again.

No one found out about jail at work. Not even Miguel or Monica, who are my roommates. The whole ordeal has ruined my nerves. At least I'm off the Antabuse since my court date. I feel paranoid and sick all of the time and want to scream and tell someone. But I can't. Ever. With the fines from court, which I've been saving for, I barely have enough money to give Monica for bills. I have to pay Monica but am running out of time to pay my fines. It will be tough to raise the $800 I've been fined. I'm saving every penny I can. I'm living in hell.

SEPTEMBER 12, 1989

That Chevy Chevette completely died on me. Overheated one too many times. I left it by the side of the road, never to return. I felt bad about leaving another car on the side of the road, so I found someone in the phone book who picks up junker cars for free. I told him where it was located and tried to get some money out of it. The tow truck driver just laughed at me and said the price of the towing should cover the worth of the car. I would just once love to have a reliable car. Why did I mess up and lose the Toyota truck? That was such a mistake. I would have done things differently had I the chance to relive it all again. I wouldn't have called the loan company until after I saved up the money to catch up the payments. That was an idiotic thing to do. Live and learn, I guess. I have learned a lot but don't seem to remember my lessons because I keep repeating my mistakes. So, I suppose it is live and not learn.

OCTOBER 8, 1989

Monica and Miguel went away for almost a week, Monica telling Keri and I as we were coming home. They were going to a gymnastic convention that Tuesday night through Sunday because Miguel teaches children's gymnastics (and so does Monica, part-time). Monica was a gymnast and a cheerleader in high school and is very limber. We didn't pay much attention until Sunday evening when Monica and Miguel got back home. Monica came in and asked why her bird's cage was still covered. Covered? Neither of us thought about the bird. It didn't make any noise whatsoever. Monica uncovered the bird and the stench was terrible. The poor little parakeet was dehydrated and hungry. I felt so terrible! Monica didn't tell us to look after her bird, and when it was covered, I didn't think anything of it. It was like we forgot she even had a bird. Keri and I looked at each other and said, "oh, no, the bird!" at the same time. Monica was so angry, she yelled at both of us, told us how irresponsible we were and that she couldn't trust us. It was horrible. There is no way that I would ever hurt an animal and we would have taken care of it if she had told us about it. I wish the bird had squawked or something so we knew it was there. I guess I thought she took it with her, I don't know what I thought.

I think the bird is going to be alright. It drank lots of water and ate some food, but it walked around weakly. Monica demanded that I put Keelie in my bedroom and close the door so her bird could get out and move around. I did it, of course. That was a real depressing night.

OCTOBER 22, 1989

Mom just left from a short visit. She took some pity on me and bought me a new Ford Festiva, the dealer's model. We were trying to keep the car payments really low so I said no to the air conditioning being added. The salesman really tried to sell me the air conditioning, but it would have added $42 more dollars a month to the car payment. I can barely afford the $165 as it is. I want air conditioning. I can add it later, right?

NOVEMBER 9, 1989

The Berlin Wall has been torn down! Since the election of President Gorbachev, he has been under pressure to remove the wall which separates West and East Berlin. You should see the news! People are tearing pieces out of the wall, brick by brick, stone by stone. It's a frenzy for freedom. Some good news in the world.

NOVEMBER 19, 1989

What a complete and total fuck-up I always turn out to be! I was one of the few people from work invited to Sylvia and Danny's wedding reception at Killearn Country Club and Inn. Only some of the employees from our department, customer service, were invited by Sylvia, and I was one of the lucky ones. I was so looking forward to a nice, classy dinner and dancing. I couldn't have been more vulgar.

I got to the reception early (Keri and Monica weren't invited) and hung out with Fran, Peter, Matt Johnson (the car seller), that frat boy Darren (he is so gross), and others. I wore my most beautiful dress, a black suede dress that I had stolen from Meier & Frank in Portland. It was real suede and zipped up the neck, had long sleeves and a full skirt. It fit and looked fabulous. I wore my hair up and put on some large black earrings. I looked so beautiful, even Keri and Monica said I did.

I only remember pieces of that night. I recall that we were offered free drinks and I had vodka with grapefruit juice. I was so nervous about being singled out at the party, being told that I looked lovely and people watching me. When I get nervous, I tend to drink fast. I had three or four right away, probably less than an hour. I was told by Fran that Peter began ordering just grapefruit juice for me when I continued ordering drink after drink. I think it was too late by then since I didn't seem to notice the difference.

I looked toward the door all night, hoping that David, Sylvia's cute brother, would arrive and he would see how beautiful I am and want to dance with me. It seemed like a long time until David arrived with his brother, Paul. They arrived after the dancing started. To my absolute horror, They both had dates. David brought someone else and looked at me for a minute, raised his eyebrows, then ignored me. I must have acted like a drunken monster, hugging all over David and tugging at him, I can remember doing that even though it is fuzzy. David must have told me to go away, went and hid or left the party because the next thing I remember is sitting at a table downing another drink. I was alone, I remember that. I was feeling sorry for myself.

The next thing I recall is Matt buckling me into the passenger seat. I think we made out in the back seat. I have some memories of doing that. Did I have sex with him? I can't remember. I'm a little sore, but I'm sore all over so it is difficult to tell. Matt kept asking me where I live so he could drive me home. I guess I told him or he looked on my driver's license. My next recollection is walking through my apartment door, Matt driving away, and Keri telling me that I ruined my beautiful dress. I looked down and saw that I was covered in vomit. My suede dress had masses of vomit all down the front. Keri brought me in and kept saying, "oh, Michelle, oh no".

This morning, Monica and Miguel were over at our place by the time I awoke. Monica started teasing me about vomiting on my dress and being so drunk. Miguel tried to shush her, but she kept going. Monica isn't mean, she likes to laugh at things in life. I didn't feel like laughing. Especially since I have seen Monica vomit more times than I have, although she usually hits the toilet.

Keri asked if I needed to get my car. I did. It was still at Killearn Country Club. Monica asked how I got home and I told her Matt from customer service drove me home, even though I can't remember much. Monica acted like she was in high school and asked if we made out. Matt is engaged to be married. I answered that I have some fleeting images of kissing him. Monica continued her rapid fire questions, catching me off guard, especially when she asked if we had "done" it. I don't know, I replied. Monica asked how I felt down there and I responded that I felt a bit sore. What a mistake that was. I don't know if I was sore from sex or just sore from head to toe from drinking too much. Monica took that answer as a "yes" and started chiding and teasing me, saying that I did one Matt and now I am doing another. Two Matts back to back. Miguel asked Monica to stop since he could see how uncomfortable I was about the conversation. I felt like screaming that her cousin Matt raped me and I may not have even had sex with Matt Johnson, but I didn't say a thing. I meekly left the room, feeling lower than a crack smoking whore. I could have melted into the floor from shame and humiliation. Thankfully, Keri saved me by telling me to get my purse so we could pick up my car. We got my car and after Keri left, I got out of the car and looked longingly at the restaurant patio, feeling a pit of regret in my stomach. Regret is nothing new for me. I climbed back into my car, sat there and cried. I didn't want to go home right away so I sat there until security started coming my way, then I just drove and drove around neighborhoods before going home. By that time, Monica, Miguel and Keri were gone. I couldn't eat and had a difficult time keeping water down so I went into my bedroom, laying on my bed right now.

My black suede dress is obviously ruined. You know, that is the final article of clothing left after my shoplifting days in Portland. Strange how each item I stole became ruined somehow. Thinking back, it all got ruined, holes, vomit, urine, and God knows what else. Karma. It must be. I didn't get caught with those items so I never paid for them. I didn't pay for my crimes so Karma came and forced me to repay.

Like many Sundays, I loath going to work. Not because of working, but having to face everyone. At least Sylvia will be on her honeymoon for a couple of weeks. I'll drag my sorry ass into the office, head down, trying to hide from the world....again.

DECEMBER 6, 1989

Stupid me got a driving without a license and no insurance yesterday. It was because I was speeding. Why was I doing something so stupid? They took me to jail and I got bonded. I am still paying for all the DUI court costs and fines. I will go to court later in February. I was driving my car from work. I was working late to make extra money. I am always ruining my life. I will probably go back to jail. I wish I was dead. I want to disappear. God, please help me. I don't know what to do. I can't tell anyone. It will all burst inside. But I can't tell anyone. I am so frightened. I feel so much despair.

DECEMBER 20, 1989

I tried to kill myself after that driving without a license ticket. I secretly took Keri's gun from her car days before I actually did anything. She didn't notice it was gone. I finally loaded the gun, took about 30 sleeping pills, drank 4 beers and walked into the woods near my apartment. I held the gun to my head, cocked for an hour or two, crying hysterically. I was hoping that I would twitch or something and shoot off the gun accidentally. I kept my finger on the trigger. I hesitated because I really didn't want to die, but I was tired of suffering in this darkness. I fired off the one bullet in the chamber into the ground because I couldn't figure out how to uncock the gun. I then laid down and faded in and out of consciousness for quite a while.

When I stumbled back home, Keri had called the police and they were in the apartment. She hugged me and said that she was glad that I was okay. I left a suicide note. I was mad at her for calling the police. They were going to either arrest me for attempted murder (of myself, can you believe that is a crime?) or they were going to take me to the mental hospital. I was so scared of going to the hospital, but finally Keri convinced me to go.

The police actually took me to the emergency room and left me there. The nurse forced me to throw up with ipecac or else they would pump my stomach. I tried and tried and finally was able to. I don't know why she did that because 30 sleeping pills is nothing for me. I knew that I wasn't going to die from that.

They put me in a room for a couple of days. A nurse called Uncle John and he came to the hospital. He called mom and she spoke to me in the E.R. Then, since I mentioned Martin Fourneir, the sales rep I had sex with, in my suicide letter, he actually called the hospital to tell me that he cares for me! I couldn't believe it. He was so nice. He found out from my boss at work, because Keri called and told them everything. It was embarrassing. She didn't know how long I would be in the hospital.

I stayed in the rehab unit for 9 days, then my insurance wouldn't pay for any more so they released me. Just when I started enjoying it, too. There were so many nice people with group and individual sessions and it felt good to talk about my experiences with court and jail. No one judged me and I got it all off my chest. We went on a field trip to Wakulla Springs and rode the glass bottom boat. They had really good food. Then I got back into my real life and that stress-free time faded quietly away.

DECEMBER 24, 1989

I'll be alone for Christmas. I wasn't invited to anyone's house so it's just me and Keelie. That's sad.

I had yet another terrible nightmare. It began with me walking along a river while the sun was shining on my face. It was a beautiful, calm day. The river suddenly started swelling and as I took a step up the hill to get away from it, the ground gave way under me and I was thrown into the rushing water.

I was able to grab hold of a branch and was tried to pull myself out of the raging river. The river was tugging at me, trying to drown me. I woke up (so I thought) into another dream. I was sitting in Monica's car. She was driving and Keri was sitting beside her. I was in the back seat. We were going down a dirt road and I knew that someone or something was chasing us.

A large river full of hungry alligators was raging to our left. The dirt road disappeared and we were driving through the jungle. We kept getting closer and closer to the water's edge. I was so terrified of falling down there with the alligators. I was actually telling Monica and Keri how much this was like a dream I had (thinking I was actually awake).

The ground began to crumble away from beneath the car. Suddenly the car disappeared and we were running through the forest. A city appeared before us.

Right there I woke up for real. Bathroom break. Shit, those alligators scared me! I went back to sleep and started the dream right where I left off.

We were in a city. A large crowd of people were running through the street. I was afraid of being separated from Monica and Keri. Men carrying machine guns were all around and they began chasing us. The crowd pushed us forward, forcing us to enter a building that was surrounded by a tall stone wall.

The next part I remember was being herded into a room within the building. I told Monica and Keri that this is what happened to the Jews before they were gassed to death. We had to get out. It was a death house. We fought our way through the crowd and finally got outside. A bus was waiting outside and we were about to board when we noticed the army men with guns again. We hid and were trying to figure out how to get to the train station so we could go home.

CHAPTER 12

1990: AGE 21

JANUARY 7, 1990

I've been having severe nightmares for weeks now. I was completely alone over Christmas again and was broke. Keri and Monica went to visit their families in Illinois. Keri and Monica are cousins, so they went together. Monica also moved in with her boyfriend, Miguel last month. Keri is just freaked out by me now.

The nightmares started on Christmas Eve. I woke up at around 6:00 am Christmas morning with the feeling that someone was there in my apartment. I was scared shitless and slept with the light on for 3 nights in a row after that.

I've been having different dreams, but in every one of them, something evil is chasing me. One dream last week started out with me seeing some old friends from Portland, Clara and Lori. They had to go suddenly and I wanted to run after them but couldn't because I was restrained by a dark-haired man. The dark man put me in a straight jacket and placed me in a dark cell inside an insane asylum. I couldn't escape. He kept saying to me over and over again that I was trapped there forever. I was so afraid of staying in that living hell.

I fought and tore at my restraints and finally broke free. I ran through a bathroom like the one at jail. I was running in slow motion but the dark man was running very quickly after me.

As I was running, I literally ran into someone that I know, but I can't remember who it was. I pleaded for him to help me. He said that he couldn't get involved, turned and walked away.

I started running again. I realized that I was outside and I could see my car. I finally arrived at my car but I couldn't find the keys. I was still moving in slow motion, like I was floating in space.

I tried the door of the car and it was unlocked. I got inside and locked all of the doors because the dark man was running quickly toward me. I noticed the keys were in the ignition but the car wouldn't start. The dark man made the locks pop up just by looking at them. He was unlocking the car with his mind. I kept locking the car doors but he kept unlocking them. I looked at him more closely and the dark man looked like he was made of plastic, so fake, like a cheap game show host in a tacky suit and stupid smile on his face. I woke up frightened.

I watched a show last night about dreams and it said that people who have recurring nightmares are usually "artistic and/or psychologically sensitive." I am both. I must write down my dreams.

I've been taking a lot of sleeping pills to stop the terrible thoughts from bubbling up to the surface. I drove over to David's apartment hysterical and I almost slipped into that "unreachable" dark place where I would never return. I spent the night with him, had sex quietly so his roommates wouldn't hear. David finally became my friend, even after the drunken escapade I had at his sister's wedding party. David makes me come in and out through his bedroom window to keep me a secret. His dirty secret.

I have a great fear of being alone. I am far too sensitive if someone doesn't call me when they say they will. I am starting to get frightened. I'm not even sure what frightens me. Life itself. I feel an ominous presence hovering over me, like a storm cloud ready to burst.

JANUARY 8, 1990

All of my anxiety comes out in nightmares. I had another Freddy Kruger nightmare. I can't remember how it started, but I knew some people were going to die horribly.

There was a room full of people watching a girl and boy kissing. The girl said, "When am I going to get laid?" I said on Easter and counted backwards from 10. Everyone else began to count backwards, too.

The man turned into Freddy Kruger and he ripped her apart with his knives. Blood spurted all over the room while the people just watched it happen. No one seemed shocked or annoyed in a way. The girl was dead and blood was dripping down her legs.

JANUARY 19, 1990

I've been able to pay off some of my fines from the DUIs. That is a bit of a relief. I still have more to pay, mainly that fence I ran over. That is the most expensive of all the fines, so it will take me some more time to save up money.

All of this stress, being alone again, is taking a toll on my sleep. I still take sleeping pills so I can sleep. I take so many now, I have to keep restocking the pills and buy more bottles every few days.

In this nightmare, I was on a river, again. Uncle John lived there, too. My mom was driving up for a visit.

I was waiting for mom to arrive since she was due in at 5:00 pm. Around 4:00 pm, a huge hurricane came up so suddenly bringing with it driving rain and winds about 150 mph. Cars were being pushed into the river. The river was raging with waves two stories high. The world was bleak and scary. I was so frightened because my mom was out in the storm.

The river was unruly and wild. People and cars were toppling into the gray waters by the hundreds. A big dog jumped up on the porch with me for protection from the storm. He jumped up two entire stories. The dog was so skinny and soaking wet. I fed him and wrapped him in a blanket.

I went out onto the balcony and saw so many dead dogs everywhere. The were all skinny, abandoned and starving. Some were still alive. I walked over to a dog who looked like he was run over. His ribs were protruding through his flesh. The poor little dog was breathing in short whimpers. He was dying a slow death. I woke up.

Why do I continue having these terrible dreams? I fear my mother dying more than anything, and drowning would be terrible. Why? It actually doesn't frighten me as much as it used to. When I was little, I was so scared that my mom would die and leave me with Jim. Now, I'm not as frightened since I have distance from my parents.

I read a book about Marilyn Monroe recently. I feel like she must have felt. Scared, insecure, confused. Will I end up like she did? Will I finally succeed in killing myself?

FEBRUARY 10, 1990

Ed Fowler and Martin Fourneir from work were in town this week. Ed is a benefits representative from South Dakota and Martin is a rep from Baton Rouge, Louisiana. I went to Dooley's Down Under with them and other people from work. We all went up to Roosters next where Martin gave me his hotel key. He is so sexy with that Cajun accent, nice clothes, and smooth talk. He is definitely a charmer. I told him that he wouldn't be able to get into his room if I had the key. We planned that I would knock on his door #108 at the Cabot Lodge in fifteen minutes. I drove around for that time and quietly knocked on his door. We ended up making love for an hour straight and then two more times that night for at least twenty minutes each time. The next night we went out to dinner and made love three times that night, too. He is a sweetie, although he is married with a daughter. He also has a college girlfriend and pays for her apartment. They both called while I was in his room. They both were jealous that someone else was in the room with him, but he kept assuring them that there was no on else in his hotel room. I laid there very quietly so he wouldn't get in trouble.

Martin invited me down to New Orleans next weekend for Mardi Gras! Yeah! I can't wait. Martin also offered me four hours of pure ecstasy. I plan on looking very sexy next weekend. I hope that I really get to go. Sometimes guys just talk. Please, oh, please, let me go. I'll be so upset if I don't. Oh! Mardi Gras! Yes!

FEBRUARY 25, 1990

I got to Baton Rouge around 3:00 pm on Friday, February 23. I met Martin Fourneir at the Benefits Management office in Baton Rouge where we had a couple of cold beers, had a quick sexual rendezvous in the supply closet, then changed into some jeans to head down to New Orleans. We almost got caught in the closet since it didn't lock and a woman came in just as I pulled up my pants.

Before we left Baton Rouge, we met a couple of Martin's friends at a local bar and tasted crawfish for the first time. You have to rip off their tails, pinch the shell to crack it, eat the flesh and suck the juices out of the head. It was spicy and had a flavor similar to shrimp. I drank a Bloody Mary before we left. New Orleans was only an hour drive so we decided to leave around 5:30 pm. We grabbed a bottle of vodka and were off.

We were driving to Martin Hanley's apartment in Metaririe when traffic just stopped. There was a car accident which held us up a while. The other Martin works in the Benefits Management office in New Orleans. He has eyes as blue as the sky and seems to have a thing for me. I don't want him, I want Martin Fourneir, even though New Orleans Martin is single.

When we arrived in New Orleans, actually Metairie, a small town outside of New Orleans, Martin Hanley had some orange juice and ice, so we made ourselves some strong drinks and headed to a Metairie parade, which is a small town just outside New Orleans. His sister, Sheila, joined us. It was not a grand parade, but I found out what doubloons are and caught a lot of cups and beads. We walked back to his apartment after the Diana parade and decide to go to Alligators bar. We drove over there and noticed that there was an extremely long line so we casually started talking to some guy and cut a little closer to the front. Luckily, everyone was too drunk to notice.

We got into Alligators and it was packed. There was a band playing and I ordered another Bloody Mary. I had quite a few there, I lost track, but so did everyone else.

Sheila went home after the parade around 12:00 midnight so it was just me and the two Martins. I noticed that I still had my camera so I was handing it to Martin F. when we dropped it and the batteries fell out onto the floor. I've done that so many times I knew the camera was still all right. The camera actually took a picture when it hit the floor. Not long after that I had dropped my Bloody Mary on someone's feet but they didn't even notice. They will when they see the stain!

After a few hours we decided that we were hungry so we went to Denny's. We ate some greasy breakfast after waiting half an hour just for the waitress. After that, we went back to Martin Hanley's apartment and I crashed on his floor.

The next day, Saturday, everyone except for Sheila woke up at 7:00 am that morning. I don't know why we woke up so early when we didn't go to sleep until 3:30 in the morning! I woke up still drunk and dizzy from the night before and stumbled my way to get some ice water. Martin F. had to go back to Baton Rouge (he lied to me and said that he was staying the whole weekend) and left right away. I ate some King Cake for breakfast which is similar to a large, round cinnamon roll with a hole in the middle with purple, gold and green colored sugar sprinkled on top. One piece has a hidden little plastic baby in it and if you get it, it is good luck and you must throw the King Cake party next year. I didn't get the baby but it was pretty good cake. King Cake is part of the tradition of Mardi Gras. It is the party before Lent and a "fast" which lasts for 40 days until Easter.

People basically give up drinking through Lent after they get it out of their system at Mardi Gras.

Martin Hanley, his sister and me alternated using the bathroom and got ready to go to the early parade, Tucks, at 1:00 pm. Martin suggested that we all have Jagermeister shots before going out. I never had one but he insisted that it would make us feel better. It was rather syrupy but it was all right.

We went Uptown but missed the parade so we went Downtown to where the French Quarter is located. We mixed a vodka and orange juice, what was left of it, and headed to Canal Street to watch the parade. We had to park very far away in a lot since nothing was available closer. We found a good place and waited for the parade.

It was incredible; there were so many people pushing and shoving to get to the front, even the nuns were pushing through the crowd! People were drinking everywhere. In New Orleans, everyone buys a beer or drink and walks down the street with it. You can even bring a drink out of one bar and walk into the next one. In most places, they have "to go" cups by the door to pour the drink into so they can have their glasses back.

There weren't many balconies on the street we were on, mostly just through the French Quarter. The parade was a pretty good one and I caught many beads, cups and doubloons. I had to fight and claw for those cheap trinkets because there were hundreds of people ready to step on your fingers or knock you over if they were given a chance.

French Quarter was savage and animalistic and I loved every minute of it. There were so many under age people drinking and the cops don't do anything to you during Mardi Gras. They just look at you from their horses and hold their tongues. I'm sure after Mardi Gras it gets a little tougher.

Bathrooms are near impossible to find so when you find one, grab it. I found a Portolet so I jumped in line and started waiting. While I was there, I started talking to the guy in front of me since we were both plastered and found out that he was a "virgin" Mardi Gras attendant, too. I had caught a red garter from a float on Isis and showed it to him. He wanted his picture taken with me so I obliged and hammed it up for the camera. He took two just to make sure the picture came out. I said that I am now immortalized.

We heard what we thought was a gunshot directly across the street from the Portolet. We looked and noticed people scattering from the noise and thought for sure someone was shot. We looked closer and saw some kid laughing in the chaos. I think he threw a firecracker. Three people were shot during the Bacchus parade so it is not very unusual for someone to be shot or stabbed there.

After the parades were over we decided to walk through French Quarter. But first, we dropped off our trinkets in the car. French Quarter was simply amazing. I never have seen so many interesting things at one time. It was only 7:30 pm when we got there so everyone wasn't totally obliterated yet. But they were wild. There were old French buildings three and four stories high with black wrought iron balconies. People had rented rooms up there or were the strippers from the strip joint down on ground level. People were standing shoulder to shoulder on the balconies and threw beads to the people below. One stripper was dancing up there in a teddy and everyone was chanting, "show your tits" over and over again. She did once and then kept showing her butt to us and shaking it.

We walked along and smelled the fragrant Cajun cooking. The rich smell of Jambalaya floated out to us along with the spicy, brown Gumbo which is poured over rice. We smelled the beignets fried in the spicy-sweet grease with powdered sugar sprinkled lightly over the top.

We were all hungry so Martin and Sheila had raw oysters on the half shell and I had some crawfish etouffee and more beer. We also had to use the bathroom and every bar required that you buy something before you can use it.

We got a table right away but had to wait at the bathrooms for a few minutes. We got back to the table and ate our food along with some French bread (how appropriate) and then walked down Bourbon Street again.

We stopped and looked at the hundreds of t-shirts along the way. There were so many brightly colored shirts it was hard to choose just one. There were many sex shops down in French Quarter with so many vibrators and sexual aids that I didn't know what half of them were. We went into a few of these shops and I saw some vibrators with prickly things on them, one that looked like a propeller, and hundreds of other toys to play with. There were female impersonators, female strippers with tattoos who were totally nude, and a few sex acts on stage. Everything you want in this part of town. There was a Ripley's Believe It or Not, Pat O'Brien's around the corner, and so many famous bars you always hear about from someone else.

There were not many costumes, they were mostly worn on Fat Tuesday since that is the big day down there. A few mule drawn carriages pushed their way through the hundreds of people stumbling about. I am surprised no one was trampled since there were people passed out on the street and one was out cold in the middle of the road!

We walked around the entire area to the Mississippi River where we went into the Jax Building. It had many clothing stores on the bottom floor and the upper levels had about five or six bars. We went to the Tuscan and had a beer overlooking the river. It was dark by this time and as I looked to my right, I could see a bridge which was decorated with white lights all the way across the top dipping down into gentle arcs where the wires hung down. I could see huge steam boats cruising lethargically down the river while the faint sounds of jazz emanated from the decks. On the other side of the Jax building was a view of French Quarter. There were many lights down there along with groups of people dancing in the streets. It was amazing how many people were out in the streets at one time. The entire city can be viewed from the Jax building along with the drifting fragrance of Cajun food and the sound of horns playing in some smoky bar. We caught the smell of beignets so we decided to go have some. We weren't done with our drinks so we grabbed a "to go" cup and walked out with them.

We walked to Cafe du Monde which served delicious French coffee and beignets. Some girl was dancing on her table and flirting with a dozen college guys sitting a couple of tables away. The beignets came fairly quickly. They are doughnut like wedges deep fried in a spicy-sweet oil. It has an unusual flavor, a little different than doughnuts. They sprinkle a little powdered sugar on top for a little more sweetness. It isn't as sugary as a doughnut but I'm sure that it is just as fattening, if not more so.

After the beignets, David, Sheila and I walked up around French Quarter again. It was getting late, or early, however you want to look at it, so everyone was drunk and disorderly. We walked down the street while men were peeing in every nook and cranny. Many were just standing there nonchalantly urinating on the street. The ground had about an inch of liquid on it consisting of urine, beer, wine, hurricanes and vomit. It had a very bad stench to it. There were no trash cans anywhere because I kept looking for one, so everyone threw the trash on the ground. Martin said they like it that way so they can see how big Mardi Gras was by how many tons of trash there was on the streets. The garbage helped soak up that disgusting mixture on the ground. No one was carded there, they don't care as long as you give them money and get the hell out of the way.

The jazz in New Orleans is unique and was playing out of almost every bar. The Mardi Gras Mambo was a popular song. The style is a little Blue Grass, a slice of jazz, a dash of blues, a bit reggae and all very Cajun. They play a lot of horns and have deep drum beats to dance to. It feels so good to be able to dance in the streets, walk around with alcohol in your hand and do whatever you want.

Our feet and heads were aching from walking and drinking for 12 hours. We decided to walk back to the car along with a few hundred other people. We gathered all of our beads and headed back to Martin H.'s apartment.

Sheila was tired as was I but I can always drink so David and I decided to go to Mirage, which is a nice lounge in Metairie, about 5 miles from New Orleans. I dressed up in a black dress and we went out to drink some more. It was an upscale place that does have a dress code. I drank some more Bloody Marys. They make them so good down there with the Cajun spices burning your mouth. We danced a little and when the song "Harlem Shuffle" came on by the Rolling Stones, six or seven people actually started dancing the Harlem Shuffle. We were watching with amazement because neither of us knew how to do it and they were dancing in perfect unison. I started to get tired and we decided to go back and get some sleep. We weren't done so was grabbed those to-go cups and headed out the door. I fell asleep almost instantly when we got back to his apartment.

Sunday morning I woke up early again at 7:30 am, still intoxicated. I only got another 5 hours of sleep that night. I took a shower earlier this time and we planned on going Uptown since I've never been there before. New Orleans is set up by Uptown, which has some old historic neighborhoods, and Downtown, which is where the office buildings and French Quarter are. Uptown is where the rich live and where Loyola and Tulane colleges are located. These colleges are on the expensive St. Charles Avenue. Yes, that is the same as the one in Monopoly. The two parades for that day were Mid-City at 1:30 pm and Bacchus at 6:00 pm. We grabbed a cooler and filled it full of beer and left again to go party. We decided to eat a real meal so we stopped at Picadilly's for lunch before the parades.

We drove down St. Charles to get there and I've never seen such grand homes in my entire life. They are huge. Most homes have enormous columns around them which are styled like the ones in ancient Greece. I was naming the architecture styles of each since I just studied that in Humanities at Tallahassee Community College, which I started recently. I was so amazed at these immense homes that I sat dumbfounded in the car. We were about forty-five minutes early to the Mid-City parade, so we just sat on the grass and drank. This part of town is the exact opposite of French Quarter. There were yuppie families with their well-dressed children and several nuns arrived from a nearby convent. There was not a nun in sight in the French Quarter. The people were not quite as viscous to get the cheap souvenirs, but human nature kicked in and a few did push and scratch. David caught a lot of things and gave me some of his pearls, which I could never quite catch. He caught a purple, gold, and green carnation and gave it to me. Those are the colors of Mardi Gras and are seen everywhere. They are also the colors of LSU. There was a building with lights that have one row of purple, a row of gold and a row of green. That is the proper order. Some lady had the gaul to accuse me of stealing her carnation out of her purse. What a wench!

She didn't even check her purse to see if it was there. Her husband had a camcorder and filmed me for some unknown reason.

We got to see the Mid-City parade from the beginning when the band was playing and everyone was smiling and marching in synch. By the time they got downtown they looked like hell and a few were crying because they were so tired. We wanted to see the Bacchus parade at the beginning also since Dennis Quaid was the king this year. I wanted to get a picture of him. We found a great parking spot only two blocks from where the parade started. Tipatina's was where the parade started which was right on the corner. We were three hours early so we continued drinking and watching the Budweiser Clydesdales being unloaded from the trucks. We were laughing how they flapped their lips really fast as if they were talking to each other. I started feeling hungry again so we walked to Tipatina's and I ordered some Gumbo. It looked disgusting but tasted delicious. It looked like a brown soupy substance with chunks of shrimp and other unknown items. This concoction is poured over rice so it soaks it up. I mistakenly added some tabasco sauce and it burned the roof out of my mouth. I learned that you don't have to add spices to Cajun food. We just carried our cooler into the bar and were drinking our own brews right there. That is the bar where the Neville Brothers played on Saturday and Sunday nights at midnight. Dr. John was also playing that night so we wanted to stick around Tipatina's for that show.

After my tasty Southern meal we went back out and it was almost time for the parade. This was the best parade I have ever seen. The floats were extravagant and beautiful. Dennis Quaid was on the second float and was extremely drunk. He kept trying to stand up as he was screaming and throwing out handfuls of doubloons. He couldn't actually stand up because someone had tied him to his chair. I think they did that because he was so intoxicated. Every time he tried to stand up he would be pulled back down. It was pretty funny. Dennis picked up the box of beads and poured them over himself. He kept looking into the crowd and smiling. I yelled, "hey, Dennis, look over here" and he finally did. He did a double take when he noticed that I had a camera and smiled that fabulous smile for me.

The floats rolled by and the bands were dancing and playing. I was the only one of us to catch a cup from that parade. They rarely throw cups out during the Bacchus parade. We decided to sit in the car with the light on while Martin smoked a cigarette. Everyone was leaving, but was stayed there. There were so many interesting people walking back from the parade. There were Black women who lived in the neighborhood, young college people, some women dressed entirely in leather, and still others dressed up in their expensive active wear who had their limo pick them up. Sheila was tired and took a nap in the car for a couple of hours. We just watched people leaving as David smoked. This was the part of town where mostly all the Blacks lived. The houses in the entire city are so close together. There was barely enough room to walk between them. When we had to go to the bathroom we walked between two of the houses and tiptoed to the back. Most of the windows were open but the curtains were closed so they could hear us if we made any noise. I started to get paranoid and held onto my beads so they wouldn't clink. I was afraid someone was going to grab me from the window or stick a shotgun in my face. I have never peed so fast in my life. I still had some toilet paper in my pocket, which was lucky. I learned very quickly to grab toilet paper whenever you see it because it is a rare occurrence down there. As we sat in the car a few hours, we got better at sneaking back for a leak. I took my beads off next time. A couple of kids finally saw us but we told them all we were doing was going to the bathroom and we weren't going to hurt anyone. When you got to go, you got to go. However, we did go elsewhere the net time we had to go to the bathroom. We sat in the car drinking our beer and toasted everyone who drove or walked by.

At 8:00 pm we decided to go to Tipatina's and get a good spot since the doors were just opening. To our amazement there was already a line which twisted around the corner. There were three or four hundred people in line already with more people coming. We were standing in the street close to the front wondering how we could cut in line when a girl right behind me was struck by a car. She didn't feel it because she was drunk, but it had to hurt the next day. It crushed the cup in her hand and knocked off some of her beads. The cops were standing there and pushed the crowd into Tipatina's, thus pushing us to the front of the line. We were inside an hour when Dr. John started to play.

We listened to him for a while but then Sheila said that she was tired and wanted to go home. We all decided to leave although I did want to stay so badly. However, the Neville brothers wouldn't be playing for another 4 hours and Martin didn't want his sister sleeping in a car by herself, so we all left. There are absolutely no chairs in Tipatinas. Standing room only. That was a bit rough.

We left there and decided we should eat at Mother's. It is a fabulous restaurant Downtown and the Bacchus parade was just ending there when we got to it. It was 10:00 pm and they closed at 10:00 pm and wouldn't let us in. Martin argued with the guy to let us in but they wouldn't. We decided to head home at that time. We got on the freeway which was a huge mistake because the traffic stopped completely. We were on the freeway an hour before we got to an exit. We got off there and were in Metairie within 15 minutes. We stopped for something to eat and by the time we were back to the apartment it was 12:30 am and we were exhausted again. I slept next to Martin in his room. We kissed a little but I didn't want to have sex. I woke up later the next day, at 8:30 am, and got ready to leave New Orleans. I collected all of my belongings and reluctantly left that wonderful city. Martin Fourneir came to pick me up since we left my car at the Benefits Management office in Baton Rouge.

As soon as I got outside the city limits I was actually having Mardi Gras withdrawals. I wanted to go back to Bourbon Street so badly but I knew that I had to get home.

Martin Fourneir and I sat in his office for a couple of hours after getting a couple of Attitude Adjustment daiquiris from a daiquiri drive through. I was amazed that there were drive through bars there. Not only drive through bars, but they were open in the morning! Only in Louisiana. I finally got into my car to leave. I had some money in my pocket and was so tempted to take the New Orleans exit and party for a few more hours. The urge was so strong that I've never felt it before. It was truly addicting. I kept driving because I would miss more school and I would be driving back all the way to Tallahassee drunk which would be dangerous. I was tired enough as it was and had to stop for breakfast in Pensacola. My eyes were crossing literally the last four hours and I had my window down in order to stay awake. I got home at 12:45 am Tuesday morning and actually made it to school. The only reason I'm in school is because my mom is paying for it. I'd never be able to afford to go otherwise.

Mardi Gras was the most fun I have ever had and I will never miss a Mardi Gras again for the rest of my life if I can help it. Everyone needs to be loose and relax for a week and a half out of the year. The world would be a happier place if there were more Mardi Gras celebrations across the United States.

MARCH 17, 1990

Back to life as normal. I made such an idiot of myself last night. The out of town representatives came to Tallahassee this week. That included Martin Fourneir. On Friday, many people from work plus Martin Hanley, Ed Fowler, and Debbie met at Dooley's Down Under for drinks. I love seeing Martin Fourneir. I had a good time, and I danced with both Martins as they bought me drinks and put in on their company credit cards. I got very drunk and started hugging on Martin Fourneir. He kept telling me not to do that because he didn't want anyone to know about us. Martin told me he was staying at the same hotel and I kept trying to talk my way into meeting him at his room later in the night. He said that it wasn't a good idea and said he would drive me home. My car was at the office but Martin thought it was best if he drove me home. Martin had Ed in the car with him so I gave directions to an apartment complex near work and said that I lived there. It was a complete lie. I pretended that my apartment was around back and told them that I would be okay now. I didn't want to go home yet and had a plan to wait for Martin at his hotel room.

Just as Martin and Ed dropped me off, I heard Ed ask if they were going to Roosters. I was crushed because I wasn't invited. Ed kept rambling on and said that Debbie was going. It hurt so much. I was still no where near home so I stuck with my original plan and pretended to go into an apartment.

Once the car left, I walked the mile and a half to the hotel. I was so drunk that I didn't feel shy and went straight up to the check-in clerk and said that I lost my key card to my room. I told the guy behind the desk that I was Mrs. Martin Fourneir and that my husband was going out with some friends but I forgot to get the room key card. It worked and the man gave me one. I told him that I was very grateful. I noticed that Martin's rental car wasn't back yet. I am sure it would be a couple of hours.

I went into the hotel and kept the lights off and got into bed, taking off all my clothes. I thought it was a good idea at the time. A pleasant surprise for Martin. I laid there for a while then fell asleep. I awoke to Martin and Ed talking and Ed asking if he could come into Martin's room. I was freaked and didn't know what to do. Maybe run into the bathroom. Then I decided to stay where I was at. I breathed a sigh of relief when Martin said he was too tired and he wanted to go back to his room to sleep. My drunk had worn off enough that I felt kind of stupid now. Martin turned on the light and jumped when he saw me. He made me get dressed and quietly reprimanded me for my foolish actions. He was so angry. Martin made me stay in the room while he went to the check-in desk to give that man who gave me a key a piece of his mind. I felt like running right then. I should have, I know. But I waited. Martin told me that he was going to take me home. I felt so humiliated. A few minutes later Martin quietly came back in the room so Ed wouldn't hear and grabbed my arm and took me to his car. He started to drive to the same fake apartment complex I had him take me to before. I was going to let that lie stay, but Martin wanted to see me go into my apartment. Since I didn't actually live there, I couldn't do that. I had to tell him the truth. Martin asked why I lied and I told him the reason; my plan the entire time to go back to his room. He drove me home to my real apartment. My car was at work but he wouldn't let me drive home since I was upset. I was quietly crying the whole time. I didn't look up very much because I was so embarrassed.

By the time we got to my apartment, Martin wasn't angry any more. He told me what I did was wrong, though, and asked what would happen if Ed or someone else had come into his room. I mumbled that I didn't know. I didn't want to be reprimanded again. Martin saw that and made me promise not to do that ever again. I promised. Anyway, he had told the check-in to never let me in again, I am sure of that. Martin said that we would plan a time when I could drive to Baton Rouge and he could put me up in a hotel and spend some time together. I was happier again and kissed him and walked to my apartment. He stayed until I got inside.

I know that Martin invited me to visit him, but I was still humiliated and devastated. I made such a fool of myself. I am so glad that no one else saw me.

Tonight, after all my pain and bitterness, at least Keri and I are going to The Warehouse to watch The Chieftain's. It is a local Irish band that plays traditional music. It sounds like fun. Plus, it is Keri's birthday on St. Patrick's Day. Isn't that strange for an Irish girl? The reps are going back home today so they won't be at The Warehouse tonight. Thank God!

MARCH 18, 1990

Last night at The Warehouse was so much fun. As usual, I didn't have much money so I didn't drink much. I did have two

Guinness beers on tap. Keri gave me money to get her one, too, since she just turned 20. She is a bit younger than I am.

The Irish music was so good! There were several other bands. When The Chieftains got on stage, Mike handed out sheets of paper with the words to the Irish songs they were going to play. That way, people could sing along. That was a great idea. They had a flutist, Harvey played fiddle, Mike sang and played the accordion, there was a traditional Celtic drummer and a guy playing a big bass. They were excellent. Keri and I stayed the entire time they played plus listened to another band who came on after The Chieftains.

They were selling corned beef sandwiches, cabbage and sausage dinners but I couldn't afford one. Keri got a Reuben and gave me half of it. It is so embarrassing being so broke. I wish I had money to do things. All of my money goes to bills and the secret DUI fines. Thank God my mom is secretly paying my car payment in addition to community college. That is so nice of her. She begged me not to tell Jim because he would have a coronary. Although, that wouldn't be a bad thing, but I don't want mom being yelled at. The silver Ford Festiva is in my mom's name, so she can't afford to get it repossessed.

Well, depressing money situation aside, Keri and I had a great time. I am glad we went. I'll have to do it again next year.

MARCH 20, 1990

I went to court yesterday for driving without a license and insurance. I got more jail time. Every weekend for three months, which could have been up to five years in jail. They are tougher on you in Florida for not having auto insurance then for DUIs. I really can't get caught any more. Even the police who pulled me over, saw my piano and college books in the back seat asked why I kept getting into trouble. The mustached, older cop said that I appeared to be an intelligent, talented girl and I should straighten myself out. He said that he hates to arrest people like me for doing nonviolent crimes. He is right. Why was I speeding when I have no license? I drive because the bus system isn't that great and I work full-time and go to school full-time at Tallahassee Community College.

College makes me so happy, the complete opposite of jail hell I will have to continue to endure. Now I will be going back to jail every weekend for three months. That place is evil and hideous. I will sneak in my sleeping pills again so it won't be so terrible. At least I wasn't pulled over again on the way back from New Orleans. I was pretty worried about that so I didn't speed very much.

I haven't told anyone about this jail hell either. It is so difficult keeping these ugly secrets inside. I feel like two people and it is very difficult to keep this charade up. I wish I could confide in someone, but I don't want anyone to know about my troubles. I'll keep it secret so people won't judge me harshly.

I start jail this weekend. Back to the horrible grind. At least it isn't during the weeknights. I can spend time with Keelie. I will have to think of some reason to tell Keri why I'll be gone on weekends. I'll think of something.

MARCH 26, 1990

I tried to kill myself again. This time, I did it secretly. I took a whole bottle of prescription Motrin (just under a hundred of them). I ended up puking it all up and had a stabbing pain in my side all night. The pain was so bad that I had to lay on the bed doubled up. I thought that I had ruptured a spleen or some other organ. Poor Keelie was so worried about me, she sniffed my face and slept right by my head all night as I tried to stay still and ease the pain. Nothing I could do helped, plus I had difficulty breathing. I had to concentrate with my entire being to keep breathing. The night crept by, seconds felt like hours. I had to crawl to the bathroom whenever the urge to vomit came up and the vomit was more like an oozing of thick bile. It took everything to vomit since it was stuck in my esophagus. My muscles were too relaxed to vomit properly. When I had to pee, I pulled myself up to the toilet and hung on for dear life since the room was spinning. I made it through the night to live another day. That was three nights ago.

Last night, I had a terrible nightmare. It began with me going into a bar. I noticed a lot of the aliens in the bar who appeared human but their expressions were strange. They were smiling too much. I was one of the only people who knew the aliens were slowly invading our planet.

The aliens surrounded me, so I ran to the door, but they had a device which rendered me unconscious. When I awoke (in my dream), I was in a single bed and in a room which was designed more like a living room than a bedroom. The room was salmon in color and as I looked around saw endless salmon-colored rooms stretching down a long hallway, all without any doors. An alien came into the room and told me that I would be staying here for six months. There were other people in other rooms, but there wasn't anyone that I knew.

The aliens gave us all new clothes to wear. The women had to wear sexy negligees with see-through dresses over them because the aliens liked to stare at us.

One by one, the women were told that they were going home and were lead into a separate room. I looked in the room and saw that the aliens were really raping the women. I was terrified and knew that I had to escape. There were few people left to lead an escape, so it was going to be up to me to save my life.

I couldn't find a way out and was stuck waiting for my turn in the torture room. Some women returned completely insane after being taken to the back room to be raped by multiple aliens.

There was a mark on people when their six months were up. One of the walls opened up to let the six month detainees go. I saw cars lined up outside ready to give the newly released people a ride home. The guards were distracted by a fight so I jumped into the back of an old pickup truck while they weren't looking. The truck stopped, went into reverse and quickly picked up speed. The open bed of the truck became enclosed like the cab of the truck. The steering wheel was gone and so were the pedals. The emergency brake was missing, too, so I couldn't stop the vehicle.

We were going down a street which had stop lights but the vehicle went straight through them. I was looking at the traffic lights and noticed a slight glitch and heard a faint buzzing. I knew that I wasn't really here, it was just the aliens playing a game with me. I knew that no one was ever released. They were just put into these games which the aliens monitored. I woke up.

MARCH 30, 1990

I have been abandoned! Keri's mother and brother snuck into town without telling me anything and moved Keri into her own apartment while I was at work. No notice, no nothing. I came home just as they were leaving. Keri, in her usual sweet way, said that she had to go and left me alone. Monica had already moved in with Miguel, now Keri left without notice. I scared her away. Her mom and dad probably think I'm a freak who would hurt their sweet daughter since I tried to kill myself before. I am going through this jail and court nightmare and am left alone. I never told Keri about it, so she had no way of knowing why I have been so stressed and acting strangely. I asked her how I was going to pay for rent for the next month, and she gave me her half of the rent in cash before she left. I asked about future rent and she suggested that I look in the paper or place an ad for a roommate. Obviously she has thought about this. I am shocked!

I don't want to be alone. They left so quickly I didn't get her phone number or new address. What a failure I am at everything. I can't keep friends, I always fuck it up. Help me.

APRIL 6, 1990

Although I quickly found a roommate in the newspaper, I still feel so alone. His name is Robert. I didn't want a male roommate, but he was the most dependable one and had money for first month's rent so I said yes. He is a Political Science major at Florida State University. He seems nice, I hope.

APRIL 23, 1990

I did something spontaneous. I went to the Jazz Festival in New Orleans and stayed with Martin Brown since he invited me to stay with him. Although I ended up having a good time, it was an ordeal to get there. I bought beer for my visit and started drinking them while I was driving. I had my windows rolled down, cruising on the interstate, heading to Louisiana, and it felt so exhilarating. I really shouldn't have been drinking while I was driving. You'd think I'd learn my lesson by now.

During the drive, after sunset, the interstate had repairs and instead of four lanes, there were only two. The lanes on the left were blocked off by cement guards which were placed only inches from the lane. It started raining heavily and I was stuck behind a semi-truck, spraying water up so I couldn't see the road. I worked up the nerve to pass the truck, bad idea, and went into the left lane with the concrete dividers. The heavy rain, the splashing up of water from the truck, and my inebriation, caused me to slide into the concrete dividers. My car must have spun around like a pinball. I have no memory of the accident since my head broke the left window. The first thing I remember is walking down the middle of the interstate and cars honking at me. I realized I wasn't in my car and was extremely confused. A truck driver stopped and got me to the side of the road and waited with me until the ambulance and tow truck came. I couldn't see my car from the truck, so I don't know how far I walked.

The ambulance came and strapped me to a board to protect my spine. It was in the middle of nowhere so it was a very long drive to the hospital since the ambulance couldn't speed with the rain. Halfway into it, I realized I really had to pee. The EMT wouldn't let me use the bed pan since it would move my spine. We were still 45 minutes from Pascagoula, Mississippi, the closest town, and I really had to pee. Still thirty minutes to go and no toilet in site. I pleaded to use the bed pan, but the EMT told me to just pee my pants. That was more difficult to do than I imagined. My bladder was so full, it hurt. I reached my limit. I told her I was going to pee and she put an extra towel down near my crotch. I concentrated and pretended I was in a bathroom and not in an ambulance embarrassed out of my head. I did it. I peed my pants and apologized profusely, but the EMT lady said it was fine, it was no big deal.

Apparently, my pupils didn't dilate correctly, implying that I had a head injury. Just as we arrived at the hospital, the police showed up since they wanted to take blood for a DUI test. I found out later the tow truck driver threw away all of the empty beer cans in the car so the police never found them. The doctor refused to allow the police to take my blood because I was going in and out of consciousness. I barely remember the hospital until I was in a hospital bed. The tow truck driver found Martin's phone number in the car, so Martin drove all the way from New Orleans to my car and brought my suitcase to me. I was hugely relieved to see him. I wasn't in wet jeans anymore, not sure how those came off. I was in a hospital gown.

The doctors said I could leave with Martin as long as he woke me up every couple of hours to make sure I didn't lapse into a coma. I got clean clothes on and my wet pants were in a plastic bag in the room.

Martin drove me to his place where I fell asleep, off and on. I drove without a license and have no car insurance, so the tow truck driver said he would hold onto my car if I chose to have it fixed. I bent the frame so it was technically totaled. I asked if he could fix it and he said he could straighten it the best he could and we agreed I would send him monthly payments until it covered the thousands of dollars worth of repairs. That made me so depressed, it was difficult not to cry at all times. School, work, what was I thinking? I will get used to riding the bus, it appears.

Since everything was so bleak, I begged Martin to take me to the Jazz Festival, which was people playing jazz in the streets, in every night club and bar in the French Quarter. People played solo and in bands. One man played an unknown instrument, so I asked what it was and it was a hammer dulcimer. Martin thought I was amazing although I planned to kill myself when I got home, so everything looked so beautiful for my last weekend on earth. The music was phenomenal and we wandered for hours. We ate dinner at Mother's (the restaurant) where I had crawfish etouffee and we enjoyed beignets and coffee at Cafe du Monde.

I should have kissed Martin more. I don't know why I didn't have sex with him, although we almost did. We slept together in our underwear, Martin holding me through the morning.

When Monday came, I had to go back home and Martin bought me a ticket on the Greyhound bus. They were having a strike, so he suggested we park and sneak into the bus station. I got on the bus early because the strikers were yelling at me and the bus drivers who were still working. It felt like an eternity waiting for the bus to move. It turned out to be a crowded ride back to Tallahassee and a guy who appeared to be high, sat next to me. He definitely was high after I noticed him tie a band around his arm and shoot up with a needle right next to me! The needle dropped to the floor. I was completely freaked out and moved seats after a lot of people disembarked in Pascagoula.

Once I made it to Tallahassee, I took the city bus home, having to make a transfer to get to my apartment. The bus comes by only once an hour, so it was a long, tedious wait. I finally made it home and was happy to see Keelie. I wasn't sure if I'd still kill myself. I keep having fears of the unknown. My life is usually miserable, but the Jazz Festival filled me with new life and determination. It could be worse. I could be that junkie.

MAY 20, 1990

I overdosed on sleeping pills. Keri happened to call me, she heard my groggy voice and thought it was another suicide attempt and called an ambulance. She began questioning me nonstop so I told her how many pills I had taken. Keri freaked out for no reason because I can take a ton of pills without hardly feeling them. I didn't know that she had actually called the ambulance until they arrived at my apartment. It's better than Robert who pretends he doesn't see me when he was here and saw me crawling back to my bedroom because I was too dizzy to walk.

The ambulance took me to the Tallahassee Memorial Regional Medical Center emergency room. I was forced to vomit rather than having my stomach pumped, then monitored throughout the night. The doctors made me go to the psychiatric ward the next day. Either go to the psych ward or jail since it is a crime to attempt murder, even on myself. That is the stupidest law on the books. Going to jail for attempted suicide.

While I was in the hospital, I had many neurological tests since I hit my head in that car accident last month. They did CAT scans, sleep deprivation tests and psychological exams. The results were actually interesting. They discovered that my waking mind works in a very similar way that my sleeping mind does. That is abnormal. They aren't sure if it is because of the accident or some mental thing. Also, they found abnormal brain functioning in my frontal lobe. That is where I hit my head. It may or may not be a coincidence. It wasn't like I was normal before the accident, so I didn't think anything was different. Of course, I did lose consciousness during the accident and was found wandering aimlessly in the middle of the interstate.

I was kept in the hospital for nine days, which is when my insurance stopped paying. The doctors gave me medication while I was there but just sent me on my way afterwards with no prescription. I don't feel any better and they didn't tell me to follow up on anything. I am not sure how it helped. It was a nice, clean hospital with good food. It was almost like a vacation. I missed Keelie, though. Poor little thing missed me terribly. She has been very affectionate toward me today and almost constantly purring. My cat is the kindest creature in the world. Too bad no one cleaned her kitty litter. It appears she was given some food and possibly fresh water. The guilt of the bird incident burns in my mind. Karma.

JUNE 6, 1990

Back to same old thing. Of course, Robert is avoiding me since we recently had sex. I guess he wants to get away from me. I didn't tell you about that, did I? While Robert and I were watching *Godzilla 1984* we scooted closer and closer together. I know, he has a girlfriend, I don't know why I do these things. I feel so lonely and isolated and want companionship. One thing led to another and we had sex. He actually surprised me by being very affectionate. I wasn't expecting that. He even got a warm washcloth and cleaned me afterwards. I know that sounds gross, but it wasn't. It was very nice, actually. We were at it for an hour, at least. Afterwards, I went back to my room and we didn't mention it again. That was a couple of months ago. Now, when I returned home, the first thing he said to me is, "now that we have this sleeping pill thing in the open, what was up with you crawling on the floor that one night?" I just shrugged my shoulders and went into my bedroom. I had to clean the overloaded kitty litter first and then spent time with Keelie. I don't want to deal with Robert now. I just want to lay on my bed and relax. I go back to work on Monday so I have this weekend to rest. Robert has gone over to his girlfriend's house. I am relieved.

JUNE 10, 1990

Keri finally invited me over to her apartment to spend the night. We made margaritas and listened to music. I told her this place looked familiar, but didn't know why. We had a fun time, I was trying on different clothes of hers, like dress up day at school. She had her door open and we were laughing. A guy stopped by for a minute and said hi to Keri. I couldn't believe it! It was Brian from a couple of years ago! The bartender Brian who drove me the long way home because I pretended I was too drunk to drive. I told Keri that I had gone out with him a few times and she was excited and said that we should go over to his place and bring margaritas with us. We went over there, me still in Keri's clothes, knocked on the door with a bottle of tequila and margaritas mix. Keri asked if we could make some drinks over there. Brian recognized me, but felt uncomfortable. I see that now, but then, we were drunk and having fun. Everyone loves Keri anyway so we stayed there a while.

Oh, my God! What happened next was beyond embarrassing. I blacked out completely, everything just went dark and I have no memory of things after that. I awoke the next morning to find myself laying on Brian's bed, fully clothed and I pissed myself. There was a huge wet spot on the bed and Keri's skirt was wet. I had a little jacket that I tied around my waist to hide the wet spot, but I was pretty saturated. I threw some clothes on the bed to cover the wet spot. There wasn't much chance of getting out of this one. I peaked out of the bedroom (the door was closed) and saw Brian sleeping on the couch. To my horror, Keri was passed out on the living room floor, fully clothed. I saw our 1.75 liter of tequila was gone! We drank the whole thing. Shit, that is a lot of alcohol. No wonder I blacked out and Keri passed out.

I tried to quietly wake Keri up while covering my wet skirt. Unfortunately, Brian woke up first. Keri started to come around and when she stood up, Brian let us have it. He told us to get out and never come by his place again. It was such a humiliating moment. Keri apologized over and over again but he kept saying get out. I don't know if I even spoke. I wanted to run from his apartment. It came back to me; this is where I came a couple of years ago. That is why the apartments looked so familiar.

Once we got to Keri's door to her apartment, she grabbed my clothes and handed them to me, screaming that she had never been so embarrassed in her life and what was she going to do now with Brian being her neighbor. I didn't know what to say. She is the one who wanted to go over there. I said that I was sorry. She then asked me to leave. I told her I would return her clothes after washing them when I see her at work. I finally was invited to visit Keri and that devastation happened. I'm afraid she'll never invite me over ever again. I cried all the way home.

JULY 6, 1990

I had a nightmare that I was living in another place and I was going to a party. It was getting close to midnight. There was a full moon that night. Three other people came back to get me at the same time I was leaving my house. We were walking through the woods slowly because of the extreme darkness. There were vines and branches grabbing at our clothes. The only light was by the moon filtering through the trees.

We continued to walk along in silence. I noticed that the crickets stopped chirping and frogs stopped croaking and we were left in complete silence. We heard something moving to our left by the river. It appeared to be very large by the sound of the bushes being trampled. We were frightened and someone said that it was probably an alligator. We headed deeper into the forest and away from the river. I asked the other people what happened to the party. No one knew. We were lost out there in the dark woods, wandering aimlessly.

By the light of the filtered moon, I could see the people that I was with were beginning to grow an unusual amount of hair. I closed my eyes and looked again, thinking it was just a trick of the moonlight. When I opened my eyes, everything appeared normal. I decided to keep walking. The others followed. We soon came across a small fishing boat on the river and decided to drift down the river until we found the rest of the people. We lifted the boat and carried it to the water. I strained my back while doing this and when I awake later, my back was actually sore.

I noticed hair growing on my companions again and was frightened to get in the boat with them but did anyway. They were werewolves and were likely to tear the flesh from my bones. I pretended to go along with them for now. As we were rowing out I jumped from the boat into the river. While I did that, I accidentally tipped the boat over. The werewolves fell on top of me in the water, so I clawed at the exposed roots and weeds trying to get a firm grip so I could pull myself ashore. That was when I woke up.

JULY 15, 1990

I keep having nightmares every night. I haven't completely paid off my court fees, my car is still being repaired in Mississippi, and am still barely making it paycheck to paycheck.

Last night, in my nightmare, a group of us came upon a swamp when a girl yelled at me to look ahead of us. There was a huge alligator out in a pond laying on a log. The alligator was the size of a mobile home. The alligator saw us and started toward our direction so we both began running toward her car. We were terrified and screaming. We stopped at the top of the hill and turned around. The alligator's mouth was open and was about two stories tall with huge white teeth that had moss on them. They resembled gigantic stalactites and stalagmites instead of teeth.

Some movement caught my eye and I noticed that five or six children were playing on the grass near the enormous alligator. There was a baby crawling around. The kids were just playing without seeing the danger they were in.

The lawn on which the children were playing morphed into a fishing boat. The alligator turned and swam toward the boat. It submerged and all was quiet for a moment. The alligator appeared from directly below the boat, picked up the boat and children into its large mouth. One child was crushed immediately by the enormous teeth and lay bleeding face-down in the water. The rest of the children were screaming as we all stood on the shore horrified.

The fear was so intense and the children's screams echoed through my head. Everything became surreal and slow-motion. I was able to zoom in on the catastrophe as if I was looking through a camera with a telephoto lens. The children were huddled together in the mouth of the alligator just before being crushed in its jaws.

One child leapt free from the carnage into the water. I was able to see into the mouth of the alligator. The children were being swallowed alive and would be dissolved by stomach acid. I was horrified as their shrill screams continued to echo in my mind. I was also screaming at the top of my lungs for this torment to stop. I awoke at 5:45am, Saturday, very frightened so I decided to write this nightmare down immediately.

I know why I had a nightmare. It is because I am going to be alone this weekend and I'm very frightened. Peter and David won't take me to the beach with them this weekend. My car is still in Pascagoula waiting for me to pay off the repairs. David actually said to me, "life's a bitch." Why is he so cruel to me? At least I don't have to spend my weekends in jail anymore.

When I was at work a few weeks ago, I asked Peter, who is highly educated and intelligent, to give me a list of classic books to read. I skipped high school so much and missed most of the required readings. Peter was happy to help since I want to learn more, not be so ignorant. He told me about *Moby Dick*, all Kurt Vonnegut books, *For Whom The Bell Tolls* by Hemingway, *Anna Karenina* and *War and Peace* by Tolstoy so far. I began with Anna *Karenina*. It is so good. I already read For *Whom The Bell Tolls*, too. Peter will think about it and give me more books to read whenever he thinks of them.

I have also asked Peter to tell me good classical music. He suggested that I listen to the classical station. I have been listening to 91.5, the Florida State University station, especially when I sleep. I was hoping that it would help the nightmares. It is nice to have the music when I wake up. They play classical 24 hours a day without commercials. It is great. They have a show called Performance Today which sometimes discusses good cds. I write down the name of the piece of music whenever I hear something I like. I haven't been able to buy any music yet because I can't afford a cd player. Someday. Shit, I wish I could afford to get my Ford Festiva. I'm very close to paying it off now. Just another couple of paychecks.

I had a nightmare last night. Peter from work was demented, attacked me and took me hostage. He was wearing a suit which is completely out of character for him. There were other men in suits who were trying to convince Peter to let me go. I was being held in a headlock.

Peter took me up to the top of a tall mountain which had sharp, jagged rocks, jutting up through the fog. The sharp rocks were pink in color. A man was trying to bribe Peter to release me, but he wouldn't accept the money. More men in suits kept approaching us, asking what Peter wanted, but he would not say. He just kept telling them to go away. I also told them to leave us alone because I didn't think Peter would hurt me. The men in suits wouldn't relent and kept pestering Peter. Finally, Peter threw his hands in the air as if he surrendered, ran up to a man and pushed him off the cliff. Several more men plummeted to their death as Peter pushed them off the mountain. I awoke.

AUGUST 16, 1990

I am excited to say I got my car back! It took thousands of dollars to get it fixed. Poor Silver Bullet (that's what a guy at work calls it because he says it looks like a Coors Light beer can on wheels). I took the city bus to the Greyhound bus station, then the tow man picked me up from the bus station. He took me back to the shop, showed me the bag full of my belongings, mostly empty beer cans, and lectured me for ten minutes about the dangers of drinking and driving. Yes, I know. For all I know, there is a warrant for my arrest in Mississippi for the accident. I didn't get anything official from the police because I left too quickly. Maybe they'll write it off. Probably not with my luck. No speeding all the way home. The car shimmies at 50 mph because the frame is slightly bent. He did a great job fixing it because I can't tell the car was totaled. I have a picture of it. Wow. The frame was off alignment by at least a foot before it was realigned. I'm home and happy to have my wonderful car without air conditioning so I sweated like a fat man in a sauna on the long car ride home.

AUGUST 25, 1990

I am exhausted. Yesterday, Martin Fourneir called me at home and asked to drive to Baton Rouge to see him and have hot sex. Not to be confused with Martin Brown from New Orleans. Martin told me to meet me at his office when I got into town. I told him that I was very broke but he said he would pay for my room and the gas. It is a long, tiring drive to Baton Rouge at 6½ hours one way, no speeding. I was so excited the entire way driving out there. I couldn't wait to see Martin and go to dinner with him. I took Friday off just to drive out there. I am so gullible. I am so smitten with him I can't see reason.

When I got to Baton Rouge, I went straight to Martin's office per instructions. It was only a little after 5:00 pm, so I was shocked to see the office was closed and locked. I was supposed to meet Martin there. I found a note left for me by the door to call Martin on his pager when I got in. My heart instantly felt relieved and stopped squeezing so tightly. I was on the verge of a complete crying binge. There was a pay phone a block from the office so I went straight to the phone and dialed Martin's pager number. I waited in the sweltering heat for 15 minutes before he called me back. It definitely wasn't a quick response. I started getting really worried when he didn't call. When the phone finally rang my dark mood lifted again into sweet birdsong. I quickly picked up the phone and heard Martin's voice. I was relieved. That was a short-lived feeling. Martin was speaking very quietly and said that his wife was insistent he stay home with her and their child that night. He said that he won't be able to get out at all this weekend. I couldn't believe it! I had just driven from Tallahassee with only a $10 left in my pocket. I was exhausted but couldn't afford a hotel room. Martin told me that he was sorry but he couldn't put me up in a room and that he would have to pay me back in the future. I didn't want to tell Martin just how broke I was. My car gets very good gas mileage so I was hoping that the $10 and whatever change I could scrounge from my car and purse would get me back home.

What could I do? I didn't hide my disappointment to Martin and my irritation at driving 6½ hours just to see him. Plus, I had to now turn around and drive 6½ back to Tallahassee. I was already tired from the drive. After waiting for Martin to call and after our conversation, it was getting close to 6:00 pm by that time. Martin said that he told the office employees to go home early, that is why the door to his office was closed. Yeah, right. He didn't want me to go into his office and make a scene. That was the real reason. I asked why he didn't call me earlier to let me know but he said that his wife only made this demand when he came home from work. I don't believe that since he closed the office early. I am sure he knew something earlier in the day or perhaps yesterday. I said a cold good-bye to Martin although my heart was aching. I felt like such a fool!

I was so hungry but didn't have enough money to eat anything. I had to drive back to Tallahassee tired, hungry and thirsty since I didn't have a penny to spare for water. I drank some water at rest stops.

My drive home was hell. About 4 hours into my drive I started getting so tired that my eyes were crossing. My windows were already rolled down so I was getting plenty of fresh air. I couldn't take the tiredness any more and pulled over at the next rest stop. Even though it was hot and muggy outside and I have no A/C in my car, I rolled up all the windows, locked the doors, and tried nervously to take a nap at the rest stop. I was very freaked out. I parked by the semi-trucks. As I laid there in my reclined seat, I got so frightened by myself. I have read of murders at rest stops in Florida. I was alone and no one in the world except Martin knew where I was. I didn't have Martin's number because out of rage, I threw away his pager number. I was completely alone. I then started to think about poor Keelie without me. I couldn't sleep. It was too much mental anguish. I decided to finish up the 2½ hours of the trip and just get home. I couldn't speed because I don't have a driver's license or insurance. I only sped 4 miles per hour over the speed limit since they don't usually stop you for doing that. I was taking a chance, but I had to get home. I found myself driving in excess of 85 miles per hour from time to time because I was so sleepy and not paying attention. Then I quickly slowed the car down to 59 miles per hour again. I didn't mean to speed so much. I just wanted to get home. The speed limit is a stupid 55 mph.

I finally made it home, hungry, thirsty and exhausted. Robert was still up watching television. He was surprised when he saw me home and asked why I was back already. I gave him the briefest explanation possible and said that Martin had a family emergency and couldn't meet me and I didn't have money for a hotel. Short and simple. Robert said that Martin was a real ass for not putting me up in a hotel at least. I agreed. I got some water and went to bed. I was hungry, but I could eat in the morning. I just needed sleep. I have eaten lunch now and am writing this sordid story in you. I feel broken inside. Crushed. Humiliated. Used. I won't do that again. That is what I say now, but if Martin asked me tomorrow I would go back to Baton Rouge to visit him. How can I be so gullible? I am manipulated by Kyle, John's hot friend, too. He calls me up for occasional sex. He comes over to my apartment after going out drinking with friends. Why do I put up with it? Because I hope someone will fall in love with me. It could happen, couldn't it?

AUGUST 28, 1990

There is a serial killer loose in Gainesville at the University of Florida. I don't like the Gators, but the crimes were so shocking, three or four nights of murder. The murderer even killed a man who was staying with his girlfriend to protect her! Five students are dead, brutally stabbed. The women were raped, and the predator broke into one girl's apartment and waited for her to return home. They all were subdued, tied up, and had their clothes cut off. They all were murdered face down, stabbed in the back. He spent time with the bodies, posing them for shock value. One poor girl had her head cut off, which was placed looking at her body.

Students from University of Florida are leaving school and some are transferring up here, to Florida State University. No one is safe since two girls were killed the same night, roommates. Can you imagine hearing your roommate murdered as you are tied up, waiting for the murderer to come and do whatever he wants to you before leaving you for dead? Serious horrors. He is being compared to Ted Bundy who finished his killing spree here, in Tallahassee. People here are afraid he'll move up the interstate to Florida State. It is chaos in Gainesville.

AUGUST 30, 1990

A man was arrested for the murders in Gainesville. It is a guy who has terrible facial scars from a car accident. He looks horrid with his scars, but he has an alibi for one of the murders, so I am not so sure he is the right person. He might be, I suppose. I don't think there is any copy cat killer since the murders took place within days of each other. Time will tell if the police caught the guy.

I am almost obsessed about this case. The thing is, the news released a description of a serial killer. They are a loner, in their twenties, have some trouble with the law in the past. So many of the traits of a serial killer sound like me! I read more about serial killers and they often were bed wetters and may have had head injuries. The difference is I'm female and I would never hurt anyone. Not intentionally. I could have hurt someone by drinking and driving. That's true. But I wouldn't purposely hurt an animal or person. I know what it feels like to be hurt, so I don't want to inflict pain on others.

SEPTEMBER 10, 1990

There was another man arrested for the murders in Gainesville. His name is Daniel Rolling and was caught in a robbery in Louisiana, which is creepy since I was just in Louisiana. We may have been going in the opposite direction. He used the same tools for the break in as in the murders. Rolling was living in a tent in the woods. Just gross. He must have smelled terrible. There were no showers where he stayed, as a homeless drifter. His breath had to be disgusting. The other scar-faced man was set free, after being touted as a killer, so his life is ruined since his picture was plastered on every news station and poster. Poor guy. He has horrific scars which caused mental illness, causing him to act a bit odd. I had a feeling he was innocent. He had an alibi for one of the murders, so it didn't make any sense to hold him and give his name to the press. I can't imagine how this will destroy his life. I can relate to him, in a weird way. We both have mental problems and low self-esteem. I'm so relieved they caught the right man. Rolling has an arrest history of robbery, peeping Tom, and other things. It seems his crimes escalated. I knew that peeping Tom we had when I was a kid in Bean was a real danger. What if he escalated, too?

SEPTEMBER 16, 1990

I'm watching a Cajun special on PBS. It shows the real people, the culture, songs, dress, love and relationships. There are old men, a mixture of French, Africans and American Indians, speaking the French Cajun and wailing their sorrowful songs on their fiddles. They know of their diverse heritage and know and love who they are. Large pots of gumbo are cooked up. They have a special confidence and a certain intelligence, not book learning, but a knowledge of the inner feelings. They are honest and honorable since they are comfortable with themselves. I feel that simple peaceful bliss at this moment. They have sorrows but it makes them strong and content. They can be alone and not be lonely. I envy those Cajuns with their families and friends all around them. I wish I could adopt that culture and then accept myself, the good and bad around me. I wish I could view my hardships as a fallen down, rotten tree which is good for nothing except for a stepping stone up to the next strong branch of a healthy, vital tree. I want to be able to see the good path ahead of me and eliminate the bad paths. Please God, let me always feel this easy, relaxed peace. The thing I must learn is to grow, feed, and nurture myself off the old, rotten, misleading ideas and become a confident human being which can handle any mishap. I can and will fulfill my dreams of being graduation from college. I see now that love of a man is not the thing that I am lacking, it is the love of myself. That is the key. I have unlocked the door and am looking through the keyhole cautiously. There is light and happiness behind that door. Hesitation restrains me from pure bliss. I will slowly open that door wider and wider until it is flung open and the light is shining brightly into my soul.

SEPTEMBER 30, 1990

I have been attending every home Florida State football game with Robert since he gets 4 season tickets as an alumni. He is a graduate student, so he buys tickets as an alumni. He takes his girlfriend, Bonnie, and his very large friend, Rob, who must be 6'-4" tall and 300 pounds. He isn't at all attractive but has a fantastic personality. The four of us go out for lunch before the game or dinner after. It is nice to be in a group of people enjoying life for a change. FSU played Virginia Tech and won. It was awesome going to The First for drinks and wings. The place was so packed it was lucky we got a table. Rob is so tall, he spotted someone leaving and got on it. Bonnie said I should date Rob, but I can't get past his extreme acne. It is so bad they are more like boils. That sounds so mean, I know. I guess I am vain. Bonnie is the opposite with skin like milk yet she won't go anywhere without full makeup. I'm not sure why she is such a princess about her hair and makeup. She dropped out of FSU. To be honest, she is really pretty but not the sharpest tool in the shed.

I didn't used to like football, only watching the Seahawks sometimes. I really enjoy college football now. I don't know what it is about the game, but it is exciting and violent. I'm really getting into it. It also brings me together with the crowd at the stadium. I feel so many people around, it makes me less lonely. I also have plans on the weekends where I didn't before. Being there in person is so much more thrilling than watching the game on tv.

OCTOBER 5, 1990

Peter asked me again what I see in his roommate, David. He knows that I go over and have sex but want so much more. I said that he is nice, and Peter said that is what all the girls say. Then Peter asked me if he really was nice, and I said yes, but maybe he knows something I don't. We have never gone out in public together, never gone on a date, only stayed in his bedroom. He never wants to go out with me, but has other female friends he goes out with. I just can't give him up. I love him. I think I do, anyway.

OCTOBER 7, 1990

I am so dejected. Florida State lost to Miami last night. We scored 22 and Miami 31. The four of us still had a good time. Night games are the best because it isn't so hot. During the day games, I feel like I could pass out from the heat. Drinking alcohol doesn't help the situation.

OCTOBER 17, 1990

Robert, Bonnie and I went tubing down the Ichetuckne river last weekend. It was so much fun even though Robert put his keys in his pocket after he was warned about losing them. Of course, he lost them. We had to wait around for all the tubers to get off the river and see if anyone turned in a set of keys. Someone actually did, after we waited for hours.

I even had a dream that we were going rafting down the river but everyone else backed out which was really depressing. I felt as if I was drunk (in real life, I was actually drunk when I fell asleep) and had a difficult time getting out of my bed because I was off-balanced and confused. My sight was blurry and everything appeared to jump around before my eyes. I couldn't walk without holding onto furniture.

The people in my apartment were a strange looking bunch. Some looked sinister, shifty and not trustworthy. I stumbled into the kitchen and noticed a trap door in the wall. I opened the door and found a staircase leading upward. I slowly walked up the secret stairs and came to a room at the top. It appeared to be a lounge with three tables and several chairs scattered around the room. I spun around and saw three more steps. I ascended and discovered a private pool. Robert followed me up there and said that it was a pool for all of the tenants. I said that I didn't know the pool was up there.

Since I still wanted to go rafting at Ichetuckne, I didn't want to be around these people in the pool. I stumbled my way back downstairs, returning to the living room.

I began feeling less drunk and more in control. I still felt as if I was walking on uneven ground when I saw a man with dirty gray slacks and a shirt with a black and white checkerboard pattern. The man was about a week overdue on shaving and wore a red hat like Humphrey Bogart's on top of his curly black haired head. He had a hunting knife in his left hand and was signaling us to come over. I screamed no but it was too late. The man moved the knife to his right hand, said that he needed a throat, and stuck the blade against my throat. I could feel the cold steel pressing against my flesh. The man asked for our money. Robert said he didn't have any but I knew he had cash. The man told Robert that he knew he was lying, and again, demanded money. I was frightened and told Robert to give him his money. Robert started slowly counting out his money as I pleaded with him to hurry. The man pressed the knife harder against my throat. I could feel the blade slicing through my flesh and blood trickling down my neck. The man just grabbed all of the money that Robert was counting and took off running.

OCTOBER 28, 1990

I am starting to feel a bit more human going to football games with friends, even though I still have a problem with small talk. I usually don't talk much, but no one seems to mind. Every night, I am filled with dread. Nightmares are all I have. I feel like I don't really fit in with Robert and his friends, so maybe that is why I have such low self-esteem.

I take so many sleeping pills in hopes of a peaceful night's sleep. I have been wetting the bed again, which is humiliating and I don't know why I go through these spells. I have to sneak to the laundry room and do laundry when no one is around so they don't ask me why I wash my sheets so often.

The highlight of yesterday was Florida State beating LSU last night, but an embarrassing fight broke out between both teams at the end. Some LSU guy started it, then the next thing we knew, both teams were fighting each other. Robert led us on the field to witness the chaos. I just wanted to go home, because I think sports fights are lame. We stayed until the dirty end. It was a fun night, in spite of the fight.

DECEMBER 3, 1990

Florida State threw the Florida Gators to the ground. The football game was fantastic. Robert, Bonnie, Rob and I went for wings and beer before the game and then the excitement of winning was ours. The Florida win was a big one after Auburn beat FSU a few weeks ago. I go to every home game and love the large crowds of people. I feel safe. It doesn't stop me from having the most horrifying dreams at night. Why is that?

In my dream I was a completely different person and was walking with a gang of five rowdy teenagers searching for drugs and alcohol. The guys wore black leather jackets, chains, dirty old black boots, and greased, spiky hair. One boy had red hair, the other dark brown with blond streaks.

The girls barely wore any clothes, except for me. One girl had on a leather mini-skirt and black t-shirt. The girls were all blonde. I looked at myself and saw that I was fat, like 180 pounds and shorter, too. My hair was very blonde. I knew that I was new to this group and was still innocent, somewhat.

"Red" ordered us all into a nearby orchard. Two girls and I sat on an old wooden fence. The boys were using their lighters to sterilize some needles. They all began to shoot heroin. I had never done heroin and was frightened. The rest of the gang pressured me into it by calling me "fatty" and "chicken shit". I finally gave in and let them stick the needle into my arm.

The boys were running around me flicking their lighters. There was a tremendous explosion. We were transported into a small room and seated around a rectilinear table with brown wooden chairs. The other girls kept fading in and out. We were dead and the other girls were dying. The walls were bare and white with only one window washed with dark paint. We knew that something was observing us, deciding our fate.

I ran over to the door but it was locked. I tried to peer through the black painted window and saw that it had steel mesh on the outside.

Everyone was crying and screaming and saying that they wanted to go back, to be alive and be better people. No one wanted to go to Hell. One of the boys yelled at the rest to shut up and stop crying. He commanded everyone to sit back down. We did.

Each person was shown all of his faults and mistakes. The visions were opened up to us through our minds. It was as if our brains were opened and a light penetrated our souls. There were two lights, one good and one evil. The good light showed us good deeds we had done. The evil light absorbed into our brains and made us all feel the worst fears ever imagined. We felt sad, lonely, petrified, worthless, and out of control. We suffered complete and total fear – fear of spending eternity trapped in morbid suffering within the black unknown.

The good light was deciding whether there was enough good to allow redemption. Two girls were selected and given a second chance and were cast back down to Earth. Somewhere the other three were engulfed into a torturous blackness which offered them Hell for eternity. The evil light got them. I was allowed another chance. I was so frightened. I didn't know what was required of me, but I certainly didn't want to be trapped in that terrible abyss.

DECEMBER 24, 1990

I am spending Christmas and my birthday alone. No one wants me to visit them. Me and Keelie alone through New Year's Eve. Robert went down to Tampa where his family lives. Everyone has family except me. I have Uncle John, and we go to the occasional manly movie, Steven Segal, or Sylvester Stalone. But when hanging out, he just watches tv and doesn't talk. Not very exciting.

CHAPTER 13

1991: Age 22

FEBRUARY 11, 1991

Apartheid has been eliminated in South Africa and Nelson Mandela was finally released from prison after 27 years. What a tremendous event. Blacks have been in segregation in South Africa, which isn't fair since the continent of Africa is really theirs to begin with. I am so happy for Mr. Mandela and his family. He was arrested for standing his ground, not for any violent crime. Leaders of the world are welcoming Nelson Mandela into their countries as a beloved guest. Happy news for a change.

MARCH 18, 1991

Yesterday was St. Patrick's Day and Keri's birthday. Keri is out of town and avoiding me still since the drunken incident with her neighbor. She drove to Illinois to visit her parents and spent her 21st birthday with her high school friends. I went to The Warehouse by myself. Hardly anyone from work went there to watch The Chieftains even though Mike and Harvey own the company. It is fun singing along to traditional Irish tunes. I was able to buy one Guinness beer on tap and one Michelob Light (which is cheaper). This time, I had enough money for a reuben sandwich.

I stayed and listened to the bands although I didn't know anyone there. There were a couple people from work that I have seen before, but I don't know them and was too shy to approach. They didn't come over to see me either. It was kind of depressing, actually. Monica is always busy with Miguel, especially since they are both gymnastic instructors at the same school. They had a gymnastic event they went to instead.

I wish I had more money for beer. It would have been more fun. I probably would have gotten out of control and puked on myself though. I guess it is for the best. I feel like I lead a very lame life. I don't ever have exciting, good things happen. I am either paranoid, avoiding police while I drive without a license and insurance or alone at home. Keri and I do things every couple of weeks when she is in town. She goes to Illinois a great deal because there is a boy that she likes. He gives me the creeps, frankly. I met him once when he came down to visit. Keri is prettier than I am, has better clothes, has more talent and guys like her better right away. She doesn't have any difficulties meeting people or dating guys. Everyone loves Keri. Even Uncle John is enamored with her, although she only likes him as an "uncle." I feel like a blank sheet of paper, always over-looked, never written on and in the end, mistaken for trash and thrown away.

AUGUST 11, 1991

Yesterday I made a complete ass of myself again. My, God! How many times in my life will I lose control and act like a complete slut?

Uncle John and Debbie, another manager from John's work, and I drove to Panama City Beach to hang out for the day. I drove the Festiva since it would fit three people. I hate driving, especially with people in the car. I feel so self conscious. Anyway, we went to the club La Villa and Spinakers. MTV was at La Villa filming a wet t-shirt contest. I wanted to stay there and try to get on television. John and Debbie left me alone to go have a drink somewhere more upscale.

I began drinking frozen daiquiris like crazy, slurping them down in quick procession. I always get excited doing something with people, going someplace, and feel nervous, so I drink fast and furiously. I was alone so I didn't know what to do with myself. I wandered around, inside and out, taking dips in the pool once in a while.

The pool was eventually cleared out for a wet t-shirt contest to be shown on MTV. I asked about participating in the contest but the MTV man said they already had all the contestants needed. I begged him to let me join and asked if I looked alright in my bikini. He said that I did but they were already booked up. I bugged him so much that he gave me an MTV shirt. I was so excited. I put it on and walked around, drinking more. I hung around so long, that when the contest was over, there were some girls still on the stage dancing, the MTV man finally let me get on the stage and dance. He said that I had to take off my bikini top and get my shirt wet and tied in a knot in the front. I gladly did as he asked, thinking, at the time, that it was a real honor. He poured water over my shirt. A college boy who I was talking to earlier said that he would hold my bikini top.

I got on stage and danced. I was finally asked to leave, I think. It gets kind of fuzzy. The next thing I remember is being on the beach in my wet t-shirt and bikini bottom, and looking for my bikini top. I found the guy who was holding it for me. He wanted to keep it, but I really needed it. I convinced him to relinquish it and put it on right there on the beach. My white t-shirt was dry by then but you could see through it pretty well. As I got my bikini top on, John grabbed my arm and pulled me aside and told me it was time to leave. Right now. He was very mad at me. I don't think I have ever seen him angry. I had embarrassed him in front of Debbie. John asked Debbie to wait in the car while he attended to me.

I'm not sure what happened next, but I had thrown up and had vomit on my shirt and woke up in the back seat of my own car. I didn't vomit in the car, so it must have been on the beach or on the way to the car. I completely blacked out so I don't know. I am too embarrassed and humiliated to ask John for details. When I saw the sorry state I was in, I just decided to go back to sleep.

What a mess I am. I can't go anywhere without making an ass of myself. I don't know when to stop drinking. I can't stop. I don't know how to have conversations with people, so I drink to loosen up. I get too loose and end up making a fool of myself. I am a complete waste of human space.

SEPTEMBER 1, 1991

Robert invited me to another football game. Robert, Bonnie, Rob and I went down to the campus hours early to park, shop at Jim's Bookstore for a shirt for Bonnie and drink beer at bars near the football stadium.

I don't know if I ever described Bonnie. She is a beautiful redhead with flawlessly white skin. She wears perfect sorority girl clothes (although she is not at FSU and is not in a sorority), has the best purses, and always has her makeup and lipstick just right. She is, however, not very intelligent. She keeps failing her classes at Tallahassee Community College and can't get into Florida State, although she keeps trying.

I also find Bonnie selfish and arrogant. She acts like she can barely tolerate me and frequently asks me why I don't date Rob. It is obvious that Bonnie thinks she is superior to me, although she doesn't have a brain in her head. She is definitely looking for someone with money to take care of her. Bonnie's claim to fame is driving her car off a low bridge into shallow water. I find it more frightening that she laughs about it. Bonnie won't ever tell me how she drove off the bridge. Also, what is so funny about totaling your car? That's Bonnie for you. Robert's other girlfriend who lives out of town and visits once in a while is much nicer and more intelligent. Bonnie doesn't know about her and Robert doesn't want her to find out. I'm sure she would completely freak.

Even though I go to the games, these people really aren't my friends. I am there to be made fun of. That is a depressing thought. Before I forget, the nightmare last night was horrifying. It began with me looking at a computer screen segmented into four windows, each leading into a different nightmare. I knew there wasn't a good dream through any of the windows. I was forced to choose one so I selected the window on the computer's touch screen which showed a doctor's office. It appeared to be the safest one of the four. I was transported into a patient waiting room at a gynecologist's office. There were a few other women in the waiting room reading magazines. The office had cheap, flickering fluorescent lights which were making an annoying buzzing sound. The walls were stained and yellow. The few pictures hanging on the walls were crooked. The wood chairs in the waiting room were rickety and creaked whenever you moved. The magazines were all old issues.

I looked around at the other women and saw there was fear on all of their faces. Suddenly the doctor's door flung open. A woman came running out half naked, grasping onto her torn clothes while blood dripped down from between her thighs. The doctor had a scraggly beard, dirty white uniform and wore one of those round reflective lights on a head strap. I could see inside his office and noticed surgical tools covered with rust. The doctor was looking for his next victim. Two enormous women accompanied the doctor, each one standing at least 6' tall and over 300 pounds. The doctor's shifty eyes scanned the waiting room, while he mulled over which woman would be next. The doctor's eyes stopped on me as he yelled, "you're next!" I screamed no as I tried to fend off the two large nurses. They over-powered me and each grabbed an arm and drug me to that dark, bloody office. The doctor was wiping the fresh blood off of his instruments onto his blood stained, grimy pants. I closed my eyes and wished myself into another dream.

I entered into another window on the computer screen where the night was dark and cloudy. I was wearing shorts and a t-shirt and was pedaling a bicycle down Monroe Street as fast as I could. I knew something evil was chasing me. I could feel an oppressive presence but could not see it, nor did I want to. It must have been very late at night because there were no cars on the streets. I came up to Allen Road and took a right. I was near my office building at Benefits Management Company, and since I had the key, I knew it would be a safe place to hide.

I arrived in the parking lot and realized that I didn't have the key on me because I was trapped in a nightmare. The unseen evil creature was getting closer, I could hear it snarling and felt a heavy feeling of dread creeping upon me. I ran up to the office building and tried to break the glass with my fists because I knew that the alarm would sound. I couldn't break the glass so I wished myself somewhere else.

The next computer window I went through was much more active. I was standing in front of a large boulder and hundreds of arrows were flying towards me. I could hear them whizzing past my ears and could see dozens of medieval archers facing me. One arrow was bearing down upon me. It was aimed directly at my chest and was coming so fast I could barely think. At that moment, Peter dove into the nightmare and knocked me to the ground. We crawled behind a large rock. Peter told me that I really should duck when arrows are coming towards me. I thanked him for his assistance and told him that I was trapped within these four nightmares. I knew that the last nightmare would be the worst. Peter pulled me out by my hand and I woke up at that moment at 10:30 am on Sunday. I never entered into the fourth window.

SEPTEMBER 19, 1991

I had a wonderful time after work. Derek drove me home (I've been taking the bus since I really don't have a driver's license). He is a musician from Miami who's deceased father left him a trust fund. He is very attractive, looking a lot like Malcolm X. Derek owns part of some record label in Atlanta, Georgia, and has recently recorded an album. It is a rap album, so not really my style. Derek is very intelligent and charming, very tall and thin. He is married but is separated from his wife. It is a mystery, he won't talk about his life at all. It is all very strange. Derek talks to his estranged wife often and pays for her bills. He doesn't want to divorce her for some reason, says he owes her something. I don't even know much of his childhood. I don't know how his father died and what his father did to make so much money. Derek is a very private person.

Basically, he came over for sex. We both knew it and talked a few minutes before going into the bedroom for some lovemaking. Derek was so analytical about the entire thing. It wasn't that long and he left immediately after. I felt a bit like a whore. I guess I was hoping for more. Hoping for a chance to have a real boyfriend. I am not after money or anything, but I think he believes that I am.

He is so suave and charming. Derek says that he may use me in a music video. I am hiding a lot from him, too. The DUI, jail time, revoked license for five years, and the huge debt I am in paying for the fines from the DUIs. I live a double life, too. I suppose we have that in common.

SEPTEMBER 28, 1991

Last night, while I was working the night shift with Peter, I almost got intimate with him. Peter and I were talking about books that he recommended to me to read and I was telling him about my nightmares. Peter also told me about his library of books at him mom's house. He has read a great deal and went to Catholic school. He often questions my interest in David, which is understandable since David's only interest in me is sex.

I was complaining how tight my shoulders were, that I had slept wrong and woke up with a huge kink in my shoulder. Peter began to massage my shoulders, much to my surprise. It was slow at work and it was just the two of us in the office. The massage turned more erotic, slower, more intriguing. Peter's hands began to work down toward my breasts. He has already said he is a breast man. Peter leaned closer to me and I was confused as to what to do. He can be so vulgar and talks terribly about women he has had sex with. On the other hand, he is intelligent and attractive. He is of Cuban decent. Just when Peter's hands were getting lower and lower underneath my blouse, Derek walked into the office to get some work. Peter instantly turned the massage into a more platonic one. I blushed terribly, since I just had sex with Derek and he probably thinks that I am a cheap whore. Even though Peter blew the whole thing off, I think Derek saw what was really going on and just gave a little laugh. Derek grabbed his work and left again, saying as he left to go back to what we were doing. We didn't. It just wasn't the same now. I thanked Peter for the shoulder massage.

OCTOBER 13, 1991

Bonnie set me up with an ex-boyfriend of hers. His name is Ed. He is pretty nice. Not bad looking, graduated from college and has a steady job and a house. Rob couldn't come to the football game so Bonnie invited Ed. He seems polite and normal. I think I'll go out on a date with him since he asked after the football game. It is nice to have a normal man interested in me. We are going out next weekend to play pool. We'll see.

NOVEMBER 17, 1991

FSU has won every game this year except for last night's game against Miami. Wide fucking right. A stupid kick lost the game. A field goal attempt failed miserably when it should have been a chip shot. Wide right, that is all I heard last night. Those damn arrogant Miami fans. They are worse than Florida fans. The game was so close. It hurts to see the undefeated National Championship contention season evaporate in the balmy Southern night air. The final score was FSU 16 and Miami 17. It is extremely depressing walking out of the stadium after a loss. They don't occur very often. There is an eerie silence in the stadium, with a general grumbling background, and some drunk Miami fans yelling how fucking wonderful the Hurricanes are. Go blow it out your nit-ridden Ibis ass. It took the fun out of the rest of the night. We all just went home afterwards. It was late, anyway. I was tired from the rum and Coca-Cola. Nothing like drinking alcohol in the hot sun. It cooled off a bit when the sun set. The next game is against the University of Florida. I am not looking forward to that game. It's in "The Swamp", too. It could spell disaster for FSU. I'm going to go back to moping around now.

DECEMBER 1, 1991

Well, as expected, FSU lost to University of Florida. It was 9-14. So much for playing for the National Championship. Two losses at the end of the season means kiss your sweaty ass goodbye, it isn't going to happen. Florida State will get a good bowl game since we draw the fans. Tallahassee, in general, is in a state of shock. A perfect season was so close you can still smell the vapors, but it evaporated at the last minute. Or last couple of weeks, really. I am being melodramatic about this. It is only football. When you go to the games in the sweltering heat or the bitterly cold nights, you really bond with college football and the fans. It is fun to follow, I really enjoy watching college football. The only thing to do now is wait for the Bowl games.

DECEMBER 24, 1991

My mom felt sorry for me and bought me a ticket to visit over Christmas. I haven't been with my parents for Christmas in eight years, I think. So much happened. I don't know where to begin. I guess the beginning.

I arrived on December 23rd and looked fabulous. I was determined to be the former Bean girl who made something of herself. I permed my hair, lost weight, and wore my best clothes. I haven't looked better to the Bean population. The first night we went to – wait, hold your breath, this is a surprise – the Bean Bar & Grill. You thought I was going to say the Bean Tavern, but that would be another night. The "right" people don't go there any more. My parents played the punch board and I convinced my mom to play darts with me. It only lasted a game until she gave up. One of their friends, Phyllis,, played darts with me. She had more energy than my mom who said it hurt her back. Phyllis was awesome and we played a bunch of different types of dart games. It was the first time I was able to go to the bar with my parents since I am over 21 now. Oh, boy, what a special event.

Jim and mom occasionally bought me tickets for the punch board during our pub visits. It is a gambling match up game where you win items. Usually extra large sweat-shirts with an airbrushed animal decorating the front. Other times, it could be something cool like binoculars or cop sun-glasses. I didn't get much. Jim was trying for a jacket with some beer company logo on it. Jim dropped $20 bills like pennies. I secretly kept track of his gambling expenditures and lost track over $120. That doesn't include beer, cigarettes, and our yummy fried dinner. Actually, it tasted pretty good, fish and chips. My parents have gone to the tavern for years. I am now wondering if Jim spends that much every night. Let's just imagine that my parents only spend $40 a night once in a while on gambling. That really adds up. All of these years, when they went to drink and play the punch board, occasionally bringing me home a stuffed frog with "Maddy" etched onto its little cowboy hat, did they spend that much money every night? All of those times Jim couldn't do this or that because it was too expensive, was it all a lie? Couldn't he have paid for a dance class or pottery shop once in a while to give me a hobby? I can't help feeling bitter and jealous. I asked my mom if they always play the punch board and she said they did.

I drank enough to go out on a limb and say that I wished they had spent more time with me than at the bar. They were too drunk to have a rational thought in their heads. Mom asked me if she was a bad mom. Well, I couldn't exactly lie. Running your child out of the house at age 16 isn't a great parent. I told her that she could have spent more time with me. She freaked out and started crying and yelling. Oh, boy. I was trying to say it as delicately as possible, but my parents were not in a reasonable mood. Jim leaped off of his barstool (showing more spryness than he had in 15 years) and confronted me face to face. Jim started his rant, telling me not to speak to my mother that way and telling me what a great mother she was. I told him that I wasn't trying to pick a fight, I just wanted them to acknowledge that they were a bit remiss in raising me, they should have spent more time as a family than going to the tavern every afternoon. Jim was furious. I overplayed my hand. They will never admit they did any wrong. Jim started telling me what a bad kid I had been and I finally got angry. I replied that I was a bad child because I had no guidance or support. They forget that I was a child, home alone. That was not what Jim or mom wanted to hear. I decided to back down and put a damper on the fire I started. I said I was sorry and told them to calm down. I said let's leave it alone. Mom was sulking on her barstool. Jim sat down on his and paid the check. Oops.

Time to go. I decided not to bring up that subject again while I was visiting if I wanted to enjoy myself at all.

The next day was Christmas Eve. Jim was invited to a party on Ft. Lewis army base at the N.C.O. club since he worked as a jet engine mechanic on Ft. Lewis. I got dressed up and we drove through the dark night from Bean to Ft. Lewis, going the back way where there were no street lights and where, years earlier, an M.P. told Paula and the rest of us to leave our party spot because they found a headless female body there. In the darkness, I saw a small white, mud-covered dog with black spots. I told Jim to look out for that dog. As we passed the poor wretch, I noticed, to my horror, that the dog was Cindy. That was our old dog that Jim dumped in the country. I sobbed, "that's Cindy Lou!" It sure looked like her. I said that maybe we should get her. There was complete silence in the car. Dear God, how can this happen? I quickly did the math and figured that, yes, it could be her. She could still be alive. The image of her matted head hanging down and her posture bent over from years of suffering has not left me, nor will it ever leave me. I was devastated and couldn't help crying. I tried to cover it up and push back the pain since we were headed to a party. Guilt has once again swept over me, eating at my soul like a cancer.

The party was sort of fun. I got a picture on Santa's lap. I put on a happy face and tried to enjoy myself. I couldn't, but pretended. While we were there, mom told me these were the group of guys that had come over for Christmas the last few years. People actually came to parties at my parents' trailer for Christmas day. What?! They had

Christmas parties at their trailer after I left home? There was going to be a party at our house and it wasn't mentioned before now. They never had social events while I was living at home in Bean. My parents are kinder to everyone except me. I am a great actor and hid my pain. Sure, I said, it is great they gave those men a good Christmas while they were away from home. Too bad they didn't do the same with me. The ride home was completely silent. I looked for Cindy but didn't see her. Poor little creature. I have seen what happens to poor, unwanted pets and will never do that to any living animal. I will care for all animals whenever I can. Even if it is a dish of food and fresh water. My heart is heavy.

DECEMBER 25, 1991

Christmas morning wasn't extraordinary. I didn't have many presents since mom and I were going to go shopping for clothes at the vintage stores in Winder, Washington. I love going to vintage stores, searching for unique items of clothings or things for the apartment. So much fun.

Mom made a ham and all of the fixings for the party. Four or five young men and their dates came over and drank lots of beer and ate as much food as they could. Jim and mom were shaking hands and hugging everyone, wishing them a Merry Christmas, giving them food to take home. I just sat back and watched, drinking beer by myself. I never got too drunk while I was there. I wanted to show my parents that a person can socially drink without getting drunk.

The party lasted hours. When it was over, my parents went to bed early, around 8:00 pm, as usual, leaving me up to watch television alone. One day of not going to the tavern. Hurray!

DECEMBER 26, 1991

The Mabreys were already at the Bean Bar & Grill when we arrived in the late afternoon and were already three sheets to the wind. Rob's parents have always liked me and Mrs. Mabrey got very excited about seeing me again and said that Rick and Rob were back in town and she would bring Rob to the bar the next night. I agreed. It would be great to see Rob. I hope I can recognize him from Rick since they are identical twins! I have always been able to tell them apart in the past, so I figured I'd still be able to see the difference.

I told them about my college experience and made it sound like I was doing well in Florida. Now that I am away from Tallahassee, I feel like I have done well. Hardly anyone from Bean made it to college. Mrs. Mabrey said Rob was taking some classes at the University of Washington but had to have surgery on his knees (again!) and was staying with them for a while. I was excited to see Rob. Mrs. Mabrey agreed to play darts with me, so we played for a long time. I put money in the juke box and played Willie Nelson, Merle Haggard, and other old school Country musicians. Doing this made the few inhabitants of the bar sentimental. Mrs. Mabrey said that she "hadn't heard that song for years", but

I was thinking it was on the jukebox the whole time, they could have just played the music.

After the Mabreys left, staggering to the door and driving home on the icy, curving, country roads, I began playing computer gambling games that mom was playing. You can play solitaire and other card games on the computer for money. If you win, that is. It was pretty addictive and mom and Jim kept feeding me coins for the machine to keep me happy. It also is their way of showing their love for me, as strange as that sounds. If they are giving, I'm taking. It's better than sitting at the bar staring at my beer.

DECEMBER 27, 1991

Today was a fun day. Mom and I drove to Nordstrom at the Tacoma Mall to do a little shopping for new clothes, not all vintage. We did much less shopping at Nordstrom, but it was nice to see the store again. I only bought one shirt. I'm supposed to be banned from Nordstrom for life, but I didn't think anyone would ever know I had once been a thief in one of their stores.

Tonight, when we went to the Bean Bar & Grill (well, not really night, more like mid-afternoon), we walked into the bar, my heart dropped seeing Rob. At first I thought that it was Rick and felt him out in conversation, but quickly realized that he was Rob, not Rick. We fell into an intimate conversation, sitting at a separate table from his parents and away from the bar where my parents were planted. Rob and

I discussed old times, the times I snuck over through the deer path in the woods. Rob said that he was going back home soon and asked if I would join him. Yes! Mom was a bit hurt that I was going over to Rob's house. For goodness sake, all we were doing was gambling, sitting on barstools, and stared at the television with some college bowl game. I asked her to understand, but she retorted, "what about Ed?" Jeez, mom, do you automatically think I'll have sex? What about Ed? We aren't married. Get off my freaking back. I only just started dating Ed.

Well, after telling Rob that he was my first (sexual experience) and he told me that I was his first, we began to passionately embrace. Rob's older brother, Ken, came home and caught us. He said that it was cool. We talked briefly before he went back out again. He had to pick something up from home. We were alone again. Rob suggested that we move it upstairs. I readily agreed, since he was my first love and I couldn't believe my luck! Rob and I made love.

After brief sex, Rob apologized and said that he had become lazy and quit school and hobbled around on his surgically reconstructed knees. He looked great to me, I don't know what he was talking about. Rob said that I looked so good, had done so much with my life, he felt guilty. That was ridiculous. His cheeks still had the pink flush of youth and he didn't look that much different than in high school, except maybe for a little belly. Not much at all. He looked good. Rob said that I gave him incentive to go back to school, to improve his life, to move to Seattle and become a lawyer (I wasn't thrilled with the lawyer part).

Here is where it gets embarrassing. Rob couldn't drive me home because the roads were so icy and his knees were still healing from surgery, so he was worried about driving a stick shift. I understood completely, because I know the high school football coach injected him with drugs in order to feel no pain, letting Rob shred his knees into paper. I called my parents' house and left a message on their answering machine stating that I would be home in the morning, that the roads were too icy and I would stay at the Mabrey's house.

I thought this would do, but was I wrong. My drunk mom called and actually woke up the Mabreys, demanding to speak to me. Mom berated me and demanded that I come home immediately. I told her that Rob's knees were healing and he only had a stick shift to drive. She still told me to come home. Like I was in high school again! For Christ's sake, just wait until the morning. Go to bed and I'll be there in the morning. But, no, my mom freaked. I guess I raised my voice, then Mrs. Mabrey told me that I had better do as my mom requested so I went home. Poor Rob struggled through pain to drive me home. The roads were icy, as I told my mom.

When I got to my parents' house, my mom reprimanded me and then went to bed. I came home for this? I could have slept over at the Mabrey's house, come home in the morning, and all would be right with the world. Mom was so concerned about Ed. My God! Who cares? She hasn't even met him. I'm not living with him, and he's not even that nice compared to Rob who is much sweeter to me. Cut me some slack. I just let her rant and go to bed. There is no reasoning with a drunk person. I could talk until I was blue in the face but she would still think she was right. I did say how humiliated I was that she treated me like a child. I told her that it was for safety I was going to stay over there. I can't believe she called the house at 9:00 pm and woke up the Mabreys! I was so embarrassed.

DECEMBER 28, 1991

The icy roads kept us home. I went out for a walk/jog to try and find that secret path to the Mabrey's house. It was overgrown, just as Rob feared. I couldn't find it anymore. I saw Frank's trailer by the pond and knew that Amber's mom was there. I didn't visit. I didn't feel comfortable just dropping by their house.

That afternoon, when my parents went to the Bean Bar & Grill, Rob joined his parents, too, and was already there when we arrived. I was very pleased. Mom seemed so jealous. She wouldn't even play pool or darts with me, saying her back hurt too much. Rob and I played darts and pool. Rob told me that he never joined his parents there, but was only doing so because of me. I was pleased. My first love! He is wonderfully kind. We only hung out at the bar together so my mom wouldn't freak out.

DECEMBER 29, 1991

It's my birthday, but it was not overly exciting, except for the fact that we went to the Bean Tavern. I had never been in the Bean Tavern, only the Bean Bar & Grill. Way to go parents for taking me to a new, thrilling tavern. Jim ordered us dinner to take home. Why we had to take it home, I'm not sure. I would have rather eaten there, but Jim doesn't like to eat anywhere except home. It was a lovely fried fish and chips with a little grease on the side. My parents would not go to the Bean Bar & Grill. I think my mom was trying to keep me away from Rob. Of course, I called Rob when my parents went to bed (by 8:00 pm, as usual). It was quite icy that night and Rob's knee was really bothering him so we couldn't see each other. I suggested the "path", but he reminded me that it was most likely overgrown. It was, I had gone down there to find it but it was lost. No one to walk through the path anymore. No use.

I did run into Paula's dad at the Bean Tavern and he gruffly said that Paula was in town and would like to see me. It would be cool to see her again. Ralph said he would call her for me.

DECEMBER 30, 1991

Paula called and said that she, Amber and Gail were going to a New Year Eve's party at a dance club. It cost $15 to get in. Mom said she would pay for it if I wanted to go. After Paula called, Amber called and said she would drive me to Paula's apartment to meet before going out. I agreed. Amber also agreed to drive me back home, if she didn't drink too much. That's fine with me since Jim would never lend me one of their cars. I don't have my license anyway, so it's for the best.

CHAPTER 14

1992: Age 23

JANUARY 1, 1992

I went to that dance club New Year's Eve party with Paula and Amber. Gail stopped by Paula's apartment for a few minutes but didn't go out with us. Gail wasn't overly excited to see me. Ever since that fateful night when I walked to Amber's mobile home instead of arriving dolefully at Gail's house, she has held a grudge the size of Texas against me. Water under the bridge.

The party was boring, basically. Amber and Paula danced a lot but I didn't feel like dancing. I sat at the bar, nursing a drink since my mom gave me $15 to get in to the club, but no money for drinks. I tried to show a happy face, but I didn't feel very happy. That wasn't what I wanted to do. The dancing, loud music, yelling to be heard, very depressing. Once in a while Amber or Paula would come over and get me to dance. I would go through the motions, but didn't enjoy it. That isn't my life anymore. It was never really my life. Bean is like a cancer in my life, eating away at my soul, leaving me hollow and unfeeling. I often feel empty inside. I can't ever truly relate to any other person. It makes me incredibly sad. I so want to fit into society, but can't. I often have to fake my emotions, so I fit in with others. I would have been happier hanging out at Paula's apartment and being able to talk to them.

Finally, Amber wanted to go home. Paula was intoxicated and wished me a teary goodbye. Amber didn't have but one drink so she was fine to drive.

I don't know when or if I'll ever see Paula, Amber or Gail ever again.

JANUARY 2, 1992

I'm still in Bean on vacation. I was allowed to go over to Rob's house again last night, one more time before going home. Nice of you to let your grown daughter go out for the night. However, mom required that I be back "home" to sleep. Give me a freaking break. What does it matter if I stay the night there? My mom still hovers over me like I am 13. However, she wasn't exactly around when I was 13, was she? Since I lost my virginity that year? Plus, I am over 21, so I should be able to do what I want to do. However, I didn't want to have my vacation end in a fight, so I complied. Rob agreed to drive me home with his bum knee.

Rob told me a disturbing story, though. He said that as he was walking around the Bean Elementary School one afternoon he came across a rape victim. He saw her laying in the grass, beaten and bloody, so he went to help her. The woman screamed and said that Rob raped her. Rob was arrested but let go from lack of proof. Rob said that he wasn't charged for rape, but it was hanging over him like a dark cloud. Rob asked if I believed that he didn't rape the girl. Of course, I believe him. Rob has never shown any aggressive or abusive behavior in the past, so I am sure he is telling the truth. Rob finished by saying what those high school football player rapists did to me was wrong. I was shocked and asked if he knew about the truth of the multiple rapes, and he said he did. Probably through other football players since Rob was one. Rob told me that he thought what happened was truly terrible. I have never spoken about that horrible night to anyone. Rob brought up the subject on his own accord and said that I wasn't to blame. I could barely speak. I didn't know what to say. I have always been blamed for being raped by three boys from school, not told that I was a victim. Only Laura said that I was a victim but she turned to prostitution and had a baby at age 14. She is lost to me. To hear of my innocence made me speechless. I'm glad he knows the truth but I couldn't speak, couldn't talk about it. I have always felt like a whore after that night. Someone else who knows the truth. It makes me feel better, somehow.

FEBRUARY 13, 1992

Now that I am back in Tallahassee, poor Rob keeps calling me but I won't return his calls. I can't. Do I want him to move down here? Do I want to move to Seattle area? Rob's parents are drunks from Bean like mine. Do I want to go back there, be stuck, trapped there forever? I am afraid. I love Rob, I really do, I just don't know what to do.

Robert is getting tired of covering for me on the phone, so I stay out of the apartment. Rob calls and calls and calls. I feel such guilt, I know I should talk to him. Thelma from work says that I am being a cold bitch, in so many words. She is right, I am. I won't speak to Rob. It is too painful and I can't get trapped back in that Bean life. I can imagine my parents and his getting into a bar fight. Mr. Mabrey would probably kick Jim's ass. He has a quick temper, is younger and thinner than Jim. Strangely, Mr. Mabrey doesn't look younger than Jim. The years of smoking and drinking have taken their toll. All of our tavern parents look older than they are. Well, Jim really is old. He is 15 years older than mom.

I don't really have many places to go to get away from the phone calls. I go to Keri's apartment once in a blue moon. I have frightened her away, I'm afraid to say. I never speak to Monica anymore. I usually go to the park and sit there for hours, killing time, making others believe that I have a real life somewhere. I don't. I should just go back with Rob and be happy. Ed doesn't make me feel happy at all. I just don't know what to do.

MAY 3, 1992

I finished up my classes at Tallahassee Community College last week. I did alright with the tests, although I only got a

C in Psychology because it was one of those stupid television courses which only came on at 7:00 am Saturday morning. Bonnie said she failed Psychology and Trigonometry at TCC. Not a surprise that Miss Priss didn't pass her tests. But I was lazy, kept missing the program and then didn't go to the library to catch up on what I missed. The last Psychology program I watched showed a poor cat tied down as they broke its spine. I can't watch things like that, it makes me feel physically ill. Whenever I see a child or animal suffering, I can't stop myself from placing myself in their shoes, of imagining their fear, their pain, their anguish, their suffering. I know that it was only a brief animal experimentation segment, but why do creatures still have to be tormented when there may be enough documentation from years of studies? That is why I only got a C out of the class. I am making excuses, I know. It was due more to the fact that it was a 7:00 am tv course on a Saturday morning. I never felt like getting up after taking sleeping pills.

On the good side, I will get my Associate in Arts degree in the mail in a couple of weeks. That is my first official degree since I received my G.E.D. I was going to into architecture but kept failing my Pre-Calculus course at TCC. I tried that class three times but failed each time. Last time I dropped the course so it wouldn't negatively affect my grade point average. It is because of my skipping in high school that my math skills are remiss. I used to be so good at math, but when I skipped classes starting in 9th grade and dropped out at the end of 11th grade, I missed too many classes and fell behind in my understanding of mathematics.

I regret it. However, I am going into the Interior Design program at Florida State University, per David's suggestion.

I had to be interviewed by the Chairman of the Interior Design program before being accepted. I did that 2 semesters ago. I brought my art from art class (in which I received an A) and the drafting work I did in the Beginning Drafting course. I was accepted but had to be put on a waiting list since they only allow so many students every semester to enter the program. I will have to wait one more semester, until next Spring, to begin classes at Florida State University. I cried when I received the letter from the registry department stating I was formally accepted into FSU. I can't believe I have come so far with college. Mom secretly paid for my TCC courses, but she is now saying that she won't pay for any additional college. I guess Jim found out about it. I am a resident, so tuition isn't too high, although it is almost double the price of TCC.

I really love learning, going to college. I didn't make any friends at TCC but maybe I can when I start FSU. I want people to respect me and not look down on me for my stupid drunken behavior and wasteful time in jail. That part of my life is embarrassing and degrading. No one knows what I am going through with court, jail and fines. It is a horrible secret that festers inside of me. I wish I could be normal and have people like me. I always scare people away. I don't know how to communicate with people and will often draw complete blanks when trying to think of a conversation starter. I am terrible at continuing conversations. Probably because my parents never had conversations, only drunken yelling.

I will try and concentrate on college. I am so proud of myself for obtaining my Associates in Arts degree. I feel so good about myself when I think about that part of my life. I will get my bachelors degree no matter what. Even if I have to get student loans to do it. I am able to get a Pell Grant, but that will barely cover any of the expenses at FSU. I'll do it somehow.

MAY 13, 1992

A few nights ago I had a bizarre dream. My life seems to be filled with nightmares. Sleep doesn't come easily, even with twenty sleeping pills. The first thing I recall is fading into a scene of people bustling around, carrying armfuls of office supplies and mementos. I stepped into the chaos from out of a thick fog. I recognized some of the people from Benefits Management Company, but others were frenzied strangers.

I walked toward the rubble of an old, bombed out building and noticed with amazement people were actually tearing it apart, brick by brick. Many people, anxious with paranoia, nervously snatched bricks from the disabled building and tucked them safely away in hidden pockets inside their coats.

Everyone wore winter garb such as coats, scarves and hats. I realized with sudden recall that this was my work building. These crumbled remains and scuttling people were draining the last bit of life from the company.

I was confused, for I was just reporting to work. I reached out and grabbed the scrawny arm of a bundled participant in this mad affair and asked what was going on. An old man with fear in his eyes and frost glistening on his old, sinewy skin, replied with shock at my ignorance, that BMC went "belly-up", bankrupt, finished. It was over.

I let the man go about his business of stealing bricks from the bleeding remains of our office building. I started laughing. I knew that this would happen someday.

I noticed Mike, the CEO and David's father, in a tattered coat searching the rubble for some specific, unfindable item and Accounts Manager Mark Stebbins telling everyone goodbye in a tearful voice.

I laughed as people pushed and pulled each other for photographs and final good-byes. I didn't care. I was glad it was over.

I turned around with mild curiosity as Mark turned over the key to some old flatbed Ford as it trembled to life. The truck rocked a little in anticipation of what was about to happen. Mark was crying hysterically as he yelled at anyone who approached him. He announced to all who cared to listen that if he could not work for BMC, he wouldn't work anywhere. Few cared. He didn't seem to notice.

Mark pushed the gearshift in directions that it didn't want to go as I heard the gears grind in disapproval. The truck lurched forward slowly but soon picked up speed. I noticed a deep ravine and realized with slight panic that Mark was headed directly into the ravine's gaping, jagged mouth. I ran to stop Mark but it was too late. The truck tumbled down the ravine and tore itself to pieces on the razor sharp rocks. No one seemed to notice but me. The mad shuffle continued.

MARCH 18, 1992

The Chieftains played at work yesterday in the conference room. They didn't go to The Warehouse this year. I don't know why. There was a bit of a party with some beer and food for St. Patrick's Day. It was enjoyable having a party at work. I didn't have anywhere to go for St. Patrick's Day. The Warehouse charges a cover so I am not going to go if The Chieftains aren't there. I injured myself at work yesterday. Our office is expanding into a larger area and I tripped over the hanging files that were stacked on the floor. It was a freak accident. I tripped on the files then fell into the sharp metal edge of another hanging file. It was such a narrow piece of metal that it embedded in the front of my ankle and hit the bone. It is a nasty wound. It is more of a gouge so it can't be sewn. I didn't go to the doctor. I probably should have but I cleaned it at work. Sylvia looked a bit nervous like I was going to sue or something. It was clumsiness on my part, so why would I sue? So I have a seeping wound for the St. Patrick's Day festivities. It hurts a great deal so it is probably best that I ended up staying home last night. I wasn't even drunk when I injured myself. Keri is in Illinois again for her birthday so I'll probably stay home by myself. Something I've been doing more and more frequently lately. It was nice having friends for a little while.

I started school at Florida State University. I am going full time and working the second shift at work since customer service is open until 11:00 pm. I'm finally moving on to the next part of my life. Now I can cheer on FSU football team as a student, not just a spectator.

JULY 14, 1992

I have been trying to call Rob from Bean, after all this time. I have written him numerous letters but he has stopped responding. I just received a letter from Mrs. Mabrey, saying that Rob's girlfriend is pregnant and he is starting a new life and to leave him alone. What a shock. Not only has Rob given up on me completely (my fault, of course) but he has already impregnated a woman. I am in shock. I am writing a letter apologizing and saying that I hope Rob has a happy family life. I don't know what else to do. I want Rob to know that I care and I am sorry. I lost my opportunity. What a loser I am. Rob is a better person than Ed, but I don't want to go back to Bean. Seattle would be great, though. Rob said that he was inspired by me wanting to improve myself and was going to re-enroll at University of Washington's school of law. He wants to be a lawyer. Why, I don't know. He is too sweet for that.

I am alone again. Rob will never contact me again. That makes me feel sad. I realized too late that I love him and had been calling and writing to him for the last couple of months. I screwed up big time. What else is new. I am really depressed again. I am stuck with Ed now.

AUGUST 25, 1992

Poor Peter from work. His home, his mother's home in Miami was completely destroyed down to the foundation by hurricane Andrew, a category 5. His mother left to safety, but his wonderful books were destroyed. All of them. Peter is heart broken. I feel terrible for him. His most prized possessions were destroyed. Peter said that he didn't care about other personal belongings, just that his books were gone, water logged and beyond use. I told him how sorry I am.

The entire town of Homestead was wiped off the map, probably forever. That is where I used to live with my mom and Jim, after they got married. Since Jim was in the Air Force, and we lived near Homestead Air Force base in a trailer park.

SEPTEMBER 3, 1992

I am taking some interesting college classes like Design Fundamentals and Survey of Interior Design. My favorite it History of Art and Architecture, and the professor who teaches it looks just like a young Vivien Leigh. Especially when Vivien played Scarlett O'Hara. I will do well in the Design Fundamentals where they teach me how to draw, use water colors, colored pencils, and markers.

There are a plethora of sorority girls in the program, especially since their sorority houses are within easy walking distance to the school. The street the school of Visual Arts and Dance is on Sorority Row. There are hardly any men in the program, mostly being gay. One guy is color blind, which baffles me completely. How can you be an interior designer while being color blind? There is an offensive lineman who plays on the Florida State University football team. His name is Mike and he is enormous. He has a twin brother who also plays football at FSU. Mike makes a point of inferring that he is not gay by talking about his girlfriend. I can't help but think him immature for worrying about being pegged as queer. The Chairman of the school and at least two professors are openly gay. I don't understand why people are intimidated by the gay population since they don't push their lifestyle on anyone else. They are in relationships where there is love, which sounds wonderful to me. I am envious of the comfort they feel in their own skin, not being embarrassed or denying their feelings.

SEPTEMBER 6, 1992

It is college football season again so I can look for Mike who is in my Interior Design classes. I wonder if he informs his fellow team mates about his major. I would be interested in hearing his conversation with another football player about being an interior designer.

While on the subject of football, I prefer the early games, but there are so many night games this year. I have never been able to stay up late into the night unless I have ingested some metabolism boosting drug. I prefer to be in bed by 10:30 pm and have always been that way. On the other hand, night games aren't as sweltering and I don't usually sweat off ten pounds and suffer from painful headaches. The ten pounds doesn't stay off since it is all water weight and comes right back as soon as I swig water.

It appears that Robert broke up with the kind, intelligent, girlfriend from Tampa. I never knew her name and barely saw her outside of Robert's bedroom. There is a point, months after you meet someone, when it becomes too embarrassing to ask the person's name. Well, the girlfriend is Bonnie full-time now. Fabulous.

Big Rob came to the game last night as he usually does. The way Bonnie and Rob treat us, it makes me feel like Rob and I are dating. I know Rob is interested in becoming romantically involved. I wish Rob would stop giving me the sheep eyes and just be a friend. It makes me uncomfortable to be under his affectionate gaze.

We all went to eat and drink before the game at The Phyrst on campus, about a mile from the stadium. The one thing I can say about going to football games is there's a lot of walking. Park far away and walk to the stadium so you don't get stuck in a major traffic jam as 80,000 people try to get home. As usual, I didn't have much money to buy food, so I spent the little I had on beer. I forget to go to the bank most of the time to get cash. I could write a check for cash at the grocery store, but I'm afraid it will bounce. I have a terrible problem keeping track of my funds. I should write down every purchase. I wish I had someone to look after my finances, or at least teach me how to save money. If I pretended to like Rob, he'd buy me food and beer before the game, but I don't have the heart to use him. He's too attached to me so I'd have to kiss him at some point. No, better to leave hungry, which I did. I only got a couple of measly wings at The Phyrst and left with a growling stomach. That may be why I get so sleepy early in the evening. On a morbidly fascinating note, The Phyrst was the bar where Ted Bundy watched some sorority girls before clubbing several sleeping co-eds viciously in the next door sorority house. Of course, it wasn't called The Phyrst back then. The name changed so people wouldn't associate a serial killer with the bar.

The football game was against Duke so FSU won 48-21. Not really a surprise about the win since Duke is pathetic at football. Duke university is highly ranked in academics, so there are a lot of intellectuals who attend Duke. Duke scored a couple of times late in the game when FSU had their third string players on the field, who desperately need playing experience. So many fans grumbled and booed when FSU didn't run the score up on Duke. A bunch of losers booing for your own winning team. Bobbie Bowden is not the type of coach to run up the score.

Since the game started at 7:00 pm, it was sweltering hot early in the evening and stagnant and humid at night. With a packed stadium, there is only room to stand and no available breeze. I just wanted to go home and sleep during the third quarter. Going to games is fun, but it is also hot, tiring, and I get sleepy from drinking so early (and not eating much). I usually get a headache and quietly walk behind the group, rarely speaking. Rob doesn't speak much either. Kindred soul, perhaps.

I am holed up in my bedroom avoiding Bonnie who still hasn't gone home. Looks like she is staying the night. She is fairly religious, being Baptist, so she doesn't usually stay the night. Bonnie lives with her prudish parents. Since Bonnie has her full make-up and overnight bag, it doesn't look good for her to leave any time soon. I have yet to see her without make-up since she refuses to be seen without full make-up, perfectly curled hair, and the most put together garnet and gold outfit to cheer on Florida State. As I said before, a princess.

SEPTEMBER 27, 1992

Ed joined us for this FSU game. Rob couldn't make the game and Ed bought the ticket from Robert. I keep referring to big Rob, not to be confused with the sweet Rob from Bean who I really was cruel to. I've been seeing Ed from time to time, but he really isn't very nice, not like my Rob, I'll call him. Going on a date with Ed is better than being alone, I suppose.

The game was against Wake Forest and we won 35-7. We all went to The Phyrst for drinks and food. Ed is a strong college football fan, often yelling at the tv when he believes a play is not called properly. It borders on embarrassing. Ed drinks a lot of beer quickly, so he bought a couple of pitchers and shared it with me. Ed is preppy looking, more like a fraternity boy but not one, wearing a baseball cap and his garnet and gold shirt with khaki shorts and white sneakers. He is mildly attractive, thin and fairly tall. Ed has a seemingly normal family, with two brothers, a mom, and dad. He asked if I wanted to go play pool tonight and I said I would. It's nice to have a normal person for a date, even if he isn't the most charming man in the world. Ed is so normal; a pleasant change from the fuck buddies that I am usually attracted to.

Maybe I found the one. I am not overly attracted to him, it is more like settling on middle ground. Does that sound horrible? I don't want to go through life in a lonely shell, isolated from everyone and everything. Maybe I could have a normal life with Ed. At the very least, a normal man on a nice and normal date.

OCTOBER 4, 1992

The date was typical with Ed. We played pool, which is something I love, and Ed took me to a sports bar which had trivia night. He didn't want to play but I convinced him and we did rather well. Ed drank a lot of beer again, at an alarming pace. I am known for drinking until I black out, so I may have found my equal. I didn't keep up with him or I would have been on the floor, puking up my wings and rings. We didn't drink by the pitcher, but rather by the beer, served in extremely large mugs which rendered the beer warm if not consumed with haste.

We kissed in his black Acura before I went inside my apartment. I got fairly trashed. Ed is 7 years older than me, so he has a steady job with the Federal government. IRS tax stuff which bored me to tears. I suppose I officially have a boyfriend, although I've been seeing him off and on for months now.

Ed went down to Miami for the weekend with his crazy friend, Doug, to watch the FSU vs. Miami game. Ed told me that I couldn't get a ticket and that just he and Doug go to away games, no girls allowed. It's some sort of man bonding ritual.

Doug is both an interesting and disturbing person. He obviously has a high IQ, is witty and can be very considerate when sober. Doug has a fatal flaw of drinking exceedingly quickly with Ed. They seem to have a contest of swigging beer as quickly as possible. After several drinks, Doug becomes sarcastic and cruel and Ed acts like the embarrassing class clown, doing physical comedy to my great horror. Doug is independently wealthy from a trust fund his deceased father left him. I believe Doug mentioned he's from the Tampa area, same as my roommate, Robert. Doug often speaks about his sister in a negative way and frequently calls her a bitch. Doug trashed Bonnie, telling Ed that she was the stupidest girl he had ever met, but Ed retorted by talking about private sexual details with Bonnie. Hello?! I really didn't want to hear details. It was cruel. Doug encourages Ed's cutting humor when they are drunk, at my expense. They hang out frequently, so I'm not sure if it's a good or bad thing. But I have to say, when Doug is sober, he is a very charming man and enjoys smoking weed, which Ed doesn't like. Doug is a real Dr. Jekyll and Mr. Hyde. I really don't know what to make of him yet. All I know for sure is Doug got a degree in some type of Management with a focus on the purchase and sale of fine wines. Can you believe there is a degree studying wine? He works for a liquor store, ordering wine and setting up displays, as well as working the counter. God only knows what they are doing in Miami. I don't think I want to know.

NOVEMBER 8, 1992

We had an annoying presidential election take place. Several sorority girls in my classes at FSU were handing out George Bush stickers and pushing everyone to vote Bush. Well, too bad, because we have the Democratic President Bill Clinton who unexpectedly won. President Bush is an incumbent, so they usually get elected for a second term. Not this time. I didn't realize there even was an election without Sorority Sue pushing Bush. It caused me to go and vote for Bill Clinton. Ed wasn't at all happy with the outcome because he is a staunch Republican and called me weak for voting Democratic. We got in our first argument. Neither of us backed down, so it was a draw. It didn't stop him from kissing me again.

It is finally a home football game again. The last few games have been on the road. Florida State University played against Maryland. We won, 69-21. I sat with Robert,

Bonnie and Rob since Robert. Ed has season tickets in the Alumni section with three other friends which has fixed seating. I can only go to games with Ed when Paul can't make it.

It was a bit humiliating sitting with Bonnie because she kept teasing me about dating Ed, who is her ex-boyfriend. The four of us didn't ride together to the game this time because Robert and Bonnie had pre-game plans, so Rob rode with me to the game in my Festiva, tilting my poor little car over to the side. Rob is so large and heavy, he actually tilted the car. We parked near my school of Interior Design, so we had a super long walk. It was the only place I knew to park and there were plenty of empty spaces. I should have parked closer.

Getting back to Ed, I believe Doug likes to manipulate Ed and treats him like his court jester. Paul, who lives in Atlanta, often joins the group when they attend football games. Paul has known Doug for years. He is really good looking but also seems to make Ed his own personal jester and Ed plays the part. Ed drinks at a faster rate than anyone else, begins talking a hundred miles an hour, slurring his speech and shifting on his skinny legs, making cruel fun at the expense of others. He waves his arms in an embarrassing way, obviously feeding off the laughter of his male companions. I feel that Doug and Paul don't respect Ed, and keep him around as someone to laugh at, not laugh with. Sometimes I am the butt of the joke or something about having sex with Bonnie, which is vulgar. I have told Ed that I do not like him talking about me that way in front of other people just to get a laugh.

I sound like I don't like Ed. I might not, but he is fairly normal otherwise. I haven't had an actual boyfriend in, like, ever. Maybe James in Portland, but he left me and never came back. Ed lives here in Tallahassee, bought a house and won't be moving any time soon. That sounds stable enough, right?

NOVEMBER 26, 1992

Today is Thanksgiving and I am spending it alone. No one invited me over. A good day to take a lot of sleeping pills and watch tv.

NOVEMBER 29, 1992

Florida State had the big game last night against Florida. The stadium was on fire, the game was almost perfect, Florida State winning 45-24. What a game! I am hoarse from the screaming, which annoys Robert.

On a different note, I have a school presentation coming up on a retail space. I'm designing a high-end menswear store located in an upscale mall. Our assignment is to research the things necessary for selling clothes, like changing rooms, checkout counters, window displays, mannequins and store display furniture.

We were given this assignment a couple of weeks ago and I have already done a lot of leg work. Other students wait too long to begin their projects and end up staying up all night before it's due. We have weeks to do the menswear store so I began working on it the day it was assigned. I notice other students working on projects together. How do they do that? Am I supposed to ask someone if I can join them? I don't know how to start conversations so I haven't gotten invited to work with anyone else. I usually work in the lab at school where it is roomy and I have access to the library. Since our building isn't very secure, we all have to leave the building by 7:00 pm. They used to leave a side door unlocked for students, but one of the professors walked in to find a homeless man sleeping, or more like passed out, in the building. It really freaked out the professor who found him and the door has been locked since.

Our school is directly across the street from the homeless shelter and blood bank so we get some unsavory characters. The Wendy's and McDonalds is also across the street, so a lot of students cross the street to get to the restaurants which are next to the homeless shelter. I usually eat at home since I don't have much money. I am still working full time in the evenings at Benefits Management Company as the 401k Specialist. I assist customers with their 401k tax-free deductions and file all the paperwork in case we are ever audited by the IRS. Since customer service is open until 11:00 pm, I can work after school. My job sounds impressive, and I guess it kind of is since I helped the programmer write the software to create specific forms for certain Family Status Changes. I work very hard. I can't fail at this. I will get the best possible grades that I can. I was lazy at Tallahassee Community College and graduated with a C+ average so I will have to work extra hard to bring up my GPA. The GPA from TCC is carried over to FSU and counts as my overall GPA. I didn't realize that. I should have done a better job before, but I am working diligently now. Even if I am not the most talented, outgoing, or creative person, I will do it, and do it well. I want to prove all those people who treated me like dirt that I am a human being with potential, who can succeed. I know that I am intelligent. My grade school IQ testing showed that. I haven't been applying myself like I could have so I am doing it now. Wish me luck. I am trying very hard not to fuck up school and work. My private life may be in the toilet, but school and work will be perfect.

DECEMBER 26, 1992

I am spending Christmas alone. Not the first time and certainly won't be the last. I will never spend Christmas with my parents again after last year. It is too painful spending Christmas at the tavern and getting drunk with my parents. I want parents, not drinking buddies.

Uncle John went over to Kyle's family's house over Christmas, and I am not invited for obvious reasons (I slept with Kyle). Ed and I aren't sure if we are serious enough for me to join him in family fun. He said I wasn't missing anything. No one ever wants me around. I have taken over a dozen sleeping pills and washing it down with rum and Coke.

Keelie is with me. She is always loyal and loving. I would kill myself if it wasn't for her and college. I can't let her go to some cruel animal owner or be put to sleep. I think she would die of loneliness without me. She loves me so much, I can't kill myself. I will suffer here and hope that something better comes along. Something positive. Like people wanting to be my friend.

I bought macaroni and cheese and corn dogs. I might as well be a glutton. I gave Keelie some milk for a special treat. I have been watching all of the great old Christmas movies. My favorite is *A Christmas Carol.* The really old one, from the 1930s. I don't like any of the newer ones. That's the one for me. I still haven't watched *It's a Wonderful Life*. I can't bring myself to watch something that I don't feel.

I have such terrible nightmares every night. They get worse and worse. Especially over the holidays when I am alone. I get so frightened, I don't know why. I sleep with the lights on, laying on the couch, with the television flickering away. I feel darkness lurking all around me although I can't see it. I can feel it. It chills my soul.

I watched a documentary about a serial killer last week and I met almost all of the criteria, with the one exception of not being male. I am aged 20-30, spend my time alone, have no feelings inside except blackness. No happiness, no sadness, no joy, no hate, only emptiness and loneliness. I don't know how to have a friend. I never have. I always frighten them away. My life is depressing enough without hurting others. I only hurt myself. I'm the only one who listens to myself, so I hurt myself. There is no one around me to hurt. Ed, but he doesn't really have a soul. He has low intelligence and only likes to hurt me, saying cruel things or blow me off.

What a lonely existence.

CHAPTER 15

1993: AGE 24

JANUARY 2, 1993

It was the Orange Bowl yesterday. Ed is in Miami with Doug enjoying a long weekend. There was no ticket for me, not even if I paid for them. Ed wants to hang with just Doug. It turns out Paul and his girlfriend Melissa joined them. How cozy for them all.

Florida State won the game 27-14. FSU got the elusive National Title so I am sure there is some partying in Miami. What do I care? I'm not down there for the game. I watched it on the television. By myself. Did I mention that?

FEBRUARY 2, 1993

This morning, Robert told me that he is moving out. I suspected as much since he has been seeing a lot of Bonnie lately so I wonder if they are moving in together. Robert is being frustratingly vague as to where he is moving. Only that he is leaving but is paying for the entire month's rent. Nice of him.

Robert said that he might go back to Daytona, where he is from, for a while, or maybe Tampa, where I thought he was from, he isn't sure. Sounds like a load of horse shit to me.

I kind of did a freak out inside my head because the cost of a two bedroom will break me. However, Robert quickly suggested that I ask the landlord about a one bedroom apartment. That was a good idea. I am not sure why I didn't think about it myself. Perhaps I secretly want to still have a roommate, someone there to end the loneliness, besides my cat, Keelie. Tomorrow is Monday so I'll inquire about a one bedroom apartment. I hope they have something available and affordable. I still work full-time while attending college full-time, so I make enough money to pay rent, as long as I don't blow my money on stupid, unessential items, spur of the moment purchases such as sunglasses, a pair of pants that are a size too small, or a dress that I thought looked good but I don't wear it because it makes me look fat.

I am still driving without a license but don't speed and don't drink and drive. I hope I don't get caught since I can't afford the insurance. There is special car insurance for high risk drivers which is very expensive. I am trying to save up money to get 6 months of insurance. I have been getting student loans for school, so I have some money, but not a lot extra. I probably shouldn't get student loans since I'll have to pay them back some day. That time is a long way away, so I don't worry about it. Getting money easily is too tempting.

FEBRUARY 6, 1993

Well, there is an apartment very close to mine that is available in June. The landlord showed it to me today. It is cute and small, but not too small. It isn't an economy apartment. It is upstairs so I'll have to move my items down one set of stairs and up the other set of stairs. Good news is the apartment opens up a few days early, so I can move my things over a bit at a time. The water bed will be the biggest pain in the ass. I shouldn't have purchased it from Keri's fraternity roommate. They talked me into it. The bed is comfortable, but is difficult with a cat who punctures holes in it, causing it to leak and soak the sheets and blankets. Not a nice feeling, I can tell you. Keelie finds pleasure in attacking the water bed. She likes the way it rolls and bounces, although it is a "waveless" water bed.

I will ask Uncle John and Kyle to help me move. I had better begin collecting boxes from grocery stores!!

FEBRUARY 9, 1993

I live in a soap opera. Robert moved out yesterday a bit early, although he has already paid for rent. He and Bonnie moved his things while I was at work on Friday. I came home and he was finishing up the boxes. I was shocked.

Robert looked uncomfortable and rushed off as soon as he could. Okay, here is the drama part of the story; today I noticed that my striped shorts were missing. I searched everywhere in my closet and dresser drawers but couldn't find them. I also began to notice other items missing, such as another pair of shorts, a skirt, a dress, and a couple of shirts. Most of the things stolen were items that were a bit too small for me and folded in the closet, but they are still mine. I know those shorts were there last week because I wore them. No one has been in the apartment except for Robert and Bonnie. I have to conclude that Bonnie took the clothing.

I didn't have Robert's phone number since he didn't leave me one but I looked up Bonnie's number in the phone book. I called and got her parents' answering machine. I asked her to please return my clothing, that she took hundreds of dollars worth of clothes. No lie! I keep finding items missing. I have called her number four times today but it keeps going to the answering machine. The last time I told her if she didn't call me in the next couple of days that I'd call the police.

FEBRUARY 10, 1993

I went to the police station today at lunch and spoke to a detective about my missing clothing. I gave him Bonnie's information, so maybe he can do something to help me out.

Bonnie finally called me after I continued calling her home and leaving messages and had the nerve to call me the liar! She said that she couldn't fit into my fat, stinky clothes anyway, but the clothes she stole were my smaller ones. Bonnie told me to stop harassing her or she will go to the police. Even Robert called me yesterday and asked me to stop acting jealous. Jealous?! I explained that this was a legitimate theft and Bonnie stole probably $250 worth of clothes. Robert didn't believe me. My heart sunk as he told me not to bother Bonnie again, that if I was jealous I needed to get over it. I never even told Bonnie that I had sexual relations with Robert! I wouldn't stoop as low as that for revenge. This isn't about revenge, it is about justice. Bonnie is a princess who is always taken care of and always will be so there is no need for her to steal from someone like me who has no one to help me financially (or emotionally, for that matter). I just want my clothes back. That's it. We'll see what the detective says.

FEBRUARY 13, 1993

Detective Johnson called me at work and said that he spoke to Bonnie at her house. Bonnie told the detective that I was the instigator and I was harassing her and her boyfriend because I was jealous. Detective Johnson told me I didn't have much of a case since there is no proof that she stole anything so it would be best to drop it and not contact Bonnie again unless I had some proof. I asked if he searched her closet to look for the items I described, but he said he didn't have the right to do that, therefore he found nothing.

How frustrating! I don't know what to do, if I'll pursue it or not. I guess I should just drop it.

It was kind of funny how Pat at work started whispering to people that the police were calling me. Pat was talking about me but Thelma told her that I was done wrong, not me doing any wrong, so that shut up the gossipers. Pat answered the phone and transferred the detective to me, so that is how she found out about it.

This entire thing is making me sick. I came home a bit early since I had finished up most of my work. I feel so beaten down.

FEBRUARY 19, 1993

Oh, my God! What a living nightmare! I called in sick on Tuesday, which was a stroke of good luck on my part because the police came to the office to arrest me! Yes, arrest me! I was in just as much shock as you are. Where do I begin?

I was sitting on my couch in my cut-off Levi's watching television when Thelma called from work. She said that the detective and another police officer came to the office asking for me. Thelma said that made a lot of people talk, but she defended me by explaining about my complaint regarding the theft of my clothing. I appreciate her calling me to tell me. I played the part with her by saying that I was glad the police were coming, that perhaps they have a lead with my case. Thelma was convinced by the time we got off the phone. I could tell at first she didn't know why the police were there, but that bit about theft covered my ass completely.

When I got off the phone with Thelma, I felt a tinge of fear in the back of my mind. I thought I took care of all my arrest shit, handled everything, but what if there was a warrant out there for something I don't remember? I considered fleeing, getting in the car and avoiding the police who were coming to my apartment. No, I thought about it and decided if it was something bad against me, then I should go ahead and face the music instead of running which will only make it worse. Of course, they may be telling me that Bonnie has been arrested and they have recovered all of my clothes. I didn't have much time while I was thinking about all of the possibilities. I looked out the window of my half vacant two bedroom apartment (because I still have until the 5th to be in the other apartment) and saw Detective Johnson and an armed police officer approaching my door.

I realized that I was wearing cut off Levis that were a bit too tight and a t-shirt and should have changed before being arrested, although I was still hoping that they were here about my stolen clothes. I let the officer knock a few times before answering the door. Dread enveloped me, although I thought that I took care of my previous arrests. What did I leave out? I didn't mean to leave something unattended.

My worse fear came to light. I opened the door and the policeman handcuffed me behind my back as he searched my pockets. I realized immediately that I looked like White Trash and felt humiliated. I was read my rights as I looked down at the ground. Detective Johnson lectured me about how I was harassing a nice, law-abiding girl and that this was all made up by me because I was jealous of her boyfriend. I couldn't believe it. I wasn't lying, but here he was, not believing my story but believing hers. The lecture went on and on as I said quietly that I was telling the truth. The detective actually called me a liar, and that with my past history, I was a sad person. What could I say? I could see they didn't believe me at all and looked at me with disdain. Who can blame them? I feel disdain for myself.

I was told there was a warrant for one of the many driving without a license arrests. I thought I took care of them all, but obviously not. It is so hard to handle all of this legal trouble by myself, not understanding the law. I only had a court appointed attorney who seemed nervous and apologetic most of the time.

I was taken to the county jail, finger printed as before, put in a holding cell and told that the bail bondsman was on his way. It seems the police felt some pity for me at the jail. I had a $2,000 bail, which might as well be $1,000,000. I was in a confused haze, not drunk, not high, not anything except numb as the bail bondsman arrived, had me sign some forms. I told him that I didn't have any money but he said if I had at least $20 that would help. I wrote a check, which basically was all of the money I had. I was thinking to myself that I cannot let this check bounce. I don't want to owe a bail bondsman money. God only knows what they'll do to me. They may come and rough me up for all I know. I don't understand, am I supposed to pay back that $2,000, or actually $1,980? I forgot to ask. I have paperwork that I can read later. I just know that I am home again and facing a court date. The paperwork will be mailed to my home address.

Although I got out of jail at 3:30 am, I went to work the next day. I was tired, but I acted as if there was nothing wrong. I didn't have class that day, thank God. I was exhausted and made it through the day making up lies to Thelma and my boss that the detectives were able to get my clothing back. They bought my lies. I acted happy as can be. I am good at acting at least. Thelma rattled on, talking about how bitches can do you wrong, and my ex-roommate should have believed me. Good acting job.

I came home after work and went to bed early, although I had to move more things into my new apartment first. I am brain dead, pretending that I am human, terrified at whatever jail sentence may be looming before me, what fines I will have to pay. I lost some of my clothes and was berated by both the thief and the police. I was telling the truth. No one knows but you, my diary. I wasn't lying. But there are bad times coming. God, I don't want to go back to jail. Please help me! I feel like a zombie. I don't even know exactly what I am being charged with because I don't remember the event. Fuck them. I'll pay my dues so I can move on in life, I hope. I am afraid of jail again. It is horrible, beyond imagining. I have to become such a tough chick to protect myself. Either that or take a ton of sleeping pills so I don't' remember it. What will happen? I am afraid to loose everything that I have going for me; work and college.

I am trying so hard to straighten out my life, but my life doesn't want to get straight.

FEBRUARY 27, 1993

I am now in my one bedroom apartment. I had a difficult time getting any help moving. Ed told me he disliked moving and wasn't going to move for anyone ever again. How sweet. John is busy working but helped out for a couple of hours. I am quite strong so I took almost everything by myself. Put a load in the car, backed it up to the stairs of the new apartment and unloaded. It must have taken twenty trips. It felt like it. I am already pushed to my mental limit, now I was pushed to my physical limit as well.

Another bit of bad news; since I had to pay some of the bail money down, I was short $175 for rent. When Uncle Jay was helping me move, I humiliated myself and asked to borrow the money. I lied about where I spent it, claiming that I wasn't paying attention to my account balance and spent more than I had. I wish that was the truth. John said that he didn't have much money himself, and I nearly broke down crying from the mental strain, so he was able to get the money, although it put him in a bind.

I already have a court date coming up for an old warrant regarding driving without a license. It's a Tuesday, March 10th, so I'll have to call in sick that day (I don't have any more vacation days left but plenty of sick time). By Jesus' tears, the police are strict in this state about driving without a license. I have gotten in more trouble from those charges than my two DUIs.

MARCH 11, 1993

Justice is swift. I have never seen the courts move so quickly, but I suppose it was because I had a warrant for my arrest (unbeknownst to me). I explained that I was unaware of the warrant and would have taken care of the charge long ago. The judge felt some sympathy for me after I explained that I was working full-time in the evenings and going full-time to Florida State University during the day. I was sentenced to 30 days in jail yet again. However, since I seemed to be straightening out my life, the judge allowed me to serve my time over the weekends. Fabulous. Also, the state of Florida has a "serve two days get one free" deal, so I automatically get time off my sentence. At least a little. I really think that criminals being allowed to serve two days in jail and get one day off their sentence it appalling. In my case, I was extremely grateful.

I have already begun jail time last weekend. The judge allowed me to begin that weekend, so I decided to get the shit over with. Done and over and never in trouble again, I hope. I live by myself now so there is no explaining to anyone and no missing work or school. The down side is the jail won't let me bring my homework to jail since I am only a temporary visitor, nor will they let me bring any book to read. I am back to the mercy of their "library" which at least has several John Clancy spy novels. It is better than the other selections which basically boils down to Clancy or The Bible. I know which direction I am going, although I probably do need to read more of the Bible since I never was around religion. Maybe later. Clancy for now. I hid the book on the back of the table under some uninteresting Born Again brochures so no one else takes the book so I can finish it next weekend.

Like before, I wore a maxi-pad, cut a small slit and inserted 25 sleeping pills. I took a couple of pills throughout the day and laid on my cot during the allotted time and zoned out or read Clancy. I didn't take a shower in the mass open shower, which is open to any police man or woman who walks through the door. We are held in a large shed, really, with one end a giant fan the size of the wall, and the opposite side has the security desk, showers and toilets, with only the security desk being enclosed. There are roughly 50 cots in there, all of them filled with mostly Blacks. I wonder why more Blacks are arrested than whites. That doesn't seem fair to me. If I was Black, would I have gotten more jail time? Probably. Most women don't talk much except for the "bullies" who hoot and cheer at the NBA game playing on the television or Soul Train which is turned up much louder than necessary.

Being strip searched and sprayed down for body lice is humiliating and degrading. Sitting in the holding cell when I check in and before I check out is a real misery, too, because I am in the general population area of recent arrests, mostly drunk men. I try and make myself look as plain as possible, but they speak their vulgarities as I do my best to ignore them. I don't want to be put in one of those solitary boxes again (for my protection, yeah, right) because there is no air movement in there and you feel like you are being suffocated. I waited my hour or so handcuffed to a cell bench which was bolted to the floor, ignoring the cat calls.

I should only have 2 or 3 more weekends left, depending on how much of Friday night they count toward my sentence. Not much longer. I need to hang in there because the end is in sight. Then, I will have no more warrants out for me. I pray to God every day that the warrant in Pascagula, Mississippi never turns up here. I don't even want to think about a Pascagula jail.

Back to school work and suffering at jail. It is almost over.

MARCH 19, 1993

Last night I went out for St. Patrick's Day. I went alone again. Keri doesn't live here anymore, she moved back to Illinois and Monica and Miguel moved to Gainesville, Florida, for a gymnastics job. It was an opportunity for them to run their own gymnastics school, which is something they both are interested in. I probably won't see any of them ever again. Very depressing. I was seeing less and less of them over the last couple years as it was. I am back to being alone, no friends. I tend to frighten people away. I know I do. Keri's mother told her not to hang around me years ago, I could tell by the way her mom treated me. As if she was afraid I would kill her and her entire family. Anyone who really knows me knows that I would never harm another person. Only myself, I guess.

I couldn't bear being home alone and Ed hates anything Irish, so I was on my own. I still wish I was with Rob from Bean. He'd like to go, I'm sure. That was my own fuck-up. I have to get over it.

The Chieftains disbanded and aren't playing anymore. The Warehouse cover charge went up so that was too expensive since I am broke, as always, paying court fines and bail bonds again. I saw in the newspaper that there was an Irish clogging party with a couple of small bands. It was in a rented hall off Monroe Street so I decided to go. They served beer.

The clog dancers were exceptional, although the hall was so overly lit with fluorescent lights there was no atmosphere. The dark cave of The Warehouse seems more suited. It was still alright, although it was more of a "nerd" congregation. Something of interest did happen. As I was sitting at the table near the back of the room a man came over and sat next to me. His name was Paul, I think. I am bad with names. He was in the state capital for a visit to the Federal prison just 3 blocks from my apartment. Paul works for the state and goes around to various prisons to inspect the conditions there. He had just inspected the prison yesterday and had another one to look at today before going back to Tampa. He was cute in a geeky way. Glasses, boring shirt, khaki pants, boat shoes. Paul was interesting, though.

We talked for a while and then I invited him to my apartment. By that time I was pretty drunk. I started drinking once I began talking to Paul since I get so nervous. I was drinking about one beer per hour before he came over (I was there all night, not wanting to go home) but started drinking one after another, especially when he started buying me beer. We danced a little before I invited him to my apartment. I live only a mile from the rented hall so he followed me home.

The home part is a bit fuzzy. I know we had sex. I am not sure how long it went on, to tell you the truth, because he went to his hotel sometime in the middle of the night. I remember seeing him to the door, but I can't say what time that was. It was refreshing being around an intelligent man for a change. We talked so much, which is unusual for me. Paul said that he was sorry we lived so far from each other but that he was glad to have met me. It was sweet. I do feel like a tramp for sleeping with a stranger. I don't know his last name and I can't be sure that his first name is actually Paul. But he was different. He didn't act like a one night stand. He was very kind, respectful, and intelligent. I wish I could find someone like that permanently.

APRIL 2, 1993

I got so angry with Ed last night. I came home from work and noticed that my light wasn't on in the apartment. I always leave one light on because I get home after dark. I felt like someone had been in my apartment. I walked in and saw a few things moved. I panicked and ran to my car, heading straight for the nearest telephone booth. I phoned Ed, explained the situation, and asked if he would come over and look through my apartment with me. It was 8:15 pm, so it wasn't too late. Ed declined to help me! I got so angry and asked if he was scared or perhaps he didn't care if someone was in my apartment and possibly hiding.

After much arguing, Ed said he would come over. He only lives 1 1/2 miles up the road so it isn't like he has to drive across town.

Ed showed up looking annoyed as I lead him up to my apartment. I asked him to go in first, and he shoved open the door and walked in, turned on the light. That light was off, the one I left on this morning. I knew it. Someone had been in my apartment. Ed walked over to the kitchen counter and picked up a piece of paper. The exterminator had come by. Oh. That was what it was. I knew someone had been in my apartment, though. I was right.

Ed made fun of my fear and looked in the refrigerator for a beer. He cringed when he smelled and saw three containers of old milk, all rotting. I just kept buying new milk and not throwing away the old. I had clothes and things all over the apartment. I never really unpacked. The apartment doesn't feel like home. I had old food rotting in there, too. I had beer, though. Actually, it was beer Ed bought last time he was here and I just happened to still have it.

We both started drinking beer and I began to get pretty buzzed and was still mad at Ed for not wanting to help me when I was afraid. Ed acted like I was some idiot, rolling his eyes and obviously not caring. It made me so angry that I lost it completely and called John at work and told him how Ed was grabbing me really hard and pushing me around. Uncle Jay came all the way over from home and told Ed to get the hell out of my apartment and treat me with some respect. I don't know how it escalated to that melodrama. Drinking too much too quickly. All because an exterminator came in and turned off my light.

APRIL 16, 1993

Last night I was abruptly awoken by a swift bolt of fear. The dream still seemed vivid in the cool darkness and trickled down to my conscious brain as I started to remember the entire, frightening ordeal.

It was a dark, starless night at the beach. The beach was in Tallahassee, although Tallahassee is actually 60 miles away from the Gulf of Mexico. A strange, bloated, yellow moon glared angrily at Ed and me. I hurriedly got into my car, advising Ed to do the same. The moon frightened me.

We drove through the dark, deserted streets of a ghost town which resembled Tallahassee. We came to a beach but the beach was sectioned off with curtains and metal folding chairs were placed in organized rows facing the mock ocean which appeared on a screen. The sound of the ocean echoed in my ears, a salty breeze penetrated my nostrils and a faint mist danced in front of my eyes. It was unnerving. Ed had rented an entire ocean movie theater so there was no one around except for an usher dressed in black with a stiff collar bearing a striking resemblance to Dracula.

Ed told me that he felt a strange tingling in his limbs. He pulled up his jeans on his right leg to look at his aching leg. The jeans began to split and Ed began to groan in agony. The skin on his calf split open grotesquely as a thin, insect-like leg emerged. Ed's skin was falling off in chunks as he transformed into a giant fly. He told me to go away because he feared harming me. Acid dripped from his mouth as he looked at me hungrily.

I leapt up quickly, grabbing the car keys and ran toward my car. The fly-creature was quick on my heels as I ran without looking behind. I could feel the evil presence breathing heavily upon my neck but was too afraid to look back. I quickly unlocked my car door and drove off as fast as possible.

I drove to a sorority house on campus where I was invited to live. I decided to live there where it was safe from the fly-creature. Perhaps, I really want to be part of the college Greek lifestyle, in my subconscious.

I was walking around the campus, wondering if I could ever see Ed again when he stepped out of the shadows, intercepting my path. I stopped in fear. I was so afraid that I would also become a fly-creature or be eaten alive by him. But the monster was gone. Ed's soothing voice beckoned me back to him. I wanted to go back but feared it was a trap. I turned to leave but he grabbed my arm firmly, causing me a great deal of pain. I turned back to Ed but he was gone again. The fly-creature emerged and looked hungrily at me as I awoke in terror.

APRIL 21, 1993

I finally decided to move in with Ed into his house at the beginning of May. My lease is up this month so I either have to sign a new year lease or move in with him. I am finished with jail, thank God!

Ed is kind of shitty because he says he is going to make me lock Keelie up in the back bedroom so she won't disturb his precious Boo-Boo cat. Keelie will certainly meow and claw at the bedroom door if she is left by herself. I don't see what the big deal is. Why can't the cats just beat it out and then live together? Ed is adamant about Keelie staying in the back bedroom. If she stays back there, so do I. I will have my own room. Ed doesn't seem to mind.

I feel such guilt about Keelie. She deserves more attention. I'll have to fix this dilemma soon. Keelie deserves better.

MAY 14, 1993

I am living with Ed, albeit in the guest room. Ed has a 2 bedroom, 2 bathroom duplex so I am moving into his guest bedroom. I got rid of my water bed, or actually, left it behind in my old apartment. It leaked terribly so I decided to forfeit my deposit for the apartment. You know, it is really the deposit from Monica way back in the day. The water leaked into the carpet so it has to be replaced. I was afraid the floor would cave in and I would be in my downstairs neighbor's apartment. I left my old couch and crappy furniture. They can carry it off to the dump for all I care. That way, I was able to move almost everything by myself. There was nothing heavy that I brought with me. I took loads back and forth about fifty times. Ed didn't help much.

It has been alright. Ed is demanding half the rent and utilities. I can start in June. Nice of him.

JUNE 20, 1993

Well, I met the parents. Ed's mom and dad drove up for one night in order to take Ed and I to dinner in order to meet me. They stayed at the La Quinta Inn up the street and took us to Applebee's. Not my first choice but it has everything for everybody.

Ed is from Lake Wales, Florida, which is a small town not too far from Tampa and Orlando. It is an old orange grove community, so there are pockets of early Florida expansion money. There are still groves outside the town.

The dinner was strange. I didn't speak much, but Ed's dad talked for all of us. He is president of Suntrust Bank in Lake Wales so he makes quite a bit of money. Ed's mom has not worked a day in her life, her husband wouldn't allow her to work. She didn't speak much, and when she did, it was agreeing with something her husband said. Then she would do a little chuckle, like she knew what the fuck she was just agreeing to.

Ed's dad is quite an opinionated guy. He talked poorly of Blacks and Latinos, saying that he wouldn't hire another one of either if he could help it. It was fairly embarrassing having him talk disparagingly about other people in such a loud voice. What was he trying to prove, at this first meeting? That I had better adhere to his rules? I can't say that I didn't argue back. He started getting on my nerves so I challenged his racist ideas. I probably didn't score any points with the family by being argumentative. But maybe he likes some verbal debating since his wife doesn't have an IQ over 100. She didn't state one idea that was her own. Ed's mother is a complete, total flake without a thought in her head. His dad is a racist bastard who likes to control all aspects of his family's lives.

I guess the dinner went well. I didn't hear any complaints. Mr. and Mrs. Floen came by our house, which they helped purchase. They didn't stay long. I offered beer and wine. Mr. Floen had beer, and so did his wife. She even ordered the same dinner at Applebees as her husband! I drank wine.

Uncomfortable conversation continued for a long, tedious hour before they went back to their hotel, La Quinta. It was only a mile up the road. Mr. Floen can pack away the beer. He can keep up with Ed. Ed is tall and skinny like his mom, while Mr. Floen is fairly muscular and looks a bit like Harvey Keitel, actually. I'm glad that is over.

JULY 2, 1993

Last night the dream was so vivid that when I reached for the ground, I could feel every piece of gravel. I looked up and noticed that the sky was incredibly blue with large, cottony clouds dotting the sky. I spoke aloud in my dream and said how real this was as I reached for another handful of gravel. This dream was so realistic that I actually acknowledged the fact that I was in a dream. I awoke shortly thereafter.

I eventually fell to sleep again in the warm, dark early morning hours. The devil appeared in my bed again (this has occurred in dreams before). In my dream, I was laying in my bed which was so realistic I couldn't tell dream from reality. I didn't know at first he was the devil. He was tall, muscular and attractive, with thick black hair – an illusion.

He kissed me softly and gently at first and I kissed him back passionately. I looked into his dark eyes and saw nothing but blackness. He then informed me who he was. I didn't believe what I was hearing so I ignored it and kissed him again.

I noticed an ugly purple scar where his belly button should be. I thought that he must have been ripped from the womb. There was a live snake darting out from between his legs where his penis should be. I became terrified as the snake flicked its forked tongue at me.

The snake turned into a large penis, 2 or 3 feet long. I told him that I could not take such a large penis so he shrank it for me. It was still too large. I feared being ripped apart internally from his enormous appendage. I could not do it.

I awoke suddenly and was released from the fear and ecstasy. He was so hypnotic, that although I knew he was evil, I was afraid I would have obeyed him, done everything he asked of me. I was thankful to be awake.

JULY 5, 1993

I just got back from the central Florida city of Lake Wales where Ed and I visited his family for the 4th of July weekend. I met Ed's two younger brothers, one of which, Donnie is married to a divorcé mother of two and Ronnie, who is still in college at Central Florida. Ed told me of his obvious disapproval of his brother marrying a divorced woman with two children, a boy, Mark, and girl, Katie. Mark is nearly blind and wears glasses that must be ¼" thick, poor kid. He's cute. Donnie's wife, Corrin, has thick glasses, too.

I was given Donnie's old bedroom because it was redecorated with a pink and blue floral motif. Ed stayed in his younger brother's room, Ronnie. We slept in separate rooms since it is a sin to cohabitate without being married in the eyes of Ed's parents.

The entire visit was rather odd. Most of the time everyone crammed into the smallest room in the house, the "family room", which really was intended as a breakfast nook. The largest room, the formal living room, was serial killer creepy. No one ever sat on the furniture, it was pristine, not a spill nor a scratch anywhere. The photographs and small figurines were arranged throughout the room. The entire weekend, no one stepped a foot into living room.

There is also a formal dining room off the formal living room. The family room is cramped and dirty, used furniture and well worn chairs. The central theme is the television which is on at all times, except for dinner. It is turned on by Mrs. Floen in the morning and left on, even when she obviously isn't watching it. We barely talked. Mrs. Floen appears to be the mom who took too many little yellow pills and nods her head in agreement with whatever anyone says, so she is one of the most boring women I've met in my life. She did some knitting, but mostly prepared food. I offered to assist, but was politely dismissed. I did a great deal of reading in the formal living room, alone.

There is an uncomfortable formality about the house and its inhabitants. The house livened up when Donnie, his family, and Ronnie arrived. The kids are rather energetic and sweet. Little Mark is extremely smart and can already read at the age of 5, even with his bottle cap glasses. He is very bookish and it is sad to see his eyesight so atrocious. It appears Donnie and Corrin are trying to have a baby together. That is important to Ed's father, it appears. He discussed it at the dinner table for Christ's sake! How inappropriate! Mr. Floen, bank president, picks his nose whenever the mood strikes him.

We all went to see the fireworks in the city's garden. It has a tower and is apparently very important to the town. We walked around the beautiful, old neighborhood where the land and orange venturers thrived in the 1930's. It is still lovely and well kept.

The biggest excitement was visiting Haunted Hill. It is a road that has a railroad crossing on it. When you park in front of the tracks, as if to stop for a train, a hill appears before you. Put your car in neutral and the car coasts all the way "up" the hill. Obviously it is an optical illusion, and we began in the middle of another hill, but it does look strange. Truly weird. I know it is logical and not a haunting but is certainly appears that the car rolls uphill.

I suppose I got the seal of approval. I didn't argue or talk much for that matter. It was as much fun as walking on a bed of nails.

I rather liked Ronnie when he was there. He is different than Ed and Donnie in the fact that he doesn't really watch sports. College football is Ed, Donnie, and Mr. Floen's life obsession. They talk about it constantly and Donnie is a high school football assistant coach, so it is nonstop talk about recruits. Ronnie tends to not speak as much, but when he does, he says something a bit unusual. One conversation explained how the Monarch butterfly travels to Mexico at the same time every year, even though the butterflies have never been there. A most interesting subject. Refreshing after football 101 all day. Ronnie seems to be more of an artistic soul. He is also quite muscular. He is really the best catch in the family.

AUGUST 11, 1993

I got married August 7, 1993 at 12:00 am in Las Vegas to Ed, the same chapel where Elvis got married. I got the proverbial cold feet and almost backed out. I felt obliged to go with the wedding since the wedding package was already paid for. What I really wanted was a vacation on a cruise. I don't know how the situation turned into getting married. I really don't know if I suggested it or Ed. It wasn't a romantic bent knee proposal, of that I'm sure. I honestly can't remember how it unfolded. I am embarrassed to say that it was most likely a drunken proposal, but I made the arrangements to Las Vegas through the AAA office while sober, so I knew the consequences.

Our wedding escapade. To continue, we flew into the always tacky, Las Vegas, on August 3 and returned home August 8. There are companies dedicated to creating the perfect Vegas wedding packages, including hotel, limo, that dude who goes into the court house and gets the marriage license, and a justice of the peace at the chapel to marry. We chose the Excalibur package. It was fabulous!

The hotel had seven restaurants and multiple floors dedicated exclusively to gambling. I sort of enjoyed the slot machines, which were quarter based. I avoided the card tables, although I floated around them once in a while, to observe. Ed and I were rarely together since he wanted to bet some money on the roulette wheel. It was too intimidating and wasteful to me. I didn't want to lose money that quickly. A quarter at a time was fine. I started off with $20 in quarters, which they dumped into a small bucket with Excalibur stamped on the exterior. I quickly discovered that the best part of gambling is receiving free drinks, even if you are playing on the slot machines. The waitresses approached me all the fucking time, and mixed drinks I ordered by the sackful. I believe I actually beat the system and drank more than I gambled. That was the only reason for gambling for me since statistically, gambling is a complete waste of money. The Excalibur was a world of fantasy. They even had an oversized wooden carved chair which was actually quite beautiful and made me feel like a Hobbit. Keeping in the fantasy theme. I got picture on the chair.

The first night we arrived, it was around dinner time but we were so exhausted we took a nap. We woke up at 1:00 am. Our first thought is we screwed up and missed our night out. I mentioned that the hotel and restaurants are open 24 hours a day, so we went downstairs to get dinner and gamble. We were hungry so we went to The Steak House at Camelot restaurant which had extremely fabulous, excellently priced meals. I had a filet mignon of grand proportions, eight Dungeness crab legs which were enormous, a baked potato and salad bar all for only $7.99. I had a little from the salad bar and barely touched the baked potato but ate the entire steak and crab. It was delicious. It was the mid-price range restaurant in the hotel. I heard food was inexpensive in Vegas, yet excellent quality.

The other restaurant we visited was Round Table Buffet. You can purchase a wrist band and have all you can eat all day, but we opted for the one meal due to its extreme tackiness in wearing a food wristband. We had the breakfast buffet which was the bomb. The food was fabulous. The most interesting restaurant was the dinner at the Excalibur medieval jousting entertainment. We went on the third night and it was an exciting experience. We were seated on wooden benches that went around the arena, all of which had a wooden bar-type table in front of you. It was mass produced and you couldn't get much special. They served a Cornish game hen (the entire thing), new potatoes and bread, all to be eaten with your hands since there were no utensils. They also provided one beer. There was no ordering a second one. The jousting was awesome, with the horses and the ribbons and the knights fighting for the honor of some women. It was a lot of fun. It was like attending the theatre since we were packed in and it was difficult to get out of your seat. The show was maybe an hour, so it was rather expensive. All of the shows in Las Vegas are expensive. That is the one thing I found.

Later, Ed found a hole in the wall gambling den which had thong and pasties wearing women. They were all dyed blonde, whether it suited them or not. That was in the old part of Las Vegas, the one with the electric cowboy. Those places were seedy and had nickel machines. Ed complained that there used to be shows in every bar along the strip which you could see for free. I don't know where he received this information, but I didn't argue. It was all part of the Vegas experience, baby.

The final restaurant of interest is the one from a James Bond movie *Diamonds Are Forever* which you can see in the background during the prolonged car chase. It was a Bavarian restaurant called Hofbräuhaus. We ate there the last day and I felt unwell but continued on through the multi-course meal. I could barely sit up, I felt so horrible. I don't know why I was physically ill. Maybe it was due to the fact that I was now officially married or most likely, too much alcohol. I didn't eat much. Of course, Ed wanted the entire multi-course extravaganza and wouldn't leave just because I was not feeling well. Those are the highlights to our dining experience. Now for the rest of the vacation.

The days were rarely seen because we began doing the vampire life, sleeping during the day and going out in the early morning hours. It was extremely exciting to get up, roll out of bed, go downstairs at any hour, order drinks and play the slot machines. Sometimes, we just got up at 3:00 am, went downstairs to gamble and have free drinks for a couple of hours, and then went back to bed. It was a great way of life. I can see why people love Las Vegas. You can dress any way you want, get up when you want, and everything is open 24 hours a day. The employees treat you like a special celebrity. I was one of the only women who dressed up in velvet evening dresses. I had several women approach me and say that I looked beautiful and they wished they had dressed up, too. I responded by saying that all of the old movies show people dressed in black tie in Las Vegas, but that is a falsity. I brought only dresses and sexy clothes, so that was the way I dressed. Anything goes in Vegas.

The new part of Vegas was incredibly opulent. When we went to Caesar's Palace, I was in awe. There was a frescoed ceiling through the mall that looked as if you were looking at the evening sky. The bathrooms in Caesar's Palace were extremely elegant. They didn't have the ordinary paper towels, but hand towels to dry your hands. Everything had the appearance of gold gilding, although I know it all wasn't gold. We didn't stay there too long, but long enough to play this silly gambling game of toy horses and chariots racing around a miniature arena. I laughed at it, but Ed was serious about it. He had been trying to win the stupid game for twenty minutes while I was playing the quarter slots. We rarely spent time together, usually going our own way once we arrived at a designated location. To prove how silly the toy chariot race, I put my $5 in quarters into the slot, selected my chariot, and waited. Ed bet on one, too, so we were in competition. To my complete amazement and Ed's utter disappointment, I won. Yes, indeed, I won $40 from the $5 I put in. I went to the counter to get the winnings. Ed wanted to leave immediately after my incredible win so we went back to our hotel to gamble.

I was elated after winning $40. My coins were getting very low and now they were replenished. I chose to get my winnings in quarters so I could gamble on the quarter slot machines, look sexy, and get free drinks all night. Ed tried his hand at roulette a few times and lost considerably. I was horrified when he placed a $100 bet on one spin. He lost, of course, so he went back to the slot machines.

For one day, we rented a white convertible to explore the desert. It was luxury unbridled, so I wore my long scarf and big hat, looking like I was out of 1961. It was hot, but not Tallahassee hot. We ran the A/C even though the top was down. For that day we explored nature around Las Vegas. We went into Red Rock Canyon and saw wild burros calmly eating grass by the road. We stopped, because of my request, and observed the herd of burros. They were the Eeyore type of animal, with the long face and droopy ears, too adorable to pass up. One burro had a calf and they let me approach them and stroke their ears. They had absolutely no fear of humans. Ed didn't care for the entire experience, but I wanted to stay for a while. How often do you get to pet wild animals? They were the sweetest things, although their hair was rather coarse. I loved them so much, my burros of the desert.

On that day, we went to Hoover's Dam, which isn't too far from Las Vegas. We got the official tour and were blown away by the sheer size of the damn place. Bad pun. The turbines were immense and still working from the 1930's government public works. We went through the small town of houses, cookie-cutter homes on streets with no trees, where the laborers lived with their families. I think it is part of the state park because it didn't appear that people lived in those duplicated houses. They all looked the same except for a different paint color. The lack of trees was really depressing.

We drove, due to my request from my X-Files fetish, to Area 51. It was on the map so we went to the base that was there. There was a very tall chain link fence which was electrified all around the base. We drove around the perimeter, looking for a way onto the base. It all looked like desert, but I know there was more to the base than that. We were quickly noticed by some military employees and we saw three black SUV's coming straight towards us. I kid you not. They were black, with darkly tinted windows, and were speeding towards us. We became frightened and left the area immediately. The black SUV's did not pursue us. It was rather creepy. It was just like the X-Files. We didn't want them catching and interrogating us. We went back to our hotel, took a nap and went out again in the middle of the night.

I never told about the actual wedding experience. A limousine picked us up at 11:00 pm. We went to the court house where the limo driver got out and nabbed our marriage license for us (after we gave him our IDs). We stayed in the limo and drank champagne. I drank most of the bottle, but there was another one waiting for us.

We went to the Graceland Wedding Chapel which included the video and ceremony. Our driver was the witness. We got married at midnight. Crazy. I really didn't want to get married but felt that I was too far into it to pull out. Plus, Ed let it slip to his mother that we were getting married. She wanted to see the wedding, but he talked her out of it, thank God! I don't know why he told her. We had agreed we wouldn't tell anyone.

Well, the wedding chapel was officiated by a female chaplain. I didn't feel that special since there was no one except the employees witnessing the wedding. Afterwards, we were given the video tape and taken back to the hotel in the limo. There was another bottle of champagne waiting, so I absorbed it quickly. I had really, seriously, wanted to back out of the wedding but it was done. When we got back to the hotel, we returned to the gambling area and drank quite a lot. That is probably why I felt like cat feces when we went to that Bavarian restaurant.

I seriously almost called the marriage off. I had a ton of reservations settling on my mind and made frequent jokes about calling it off. Ed wouldn't have any of it since it was already paid for. The drunken ogre. I became positively terrified before we were picked up in the limousine. Not nervous, but I felt that I was making a huge mistake. Does everyone feel that way, I wonder? We often have terrible fights. I get so angry, I can't control myself. Ed is of a lower intelligence than I am. There it is. The center of it all. He is borderline stupid. What did I do? I thought Ed was nice, but is he?

AUGUST 29, 1993

I started back to school last week. I am excited to begin a clean slate, learn and absorb as much information as possible. I wish I could attend college for another ten years! There are so many different courses which sound so interesting, whether it be in art history, music, theatre or art. I can only take a few electives, so I can't do too many courses outside of my curriculum. I couldn't get a music class anyway because I would need to audition. That is not possible. I am not that great of a pianist.

When I began classes, in studio I mentioned to Stacy that I got married in Las Vegas and she started calling everyone in class over to look at my ring. Mike, the football player, asked if marrying in Vegas was legal. Yes, of course it is, dim wit. I said we got married where Elvis and Priscilla allegedly got married. It caused a minor stir but I didn't keep conversations going so they soon lost interest in me again. I sank back into ordinariness. A married boredom.

Yesterday was FSU's first football game of the season. We played Kansas in New Jersey and won 42-0. Ed didn't go to that game since he doesn't want to go anywhere near New Jersey. We watched it on television together. What a fabulous, endearing time. Sense the sarcasm.

SEPTEMBER 4, 1993

I lead two separate lives. One is the drunken, drugged, crazed Leigh who gets in trouble with the law, and the more responsible college and work-dedicated Leigh. People have caught glimpses of the crazed Leigh, but no one, not one soul who knows me is aware of my jail life, DUIs, and driving without a license most of the time. Every person surrounding me is unaware that I have to buy the most expensive and sketchiest auto insurance on the planet, meeting the salesperson in a small rental house. No one knows how paranoid and afraid I am most of the time, looking behind me for police lights or worrying about that one bounced check I forgot to pay. I am trying to hide the bad Leigh and concentrate on the good one.

I am doing so well at school, I am getting either A's or B's. My GPA is almost perfect. I work very hard to do well in college. I am getting mass quantities of student loans, so I hope it pays for something useful.

I really enjoy my classes. I am taking History of Interiors II this semester, which is Renaissance architecture and furniture. I take good notes in all of my classes. When I get home, I type my notes and print them. Typing my notes gives me an extra chance to remember the lesson from the day, but also keeps my notes in compact, easily readable pages. I am extreme in my personality. Even I know this. No one notices.

I haven't actually made friends here. Acquaintances, sure. I know just about everyone in the program since the program doesn't hold a great deal of students (around 100 at one given time). I hear sorority girls talking about Rush, and girls sharing phone numbers so they can work together. I don't know how to do the social thing. It is the small talk. I feel like it is a complete waste of time. However, I do not know how to do small talk since my parents didn't talk to me very much.

I want to make friends, I really do. I don't have Keri or Monica around anymore.

Today FSU plays Duke at Duke, and I was not invited by Ed to attend the game since it is an away game.

Doug, Jim, and Paul, his college friends, are going to the game. He says it is only "the guys" but I am not so sure. That is alright, I don't feel like driving up in a car full of people while I am under so much stress. I don't know how to have small talk, a normal conversation with people so I'm usually not the life of the party (unless I have one too many drinks, then I am the life of the party, in a bad way).

I have only the basic cable so I should be able to get the game since Florida State is so highly ranked. It should be on one of the main stations, NBC or CBS. I hope it isn't on ESPN because I do not have the bonus package. I don't have much money due to court costs and fines. Ed is too cheap to buy the bonus cable package since we go to most games. If it happens to be on ESPN, we go to a sports bar. Well, I'm going to see if I can find the game on television now. Bye.

SEPTEMBER 12, 1993

I went to the Florida State game yesterday. We played Clemson and completely annihilated them 57-0. FSU won against Duke, too, 45-7, so Ed came back happy. Ed got me a ticket to the game from his friend, Doug. We went to the Phyrst before the game and they ordered pitcher after pitcher of beer. Ed is such a tight wad, he rationed my beer since I didn't have the money to buy a pitcher, even though we are married. He wouldn't buy me anything to eat, either. He's my husband and he won't buy me dinner and drinks. I suppose he really isn't a gentleman, although he shared some of his fries with me.

Both Ed and Doug snuck in rum to mix with a Coke once we got into the stadium. Doug puts his rum in several ziplock baggies. Ed said that he is brave to attempt such a thing. Why doesn't he get a flask like the rest of the world? He has the money for it since he inherited money from his father.

After the game, we went back to the Phyrst. I really didn't want to go, but I could at least order water to make me feel better. Ed gave me a couple of drinks from his pitcher, the miser.

SEPTEMBER 19, 1993

Ed went to the North Carolina game to see Florida State beat them 33-7. As usual, there was no room for a female.

Oh, I forgot to mention that I was nominated President of the Student Chapter of ASID (American Society of Interior Designers) at FSU. Christopher is Vice President and a lot of fun. I'll schedule guest lecturers, meetings and school events within the Interior Design Department.

OCTOBER 3, 1993

I went to the Georgia Tech game here in Tallahassee with Ed and his friends. Paul brought a girlfriend, I forget her name. She seemed a bit arrogant and I could tell that she and Paul were making fun of Ed. She lives in Atlanta with Paul. I'm trying to remember her name. I'll find out next time.

Florida State University won the game 51-0. More drinking at The Phyrst before the game. It was a late game so we didn't go drinking afterwards, which was a relief. I was exhausted and didn't feel like watching Ed get so intoxicated that he slurred his speech. That is a bit embarrassing. Now I know how people felt about me when they see me drunk. I have to be non judgmental.

I slept in the guest bedroom again, which is rather nice. Ed has a two bedroom townhome so I've been sleeping in the spare room, citing the fact that my snoring is most intrusive to Ed's sleep. I like having a bed all to myself. My own private universe with Keelie.

I had another Marilyn Monroe dream. Almost nightly I am her, or see scenes from her life playing back; scenes that are private. I should write them down. I am her reincarnated. I am certain now. But I can't tell anyone or they'll think I'm crazy - again. As I research, I am finding that we have so much in common. I feel alone and confused but long for more dreams. They are becoming more revealing.

OCTOBER 10, 1993

Last night was the incredibly big FSU vs. Miami game, on Prime Time ESPN. The stadium was packed to overflowing but it was at night so it was only sweltering during the first half. By the end of the game it was bearable. That many people packed together produce a great deal of heat. It was a close and exciting game until the fourth quarter when FSU scored several touchdowns to win the game 28-10.

I sat with Ed and his crew, but this time, at Doug's house, we drank and smoked weed. Not Ed, of course. He despises it to his core and leaves the room when we do it. Of course, he doesn't want to get out of their good graces so Ed stands at the edge of the room, trying to be the class clown to get everyone laughing. I agreed to smoke some pot while Ed was in the bathroom. He saw that I was high and gave me the cold shoulder. Doug, Paul and Melanie (I discovered her name!) harassed Ed about me getting high, telling him to lighten up. Thank you.

I came home and went straight to my bedroom and went to sleep. I had another one of my Marilyn Monroe dreams. They don't feel like dreams but they must be. These things can't be happening for real.

OCTOBER 17, 1993

I am so busy with college work, it is exciting. My brain throbs as it absorbs new information. I decided to reduce to part-time at Benefits Management Company to concentrate on school. I will be working 20 hours a week, and had to give Thelma my 401k work, which was my baby. I left the department better than when I started, so that makes me feel good, although it feels like I'm giving up a huge responsibility.

The work I'm doing is now the paperwork that Thelma used to do. We are basically switching positions, so I am swallowing my pride and not making an issue of it. My manager wanted a full time employee for the 401k. My hours are flexible, I can do the paperwork any time until 11:00pm, when the office closes. At least my income there will cover my bills with Ed. He is splitting the bills down the middle like any other roommate.

I went to the FSU football game again yesterday. It was against Virginia and we won, 40-14. We did the usual pre-game drinking, but since the game ended late, lots of penalties, Ed and I left and stopped at IHOP for a late night breakfast. That entire experience was a nightmare although I found some humor in the situation, since it was like out of a movie. We were at IHOP for 2½ hours. Everything went so wrong at that restaurant. It was a busy night, lots of people were hungry after the football game and stopped to eat. We were excited when we got a table in ten minutes. That was the only good thing which occurred at IHOP that night, because that is when they still had staff.

It took forty minutes for our waitress to take our order as Ed and I sat in silence. We always sit in silence. She was the only waitress on duty. Yes, you heard correctly. In the entire, jammed to capacity IHOP, there was only one waitress and the manager waiting tables, telling us that a few people just walked out on their jobs because of some managerial conflict, so they were scrambling to get to all customers. We were assured that the food would be coming soon.

Another forty minutes went by, we continued to sit in silence, like always. We don't talk very much, I'm ashamed to say. Ed doesn't know how to do small talk, either. Other people were grudgingly leaving, grumbling, throwing down money on their tables for their sodas and walking out. Others held tight, being hungry, like us, and IHOP being the last open restaurant on the way home. Our poor frazzled waitress came by to refill our sodas, said that our order was coming up soon. We decided to wait in our typical silence. We waited until the restaurant was almost empty and finally got our food. Ed and I were so hungry we devoured it immediately. As soon as the waitress brought the food to the table she disappeared. I was going to ask for the check right then. But, no, she didn't come by for another half hour saying that she was getting our bill. She forgot, or got sidetracked, so Ed, who wouldn't yell at anyone to their face, went up to the waitress and asked for our bill. He came back and sat down for a little while, realized the waitress was not coming back to pick up the money. Ed needed to have a twenty dollar bill broken down. He wasn't going to leave her an $8 tip.

Finally, we decided to go up to the counter and pay the bill. So did everyone else. The line was slow because the manager was working kitchen, waiter, and greeter (people were still trickling in) so we waited, and waited in the line at the desolate cash register counter. We couldn't walk out, well, yes we could, but we felt obligated to pay for the food we consumed. So did most people, although some left without paying as they threw their checks on the floor. I felt fine once I ate, not in a rush to get home. It was the waiting for the food that was torture. We finally paid for the meal and went home in silence.

NOVEMBER 7, 1993

I've been working on several school projects, but the most enjoyable is the residential design retro-fit into an old African-American church in downtown Tallahassee. The structure is real, a church that was turned into a residence that my professor. We got a tour of the residence and it was gorgeous. The stained glass windows are still there, walls structured around them, and the clearstory windows were beautiful in the living room. The bedrooms were above on the perimeter, so there was a gallery from which you can look down upon the living room.

This project is a challenge due to the fact that it is a historical building and the outer walls and fenestration cannot be changed. Only the interior can be altered. The church is fairly long and narrow, like a shotgun house. We are not subjected to a budget, as long as everything we design is physically possible to construct.

I have other projects, also, and am always studying for History of Interiors with Karen. I have never seen Karen wear pants, but mostly wears very long skirts with a simple shirt. She is very delicate and feminine and used to dance ballet. She looks like she still does ballet by the way she dresses and walks.

I do well in Karen's classes because I take excellent notes and retype them on my computer. I have gotten A's in her classes, tests and essays. I do extra credit work, which she offers, just to be sure that I get an A. I wish more instructors offered extra credit. It is very helpful when there was a particularly difficult test on which I received a B. I've been on the Dean's list every semester since I've been at FSU. My main GPA is slowly increasing.

Ed will be getting back any time from Maryland. I watched the game and FSU won 49-20. Maryland scored a late touchdown to make the point spread less impressive. Also, Coach Bowden put in the backup players when the game is obviously over, so there are bound to be some points scored against second and third string players.

Time to take some sleeping pills. I want to be asleep by the time Ed gets home. He'll be tired. He is 7 years older than me so he is kind of old and tires out easily. Plus, he doesn't exercise at all. Not that I am in stellar shape myself. I am such a yo-yo person, gaining and losing weight quite often. I can gain or lose twenty pounds in a month or two. When I get stressed, I binge eat. I admit that I hide food in the house. I buy Vanilla Wafers, or Captain Crunch cereal and can eat almost the entire package in one sitting. Captain Crunch with Crunchberries has been my favorite lately. I am ashamed of my hidden binge eating. Sometimes I try to make myself vomit, but it is difficult to do! I am overweight. Not severely, but enough so my pants are all tight, with the buttons bulging or I use a safety pin to hold them closed. I have burst open a few zippers. That is humiliating when you are at school or out in public. I have been carrying around safety pins so I can at least pin my pants closed and pull my shirt down.

I still have a hidden life. I always have and I guess that I always will. No one knows everything about me. I am always hiding, or lying about something. Sometimes I lie for no apparent reason. A new credit card "co-signed" by Ed (forged by me, to be honest). I have a couple of department store cards but I always end up buying clothes without trying them on or buying a size smaller so I am forced to lose weight. That ploy doesn't work. I basically have a closet full of clothes that I can't wear, and many that I've never worn at all. I know I should purchase clothes that fit, but I hate to get a size 14. A size 12 sounds much better. I've been wearing long, flowing skirts. It hides some, but not really. I look like shit. I color my hair to be the blondest blonde but I look like a fat Marilyn want-to-be.

Alright, I am thoroughly depressed now. Good night.

NOVEMBER 14, 1993

Oh, boy. FSU had an away game at Notre Dame. FSU lost 24-31. Unbelievable. Ed didn't go to that away game because his friends didn't want to spend that much money and drive so far for the game. We went to AJ's to watch the game and Ed drank pitcher after pitcher of beer, getting angry, swearing, throwing his hat down, and acting like a complete embarrassment to me. It is a football game, not the death of close friend! Ed gets so angry when FSU doesn't play well, and acts like an asshole in public. I just sit there as quietly as possible until we go home. Ed embarrasses me a lot, although he rarely takes me out in public. He is so lame about taking me out. We have never gone to a movie together because he hates them. We haven't been to the beach because he hates sand. We rarely go out to dinner and the only entertainment is playing pool at AJ's Sport's Bar because they have $3 32 oz beers on tap. I can down two of them, although it makes me tipsy and argumentative. Ed drinks 3 or 4 of them. I can't drive home because I have no license and Ed said that he would never let me drive his car, even if he was unconscious. That was a mean thing to say. I didn't tell him the entire truth about my license suspension. He doesn't know that I got three DUIs and all the driving without a license charges. I said that I got one DUI. He doesn't care to know anything else about me so I don't tell him.

I am busy with my college work since Ed is in such a bad mood after yesterday's loss to Notre Dame. What a big baby. I didn't think he would stay so angry, but he did. I wish I could smoke pot. Sometimes I get some from John and smoke it when Ed isn't around. I really hide it because he would give me the third degree.

It was a nice excuse to go into the lab at school to work. I found out there is a trick door on the front of the building. It feels locked when you pull on it, but if you really pull hard, it will open. The instructors told us that trick since the doors are supposed to be locked when a teacher is not in the building.

Truth is, I shouldn't be driving at all. I lost my license for 5 years, and I have 3 more to go. It is difficult hiding that fact from a roommate, but Ed doesn't ask many questions. I drive the speed limit, I can tell you. I park legally and have a hell of a time keeping expensive auto insurance. I still have to go to those hole in the wall places and pay through the nose for insurance. I only do that when my tags come up for renewal every two years. The rest of the time, I am uninsured, so I drive defensively and at the appointed speed limit. It is stressful looking in the rear view mirror every 30 seconds to see if there is a police behind me. When it does happen in traffic, I pull in to the first gas station or convenience store to let him pass. I've done that several times. I try not to drive at night when I am more likely to get pulled over and I don't drink and drive.

Back to work.

NOVEMBER 21, 1993

I received my sexy feather and silk negligees from Victoria's Secret last week. There are several shirts and pants from there as well since I have a credit card through them. I also have a Nordstrom account. I love having clothes delivered to me. I dress up in them when I am alone, not for Ed. He doesn't know about them. It makes me feel sexy when I wear them, like I am Marilyn. I have dropped a pant size, by the way. I look much better.

Another FSU football game yesterday against North Carolina State for the ACC Championship. FSU demolished NC State Wolfpack 62-3. Our third string quarterback was in for most of the 4th quarter and we still kept scoring. It makes Ed quite happy, but the Florida game down in the Swamp looms large next week. That is one away game I do not want to attend. I've been down there on business and people are hostile against FSU. Some people take it way too seriously. If FSU loses, then it will be a humiliating walk back to the car. Let Ed go if he has the nerve. He probably will go with Doug. Good riddance!

NOVEMBER 30, 1993

It was an interesting Thanksgiving this time. Jim and his wife Jean, who recently purchased a nice country style home in an established neighborhood. Jean is a wonderful, kind woman. I can't judge how old she is. I think she is the same age as Jim, but she looks much older. She tries to look young, but it makes her look even older. Ed has told me repeatedly that she cannot have children and Jim is fine with that, but I truly believe it is breaking Jean's heart. She wants to adopt, but Jim still thinks he is a hard-drinking college student with no responsibilities.

Jim is a good looking man, who enjoys drinking and is a happy drunk. The more he drinks, the more kindness oozes from his slurring mouth. He doesn't have a mean bone in his body, but he always gets sloppy drunk, running into furniture, falling and spilling beer or whiskey and Coca-Cola. Jean enjoys inviting her sister and friends over to watch the FSU away games or any other excuse for company. Jean prepared a wonderful Thanksgiving dinner, although it was a Thanksgiving grill-out. It was excellent, with hamburgers and hotdogs being cooked by a tipsy Jim, and many dishes of potato salad, broccoli casserole, bean dip with tortilla chips, coleslaw, and a variety of other tasty delectables. Jim and Jean provide alcohol, but Ed at least brings a six pack. It's a nice gesture, but he will drink 4 to my 1 beer, almost racing with Jim.

Some other people were at the party. Jim's pride and joy, Odell Haggins, Tight Ends, Offensive Line Coach for the Florida State University football team, showed up. Jim took some classes with him in college, they were friends, and when Odell became an assistant coach, Jim was overly excited.

Odell arrived late with his wife, and didn't stay long. It was a courtesy call because poor Odell was completely embarrassed by Jim reciting his entire football career for everyone. Jim slapped Odell on the back and said that this is the biggest man he had ever met and to check out the size of his neck. Jim talked of nothing else except Odell while he was there, and Odell was obviously uncomfortable being the center of so much drunken attention. He stayed twenty minutes then politely left. Jim was pleading with Odell to stay, but Odell, very nice man, was kindly telling Jim that he really couldn't stay. Odell obviously was friends with Jim, but not with the intoxicated Jim.

Oh, yes, the FSU football game. FSU played Florida in the swamp and won 33-21. Odell left before the game began and Jim began vomiting in the bathroom at the end of the 4th quarter.

DECEMBER 28, 1993

We are back from Lake Wales, Florida, for Christmas. Ed and I were given a room together now that we are married. How 1950s of them. Ed's brothers showed up and his sister-in-law and her children. Corrina is pregnant and Donnie is so excited, talking about how he will teach him football and baseball so he can become a professional athlete. Hello? She is only a couple of months pregnant. It may be a girl. I guess he would be crushed by that fact. Donnie and Ed are so much alike, except for the fact that Ed wants nothing to do with children. Of course, I have always wanted a child, but the home life needs to be stable and happy. I don't want to continue the cycle of abuse and neglect. It would be nice to have someone who would love me unconditionally. I would always have a friend.

The Floens did Christmas in the formal living room, which is the only time the room is used. We each opened a gift, one at a time.

I got a kite from Ronnie. He likes to purchase a gift that is either functional or entertaining. Ronnie is the youngest, but acts older. Some of his family teased him about his functional gifts, but I think it is a great idea. If you are going to give someone a gift, why not get them a gift they will use? I mentioned at Thanksgiving how I'd like to try flying a kite.

Ronnie must have heard me and purchased one for me. It is the kind with two handles to do tricks. It's a nice one. I'll have to try it the next time I go to the beach.

I read a book most of the time, or did cryptograms alone. I drank wine when it was offered and tried to find the nice happy medium alcoholic intoxication that would make the boring times more enjoyable, but not too much to vomit on myself in front of the entire family. I really don't want to make a fool of myself in front of the Floens. Mr. Floen is so fucking conservative, he enjoys watching the Rush Limbaugh show. Ugh, how painful. Ed watches it, too.

It is my birthday tomorrow. Ed is going to take me to the restaurant of my choice, except for the French restaurant. He doesn't want a violinist bothering him while he is trying to eat dinner.

CHAPTER 16

1994: AGE 25

JANUARY 2, 1994

What a great way to begin the new year. Florida State University won their New Year's Day game against Nebraska 18-16 and became National Champions! It was a nail biter. Ed and I watched the game at home, just in case FSU lost the game. It was for the best since Ed swore like a sailor, and drank like one, too. He is sick as a dog today. I am a bit hung over, but I drank to deafen the uncouth language. Not that I am a prude, by any means, but must the profanity continue with every football play? Maybe it wasn't constant swearing, but it was constant negative energy. Keelie hid under the bed early on and I sat at the other end of the sectional, drinking my wine coolers. Ed is frequently negative, and frankly it is embarrassing. Thankfully there was no one around to see him this time. If the conversation isn't about FSU football, it dies off. I don't even talk about school with him, now that

I think about it. Ed never asks about my course work so I haven't mentioned much except for the occasional award or something special.

But this is all normal, isn't it?

JANUARY 14, 1994

Oh, my God! I went for my annual exam and found out that I am pregnant! I have been taking my birth control pill but I missed just one and see where that landed me. The doctor noticed that I wasn't extremely excited, but he talked me into being happy. I was planning on going to graduate school after I graduate this year and this will change everything. I haven't told Ed yet. I actually enjoyed sitting in class knowing that I had a baby growing inside of me. It isn't actually a fetus yet, since I am only two or three weeks pregnant. I had a normal period last month so I am not far along. I have been sick to my stomach, though. It isn't just in the morning, but can hit at any time. I eat something starchy which makes me feel much better. I called and told my mom. I am getting excited about having a baby. I don't know how Ed will feel about this.

JANUARY 22, 1994

What a misery I am in. I told Ed last week that I was pregnant and he wouldn't even discuss it. I must get an abortion. He said he'd pay for it and there is a clinic near by. He had taken Bonnie there before. That's not what I wanted to hear.

We went out to dinner last night and I started feeling sick from the smell of the cleaners being used in the restaurant. Ed couldn't smell them but I could. We had to go home. It was made even more depressing by the fact that I knew that I would be aborting this child. I don't want to, but I was an unwanted child. I don't want a father not to want his baby. I couldn't raise a child by myself. I think it would be too much.

I made the appointment for the abortion. Well, I have to go in and be interviewed to make sure that is the choice I want to make. I'll be going in on Monday to speak to a nurse.

FEBRUARY 15, 1994

I got the horrible abortion done yesterday, on St. Valentine's Day. Since the fetus wasn't that far along, it was fairly easy. I didn't have to be induced like some other women were. I had to go through the whole process alone. Ed wouldn't come with me. I didn't want to ask if he had gone with Bonnie during her abortion. That is more than I care to know.

My mom was sad for me since she knew that I really wanted to keep the baby. I'm too messed up to try it by myself. I'd hurt the child and they would end up hating me and running away forever.

I didn't realize until I was leaving, after the medication was wearing off and I had to sign myself out of the building that it was St. Valentine's Day. Ed didn't get me a card, a flower, or chocolate. He didn't even wish me a happy Valentine's Day. He forgot about it. Now I'll always have this horrible memory on St. Valentine's Day for the rest of my life.

MARCH 24, 1994

I received a ton of boxes from Neiman Marcus today. Lots of perfume, clothes, dresses, things I can hopefully wear. My favorite are the Gucci rain boots. I bought them with my secret Neiman Marcus credit card. Ed is a "co-signer" for it, and it is very difficult collecting the mail before he does on the weekends. I can't let him see any of my credit card bills. I'm making payments, but I love to spend money and get beautiful things. Maybe it is because of the sad month I had in February. A little happiness in my life.

That little happiness was marred by the UPS delivery man. I see the same man for each delivery and have spoken with him a few times. I answered the door in tight white leggings, a sheer white burned out floral motif shirt with a camisole underneath. Oh, and my see-through shoes that look like glass slippers that Barbie would wear. I felt like I looked like a 1963 housewife, but kind of sexy. When I took all of the boxes he delivered, he brought the largest box into the house for me (it is a winter coat, yes, I know, it is only March but it was on sale and it is white with a furry collar). I thanked him for his assistance and as he was scanning the packages into his hand-held device, he asked me if I was pregnant. I kept a smile on my face and laughed it off, saying that I was wearing an oversized shirt and, no, I was not pregnant. I wanted to tell him that I was pregnant, deleted the poor little glob of cells, and have been eating stashed cookies and doughnuts and malted milk balls ever since. All that came from my lips was "no". The UPS driver was obviously extremely uncomfortable and embarrassed. I assured him that it was okay, I know I need to lose a little weight. He turned his red face away from mine and walked quickly out the door.

After he left, it was difficult to revel in the things I just purchased. Plus, I had to hide it all quickly, before Ed arrived home from work. I tore the tags off, broke down boxes into just one, and hung up some of the new clothes but kept the others hidden away at the back of the extra bedroom closet, behind my unpacked boxes from the move. I have to be quick about it because the UPS is delivered around the same time Ed gets home from work.

I don't want to be fat any more. I must do something. Starving myself is not the answer. I will begin by walking around the neighborhood with light hand weights. I can drive it to see how far it is, so I can be sure to walk 2-3 miles a day. Yes, I need new sneakers, a sports bra, and workout clothes. I better buy some. I've got to get out of this funk. Ed certainly hasn't been trying to cheer me up. Maybe I can talk him into going to the French restaurant, Chez Pierre. They usually have a musician or two there, playing the guitar or violin while patrons are dining on escargot, lamb, and other delicious delicacies. A little excitement would be very much appreciated. We'll see if he goes for it. If I offer to pay for half of the bill, then Ed will probably say yes. Wish me luck. Got to go. He's home. Fuck.

APRIL 6, 1994

I was nominated by David and received the Academic Leadership Award for the entire School of Visual Arts and Dance. I received the award last night at the Leadership Awards Night celebration. The Dean of the school presented it to me. I am sure I looked pregnant in the photographs that David took. He was my cheering section. Ed did not want to attend the ceremony.

There was a brief mention of my award in the Tallahassee News Tribune. David nominated me because I have made the dean's list every semester except one while being at FSU. Also, I am president of the student chapter of ASID (American Society of Interior Designers). I am also a member of the Golden Key National Honor Society.

I sat with David. The event only lasted less than an hour. There were other awards handed out but no one gave any long speeches. I still am in shock at receiving this certificate. It means so much to me, especially since it is for the entire School of Visual Arts and Dance which includes Art, Art History, Dance, Theater and Interior Design departments. That covers a lot of students. How amazing. Me, succeeding in one segment of my pitiful life.

APRIL 17, 1994

Last night I was invited to the Golden Key National Honor Society dinner party. It was a formal event so Ed came with me this time. Of course, he will accept the events for which he can get a free meal. There were several speakers and a classical quintet playing off and on through the evening. Toward the end of the evening, I received a certificate stating that I am a member of Golden Key National Honor Society and giving me the rights, honors and privileges it entails. It is another piece of paper that can be framed to go along with the Academic Achievement Award and degrees. I won't be graduating summa cum laude because my TCC grades are averaged into the mix. I won't even be able to make cum laude because I had a C average at TCC. I was very close to bringing it up to high enough to get cum laude, but just missed it. I did some calculations, and if I continue receiving 3.85 gpa, I should be able to make the magna cum laude for my Master of Fine Arts degree. I will work hard to get that recognition, too.

It's pretty impressive being on the Dean's list every semester except for one. That one semester was my first one when I was still getting accustomed to college life at the higher level. I didn't make that mistake again. The judges and police who have dealt with my other side wouldn't believe it. Nor would the people who have seen me drunk, vomit on myself and pass out. I'm always treated like a stupid blonde, someone who doesn't have a brain in her head.

It has always upset me that I am treated with such contempt by society. I am doing every thing I can to rectify that. I will be respected. Even if it kills me!

MAY 1, 1994

April 30th was graduation day. I walked with my cap and gown for the first time in my entire life. I never graduated from middle school or high school. I received my Bachelor of Science degree in Interior Design. I was only one stupid class short of receiving a Bachelor of Arts degree. If I had known earlier I would have taken it. There was some poor advise given to me during the course planning stage. I would have taken one more class to get the BA instead of the BS degree. Well, I shouldn't worry too much since I am continuing on to the Master of Fine Arts program. It is a 2 ½ year post professional degree that falls between a Masters and Doctoral degree. It will enable me to teach at the college level. I would love to teach some day. That is my goal. I would have so much respect from people, from strangers, people who don't know who I really am but seeing a glimpse of what I could be. That would be the best thing that I could do is to gain respect from people.

I also was voted by the other students in my Studio IV class "Best Space Planning/Design" for a restaurant/retail space. That was a nice bonus. Not everyone received a certificate. In fact, only 6 of us got one. That makes me feel good.

I went to my graduation with Ed and Uncle John, although I had to sit with the students. My parents didn't come because they didn't want to spend the money on airline tickets. They said they would wait until I receive my MFA. That will be another 3 years from now since I am taking the summer off. I am so pleased that John was able to make it. He was so happy that I received my BS degree because I am now officially the highest educated person in my family, on both sides.

My parents did send $300 to go toward a piano for me. I'll have to get a used piano somewhere. I have been practicing at FSU's School of Music across the street. I discovered the practice rooms over there and go during the less busy hours. There are so many rooms that they rarely fill up, unless it is close to the end of the semester. I practice whenever I can, usually Saturday mornings. It will be nice to play the piano at home. I invited Ed to listen to a Mozart piece in the FSU practice room once. He didn't seem to care at all, so I haven't invited him since. Nor has he asked. I wish he would encourage me just a little. It is depressing to play for no one. I have no audience. I feel that I play well, too. It seems so wasteful not sharing my talent with others. Maybe I'll find someone who enjoys listening to me play. Katie in Portland use to request me to play quite often so I know there are people out there who enjoy listening to piano music. I just need to find them!

JUNE 20, 1994

In my dream, I was dying, yet wanted to live. People were around me, helping me. I kept coughing, my lungs were filled with fluid. A tall handsome man whom I love, and who loves me in return, was helping me, supporting me. I was saying good-bye to my friends and family.

I saw Ed's grandmother going into the movie theater where I was collapsed on the floor. She was dressed up and seemed very happy. I looked around and saw a man who was dead laying on the floor near me. No one seemed to notice that a dead man was there.

I felt that I must accomplish more before I die so I decided to fight death. John was there helping me because I was so physically weak, yet mentally strong. I awoke. I realized that I was actually Paige and the kind man was Todd, her husband. I know I had the dream because Paige just died in surgery while having a double lung transplant. She had Cystic Fibrosis, a horrible disease where your lungs are constantly filling with fluid, requiring someone to hit your back to loosen the phlegm in order to expel it. Todd or a friend had to cup their hands and strike Paige on her back a few times a day to prevent her from drowning. It was like having pneumonia constantly. She couldn't even sleep all the way through the night without having her back beaten. Paige could never lay down flat on a bed, either, she had to be propped up with pillows so she wouldn't drown every night.

Paige was also extremely emaciated because her body couldn't break down the nutrients from food. I don't think she even weighed 90 pounds. She was never hungry anyway because of the fluid. She was always coughing and shaking and her fingertips had a slight deformity, they flattened out. It is also part of the disease, I looked it up on the internet.

She told me that she had Cystic Fibrosis when I mistakenly thought that she had severe asthma. She angrily retorted that she didn't have asthma, but C.F. I felt ashamed for thinking that it was only asthma. I had never seen a C.F. before.

Apparently, Paige, when she died, was the oldest surviving C.F. person on record, so I have been told. She was 27. We weren't friends, she hated me because I hung on men and they were attracted to me for sex. I am ashamed of that. I don't like being the loose woman. I want to be respected, that is why I am going to college.

Even though we weren't friends, once I found out how horrible that illness is, I really wished that her double lung transplant would work. She only had a 50% chance of surviving the surgery. However, if it was successful, she would have lived much longer with healthy lungs, something she had never known. It is a horrible disease, I can't even imagine the suffering involved. I have had severe bronchitis before and it is bad, and her illness is much worst than that. I do wish there was a cure for C.F.

I feel that Paige's spirit is trying to communicate with me, not because we were close but because I am more open to the spirit world. I have felt her so strongly that I used a Ouija board by myself. I know you shouldn't do that, but I felt pestered by Paige. One of the things Paige told me was that she and Todd honeymooned in Greece but she didn't like the food. I haven't been able to verify this because if I ask anyone, they will think I am crazy. Paige also told me that Todd is seeing someone else. This, is true. Todd lives only a couple of miles from here (John mentioned it one time) and I have seen him in the grocery store with another woman. Paige was bothering me so much I have now refused to speak to her. There is nothing that I can do to help her. I don't know what she wants, either. I hope she finds peace.

SEPTEMBER 11, 1994

I have the house to myself since this week we play Maryland, which is an away game. Keelie and I drink cocktails in expensive clothes. By the way, FSU won 52-20. Ed went with Jim to the away game. Jim is like me and drinks until he is so shit faced that he vomits or does something stupid and doesn't remember it. Ed told me how he got a DUI one night after going to the Phyrst and Jim drove the wrong way down a one way street, Piedmont. What a stupid thing to do. There are signs everywhere saying "wrong way" but he was obviously too drunk to see them. I can relate. I am not going to judge the poor guy. Ed wasn't with him during the DUI but picked him up from the police station.

SEPTEMBER 16, 1994

I had a feverish dream. I had a cat bite in my dream, a bite from Keelie when she attacked me because she was being tortured by people. Unknown assailants were burning and cutting Keelie as I fought my way through them and released Keelie from her bondage. That is when she bit me in my dream.

In the next dream, I was transported to a laboratory with a large robotic computer hovering above me (like at the automobile factories). The robot was on wheels so it could maneuver quickly around the room. I was with Susan Sarandon again (why, I don't know; let's do the time warp again), a man and we were locked in a lab with the robot. The oppressive robot was angry with humans for experimenting on him so he wanted revenge. He had selected a few humans to torture, including me.

All of the doors were locked and there were no windows in this metallic lab. The doors were actually locked with large dead bolts that went straight into the wall and were controlled through the computer security system. We all tried in vain to pound on the locked metal doors.

The robot started his twisted work on the other two people first. I had to watch them being tortured so I tried to find a hiding place. There was none.

First, the robot trapped the victim by pinning him to the floor with his arms. He had many arms, each of which held his victim's limbs in place. The victim was screaming and writhing under the robot, but there was no way that they could free themselves. The robot had another arm with a fine point at the end and gouged out their eyes. I saw blood pour out of the sockets as the tormented soul screamed to a frenzied pitch. I felt complete horror and was frozen in place. The robot punctured one eardrum with the point but stopped before puncturing the other when he saw his victim struggling convulsively. The robot was afraid of injuring the victim's brain. He wanted his victim to be aware, conscious of all of the pain.

The robot suddenly emitted a high piercing sound which ruptured the other eardrum of the first victim and both eardrums of the second victim. I covered my ears as hard as I could to save my eardrums.

I saw the door unlock momentarily so I ran out of the lab and ended up in an observation room. I was cornered and forced back into the lab to watch the torture.

The robot used a laser to cut off the victim's arms and legs in order to render them completely helpless. The laser seemed to seal the wounds so they wouldn't bleed to death.

Finally, as the victim was blind, deaf, and without any limbs, the robot attached computer wires to their heads and stumps of their limbs. He sent an electrical current through the wires, but not too much to kill them or render the victim unconscious, but to be as painful as possible during every waking second. The robot wanted them to know what it is like to be a computer all of the time like his own enslavement.

The robot turned toward me. I screamed and clawed at the metal door. It wouldn't open so I tried to flatten myself to the wall and be as still as possible so maybe he could not locate me. This tactic did confuse him at first, but his massive arm swung around and pinned me to the wall. I screamed with pure terror. I could see the other arm with the point coming toward my eyes. The robot was about to gouge out my eyes when I awoke. It is raining and dark. It is 8:30 am on Friday. I am alone. I still feel panicky. I keep telling myself that it was only a dream, it was only a dream.

SEPTEMBER 18, 1994

I am alone again this weekend. Ed went with Doug to Wake Forest for the FSU football game. Of course FSU won 56-14. I watched the game on television. I have to tape all games for Ed, cutting out the commercials, because he likes to watch the games again later. I think that is rather strange for a nobody game. I can understand, perhaps, the reasoning for recording big games like Florida or Miami. I do my duty.

I bought some orange cream alcoholic drink to make at home and I am sipping on it now. It is so good, it tastes just like orange sherbet. I am watching the movie *The Double Life of Veronique*. It is a fabulous foreign film. The music by Priesner is hauntingly beautiful. I enjoy renting classic films and foreign films in order to broaden the narrow life in which I currently exist. I can see other cultures, ideas, places, and imagine that I am visiting a foreign country. I wish I could do the Study Abroad program, but it costs so much. I would so much like to go to Florence with Karen's class. It is only a dream, I fear. I would worry about Keelie, too. Bad idea.

Another city I want to visit is Prague. Architecturally, the city is ancient and concentrated in one area. There are so many twists and turns in the city, narrow streets and walkways, restaurants and shops. At least, that is how it appears in photographs. I wish my life was destined for world travel, but I fear I will be permanently affixed to the United States. I can dream, though. I will dream and drink more creamsicle drink. It is so yummy and I want to numb my mind and body. I have already finished a third of the bottle. I am going for a record. Watch me now.

SEPTEMBER 25, 1994

Yesterday was another FSU home football game. This time, the punching bag was North Carolina with a win 31-18. The entire group attended, except for Paul's girlfriend. We drank over at Doug's house, all sitting around the only furniture in the living room; an enormous wooden dining room table that seats ten, easily. He kept it from his parents' estate but got rid of the couch and other furnishings that were not his style. "Old woman" style, I believe Doug called it. At least I was able to get high again. Doug and Paul both had some.

Some time during the post game party, Doug or Ed started a conversation about Bonnie, his ex-girlfriend. I inquired about the subject, then told everyone how angry I still was at Bonnie for stealing my clothes (and starting the ball rolling to me getting arrested for some outstanding driving without a license ticket). As I was talking, Ed interrupted me and told me to shut up. Doug let out a loud "oooowwwwwww" as his sparkling eyes turned to me. I told Ed that was a shitty thing to say to me and the he was being cruel and cold. Ed retorted by saying that he knew Bonnie before I did and he was the one who fucked her, not me.

Needless to say, it was humiliating being spoken to that way just so Ed can swagger in front of his friends.

He would never have said that in private. I couldn't even defend myself because I would be sounding as vulgar as he was. I stopped speaking for the rest of the evening and tried to blend in with the background. I became a camouflaged chameleon.

When we got home that night, I just wanted to go to bed in my own room and didn't say much except that was a cruel thing to say to me in public. Ed blew me off and acted as if my feelings were unimportant. I'm on my own, except for Keelie.

NOVEMBER 7, 1994

I was actually invited to attend the Georgia Tech game in Atlanta last weekend. What an experience. Ed and I met up with Jim and Jean in a hotel just a half mile from the stadium. We drank at the bar on the first floor of the hotel and got pretty trashed. We walked to the game, and I was drunk. I looked behind me to see what our hotel looked like, just in case, and made a mental note of our hotel room. Only Ed brought the room card, and I was wishing that I had brought the other card. I felt an ominous feeling of what was to come. Here is how it went down.

We all walked to the Georgia Tech game, going past The Varsity (I didn't want any of the fried, heavy food), went down the area of Georgia Tech where they celebrate before the game with their old car, some vehicle from 1930 or something. The Rambling Wreck, it is called. The band was marching around, parading the fans and the Rambling Wreck to the stadium. We joined the Georgia Tech fans then went with Jim and Jean to our seats.

The Georgia Tech fans were cordial, and kind, especially since they knew they would lose. Yes, FSU won 41-10. Since we brought rum with us, I was getting even drunker. It was the first road trip I had been invited on, so I was enjoying Atlanta.

Halfway back to the hotel, the foot traffic was thick and I had to urinate. Badly. There were Portolets nearby, so I told Ed I was going to use it and come back where they were going to wait for me. I was adamant that they wait for me since I didn't have a key to the room and was drunk. I would have pissed my pants had I waited.

I waited an eternity but finally got a Portolet and relieved my tight bladder. When I walked out of the Portolet, I looked around and could not remember for the life of me where Ed, Jim and Jean were waiting. There were so many people around, I searched and searched, at least for thirty minutes. I couldn't find them, but could see our hotel, so I decided to head back to the hotel. That is the reasonable choice, right? The hotel loomed large about a quarter a mile away, so I walked toward my haven.

I made it back to the hotel, looked in the bar for Ed, Jim and Jean, but did not see them. After waiting a few minutes with no money and no ID, I decided to ask the attendant to let me back into my room because I had lost my friends. He let me into my room (I had to give my name and he found me on the list because I forgot the room number).

When I got to the room, it was empty. I was exhausted. I laid down on the bed and fell asleep.

I have no idea about how much time went by, but at some time in the night, Ed slammed the door, yelled at me to wake up and began lecturing me about leaving the group. What the fuck? I am an adult, right? I told him the truth about how I looked for them for at least a half an hour but couldn't find them so I did the smart thing and went back to the hotel. Ed said that they searched for me for an hour and a half, even though Jim kept saying that they should go back to the hotel since that is where we agreed to meet up. Ed yelled and yelled at me. What could I say? I got lost and came back to the room. After he was done yelling, he called Jim and met him at the bar downstairs. I couldn't believe Ed was so fucking mad! He treated me more like a child than being worried about me. I was grateful when Ed went downstairs to the bar because I was really sick and tired of the thirty minute lecture.

DECEMBER 29, 1994

Ed and I went to his family's house for Christmas and are still here. It has been dull as dirt, as usual. Since the weather down here is warmer, I've been going out for walks, going to the historic part of town. Ed would yell if he knew. He won't know, the twat.

I've also been doing a lot of reading. I don't drink much in front of his parents or I'll get drunk and do something stupid. I keep the drinking to a minimum. It sounds like I'm a healthy person, but I'm not drinking so I don't throw up in the formal living room or pee my pants at the dinner table. Happy fucking birthday to me. And New Year. Yay.

CHAPTER 17

1995: AGE 26

JANUARY 10, 1995

It has been a hectic day. Today was the first day of classes for my Master of Fine Arts and I was almost late because of a squirrel. Our neighbor's cat, Mr. Grey (his owner never named him, so he goes by "cat"), was holding some critter in his mouth, growling low and getting a thrill from the struggling animal. I was heading to my car to get to class early, as I usually do, when I saw Mr. Grey with something in his mouth. I ran over and scared him away and saw a newly born squirrel mewing loudly on the ground. Its eyes were closed and it was terrified. I couldn't leave any creature in this much agony. I didn't know if it would live, but I took a chance. I found a shoebox, grabbed my furry teddy bear and got an eyedropper full of slightly warm milk. The squirrel, which I quickly named Warrick, was greatly comforted by the teddy bear. The poor little critter nuzzled into the artificial fur searching for a nipple. I attempted to feed it with an eye dropper, but it kept squealing. Keelie was going ballistic so I had to take the squirrel into the closet. I thought a nice, dark place would sooth its nerves. It did, but Keelie was clawing at the door, wanting to attack the little thing squealing in pain and fear. I had to get to class. Nothing around it, especially since this squirrel probably won't live.

When I arrived back home after my two short classes, poor Warrick was deceased. I figured it would be so, but he was clutched to the teddy bear. I couldn't bring myself to remove the squirrel from the bear, so I buried them both together. I know, it is strange. Ed thought I was a fool when I told him the story. What does he know? Poor little creature. At least it was calm with the teddy bear. I think it died peacefully, clutching onto the artificial fur of a teddy bear. That damn cat! I have written notes and even knocked on the door of the neighbor tonight who owns the cat and pleaded with him to neuter his cat. The cat is running around all day and night. Mr. Grey is a very sweet cat, don't get me wrong, but he needs to be spayed. I feel like I am being a bitch to my neighbor, but I sincerely believe that everyone needs to spay and neuter their cat or dog. There are millions of unwanted cats and dogs being put to death each year while stupid people like my neighbor let their animals breed. It is appalling. Poor little Warrick, named after the great running back, Warrick Dunn here at FSU. I was hoping it would make him a fighter. Alas, it is probably for the best.

JUNE 3, 1995

I am so humiliated. Not the first time. Doug was in town last night and Ed wanted to hang out with him. I let him go. I wasn't really invited, actually. I rented another foreign movie and bought some creamsicle drink mix (alcoholic). I watched the movie, cried and drank rapidly. I want to have another life. I feel so trapped living here with Ed, he makes me feel angry from his strict conservatism and closed mindedness. I want to be free. I watched the movie twice and then watched *Jesus Christ, Super Star*, singing at the top of my lungs. I drank hard and fast, searching for a method of escape. Ed is always late when he goes out and comes home so drunk he stumbles. What does it matter if I get overly intoxicated? However, I woke up this morning with the last image of *Jesus Christ, Super Star* on the television, frozen for posterity. I was laying on the floor with vomit on me. It appears I made it to the bathroom because it wasn't on the couch. Just some vomit on my shirt, hair and face. I also pissed my pants. I was wearing jeans and they were plastered to my body. I slowly raised myself up to a sitting position and looked around, a little dazed. It was morning. Fairly early, too. I slowly got to my feet and was relieved to see neither vomit nor urine staining the carpet or couch. I needed water and a good toothbrushing. I washed the vomit off of my face and changed clothes, walking quietly into the extra bedroom to sleep. I felt like shit on a skillet. I was able to sleep a couple more hours. It took a while to fall asleep.

At first I was glad Ed left me alone. But I started thinking, you know, he has passed out on the couch and I covered him up and took care of him. I shouldn't I know, but I was as helpful as I could be under the circumstances. We spend more and more time apart. I actually ask Ed to go out with his friends. He sometimes goes over to Jim and Jean's house without me, too. I am terrible at small talk. I can't stand small talk because most of it is vain and superficial.

To get back to my drunkenness, I started to be annoyed that Ed didn't at least cover me up and turn off the television. He just left me on the living room floor, passed out and miserable. Again, I thought he was nice, but he really isn't. Ed probably came in so drunk he can't remember. I hope he can't remember I pissed my pants. That is humiliating.

JULY 16, 1995

In a moment of self loathing, I have decided to lose weight. I ordered the Kathy Smith complete weight loss package. It has a weekly diary, a book with inspiration and recipes, three workout VHS tapes, twelve cassette tapes to listen to each week (one a week), and a hypnotic/relaxation tape. It cost me a pretty penny, but I spend so much on crap anyway, I might as well do something positive. I didn't tell Ed about the purchase so he wouldn't make fun of me.

The system is awesome. There is a chapter a week which focuses on making some small change in my lifestyle.

Nothing drastic. I am starting out by just writing down in the diary provided every morsel of food and drink that passes my lips, when I ate or drank that item, and how I was feeling (depressed, happy, etc.). I am also supposed to write down if I was sitting or standing, if I ate at a table or in front of the television. It is designed to show me my poor eating habits and how I might be able to correct them.

I just started, but I feel positive. Each week, I listen to a new tape, read a new chapter, and start measuring out my food. Kathy Smith follows the diabetic or nutritionally balanced meal approach. There is a section in her book about food groups, how to substitute foods, and eat healthy when at a restaurant. There is one drawback; I must quit drinking. Yes, I know, it is going to be difficult, but I don't want anyone else to ever ask if I am pregnant again when I am not. I will get in great shape and then leave Ed. I hide everything from him. He doesn't care, anyway. Wish me luck!

AUGUST 9, 1995

My Kathy Smith lifestyle change package is really starting to work. I have stopped drinking, which was easier than I thought, began a variety of exercise, and prepare meals that are nutritionally balanced, weighing and measuring everything I eat. I preplan a menu for the week and follow it to the letter. I feel and look better already. I am thrilled that I purchased this system. The best part is the relaxation tape. It always hypnotizes me because I have no memory of the tape and wake up when I hear the cassette click off. It truly relaxes me, and is supposed to have inspirational messages, although I don't consciously remember them.

I do a variety of workouts, walking daily plus doing one of the free-weight workout tapes. I either walk in the neighborhood or go to a local park where there are hiking trails. Luckily, there is one just up the road at Jim Brown Park. It has some beautifully secluded forest trails that go over streams and through dense underbrush. It is nice and cool on a hot day.

I do a weekly body measurement and a monthly weigh-in. I am not supposed to focus on the weight since I am building muscle through weight training. My clothes are starting to fit loosely. I am thrilled!

SEPTEMBER 1, 1995

Luckily, the fat is burning off me quickly. I am getting in great physical shape, which probably saved my life.

I went to Jim Brown Park as I do almost every day for my brisk walk through the woods, wearing leg weights to increase the challenge. The trail is an elongated figure eight and goes straight back into the woods from the parking area. It is very dense and beautiful, but is a bit isolated. I don't always see people on the trails.

Today, I had the scare of my life. I was probably 1/3 of the way through the trail, wearing my headphones, listening to classical radio, when a woman stopped me and told me there was a very creepy man further on the trail and to be careful. I thanked her, but kept walking since there were a few other people about.

Within minutes, a terrible thunder storm rolled in, sending in frightening gusts of wind and black clouds. This doesn't usually bother me in the woods, but I instantly noticed that I was alone. The couple walking their dog was gone. The woman who warned me about the man was gone. The old hippy man was gone. I was at the halfway point through the trail and realized my mistake. That woman pointed to the direction I was walking when informing me about some nutter. He could be anywhere!

I put my headphones in my fanny pack so I could hear better. It was dead quiet. The birds and insects stopped their lovely songs. All I could hear was wind in the trees. I decided to turn back the way I came from. There were many little side trails that unnerved me. I had barely taken a few steps when I heard a stick crack. I still had not seen the creepy man but now had an overwhelming feeling of dread, and felt as if I was being watched. The air was heavy. I began jogging back to the parking lot. My intuition said there was someone following me although I still didn't see anyone.

Just as my terror began to mount, I emerged from the trail. The sky was so dark it looked like night. It wasn't raining yet, but the wind was fierce. When I emerged and got a few hundred yards from the trail entrance, I suddenly felt silly. There were no other cars in the lot. I was indeed alone. That means the other creepy man was gone. I never saw him anyway, so I began to relax. I stopped jogging and walked over to the swing to enjoy a little play time.

I was on the swing only a minute or two, facing toward the trail when I felt the hairs raise up on my arms. I thought I saw something dark moving by the trail entrance. It could have been my imagination, I couldn't be sure. I felt it more than saw anything. The rain started falling so it was getting hard to see. I love the warm summer rains, so it never bothers me to get soaked, although I had my rain jacket on with a hood so I didn't get too saturated.

I slowed my swing down and looked more closely at the moving bushes. To my complete horror, a man emerged fairly close to me, wearing a black hooded sweatshirt with the hood pulled tightly over his face. I couldn't see the man's face, but I knew instantly that this was the creepy man that two hikers warned me about (that woman and another man mentioned a creepy man). My car was several hundred yards away. I jumped off the swing and started walking briskly toward my car, digging around my fanny pack, trying to find my car keys. I glanced over my shoulder and saw the hooded man start running toward me! My God, he wasn't that far behind me. I ran as fast as I could and unlocked my car, afraid to look around until I locked myself in. What seemed like three years passed before I finally was in my car. The man was only a few hundred feet away and darted back into the woods once I was locked in my car. I started the engine and drove very quickly past where the man hid in the woods. I looked in my rearview mirror but saw nothing. I sped through the park, got home and changed into dry clothes. I am still so frightened, I keep looking out my window. I know he couldn't have followed me since he didn't have a car in the lot.

I feel that I have escaped a life-threatening event. I am still shaking from fear as I write this entry in my diary. It will be a long, long time before I go back to Jim Brown Park.

OCTOBER 3, 1995

My Photography II class is going so well. It is an elective for my Master of Fine Arts program. We are doing a self-portrait series so I try and find my most vulnerable or stereotypical poses. I take my camera everywhere in case there is a photo opportunity. Once I stopped by the side of the road when I saw a cornfield swaying in the down burst of an upcoming storm. I hurriedly set up my tripod and snapped some pictures of me cautiously entering the cornfield. Good shit.

When I went down to Sarasota for my Susanna and Her Elders research for Art History: Renaissance, I received a wonderfully tacky Florida hotel room with a wall painting depicting a Florida beach. I brought my sexy baby doll pajamas from Victoria's Secret and posed in the most seductive manner.

I thoroughly enjoy my work in the dark room and often go to the dark room at the Student Union since it offers more hours to work. I prefer the school lab in the Art Department since I have been using it for a while, but it's quite nice over there at the Student Union.

There are so many tricks one can use to get completely different developed photographs. You can enlarge an image to almost any size, within reason. I saw a student who did their photo on dozens of photo paper, she put them together and created a large image of the Virgin Mary and erotic art. She is a photography major, so she knows much more than I do. My professor, Amy, told me that I have a real gift at photography and I should pursue it. She told me how most people don't succeed because they don't try. They stop doing the art they once loved, leaving behind a husk that once was their creative soul. I agreed with her. Amy also said that my work was very similar to Cindy Sherman. I'll have to check it out.

NOVEMBER 12, 1995

I have been interning in a fabric store called Chrysalis this semester. It was the only slot of interest left available to me. I wanted to go to an interior design or architectural firm, but selling fabrics is helpful. I have been learning a great deal about fabric construction and the right fabric for the job. I work with a blatantly gay man, Joe Munroe, who is an architect driven back home by his mother's guilt. He had lived and worked in Washington D.C. for many years and loved it so much, but his mother, a Southern Belle, wanted her favorite son near her in her later years. He reluctantly submitted to his mother's request. He comes from a family who made their wealth from Coca-Cola and land in north Florida.

The owner of the store, Mrs.Windle is a fascinating woman. She is a lady, a friend of Mrs. Munroe's (Joe's mom) since childhood. Her husband is an opera singer who travels frequently to other cities and her son is a fashion designer in New York. She is exceedingly proud of her son. He frequently sends her dresses from famous designers. He sends it to the office so we can all view the dress with envy. Mrs. Windle lights up like a lightening bug each time her son calls or sends her a gift.

DECEMBER 23, 1995

The Windles had a Christmas party at their home, a mansion in north Tallahassee. Their house was decorated to a southern lady's desire, with brocades, velvets, high backed chairs, roaring fireplaces, vases that appeared to be from China. There were many hors d'oeuvres to devour. Most of the time I just observed the others who attended the party. So many aging, wealthy couples from Tallahassee and the surrounding areas wearing dresses that sparkled and shirts which crinkled under the heavy starch press they just received.

I was so excited to be invited to such an extravagant soiree. I wore an evening dress and Ed wore a blazer, shirt and tie. I pick out most of his clothes now, buying them so I can have him looking dapper.

DECEMBER 15, 1995

I love attending a liberal arts university. There are free concerts quite frequently in the Music Department, mostly students giving free shows. The music is usually classical, but is jazz from time to time. I've seen many string quartets, piano recitals, duets, trios, all combinations of musical groupings. I attend as many as I can to take advantage of the excellent music at a free price.

One of the evenings shines vividly in my tired brain. It was a night of Shubert. A professor stood up on stage and gave a physical description of Franz Shubert, then treated the auditorium as a salon.

Seeing Mendelsson's *Messiah* choral work conducted by Robert Shaw and sung by Florida State University singers was one of the closest times I have ever been to God. The beauty of the music, the tears of joy flowing down the face of the soprano. I got tickets so close I could hear the oboe and bassoon clicking while being played. Just a few rows back. I went to the Theater Department and purchased the tickets immediately once they went on sale.

A very bored and sober Ed attended the concert with me. I didn't want him there. I wanted to openly cry, kiss, love, but not him.

CHAPTER 18

1996: AGE 27

DECEMBER 18, 1996

I received my MFA degree on December 14. Not that I actually got my degree. FSU is going to hold it until I pay the over $120 in parking fines which are outstanding. They charge interest. The amount keeps going up. Ed won't pay it so it may be a year before I can pay that bill and get my paper degree. I almost messed up with the cap and gown and waited too long to get it. They didn't have a cap small enough to fit my pea head so I had to get one that was close. I kept my tassel this time because a student told me that I can keep it. I didn't know that! Ed never told me at the first graduation, and he was there when I returned my cap and gown. How am I supposed to know I can keep the tassel if I have never graduated in my life? I would have kept the last one, too.

Also, my calculations say that I graduated magna cum laude, but the registry office told me that I was suppose to apply for it. I thought they automatically included that information on my degree when I graduate, but apparently not. That made me so angry. They won't do it now and I wasn't announced as being one of the magna cum laude during graduation. I almost cried when I found out. I worked so hard, almost receiving straight A's for years, and they won't type magna cum laude on my degree because I didn't apply for it. I wish I had known! Why didn't anyone tell me?

The graduation was alright. My parents came and then we all went to Orlando for dinner and drinks and to introduce my parents to Ed's parents. They live near Orlando in Lake Wales. We stayed in a hotel room in Kissimmee where it is cheaper. Of course, my parents were too cheap to go to Disney or Universal. I should be grateful. I got nice and drunk that night and had a good time at the piano bar in Orlando. They had a blues singer and dancers on stage. We only stayed the one night and came back to Tallahassee.

We rented a movie and Jim complained about it. I shot back at him that it wasn't as wonderful as the superb acting of John Goodman (whom Jim raved about for 15 minutes). Jim said that I was being mean and I quickly replied that I learned from the best, meaning him. Nothing I do is good enough for them. I am overweight. I know I am, but my mom doesn't have to tell me and go on and on about how beautiful and thin other women are.

On top of that, now, I am in way over my head and in debt for $108,000! Why did I get so many student loans? That was my fault, not my parents. I was turned down for a few scholarships because my parents made too much money (even though they weren't supporting me at all). I was turned down time and time again on scholarships because I had to prove my parents' income and it was always too high. That proves they could have helped pay for college. It's my fault for going on to FSU. I could have gotten by with my associates degree. I shouldn't blame my parents for my huge debt.

My graduation present for this time is my great Uncle Tom's writing desk. But, they didn't bring it. They said they will some day. Maybe in 4 or 5 years. I am not lying, that is what they said. "Next time we visit, in 4 or 5 years, we'll drive out and bring you the desk." Thanks.

On a positive note, I have my driver's license and car insurance. I have been legal for a few months now. I worked hard at cleaning up my driving record so now it is spotless. Ed still won't let me drive his car. His perfect Acura is his baby. I'm his wife, so I should be allowed to drive his car which has air conditioning.

Why did I marry this asshole? I thought he was nice, but he isn't. Ed is stupid and selfish. He won't even try to improve himself. Ed complains about his job, about his wanting to write for a sports magazine and I have told him countless times that he can do anything he sets his mind to. I have even suggested that he volunteer with the FSU Athletic staff in order to get his foot in the door. No, he won't actually do anything about it. He will only complain. Lazy, good for nothing asshole.

Listen to me, I should be so pleased with my accomplishments but I am going on a rant. I am so proud of myself for finally receiving my MFA after the year of thesis work. My major professor thinks that I can get a condensed version of my thesis published in Interior Design publications. We will begin working on that next semester, when I begin my teaching job. I will be co-teaching Advanced CAD course, correcting tests, grading projects, next semester. I will be paid, too, but only minimum wage. That is all they can afford right now. I can work my way up to professor with time and patience. I am so excited about that. I'll finally get the respect I crave.

One shocking thing occurred. While my mom and John were talking the one evening they could spend together, they began to talk about Trent, Grandpa's wife, Denise's son. The one with whom I had a sexual relationship when I was 16. I nearly fell out of my chair when they said that Trent is probably the illegitimate child of Grandpa's because he was having an affair with the married Denise at the time. Apparently, Denise told grandpa that Trent was his child. This may or may not be true. Denise is a gold digger who will use any strategy to obtain more wealth. Using a flesh and blood child as bait is something she is more than capable of. However, if it is true, then I had sex with my uncle! Yuck. I pray that Trent is NOT Grandpa's illegitimate child. I suppose there is no way to know for sure unless there is a paternity test. Denise and grandpa never told Trent until after grandpa died. That would account for grandpa being so adamant that Trent and I not get romantically involved. He stressed it at least three times that Trent must act like a brother, a complete gentleman. I feel repulsed. We didn't know that we might be related!

CHAPTER 19

1997: AGE 28

MARCH 6, 1997

I met Hemingway. In a dream, of course. Well, I met an older, grey-bearded Hemingway, slightly sagging. I am, after all, reading *A Farewell To Arms*.

I walked into a house by the water where there were lots of people gathered for a party. In the center was Ernest Hemingway in a big side chair, with large arms and an enormous back. He was in jeans, worn and light blue, and a t-shirt. He seemed to recognize me and called me over, waving his bronzed arm.

Hemingway stayed seated. Without speaking, I sat on the arm of his worn, leather armchair. He suddenly hugged me, putting his large arms around me. I felt so secure. I kissed his bristly face and he kissed me back and smiled at me. His face lit up when he smiled, and crinkled in a nice way around his eyes. I loved his smile.

I introduced myself quietly, a little embarrassed. He whispered, "I know." I told him that I had always wanted to meet him and that I was currently reading *A Farewell To Arms* and he said that it was his favorite book. We started into a conversation about it, and then he took a drink of his whisky, leaned back in his big, overstuffed leather chair, and said that he wrote it in one day. I leapt back in amazement and said that it must have taken longer than a day. Hemingway started laughing, spilling his drink on his right leg.

I stood up and went to the coffee table where my book, *A Farewell To Arms,* was still lying. Hemingway was laughing and motioned me to come back. I came back over, less bashful this time, with my book and sat right in his lap. He wrapped his arms around me and kissed me again. It felt so calming, so comfortable in his arms. I then asked timidly if he would sign my book. He said, sure, and opened up the blank page at the front. I handed Hemingway the red pen I happened to have in my hand at the time.

Some guy came up to Hemingway and I suddenly felt uncomfortable. I felt like I shouldn't be there, so I got up and stood in the shadow.

A beautiful woman with long, black hair, and gorgeously bronzed skin came into the room. She glared at me and then at Hemingway. Sparks seemed to fly from her jealous eyes.

I suddenly noticed another woman looking directly at me. She was an older, plain woman wearing glasses with casual, graying hair, and was sitting quietly in a nearby chair.

I didn't know anyone at this party, so I approached her. She looked the kindest. She smiled gently at me. I felt so tired now. I needed to sleep.

The older woman motioned me to the floor next to her. She placed some pillows down for me and I curled up. As I was drifting off to sleep, I mumbled that I really wanted to meet Ernest Hemingway. She said that I had already and that I was lucky he treated me like his children. I noticed Hemingway crossing the room toward the bathroom. I wanted to run over to him, to put my arms around him. I didn't move since I was tired and I really didn't know Ernest that well.

When he returned, Hemingway seemed a little more tired. He stared belittling a somber man for something he didn't do. I seemed to know that he didn't do whatever he was being reprimanded for. This other guy looked so quiet and shy and wouldn't defend himself, only looked down at the floor. I felt such pity for him. Everyone remained quiet, afraid to speak. I knew what the older woman meant. If he didn't respect you, he hated you. I felt good inside that he liked me. I felt so special as I looked at his autograph in my *A Farewell To Arms.*

MAY 9, 1997

I finally found a wonderful job. It is in Atlanta, Georgia. I was "head-hunted" by Thompson, Varnes & Associates (TVA), an architectural design firm listed in the top 40 in the country! They called our department and asked for recent graduate recommendations and David recommended me. I went to the first interview in March and didn't hear anything back for almost two months. Then, out of the blue, they called me for a second interview. Both times I couldn't afford to spend the night so I had to drive back home after the interview. Thanks, Ed, for caring. It is a 4½ hour drive one way. Ed wasn't about to pay for a single night hotel room. I admit, it was tiring. However, I was hired during the second interview and I start in two and a half weeks, on May 26th. I have to find a place to live right away. I got the tour of the building in Midtown and it is phenomenal. They designed the building and I will be working on the 27th floor. I am still in shock. So many young, talented people working diligently on creative projects. I am frightened but excited. I started looking on the internet for apartments in the area. I don't want to be very far from the office so I have limited my search. There are a few available rentals that I will have to drive up and look at. I don't know Atlanta at all, so I definitely don't want to rent until I see the place. I don't want to move to the hood. There are some rough parts of Atlanta.

Ed was not happy at all. I have already told him that I want a divorce and I was waiting for a job. I am sure that is why he didn't pay for my hotel room. He keeps begging me pitifully to stay in Tallahassee with him, to take one of the sales jobs that I was offered through Knoll. I don't want to be a salesman. I don't want to stay in Tallahassee. I have been looking for a job locally since I graduated and there is nothing. The market is saturated with graduates. I have literally tried every conceivable design studio and they are not hiring. I was hoping to get a job so I could move out and continue teaching at FSU. I have also sent my resume to large design firms in Seattle and Portland, just in case. I love Seattle. That would have been great. Well, this worked out better. I will live in a city again. I am still in shock. I will have to put every penny from my next paycheck into deposits. I have been saving a little money, so I'll find a way.

I have so much to do.

MAY 26, 1997

I found an apartment just in time. It was fate, I feel it. This is meant to be. I moved in last Friday and Saturday and started work on Monday. I still have a few more car loads in Tallahassee. I am leaving all furniture and taking only my books, clothes, and personal belongings. That piano doesn't work anymore, so there is no need dragging that to Atlanta. My Festiva is roomier than it looks, the Silver Bullet. I don't have to rent a truck. I can't afford it any way. The apartment is sparse, but I love it that way. I have stacked my books around the perimeter of the living room. I don't even have a bed. I am sleeping in my sleeping bag, on top of the comforter and blankets. It is warm right now so I only need a light sheet over top of me. It is actually a pretty comfortable pallet. I will start fresh. Like the movie *Blue*. I don't want any relics of the past. Although I hope I don't get as depressed as the character in the movie.

Keelie wasn't thrilled with the car ride here, but she is happy now. This place is great and is only 4 miles from work. I am living in Buckhead and I work in Midtown. I live near the restaurants and bars so I am within walking distance of a wide variety of eating establishments and a grocery store. I don't have any money right now, so the smell of cooking food from the restaurants drives me crazy. I spent every penny on deposits. The building I am in is brick with a central courtyard, hence, Peachtree Courtyard Apartments. It is very reasonable rent, especially for this location. It is a one bedroom apartment and is quite spacious. I am so lucky to have found this place. Every other apartment I had on my list was in the hood. This one was last on my list and I fell in love with it immediately. The landlord, Fred, didn't even charge me for a cat deposit. The deposit is usually $200 and I asked if he could split up the payments over a few months. He said that he wouldn't charge me for it at all. That was very nice of him. Fred also said that when people move out they almost always leave belonging behind so he'll inform me when this occurs and give me second pick to the items (he gets first selection). That sounds like a good deal. Free items. I am happy in this sparseness. I will paint the horrible fake wood panelling. I asked if I could paint and Fred said that I could. There must be a way to paint over wood panelling. I know it is a slick surface so it may not be easy. Perhaps I could sponge apply the paint. Once a coat has been put down, the rest should go on much easier. I'll look at color chips at K-Mart.

I spent all day in training so I haven't started working yet. I will be in training two more days. They are teaching us their phone system, email, file and name saving procedures and all the technical and boring things that we need to know. TVA has an attached covered parking deck which makes getting to work a breeze. TVA validated my parking ticket today so I didn't have to pay the daily amount. I have gotten a parking pass that is partially paid for by TVA and the rest is deducted from each paycheck. If I didn't have a car, TVA would give me that money toward a MARTA pass instead. The building is located right next to the High Museum of Art so I can go over there at lunch. There are two floors of studio space and hundreds of TVA employees here. They have a wonderful library and gorgeous, expensive furniture in the lobby. Definitely a high-end commercial design firm. They have been in Architectural Digest as well as numerous other publications. I still can't believe that I am working for a firm like this. A trailer park girl in the big city. I will need to buy a better wardrobe. All of the young employees dress so hip. Mostly wearing black. I have quite a bit of black already. I feel that I am in a dream.

On each side of the floor is a kitchen with a soda dispenser, coffee, refrigerator, microwave and seating area. I don't drink soda but I can get an occasional one. It is so luxurious. I have definitely made it now. Wish me luck!

JUNE 2, 1997

I have to go down to Tallahassee every weekend and fill up my Festiva with personal affects, most of which are books.

Ed keeps trying to get me back. It is pitiful. I sleep in the extra bedroom as I pack up my belongings, and he tries to lure me into the bed with him. I don't think so. Ed has begged me to stay with him. I told him that I won't stay with him, but he seems to hold a misconception that I may return to him. I don't want anything to do with him, but I keep that part quiet until I retrieve all of my belongings. I have purposely not brought any furniture. I want to feel nothingness and build from it. Ed wants to visit me. I guess I'll let him, if he brings a load in his car. Poor Ed is trying so hard to get me back. He doesn't believe in divorce. I remember Ed saying more than once he would never marry a woman who had been divorced. Now that he will be divorced, he is scrambling to try and keep me. I don't think so. His intelligence is on the low end of average, way too low for me. I need someone more intelligent.

JUNE 13, 1997

Holly invited me, Justin and DJ to join her and Keith and some of her friends at Piedmont Park to watch *Casablanca* at the film festival in the park. Holly used to be a pastry chef, and loves to have the complete layout, bringing wine, beer, and hors d'oeuvres. We sat a fair distance from the screen, but we had all seen the movie (except Keith). We were there mostly to socialize and relax. It was wonderful. Holly is so social and normal. She has a very romantic fiancé, Keith. For their dating anniversary, he sent her 4 red roses and one white rose to the office; the four red roses, he explained in a note, were for the four fantastic years they have been dating. The one white rose shows the love he has for her and hopes for many years to come. That was so romantic. Holly cried. Keith is an architect at another large architectural firm in town.

I shyly drank their wine. It was BYOB, but I didn't bring anything because I am broke, as always. Keith was so nice and gave me wine and beer. He is a good catch for Holly. Very intelligent, kind man. He is 7 years younger than her, and Holly feels embarrassed by that fact, but Keith tells her repeatedly that it doesn't matter. He told her if the age difference was the other way, Keith being 7 years older, then would Holly be so concerned? She capitulated and said that it wouldn't be as big of deal. Keith caught her being stereotypical and brainwashed by society into believing that the female must be younger than the man.

I got fairly buzzed, but not trashed. I didn't want to drink all of their alcohol. We walked back as a group to the office to retrieve our vehicles. Keith said he still hadn't seen *Casablanca* because we were all talking and drinking so much he couldn't concentrate on the screen. Holly said that she would rent it.

I went home and contemplated the evening. I talked to DJ quite a bit, as well as Justin. DJ is a tightly buttoned man who always wears a bow tie and speaks in a slightly condescending way. He views me as his equal, so I am not looked down upon. He makes and plays ancient instruments, like the lute, mandolin, and guitar. He also paints life-sized portraits. He will show me photos of them sometime. Justin is more down to earth, and we are more alike than me and DJ. Justin is a gay, well-dressed architect who is utterly charming. Apparently, he used to be overweight, but lost a great deal of weight during college when he joined a fraternity. He seems so unlike fraternity material, it baffles my mind. You wouldn't know he was ever overweight. He looks terrific! So kind.

JUNE 22, 1997

Ed came and spent the night with me. He tried to slip his way into my bed, but I wouldn't have any of it. I don't want to ever have sex with him, and more importantly, I don't want to mislead the poor guy. I want a divorce, so give me one! I didn't force him to visit me. It was his choice. He is pitiful, though, the way he pawed at me and tried to sleep with me. He doesn't want a divorce, but it is already in the making. I wish it was finalized. I just want to be split forever from Ed. I only have one more load from Tallahassee.

JULY 5, 1997

Last night, I went to the TVA office to watch the fireworks with some other people. DJ invited me, and Justin showed up too (thank goodness!) It was a perfect viewing point to see the fireworks from Stone Mountain (except for people at Stone Mountain). It was moderately entertaining. No alcohol or drugs, so how fun can it be?

I feel so liberated. I just started over here in Atlanta. Holly acts motherly and offered me their extra bed. I turn her down politely. I don't want furniture right now. I want empty space, although I accepted a large vase and two lamps from Fred, the apartment manager. Fred offered me the bed, but after taking one look at it, I turned it down. An old woman had died in that bed, and the urine stains were still fresh.

I want a barren apartment. I painted the wood paneling black with ochre undertones using a sponge. It took about 5 coats to get it to stick on that horrible wood paneling. I also painted the upper part of the wall purple and the bathroom green. It looks so much better. I probably just lost my deposit, but who cares. It looks so beautiful. I placed my books all around the living room, encircling myself within my hundreds of books. On the weekends, I listen to the jazz show on the radio and listen to the sounds of the Buckhead clubs and the delicious aromas from the surrounding restaurants. I can't afford crap. Although, for dinner, I sometimes buy some brie, bread and wine and sit on the floor doing a jigsaw puzzle on the dining room floor.

JULY 13, 1997

Justin and I have really hit if off. He invited me to go to Backstreet, a gay dance club last night. I spent the night at his apartment, sleeping in the bed with him. His bed has feather padding and feather comforter so it is so comfortable. I feel so safe and relaxed around Justin. I put my arm around him and just laid next to him. To my complete horror, I wet the bed. It wasn't a lot, but enough. I got one of his towels and laid on it. It seemed to soak up most of it, thank God. Justin never noticed. I slept in my underwear, so I just got dressed and stuffed my underwear in my purse.

Justin wants to come over for dinner tonight. I invited him and he agreed. I'm going to make stuffed pasta with pesto sauce with spinach, as per Justin's recommendation. Sounds great to me. It is nice to have such a close friend.

I am about to go visit my parents. It has been a while. I bought some inexpensive tickets from ATL to SEATAC. Great prices from Atlanta, really. I bought the tickets months ago, my mom helped me to pay for it. I am not supposed to tell Jim that mom helped me pay for the tickets. He is a real prick who is an extreme tightwad with money unless he is gambling and drinking, then he'll dump a wheelbarrow full of money into his vices. We'll see how it goes.

JULY 27, 1997

I just got back from my exciting Seattle adventure. My parents have moved to a modular home on a pond. It is the home they moved to and forgot to tell me for months.

July 23rd proved to be more adventurous. Mom and I went to a couple of great vintage stores where I found a fabulous faux leopard print coat, three-quarter length. As

I was trying it on, a girl who was around ten years old said that the coat looked awesome. What was better than that? I bought it for $12. I found some jeans and shirts for dollars each. I also found some great vintage fondue pots, one orange and one green. I got a great serving tray for $1. Loads of fun. No, I'm not being sarcastic, it really was fun going through the vintage shops.

When we got home, my mom wanted me to show Jim what I bought. Just like old times, but this time, I'm not hiding any purchases since they were all inexpensive. I wore a "new" outfit with my fabulous faux fur coat to the Bean Bar & Grill. Might as well look good in the old home town. Barf. Home town.

One of the most surprisingly gorgeous part of the journey was an unexpected gift from my mom; three tickets on a train to ride the Mt. Rainier Scenic Railroad. It went through the foothills of Mt. Rainier and left and arrived back in Arla, a small town not too far from Bean. My mom said that she and Jim have been on it before and wanted me to experience nature. Jim joined us, but sat in one of the cars the entire time. It would have been nice if they took me on this train ride in high school.

There is nothing compared to the beauty I encountered through hills, over rivers, to a turnaround on Mt. Rainier. We saw a herd of wild elk. Something one doesn't see every day. They were lazily grazing on the grasses of someones property since it was fenced in. The elk can easily leap over the fence. The sound of the train only made them moderately curious.

My mom went out onto the observation car where it was completely open to the wilderness, making me feel so intimate with the Pacific Northwest. I miss that area dreadfully. It is painful to my soul not to live near the splendor of the Pacific Northwest. It was slightly chilly outside since I had on only a shirt and pants. Yes, even in the summer, it can get chilly in the evenings or on a moderately fast moving train. My mom was game about staying on the observation car so we photographed, gawked and awed at every waterfall, at each tall bridge over dried river beds, and wildlife appearing at regular intervals. Mostly more elk. They must really enjoy the scenery as much as I do. I am thankful to have seen wild elk. It isn't something I can say I've seen frequently. We also were a train car away from Jim which is always a heart-lightening feeling.

There was a pleasant fifteen minute break at the turnaround where we could stretch our legs and wander a round a little. I took some photographs of the train and myself in front of the train. The train track actually did a loop and someone had to switch the track over to return whence we came. We traveled the same stretch of railroad back to Arla, which was spectacular. I knew what hidden surprises lay in store for me and was ready for every fleeting moment.

The glaciers loomed large above us, and the river bed was dry and in need of some moisture. The small waterfalls that we did espy were not large enough to fill any reservoir, unless you waited fifty years.

When we returned to Arla, about two hours later, it was refreshing and exhilarating. On one of the tracks was a restaurant car where people were devoured deli-styled food. I wanted to eat there, so we went inside and just barely got a seat. I ordered a turkey sandwich with some avocado and chips. The food was not to the liking of Jim. He complained about everything; the lemon wedge in his water, the high price for "just a sandwich and chips", and the service. They didn't check on Jim enough because he needed a beer every 3½ minutes. Jim preferred draft beer over the bottled beer that was brought to him. It was one of the most depressing lunches I have ever sat through. Jim needs to seriously lighten up and enjoy life even a small percent. Unless it is a smoky tavern that smells of stale beer, vomit, and piss, it isn't to his liking.

Mom asked if we should go to Paradise on Mt. Rainier. No, no, Jim moaned. You two can do that another day. Mr. Excitement. We did. The next morning.

We also went to Olympia, Washington, to visit the vintage shops and see some new and exciting place. It has been forever since we've been there, so my mom thought it was a good idea. It was. Olympia is so cute now. It is so like a mini Seattle, with its vintage stores, hip shops and pubs.

AUGUST 10, 1997

I got back a couple of hours ago from our company white water rafting and camping trip. I had so much fun. Dawn, a very large and abrasive woman, headed up the excursion. When Holly asked when we were leaving, Justin said "at the crack of dawn." Holly shivered and said that she had a horrible image of Dawn's crack. We all started laughing hysterically. I thought I was going to wet my pants.

Dawn was in charge of cooking all of our meals. Of course, she complained about cooking for everyone this morning while making breakfast. No one asked her to cook for us all. Most of it was wonderful, but there were a few disastrous moments.

I brought my pup tent, Justin slept in Dawn's four person tent, and about a dozen other architects and designers from work arrived with their camping gear. Most of the people that were there I had only seen in passing. There was that wonderfully, sweet, attractive architect named Jimmy who works on Merrill Lynch with Justin, Holly and I. Jimmy often talks about Téa Leoni dating David Duchovny, and being highly disappointed when they married last month. I'm disappointed, too; David Duchovny isn't available any more (like I had a chance in Hades) and Jimmy is more attracted to an unobtainable actress than me, a low born, white trash hussy. He doesn't even acknowledge my existence.

Enough of that trite nonsense. We stayed one night, and went rafting soon after arriving to the north Georgia location. It was a partially man-made river that was enhanced for the Olympic Team when they competed in the Atlanta area in 1996.

It was the Ocohee River located in Tennessee, just over the border, although we camped at one of their approved campgrounds in North Georgia. A bus picked us up and brought us back to our campground. We were booked for a half day trip down the Ocohee River with its class III and class IV rapids. Halfway through the rafting experience, we stopped for snacks and juice. Mostly granola bars and fruit.

We were all crammed into the bus for the 45 minute drive, me sitting next to Dawn and Justin. Dawn took up so much space it was very tight. I was glad to get out of the bus. It felt so claustrophobic and held other rafters who were not in our group.

Once at the rafting location, there was more waiting. We were all fitted with helmets and vests. The guide had a hard time finding a helmet to fit my small head. It was embarrassing, really. Justin had the opposite problem, they couldn't find a helmet big enough to fit his large head.

The two people who were to be our rafting guides went around to everyone and tightened their life jackets. I could barely breath but it has to be tight to work properly. Our TVA group was going to take up two rafts.

After an hour of boredom, it was finally our turn to head out. Everything picked up speed from that point onward. As we headed for the raft, our guide asked who wanted to be in the front. I volunteered. What an idiot. He asked if I was sure, and I said I was. Dawn wanted the front. I should have given it to her since her weight would have balanced the boat better, keeping the front down.

The top part of the course was extremely enjoyable. Our guide would shout to duck into the boat or lean one way or another. I had to be on top form, pay complete attention since there were some intimidating rapids. I performed well and felt exhilarated. When we reached a pool, the guide would tie up the raft and let us all swim. We had two boats in our group and we kept in close contact with each other.

About an hour and a half after setting off on my white water adventure, we pulled over to a pit stop for some juice, fruit and water. It was our lunch. Some people jumped into the water and swam, but Dawn became very bossy and said that we should leave soon. Is she now our guide? She bugged our guide until he relented. I offered the front to Dawn. She wouldn't take it. Not now. She wanted it before, so she acted spurned. I asked if anyone else wanted the front but they all declined (it was a bit perilous and required a bit more work than the center people). I kind of wanted someone else to get to the front so I wouldn't have to keep an eye out for the rapids, but I willingly went back to the fore position. Our guide told us that we already went through the Olympic rapids, and there were only a couple of class IV rapids left. The second part should be easier, more relaxing and more swimming.

We drifted back onto the river and made our way to the white water. There were a couple of successful rapids and we were approaching only a class III rapid (still big in my opinion) when it all went wrong. I saw two large rocks ahead and yelled back to the guide. He said to steer toward the middle. Everyone tried to go through the middle, but we got turned around and were heading right toward a rock. I ducked and we missed it. I sat back up and didn't hear our guide tell us to duck again. It seems so surreal now. It is true that during extreme stress, time seems to slow down. The seconds seemed to stretch into minutes. I suddenly became aware that I was no longer in the boat, but UNDER the boat. I didn't take a breath before going under so I felt desperate to get to the surface. I pounded on the bottom, trying to find the edge to get to the surface. I still had my paddle in my hand so I tried using that as a rudder. It wasn't working. I was still stuck under the raft. I felt Death hovering again over my shoulder. I have been near to death before and Death's fetid breath was upon me once again. I began to feel panic. Why wasn't I getting around the raft? Why was a stuck under it?

I finally made it around the raft and fought to the surface. I was able to get a quick breath and swallowed some water, but I couldn't stay above the surface. I was pulled under the water again, pushed onto my face despite my life jacket. I used the oar to turn myself around to the surface, but to no avail. Every once in a while I would get a glimpse of the raft, too far away from me, and then got pushed onto my face again. I couldn't catch a breath. There was no breathing and my lungs were screaming for oxygen. In my panicked state, my mind considered death. It would be so easy to inhale the rushing water but I wanted to LIVE. I needed a breath. Every here and there I could snatch a small breath but got sucked under too quickly. I never could get a full breath.

I still fought for life. I am not exaggerating. I am sure you think that this is a tall tale, but it is not. Finally, when I thought that I couldn't take this anymore, a hand reached out and pulled me to the surface. It was our guide. I was still clutching the oar and the guide told me to drop the oar because they couldn't get me into the boat. I didn't realize that it was still in my hands to be honest, and released the oar once it smacked me on the bridge of the nose. I felt dizzy from the strike to the nose and dizzy from lack of oxygen. My nose felt like it splintered, but it was still there.

I suddenly felt like I weighed 200 pounds. Multiple hands were clutching me but they couldn't get me into the boat. Our guide told me to kick with my feet. I was so exhausted that I had to expend the rest of my energy just to kick. Suddenly I was in the boat gasping like a fish out of water. I couldn't stop coughing, the water that got into my lungs and the lack of oxygen. I don't really remember much after that until a few minutes later. After they retrieved my oar, we continued on our way, albeit on a sombre tone.

Our guide told me that he didn't know where I was until someone in the middle felt me under the boat. He said that he tried to move the boat only to discover that I drifted 20 feet or more from the boat and was being tossed against rocks and tumbling face down into the water. Justin said that I was under water for quite a while. I thought that it was a long time, and that confirmed it. I was fighting for my life.

I huddled in the bottom of the boat, afraid to even look out. I felt like I let the group down because I wasn't allowed to row again. I was told to rest. I curled into a ball and glanced around once in a while at the beautiful scenery. I wanted out of the boat but there was still an hour to go. It went by so quickly. I felt scared and withdrawn, my nose and body hurt from being hit by the oar and rocks.

We finally pulled into the shore, completing our white water adventure. I was stripped of my helmet and life vest (not that it did much good on such a tumultuous river). I stumbled into the sales office and a woman tried to push some photos on us. I looked terrible. They had a camera at one of the bends that I never saw. Justin thought it was good and ordered one. As always, I had no money to buy a photo. I wanted one, but was broke. Justin bought one. He couldn't buy two so I was screwed. I'd only get to look at his photo.

We finally climbed wearily onto the bus to take us to our campground. The long trip which was such torture the first time on the bus with the tight group of sweaty people flew by on the way back. I sat next to Justin and just vegetated there.

I became invigorated at the campsite after getting dinner (which Dawn complained about every second while cooking it). I told my story around the camp fire. I started feeling better. Then, Jimmy wanted to go for a swim. I agreed, but of course, he was trying to get some other prettier girls to go. Four people agreed to go and off we walked the mile to the lake. Once in the water, we all gazed in amazement into the sky. There were no city lights or any lights whatsoever except for the light of the moon (which was almost full) and the stars. It was so dark that you could see the Milky Way. So amazing. Jimmy talked about the stars, saying that he wished he knew the different constellations. I did some verbal bantering as I swam closer and closer to Jimmy. I might as well been Roseanne Barr. Jimmy swam away from me when I got too close. I thought we were enjoying each other's companionship, but I was wrong. Someone wanted to go back to the campsite and I agreed. What was there for me here?

I was exhausted by the time we got back to the campsite. I just wanted to go to bed. I asked Justin to sleep in my tent but he insisted on staying in Dawn's tent, since he already told her he would. Plus, she had a four man tent and I only had a pup tent. I went into my tent and fell quickly asleep. No alcohol was brought since none was allowed. No one broke the rules and I was really disappointed.

The next morning, I awoke to the sound of squabbling. Dawn refused to cook one more meal (although she is the one who volunteered in the first place). People were discussing who was going to cook and what we should eat. It was decided to eat the cold grilled shrimp and have some yogurt for breakfast. Great. That was fine by me.

As we were sitting around in a circle, eating our light breakfast, someone who was playing the guitar the night before asked everyone who the hell was snoring last night. He said that someone was snoring like a sailor and woke some people up. They all said they didn't know who it was, but I knew who it was. It was me. When I am tired or drunk I snore. I was exhausted after the rafting experience and the near death fiasco. How humiliating. I felt the same feeling when I was a child and wet the bed at a friend's house while staying overnight. I concentrated all I could not to piss my sleeping bed and ended up snoring like a drunken sailor. I wanted to crawl inside myself. I was ready to go home. I don't know how much time went by, but finally we were packed and ready to go home. I packed my tent early and was waiting to go back to Atlanta with Justin and Dawn. Just get me home!!!

I had a great time, no doubt, but the near drowning experience along with my humiliation of being made fun of for five minutes about my snoring nearly destroyed me. I felt so elated when I arrived but felt cold, despondent and isolated on the way home. I arrived home and got out of the truck as Justin called after me that he would call me later. Dawn was driving her SUV and quickly drove off.

I got back in my apartment after only a day and Keelie attacked me for attention. I collapsed on the floor. I soon made a palette to lay on and cuddled on the floor with Keelie. I was so tired and completely freaked by the fact that I almost died. No joke, but for real. It could have gone the other way. I would definitely go white water rafting again, but I would sit in the middle and NOT the front.

AUGUST 17, 1997

Justin and I have been spending every weekend together. We have been going to Backstreet Saturday nights. I am not a real dance club kind of girl, but I am being invited to do something with someone, so I am definitely going. Justin has a bartender there who is a friend, Bart. Bart is so sexy and outgoing. He sometimes shares his Special K, although I have to nag him about it. I offer to pay him, but he says he doesn't want me to become an addict. Why do people feel compelled to protect me? I want the fucking drug. It makes time slow down at first and then makes me feel like I am in a bubble. A little like LSD. Apparently, K is actually a horse tranquilizer, and Bart doesn't want me to overdose. I won't, for goodness sake. I am a well conditioned addict. I can take any drug.

I slept at Justin's apartment again. I have been spending every Saturday night with him for weeks and spending every evening with him. Sunday, we usually have lunch somewhere and he often comes over to my sparse apartment to paint or do something creative. We worked on the Artfest birdhouses at my apartment. I painted a birdhouse red and made it look like a bistro. I called it "The Beatnik Bird Bistro" and had a blue jay with a beret looking out a window and a cardinal playing the bongos. It turned out that my birdhouse went to private auction, which is an honor. It went for over $200! The money goes to Habitat for Humanity and was encouraged through TVA.

Justin built a metal and wood birdhouse from scratch, an architectural masterpiece. It didn't go for silent auction, but sold for $75. That is really awesome. Most of the houses sold for $15 or $20.

I love spending every weekend with Justin. He is so creative and fun. Sometimes we walk up to a Buckhead restaurant and have lunch and a pitcher of beer. It is awesome.

SEPTEMBER 6, 1997

Justin and I went out Friday night this time. We went to Nikimoto's in Midtown. It is so beautiful. Architecturally, it is a masterpiece. Everything is custom made and they have the best sushi and a very attractive bartender. Justin is an expert with bartenders. He will order a drink, and give a $5 tip or more. After that, the bartender remembers him and makes our drinks stronger. It's a good ploy. The vodka tonics got so strong there was only a splash of tonic by the end of the night. Justin wants to go next Friday night, too. He will often pay for my dinner since I am desperately poor, barely paying my bills because of all the credit card debt I have. It is so sweet of him. I try and pay when I can. We had a great time. Justin flirted with the bartender, although I think he is straight. It doesn't matter. He likes the large tips Justin leaves, so he is amiable. Loads of fun. We went across the street to a gay bar. It is more low key and not a dance club. It was a nice place. They have drag shows there. I saw Raven, a gorgeous brunette scantily clad. She is incredibly beautiful. I can't tell that she was ever a man. She had breast implants. Justin says that she is a friend of Bart's and she still has her penis but tucks it up.

OCTOBER 7, 1997

That Jessica is a real bitch! She was talking about Jimmy. Jimmy was not in the office at the time and Jessica said that men who change their name from Jim to Jimmy are quite charming, but Jimmy was not charming. She said that he was a freak, a real weirdo. I felt crushed. I have always been attracted to Jimmy, although he has never acted that I exist. He wants bigger and better fish than me. I am so ignored by Jimmy. His beautiful blue eyes only glance my way from time to time. How dare Jessica talk about Jimmy like that. Why is he weird? I don't see it at all. I so want to go out with him. I have come to the conclusion that I am not good enough for Jimmy, but I will not speak badly about him, because he has always been nice to me. Apparently, to my disgust, Jessica said that Jimmy was drooling all over Holley H. Yes, she is a petite, sparky beauty. I am not. Holley told Jessica that Jimmy was a slobbering freak and Jessica quickly adopted her view. How crushing, on many levels.

On a somber note, my credit card debts are crippling me. I felt so guilty about getting so many credit cards forged with Ed as co-signer, that I agreed to take all of the cards under my name and pay them off in the divorce settlement. Holly told me I was stupid for taking on all of the debt from the marriage, but I am the one who spent all of the money, so I feel it is my responsibility. I took more than I can handle, just barely paying my bills with nothing left over.

DECEMBER 20, 1997

Well, I won't be alone for Christmas this year! Justin has invited me to visit his mother and stepfather in Arkansas. We are flying out on the 23rd. I am so excited! Justin's mother is so sweet, I met her a few months ago when she came with Justin's sister to visit. While we are in Arkansas, Justin wants to visit his ex-boyfriend and cousins in Little Rock and his other high school friend in Oklahoma City. Justin said that he will take me on the Pig Trail, the historic windy mountain road where the pigs used to be driven for sale in town. It must be very picturesque in the Ozarks.

I have already started packing. I can't believe it! At least airline tickets are inexpensive from Atlanta. I purchased my ticket three weeks ago, I just forgot to tell you about it. I am so relieved not to spend Christmas alone like last year.

CHAPTER 20

1998: AGE 29

JANUARY 5, 1998

I had a great time at Christmas. I was very impressed with Little Rock. It is such a hip little city. Very artistic and modern. I had the misconception that all of Arkansas was in the Ozarks. Justin has so many aunts and cousins it makes me dizzy. Mostly female and they all love him. Justin is very kind and gentle and everyone falls in love with him.

There was one mind-boggling relationship that I must share with you. Justin's mom has a plethora of sisters. They grew up in the Ozarks very poor and are descendants of the Cherokee who suffered through the Trail of Tears. Some of Justin's mom's sisters had the same father, but others were from step-fathers after the father died. The youngest daughter, Angie, is in her early 20's, which makes an aunt younger than Justin. Angie is mostly shunned by the other sisters because when she turned 14, she ran off with her step-father. It was very confusing for me hearing about all of those fathers and step-fathers and sisters. Well, that is the one Arkansas story that I have to relate, although Justin would kill me if I told anyone.

I also found out about Justin's real father. Ever since Justin came out of the closet (in college) his father won't have anything to do with him. All I could find out was that Justin's parents divorced while he and his sister were in their early teens. Well, once Justin discovered that he was indeed gay, his father told him that he was disgusted and never wanted to see his son as long as he lived. His father went one step further and said that in his mind, he didn't have a son. Therefore, Justin never sees or speaks to his father. It is certainly for the best because he sounds like an abusive asshole. He has that Irish temper and is a heavy drinker and used to hit Justin's mom. She finally left him and went to work full-time for the first time in order to support her two children. A quite remarkable story, really. Justin's stepfather is much nicer, although he is a bit stand-offish. However, he is not a mean, bitter man, which is the important thing. Enough of the family history.

Justin and I stayed two nights in Little Rock and then went back to his mom's house 3 hours north. Justin took me by the Popeye Spinach plant and showed me the giant Popeye statue on their front lawn. We also went by the owner of Walmart's house and his wife's house. They live in separate mansions about 5 miles apart. The owners of Walmart have so much money that they can afford two houses, one for the husband and one for the wife.

One day, we went to visit a "cousin" of theirs who lived way out in the Ozarks. They weren't really related but had grown up together. On the way to their house (I can't remember their names) we drove at least 20 miles on dirt roads, passing by dilapidated one room structures that had no electrical lines going to them. I could tell people still lived there since there was a lantern lit inside. It was a cold snowy day. I guess they burn a fire for heat. There were many small shacks that had no electricity. Dorothy said that they had outhouses in the back, too. I love the modern toilet. I can't imagine going outside in bitterly cold weather to go to the bathroom. It amazed me that people are still so desperately poor in the Ozarks.

The "cousin's" farm was very nice with a gorgeous wood cabin as the main house. It was a very spacious wood cabin that they built themselves. While I was there I saw their pigs, Wynonna and Naomi. The fatter one was Wynonna. They lived in a nice pen and are frequently petted. Yes, then slaughtered. Well, bacon is darn good. They slaughtered the pigs themselves. We weren't around to see that, thank goodness. While I was there, I completely solved a Rubik's Cube! I was in the "zone" and could see all of the moves ahead of time. It took me only 20 minutes. That is the first time I have solved a cube by myself without using a cheat book. I was amazed. No one else seemed to be as amazed.

There was some snow the last two days of our visit in Springdale. I got to see some after all. There was snow in Atlanta, too, I heard. I would have gotten it either way. Whew! I'm tired of writing. Later.

FEBRUARY 22, 1998

I had the most unusual experience last night! Justin and I went to Blake's again, a gay bar in Midtown. To begin with, Raven dressed in the entire Wonder Woman outfit and danced around the bar. Then, to everyone's surprise and enjoyment, she went outside to stop a bus, like the real Wonder Woman. We couldn't believe it. Stop a bus? Well, we all ran outside and waited for a Marta bus to come by. Sure enough, within ten minutes, a bus came by. Raven jumped out into the street right in front of the bus in her Wonder Woman outfit. The bus driver was asking what the hell was going on. Raven explained that she was stopping a bus like Wonder Woman. Raven then grabbed her gold lasso and started to circle it above her head. The bus driver was laughing and the passengers were standing up and gawking at the scene of gay men cheering on Wonder Woman. After a few minutes, the driver said that she had to go. Raven thanked her for stopping and being so open about the whole incident, and the bus driver said that it made her night. We all cheered Raven.

When we went inside, I was coming from the bathroom and Raven passed by me. I told her she was awesome when she stopped that bus but she completely ignored me (although she had to have heard me). Bitch.

That was the beginning of the excitement. Justin said that he had to go to the bathroom and put his bulky wallet on the table and asked me to watch it for him. I agreed.

I put my head in my hands as I was thinking about how Justin and I were growing apart due to my obsessive nature. I want to spend every day and every minute with him on the weekend and he spends more and more time with his other female friends.

As I had my head down, I saw a hand dart forth and grab Justin's wallet. I was infuriated! I was asked to watch Justin's wallet, and watch it I was going to do. I ran after the 6'3" man and grabbed his arm and demanded Justin's wallet back. He said that he didn't know what I was talking about and pushed me away. I started screaming for help and said that this man just stole my friends wallet. About a dozen gay men encircled us. They didn't help me, but they stopped the thief from running away. I grabbed for Justin's wallet and clutched on for dear life. The man tried to push me away and was about to hit me when the boys around us closed in on him. I hit the thief over and over, telling him to release the wallet. He said that it was his wallet and that I was the freak. No one believed him so I kept hitting him. Finally, he let go of the wallet and ran off. I told the bartender that a man tried to steal my friend's wallet and I pointed him out. The bartender told me that they had trouble with that man before and sent the bouncers to throw him out, telling him if he ever returned, he would be beaten to a bloody pulp. The man left, calling me bitch.

Once the man was expelled, the men who formed a circle around us applauded me. I was patted on the back and treated like a hero. I was shaking all over. Justin had come back from the bathroom and wondered what the commotion was. I explained what happened as I shook uncontrollably. An unknown man bought me a drink and patted me on the back. Justin proceeded to buy me a few more drinks for my bravery. His wallet had almost been lost but I had saved it by clutching onto a man who was almost a foot taller than me and outweighed me by at least 75 pounds. I wasn't afraid, I was mad. It took a while for me to stop shaking. I was approached by some men and told how much of a hero I was. I couldn't believe it. I wasn't trying to be a hero. I was asked to guard Justin's wallet and was doing my job.

MARCH 8, 1998

Justin has increasingly been making excuses not to see me. Ever since Jessica started working at TVA, he has been spending time with her and her friends. She is an architect who graduated from some college in Texas. She invites men to lunch every day. They sit in the garden and eat their lunch together, not inviting me of course. I used to eat lunch with Justin and Holly, but Justin doesn't offer for me to join him and his new friends at lunch. It really hurts. Why doesn't he want to invite me?

Jessica has several friends in town, another guy named Justin and his ex-girlfriend, I forget her name, but she is another new friend Justin spends time with. I mean every weekend, almost every day and evening. If it isn't that group, then it is the fat, bossy Dawn.

Dawn is a nasty thing who is an interior design supervisor on many jobs. Dawn is the type of person who will verbally belittle you in front of the entire office if you make any mistake, no matter how small. I have heard her do it several times to other people. She tried to do it to me once, for some trivial matter, and I told her not to treat me like that since I worked so hard. I suggested to her right there that she discuss these matters before blowing up at the person. Then she wanted to speak to me in a private conference room. Dawn started another tirade about me "back-talking" her. She isn't my boss. Also, she shouldn't treat people that way. It isn't necessary. Most of the things she gets upset about are so trivial, like putting seating for six instead of eight on the floor plan conference room for some project. I kept calm throughout the tongue lashing, answering her in the same way; telling her that she has no right to speak to me that way. Being calm aggravated her and she started crying. I told her that I will make the corrections, but I don't appreciate being embarrassed in front of the entire department for such a small matter. It isn't like our job is brain surgery and someone loses the use of their right arm. It is interior design, space planning, work on the computer which can be easily corrected. What a psycho.

Later that day, Dawn must have spoken to Justin, crying over my reaction to her "management". Justin spoke to me at lunch and told me how much he respected Dawn for being a woman in a man's world, blah, blah, blah. What does that matter? Does she have to be so rude to everyone? I told him she is a hot-headed, irrational bitch who shouldn't be managing any job. Justin then tells me that I don't know the real Dawn, that she is actually kind and sweet and puts on a façade while at work. Is that necessary? To smooth things over with her, he said that I should go to Dawn's house with him after work, to see her at home. I agreed to that arrangement. I don't want a departmental grudge. I just want to do my job and be treated with respect. I went over there for a short time, saw her 4 cats, had some ice tea and then we left. I have to admit, Dawn acted much differently at home. She acted sweet and child-like. Why doesn't she act that way to her fellow employees?

Due to my complaints that Justin and I never do anything, nor am I invited to any of the group activities, he planned a movie excursion with Dawn and myself. We went to see *Titanic*. They had both seen the movie before but I hadn't. It was still hanging around theaters because of all the accolades it received. It wouldn't have been my top choice of a movie. I'd rather go up to Garden Hill Cinema and see a foreign or independent film. The movie was alright. Dawn sobbed uncontrollably through half of the movie. On the way home, Dawn said that she wouldn't mind dying in freezing water, that it would be a fast death. I was kind of shocked at that opinion. Didn't she see the suffering on the screen? When ever you put your foot in ice cold water, it hurts. Your body hurts from cold. It doesn't sound like a pleasant death to me. Sure, it beats burning to death, I suppose, or being hung, drawn and quartered.

That was the only time I was invited with his other friends. It makes me feel angry and jealous toward them, which isn't a pleasant feeling. They invite other people during these weekend escapades, so why not me? It has been weeks since Justin and I did anything together. Excuse after excuse. I feel like he used me like all of the men in my past. We would do everything together before. Now he is cold and callous.

MARCH 24, 1998

I am in so much anguish. I can't think straight and have been calling in sick to work. I can't stand to face Justin and Jessica. Last weekend Justin and I went to Backstreet, something we hadn't done in a long time. I stayed the night, as I usually do. I love sleeping next to Justin. I feel so intimate with him, like we can almost read each other's mind. Or, so I thought.

Sunday morning, as we were lounging around his fashionable Midtown loft on his white on white feather mattress and comforter from The Pottery Barn, the phone rang. Nothing new there, Justin gets a lot of phone calls from his many friends. It sounded like it must be Jessica. He was planning a Sunday brunch and evening get together with Jessica, Jason, and Jason's ex-girlfriend, whose name escapes me. Fabulous. It was the next bit that struck a knife through my heart. Justin and Jessica were going to look at houses to rent together! Move in with her? I'll NEVER see Justin then. I had been asking Justin for ages to move in together but he kept saying he wanted to live alone. That was a lie. He didn't want to live alone, he just didn't want to live with me.

I completely broke down. I kept screaming of his betrayal and asked why it had to be with her. I was crying so hard and Justin was shaking, saying over and over again that we would still do things together. Like we are now? We barely see each other. Even at the office, Justin takes every lunch with Jessica and Glen, another architect who is under Jessica's influence. I am never invited to lunch with them, so how will it be better once he moves in with the vile bitch?

To make matters worse, Jessica's mother is mentally ill, bipolar, so Jessica wants Justin to steer clear of me. Jessica has told him horror stories of her drugged out mom breaking three vacuums on the stairs, not cooking dinner, acting like a zombie, and other cheerful stories. I really think she is undermining our relationship. Justin is gullible not to see her manipulation.

The final stab through the heart is when Justin told me that Jessica has a sister who is gay, and most of her friends are gay, so she understands him better than I do. What? Most of my friends are gay, too. I went to interior design school. The few males in the program were almost all gay. The Chairman of the department was gay, as were several professors. That was complete bullshit. Justin denies saying this today, but I heard him tell me that I don't understand him as well as Jessica. That is when things got fuzzy. I became hysterical and was crying my heart out.

I can't remember everything during my break downs. I remember crying in the hallway of his apartment, leaning against his door because I had left my purse in his apartment. Justin brought me back in and comforted me, promising me he will continue our friendship, that he will invite me to do activities with him more often like before. I didn't believe it. Nothing he could say would convince me, but I calmed down and Justin drove me to the offices' parking deck to retrieve my car.

I am a broken person. I have missed a great deal of work, close all of my curtains so no one can see in, and am getting very paranoid every time someone walks by my door. I am in my apartment with Keelie, my one and only true friend. Keelie is always there, always loves me, always needs me. I don't want to leave the apartment, to leave Keelie. I often disconnect the phone and even have missed work a couple of days without calling in at all. I am sure I will be fired. That will make matters worse. But I can't face them at work. I am so humiliated and embarrassed. Betrayed and ignored.

MARCH 28, 1998

I had a strange nightmare. I was living in a house that I have never been to and had a brother who never existed. My mother was my real mom. Here it goes.

I lived in a farm house with a chicken house out back. There was also a brilliantly blue swimming pool. The house was painted pristine white and the green grass glistened in the morning sun.

I was around 10 years old with an older brother who was 17. It was a school day but I was allowed to stay home sick. My brother's friends pulled up in a Dodge Caravan to pick him up for school. My brother ran out to meet his friends. I followed him out, asking him to stay home with me. He couldn't, he said. He had football practice after school. But something was not right with his friends. I was not sure what was amiss, but I noticed that he sensed it too just before he got into the van.

My brother hesitated at the door of the van. His friends grabbed his shirt and pulled him into the back. Mom thought it was just roughhousing. I didn't think so, and started to cry. Mom told me to get back into the house since I was sick. I obeyed.

A couple of hours went by when I heard a knock at the door. Looking out the window I noticed that it was the local sheriff with a younger man I did not know. I had the same ominous feeling as before and begged mom not to open the door. I felt something was wrong. Mom said that I was being silly, but she didn't advance toward the door, nor did she unclasp the lock.

Almost reluctantly, mom finally opened the door. The sheriff said that he wanted to introduce us to his new deputy. Mom and I exchanged glances. Something was wrong, she sensed it too. We both looked at the men, me hiding behind mom, and they both just kept smiling blankly at us with their overly large smiles emphasizing their unusually huge, bulging eyes.

Mom told the sheriff that she was busy today and started to close the door. The new deputy put his foot in the door and asked to come in. His voice was low and gravely. My mom told him no right away and pushed the door shut.

I helped put my weight against the door as we quickly fumbled with the dead bolt.

I suggested that we go through the house and make sure all the doors and windows were locked. Mom agreed. We had just begun our errand when the chair from our front porch came crashing through the front window. Glass shattered in all directions, glistening in the morning light. The sheriff and deputy were not quite in the house yet because they were struggling with the shards of glass still embedded in the window frame. The sheriff grabbed another chair and swung wildly at the remaining glass in order to clear an opening.

Mom and I decided to run for the car. We opened the back door and ran toward the car. Suddenly, mom screamed. I froze in terror, fearing that the man-creatures had attacked her. Instead, she was crouched low to the ground. I asked her what was wrong. She had the shits. She had to go. I told her she better shit her pants because if she went back into the house she would be murdered. Mom told me to run and waved me on. I stood there for a few seconds, then bolted for the car.

Suddenly, the young deputy, wearing his khaki wind breaker, Levi jeans, and a crisp, white, Izod shirt came running through the back door, right toward my mom. His greasy, shoulder length blond hair was matted to his sweaty neck. He still had that stupid smile on his face as he changed direction and began to run toward me instead of mom. He caught up to me in a flash and slung me over his shoulder. I struggled in his tight grasp, but could not free myself. He told me that he loved me and planned to eat me. Of course, I was petrified.

The demonic deputy ran toward the chicken house. There were a lot of tools in there. Tools which could easily chop up a body. I realized with horror that the body would be me.

I broke out of my daze and reached around and gouged out his right eye. It gave me enough time to wrestle myself from his grasp. I fell to the ground and leapt up in an instant and began running toward the neighbor's blue farm house. As I was fleeing this hell, I noticed something metal glistening in the grass. As I approached, I saw it was a screwdriver with a long, yellow handle. I snatched up the screwdriver, turned around, planted my feet and thrust it through the throat of the oncoming deputy.

Some creature slithered out of the wound in his neck and bit into the fleshy part of my right hand. You know, the place between the thumb and forefinger. It's jagged teeth ripped the flesh away from my hand. I screamed in pain and terror, but kept stabbing the deputy with the yellow, bloody screwdriver. The deputy finally dropped to the ground and began convulsing on the grass by the chicken house. His hands fumbled with the screwdriver in his neck, trying vainly to remove it. He didn't seem to have control of his arms, which were flailing uselessly. Finally, his strength began to give way and he lay there twitching. Blood and saliva were oozing from his mouth. Evidently, he was dying. I stood watching him, making sure that he was really dead.

I ran back to the house, searching frantically for mom. She was standing in the kitchen, blood covering her. She pointed lifelessly into the kitchen. I entered the kitchen very slowly, peeking fearfully around the corner. The sheriff had our best butcher's knife embedded in his forehead. He twitched lifelessly. I ran up and hugged mom.

I expressed my concerns for my brother, who, I felt, was in grave danger. I insisted that we try and find him immediately. She agreed and grabbed the car keys from the hook in the kitchen. We were almost to the car when we suddenly noticed the neighbor's young hired help only a few feet away, running toward us with a gruesome smile on his blood-streaked face. He had a bloody machete in his right hand. He raised up the machete! I awoke.

APRIL 13, 1998

An Easter nightmare. Justin finally invited me to hang out with him, Jessica, Jason, and Julie (Justin's ex-girlfriend). Jason (the wonderfully hot, bisexual friend of Jessica) invited us to his new home near the baseball stadium. Jason is extremely attractive and charismatic. His entire neighborhood is new and is completely Black. He is the kind of man who doesn't care what other people think, and makes friends everywhere he goes. He just bought this house (it is really cute inside, although each lot is quite small with a large front porch taking up most of the front yard), he is thinking about moving to Detroit with his current girlfriend who recently moved there. That is unfortunate. He is an incredible guy.

It started out wonderfully. We were all supposed to bring some cd's to listen to, something unique. I brought Ella Fitzgerald, Billy Holliday, The Squirrel Nut Zippers, Frank Sinatra, and the Brian Setzer Orchestra. All popular choices. Julie showed up late for Easter dinner, everyone brought a covered dish (mine was squash casserole). I can't believe that Jason used to date Julie. She is a hyper, bug-eyed mess. I swear, she never blinks when she talks to you. She was all up in Justin's space, monopolizing his time. Apparently, they have become quite chummy. Some other guys showed up, friends of Jason, and we were all drinking and having a good time. All except for me. I was ignored, as usual. It is probably my fault since I am terrible at small talk. I see small talk as a complete waste of time. I need to learn how to do small talk because people avoid me. I talk a great deal when I am around one person I trust, but when I get around a group, I freeze up. I did alright after several drinks.

The food was put out on the counter and people just ate whenever they wanted, carrying plates of food around the house or out onto the porch where Jason interacted with every person who walked down the street. He had already formed friendships with several Black families around there. Jason picked up his small three bedroom, two bath home in downtown Atlanta for minimum amount (I don't know how much he paid, but he said that it was very inexpensive).

Jason and Julie, who is a graphic designer, talked extensively about her moving into his home, Jason moving to Detroit, and Julie basically renting the house out for the price of the mortgage. That way, Julie can have her business in one bedroom and have two bedrooms left over. You know, computer, printer, etc. They came to a deal and Julie said she would move into Jason's house in a couple of months. She was slightly concerned about the neighborhood, but Jason, in his sweet drunken state, went to a few neighbors' houses and introduced Julie to them.

Hours into the partying, Jessica wanted to go dancing at the Armory, but everyone wanted to wait until dark, at least. I was wandering between various groups of people since Justin was completely enamored with Jessica and Julie, ignoring me the entire time. Why was I invited if I was just going to be ignored? I tried to edge into their conversation, but I got the definite impression that I was the "third wheel". I drank more and more because of the almost physical pain I felt from the rejection. My heart breaks every time Justin does that to me; monopolizes his time with only one or two people all night.

I finally got to the drunken state where I told Justin he should talk to ALL of his friends, not just those two. We argued a bit and I hit him on the arm, in a half joking manner, so I thought. Jessica came up immediately and told me not to hit Justin. I said that it really wasn't any of her business. The beginning of the end.

We all finally went to the Armory, and Jessica kept pulling Justin onto the dance floor. It was as if I wasn't there. One of the other Jason's friends, I can't remember his name, saw my deep depression and painful look on my face as I asked Justin to dance with me, too, but was rejected. He and I danced for a bit. Jessica was hanging all over Justin and kissing on him, laughing in her drunken stupor. It is devastating to me now to write about it. We all finally went back to Jason's house and went home. Justin and I had come together, leaving my car at his apartment complex so we had a silent ride back. He didn't invite me in so I went home. I am so humiliated, again. Now Jessica will never want to invite me to any of their events. She already acts cold towards me, but now it will be unbearable. I can't stop thinking about it, tried to call Justin, left messages on his answering machine. He won't answer and won't call back. I know he is home, he is just ignoring me. As usual, I fucked things up. I just don't know how to make and keep friends. I don't know how to communicate with people in a "normal" manner. All of my friends drift away, abandon me, leave me isolated and alone. The anguish is almost physical. I will take some sleeping pills so I can try and get some rest. My mind keeps running in circles, going over all of the events, leaving me bitter and sad. Hopefully I can sleep now. I am feeling a little tired. Keelie is here, my faithful little furry friend. My only friend.

APRIL 15, 1998

I had an overdose tonight. During my anguish, I called Justin but he hung up with me and called an ambulance who came and checked me out because I was having trouble breathing. By the time they got there, I acted like I was alright. They stayed with me for a while, I am unsure how long they were there, talking to me kindly, asking me about my interests in the piano and reading since they saw the hundreds of books stacked all over my apartment. The paramedics finally left, after I started to feel better. They gave me a shot of something, but I can barely remember it and don't know what it was. Thank God they didn't take me to the hospital. That would have been a nightmare.

APRIL 18, 1998

Last night, Justin and I went to Backstreet again. I convinced him to go out. While I was there, and Justin was dancing with shirtless men, a tall, somewhat attractive man approached me and asked me to dance. We did dance for a while. He seemed like a nice guy, so I gave him my phone number. I wasn't going to go home with him that night. I think his name is Wade. At any rate, he is going to call me tomorrow, Sunday, to plan a date. We'll see how it goes. I hope he is decent looking, because sometimes, at Backstreet, someone will look attractive in the dark smoky environment but turn out to be ugly. I'll let you know how it goes.

APRIL 19, 1998

What a strange date. Wade called me and came by my apartment so we could walk up to Fellini's for dinner. Wade was alright looking and kept talking about the movies *Blue*, *Red*, and *White*, after I mentioned that *Red* is my favorite movie. He got some of the information wrong from the films, so I knew he was lying to me, trying to act like he knew what the fuck he was talking about. No need to lie. Just say you haven't seen the movie. We hung out for a short time at my apartment before going to the restaurant. I started having doubts as to whether I should have met him someplace instead of giving him my address. Something about him was strange.

Wade and I walked to Fellini's since it is only a mile away. After much unnecessary arguing, we decided to each order a slice of pizza and a beer but he made me pay for my own pizza and beer. That is strange for a first date.

As we were drinking beer, Wade told me an unnerving story about his stint in the Navy. Wade said that he hated the Navy and disliked living on a small ship so close to men. Well, what did he expect? I sat in disbelief as Wade told me his Naval story. It appears that he may be gay after all, or bisexual, accounting for the fact that I met him at a gay bar. I was wondering about his orientation. No big deal. But to deny attraction to males in such harsh language was shocking to me. Wade started talking about "fags" in the Navy who hit on him, how he was locked in a room for his conduct, and how he became so enraged he hit the metal door until it bent. Wade then continued the story, saying how hard it is to bend an iron door. Well, I should say so! He said that he blacked out from his rage, a rage he gets from time to time where he just beats the crap out of anything in his way. That didn't make me feel very warm and fuzzy inside. Surely he must be exaggerating his story. How can anyone bend an iron door?

I tried to change the subject by asking why Wade was at Backstreet (since he is obviously homophobic). It was as if I didn't speak, and Wade started telling me more frightening stories about the Navy. He was kicked out, dishonorably discharged. Wade seemed to be proud of the fact, but I was very embarrassed for him. It isn't anything to be proud of. Wade swaggered that the Navy is full of queers. I was wondering if he wasn't gay and was overly sensitive to other gay men.

Wade wasn't buying me another beer, so I suggested that we go back to my place where I had vodka tonics. If I wasn't so lonely, I would never invite such a freak over. I soon was sorry I had.

When Wade and I got to my apartment, he started talking about the Navy again. I interrupted and told him to take his clothes off. I might as well fuck him, even if he is a loser. We were on the floor, rolling around, but he couldn't get it up. I rubbed his dick but to no avail. I knew then he was gay but didn't want to admit it. We tried a few times, but he could never get it up. Wade began to get angry, and I didn't want that black anger to arise, so I said that I was tired. Wade was really dejected because he couldn't get it up, but I just wanted him to go. Finally I got him out the door. I hope that is the last time I see him.

APRIL 23, 1998

Wade keeps calling me. I let it go to my answering machine, but he called me at work, too. He wants another date. Not a chance. Justin thought that I was crazy for trying to have sex with a man that I despised. I told Justin that I might as well get something out of the date since I didn't get a dinner. Justin just laughed about it.

APRIL 26, 1998

Justin called to tell me that both Friday and Saturday nights, Wade came to Backstreet asking where I was at. Justin said that he didn't know. Wade even harassed Bart, asking where I was. What a freak!

MAY 6, 1998

Last night, Tuesday, I walked around Buckhead looking for some escape. I first went to the Irish pub and sat in an area where someone might approach me. I have done this numerous times before. What I do is sit wistfully at the bar, scraping together my change to buy a beer. Some lonely man will approach me and ask if he can buy me a drink. Bingo.

It is usually a business man who wants to see a little of the Atlanta nightlife. I might as well give it to him. No sex, just using him. I know, it sounds terrible being so blunt. If he is unappealing, then I will get a drink or two out of him, say that I am going to the bathroom and sneak out the back door. I have done that a few times. Poor guys. Completely used. I feel only slightly bad about it because I have been used by men so many times in the past, it kind of feels good to use one back.

I did my usual "go to the bathroom, sneak out the back door" trick and went over to Cafe Tú Tú Tango to see what was going on. I walked through the door and was mesmerized by a brilliant artist painting a jazz scene on the center stage. They often have artists and palm readers, belly dancers, or something else unique.

I approached the bar that was near the artist, so I could watch him at work. His paintings were incredibly brilliant. I bought one of their drink concoctions with the few dollars I had left. I drank it up greedily so I could get a buzz and loosen my inhibitions.

I asked the artist his name and he told me that it was Clifford O'Brian. He looked so dark and bohemian. Shoulder length, naturally black hair, blue eyes, well dressed and handsome. He made a living from his painting, which I think is fantastic. I went back over to the bar to finish my drink. The bait was taken. After Cliff's session he came over to talk to me. I found out that he is from Miami but goes between New York, Atlanta, and Miami. He met Woody Allen in a jazz bar where Woody was playing clarinet. They started talking and Woody bought a painting from Cliff. Woody Allen was being filmed at the time for a Jazz documentary about himself and the band he was in. Looking around, I saw many Cliff paintings in Cafe Tú Tú Tango.

I don't know why, but I told Cliff that I was up there drowning my sorrows because I had just found out that I am bipolar. I recently landed a few nights in the psych unit after overdosing on sleeping pills. Justin called an ambulance and they took me to the hospital. Amid the chaos, and the few days I stayed, I was finally told I am bipolar. Cliff said that was interesting because he had a high school friend just tell him days before that she had been diagnosed schizophrenic.

It probably was a mistake telling him. I am bipolar.

As Cliff was packing up his painting supplies and canvases, he asked if I wanted to come over to his loft downtown. I agreed and went with him. I walked to the bar, so I drove with him in his minivan. It was necessary for all of the canvases that he had.

We arrived at his loft downtown, entering through a private garage. It was around 2nd street and was in a really sketchy part of town. But the lofts were phenomenal. A true artist's loft. However, there were boxes and groups of paintings stacked ready for removal. Cliff hired a moving company to pack his belongings and move them to a house he bought in Virginia Highlands. He said that he thought the artist loft thing would be cool, but it really sucked in Atlanta since there was no where to walk to and he bought a home with a yard. Of course, he couldn't quite afford to buy a loft in New York. But he obviously had money because he had the movers packing all of his belongings.

It was a wonderful night. Cliff played guitar and sang to me. I was in complete heaven to be around such a bohemian. I felt energetic and danced around. He said that he had never met someone like me before. We listened to old jazz and blues records for hours, smoking a bit from a joint. He recently quit (mostly) because of a serious heart defect he has. He may have to get a transplant. I smoked and drank enough for him and me.

After hours of dancing, talking, singing, being completely happy, we went to bed. We were both nude and he was on top of me about to enter me. Dumb me, I said at that exact moment that it had been over two years since I had sex. Cliff completely stopped, much to my disappointment. He asked why I hadn't had sex and I said that since my divorce, I only wanted to have sex with someone that was special. Cliff thought that was touching and didn't want to ruin it for me. Damn! What an idiot! It is true, but STILL. I practically begged him to have sex, but he wouldn't. He looked so darn attractive, I wanted to lay on top of him but still denied. His penis wanted to have sex.

Soon afterwards we went to sleep. The next morning, I was hung over and wiped out. Cliff said that I snored. I was so ashamed and apologized for snoring. He said not to apologize because he thought it was cute. Oh, great. I usually only snore now when I am drunk. Since I have lost weight, I don't snore as much.

Cliff took me home and said that he would get in contact with me after he moved. I guess I'll have to wait. What a shame! He was everything I want in a man. An artistic, outgoing, fun, exciting and kind. I really hope he calls me because I LOVE him. He is so bohemian.

Here's to hoping Cliff calls me back.

MAY 8, 1998

I went up to Cafe Tú Tú Tango to try and find Cliff again only to find him absent. Then, I latched onto a bartender who happened to want to come to my apartment after he got off work. I got two free drinks, which were incredibly strong, specialty drinks. He was showing his bartender skills and I was the willing test subject. The bartender came home with me, but it is only a blur. I remember sitting in his lap in my Le Corbusier and fucking him with excessive energy.

I discovered the next morning to my horror that there was vomit down the back of the Corbu chair. I was sitting on him and vomited sometime during sex. I don't remember when. He left his ring. I called him at work but he never picked up his ring so I threw it away. I can't remember anything else about that night. How terrible. I may have been passed out for all I know. Anything could have happened, not that I really care.

MAY 23, 1998

Cliff called and asked to go to see *The Red Violin* right now. I was a bit drunk from an after work rep party and told him I may not be the best company. He insisted, so I capitulated and let him pick me up and see a movie.

The alcohol made me tired, so I was half falling asleep through the movie, although it was a very beautiful, moving film. It was incredibly long, which didn't help me. I ended up being lame and going home and going to sleep. I couldn't stay awake.

MAY 24, 1998

Cliff took me to a sadomasochistic leather bar which had half naked people chained up and being lightly whipped. It was a turn on, but I have been feeling spiritless lately and didn't give Cliff the show I know he wanted. I was trying to think of some way to get his attention but couldn't think of anything except some stupid comments on the dancers' attire.

I could tell I was being evaluated by Cliff. My strengths, my weaknesses. I knew I was failing the test since I have been spaced out a bit with my medication and find myself staring into the distance. Not the best date material.

We drank a few drinks then he took me back to my place. Cliff didn't want to come in, so I went alone. I can be so much fun to be around and other times boring as hell. Last night I was boring and I hate that it's happened twice in a row now. I want to call Cliff and let him know that I'm not boring.

JUNE 6, 1998

Cliff hasn't been answering my calls and finally called to tell me that I was freaking him out, to be honest because I'm calling too often. I said I wouldn't call him any more, tried talking to him, but was cut off abruptly, heard a click then was alone again. I scared someone else away, someone who may have been a perfect partner in life. I don't know how to be social all of the time. Sometimes I have so much energy, I light up the room and people want to be around me. Other times, I am so tired and listless and can't think of a single thing to say. I can be so boring. Maybe it has to do with being bipolar, like my doctor said I was. I'm supposed to go see a specialist but haven't yet.

JUNE 13, 1998

I walked up to the Irish pub in order to scam a few drinks from some men. I don't dress up at all. I have old ripped Levis, an Old Navy ringer t-shirt and sneakers. I don't brush my hair in the least. I have a great haircut so it looks good messy. I usually don't even put on makeup. It doesn't matter, because I will always find a man to buy me a drink. Some men like the grunge look, so it's a turn on. That's cool. I just walk out of my house with an ID in case I'm found dead and a few dollars to start a bar tab.

Last night I lingered long enough to meet a hot guy named Selby who does landscaping. We hit is off quickly, and he invited me to his place. Sure, why not? I got into a complete stranger's car and went to his apartment. He was a professional, that was quick to see. He had condoms strategically placed throughout his apartment. Under cushions, behind pillows, inside books. I laughed at this but he didn't see why it was funny. It was hilarious because he obviously plans these trysts with other women.

He had a couple of sexy tattoos along one side of his body. Celtic or something along that line. Shelby was fit, perfectly proportioned, extremely handsome man. During sex, he asked me what sports I play, since I have such a smoking hot body. I said I don't play any sports. Oh, his girlfriend plays soccer, that's too bad I don't play. Small talk while having sex. A new experience for me.

This is the third time I've had sexual dates with Shelby, at his place. It's a nice condo, aesthetically pleasing decor, with a bit of Pottery Barn thrown in for balance. Shelby is just so darn charming, I don't mind being used only for sex. He talked about me to his friends when we were at the Irish pub. When I was walking out, they walked behind me, and he said what an ass I have. The perfect, firm ass. Shelby said it in a way that wasn't demeaning, so I rather liked it and shook my ass.

We have had sex many times in different positions. Selby was the director in our sexual escapade. Bend over this way. Sure. Sit down like this. Okay. Hours of sex. He said he just broke up with a long term girl and he's playing the field. Selby thanked me on the way home for helping him to see that he still loves his ex-girlfriend. You're welcome.

JUNE 14, 1998

What another crazy night I had. Justin finally invited me over to his apartment to go to Backstreet and spend the night. I was elated. We decided to have dinner first at the Vortex, which is on the ground level in his apartment building (soon to be condos). I left my car at work and went with Justin. He lives about 1½ miles from the office building.

After dinner, Justin and I had some vodka tonics at his flat in order to kill some time before going out. We rarely go to Backstreet before 11:00 pm, but last night we went around 10:00 pm. We went down to the dance floor to say hi to Bart, the very sexy bartender who is so charming. We talked to him for a while, all the time I am trying to hint at buying some "Special K" (Ketamine, a horse tranquilizer). I finally got him to give me a hit but he won't ever sell any to me. It really sucks. He didn't give me much, but it was pretty good. Justin doesn't like to do it because it can be dangerous. That won't stop me. Of course, Bart said that Wade stopped by last night looking for me. Bart says Wade comes by EVERY night looking for me. What a freak! I told Bart not to tell him anything about me, that I am not interested. Bart agreed, and said that he already did. Bart said that I could do better. No kidding.

Justin and I went upstairs to watch the drag show. I prefer this over dancing, but Justin likes to dance. It is always painfully crowded up there and you can never find an area to stand in where you won't be bumped and run into all night.

Justin and I went back to the dance floor. I went to the bar and smoked a cigarette. I bought another drink from Bart since he makes them deliciously strong. Justin was happily dancing between two men.

Around 12:30 am, Justin said that he wanted to go home. I agreed, since I am usually bored while he dances with bare-chested young men. We dance together sometimes, but Justin is trying to find a man so he doesn't want me busting up his shit. We walked across the street, past Bulldog's (a surprisingly cool sports bar which frequents gay, Black men) and to his apartment. Justin lives across the street from Backstreet. Convenient.

We had one more drink and went to bed. I thought all was well and good. No problem. Not until I woke up at 2:30 am and saw an empty bed. Justin was gone. No note, nothing. I knew he went back to Backstreet. I tried calling Justin on his cell phone, but got not response. By 3:00 am, I was severely irritated. I would have gladly gone back with him had he asked. I built up my nerve and went back to Backstreet. I still had my stamp, so I got in again without repaying the cover price. I searched the bathrooms (where groups of men were huddled in the stalls of the women's bathroom doing drugs) but didn't find him. I was the only girl, I think, at that hour in the morning. Men went into the women's bathroom openly doing drugs. Justin would not be found there. I went to each bar, upstairs and down, but found no Justin. I searched for Bart and finally found him filling in at a different bar. Bart told me that Justin had come back to Backstreet but left with a man. Shit. Why didn't he tell me or leave a note? I got another drink from Bart, luckily for free since I was broke. I hung around for a while, hoping Justin would come back. I couldn't go to his apartment again since it had a code to get in. I kindly had locked his apartment door when I left to Backstreet (knowing I couldn't get back into his apartment).

When I left Backstreet, I was at a loss as to what to do. I had tried Justin's phone again, but I knew it was turned off. I couldn't go back to his place, so I decided to walk the 1½ miles to my car back at the work parking garage. I was furious with each step I took. Why didn't Justin tell me he had planned to go back out? He didn't want me to go, so he snuck out after I fell asleep. What a shit. I got angrier and angrier as I walked through the sketchy part of Atlanta (Downtown) at 4:30 am. I walked past the prostitutes who were shivering at the morning coolness in their miniskirts. I always feel such sympathy for prostitutes. I know they are most likely desperate and probably drug addicts who hate themselves most of the time. I never look down on them or feel like I am better than they are. We all have our ghosts, but theirs are more needy than others.

While I became angrier, I was shocked into reality when a pimped out white Cadillac with gold rims pulled up on the sidewalk directly in front of my path. I should have been frightened, I know. I was intoxicated, bipolar, and didn't give a shit. Probably the best attitude I could have in the circumstances. A Black man with a gold and white silk shirt and purple hat stepped out of the backseat and blocked my path. He asked if I wanted to work for him. I told him to fuck off and get out of my way. He laughed at his friends and looked at me again and asked if I would work for him. The cheek of the man! Here I was, devastated that my best friend ditched me and he was trying to drum up new girls. What an asshole. I know, I should have been frightened, because he could have easily abducted me, but I was angry. I told him I would never work for him and to get the fuck out of my way. He stood there with his driver and another man staring at me. They were parked on the sidewalk in front of me, so I started walking around the car. The main man tried to stop me, but I turned on him and told him not to fucking touch me, leave me the fuck alone, I would never work for him. They started laughing again, but I was furious at the delay to my vehicle. I kept walking as they stayed parked on the sidewalk, watching me walk away. The prostitutes shifted uncomfortably on their stilettos, so I figured this was their pimp. Fuck him. Just try and take me. I'll fight you tooth and nail until one of us dies. I heard screeching tires behind me after another block. They drove off. The sun was making its way to the sky. The hazy morning looked forlornly at the ladies of the night.

I made it to my car and drove home. I drank and smoked some weed until I was totally wasted, then went to sleep. That fucker Justin. I have already left numerous messages on his voice mail. I could have been abducted by a pimp. He doesn't care.

JULY 13, 1998

I went to Backstreet by myself last night. I was looking for Justin, to be honest, but he wasn't there. I talked to Bart for a while and he said that Wade STILL is looking for me. What a freak. He just won't take "no" for an answer.

Justin is avoiding me again. No sign of him all weekend at Backstreet. Damn it all to Hell! It is so depressing. I just came back home and drank and took pills until I fell asleep.

AUGUST 16, 1998

I never mentioned but I was taken to the hospital for a few nights again. I hated the stupid detox. I overdosed on some sleeping pills, Justin called the ambulance again, but this time, they took me to the mental ward. Not that's it's new for me. This is my fourth or fifth time, I just don't write about it because it's embarrassing and depressing. Nothing special happens except I'm given their drugs and wait for my release. Justin did pick me up from the hospital and drove me home, which was a really nice thing to do. Poor Keelie was hungry and wanted some attention. I was only gone two nights. It wasn't the nicest psych ward I've been to. It was at Northside Hospital, which looked beat up and abused. People are always nice in those places, so I basically chill on their meds and watch tv with a bunch of strangers who are strung out or bored like me. This time, I need to attend some kind of therapy in order to be released. I need therapy, so I'll do it.

AUGUST 25, 1998

I started seeing a new therapist. There are some partially covered under my Blue Choice medical policy. The copay is $20. She is a very nice lady but she isn't a medical doctor and has set up an appointment with a psychiatrist for medication on August 27. His name is Dr. Jacobs. I will do it, I guess. Fran is adamant that I go see him. She feels that my illness is far worse than just handling through therapy. I will be seeing Fran every week at first and then I can drop back to every other week, once the medications are beginning to work. It is all very expensive, but at least it is mostly covered. I have to pay these $20 copays each time though. I'll try. I feel miserable all of the time and it is hard for me to keep friends at work.

Holly has strongly encouraged me to seek help. She has a friend who suffers from depression and Holly said that she had to be tough with her friend in order to get her help. Now, her friend is doing well with a family. Holly is a nice girl. I go over to her house once in a while. She is living with her fiancé now. She just moved into a house that he bought off Grant Park. Holly invited me to her clam chowder party the weekend after Thanksgiving. That will be fun. She has so many friends. Holly's life could be straight from that show *Thirty-Something* because she has so many nice, normal mostly married friends. Justin has been invited also so I have someone to go there with. That will be enjoyable.

I am tired. Therapy is painful and tiring. Fran delves right into my childhood which is bringing up horrible memories like bile. I hope therapy helps in the long run.

AUGUST 28, 1998

I saw Dr. Jacobs yesterday. It was a 15 minute appointment which feels disappointing. I don't know what I was expecting, but I suppose I thought it would be like the psychologists that I see on television which will hypnotize you and make you feel instantly better. Dr. Jacobs prescribed a couple of medications to combat my depression. He said that I may be bipolar so he will keep an eye on the meds and wants me to come back in a month. I'll take the medication. If it helps, I will gladly take the medication. If it doesn't, then screw it. I will honestly try.

NOVEMBER 14, 1998

Polly at work invited me to her parents' house for Thanksgiving. Polly is an Administrative Assistant for the Interiors Department. She has such a humorous side to her. Polly's parents used to live in Tallahassee but now live in Marietta, just north of Atlanta. It isn't that far to drive. That was very nice of her to invite me. It will be better than staying in my apartment by myself eating macaroni and cheese.

NOVEMBER 28, 1998

Thanksgiving was very enjoyable. Polly's father is a professor who used to teach at Florida State University. Tallahassee is where Polly grew up. Her brother is a top chef and the other is an electrical engineer. I don't want to be judgmental, but both of Polly's brothers are very well educated but Polly never went to college. Her parents wouldn't pay for it. I hope it isn't because she is female. That disturbed me because Polly does hold a grudge toward her parents because she did want to attend college. How can an educated and well-read man like Polly's father not want to encourage his daughter to greatness? I admit that Polly's mother is very matronly, has been a housewife her entire life. I am afraid that it is a sexist thing. Other than that one major flaw, her family was very interesting and had a great sense of humor. I'm glad I went.

DECEMBER 18, 1998

I have been invited again to Christmas in Arkansas. I had a great time last year so I am very pleased. Justin's mom bought me so many gifts last time, she really didn't have to do that. She is a very nice lady. It makes me happy to have friends. I don't feel so lonely now, even though I am still having depression. I should be happy all of the time. I don't know why I am not. I will do a little Christmas shopping for Justin and his parents.

DECEMBER 29, 1998

I am getting a tattoo tonight! I went to the tattoo parlor in Buckhead and the biker tattooer said that I must wait 4 hours before getting my first tattoo so I have time to change my mind. It is his policy. I am going up there at 7:30 pm. I will stop by the bar on the way and have a couple of vodka tonics first. I am getting a small butterfly on my right ankle. I wanted the butterfly to symbolize rebirth. It is my 30th birthday present to myself and I want this year to be much improved and happier. The tattoo artists looks like a young Michael Madsen. I am looking forward to it. I have always wanted a tattoo. He said that I have the perfect skin for tattoos because it is so white and smooth. No, I don't have perfect skin on my face, but the skin on my body is much nicer. I didn't really think much of it before. He specializes in color so he has such creative ideas about the shading of the butterfly. I'll let him do his thing. The pictures of his work are phenomenal. I trust him.

DECEMBER 30, 1998

I got the tattoo. It looks fabulous. It is bandaged now and then I will have to soak it in salt water twice a day and apply Vaseline to it with a Q-Tip every night. That is easy enough to do. It will take a couple of weeks to heal. There is some swelling and redness. It did hurt. I have to admit that it did. It took an hour and a half. Whenever the needle hit a nerve the pain was excruciating. That didn't happen very often. I just concentrated on a spot on the wall and it was fine. The tattooist played Rob Zombie cd's because that is what he likes to listen to when he tattoos. He stopped for a cigarette break half way through and we went outside to smoke. It was bitterly cold outside! It was a fast cigarette!

CHAPTER 21

1999: AGE 30

JANUARY 1, 1999

I can't remember if I have enough gas in my old rattle and hum car to get this boy to his apartment. I can't remember his name, although I am not sure I ever asked. After all, it was New Year's Eve. It is now 1999 and I don't even know where I am driving. The Boy gives me directions as I drive, his shirt left behind in the battlefield of spilled beer, sweat, confetti and vomit that was the Backstreet dance floor. Turn right. Next light, turn left. Go around the bend and it will be on the right. I just want it to be over. How much farther is his apartment? What is the address? He tells me I don't need to know the address. We hardly speak at all. Dead silence. I can't get anything on my car radio because someone broke off my antennae. Static radio and a cassette deck. I have a Depeche Mode tape somewhere, but it isn't easily found, so I opted for no music.

Bitter alcoholic bile rises in my throat as I try and remember this boy's name. Is he bisexual? Backstreet is primarily a gay dance scene, especially after 3:00 am. After 3:00 am, all bathrooms become male and female, male couples cramped into stalls snorting coke, special K or exchanging a blow job for ecstasy. I tried to interject myself into one of those private drug parties, but shoulders pushed me out, bathroom stall doors slammed in my face. If this was a straight bar, I could dangle sex before a horny man's eyes in order to get my drinks paid for or a sniff of K.

Gay bars are different. Men don't buy girls drinks and certainly don't share their drugs with one. I should have dressed more like a drag queen, then maybe I'd get somewhere within the drug scene. At least Bart, the bartender downstairs near the dance floor, cuts me some slack and gives me a complimentary drink from time to time. Vodka tonic. Top shelf vodka only. Sometimes if I pester Bart enough I can score a line of K, but he won't ever sell it to me, saying he doesn't want to be responsible for me becoming an addict. What the fuck does he care if I'm an addict? Don't I have the right to be a junkie if I want?

Justin, is a long, painful, complex story that cuts me to the bone. He is gay but I want him to myself. I want to show Justin how a woman can love. I only frightened him away, leaving him freaked, frail and shaken. I pushed him too hard. I am sorry.

Sometimes I get thoughts hooked in my mind and I can't detach them, as if written on my brain with permanent ink. Some single minded idea becomes lodged in my brain like a bone in my throat, a broken record that keeps replaying for eternity. I become obsessed with something and I can't stop. I end up calling the person of my focus too many times in one night, or stopping by their apartment unannounced once too often. It always happens. I frighten everyone away eventually. I am just some freak who doesn't know moderation, who wants a person all to myself, not to share with anyone. Obsessed behavior tends to freak people out. I can't stop the thoughts, can't they understand that?

Finally, Boy tells me to let him out of the car, he can walk the rest of the way. He is shirtless, for God's sake. He would rather walk half naked in winter then let me find out where he lives? Is January first even winter? I won't stalk him, but he doesn't know me from Adam even though we have been fucking for five hours straight. Okay, get out, then. Walk to your goddam apartment. I need to get home before I run out of gas. I don't tell him any of these things because my shame silences me, it stands before my eyes like a heavy red velvet curtain. I loathe myself after fucking a stranger, so why do I keep doing this?

The Boy didn't wear a condom and I don't keep any around. Fucking AIDS or some STD. I hope not, but I am too exhausted to care. His waxed, tan, muscular chest glistened at the multi-colored nightclub lights while I waited in a long line to buy a pack of cigarettes. I didn't have dollars for the cigarette machine, so I had to wait in the serpentine, slow line where they sell cock rings, glow sticks, wigs, bongs, pipes, and cigarettes. I wanted a cigarette so badly I could have picked up a butt from the floor if the wasn't so bloody repulsive, slick with bodily fluids.

Shirtless hot Boy met eyes with me and slid next to me in a hot embrace, kissing me hard and searching me with his tongue. I think he only wanted to move up in line. His chest was hairless and completely buff and looked every inch a gay man. Fuck it. First attention I'd had all night, so why not? I'll play the game. I could feel his hard cock through his jeans pressing against my moist loins. He whispered to me that he was flying high on ecstasy. Do you have any to share? No, of course not. Prick.

I haven't tried ecstasy yet. I'd like to try it. I'll try any drug, except heroin, only because it requires a needle and I morbidly despise needles. My fear of needles has a date and location; 1974, Philippines. Endured the sickening aching pain of rabies shots, three the first day and one each and every afternoon for 27 more days. I was six years old and living on Clarke Air Force Base. My stepfather was in the Air Force. Jet Engine Mechanic. I wasn't even attacked by an animal, which is the most confusing part. A stray cat in the neighborhood, which I fondly petted, as did all of the other kids. The cat freaked out one day and attacked a young boy then ran off. The description of the cat could fit rabies, but the cat was never found. It just disappeared. A nice cat to play with one day and gone the next, dying a miserably painful death alone and afraid.

The strangest part of the memory searing ordeal was the unfortunate native Filipino who was in the ER when I arrived at the hospital, screaming and slobbering, acting like a frenzied madman. Nurses blocked off groups of people, bravely facing the frightened man who was suffering from none other than rabies. Rabies. I was at the hospital for rabies shots. I lost it completely and started crying and trying to escape the madness. I thought for sure I would end up like that madman, that I would suffer the cruel fate of rabies, too. I finally calmed down when I remember my mom softly telling me that the shots will prevent rabies and I won't become like that man. She knelt down in front of me, holding and rocking me, consoling me before the tortuous shots began. Not only were the needles unnecessarily enormous, but my joints swelled and muscles ached and I felt a little feverish for the next month. Stomach, back, thigh, arm, all in rotation every day. God, the fucking needles. I still remember the huge flesh piercing needles full of serum to pulse through my veins, muscles, sinew and bone. Never will I shoot heroine. No fucking way.

The smooth, shiny bare chested Boy didn't have any ecstasy to share but was willing to put his cock in me. I think he would fuck anything that was warm with a pulse. I told him we could drive to my apartment. I hadn't had a drink in half an hour, so I was fairly steady. I would have been drinking if I had enough money. It was either cigarettes or a drink. I chose cigarettes and it got me laid. Sure, I could drive. I have a soulful blue convertible, a crappy Chrysler Lebaron that Justin sold me for $500 even though he won it with a dollar in a lottery at another gay club, to which I was not invited. Justin already had a Volvo, so he had called me at 2:00 am a few months back to inform me he was giving me this convertible, for only half a grand. I giggled into the phone my sweet appreciation of his loving me so much he would give me his newly won car. My own car, a Ford Festiva, was a dusty heap in the parking lot of my apartment complex. Poor car needed a new transmission. Like that was going to happen. Pull money from where, my arse? I haven't actually accepted money for sex so I am not getting an income, caught in the unloving arms of manic depression. Buy me a few drinks, well, I might be your girl for the night. Sad, really. Drinks instead of money. I think I'd do better asking for the money.

There were enough gas vapors in my car to get me back home. Of course, Boy didn't offer to give me money for gas. I wasn't sure if he thought it would be rude to give me money after fucking or if he was really a selfish asshole. I'll never know. I'll never see him again.

I wouldn't have dreamed of bringing in the new year violently fucking a stranger. I can't say it was all pleasurable. The Boy couldn't cum because of the ecstasy and alcohol, but he was tenacious. He pumped for hours, me on top, then him throwing me over onto my stomach as he fucked me from behind. The boy penetrated my anus, which wasn't the most pleasant feeling in the world, so I guided him back into my vagina. He was having none of it. The Boy grabbed both wrists in his hand and pinned them over my head. I couldn't move, I was trapped. I had become dry and out of the mood after the first hour, but he kept pumping me for four more hours. I told him several times that I was done but was ignored. My orifices were raw and painful but he was unrelenting. I finally got to the spot in my mind where I wasn't in my body anymore, but in a safe, private place, deep in the recesses of my mind. I learned how to escape when I was seven after my two cousins died in the fire.

At the funeral, I had a rising feeling of laughter bursting from my body. It bubbled up from my gut, into my mouth and out into the air. I laughed and laughed and laughed and could not stop. I wasn't laughing inside, I was crying, but on the outside I was laughing. Doug told me to shut up, it wasn't funny. My mom didn't notice my hysterics in her grief, so I backed away from the circle of mourners, fading into the grass, blending with the trees, escaping from the pain and the terrible looks from Doug. No adult ever knew, never saw what happened to me that day. Hysterical laughter at a funeral from a 7 year old should be a sign of danger ahead. Cracked ice spotted. Don't wander out too far onto the frozen lake or you will drown. There was no one to stop me from falling into the black void that had become my soul.

Returning to my disheveled apartment on New Year's day was dismal. The Boy and I had knocked over furniture, sheets, blankets, and clothes scattered everywhere. What have I done? I must test for AIDS. How long do I wait to be tested?

I didn't anticipate the escalation of violence which occurred in my room. Part of me liked it, in my highly sexual manic state, being forcibly sodomized gave me a little thrill. The thrill was short-lived. An hour and a half of sodomy was beyond the enjoyment I had envisioned. I hurt all over and it is difficult to sit. A long hot shower to cleanse myself. I sat down in the tub and let the shower rain down upon my head like a rain storm. Washing away the sweat and shame.

My cat, came crawling out of her place of hiding deep in the recesses of my closet, behind the shoes and piles of clothes. It was safe again to come out. I was stunned at the look of fear expressed in my cat's body language. Keelie crept low to the ground, turning her head left and right, sniffing the air for any scent of the Boy. She had the right idea. If I could have hidden in the closet, I would have.

I sadly collected the sheets, remaking the bed with fresh linen that didn't smell like the Boy. Wash it away, tuck it up my sleeves. Only a memory now, but it was the first memory I had of 1999. What fresh hells will this new year bring?

APRIL 5, 1999

It was Easter yesterday. I invited Justin over for dinner, but he had already been invited by Dawn. Of course, Dawn wanted it to be a special, private dinner without the annoying me around. Not invited. How horrible. It is probably because of last year's Easter disaster. I pleaded with Justin so much that he got me an invitation to go with Bart (bartender from Backstreet) to a gay Easter rave dinner. I agreed, only because it sounded like so much fun. I would have rather spent Easter with Justin, but he repeatedly said that he was envious that I was going to that dinner party and he wasn't.

It turned out to be lots of fun. I went over to Bart's house early as he got ready for the party. Bart was extremely hyper and talked a hundred miles per hour. He told me a story of a date gone wrong, but asked if I would be offended. I told him that unless he told me I looked like a tramp, I wouldn't be offended. Just a few nights before, Bart invited a sexy boy that he met at Backstreet over after work. By that time, it had to be early in the morning. This boy, who Bart admitted didn't know what his name was, asked if he could clean up in the bathroom first. Bart said he could. The boy apparently used an enema to clean himself out before sex, a practice that some gay men do. Bart was laying naked on the bed when out this rave boy came. They were rolling around on the bed, the boy got on his knees to do some genital gratification, when all of a sudden, a piece of feces shot out of his ass. Bart was laughing hysterically but the boy was so embarrassed that he got dressed and ran out of the house. Bart told him not to be embarrassed, that he didn't care, but the boy was too humiliated to listen. Interesting story. Pretty gross, but interesting.

I knew that Bart was doing drugs in his bathroom and was so hoping he'd offer me some. He didn't because he felt guilty giving me K. I don't know why he felt guilty. Give me some!!!

After a couple of hours at Bart's house and waiting around as he received countless phone calls, me watching television with Bart's roommates, we finally left.

The dinner party was at an upscale condo of a friend, Tim, I think. He was going to have the entire Easter dinner set up. By the time all of the arrangements were confirmed, it was Sunday so I couldn't buy any alcohol. What a dumbo I am. Bart said not to worry about it, that Tim would have a stocked bar.

The condo was all white on white with glass tables and a back porch overlooking a midtown neighborhood. It was swank, definitely. It began calmly enough as I sipped on vodka tonics. After several hours, the place filled up with gay men. There must have been 20 or 30 people in the small condo. Being the only girl, and I dressed to kill in my knee high black boots and black feather trimmed sweater, I was actually quite popular. I dressed correctly.

I felt like a mooch, though, because I didn't bring a dish, didn't bring alcohol, and bummed cigarettes from people. I apologized every time I had to bum something, but the guys were getting so trashed that they said it wasn't a problem.

I started to notice a line of boys going in and out of the master bathroom. Very suspicious. Drug use, most assuredly. I slowly made my way back to the master bedroom, pretending to wait in line for the master bathroom. I spotted Bart and begged him to share some drugs. It took some work, but I was able to get some K and a few lines of cocaine. I was bouncing off the walls after that. I had so much energy I felt like I could devour the world.

The rest of the party was much more enjoyable, as I became a social butterfly, approaching men and coming up with quick conversation starters. I wish I could think of conversation starters when I am sober. I don't think my parents had a real conversation the entire time I was growing up. Mostly demands and grunting. A family of baboons, scratching their ass and picking their fleas, screaming or sleeping, until the day they are called on a journey away from home; the tavern.

Bart had some plans that evening (which were private, for men only) so he was going to go back to his house to change and let me get my car. The SUV was full of men, I didn't know any of them except for Bart. Bart had some idea about seeing some prostitute, I believe, for drugs. We drove around the shady part of town, Bart asking out the window for someone. Finally, the person in question was spotted. She looked female, but I was wondering if she's a transvestite. Bart grabbed her and sat her on his lap and told us all that she is the most unique person he has ever met. She was from somewhere in South America, I can't remember which country, but the truly remarkable thing about her is she is a true hermaphrodite. She casually exposed her breasts, and Bart wanted to see her pussy/cock. Apparently, the penis emerged from female genitalia. I wanted to see it, too. She said that we'd have to pay for it, but still wouldn't do it when Bart offered to pay. I think she had some drugs on her because Bart and the hermaphrodite appeared to be exchanging something. I couldn't really tell what was going on. I was completely enthralled with meeting a real hermaphrodite. Unfortunately, she was a street prostitute.

Shortly after, I was dropped off at Bart's house. He ran in the house, saying his good-byes, as he hurriedly ran to his bedroom to change clothes. I new my invitation had expired, so I got in my car, cruised by Justin's house to see if his car was back yet (it was) then went home. I was so wired from the K and cocaine that I maniacally cleaned my bedroom closet. I removed everything and reorganized it, staying up until 5:00 am or 6:00 am. I just couldn't close my eyes. I felt like I would jump out of my skin. I guess it was the combination of the multiple drugs that caused this feeling. At least I got a clean closet out of it, organizing all clothes and shoes by color. I began with red, then orange, yellow, green, blue, purple and black. It looked like a rainbow of clothing terminating into a black abyss.

APRIL 7, 1999

Justin called me on Monday to inquire about my Easter excursion. I had finally crashed and missed work again. I was up way too late, or early, to be able to do anything with any accuracy. I feel so guilty about missing so much work, but to be honest, the Washington D.C. Convention Center seems to have enough people working on it. Liz, the architect in charge of the project, is extremely sympathetic and kind. I have been honest about my mental problems, so she is taking the work load off of my shoulders. Liz even said not to worry, just work whenever I can. I don't deserve such kindness.

I'm glad Justin called me. I didn't expect him to phone me, and he did sound a bit distant, but was trying to be kind and upbeat. I told him about my closet cleaning and he thought that was hilarious. I told him he should come over to see my newly organized closet. He wavered and wouldn't pin down a date. Instead, he suggested, again, that I seek psychological treatment and stick with it. I've been trying, but it seems like my medication makes me have very rapid mood swings. I can be depressed one day and literally the next day be a live wire of energy. Rapid cycling, it is called. I feel out of control still, even with medication. That is why I keep drinking and doing any type of drug that I can get my grubby little hands on. I feel like I am going to explode if I don't self-medicate.

Justin hasn't been coming over, always making excuses, or flat out telling me that he won't be friends with me until I am more stable. But this is the time I need him! He doesn't see it that way because I often yell and cry when he is around, reprimanding him about his spending all of his time with Jessica which only invokes his anger. I just can't win.

Cirque Du Soleil. Justin went with Jessica and didn't invite me. I was devastated. I cried, screamed, and pleaded to go but to no avail. He just kept saying that he wanted to go with Jessica. How could he? Why can't we all go together? Doesn't he realize that the more he separates me from him and his other friends, the more jealous I get?

Justin bought tickets for me and him to see *Quidam.* I guess he felt guilty, and told me that the story reminded him of me. I felt better about being ditched the first time. I am so excited to go. I cried when he invited me. We haven't done anything together for so long, I crave his friendship.

Thank you, Justin! I am so happy. I wish I would be invited while other people are around, though.

APRIL 23, 1999

I screwed up again. I have been having real problems with my medications, nothing seems to help. I get so restless and crave alcohol and go up to the bars in Buckhead alone at all hours of the night. Three days ago, I got extremely depressed and called Justin. He has been spending most of his time with Jessica and the other half with Dawn. Justin won't hang out with me at all anymore. Therapist Fran keeps asking me if I am in love with Justin because I am obsessing about him. She doesn't understand. It isn't that I am in love with him, I think it is more the fact that for a while we did everything together. We hung out every weekend and several nights during the week to paint or go walking. Then, everything stopped. It hurts to be shut out like that. I admit that my moods swing wildly and I have been acting more aggressive. I am not usually violent, but I have been prone to slapping Justin. That is a terrible habit to get into. I don't know what comes over me. I get so angry and hostile that I can't control myself. Of course, that drives him away even further.

Doctor Jacobs put me on yet another medication. I can't even remember what it is called. I just seem to get worse, not better. I actually crave alcohol now. I feel so restless that I wander the streets at 3:00 am alone, almost hoping to be murdered. It was in one of these black moods that

I took some sleeping pills. I took some and when I couldn't rest, I took some more. I continued doing that until I finished the bottle. I didn't feel suicidal per se, but was looking for relief.

While I was in this drugged, black state, I mistakenly called Justin. He reprimanded me and told me not to call him. Justin hung up on me. I was devastated. I laid on the floor crying for the longest time. I don't know how long I was laying there, but I heard a knock at my door. I staggered to the door and answered it and it was the police. Justin called the police on me, for the third time. To help me or something. Not an ambulance but the police. I tried to tell the police that I was fine but they didn't believe it. The pressured me to tell them what I had taken. They were walking around my apartment opening things, looking for pills or empty bottles, so they said. I didn't like them doing that so I just told them what I had taken. To make a long story short, the police drove me to West Paces Medical Center. They didn't cuff me, they just drove me over there. That hospital is a little on the frightening side. They sent me to the psych ward in order to "dry out." They monitored me for a couple of days and forced me to stay in their horrible psychiatric ward. It was dirty and dingy and people were screaming at all hours of the day and night. I was fed medication every few hours as I "detoxed." I asked several times what the medication was they were giving me but they wouldn't tell me. That seems illegal, doesn't it? I was just curious, but they wouldn't tell me. The nurse even went so far as telling me that they would force me to take the pills if I didn't cooperate. I took the pills, I was just bloody asking what they were!

I tried to act as normal as possible to get the hell out of that hospital! That was not a place I wanted to stay. I think it was too close to downtown and had a wide assortment of crazy people. I was released last night and Justin was nice enough to pick me up and take me home, but he wouldn't stay. He told me to get help. Then, maybe, he would be friends with me again.

MAY 9, 1999

I was in Piedmont Hospital two nights ago for overdose of sleeping pills, again. I felt so depressed. Justin doesn't want anything to do with me any more. I wasn't exactly trying to kill myself, I just kept taking more and more pills so I could pass out. It is hard for me to sleep on sleeping pills. I don't know how many I took, maybe 30 or 40. I started having a hard time breathing and called Justin. He told me to call 911 and hung up. I didn't call but Justin must have. The ambulance got to my apartment and they had to stabilize me for a bit before they took me to Piedmont Hospital. I was taken to the emergency room and monitored for several hours. Then a doctor discussed possible therapy that I should receive. After being there for 6 hours or more, I was finally allowed to go home. I had no way to get home so I called Justin. He picked me up and took me home but left right away. He said that he didn't want to be around me if I didn't get treatment. Again. *Groundhog Day* for fucking sure.

MAY 20, 1999

Fran, my therapist, has just told me that she doesn't think she will be able to help me. She says that I am much worse than she can handle and that I need to go into the hospital for treatment. I knew it was heading toward this. I have become worse through therapy. I am not sure if it is because I have to rehash my childhood or what. It is very depressing when your therapist tells you she can't help you. Fran has told me to continue seeing Dr. Jacobs about my medication. I will, although I have not gotten any better with his treatment either.

JUNE 30, 1999

I had a devastating experience at Dr. Jacob's office today. Apparently, the check I wrote for my last copay was returned and Dr. Jacob went through the roof. I honestly didn't know. I assured him that I will take care of all charges immediately. He didn't care. He berated me and told me that I don't respect him for passing a worthless check. He didn't believe me that my account is barely covering my bills and the slightest miscalculation will cause a bounced check. I swore to him that I didn't do it on purpose. I really didn't. I wouldn't do that. I am trying to get my finances in order but I am barely making ends meet, especially with the twice a month Dr. Jacob appointments. He told me to mail in a money order and that he never wanted to see me again as long as he lived. I can't believe he reacted so strongly. I told him that I would pay cash in the future but he wouldn't listen and kept telling me to get out. I feel completely worthless, just like the check I accidentally passed to him. I even have to pay for today's appointment even though he didn't treat me. It is so painful. I trusted him and I feel so betrayed.

JULY 25, 1999

I have just gotten out of Peachford Hospital. I feel much better for having gone there although I was pressured by Justin to go. I have been on short term disability income and now am on long term disability income. I am very relieved that I paid the additional monthly premium to have that coverage. It has saved my life. Plus, most of the hospital stay was covered by my medical insurance. Due to my limited income, the hospital actually wrote off most of the bills so I have to pay less than $200. They have even set up a $20 per month payment plan which is an amount that I can afford. Two different doctors there diagnosed me with being bipolar. They are still working on the right medications for me, waiting to see if I have any adverse reactions to the meds I am on, and whether they are helping or hindering my illness. I have already been on several, some of which make me manic or lethargic. Dr. Asaf said that it may take a while to find the right combination of medication for me. Even then, my body may become used to the medication and will have to be altered from time to time. Right now, that is the most difficult part. I will take the medications that are prescribed to me. I am sure they will help eventually. I won't give up this time and will completely listen to Dr. Asaf. He is very knowledgeable in his field and is well published. He is also a modern doctor who researches the newest medications. It is no longer necessary to prescribe large doses of lithium when there are better and more specific medications on the market for manic-depression.

I have been instructed by Doctor Asaf to continue going to group therapy at the hospital. I was given an assignment to write down how I am feeling and goals for the week. Maybe Justin will start to speak to me again.

GOALS FOR WEEK

- Don't drink
- Walk/exercise 5 days
- Take vitamins daily
- See Dr. Asaf about meds
- See Dr. Kelly (therapist) at hospital about depression
- Organize bills
- Practice piano daily
- Be myself, no masks
- Get sponsor

IF DEPRESSED

- Go to meeting

- Play piano
- Paint
- Take walk (not to the bars)
- Call friend (not that I really have any)

– Treat myself as I would a friend in need. Would I say mean things to them?
– Don't depend on others.
– Write down ALL negative thoughts.
– Don't expect anyone to understand what I'm going through, I need to understand myself and just BE.
– Don't be codependent - don't please others to feel worthy - don't try and control the world around me.

RELAPSE INTO BAD HABITS HAPPEN WHEN:

- hurt
- self pity
- loneliness
- lack of life structure
- isolation
- hungry
- no money
- angry
- pain
- tired
- bored

- resentment
- too confident
- guilt
- relationships
- fear
- stress
- negative thinking
- rejection
- anxiety
- grief
- lack of self control
- travel alone
- shame
- betrayal
- uncomfortable

THINGS I AM GRATEFUL FOR:

- Healthy physical
- Roof over my head
- Getting treatment for my mental health
- Birds are singing
- My talent on the piano
- My intelligence

I must call the electric company to get my electricity reconnected up this week. Also, call Check Care about that bounced check. Call IRS to arrange payment plan. Contact a lawyer about filing bankruptcy. I must get out of this perpetual debt that I am in!

AUGUST 29, 1999

Justin and Jessica had their party. It was a bit overwhelming spending time again with Justin and seeing him go into isolated conversations with Jessica and Julie, shutting me out. I didn't drink because I was afraid of losing control, but it was so difficult. Everyone was getting drunk in front of me. Justin acted kind to me but when he started getting drunk, I put up my defenses like I did with my parents. Since it was his party, Justin had to go around to everyone and talk to them, leaving me isolated and alone. He would come back and see how I was doing which made me feel better.

Jessica hates me because she doesn't like her mom who is bipolar. Since she lives with Justin and spends all of the time with him, it makes it impossible for me to feel comfortable. The party made me feel so scared, especially being alone. I felt like I was outside of my body like I used to feel when I couldn't take any more hurt as a child. I felt sad, angry and betrayed.

Now, I'll never be able to visit Justin or spend the night like I used to because Jessica wouldn't allow it. I know that he won't invite me over much anymore.

AUGUST 30, 1999

Another weird dream. I was at work and there was a girl named Maddie, a mean little woman with light brown hair, unlike my current red hair. She followed me around and made my life a living hell. She told my boss that I wanted to be transferred back down to Interiors, which I don't. Steve, the architect in charge of Interiors, wanted to speak to me because he heard from Maddie that I hate him and will never work in Interiors again. Steve was angry with me and I was reprimanded for the lies that the mean girl Maddie was telling everyone.

Then I saw Maddie talking to Justin. She was yelling at him and saying cruel things. I ran over to stop this evil woman but Justin stormed off and wouldn't speak to me. I tried to confront Maddie, but she only sneered and avoided me. She laughed at me from across the room. I think this is my other side.

AUGUST 31, 1999

I had an auditory hallucination today. I could hear Justin calling my name, but there was no one around. I looked everywhere to find the source of the voice, but there was no one.

I woke up this morning at 7:15 am from a nightmare. I was living back home with my parents. A storm was raging and water was pounding against the house. My parents came home drunk as usual. I was watching TV, but Jim turned the channel from a movie I had been watching when it was almost over. This part actually happened in real life many times. I hated him for the utter rudeness of it.

My parents had rented a porn (which they have done before when I was in high school) and wanted to watch it. I took the tape and threw it against the wall but it didn't break. I felt the fear I always felt of not knowing when I would be hit. Jim got up out of his chair and I knew I was in for a beating. My mom left the room, as she always did. I screamed at the top of my voice at them and ran toward my room. I woke up afraid.

I slept again from 9:00 am to 11:00 am after that. Felt depressed. Wet my bed during the horrible parent dream. I am so tired I want to sleep all day. I forced myself to get up and get ready for work. Justin called but I didn't answer.

I probably had the parent dream because my mom paid to re-hook up my phone. She used a credit card secretly without Jim knowing. He has always hated giving a penny to me. It rarely happens that mom helps me out financially. Mom said not to pay her back. I felt disgusted that Jim would get mad about giving the phone company $200 to get my phone connected again.

I found out that Justin is going hiking with Jessica. Why didn't he want me to go?

SEPTEMBER 6, 1999

My mom called me, I hung up accidentally so I called her back. She wanted to check up on my psychiatric care. She was drunk and rambling. I felt like I used to feel as a teenager. It was 9:30 pm here, so it was only 6:30 pm there. I went to sleep afterwards. All through the night I had dreams in which I went up to people that I know and have known and they were all too busy to do anything with me. No one had time for me, even old friends and acquaintances. Yeah, like that is a lot. Really, how many old friends do I have? Exactly. Zero.

Later in the dream I walked into a dark classroom. The students were watching a film but I didn't notice this at first. Justin and Craig, a gorgeously bisexual architect at work, both started yelling at me to get the hell out, to leave them alone, that they didn't want me around. I went back out through the door and collapsed in a heap, crying hysterically. Craig came over to ask if I was all right. He then said it was best if I left. I felt like everyone doesn't want to spend time with me. Like reality.

SEPTEMBER 10, 1999

Self first. Love self. Reorganizing. Communication. Not there. Evasive. Feel like separated from other people. Changed, moody.

SEPTEMBER 11, 1999

Horrible stressful event last night. I am still so frightened I can barely concentrate. I went to sleep around 11:30 pm since I've felt sleepier lately. I didn't want to go to bed too early. I tossed and turned but finally fell asleep. Around 1:30 am, I was awoken by Keelie. She was crouching on my bed, on the window side, and growling in an unnatural way. It took me a minute to get oriented but when I realized that Keelie was growling at the window, I sat upright and froze in terror. That is when I heard the window being jiggled from outside. Someone was trying to open it! There is no light on the back side of the apartment complex, so I couldn't see a shadow through the blinds, but it sounded as if he had a screwdriver and was trying to pry the window open! Luckily, I bolted my window shut that night. The landlord had drilled holes into the metal window casing into which I could screw a bolt preventing the window from being opened from the outside. Fred did that only months ago because of the Northside Rapist who has been stalking the area. Up until that time, the window could be easily opened from the outside.

I know it sounds like a movie, but I was literally frozen in terror. I couldn't move, scream, get up and run to the phone, nothing. Keelie's growls grew louder as the man struggled with the window with more fervor. Keelie crouched next to me offering her protection. I could feel the room spinning, my breath coming short and difficult. I must have been having a panic attack. The man began to jiggle the window even harder and the fear of it breaking seemed to shake me out of my trance. I got to my shaky feet and tiptoed into the living room, searching around me for a weapon. I didn't dare turn my back to the window. There was no light on inside, so he probably didn't know that I was moving. I backed out of the bedroom and closed the bathroom door since there was a window looking directly into my apartment in there. From the living room, he couldn't see me through the window but he could through the bathroom. I was too afraid to close the bedroom door so that I could calculate where he was at all times. Keelie stayed close by my side.

I turned on the kitchen light and rummaged through the kitchen drawer and got my claw hammer. Then I spotted the mallet leaning against the wall. It was much heavier and would do much more damage than the hammer, although I didn't want the man to break in. I didn't want to struggle for my life or stop the predator from raping me. He was known to carry a gun.

My mind was still fuzzy from the fear and everything felt like slow motion. I could no longer hear him hitting and jiggling the bedroom window. I was standing in my nightgown, wondering if I should call the police or not when to my horror, I could hear him trying to open my bathroom window! The door was closed, but I definitely could hear him trying to pry it open. That was enough. I grabbed the phone and backed up toward the front door, ready to flee if I had to. I called 911 and told the woman my name, address and the current situation. The bathroom window was still trying to be pried as I spoke to her. The operator kept me on the line until she contacted an officer in the area. She told me that an officer would be here in ten minutes or less and that she wanted me stay on the line with her. That was fine with me.

I don't know if he could hear me talking on the phone, but the window jiggling stopped. I turned off my kitchen light so he couldn't see where I was at and crouched in the hallway, listening for any noise from the back. Either it was a fast ten minutes or the police arrived very quickly, but I heard a knock at my door. A vision went through my mind of the predator trying to trick me by knocking on the door. I tiptoed to the door and peered through the peephole. To my relief there were two officers standing by my front door. I quickly opened the door and let them in. When I said that the man was in the back, one of the officers immediately went to the back of the complex.

The rest is a blur. The extreme paralyzing fear had left me exhausted and mentally numb. The police searched the area for about half an hour. One of the officers came back and said that he found a wrapped condom dropped on the ground by my window and saw a used condom nearby as well. From the disruption of the leaves, he said it was fresh. The officer suggested that I get the landlord to install a light in the back of the building since it is pitch black back there. A policeman gave me his card and wrote a case number on it and said to call him if I see or hear anything else. They left me alone again.

I couldn't sleep in my bed, I was too petrified, so I pulled the comforter into the living room, got my sleeping bag and made a palette on the floor where I could sleep without being seen from any window. I put the hammer, mallet and phone right by my palette. I laid there for hours unable to sleep, listening to every footstep and noise. I kept waking up every half hour and didn't get a good night's sleep. I gave up and have been huddled here in my living room, afraid to move. Thank God Keelie woke me up. She is so protective of me.

SEPTEMBER 16, 1999

A hand print seems to have appeared on my bedroom window. I called the policeman who gave me his card and asked if someone could dust for fingerprints, since they didn't do that the first time. He said he will send someone over tomorrow after work. I have still been sleeping in the living room. I have too much fear in the bedroom and I keep the bathroom door closed when I am not using it. I don't want him to look in and see what I am doing. He probably won't return, but I don't know. The stress is taking its toll on me. I have started showing signs of rashes and hives on my body. I made a doctor's appointment so he can give me something for the itching.

SEPTEMBER 19, 1999

The print turned out to be a smudged handprint on the window. An officer dusted the window pane pretty well but she said that the handprint appeared to be rather old. Due to the smear patterns in the dust on the exterior of the window, she thought the perpetrator wore gloves. If it was the Northside Rapist, then he would be wearing gloves. The officer was nice but nothing more could be done. I don't want any woman going through that horrible fear. I have never been so frightened in my life. I am not exaggerating. It would be a tortuous death to be raped and murdered. The fear I feel would permeate my brain, unrelenting. I can even envision an intruder breaking through the window, binding me before I could get a weapon, raping me, choking me, killing me. I see this image every time I close my eyes. It is difficult to concentrate at work.

I have called the landlord about installing a light out back. It still hasn't been done and I haven't heard anything. Holly, whose father is a lawyer, told me to fax them a letter with the police case number and request immediate action. I wasn't going to at first but she kept bugging me about it all day Monday and Tuesday, so I did what she said today. Maybe a light will be installed now.

I went to Doctor Marcus, that wonderful General Practitioner that I see, and he said that I have shingles. I had no idea what shingles actually was, but it is brought on by stress to someone who has had chicken pox in the past. I had a case when I was three. It has been affecting my nervous system and I must be careful not to let it get more aggravated. On top of the shingles, my bipolar has been getting worse. The medications aren't working well and I feel so depressed. The current situation is making it come back.

Susan from work asked me to move in with her but she lives in Marietta, much too far for driving with an undependable car every day. Right now, I am only 4 miles from work and on a direct bus line to the office. Plus, Susan has two cats. I don't want a bad experience for Keelie.

SEPTEMBER 21, 1999

The light out back was installed. It is pretty bright so it should stop people from hanging out back there, jacking off.

SEPTEMBER 30, 1999

Very up and down. Still sleeping in my living room. Asked to stay with Justin a few days to get some rest but he made some excuses. He did let me sleep over one night. No more than that.

OCTOBER 1, 1999

I am feeling depressed and manic. I went outside and cried at work, feeling like I have no friends. The lack of peaceful sleep is taking its toll on my well being. I stupidly went out alone until 3:00 am even though the predator may be out there. I went back to roaming the bars again, getting free drinks and adoration. I didn't bring anyone home this time. I had several opportunities to be with a man, since I had several drinks purchased for me. I was tested and don't have AIDS or a venereal disease, so I don't want to get one now. I've been worried about the Boy I brought home on

New Year's Eve, so I finally got up the nerve to be tested. I really need to be more responsible, although I'm out walking alone, with an ID and a few dollars in my pocket. My ripped Levis are the only pants I wear anymore.

OCTOBER 2, 1999

I felt generally happy until no one called. I have been getting little sleep. The shingles are getting better with medication. I am sleeping in my bed again, although I have the mallet right by my bed and the hammer under my pillow. I also moved my bed away from the window.

OCTOBER 3, 1999

I called Justin but no one is home. It makes me so lonely. I went for margaritas alone, but before I got out of the apartment complex, I ran into the sexy neighbors smoking a blunt in the courtyard. I was invited to join in with the blunt smoking. They also gave me a beer. I had sex with the extremely sexy boy in my apartment building. He is about 6'3", muscular, and has tattoos from his neck down. He's gorgeous. The sex was quick and unrewarding, unfortunately. He practically kicked me out afterwards, or at least his roommate did. His roommate doesn't like me after I laughed at his baseball superstitions. He is a Yankee's fan and thinks I am bad luck for the games. How stupid. Maybe I'll get a little sleep now.

OCTOBER 4, 1999

Very negative. Feel like no one wants to do anything with me. Especially group outings. I'm not invited. Didn't cry, not really depressed, just agitated, felt like breaking things, yelling. Slept like the dead. Wet the bed.

OCTOBER 5, 1999

It is technically October 6. I need to ask my doctor about medication, Vaproate. I think I am having rapid cycling again, swinging viciously from deep depression to frenzied manic. I am taking Depicote, 500mg and Prosak 20mg. I have such guilt over sleeping, no, fucking so many men. I wish I could stop. Sunday I slept with someone again. It was very unsatisfying and he made me feel cheap. He didn't know that I am educated. I picked him up in a Buckhead bar in my usual way, by purchasing a drink and sitting alone, waiting for some man to approach me. He was like all those teenage fucks years ago. He actually told me not to tell anyone about this because he has two girlfriends. I don't care. Who am I going to tell? I fucked him anyway because he is so damn cute and well endowed. He meant nothing to me. But, shit! It was only about 5 hours after church with Kelly.

I only go to church with Kelly because I want to have a female friend. I don't care about church. It is typically full of shit, although there are many different types of religion, so I should keep an open mind and look into other possible churches. I know Kelly is trying to help me find religion, so something can help me out of this funk. She grew up religious, like so many people. Kelly is teaching me about the Bible and gave me a student Bible to read which is easier than King James Bible. She gives me reading assignments, which is kind of fun, reminiscent of college, then we have intellectual discussions about passages I read. I question so many of the stories, I'm probably getting on her nerves.

Tonight, or was it last night now, I was reading *Moby Dick* at home, but wanted to be around real, in the flesh people, so I went out again for a few hours. I like eaves-dropping on conversations in the bar. The discussions are superficial and bland, talking about football, baseball and beer. I didn't see an easy target last night, and didn't feel like interacting with another man, so I went home.

Some hours I am in my manic cycles while other nights I slip into depression and sleep like the dead. During the manic nights I can't sleep. I embarrassingly wet the bed again. I had so many vivid dreams but I can't remember them now so they must not have been too vivid. I might think of them later. I've been listening to a cd of Adagios for an hour. So beautiful, so sublime, although they are kind of depressing. I had a difficult day at work today, Tuesday. I found it hard sitting still and concentrating. I feel that I am so damn bored I want to scream!

I wandered into the 8:00 pm Peachtree Christ Church Emotions Anonymous meeting. My therapist suggested I attend some group meetings. It really wasn't my scene, so if it isn't court ordered, I'm not doing it. I sometimes attend AA meetings which have larger groups of people than the Emotions Anonymous meetings, which have a few sad individuals, too few in number to feel like just listening and not sharing all of the time.

The old man Joe and I are becoming good friends. He is my neighbor who laughed at my Chrysler Lebaron convertible because he said that is one of the biggest lemons in car history. I think he's right because it has given me problems. Nothing major, just small things so far, but they are getting expensive. I often hang out with him, watch tv, he gets me completely stoned, and we talk about whatever government plot is currently being hatched. He is very paranoid about the Illuminati, which is something I only heard about on the *X-Files*. I talked about how broke I always am, so Joe said if I'd wash his dishes every day, he'd pay me $50 a month. That's actually easy money. He eats some packaged foods and I wash the dishes.

I think Joe may be bipolar, too. He is an interesting, intelligent man but not easy on the eyes. He is missing most of his teeth, doesn't brush his hair, and goes shirtless most of the time. He also has plaque psoriasis which looks more painful than it is, but that's why he goes shirtless, to let air get to his psoriasis. It isn't anything sexual this time, just an interesting person to speak to on a regular basis. He told me that I was special, intelligent, beautiful, loved my piano playing and said that I am very kind and he usually doesn't trust people and he hesitated to trust me. He has not completely yet. He had an abusive home life. Now it is Wednesday morning 1:45 am. I will try to go to sleep now. Until later.

OCTOBER 12, 1999

I am back to my isolated self, like all the years of my past. I always think things will be different, find some friends, then lose them because of my bizarre behavior. I don't know if that is the reason, or if they find me boring to talk to since I have a problem with small talk.

I have nothing else to do so I organized my closet again until 3:00 am or 4:00 am. I forced myself to sleep. I'm having difficulty falling asleep. I listened to my relaxation tape and it helped.

OCTOBER 13, 1999

My addled mind only allowed me about 3 hours of sleep, although I feel calm and positive today. A bit hyper. I started my period so I should feel like shit but don't. I had a deadline at work and didn't panic. I'll do what I can do. I feel very content. I was very productive at work today, which is a rarity. Maybe my medication is helping after all. I actually went to lunch with Ted. He asked me for the first time.

Some people from work were meeting for drinks after hours and I was invited. I stupidly told Mark from work that I was manic then I kissed him and invited him over when some of us from work were having drinks. He didn't kiss me back or come over. I didn't apologize although I should. I should be embarrassed but I don't feel like troubling myself with guilt. He treats me with respect unlike most other guys.

The following is a quote from *I Shot Andy Warhol*:

"Dear Diary,

I try to get what I want. I always have found that socially unacceptable people make better lovers because they are more sensitive. I can be happy and fulfilled. I will never doubt it. I cannot afford to. Each thought, each movement tuned to some great, moving force. - Candy Darling"

OCTOBER 14, 1999

Justin told me, when I needed him most through my medication change, that he and I need to go our separate ways. He is my best friend, so I thought. I did freak out over the weekend. I get so frustrated with all of my "friends" not inviting me out in group activities. No one calls me and no one invites me places. What is wrong with me? I take my medication to help with being bipolar, but what is the use if people still don't want to hang around "the freak." What hurts the most is Justin never invites me with his group of friends. He and I do very little together and I got upset over this.

I went over to my neighbor, Joe to visit. He always has weed so we drink and get stoned while watching tv. Joe is on the fringe of society like me, and sees conspiracies everywhere. He shows me websites which claim to know the truth about so many political scandals, wars, and news stories. I read it to humor him, because most of the stories are far fetched. It's like living in the *X-Files* and the smoking man is really out there changing history. Joe is big into the Illuminati which he claims goes back hundreds of years. Some of the stuff seems possible, but over all, I think his obsession is a bit strange. Who am I to judge, though?

OCTOBER 20, 1999

I have missed 5 days of work since Justin told me again over the phone that he doesn't want to see me at all for a long while. I was devastated again because I thought he would change his mind once I delved into therapy, seeking the help he insisted I receive. I went out drinking alone at the bars when I felt that I had enough. I didn't want to use a man for drinks and slip out the back door. I had the urge to escape, so I ran home as fast as I could, barely being able to see in the darkness, when I fell so hard on the pavement that I tore my pants and have a deep wound on my knee and both hands. My hands look like a stigmata. I just don't care anymore but don't want to bring home any men.

My dreams are bizarre and cruel. My "friends" were all standing around me, their faces melted like wax, while they were laughing at me. Another night, I dreamt that I was in an enormous yacht, my friends were swimming, we were all laughing, enjoying ourselves. A few at a time, my friends swam over to another boat and didn't come back. The boat that I was in turned into a rubber raft and began deflating with me and my mom trapped inside. The waters turned into white water rapids. My mom tried to save us by jumping onto a passing dock. She couldn't grab the boat and I was swept away. I went through alligator infested waters as I was sinking. I had to throw the alligators off of me as they crawled over each other to get to me. There were so many alligators that I couldn't look in all directions at once and they surrounded me. Suddenly, I was awake. I have a lot of alligator nightmares, don't I?

Last night I filmed our Halloween movie with some guys from work. It was the most fun I've had for a long time. We did an architectural version of *The Blair Witch Project*, called *The Baer Witch Project* (named after an architect in the office) making architectural deadlines seem so ominous. I played the only female role. I did a good job. I was pleased Justin recommended me for the part. I even did the solo crying scene that the woman did in the movie, but went into a bathroom stall. I cried and said that I couldn't make the deadline and was afraid. I went on and on, making it like the movie. The guys said I did a good job at improvising. Acting isn't a problem for me. I LOVE to act. I wish I had gone into acting instead of interior design. Maybe I would be mentally healthier and be able to become someone else.

God help me through the next few weeks. I am off Depecote because I got a body rash from it that itches terribly. I have to go a week without medication until the rash is gone, then try yet another medication. I am afraid because I have no friends around for support. I am alone. My worst fear.

OCTOBER 22, 1999

More horrible dreams. I was in a swamp, trying to get onto land. There were other people, whom I did not know, yet they seemed familiar. There were alligators and snakes. Poisonous water moccasins. The snakes attacked us all. I was bitten twice, once on my left forefinger and once on my right arm. Other people were stricken with poison as I crawled on shore screaming and trying to shake off the snakes which held on fast. The poison felt like fire in my veins. I was in excruciating pain, then my muscles became extremely stiff. I laid on my stomach suffering in silent agony. The pain wouldn't stop. I laid as still as possible so the poison wouldn't course through my veins as quickly. There were other people who were in extreme suffering as well.

We were all suddenly in a school bus. A tornado was spotted ahead, a little to our left. I knew the bus couldn't outrun it, so I told everyone to get under the seats. Keelie was scared and alone on the back seat. I crawled to Keelie, grabbed her and got under a seat. The bus tipped over and skidded but we were all safe, just frightened. Next, I was back at the swamp. This time, in addition to the snakes, there were alligators and a very large tiger. To get out of the swamp, I had to go by the tiger. There were some people around, including my mom.

By the side of the road a person was selling jewelry so I stopped to buy some. The tiger, who was laying down between me and safety, ran toward me. I was afraid, but the tiger turned out to be just a tiger cub who jumped up on my lap.

I haven't been to work all week and my phone has been disconnected again. My rash is slowly going away. I must reconnect up my phone. Even before my phone was shut off yesterday, no one had called but collection people. I am behind in paying for my credit cards. Joe suggested I file bankruptcy. I hadn't considered that option but may have to since I will have my student loans coming due soon. I really shouldn't miss so much work. It is difficult getting there with my sleep schedule all over the place. I need a phone first. I can't do anything until I go to the phone company and get it reconnected, again. This will make it the fourth time it's been disconnected.

OCTOBER 23, 1999

My neighbor, Joe, knocked on my door today. He couldn't call since my phone is disconnected. He asked me to come over because he had something to tell me. It sounded important so I went. Joe said that last night, when he was laying in bed watching television, he heard someone slide open his bathroom window. Joe keeps a Magnum by his bed so he grabbed it as he got out of bed. He heard a shampoo bottle fall from the window sill. As soon as he heard that, he began swearing at the motherfucker, telling him that he was going to shoot his mother fucking head off. By the time Joe got to the bathroom window there was no one there. That was around 2:00 am. The reason he told me was because his bathroom window is right next to mine. The intruder may have gotten the windows mixed up. The Northside Rapist just recently struck again and Joe swears that it was he who tried to get me again. After all, Joe has lived in that apartment for 15 years and no one has ever tried to break in before. Even with the new light installed back there, someone tried to get in. I wonder if it could be the predator. I don't know. Could it just be a coincidence?

After speaking with Joe I went around to the back of the apartment building. I counted over windows, finding mine. Since our apartments are right next to each other, our bathrooms are back to back. The windows are only a foot apart. It is true, someone could have mistaken the window and went one too many over. It could be. Just to be safe, I am going to put a palette in the living room again to sleep on. I don't want to be in that bedroom right now. Just when the fear was melting away it comes back like a stabbing bolt. I feel almost paralyzed with fear again. Has he been watching me? I must be more cautious again.

OCTOBER 25, 1999

I am socializing with Ryan from work. I think I love him. It is just a feeling I have. He is such a nice person. He just graduated from college so he is younger than me. He has a lot of friends, which is a good sign to being a normal person. I enjoy hanging out with him. He has come over to my place and we talked and listened to music. I actually was talking. He takes Marta to work instead of driving. It is better for the environment. He says he has the series *Twin Peaks* that he's watching with a friend. When he's done, he said we can start watching it together. I'd love to since the show is supposed to be curiously bizarre.

I had horrible dreams last night. Mostly about being chased or raped. I was so afraid of going to work. I was tired but couldn't sleep. Finally slept, but horrible nightmares. I was in a city hiding. I was a Jew during World War II. The Nazi's found me. I was tortured and ended up being led to the gas chamber. I was so frightened the entire time because I knew bad things were going to happen to me. Many other nightmares all night but I can't remember them. I woke up scared and sweating even though it was cold in the apartment. I'm going to the doctor now. Keelie has been very affectionate. Whenever I woke up from nightmares she was there. Like Saturday night with Ryan. I love laying next to him. My tv is in the bedroom, so we lay on my bed to watch it. We haven't had sex, he is the type who likes to wait. He is so smart and talented. I hope I don't scare him away by wanting to spend every day with him. I'll try and give him space. I didn't tell him how scared I am to go back to work. I wasn't scared while he was here. I am now.

I was so restless on Sunday when I was by myself. I tried keeping busy, but I feel angry, restless and agitated. I took a walk in the neighborhood, away from the bars, and felt much better.

NOVEMBER 1, 1999

My part in *The Baer Witch Project*, a parody of *The Blair Witch Project* was accepted as a classic. It was a huge hit in the office at the Halloween party. Baer is an architect from Europe whose hairstyle looks like A Flock Of Seagulls. A huge sweep-over. He acts like he is God's gift to humanity. We pretended that a project was due in a stressfully short period of time. Ryan, another Ryan then the one I've been socializing with, edited the film and did a great job. It was hilarious. I asked for a copy. I hope I get one.

After work, Susan had a Halloween party at her house in Marietta last night so I got dressed up as a hippy and went by myself. Justin and Ryan both had other plans. There were people from work, so it was pretty fun. I even bought oregano and rolled some "joints" and put some of my medication in baggies, taking them out occasionally and asking people if they wanted "an upper, man." Two people thought that they were real and said yes but I told them it was only Tylenol. The joints looked real, too. It was fun. I didn't want to drink too much because of the long drive, but had many jello shooters. They actually got me intoxicated. I ate the food, too. Food is necessary when drinking. I don't ever want to have a drinking blackout with people I work with. I try not to have that situation anymore. Susan asked if I needed to stay the night, but I wasn't very drunk by the end of the evening and went back home.

I got to my apartment around 2:00 am. Where I park, there isn't much light and I suddenly became terrified. I felt like someone was watching me. I sat in my car with it running for a few minutes, looking around to make sure it was safe. I still had the feeling of being watched. I didn't have a weapon at hand so I quickly turned off the car, locked the car door and was about to run to my apartment when I saw a man dressed in black with a black toboggan hat duck behind the dumpster only 7 feet away! I saw him. I know I did. It wasn't just paranoia. I ran to my door, unlocked it as fast as possible, and got into my apartment. Not only did I lock my door but I pushed furniture up against the door. I closed the bathroom door and remade a palette to sleep on in the living room. I had just started sleeping in my room again because my back was starting to hurt.

Is that him again? The Northside Rapist sketches look just like the man I saw; a man wearing a black toboggan and black clothes. Has he come back for me? Did he target me before and still wants me? The fear is back again. I wish he would be caught. Does he live near me and periodically check on me? There are so many apartment complexes nearby that it is a real possibility. What a nightmare!

DECEMBER 17, 1999

Justin bought me a ticket to go to Arkansas for Christmas with him! I can't believe it. He has been telling me that I can't go with him but he ends up buying me a ticket. I hope this will heal our friendship. I am so relieved and happy that I cried when he told me. Maybe it was his mom's doing. I don't know. I am grateful, none the less. I wasn't looking forward to being alone for Christmas, especially with that stalker out there. Who knows if he is still watching me. I feel like I am being watched so often now. I think paranoia has set in.

DECEMBER 30, 1999

I just got back into town on the 29th when Holly invited me to dinner for my birthday last night. I can't believe she remembered! I met her at the posh Harry and Son's restaurant which serves excellent sushi. There were several people there. Justin is still in Arkansas, I came back earlier, alone. But strangely enough Jessica was there. That was a shock. Also, Kelly, Dawn P. (the nice Dawn), Ted, and Keith (Holly's fiancé). It was so sweet of them! I got so many great gifts. I wasn't expecting that at all. However, the evening started off with a shock. As I was getting into my car at 7:15 pm (for a 7:30 pm dinner) I saw that man duck behind the dumpster again. He was wearing black with that black toboggan. It gets dark early because of the time of year, but I definitely saw a man move from in front of the dumpster to behind it. I started my car, locked the doors and backed up, searching the shadows for a sign of someone being there. I couldn't see anyone. I was never expecting to see him again, especially that early in the evening! The other events have been between 1:30 am and 2:00 am. Did he see me come back into town? Was he stalking me again? I didn't tell Holly or anyone else what I saw. They probably wouldn't believe me. I got a look of disbelief from Holly last time I told her of the man ducking behind the dumpster on Halloween night. I know, it sounds far fetched. But what if he does live nearby? He may be able to see me from his apartment. The Northside Rapist has still been active and his sketch is on the news. I am sure that Holly thinks that I have paranoia from being bipolar. I do have paranoia. Why would a tenant, throwing away their trash, hide behind a dumpster? There is nothing behind the dumpster except the shallow woods behind my apartment complex. No one would go that way because it isn't an easy route. There is a 3 foot wall you have to climb up before getting to the wooded area. It just doesn't make any sense. I am not going to call the police again unless I see something more definite or he tries to break in again. They will just come out here, look around, find nothing, and go away. I will just be cautious.

CHAPTER 22

2000: AGE 31

JANUARY 3, 2000

I never told you about my Christmas excursion. We stayed in Little Rock with Mike for a few days, Justin's ex-boyfriend. Mike had a sweet girl over named Melanie. I was attracted to her but nothing happened. I found out afterwards that she thought I was attractive, too. I guess it wasn't meant to be. We had a good time, going to a bar only blocks from Mike's downtown apartment. I had a great time.

Justin went to stay two nights with his friend Heath from Tulsa again, but I was prepared for it this time. He informed me about it before we even left to Arkansas. Dorothy and I went shopping and ate lunch. I had a good time with her, talking and playing cards. Her step-daughter, 9 year old Ashley, was there and she did some homemade ceramics that can be kilned in the oven at home. One of those kid sets. She made me a lopsided ashtray. It was very sweet of her. Ashley's mother is a freak, though. Ashley is all about the Spice Girls and is collecting their dolls. She already has Posh and just got Ginger. Ashley keeps saying that I look like Ginger Spice. The freaky thing is, her mom won't let her take the doll out of the packaging. She didn't let her take out Posh, either. Her mom says that the doll will be worth more in the future if it isn't opened. The poor girl can't even play with her own dolls! That is the strangest thing I have ever heard. Will the Spice Girl dolls really be worth that much money in the future? Come on, lady. Let the kid have fun and dress up the dolls.

I didn't do anything for New Year's Eve. People had plans and I didn't want to interfere. I went to dinner by myself and made some drinks at home and hung out with Keelie.

I have been doing pretty well this week. I feel much calmer and am relieved that Justin and I are friends again, even if it is on a tentative basis. I have been trying so hard to be normal around him. I know that I can get out of control sometimes.

No sign of that stalker again. Thank God.

APRIL 23, 2000

A small victory, of sorts. Justin invited me to his and Jessica's Easter party. I was allowed the privilege of arriving hours early in order to help Justin set up trays of delicious hors d'oeu-vres, strategically placed scented candles and flowers throughout the house, porch and yard. Jessica was running errands, collecting alcohol, mixers, and other party necessities. So, it appears I was invited over to the house during a time frame when Jessica wasn't there, on purpose. I am sure it was Jessica's request so she wouldn't have the "torment" of my contemptuous bipolar company. I was being appeased, not invited because of our endearing friendship, but allowed to join in Justin's life after I had been a good girl and stopped "stalking".

Any joy I had for the Easter party quickly evaporated. I stood in the kitchen, numbly putting flowers in a vase, feeling hollow inside again, seeing life through a movie camera, not my own eyes. I had been abandoned, again, and manipulated. The pain and humiliation was almost too much to bear, especially when Jessica stopped by for three minutes to unload some party items, whispered a few words to Justin in the corner of the kitchen about selecting music for the night and quickly leaving the house again after hugging Justin and telling him how happy she was that they were roommates. It was done on purpose, it had to be. Cruel fucking bitch. Justin seems oblivious to Jessica's obvious manipulation and hatred of me because I am bipolar like her unloving, uncaring, drugged mother.

I had to keep a friendly, happy face so I wouldn't be rejected outright. I went to the solace of James' super hip upstairs bathroom to cry. I tried to muffle my deep wrenching sobs so no one could hear. It should be me living with Justin, not Jessica. Justin and I were best friends until she showed up and greedily kept Justin all to herself, poisoning his mind against me.

The Easter party turned lively and crowded, Jessica swing dancing with a man from work. I needed a smoke and I wasn't allowed to smoke in their house. I threaded my way through the popular crowd to the front door and settled myself in the shadows of a large protective bush in the front yard. I stayed at Jessica and Justin's house until late at night, almost enjoying the pain my exclusion was causing me. I wasn't going to give in to her. I wanted to show Jessica that I was here to stay, she couldn't get rid of me so easily.

It didn't turn out that way. Jessica flitted amongst her friends, laughing at a joke here, swing dancing there, being the center of attention, center of life and all things living. I was skulking in the shadows, talking to no one because I don't know how to just talk to someone. My borderline personality disorder is to blame, the doctor says. Bipolar with a borderline personality disorder. Sounds like a concoction for disaster. It is. My life is a disaster. I live like a rat in the gutters, on the fringe of society. I want to be the happy girl who attracts the normal people, people with dogs and jobs and mortgages. I want to be the flame for the moths. In truth, I am only a small sickly green flicker that attracts the misfits and freaks who are also shunned by society. I was completely alone at this party, talking to no one. No one wanted to talk to the creepy, quiet girl smoking alone behind a bush.

I had to leave. I walked slowly to my car, no one noticing my absence. I hoped Justin would notice, but he didn't. I could still hear the upbeat laughter of Jessica and her life-loving groupies. I hate them but long to be them. I didn't say goodbye to anyone because there was no one around me to say goodbye to. Justin was busy with his guests, making sure everyone was entertained, refreshing their drinks, lighting cigarettes.

Tears streaked my face as I drove away from the candle lights, dancing, laughing and singing. I wasn't hysterical, just crying with no emotion. I don't belong there. I belong in the gutters with the working girls.

MAY 20, 2000

No sign of the Northside Rapist. There haven't been any attacks here for a while. The police didn't catch him so he must have either moved away or got arrested. I hope he got arrested. I wouldn't want him to move into another city only to start stalking again. Maybe I can get some peace now.

My medication gets better and worse. It will work well for a few months and then stop working. I either get manic or depressed. I had to start on new medication which makes me suffer with side effects. It is difficult to concentrate at work. I get so distracted and forget what I am doing. I don't want people to know how difficult it is getting, but I think Liz can tell. She has asked if I have been alright.

Sometimes at lunch, I just walk around and cry. Few people want to be around me and I can't blame them. My moods will swing so drastically. I am happy one minute and in tears the next. Sometimes I talk up a storm and other times I can't think of anything to say and sit quietly, boring the other person to death. I feel so needy and can't help but obsessively email Justin or Craig. I am starting to anger Craig so much that he came to my desk one day and told me to leave him alone. Not to email him so much. I felt so embarrassed.

I have been seeing Ryan, though. We started watching *Twin Peaks* or go have coffee somewhere. Sometimes we just hang out. He doesn't seem put off by me. I try and act normal. Sometimes I get so obsessed about one idea and I can't get it out of my head. I hatch some stupid plan and bug someone to death, trying to get them to do whatever plan I have devised. Like with Craig, he said once that he wanted to paint me. Now, I keep bugging him about it so much that he will never paint me, forcing him to tell me to leave him alone. We were talking about going to Amsterdam next year for Christmas since he goes frequently, but he has told me that he doesn't want to go with me if I act like this. The only way I can go now is to straighten up my act. But we would need to buy tickets soon so they aren't too expensive. I think I lost my chance of going to Europe. I really couldn't afford it, anyway.

MAY 30, 2000

I'm still seeing a therapist, which is going only moderately well. She recommended that I tell people I'm bipolar. I also got the idea from Patty Duke's autobiography, *A Brilliant Madness*, which she put down all of her darkest secrets in a book. I thought that was a fantastic idea, so I got the notion in my head that when I went to work, I emailed everyone in the office, every person at work, that I am bipolar and gave a brief description of the disorder. I got mixed reviews by people from work. Some people said I was brave while others ignored me completely. I knew I made a mistake afterwards and regretted my stunt. When I told my therapist, she was horrified and asked why I did it. I thought she wanted me to, I was so confused. Now everyone knows I'm bipolar with a borderline personality disorder, which I felt compelled to also describe. Going to work is even worse than before. I'm like some freak. Nice going.

JUNE 16, 2000

Gloria from work has strongly urged me to quit my job. I feel devastated. I haven't been fired, but since I am on disability income, she suggested that I try and get Social Security Disability. It looks like I won't be able to work full-time any more. The strain is too much on me psychologically. I feel like such a weak person! Gloria told me of an obscure regulation stating that my company stock becomes vested if I am permanently disabled while employed under 5 years. I will get the $30,000 distributed to me over the next 5 years, starting next March. That is good news. It was very kind of Gloria to tell me about that. She didn't have to and I wouldn't have known the difference. It will help in the future, but not right now. I am completely broke, paying my rent and letting the electricity, gas and phone get cut off on a regular basis. I can't afford to pay all of my bills on the disability income I have from TVS. Gloria has been so helpful, and so has my boss, Liz. No one seems to hold me any ill will. That makes me feel much better. It still doesn't stop me from feeling like a failure. I had it all and lost it.

I have become bipolar and my life is not my own. I am betrayed by my own mind. What will become of me? I don't want to sit around the apartment on disability all of my life. I didn't work that hard through college to end up destitute and alone. It greatly saddens me that I will no longer be a part of the enormous creative wheel of TVA. I am so proud of the projects that I was a part of. Especially working on the conference center. There are no favorites, there are only promotions based on experience and hard work. I know that my work was more architecturally based there, but I was happier to be part of a team.

There is good and bad at TVA, but definitely more good than bad. The company often had parties in their conference rooms, invited the most prestigious guest speakers, had informative free luncheons, showed documentaries and pertinent movies during the brown bag lunches, had interaction with the community through Habitat For Humanity art donations (for which I donated artwork every year), amongst the many other benefits. I am sad to leave it behind. What can the future possibly hold for me now?

JULY 14 2000

My mom felt sorry for me and purchased airline tickets to visit her for a week and a half.

Then the Seattle extravaganza! We stayed at the Best Western Executive Inn that was almost under the Space Needle. It was a block away and directly across from the new and thrilling EMP (Experience Music Project) designed by Frank O. Gehry.

One of the first things we did in Seattle was take the monorail to the end of the line, only a mile or so. We went through the heart of Seattle, slicing through a building and hovering over the streets. We got off the monorail and walked in and out of some shops along the streets, going up and down the blocks, perpendicular to the wharf. We perused vintage clothing stores, hippie shops, stopped for an occasional beer at a pub, and generally enjoyed the day. We discovered that the buses were free during the weekdays in Seattle, so we could use them at will. Even to go up a couple of blocks.

My mom and I decided to do the Underground Tour which strolls through the original level of Seattle before a devastating earthquake and fire destroyed it over a hundred years ago.

I've done the underground thing before, but it is such fun. The old saloons, storefronts, sidewalks, and homes are seen in the darkness and kept pristine for prosperity. You can even see the occasional rat flit in and out of the darkness, out of the corner of your eye so you are left wondering whether it was truly a rat or perhaps a suffering soul trapped in the rubble for eternity.

We emerged from the bowels of Seattle, crossed the park and went to a pub to have another beer. Why not, since we are on vacation. Mom and I decided to take the waterfront trolly to Pikes Place where we could meander through the gift shops, thrift stores, and souvenir stores.

Once we tired of that scene, we walked down to get excellent clam chowder and seafood at the nearby Seattle seafood staple, Ivar's Seafood Restaurant. The outside seating was infiltrated by seagulls fighting over every scrap of bread or french fry. Therefore, we sat indoors in the relaxing restaurant overlooking the Puget Sound.

Mom and I decided to walk back to the hotel and take a rest. We actually picked up the wharf trolley (since our tickets were still valid) and got a bit closer to our final destination. Of course we had to traipse up the hill past the Space Needle to the comfort of our room.

We dragged our tired, smelly carcasses back to the hotel where we relaxed with a cigarette and a beer (which mom brought with us and placed into the security of the mini refrigerator). We slept enough to wake up hungry and invigorated. We decided to walk in the opposite direction from downtown, which was go by the Space Needle and turn right. We discovered a bohemian sanctuary of bookstores, Seattle's Best Coffee (which is much more popular than Starbuck's) and pubs. We decided to head over to an English styled pub after perusing a small bookstore.

The English pub was relaxing and a perfect finale for the evening. We consumed some delicious shepherd's pie, guzzled some alcohol, and walked leisurely back to the hotel. The first day was glorious and I felt free, relaxed and invigorated. I long to live in downtown Seattle, but unless

I win the lottery, it ain't going to happen. So few homes in a small area of downtown due to natural construction constraints. We walked from one end of downtown Seattle to the other end in about 40 minutes without rushing. It is a small city proper with congested freeways proving how many people commute to work in Seattle from the suburbs.

The second day was planned for Experience Music Project, or EMP. EMP only just opened this year so I am one of the early visitors to this fantastic musical anthology and history. That museum is mind-blowing and unexpectedly enjoyable. There is a room where you can play instruments and alter the sounds with switches and knobs. There were different rooms going through the history of the electric guitar, being brought to life by a digital audio system that is loaned to you when you walk through the door.

There was memorabilia, posters, records, and a half ton of guitars of every shape and color. Mom was pleasantly surprised by the museum and enjoyed it tremendously. We left after a few hours because of fatigue. We didn't visit the entire thing, but were so tired we got our fill of EMP.

I searched long and hard at the gift shop and purchased a man purse for Ryan and a silver book bag for myself. My mom encouraged me to contact Ryan often, although I would forget and called only a couple of times. We had a coffee in the cafe and rested our aching feet. Mom was complaining about her back and said that she couldn't do much more. I was a bit wistful, thinking of the rooms of EMP we hadn't even seen yet, but reluctantly agreed to leave. I was fairly exhausted and over stimulated mentally, too. It was an intense two nights and almost three days in Seattle. We filled every minute. We even went to the amusement park under the Space Needle and rode the roller coaster and a couple of other old rides. We were too tired and broke to go to the Seattle Science Center. We had been there so many times before that we decided to skip it this time.

Mom and I contemplated going up to visit Jim's mother, Grandma Johnson before heading home, but since that is another couple of hours north toward Canada in Sedro Woolley (where we used to live) we decided to head back to her house. Part of me felt guilt for not visiting Grandma Johnson, but I was exhausted and we didn't really want to stay the night with her. That sounds cruel, I know. I personally can't take too much Lawrence Welk. She loves Lawrence Welk and I have been tortured watching episodes in my childhood.

We went back to Bean to finish out the last two days, gambled and drank at the Bean Bar and Grill. There was no sign of Rob. He lives with his girlfriend and has a baby. It is for the best. Mrs. Mabrey gave me the cold shoulder, although I tried to soften her heart a bit before she left. I succeeded. I would crumble if I saw Rob. I screwed us up before when I visited and didn't return his calls when I returned to Tallahassee. Rob didn't want to be burned twice.

Nothing else of note occurred in Bean except played pool, then darts with Velma, who's still fucking alive, drank beer and gambled on the punch board. I didn't do much gambling since I see it as a useless activity. The odds of winning are so low, so what is the fun of that? You spend money, win once in a while, and spend the money again. Jim shells out the money like candy. I saw twenties being passed to the bartender frequently and heard profanity from Jim's mouth, so I knew he wasn't doing well. Of course not, it is all about statistics. It is just too risky for me. I already have enough vices, I certainly don't need gambling.

AUGUST 13, 2000

I walked up to Fellini's Pizza for some beer in the mid afternoon, spending money I don't have, not intending to pick up any man. I was sipping on my second or third drink, reading *War and Peace*, trying to forget Justin's betrayal, his avoidance of me, his spending all of his time with Jessica. An attractive Italian man and another man were sitting outside on the patio, too, and kept looking at me and obviously talking about me. I was the only other person on the patio. It was a hot day and people were still at work since it was only around 3:30 pm or 4:00 pm. I periodically glanced in their direction, still not intending to go out with any man. Eventually, the other guy (not the attractive Italian) came up to me, introduced himself as John and said that his friend and business partner wants to buy me a drink and that he is very wealthy. I said something like, "that's nice for him" and returned to my reading. I wasn't in the mood.

John went back to his table and probably told the handsome Italian that I blew him off. Shortly, the Italian came to my table and said that his name was Tony and he wanted me to join them at their table. I told Tony that I wasn't there to pick up any man but Tony kept insisting until I relented. I went over to his table and received another drink. Tony and John started telling me about their business, and that John was Tony's accountant because Tony made so much money doing infomercials, or something like that. You know, one of those people who are hired to give pep talks or tells someone else how to win customers. Basically, a salesman. I told them that I wasn't interested in hearing about his money, his cars or his houses. I thanked them for the drink and got up to leave. John apologized and said that he didn't mean any disrespect and asked that I sit down again. I stood there for a minute contemplating my options. I thought, what could it hurt, a few drinks, walk home and not worry about it. I sat down.

We had general conversation, asking what business they were in and telling about my interior design career (omitting the string of problems I have been having). About a half hour later, John shook my hand, said he was glad to meet me and excused himself, saying that he had work to do. It was a lie. I could tell. I was thinking about taking off too, but Tony was an interesting person (after all, he is a salesman) so I stayed for another drink.

I am not sure how long we were there. I had many drinks and remember eating some dinner around sundown. Tony invited me to his condo a mile away. I accepted his invitation and we had lots of great sex. He liked to change positions and went on and on. Truthfully, I would rather it be shorter. It starts to hurt down there.

I can't remember when I fell asleep and what went on exactly. Back to my old stupidity. But Tony really was nice to me, saying how different I am from other women, not wanting gifts from him. I informed him that I am not one to be purchased and he laughed. We were still naked, he said I have a beautiful body, a girl with curves. More sex. Oh, boy. I really did it to appease him, but he is an extremely sexy Italian man.

After the morning interlude, I was invited to go to Pensacola with Tony. He had some business down there and told me that he would pay for all of it when I told him I couldn't afford an airline ticket. Tony tried to persuade me to go, but I told him firmly "no". I didn't like the sound of trusting a stranger taking me to another state and who might think I am a prostitute. I may choose to have sex with men, but I don't want to be a kept woman. I have my pride to think of. I did consent to spending one more day and night with him since I had nothing else to do. I told that I had to feed my cat, shower and change. Tony said to take his car (since I never had one that night). I didn't feel right about taking someone's car so he drove me home and I told him I would come back over to his place in an hour or two. He offered to pick me back up, but I wanted my own transportation. You never know what situation may come up. Tony reluctantly agreed. He is a very big on old fashioned manners, opening my car door, offering to walk me to my apartment.

When I went back over to Tony's condo, we went to out to El Azteca for dinner and margaritas (for me, anyway).

I drank quite a bit and don't remember that night much. However, I did end up staying the night again with Tony and woke up this morning naked. Tony asked me to scratch his back because he gets it shaved every few days by a lady. Tony said he didn't want a hairy back and I agreed. I know, strange conversation. Tony tried again to convince me to fly to Pensacola for a couple of nights, but I still refused. He said again how unusual I am, that he had never met a woman who wasn't after his money. Tony wanted to call me, meet up with me again, but I was being vague. I didn't want a relationship with him. He was very kind and funny, but we really have nothing in common. He wasn't book smart and didn't ooze intelligence. I shouldn't say it that way, he was street smart, but wasn't well read, didn't listen classical or jazz music. I could tell it would drive me crazy to get into another relationship with a man who is more interested in material things. I didn't want to start a doomed relationship. I called it a day and told him I was going back home. Tony seemed to truly like me and asked to call me again. I told him no, even though he pestered me. It was exciting, though. A Pretty Woman experience. I broke down and called Justin. I am so weak. We met for coffee and I told him about my experience. He didn't care. Just said that he didn't have much time. He had to meet Jessica, Justin and the graphic design bitch for dinner. I can't remember her name, but she has intense eyes that seem to never blink. They are always wide open, like she just did 5 lines of cocaine. I wasn't invited, as usual. Well, fuck him. I came back home and watched tv. Another exciting couple of days.

AUGUST 12, 2000

I drunkenly stumbled through the streets and alleys surrounding my apartment and the plethora of bars where I can find lonely losers who want some company. I actually had a life for a short time, but even then, it was an empty cardboard box waiting to collapse upon itself. I worked full time in a lucrative career where I could have thrived if only I knew how to be a real, tangible human being instead of this empty void of nothingness.

I mistakenly signed my name to every grant and loan which was placed before me in college, creating the colossal sum of $108,000 in student loans. Although my rent for my modest one bedroom, one bath apartment in the city is only $580 a month, my looming monstrous loans could no longer be postponed and payment was soon eminent. For only $800 a month over 30 years, I could buy my life back. How could I get in so much debt? I wish I had a mentor, anyone who could have advised me about which forms to sign and not sign. I spent most of my money on chic clothing from Neiman Marcus and Marilyn Monroe Bradford Exchange plates stacked neatly in my closet. I purchased Gucci rain boots and sexy evening gowns that I could never wear because I had no place to wear them.

My looming student loans created cracks in my psyche, strained my mental stability. Cold fear, like ice water flowed through my brain every night, causing me to awaken nightly in sweaty panic. I believe that was the beginning of my most recent mental breakdown, the worse one yet. I was barely scraping by with my bills, ending up filing bankruptcy to put a quick death to my enormous credit card debts and collection agencies where bounced checks were collected with interest. I thought that bankruptcy would clear up enough cash to cover my upcoming student loans. Ha. It didn't even come close. There was no choice but paying whatever I could on the student loans and most likely default on them, destroying the remnants of my credit. I have a Master of Fine Arts but am worth nothing. Never will I have a house, a car built in this century or anything else because of my ignorance and stupidity.

I am now am a suckling pig on society, a fat tick drinking the blood and sweat of the working classes. Living off Social Security Disability Income. I am ashamed of myself and a failure at everything I try to do. My old, drunken neighbor, Joe, is the one who guided me down the disability path, suggesting that might be the answer to my student loan dilemma. Maybe, just maybe, I could get my doctor to sign documents saying that I will never be able to work the rest of my life, never becoming a productive a member of society. Well, Joe was right. With tenacity, I was able to get the paperwork in order and get my $108,000 student loans written off like it was a bad dream. Bankruptcy and failure to pay my student loans. Could I sink any lower? Joe told me that I had beat the system, with the rest of my life ahead of me with no expectations to fulfill. I'd have the whole day to do whatever I wanted.

What did I want to do all day? Sleep after my long nights wandering from bar to bar, drinking until I vomited, fucking nameless, faceless men. I can't remember the name of my latest victim. He was another long-haired bartender at a local bar who fattened me up with hurricanes (the drink) until I stumbled home, leaving my door unlocked for his entry after his shift. As usual, I paid for my first drink, but the rest came freely when he realized that I was an easy target. Promises of sex for two or three strong drinks. I've done it before.

I can't remember coming home, but I remember when he arrived, waking me from my drunken stupor. I was a rubber doll, stripped and fucked. I must have been bent over my le Corbusier chair, again, because there is vomit all over the back side, again, dripping down into the cushions and onto the carpet beneath. I faintly remember him still continuing the brutal fucking while I vomited and pushing me down on the ground to steer clear of the puke. My face was pushed into the carpet as he banged away at me until he was finished.

I don't remember him leaving, but I woke up in the living room, naked from the waist down, my face in the ugly beige carpet. My front door was still unlocked and he left a pair of earrings on the table next to my chair. Ugly, black, bulbous earrings. What was his name? I know where he worked, at any rate. I should be able to track him down to return his earrings.

My hangover is epic. The multiple liquors which make up the Hurricane are brutal. Especially when they are mixed with the three meds I am currently taking to ease the manic states. Of course, I am not supposed to drink alcohol while on the medication. Recently, I have begun having a muscular twitching of my face and shoulder. It is a freaky thing, so I stopped taking the anti-convulsing medicine which is to blame. It is one of the many strange side effects I have encountered over the course of my medicinal experiments. Luckily, no one saw the bizarre face twitching. I don't think I could get free drinks anymore if I was twitching on the barstool.

I still haven't cleaned up the vomit. It is dry now, so cleaning it up will be disgusting. I can do it tomorrow. Today, I feel too nauseous to go anywhere near that stinking mess. If I leave it there long enough, maybe I can just vacuum it up.

I tried calling up the bar and delicately inquiring about the long-haired bartender who worked last night. What was his name? Jim, they think. It sounds like Jim, but there are a couple of men who worked last night with long hair. I explained that this one wore black earrings. Yes, it was definitely Jim. He just filled in for the night and wasn't a regular bartender. The girl didn't know when he would return. Hmmm. I wonder if he told her to say that or if it is true?

Going through my piss-soaked jeans, I found a scrap of paper with "Jim" and a phone number. Bingo. When did I pee in my pants? Did Jim see me with wet pants? Fanfuckingtastic. Pissed my pants and vomited all over myself again. Apparently, it wasn't enough to deter him from fucking my brains out.

I tried calling Jim and got an answering machine. I told him I had his earrings, so if he wanted them back, he could come over. I still haven't heard back from Jim. I called the number 3 or 4 more times, just to be sure he wasn't home. If he was, he probably wasn't answering his phone. Why would he want to ever see a girl who pees her pants and pukes on herself? If I don't hear from him by tomorrow, these ugly earrings are going in the trash. Fuck him, the loser. Ow, my aching head. Wait, Jim thinks I am the loser, doesn't he? That is why he hasn't returned my call. I even tried calling the bar again a few times. Still no Jim. He wasn't working that night and the girl didn't know when he was going to work again. Same girl as before, I think. I have a sneaking suspicion that she is not telling me the truth.

After ten phone calls, I have given up. Jim will ditch his ugly earrings. It wouldn't be worth his time to see my skanky ass again. Jim is cutting his losses. Better to lose the earrings than seeing this crazy bitch again.

What a fool I am, again. It has taken all day for me to realize that Jim doesn't want to ever see me again. Did he use a condom? I can't remember. I never remember. I should keep some around, but haven't purchased any before.

Hungover and humiliated. I feel two notches lower than yesterday, if that is possible. If I get enough energy, maybe I'll go back up to the bar and see if Jim is working. Should I? Probably not, but I am so desperate and lonely, what do I have to lose except my dignity? I lost that a long time ago.

I keep finding myself in this cycle of drunken sex with strangers, forgetting their names, and feeling disgust and remorse. Please help me, someone. Justin? He hasn't returned my calls again. I only get his and Jessica's answering machine and I'm sure she just hits delete. I've lost track of all of the times I've phoned their house. Too many, most likely. I'm probably stalking him again and frightening him away. Am I the predator or the prey? I am so confused and sad.

I should try one last time to find Jim and return his earrings. I'll go up there in a few hours. What is a little more humiliation? I may get a few free drinks out of it.

DECEMBER 30, 2000

I can barely remember Christmas. It was a blur. Just me and Keelie. I ate some Hawaiian bread and smoked salmon. Drank lots of wine. Yay, for me.

CHAPTER 23

2001: AGE 32

JANUARY 12, 2001

Keelie died! I am ripped apart. It came on so suddenly. It was late at night and she started panting and hid under the bed. I knew that something terrible was wrong. I couldn't afford her thyroid medication and now poor Keelie is paying the price. God, why didn't I get that medication by hook or by crook? It is so expensive. I don't have a car anymore so I had to call a taxi. A taxi, in an emergency. It probably cost her her life.

We made it to the veterinarian's hospital that I found closest to the apartment. We were there an hour or two as the doctor listened to Keelie's heart and lungs. She was given something to slow her racing heart and told me to wait in the lobby as they put Keelie in a quiet, dark room. Time didn't register with me. The vet came in and told me that Keelie's heart rate was down and her breathing much more regular.

When I saw Keelie, she was still panting and asked if she was really okay to go home. The young vet told me she was fine, her heart and lungs sounded fine. What a lie. I asked if they could wait a week on the bill until payday, and they said it was fine. I get Social Security Disability now and the deposit was coming in a couple of weeks. I called a taxi again.

Within minutes of returning home, Keelie began acting the same way as before; panting heavily and hiding under the bed. I was out of money! I had no more cash on me for a taxi and no more money in the bank. I haven't had a credit card for ages because no one will give me one, I was so desperate. Keelie needed help but I was broke without a usable car. Two cars which don't run.

I decided to literally run up to Publix and cash a check. I knew it would bounce. I don't usually do that, but since Keelie's life was on the line, I did it. I don't even know what time it was, and was hoping I could still cash a check. I ran up the hill to Publix and saw that Customer Service was closed. Of course, it is pretty late at night. I had a split second to decide, so I chose to purchase some beer and wrote the check for $20 over the amount. I might as well have beer for the horror unfolding before me.

I ran down the hill back to the apartment and Keelie was still in bad condition. I called a taxi and went to grab Keelie. The taxi arrived within minutes and I hadn't caught Keelie yet, so I grabbed her by the scruff of her neck and thrust her into the cat carrier, apologizing to her as I crammed her in.

The moment I got in the taxi, I felt a tremendous "thump" in the carrier. I told the driver the destination; the animal hospital again. I opened the carrier door to check on Keelie and calm her down. She was completely limp. I knew she was gone. I grabbed her, sobbing uncontrollably, and tried mouth to mouth. I also tried shaking her lightly and slapping her on the back. No response. She was gone. I knew it was too late. I couldn't speak but could see the taxi driver looking in his rear view mirror at me with a look of sadness on his face. I appreciated that look. I told him to drive to the hospital anyway. What do you do with a dead cat? I held her the whole way, crying into her fur. I am so sorry that she suffered such pain. I was sorry for shoving her into the carrier so forcefully. I was sorry I didn't have a car or money. I was sorry that the vet told us to go home and didn't help her earlier.

I couldn't speak. I paid the taxi driver and got out. I remember he opened my door and also escorted me to the door of the emergency room. It was so kind of him. Most taxi drivers are callous to help their customers. I whispered a thank you and entered the building carrying Keelie in one arm and the pet carrier in the other.

As soon as I walked in, I saw a little boy, his mom and dad with a small, limp dog. The poor little boy, around 7 or 8 years old, was sobbing hysterically, calling out the name of his deceased dog. He was pleading with the doctor to bring back his dog, but it was too late. I stood there holding my dead cat as their drama unfolded. I couldn't possibly interrupt that poor boy who lost his dog. I waited calmly now, knowing it was over. I was alone.

There seemed to be only the one veterinarian on duty so I had to wait. She noticed that my cat was dead and finally came over. I told her that she died in the taxi. Was her spirit going to find her way back home? I hope so. They took Keelie to be cremated. I couldn't afford the pet burial, plus, it is not necessary. Why does Keelie need her body now? Unless they could bury her in *Pet Cemetery*, there was no purpose. I would never be able to visit her grave. The pain cut too deeply.

The veterinarian asked if I wanted to buy an urn with the ashes. No. Even if I had the money I wouldn't do that. It isn't Keelie anymore. My beloved cat who had been with me since Portland, traveling with me, my only friend. She was always happy to see me, she loved me unconditionally.

The next day, I called Ryan on his cell phone at the recording studio where he was with Trey and friends. Ryan said that he was sorry but it felt hollow. I don't know what I wanted. I can't sleep or eat. I watch tv to numb my brain. I drink and smoke. I wanted Ryan to drive home to see me that night, but he couldn't. He'd be back in a few days. Days. Time doesn't matter anymore. I call to Keelie's spirit so she knows where I am. Please stay with me, Keelie. I love you so much.

SEPTEMBER 11, 2001

I can't believe my ears and eyes! The World Trade Towers were destroyed by two airplanes. Also, one hit the Pentagon! I knew this was coming because of Joe. He had predicted this for months. He said that President G. W. Bush would find some way to start a war with Iraq. It happened. Joe and I both believe that President Bush knew about the attacks ahead of time but let them happen so we could get involved in a costly war over oil. He owns oil wells so of course he wants cheap oil. A couple of thousand died, God bless their poor souls, but not tens of thousands like it could have been if the attack was during the busiest part of the day. The attacks were at a time when the fewest people would be at work. I hate to see the destruction of innocent lives, yet I can understand why foreigners hate the World Trade Organization. Basically, the United States is buying from large corporations overseas who are inexpensive. I hate the WTO, too. The WTO opponents in Seattle were blasted out of town. The government doesn't want to mess with cheap foreign labour. But bombing the towers is beyond all understanding. Airplanes crashing into the towers and Pentagon. I am so sad but can't cry. It's like the pain is so horrible.

I drank early with Joe. We smoked some weed and drank coffee and beer. It is the end of our civilization as we know it. Paranoid Joe suggests that I stock up on supplies and get lots of cash in my house for when the electricity and all electronics are cut. He thinks the satellites will shut down, ATMs will close up shop, gas stations will run dry, and grocery markets will run out of food. He predicts fights and evilness. I said that I would camp out in my tent in the middle of South Dakota if I had to. He agreed. Of course, he has thousands of dollars in his fireproof safe. Also, bags full of weed which he keeps primarily for me, to keep me coming over and to pay me with weed for the cleaning I do around his apartment.

This is fucked up. I can't watch any more. It is too distressing.

SEPTEMBER 29, 2001

I heard a cat meow last night endlessly. The last few weeks I have heard that cat meowing pitifully through the night. I have covered my ears with the pillow, but her cries are heart wrenching. I couldn't take any more and went in search of the cat cries last night. I heard them coming from deep inside some bushes behind my apartment complex. I ran back to my apartment and got some cat food. For some reason, I kept the cat food but threw away Keelie's kitty litter. I often feed stray animals, so I kept it. I put some on the ground, hoping to satisfy that poor crying cat.

As I was waiting for the cat (I had nothing else to do since Justin is a complete prick and won't do anything with me on Friday and Saturday nights) a young couple came out to join me. They told me that they have been trying to capture a little grey kitten for weeks but with no luck. They told me about a tenant in our apartment complex who threw his cat and kittens into the parking lot before he moved. They saw one other grey kitten, as far as they could tell, and were trying to catch them, although they already had two cats of their own. I told them of my sad story, how Keelie died at age 13, happy until her heart failure.

By the end of the evening, as I was sipping on my huge vodka tonic that I mixed while I was waiting for the kitten to come out, the couple said that they were going to set a trap for the kitten next weekend and they would give the kitten to me. I was ecstatic! Yes! I want the kitten. I was grilled as to whether I would care for the kitten, keep her and take care of her. Yes! I will take care of the kitten until she dies of old age. This kitten could be Keelie reincarnated because there is enough time between her death and the creation of this kitten for it to be true.

This kitten never came out, so I left the uneaten cat food and went back to my apartment. I heard the sad cries of the kitten that night, too.

OCTOBER 5, 2001

I had a wonderful surprise last night! It was fairly late, around 11:00 pm when Ryan and I heard knocking at the door. The knocking persisted so I walked lightly to the door and looked out the eye hole. What did I see but that couple who had been trying to catch the kitten. I quickly opened the door and to my delight they held a squirming bundle of gray fluff in their arms. The guy asked if I still wanted the kitten. I said I do! I'd love to take the kitten. He was very stern with me, quizzing me about how I would care for the cat, and it was something that I must do for the rest of her life. I also said that I would find another kitten to keep her company. They seemed happy about that and gave me the clawing kitten. I thanked them and they left. I quickly got a bowl of fresh water and cat food. I didn't have a kitty litter so I took my only cake pan and shredded newspaper in it for a makeshift kitty litter.

The kitten was frantic and terrified, and as soon as I put her down, she ran under the bed. I brought the food, water and litter into the bedroom and gently coaxed her out. Eventually she came out and devoured the food. I refilled the bowl and she ate more. I thought she may burst at the seams, but didn't.

I didn't want her to keep going under the bed, so I set up a nice, cozy cuddle area with my velvet comforter, placing the food and water up there, too. The kitten seemed to like the nest I made for her and snuggled down and let me pet her. She soon attached herself to me, not leaving the bed. I can't convey how ecstatic I am about receiving such a special gift. I love her so much. She acts like Keelie. That makes me feel much better.

OCTOBER 18, 2001

The couple who caught the cat dropped by unexpectedly last night to see how Moya was doing. That is the name Ryan and I came up with. The name is from *Farscape*, the science fiction series. Ryan was in the bedroom watching tv and I invited the couple in, not remembering their names, as usual. I am terrible with names. I can recognize faces but don't ask me to recite names.

I was able to capture the frisky Moya and tried to hold her for them to see, but she was very squirmy and didn't want to be held. She was also very skittish of other people. Moya has formed an attachment to me and trusts me. Especially during those first few days and nights. She realized that I was helping her. She had been potty trained because she used the paper litter box.

Moya is now so hyper she jumps precariously from bookshelf to bookshelf, frightening me completely. She has no fear of heights and no fear of anything except for humans.

NOVEMBER 25, 2001

I adopted another kitten. I wanted to give Moya a friend. I think animals enjoy being around their own. Moya's veterinarian said that she had a flyer about free kittens. I told her I would love to get a friend for Moya. The vet also said it would be a good idea, especially while they are still kittens.

I went over to the house to look at the kitten, bringing the cat carrier with me. The house was located in Buckhead, just a block from the Governor's mansion. Her house was enormous with a grand piano lounging lazily in the living room next to the 12 feet Christmas tree.

The nice Buckhead lady picked up Tiger and handed him to me, saying she wanted him in a caring home. She was glad that I had another cat since Tiger loved his siblings and mother so much. Tiger loved me at first sight. I had my faux leopard print coat on and he attached himself to it and wouldn't let go. He is kind of comical looking, with a huge head and small body. His paws are enormous. He looks unnaturally disproportionate.

I am trying to get the two cats acclimated. I read on the internet not to scold Moya for hissing and attacking Tiger, because she will associate scolding with him. I have instead praised her good behavior. That is all I can do. I hope they like each other soon.

DECEMBER 16, 2001

Finally, Moya is tolerating Talyn a little bit. I renamed him to the name of a character from *Farscape*. Ryan helped me name him. We both love *Farscape*, the science fiction show of SciFi.

CHAPTER 24

2002: AGE 33

MARCH 5, 2002

I finally did it. I moved to Athens with Ryan. Ryan and I have been getting along so well, and I really missed him when he moved from Atlanta to Athens to be near his childhood friends. Ryan joined their band. They grew up together so they've known each other for a long time. Ryan is a gentle soul, intelligent and kind. I found someone who loves me and is normal.

I hired a moving company, Peachtree Movers, to get all my things here. I used money from my TVA annual installment of money for my company stock and went the easy route. I drove the cats to Athens on Thursday, along with the comforter from my bed. I wanted something familiar for the cats to cling to. It was a good thing, too, because they were completely freaked by the move, and the long car ride. I thought that I was going to scream listening to the cats meowing pitifully the whole time. It really tore at my heart strings, yet simultaneously tugged at my nerves.

I spent a little time with Joe before the final move, and he was emotional and sad that I was leaving. You know, looking back, I will miss him, too. He was always there, next door, ready for a beer and a joint. Sure, Joe is paranoid, crass, rude, uncouth, but he is intelligent and mostly kind. He has his moments. Joe can be sweet as pecan pie one day and a real mean bastard the next. I have to give him some slack since he grew up in the rough neighborhoods of Washington D.C.

It is so nice living in a house. Already, I feel so much freedom; freedom to blast the stereo, watch a movie with the bass until 2:00 am, vacuum at any hour, and hammer nails whenever I want to. The house is a cute little rental. It is owned by a church and backs up to an apple orchard. There is a small front porch where Ryan and I can have an occasional cigarette and watch people walking by. It has three bedrooms, and we've made one a music room where the instruments are set up for use day or night. We are so close to downtown that we can walk or bike. It's definitely a walking town and has so many great restaurants and venues for shows, which Ryan loves to attend.

It is great living the slow life again. The traffic is light here. The neighborhood is also gorgeous, the Cobham District. I am quite content. I think I found the good life. All of those years of unhappiness are finally over, I can start my life fresh and new and live with being bipolar. As long as I keep my medications in check, I feel that I can be happy.

My medications have finally balanced out so my mood swings aren't so drastic. My heart feels lighter already. I've finally reached the point in my life where I might actually be a normal person in a normal relationship. Wish me luck!

AUTHOR'S NOTE

In 1998, I was diagnosed Bipolar with Borderline Personality Disorder. When does mental illness manifest itself? Is there a specific point in one's life when sanity disintegrates and insanity begins to fester? I have found the only true expression of my deepest feelings through written word. As a child, I kept meticulous diaries. Later in life, I wrote down my thoughts and feelings on scraps of paper, torn from old notebooks, often undated and shoved into an artistically painted desk drawer. I went so many years undiagnosed and untreated, my life, for the most part, was interconnected by tangled threads of unhappy events, disturbing and frightening situations from which I did not know how to escape. Did I mention a crippling debt which surpassed many third-world countries due to manic spending sprees for unnecessary items which were often left in their packages, tags dangling lifelessly?

Since my diagnosis, I rapidly cycled from black depression to fearless mania. For years, my psychiatrist tried countless combinations of medications, one to ease my anxiety, another to reduce manic cycling, another to prevent the frequent paralyzing, black depression which would sink me to the floor, huddled into the corner of my apartment, smoking cigarettes and talking to my cat, my only friend.

After settling into the lazy, hazy pace of a small town, I decided to put my diaries, notebooks and scraps of paper into some sort of chronological order. This turned into a tedious task since nothing was dated. I had to guess the year of those intriguing rants. After organizing the writings, I began to type all entries into the computer for posterity, in case anyone was the least bit interested in my lascivious lifestyle.

Once my warbled memories became a typeface on a computer screen with chapter headings and dates, I noticed huge gaps in my life, especially between my multiple mental breakdowns and subsequent hospitalizations. These institutionalizations occurred from one coast to the other, criss-crossing the United States like the a pin in a map of a serial killer denoting each victim. There were so many life-altering, momentous events in my life that were missing, gaping voids like the wounds of a dying animal, many of which probably had a direct link to my mental illness and needed to be documented. My various personalities of adulthood, swelling with fragmented thoughts and experiences matching my psyche, were documented as I lived my life; a complete and total mess. Thankfully, my childhood diaries were dated, organized, and legible. Those early diaries turned out to be the stuff of nightmares, not far removed from the nightmares I endured almost every night of my life. The next task was to fill the voids, to complete my story.

I retraced my steps, or rather, my life, and created new "diary entries" from actual events which occurred. I clung to a stash of medical bills sent to collection for hospital stays which pinpointed specific dates on my timeline. Since the bills listed my residence, I could reconstruct my living situation at the time, my roommates who were equally confused by my actions. I began to remember events which led to the hospitalizations and the chaos which occurred afterwards. I refined the entries by researching the dates on the internet, finding major news events which lined up with my breakdowns, in order to get the most realistic "diary entry" possible.

Most people do not really know the definition of mental illness, but rather envision it as a rambling, neurotic, dirty, smelly person with no direct contact with reality. Sometimes this is true, but it is not the case for most mental illness. We often come across as rational, intelligent, creative beings who don't share our true feelings so we won't become alienated by society and labeled as a freak. We are good actors. We know what you expect to see and hear and will deliver an Oscar-winning performance.

With my book, I want to rip a hole through the veil of mental illness so that others may understand and help their loved ones who may be suffering in silence. Don't be afraid to ask questions. Being ignored and neglected is a much worse fate for the mentally ill than having a caring friend asking questions in order to understand.

Now that my reasons for writing this book have been laid bare, I must inform you that names of people, identifying features, and cities have been changed in the retelling of this story to protect the identity of those who may not want to become entangled in my memories. I have taken artistic liberty in writing my memoir, sometimes combining separate events into one or merging two people into one for clarity of reading. Thank you for reading my story.

Bipolar Disorder: "Bipolar disorder is a serious mental illness in which common emotions become intensely and often unpredictably magnified. Individuals with bipolar disorder can quickly swing from extremes of happiness, energy and clarity to sadness, fatigue and confusion. These shifts can be so devastating that individuals may choose suicide. All people with bipolar disorder have manic episodes—abnormally elevated or irritable moods that last at least a week and impair functioning. But not all become depressed. Adapted from the Encyclopedia of Psychology[1]"

Borderline Personality Disorder: The symptoms of Borderline Personality Disorder can be summarized as instability in mood, thinking, behavior, personal relations, and self-image. Individuals with the disorder may: demand constant attention and make unreasonable demands; avoid being alone by acting out a crisis or dramatizing a problem; display provocative behavior; go on eating or spending binges; threaten or attempt suicide; cut, burn or scratch themselves; have mood swings, brief periods of severe depression or anxiety, or intense anger over something minor; engage in self-destructive behavior like reckless driving, or abuse of alcohol and other drugs; say they are bored, life is empty, and they do not know who they are; have delusions and slip temporarily into a psychosis.[2]

[1] American Psychological Association
[2] Mental Health Association

www.ingramcontent.com/pod-product-compliance
Lightning Source LLC
LaVergne TN
LVHW052202200926
848481LV00001B/15